Empress

EMPRESS

by

Evelyn B. McCune

FAWCETT COLUMBINE / NEW YORK

A Fawcett Columbine Book
Published by Ballantine Books

 Published in the United States by Ballantine Books, a division of Random House, Inc., New York, and simultaneously in Canada by Random House of Canada Limited, Toronto.

Library of Congress Catalog Card Number: 94-94061

ISBN: 0-449-90749-X

Designed by Ann Gold

Cover design by Judy Herbstman
Cover illustration by Jeff Barson

Manufactured in the United States of America
First Edition: August 1994
10 9 8 7 6 5 4 3

In memory of the pioneers in Asian studies in mid-century at the University of California: Peter Boodberg and George Lantzeff from Russia; Otto Maenchen, Ferdinand Lessing, Wolfgang Eberhard from Germany; Hu Shih from China; and from the United States, two young scholars newly released from service in World War II, Delmer Brown and George McCune—"Mac"—my husband, who saturated himself in historical materials, mocked them, and relished it all as long as he lived.

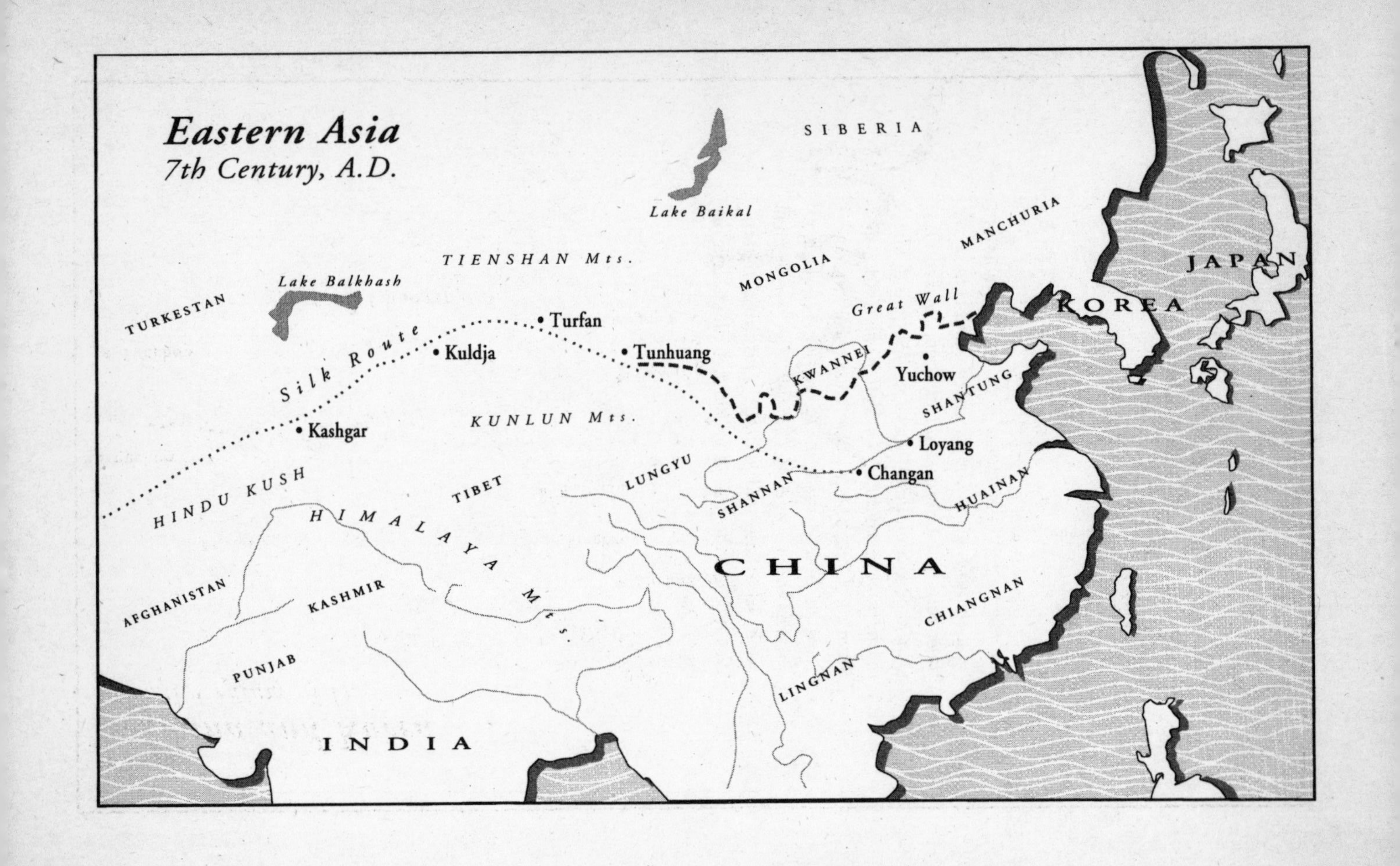
Eastern Asia
7th Century, A.D.
SIBERIA
Lake Baikal
MANCHURIA
JAPAN
KOREA
TIENSHAN Mts.
MONGOLIA
Lake Balkhash
Great Wall
TURKESTAN
Turfan
Silk Route
Kuldja
Tunhuang
KWANNEI
Yuchow
SHANTUNG
KUNLUN Mts.
Kashgar
Loyang
LUNGYU
Changan
HINDU KUSH
TIBET
SHANNAN
HUAINAN
HIMALAYA Mts.
CHINA
AFGHANISTAN
KASHMIR
CHIANGNAN
PUNJAB
LINGNAN
INDIA

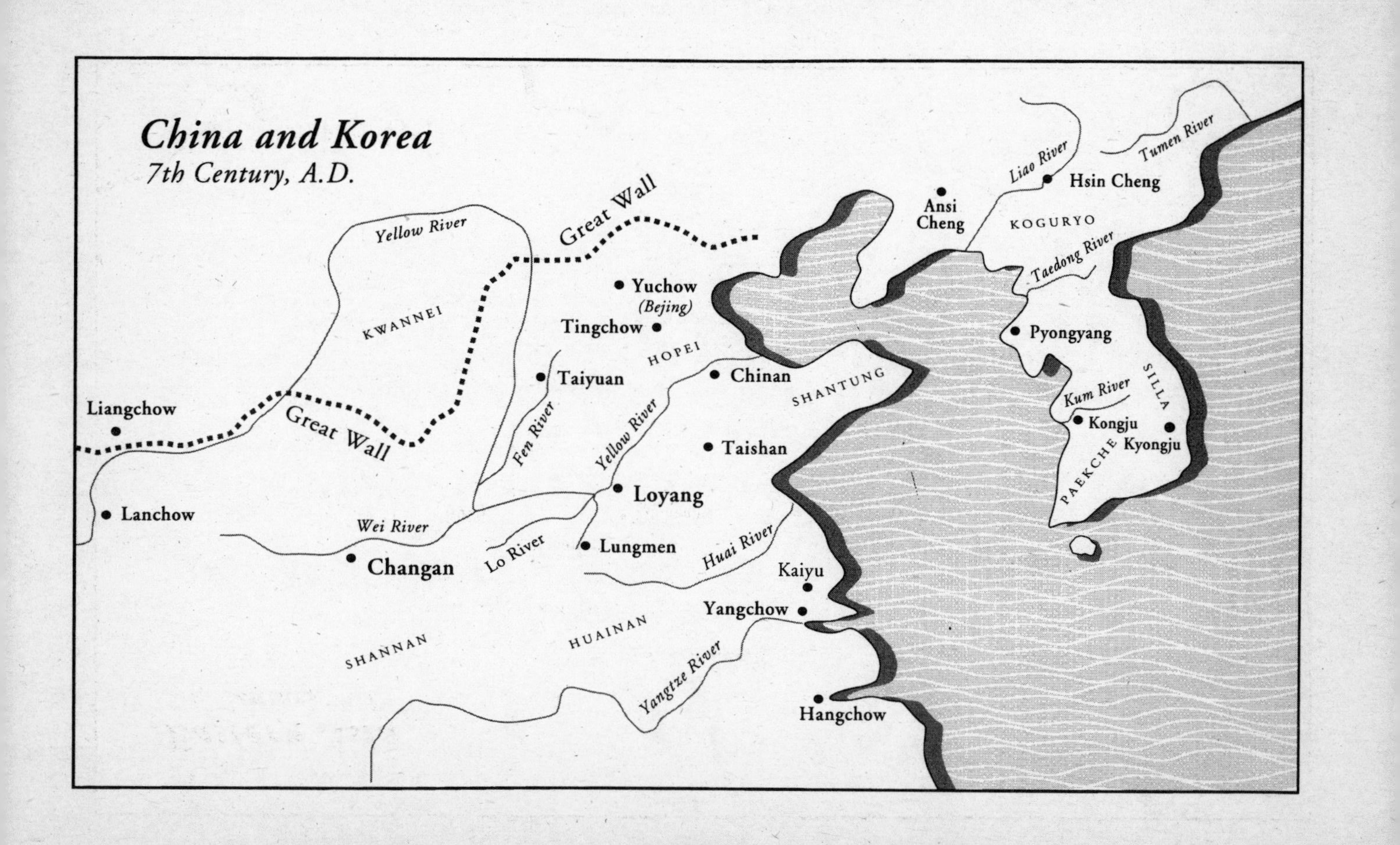
China and Korea
7th Century, A.D.
Yellow River
Great Wall
KWANNEI
Great Wall
Liangchow
Lanchow
Wei River
Changan
Lo River
Fen River
Taiyuan
Tingchow
Yuchow
(Bejing)
HOPEI
Yellow River
Loyang
Lungmen
Chinan
Taishan
SHANTUNG
Huai River
Kaiyu
Yangchow
HUAINAN
SHANNAN
Yangtze River
Hangchow
Ansi
Cheng
Liao River
Hsin Cheng
Tumen River
KOGURYO
Taedong River
Pyongyang
Kum River
Kongju
SILLA
Kyongju
PAEKCHE

Chapter One

Caravan leader Ko stood in the doorway of the kitchen courtyard and eyed the clouds piling up on a darkening horizon. The big man exuded strength and confidence, but his lined, normally good-natured face was troubled. "Couldn't be snow, but looks like it—and feels like it," he murmured thoughtfully.

He turned to eye the maids, who were hurrying past on their way to breakfast, screeching because of the wind in their faces and the ice underfoot. "You there," he shouted to the nearest one. She was clutching a coat over her head, and lifted it reluctantly.

"I?" Nurse Wang asked chidingly.

"Who else?" Ko was disappointed that he had gotten the older woman. "You look as if you know what goes on around here. . . . Will you tell me where to find the masters?"

Nurse Wang nodded and pointed with her chin. "There," she said.

Ko aimed his eyes at a couple of vehemently arguing figures standing toe-to-toe at the far end of the court. "Those are the masters?"

"Those," she sniffed and hurried on.

He'd started toward the two men, when he was nearly knocked off his feet by a boy who slipped on the ice. Another small figure crashed into the first. "Here now, you two, watch where you are going!"

" 'Scuse," panted the boy.

"Yes, pardon us, *lauban*. Did we hurt you, sir?" asked the girl, breathing heavily as she scrambled to her feet. Unabashed, she erupted in laughter, dimples appearing enchantingly under red cheeks and sparkling black eyes.

"Are you calling me *lauban*!" Ko exclaimed, pretending to be affronted.

"No, no. You are certainly not old," the boy said quickly. "She means to be polite, but she is only a girl and makes mistakes, and so what can you expect?" He was tall for his age, small-boned and wiry, with quick, inquisitive eyes. "Are you the caravan leader?" he asked impatiently.

"How did you guess?" Ko replied, looking with amused interest into two pairs of dancing eyes.

"From your nose. Like a hawk's beak, different from Chinese noses," the boy answered. "But what we want is to see your famous camel."

Ko raised his eyebrows and frowned. "My nose? Ah yes, my handsome nose . . . thanks for your compliment! As for the camel, difficult. Yes, very difficult, I must think about it. Who are you? I don't show my priceless camel to just anyone." He looked solemn to tease them.

"We aren't just anyone," the boy protested. "I am Dee Jenjer of the Taiyuan Dee family, and here is Wu Jao of this household. She's important too—I'm not sure why. You are taking her to the Inner Palace in Changan. So now will you show us your camel?"

Ko stared at the girl, enchanted. Young as she was, her beauty was electrifying. Every feature was exquisitely proportioned to grace a piquant, small face; and her figure, apparent even through her layers of quilted jackets, was already mature. Her movements were graceful and the proud way she held herself made her seem older and taller than she was.

Ko recalled himself abruptly. "Dee? Your family is illustrious. Are you going to be a magistrate like your father?"

"It is to be expected," Jenjer replied. "Now you should tell us your name and who you are."

Amused, the big man responded patiently and politely. "I am Ko, from Tunhuang oasis. We are camel owners and caravan conductors, the best in the business. That's why I am here now. All my camels are good, but my lead camel, Desert Runner, is special. He and I grew up together. I would trust him with my life . . . have done so several times. Is he the one you want to see?"

"I have heard about him," Jenjer said solemnly, "and that's why I'm asking."

Ko pondered, then agreed, nodding importantly. He led the way across the court to the stable and through the heavy door. Inside, a line of feeding camels raised their heads suspiciously.

Ko passed a soothing hand over the rump of the nearest camel. "This is Desert Runner," he said simply. The camel was a champion, and looked it. Over a hand taller than the other camels, Desert Runner had a coat glossy from brushing. Even his hooves were free of dirt. He eyed the children and planted his feet as if to let them know that he was aware of his superiority. Ko gazed at him with pride, while the young ones stared, awestruck.

"There. That is where you are to ride . . . up there," Dee muttered to Jao.

She directed a somewhat intimidated smile at the animal, who, ignoring them all, had returned to his meal. "I'll love it," she said.

Jenjer stared. "Aren't you afraid?"

"Should I be?" she asked.

"Yes," he said flatly. "You can see for yourself, Desert Runner isn't for girls." He turned to Ko.

"Do you know why they are sending this *kuniang* here to Changan in such style?" he asked, referring to Jao as a young woman, and trying not to show his jealousy. Ko scrutinized him and then Jao. She was the same height as Jenjer, although, at thirteen, she was five years older.

"She is important," Ko said, "because she has been chosen by the emperor for the palace."

With this new insight, Jenjer looked at Jao consideringly, but shook his head. "I don't see it. Why should she get to ride on Desert Runner? He looks mean, and it's a long way down and she might fall off." Dee sounded as if he hoped she would.

Jao's laugh rang out, startling the camels. "I won't fall because I'll be sitting in a basket saddle. What a glossy coat Desert Runner has, no saddle sores or patches of hair falling off."

"Not on my camels there aren't," Ko replied. "Camels like mine have to be cared for like kings. They will carry heavy loads if they are happy and are taken on interesting expeditions, but only because they like to travel. A camel like mine does what he wants to do, but nothing else. Fact!"

The children studied the camel curiously and keenly, but Desert Runner was not friendly in return. He was snapping his jaws and shifting his feet ominously.

"See," Jenjer said, backing off. "He's dangerous, I tell you!"

"Hold still," Ko commanded, and Desert Runner, understanding that he was not to stamp on visitors' feet, gave them a menacing look and went back to feeding.

"Why did you say that you can trust him with your life?" Jao asked after moving judiciously back.

"Because in the huge deserts that we cross, killer sandstorms arise in seconds, and if it were not for a camel like Desert Runner here, we would all be suffocated. Only the experienced camels know when such winds are about to fall on us. The camels snarl and bury their noses in the sand. We cover our own noses and mouths. The winds whirl madly for what seems an endless time and then are gone. If it weren't for the camels, we'd all die."

The children fell silent, staring avidly, and Ko chuckled. "Have you seen enough? If so, please go out in front of me."

He opened the door and the three of them went out into the yard. It was empty now except for the two masters of household, who looked up when the stable door squeaked noisily on its ancient hinges. Jenjer started to laugh. "Look at your brothers! They glare at us the way the camels did. And their lips are long and chew sideways like the camels, and they sway their heads. . . . so." He imitated, thrusting his thin neck in and out.

"Don't!" Jao said giggling. "The Elders will hear you . . ."

Ko gave a crack of laughter, which he quickly swallowed. "I must leave you now," he said hurriedly.

"Then we must go," Joa said. "*Wanfu!* A thousand thanks for your courtesy!"

The caravan leader salaamed in farewell, and Dee saluted, gratified. Ko said to Jao, "I hope to see you again in a few hours, the fewer hours the better, as I shall be in charge of your safety until you reach the palace."

"Why do you say 'the fewer hours the better'? When do we really leave?" Jao called to his retreating back.

He paused. "Hard to say . . ."

Jao persisted. "Why hard to say? You are the caravan leader. How can you say you don't know?" she asked in a soft voice.

Ko turned again, to look into bright, appraising eyes. "We have to wait for someone to decide the lucky hour, the most propitious hour," he stated stiffly.

"What do you think is the lucky hour, then?" Jao responded.

"Today . . . tonight . . . as soon as the men and animals are fed and rested, at the most ten hours from now," he said impatiently.

Jao counted on her finger. "Ten hours, the hour of the bull. Why is that lucky?"

"Er . . . because the bull is tough and enduring, of course, and that's what we need on a trip like this one." He eyed her curiously. She looked a child, and yet her questions were not childish. "Because the wind has shifted and the air is heavier. We should get out of here and down into the protected Fen Valley as soon as possible. Seven hours for rest, one for feeding, and two for loading. Yes, the hour of the bull is the lucky hour."

Jao nodded. "Our family soothsayer is my friend. Shall I ask if the hour of the bull is lucky? And get him to explain to Elder Brother?" Her expression was bland.

"Would you?" Ko replied, pleased.

Jao showed her dimples. "I will go now. And I'll give him a package of the new ginger tea, which he loves, and a jar of honey because he has no teeth."

Ko grunted appreciatively. "It would be a good thing to have the masters know the lucky hour, but . . . would knowing it hurry them?"

Jao threw her heavy braid over her shoulder. "If Ko can handle Desert Runner, he can handle Elder Brother. After I have done my share . . ." she said sedately as she walked away.

In Lady Yang's room all was confusion. She was trying to supervise the sorting and packing of Second Daughter's clothes while First Daughter Holan lay among the fur rugs on the *kang*, the heated sleeping platform. A slender matron, Lady Yang looked young and comely for her thirty-five years. While her second daughter, Jao, had inherited her heart-shaped face, fine bone structure, and graceful movements, her elder daughter had the narrow head, large features, and stocky build of the Wu family.

Her sister's departure for the palace made Holan restless, and she could not stop talking. "There's some kind of a mix-up down there," she said. "The emperor's new List of Genealogies includes all the aristocratic families in order of importance, and neither Wu nor Yang is high on the list. Disgraceful."

"Not high?" her mother replied distractedly. "How much higher can you get than the Yang imperial family?" Related to the Yang emperors, Lady Yang had been brought up in the palace. There, she had been carefully schooled in court etiquette. But after the downfall of the Sui dynasty, Lady Yang had been summarily married to the elderly General Wu as his second wife. This social denigration, and the disgrace of giving birth only to daughters, had lowered her status to the point where her opinion was never sought and her person little noted. Nevertheless, she maintained her dignity. Her silk clothes might be threadbare, but she wore them with an air.

"Mother," Holan scolded, "the Yang Family of Sui have been in disgrace these twenty years, and the Li Family of Tang are now ruling. You must be more careful what you say."

"Yes, of course," Lady Yang replied apologetically. "I will take care. What were you saying about the current families of importance?"

"The Wu family and the Holan and the Changsun family of the empress—none of us are listed very high," First Daughter complained.

"That is to be expected, don't you think?" Lady Yang continued, folding scarves and sorting the piles to be packed. "The Wu lineage of your father is only from Wenshui military people, and the Changsuns are the same, of mixed blood, Tartar and Chinese. But then, it no longer seems to matter—now that the present emperor has so little Chinese blood. The fact that he is the emperor is what matters."

"Even the emperor's family of Li is only listed third!" Holan said angrily.

"Who are the first families now—since the old ruling families are no longer important?" Lady Yang asked neutrally.

"Four 'pure' Chinese families from the plains—although the senior members live in Changan, where they have a better life—the Tsui, the Lu, the Cheng, and the Lunghsi Li. And now you have heartlessly turned over Second Daughter to the mercies of the Tang court, who made this list and doubtless look down on us all!"

Lady Yang opened her mouth to deny the accusation with indignation, when Holan changed direction. "How do they deliver girls to the emperor anyhow? Do the girls just walk into his presence, or are they carried in naked, wrapped in a scented quilt?"

Lady Yang shut her mouth again, regarding her first daughter with distaste as Holan rattled on.

"No girl should be delivered to a man like a package, not even a dancing girl. She should be able to choose, to be pursued . . . captured . . . carried off in triumph."

"That is nomad custom, not Chinese," Lady Yang said peaceably. "You are just jealous."

"You are not listening to me!" Holan exclaimed, tumbling the furs onto the floor as she sat up. This upset her poodle into a fit of barking, which was answered by more barks from outside as Jao dashed into the room, followed by her own dogs, Nurse Wang, and a rush of cold air.

Lady Yang frowned and sat down, distracted, her hands over her ears, while the dogs chased each other around, upsetting all the piles. When at last they were under control, she said firmly, "Out. Everyone out of here except Jao. Holan, go see Elder Brother and find out when the caravan will start—tomorrow, the next day . . . when."

Holan hesitated, but realized that her soft-spoken mother was serious. She went out. When the door closed behind her, Lady Yang turned to Nurse Wang, who had ignored the order and was inspecting with curiosity the goods that had been laid out. "And you too . . . Go on," she repeated as Wang hesitated. Finally, the nurse obeyed, as slowly as possible, letting in a great deal of cold air.

"Now," Lady Yang said to Jao. "We have to decide about your clothes and other things, and I don't want anyone in here to listen to what I say and to pass it on to the neighborhood. First, I have laid out some jewelry for you, and a rabbit-fur coat and hood—you won't be allowed to wear more expensive furs yet. Here is a pile of embroidered shoes, enough for some time. And this lacquer box holds the jewelry. I won't open it now, but take care of it. Don't let it out of your sight while traveling. One of the pieces is the large pink pearl set in Silla gold that your father gave me."

Jao's mouth fell open. "B-But that is your best pin and you have never parted with it—the one that father gave you on your wedding day."

"Nevertheless I am parting with it now," Lady Yang said firmly. "Several necklaces of lapis lazuli and amber, and one of Khotan jewel jade are also inside. There by the bed are boxes of delicacies to share with the others in your house: Taiyuan raisins and jars of dried ginger. And as a guide for good manners, I am putting in my own volume of Lady Pang's etiquette book."

"I know it by heart, so I don't need to take it," Jao said hastily, but her mother stopped her.

"You will need to refer to it from time to time. I fear for you because of your impulsive nature . . . and because of your habit of saying whatever comes into your head. You may make enemies by your tongue without realizing it. You are apt to disregard people who seem . . . uninteresting to you."

"Dull," Jao supplied.

"What? Well, yes, I suppose so. You never seem to care what people think."

"I don't really," Jao admitted.

"You don't what?" Lady Yang frowned.

"Care," Jao replied.

Lady Yang gave a little shriek. "That is what I mean. You must care

. . . or seem to care. If people's feelings—their self-importance—is hurt, they want revenge, and will go after it in small, deadly ways. The palace is full of people like your elder brothers."

"Half brothers," Jao corrected.

"Half brothers, then," her mother said. "Well, we won't talk about them. You know very well what I mean. But now I want to talk about the most important thing of all—about pleasing the emperor."

"I won't even try," Jao said softly.

Lady Yang put her hand to her mouth, her eyes staring. Jao's eyes were remote.

"I won't even try," Jao repeated.

"Whatever do you mean?" Lady Yang quavered.

"Look at what has happened to me in this household. I have tried and tried to get good treatment from my elder brothers, and nothing I do ever has any effect. If the brothers are in good temper, they have time for everyone except me. If they are in a bad temper, I attract their attention, I am ordered about and slapped. When I am with you or any of the women, I am treated properly, but with men it is better to be small and invisible and stay out of their way. Not to try to get any attention at all is safer. Better."

"I have not brought you up correctly!" Lady Yang moaned. "Here in this northern country, doing what you think best is masculine conduct and is accepted in a girl because we are all half Turkish. But for the Imperial court it may be—will be—all wrong. When you say that you will not try to get the emperor's favor . . . when forty concubines in ranks above you are exerting all their efforts and wits to obtain it, and you just stay in a corner, that is where you will remain—in a corner."

Mother and daughter looked at each other in consternation as they considered the possibility of isolation and ostracism. For differing reasons, both were appalled at the thought. Then a look of merriment came into Jao's eyes and she threw her arms around her mother's neck.

"I'll not stay in any corner," she assured her parent. "You'll see. All I meant was that I can't follow Holan's way. To scheme and fawn, to plan a campaign for a man's favor, smiling, smiling, with female guile . . . If the Son of Heaven is so stupid as to be taken in by such tricks, I will not have a chance—I'm no good at acting. So . . . better not to try."

Lady Yang looked half relieved. "If that is all you meant," she said, "maybe you have a point." They looked at each other, and Jao flung her arms around her mother again.

"Not to worry, dear parent," she said cheerfully, then pointed to the debris on the floor left by the dogs. Most of it she did not recognize and was sure she did not want. "What are you going to do with all this?"

"There are four red lacquer bride chests of the same size, so that they will balance each other on the backs of the camels. See them stacked over there? Open them all and we will pack what is proper in each one. Here in the first one go those ten jars of honeyed ginger from Yangchow. If you are regular about taking it, you will have a lovely, soft complexion. Those boxes of figs are from the West somewhere; they are also good for the skin. The ginseng and calomel are for infections and stomach trouble. And three jars of cloves, nutmeg, and cinnamon for fevers. I'm not putting in the sulfur for skin disease because you won't get any such thing in the palace."

Jao eyed the bottles and jars dubiously, but dutifully packed them away, wrapped in silk underwear. They filled up one chest, which she closed and locked with its brass padlock, putting the key safely away in a silk purse. By the time she was finished, Lady Yang had everything else sorted into three piles. Jao looked at them without enthusiasm; some of her sister's hand-me-downs, she thought. Her mother saw her lack of interest.

"Clothes for the four seasons in those two boxes," her mother said. "Bedding, towels—those new thick cotton ones from India—and bolts of silk and felt for new clothes."

Jao brightened, new clothes were acceptable. She packed them all tightly and sat on the lids. "What is that?" she asked, gesturing at the last pile of folded cloth and tree floss from distant Szechuan.

"That? Oh, that's a layette with the latest thing in diapers." Jao looked nonplussed. "Pack it," Lady Yang said, and then sighed. "I doubt that it will do you much good. The emperor already has about thirty children, two or three sons by the empress, and many more sons by mothers higher-ranking than you. I don't suppose that if you are lucky enough to have a son, he will ever become emperor. It would be impossible. Especially with all those other women, a hundred or more, all striving for the emperior's attention, fighting each other to get first place, or some other high privilege. And yet he's only thirty-eight years old. You must—you simply must—try to please him."

"Mother," Jao chided, "You have said all this before."

Lady Yang stared at her daughter in silence, twisting her scarf around her fingers in her dejection. Jao jumped up to run to her mother to comfort her, when the door opened and Holan came in with Nurse

Wang at her heels, both ready to organize Jao's dowry, both crestfallen when they found that it had all been done.

"Everything is packed and ready to go," Lady Yang said. "What did you find out about the time to leave?"

"Elder Brother has not yet made up his mind. He said that he'll be in soon to give you your instructions," Holan said, looking speculatively at the locked chests. Wang looked at them, too. "I'll have to repack," the nurse said. "Jao does not know how to do it properly."

"They are ready to go as they are," Lady Yang said firmly, "but thank you anyway, good nurse." She turned to Holan. "Jao and I have had a chat, and I am satisfied that she knows what to expect in palace life and that she knows how to behave."

"I doubt it, but it's too late now," Holan replied. "You should never have agreed to send her."

"I was never consulted. It was all arranged by my stepsons, who are not in the habit of paying the slightest attention to my wishes. But that is over and done with. What we have to do now is to look to the future. If Jao should please the Son of Heaven—Why do you laugh?"

"Because Jao's idea of how best to please a male is to challenge him to a horse race or talk him deaf about dogs! There is nothing in the world harder than to try to please a sovereign. 'To attend the emperor is like sleeping with a tiger,' as the saying goes, and—keep still, you fool!" she yelled at her poodle, who was once again barking. More barks from the outside had been added to the din when the door flew open and Elder Brother entered, accompanied by his muddy hounds.

"I have come myself," he announced, "to give you your orders. We leave tonight at the hour of the bull. You must be ready because this is the most propitious time to start. What was that?" He looked sharply at Jao, who had clapped her hands, and then with even more disapproval, he glared at her mother. "Lady Yang, you are always late, but do not delay things this time. Have Jao ready. At the hour of the bull! Come," he shouted at his dogs, and departed.

"At the hour of the bull!" Jao mimicked, striking a pose. "Come!" she thundered at the poodle, who scrambled under the bed. The others laughed, turning off the flow of tears that had started when the door closed. As the merriment died down, Lady Yang smiled, and wiping her eyes, said resignedly, "Not much time left, then. Let us have our festive dinner in the main hall at the hour of the dog and enjoy ourselves while we can. Holan, go stand beside Jao. I want to have a last look at you together."

"Come here, Jao, see if you are as tall as I am now." Holan laughed, pulling at Jao.

"Jao is taller," Nurse Wang exclaimed. "You look like a pear and she looks like a double fall of wisteria!"

"What on earth do you mean?" Holan said crossly.

"She means that you have graceful lines like a pear, with your bust slightly smaller than your hips and the flow from shoulder to knee smooth and attractive," Lady Yang interposed hastily.

"I've had two children—" Holan began.

"And Jao has had none. That is why I have had trouble fitting Jao gracefully into her palace clothes. She looks both fragile and tough—like wisteria."

"Like a wasp," Holan said unkindly.

Jao giggled and pulled her sister closer, while Lady Yang studied them both critically as they stood together before her. "You are both lovely," she mused. "With those heart-shaped faces, narrow little noses and big eyes. Satiny white skin too. I don't know how I ever produced you."

"Nonsense!" Nurse Wang interrupted. "You are more beautiful than either one. All the Yang women were beautiful, with strong, lithe bodies! And here are the three of you, best in the province, maybe in the empire. I know what I am talking about," Wang insisted, despite the jeering laughs she received. Nevertheless, they all felt better at her bantering.

The courtyard gong sounded, and Lady Yang, startled, said, "It's time! You, Holan, and you, Wang, attend to your duties in the dining room and kitchen so that we may have dinner just after sundown, during the hour of the dog. Jao will stay here with me for a while." Anticipating a feast of special treats ahead, Holan and Wang went off briskly.

Lady Yang sighed. "I want to see you alone for a few more minutes because I have something more to say to you."

Jao stopped pulling the dog's ears and fixed her eyes warily on her mother.

"First, in your beginning months at the palace, listen much and say little. Find a friendly older concubine—preferably one of the high-ranking Fei—and serve her. And don't be afraid to ask her what to do when you don't know. It is better than making a fool of yourself. Second, don't probe. People will think you are aggressive if you ask a lot of questions. . . . Yes, yes. I just told you to ask questions. You have to use your head about what questions to ask safely, that's all. And lastly, don't get familiar with subordinates, like you do here, if you want respect. I am anxious for you. You must never, night or day, forget about this danger."

"What danger?" Jao asked hopefully.

"The danger of offending people, of course! You are such a child—only thirteen years old."

"Fourteen," Jao said. Her mother shrugged. "In ten days, at New Year's time, you will theoretically be a year older. The point is that you will be so far away that I can't help you. I can only beseech Kuanyin Bodhisattva that no harm comes to you."

"Maitreya Bodhisattva . . . Milo," Jao offered.

"Why Milo?" Lady Yang asked, diverted. "Sakya or Amitabha Buddha are the great Buddhas. Or if you want a bodhisattva, surely the compassionate Kuanyin is the one."

"Maitreya is the protector of the small people who are in trouble, the ones that Kuanyin is too grand to listen to," Jao said.

"Wherever did you get such ideas!" Lady Yang cried. "Kuanyin is the only one for a woman. She is female herself!"

"That's why I want Maitreya, he's strong and close to small people," Jao answered, with what she thought was clear logic, but which only confused and distressed her mother. Lady Yang was a devoted Buddhist of the Tientai persuasion, in which Maitreya was only a minor deity.

Lady Yang studied her daughter in silence, then went to the alcove that housed her small shrine, a recent work of art featuring a Sakyamuni Buddha flanked by a Kuanyin and a Maitreya, each figure carved out of Khotan jade. It was her greatest treasure. She selected the Maitreya and presented it formally, in both hands, to Jao, who jumped up to receive the lovely statuette.

"I bestow this Maitreya upon you, since Maitreya is the one who moves you to reverence. Commit your welfare to him and be saved from harm."

Jao, not religiously inclined, was at this moment deeply touched. Tears came into her eyes. "I accept—I promise—I will keep this treasure of yours with me all my life and pray daily. Because of you and Maitreya to remind me, I promise to learn more about the great mysteries and be more serious."

"You may be sure that I shall be doing daily petitioning also. For you, to keep calamity away from you. You may be sure of that. I shall burn rare incense while doing my devotions, and I shall contribute without fail to the monks and monasteries in Taiyuan on your behalf."

Lady Yang dried her cheeks. "And now there are clouds and rain to talk about. This is what you are in the palace for—to please the emperor in bed. To give satisfaction. To give yourself willingly to this man."

"What do you mean when you say 'willingly' in that tone of voice?" Jao asked.

"I mean that you must not hesitate for an instant or even flinch the tiniest bit, whatever he might do—painful or unpleasant. But you must show more than willingness. You have to . . . you have to . . ."

"Be seductive?" Jao volunteered. "That midwife from the head eunuch's office who came here to look me over to see if I was healthy and whether I had had my moon flow yet, she said the same thing. I knew it all anyway."

"You did? You do?" Lady Yang exclaimed. "What exactly do you know? Observing animals is not what I am talking about. I don't mean the physical thing, but the personal thing. You can't be coarse or aggressive, even though the emperor might be. If you behave in a vulgar way, you will certainly fail to please. And that could mean, it probably will mean, unhappiness."

Jao cocked her head thoughtfully. "I have not thought much about how love is done before," she admitted soberly. "I have just accepted it. Now I shall make this a great skill, I promise you."

"I cannot think of anything more to say." Lady Yang was on the verge of tears again. "I have said it all. And have done my duty . . . more than anyone ever did for me." The tears began to roll down her cheeks, and she did not try to stop them. Jao knelt before her mother and gathered her hands within her own.

"To be admitted into the presence of the Son of Heaven! How can you tell that that means unhappiness? Why are you crying like a little girl?"

Lady Yang looked down into the small face so close to her own. The possibility of happiness of any sort among the spoiled women living unnatural lives in the palace seemed remote to her. For Jao's sake she smiled and wiped her face whereupon Jao jumped up and did a happy pirouette.

"When I am promoted from Rank Five to Rank Four—or higher!—I shall send for you to come and live with me," she cried.

Lady Yang just nodded and kept on smiling as Jao flung her arms around her.

"And another thing to keep you from worrying," Jao said. "Even if they send a girl home in disgrace from time to time, I promise it will not be me!"

A cock crowed sleepily. A candle was lit in the kitchen and soon after in the gatehouse. Then the servants and stablehands began to stir. A great rustling and stamping started in the sheds as the animals were roused, watered, and fed. Jingling bells mingled with the noises of men shouting and running about as they finished their harnessing. When Ko was satisfied that the animals were ready, he gave the order for them to be led into the first courtyard, where the baggage was piled.

A brazier of hot charcoal was brought out and a pot of boiling deer meat was hung over it. Torches were lit. Grooms struggled to balance and rope the loads over the humps of the restive animals. Moving about briskly in spite of the dark, men and animals cast long shadows upon each other. A steady chorus of snorts, growls, and foot-stamping accompanied all the activity. When loading was completed, the men collected around the fire, anxious to fill their stomachs with hot food while they could. Each one carried pouches of parched barley to sustain himself en route, but such fare, though routine, was not very attractive to the more sophisticated.

Shutters clanged open as the two Wu masters, swathed to the eyes in fur-lined mantles, bustled into the yard. The grooms lapsed into silence, making haste to empty their bowls while they still had time. Shuddering when the cold air hit them, the Wus moved rapidly to the gate, where their mounts were being held by the grooms. Ko gave a last pat to Desert Runner and hastened forward to greet the masters.

"Is Wu Jao loaded?" Wu Yuanshuang asked, peering into the darkness.

"She is coming now," Ko answered, at the sound of another set of doors opening. The women of the household, with wraps thrown loosely over their shoulders, were bringing out the girl Jao, almost hidden among them.

"Here," Wu Yuanshuang shouted. "Make haste. Enough of your farewells, we must be on our way, no more of that wailing either."

Ko was already in position at the head of the line, but seeing the agitation on the porch, he dismounted, shouted apologies, extricated the girl from the women and threw her expertly into her seat. Raising his whip, he gave the order to start. His shout echoed down the line, triggering answering commands from the drovers. A shuffling of hooves and creaking of harness began as the loaded animals fell into line. The women threw their aprons over their heads, their cries rising shrilly above the other noises.

Lady Yang, who had stayed close to Wu Jao, looked up at the small figure leaning down to grasp her hand. She intertwined her fingers while the orders to move rang out. Jao held on until their fingers broke apart and Lady Yang at last let go.

"We will meet again . . . again, Mama!" screamed Jao over the noise of the wind as her mount lumbered over the sill of the gate into the cold wind.

Jao tied her scarf over her face and settled into her seat, pulled on her fur mittens, adjusted herself to the motion of her animal, and discovered almost at once that she was not terribly sad at leaving home, but was exhilarated and full of the sense of adventure. The darkness, lit only by the flickering lanterns, the feel of the animal beneath her, the movements of the animals in front and behind, their snorts and rumblings, the sense of freedom and enjoyment . . . this was life! This was it! A feeling of being supremely alive and supremely happy suffused her.

The trip began well. The ground was hard and the caravan made steady progress. The way was lit for each animal by the lanterns of the grooms, and there were few ruts in the well-traveled streets to slow them down. Taiyuan's south gate was opened in spite of the early hour. The caravan passed through, and the gate was speedily closed again. Then the line of animals settled into a steady jogging pace as they descended from the windswept heights into the Fen River valley.

The hours fell away until a pale dawn lightened the eastern sky. They continued down the valley which they were to follow until it ran into the wide plain of the Yellow River at the point where that great river turned eastward. There, they were to turn into the Wei valley and travel on to Changan. If all went well, it would not take more than a week.

Muffled warmly, the brothers guided their animals behind Ko, secure in their belief that they had started out at the most propitious hour. Their feet, however, were getting numb with the cold, and the wind was increasing. Ko kept testing its direction and urging greater speed. It was becoming obvious that a storm of some magnitude was almost upon them, and that they were going into it rather than away from it.

At length Wu Yuanching, riding close to Wu Yuanshuang, shouted uneasily, "I hope this wind will . . . ease off."

"You worry too much," Yuanshuang scolded through his wrappings. "This wind is no great matter. Remember that we have bull protection. Just beat your feet against your mount and bang your hands together to warm them."

The wind continued to rise, and when they reached the bottom of the warmer valley, snow flurries started, blurring vision and slowing the pace. The caravan struggled on through the hours, bells jangling and harnesses creaking. Acute discomfort set in. Leaving Jao to the care of her groom, who now had to hold her in her seat because of the strength of the storm, the brothers finally rode up, one on either side of Ko, and angrily accosted him. He responded calmly. "What I expected," he shouted. "In another hour we will halt and take shelter until this blizzard passes. After that, when there is no wind, we can continue easily in the snow. Your Honors insisted that we be in Changan by New Year's, so we have to take our chances."

To Jao, the effort to stay in her seat and to keep her face from freezing seemed endlessly prolonged, almost unendurable. At length, however, the cries of the drovers rang out sharply and the caravan came to a halt. Jao looked around but could see nothing except a blurred gray-white landscape. Her eyes watered in the cold and she hurriedly covered her face again. She could hear the baggage being unloaded and her groom saying "*Kuniang*, please get down now. I will catch you." She struggled to lift her legs and then to slide down to the ground, but her legs were too numb for her to keep her balance. The groom steadied her while she stamped until sensation returned.

Everything around was ghostly white, the land, the sky, the dim outlines of the caravan. She could see nothing at all, no lights except the few ragged lanterns of the grooms, no shelter of any kind. Then she saw where the drovers were leading their animals, into what looked like a black hole in a snowdrift. She saw her brothers disappear into it, and then Ko coming back to her. She shook her head when he asked whether she was too numb to walk, and followed him into the mysterious hole.

Inside, the noise of the storm was suddenly cut off, and she saw that they were in a large cave filled with horses and camels. Grooms were unsaddling and rubbing down their animals. Other caravan servants were piling baggage along the walls. A pot of coals in the middle of the cave and a few torches gave light, the smoke escaping in some indirect fashion above. Jao saw a small door about three feet high on the rear wall through which her brothers were disappearing. Ko steered her toward it, and she stumbled through its leather curtain into another smoke-filled room, but this one was lit by oil lamps and occupied only by people, some rolled in their felt blankets, asleep, some squatting companionably together, sharing handfuls of parched grain. A wizened woman in a loose caftan was building a fire with twigs to heat water in a caldron hung over it. In front of a sleeping *kang* along the back wall were baskets of onions, parsnips, turnips, cereal.

Jao's brothers were pulling off their mantles and making room for themselves on the warm *kang* when Nurse Wang came in, red-nosed and half frozen. She looked around belligerently and quickly caught sight of Jao standing wet and uncertain in the middle of the chamber while her brothers ignored her. Wang hastily took the girl's arm and steered her toward yet another small door. Bending almost double, the two women pushed aside a heavy curtain and entered a third cave. This one was small and cozy, with colored felts and cushions. It was lit by one flickering light and harbored only a few women, all asleep. Jao's teeth were chattering, but after Wang pulled off her wet clothes and rolled her into a nest of furry coverings, the chattering ceased. Within minutes Jao was asleep. The old woman unrolled her own felts and, groaning with exhaustion, watched the shadows on the ceiling until she too dozed off.

Jao opened her eyes and looked around. The cave was still dark but the women were stirring, combing their hair and rolling up bedrolls. An elderly woman—about fifty—with a dignified mien was being dressed by her maid in felt garments embroidered with Taoist symbols. Another woman, a middle-aged nun, was seated cross-legged against one wall, immersed in her morning devotions, the light from the lantern shining on her bald head and tranquil face.

Jao glanced at them. "Such company . . . one old and one religious," she said aloud. She looked at Nurse Wang, who was softly snoring, and again at the nun and her acolyte, and saw that their rising intonations heralded an end to their prayers.

"Good morning," the nun said to the Taoist matron. Her voice was cultured. She had completed her meditations and was back in the real world, although as a Buddhist, she called it the world of illusion. The old lady responded politely, and the nun turned to Jao to greet her as well.

"Good morning," Jao replied stiffly.

The nun smiled but turned to the matron again. "Since we are to be together for a day or two, we should introduce ourselves. Will you tell us your name and where you come from?"

Nodding amiably, the matron obliged. "My family name is Sun and we come from Shensi, near the capital. Hua-erh is my personal name. I am mistress of a Taoist hostel for women. I'm returning to Changan from Taiyuan, where I was attending an important lady in her first child-birth, Li Kahua, daughter-in-law of the Fang family."

"Is it possible that your brother is the famous physician, Suntzu Miao? And are the Fangs of Taiyuan any relation to Minister Fang?" the abbess asked.

"Suntzu is my brother, and Fang of Taiyuan is the son of the finance minister," the matron began.

Jao broke in. "I know Kahua, she is a friend of mine and we did many things together before her pregnancy. Then she was sick all the time. I have recently attended the month-feast of the baby, which was a great occasion because the Fang family were so delighted to have a healthy boy, the first in his generation, grandson of Minister Fang. . . ." She paused, but the women were not listening to her.

"How is the girl?" the abbess asked.

"She had a hard delivery, very hard, one of the most difficult I have ever had to deal with. I did not think that she would live, or the child either. There were three days of labor and the child did not come. It was large and had been very active and was turned the wrong way. And the room where the girl lay was so filled with midwives and shamans, and the din was so exhausting, that I could not attend her properly."

"Ah," the nun said knowledgeably. "It must have been impossible for you—as an outsider."

"Yes. But the time came when it was matter of life or death for both. I asked to see the husband—told him that I could not be responsible unless I was in full charge. He told me to do what I could to save the lives of both infant and mother. So I chose the most skillful of the local midwives to help me, and the husband cleared the rest out of the room. I had braziers of hot coals brought in to keep the girl warm and a kettle of water heating. I washed my hands ritually and had the others do so. Then I rubbed them in hot, freshly pressed sesame oil to handle the infant. Fortunately, both mother and child lived. I have developed my own methods after studying with my brother."

"You must know exactly what you are doing to manage a frightened and exhausted girl like that," said the abbess said. "Not many midwives have the strength and skill. I congratulate you!"

The matron looked pleased. "So you recognize that to make an easy delivery is no simple thing? It took me a long time to learn my skill. Thank you for your kind words."

"What happened to the girl?"

"She has recovered and is very proud of her boy-baby. But still weak, thin. She cannot have another child for two years, and so I told Master Fang."

"How grateful the two families must be, the Fangs and the Lis," the nun said with warmth. "You have saved two lives, and they are important ones. Kahua is the daughter of Emperor Taitsung, and the baby is his grandson. You are sure to be handsomely rewarded!"

"Kahua is normally thin and normally not strong," Jao broke in. "Nothing was wrong with her or with the birth. The proper characters were painted on her stomach, and the proper incantations were chanted by the local shamans, and the birth came at the appointed hour, and so it all happened by their efforts. I have heard all about it from Wang."

The older women fell silent. Then the matron said, as if she had not heard Jao's remarks, "The Fangs were very grateful and rewarded me suitably. There is no need for any gift from the emperor. My report shall go to him because the child is his grandson."

Abbess Li listened carefully. "That is as it should be. Well done, Madame Sun!" she said with approval.

Jao felt disgruntled, made small by the turn the conversation had taken, and she let her feelings show in her face. Neither woman seemed to notice. The older woman crossed her hands over her stomach and resettled herself.

"That is enough about this humble one," she said. "What is your ancestry, Reverend Mother?"

The abbess responded politely. "I am a Li, cousin and close friend of the emperor's sister, Shih."

"Cousin of the Son of Heaven! You are indeed an exalted person," the matron cried excitedly. Jao stared, confused.

"Years ago when we were children and the Duke of Tang, Shihmin's father, was a frontier governor under the Sui, Shih and I played polo with our brothers and cousins and we took each other for granted, never dreaming that out of all the duke's children, Shihmin would be the one to launch a new empire," the abbess said.

The matron and maids in the cave were now listening with flattering attention.

"Po po po," the matron exclaimed. "You are so high-ranking that the taboo about the emperor's name does not apply to you?"

"Yes, it does. But I am so used to calling him by his whole name, through all those war years as well as in childhood, that I forget. His sister and I were in the wars ourselves. We sold our jewelry to hire soldiers, and succeeded in consolidating all the villages south of Changan for the Tang. There were twelve contenders for the throne at that time. We rode with our troops like the men, and secured the loyalty of at least the one region." At this the women clapped their hands in their excitement and the nun smiled.

"A woman warrior, you! Then what happened that you are now a nun?" Jao exclaimed out of her confusion. "Why of all things . . . a nun?"

The abbess shrugged. "Why not? Or a Taoist healer in charge of an important hostel?" She gestured at the matron, who smiled with gratification. "What better way is there for a woman to run her own life and to have responsibility for an establishment, like a man? Acquiring merit by one's own efforts? But I digress. During the wars I was captured by the enemy, by General Li Mi. I had a bad time and would have taken my own life had I not been rescued by Shihmin. I decided to become a nun in gratitude, and am now the Abbess of Kanyeh Convent in Changan."

"Ah," the old lady murmured. "We have all heard of Kanyeh-ssu and Hunfu-ssu, those great monasteries that the Son of Heaven founded in honor of his mother and wife. And, of course, he also founded Taoist temples. We religious are fortunate. To have peace and a united empire and a generous Son of Heaven. We are lucky in our lives these days, compared to what it was like twenty years ago." She stopped, realizing that she was being garrulous.

The nun was silent. She finally replied in a reflective way, "No, don't stop, I like to hear your opinions about the condition of our country now that it's under Tang rule. After ten years on the throne, the emperor has proved himself not only a great warrior, but also a good peacetime sovereign. He reorganized his armies by throwing out the incompetent. He reshaped the government by sending away hundreds of lazy and dishonest magistrates from the provinces—to the relief of the people there. It's no wonder that the population reveres him. He is one of the two great men of our time . . . and I should not wonder if history remembers him as one of the greatest of all."

She broke off and the women smiled and clapped again. The abbess was pleased. "Is it not time for us to have a meal? Can you go now for hot water?" she asked her novice.

The girl padded out, waking Wang, who bestirred herself to fold bedding and unpack gear. When Wang located Jao's brass basin, she started out the door, announcing, "I am getting snow to wash you."

The nun chuckled and then turned to Jao. "How are you feeling today? A little homesick perhaps?"

Jao looked at her. "Why do you think that?"

"The way you act. I understand that you are en route to the palace. I heard it outside when I was trying to buy a couple of donkeys. Mine have both died."

"What a calamity," Jao said in quick sympathy. An animal's welfare was still more important to her than a human being's. "What happened to them?"

"The wind and the cold were too much for my poor beasts. They were old and not strong. Now I shall have to wait until someone lets me have an animal or two. They say this storm is the most violent in twenty years. We shall be holed up in here for three days at least."

"Three days!" Jao wailed. "What can we do? We shall be late in getting to Changan, and my half brothers will be angry."

A twinkle appeared in the nun's eye. She had smile wrinkles, but otherwise her ivory skin was smooth and healthy. "We can play games," she suggested. "And I can teach you."

Jao looked apprehensive, and the nun laughed. "I won't be teaching you about religion until, and unless, you deserve to hear. I meant that I can teach you to play a new game. Do you know any yourself?"

"Finger games and hopscotch and jump rope."

"No jump rope in here, please. How about pachisi?"

"What's that . . . if I may ask?" Jao queried. She had decided to mind her manners before a Li.

"It is a new game from India. A friend brought me a folding board. . . . But here is your nurse with snow for your morning wash, so we will play afterward. It is a good game, just right for making the time fly."

"Thank you, then. I'd like that," Jao agreed, spluttering while her face was swabbed with snow.

Wang then served her a bowl of mixed cereal porridge, and waited until she finished before presenting her with a paper of salt and a twig for cleaning her teeth. "Your mother said that I must keep your teeth like pearls, also comb out your tangled hair and brush it ten tens every day," Wang said in a loud voice while seizing a bamboo comb and starting to unbraid and comb out, none too gently, Jao's mane of heavy hair.

"You see," she said to the nun, "what a child this one is. She is going to the palace, where she has now the rank and title of Elegant. Elegant! She does not know the first thing about elegance and won't learn!"

The abbess chuckled as she saw Jao frown. "I was infatuated at one time with the idea of being beautiful, myself," she said. The women in the cave looked at her in surprise. "I once had nice hair like yours and took delight in fashionable ways of arranging it." The silence in the room was so eloquent that the nun laughed merrily. "That was a fact . . . once."

She turned to rummage in her saddlebag, which she had been using as a pillow, and drew out a board and a silk bag of counters. "Beautifying yourself is of first importance if you want to become an elegant tsairen," she commented lightly. "Of first importance, along with your daily meditation. Now then, let us play pachisi."

Jao hitched herself closer, crossing her legs under herself as she faced the abbess who had laid out the colorfully patterned board between them. She listened carefully while the abbess explained the rules, her restlessness gone. The nun studied her as they played, interested in gauging the girl's capacities. She knew the life that was behind the girl and the life that was ahead of her, and several times she sighed softly.

The time passed rapidly as the day wore on and Jao began to gain expertise in the strategies of pachisi. Finally the older woman closed the board. "Enough," she said. "We'll have more tomorrow. Now let us stretch ourselves."

At this suggestion, Jao stood on her head, and then, because there was no room to somersault or cartwheel, went into the more controlled forms of her martial-arts routine while everyone else in the room moved hastily out of her way.

Abbess Li also stretched."We all need to warm up, especially our hands and feet, or the damp cold will penetrate in spite of this small brazier."

Matron Sun nodded vigorously. Restoring one's strength was a major Taoist precept and practice. She joined in with her own routines.

When they seated themselves again, the nun said to Jao, "Let us now talk quietly for a while," Jao was surprised at the hint of command in the nun's voice, but did as she was asked.

"What shall we talk about?" she ventured.

"You," the nun replied "and what you are going to do when you are grown and have a high position in the palace, what you are going to do in compassion for the people of this poor world."

"Me!" Jao exclaimed. "I am destined for the palace, not a nunnery!"

"And do you think that kindness should be confined to a nunnery?" the nun asked placidly.

Jao looked at her resentfully, not wanting to listen to a lecture. "When you put it that way, of course I agree with you, or rather, with my mother's teachings about Kuanyin and the accumulation of merit by kind deeds. But I am not going to make a business of it! Why do you ask?"

"Because you have inherited from your ancestors a very strong body." Jao lifted her head proudly. "But your spirit is weak," the nun added, and Jao stiffened.

"I am not an ignorant person," Jao protested. "I have been well-taught, for a girl. I can read the classics, I can do calligraphy—"

"I am not talking about your mind. One's mind can be so full of knowledge that it crowds out more important things. It often hinders one from becoming conscious of what is really going on," the nun replied, watching Jao closely. The girl's face was red with anger. "I am talking about whether you have intuitive understanding, that is, any comprehension of what lies below the surface of things."

"If you mean, do I understand a lot of things without being told, yes, I am intuitive. If you mean the Four Truths and Eight Paths, I know all that. If you mean do I know what you are lecturing me for, I don't."

At this abruptness in the young girl, the other women in the room looked up in surprise. They all knew who she was and where she was going, and they expected good manners from her.

"Jao," Wang protested warningly, and Jao murmured "Sorry . . ."

"Yes," the abbess murmured kindly.

Madame Sun picked up her well-thumbed book, the I Ching book of days. "This week deals with the last days of the year, and the *kua* for today is . . . let me see . . . 'He who possesses something great must not get too full of self-importance,' hence this *kua* of modesty. Nature fills what is empty and reduces what is full. Today's command is as follows: A difficult enterprise is made easy when it is dealt with without delay. Also it is made easier by an unassuming attitude."

Madame Sun closed the book complacently and the abbess applauded. "Very suitable for the fix that we are now in; difficult enough, but made easier by, ah, the right attitude."

Jao felt her cheeks grow hot. These old women, how dare they offer criticism? Especially of me, Wu Jao, newly invited into the Inner City! she thought to herself.

A silence fell on the room. No one smiled and the silence lengthened while one by one the women composed themselves. Even the garrulous Wang had nothing to say. She covered her mistress and curled up in her own pallet. Overcome by fatigue and poor air, the women soon drowsed off. Jao was the last. As she dwelt upon her hurt feelings, she suddenly realized how much she was being like Elder Brother, and it struck her as funny. She gave a small giggle and then she too slept.

CHAPTER TWO

The next morning Jao, bright-eyed once more, yielded meekly to Wang's ministrations, eating her porridge and drinking her barley water, while eyeing her roommates warily.

"Good morning," she said to the nun politely when the opportunity came. "Would you like to play a game of pachisi this morning?"

"This afternoon, perhaps," the nun replied good-humoredly. "I plan to spend the morning today in meditation."

"What's that . . . may I ask?" Jao asked, bent on improving her conduct.

"If you watch, you will see me become still and remote from the realities in this room, my mind disciplined to free my spirit. This is a Buddhist practice that is more familiar to me than the southern practice of worship through sermons and prayers to the deities. Meditation is northern."

Jao nodded her thanks, not wanting to hear any more, and turned to Matron Sun.

"Good morning," she said. The old lady bowed and returned to her reading.

Jao fidgeted, rocking idly on her seat, feeling isolated. Wang, busy mending a tear in a saddlebag, was uncommunicative. Jao wished that she had her dogs to play with or could go outside to ride. Two hours passed. When the nun opened her eyes, took a drink of water from her bowl and looked around the room, Jao's eyes brightened. The abbess, however, addressed herself to the old lady sitting tranquilly against the wall.

"Sister Sun," she said. "Did you sleep well?"

The old lady smiled. "Indeed yes, because of the exercises." The nun nodded. When she picked up her rosary, Jao realized that she was not preparing to play pachisi.

"Yesterday," Jao said, not wishing to be ignored, "Yesterday you mentioned that there were two great men among us, one the emperor, for whom you have such family loyalty, and another. Who?"

A twinkle appeared in the nun's eye. "I must be careful how I present new information to you because you already have strong ideas about what you will listen to and what you won't listen to."

Jao was taken aback. "I beg your forgiveness if I am difficult to teach. I don't seem to be good at exchanging thoughts or conversations the way you are."

"Exchanging thoughts as equals is not easy to do. Madame Sun and I know how because we are independent women who are in charge of many others and are responsible for them. There is no true communication unless people feel equal."

"Equal?" Jao returned, lost.

"There are four ways to control people, according to our teachings: persuasion, custom, law, force. The best is the first—but I won't go into all that now. Since you ask, let me tell you about the second great man: He died the year before I was born. This man was as different from the emperor as anyone could be, but the two share the honor of being the ones, more than any other, who unified this empire and pulled it together so that it can never fall apart in the old way again. The one conquered by arms, the other by persuasion—by harmonizing the two totally different practices of Buddhism in north and south and unifying the country by a common religion. Taitsung and Chihyi used the best and the worst ways to deal with people. One kept the peace by force and by hard laws in the name of justice and order. The other sought peace and justice by aiming for people's hearts, to induce them to change their attitudes."

"That sounds like the Taoist *kua* that Madame Sun read off yesterday," Jao replied.

"Not really. The Taoist commands are for ensuring success for oneself—they are good, of course." The nun stole a glance at the straight-backed old lady who was listening intently. "But what this man Chihyi did was to shift the attention from what one can do for oneself to what one can do for others. Between understanding and action there is this thing called attitude: If your attitude is correct, your actions will be correct, if your attitude is harmful, your act will be injurious, to yourself as well as others. Intuition is the key to forming the right attitude. . . ." Her words trailed off.

"Intuition?" Nurse Wang repeated. "What's that? Heart?" She thumped her broad chest. "The Lord Buddha will listen to someone like me, only a woman, if I pray from my heart. I am not learned enough to read sutras and I don't understand what is meant by salvation and karma and nirvana and all that, but I understand my heart well enough!"

The nun looked at her thoughtfully. "You have put your finger on the central idea in our Tientai teaching, that the heart can show you a way to salvation . . . but we might discuss that later," she added as Jao stirred impatiently.

"May we play pachisi now?" Jao asked.

Without another word the nun got out her board.

The third day in the shelter passed more rapidly than the previous two. The women were told in mid-morning that the caravan could leave sometime during the night. This raised the spirits of all except the Buddhists, who had no transport. Most of the women were tired of cramped quarters and were eager to go. Jao, leaving packing to Wang, began practicing her t'ai chi rhythms to pass the time.

"Just like a boy!" Madame Sun exclaimed with admiration. "All those smooth movements, one into another, using her body in a flow of patterns, like a bird in the wind . . . strong too . . . see her lunge!" She clapped her small hands.

This was much to Jao's liking. She preened. Perhaps the Taoist matron was not such a bore after all. She cast around in her mind for something pleasing to say and remembered the calendar.

"Is Matron Sun willing to read out the thought for today?" she asked.

"I suppose so," the matron answered in surprise. "I am sure I am happy to oblige. Let me see now, the third day before the New Year, here it is, 'There is a measure to all things. It is ignoble to pretend to be doing honest work by hiding behind the letter of the law and shirking one's responsibility.' "

"Now that is something I understand. My brothers . . . rules and regulations and no heart. Ignoble is right! That reminds me—I must ask my brothers if my baggage is safe. Wang, go out into the storage and see. There should be four lacquer trunks, six boxes, two rolls of bedding, and one bale of silks. Now, please."

"I have already counted and they are all there except . . . there has been a change."

"A change? What do you mean?" Jao asked, startled.

"Er . . . Ko tells me that the Wu masters have opened everything," Wang replied, "and done some rearranging. They left the first leather trunk with the layette and such untouched . . . except they removed the lacquer box containing the gold and silver jewelry and jade Maitreya. Elder Brother put it for safety into his own saddlebags."

Jao stared. "Are you sure?" she demanded.

"I paid Ko to watch the baggage himself, because he is the one responsible and your mother wanted him to take special care of your things. Which he was glad to do," Wang added virtuously.

Jao frowned, thinking, while the others watched her curiously. Then she shrugged. "There goes all my mother's care in keeping her gifts to me a secret. How did my honorable brothers get the locks open, since I have the keys?"

"Broke them and supplied new locks. They've had time to do it. They went through your bride's luggage behind a screen of their own. Ko saw them."

"Can you or Ko secretly remove the lacquer box from Elder Brother's bag," Jao asked, "and bring it to me?"

Appalled, Nurse Wang stole a glance at the older women's faces, but could not read their expressions. "The masters! You must yield to them. If they wish to repack your baggage, that is their right. You can't go against them," she scolded.

Jao marshaled her wits. It was vital for her to deal with this crisis correctly. She understood better than before the purpose of her mother's fussy plans over presents to give to the people she would be dealing with in the palace. Such gifts would ease her entrance into her new world. Now it appeared that the valuables would not be delivered to the palace, and she suddenly realized how much she would need her resources.

"Wang, good soul, listen to me. There is a misunderstanding on the part of the Elder Brothers. This lacquer box was left to me by my father, and it was intended to come into my hands when I left home. My mother transferred it to me as the dowry that every girl has to have. I must have it. But if my brothers decide to take my lacquer trunks, well, let them go. The clothes were intended for my use in the palace, but I have money and I could get more, somehow. See, here are my keys."

Jao opened her purse and displayed her keys while everyone in the room watched avidly. Her possession of the keys convinced everyone in the room that Jao alone was entitled to her baggage.

Jao spoke to Wang, "You are the only one who can get justice for me. I can only receive my father's legacy if that lacquer box is restored to me. Secretly. Elder Brothers did not intend for me to know what they have done, and so they will not undo the wrong by themselves."

"Difficult . . . and dangerous . . . impossible," Nurse Wang said immediately. Then she noticed that Madame Sun was shaking her head and that the abbess was looking like a thundercloud. The silence in the room lengthened. It seems they are both on Jao's side, Wang thought, much perturbed.

"It would cost you," she began in a different tone of voice.

"Find out how much," Jao interrupted.

"Too much," Wang returned. "And now you don't have the money to pay." At this, both the abbess and the matron looked up sharply.

"I have some silver in my saddlebag that you don't know about. Find out how much Ko wants," Jao ordered stiffly.

Wang stood her ground, however; she did not want to believe the worst. "The masters surely know more about what is to be done than a thirteen-year-old," she muttered, but noticed that every one of the listening women seemed to be sympathetic to Jao, as Wang was herself when all was said.

"I'll speak to Ko," Wang said huffily, and left the room.

After she had gone, Jao, embarrassed about having exposed her family affairs, cast about for something to divert attention. She dug into her saddlebag for a packet of tea. "As soon as Wang can get us some hot water, we might refresh ourselves with this Dragon tea," she said invitingly.

The atmosphere in the room brightened at once. Everyone wanted a sip of the novel drink.

"This new drink of tea—it comes from India, doesn't it?—it refreshes the whole person," the abbess said. "It warms the body and awakes the spirit. We've been using it in our religious activities. It is a gift from heaven."

"I'll send my servant for hot water," Matron Sun suggested. "We need not wait for Wang."

Pleased that her tactic had worked, Jao nodded in agreement. As the matron's servant was leaving, Wang returned.

"Ko has agreed . . . five pieces of silver. Now Elder Brother wants to see you," Wang recited.

Jao stood up in alarm. "Does he know? About . . . ?" Wang shook her head, and Jao said, "I'll go at once—but do you know what he wants?"

"The master wants you to receive instructions. Now."

"What instructions? What about?"

"Don't argue, just obey," Wang responded mechanically.

Jao rearranged her clothes, donned her kerchief, and feeling alarmed and uncertain, went into the next chamber, where she found her brothers playing chess. "I am here," she said, standing at attention.

After some time Elder Brother spoke, without looking up. "We leave tonight. Hour of the dog. Be ready. You will be riding in a light sledge."

Jao absorbed this news. "Then there is room in the sledge for another, so may I invite the Reverend Abbess Li of the imperial family to ride with me? She has lost her donkeys and is stranded."

"No," Elder Brother said.

"She is Abbess of Kanyeh Convent. If she can ride with me in the sledge, why not take her?"

"No!" Yuanshuang roared.

But this time Younger Brother Yuanching looked shocked. "But an abbess, member of the imperial family? It is a chance to get favor," he protested.

"I have said no. We do not need to curry favor with an obscure relative, a female, now that our family has been recognized by the emperor himself. No."

Jao remained at attention, studying Elder Brother, but he ignored her. Younger Brother stirred uneasily.

"Am I dismissed?" she asked. Elder Brother waved her away impatiently, and she left.

Back in the inner room, she found a chattering group watching with eagerness while the hot water was being poured over the tea leaves.

"Reverend Mother," she said to the nun, "please have your saddlebags ready at the hour of the dog tonight. We are leaving then, and you are invited to come with us, riding with me in a sledge. Your assistant can ride with Wang and the baggage in another."

The abbess looked up in surprised relief and put her palms together in a gesture of gratitude.

"How fortunate! How good! Now I can be with my sister nuns for the midnight mass on New Year's Eve. It is an occasion that I cherish, an important ceremony for our whole convent. Last night I made special prayers to Maitreya to come to my assistance at this time. Maitreya helps travelers, and I have been granted my prayer!"

"Maitreya is the best of them all," Jao replied, then with diffidence, "don't you think?"

The abbess nodded approvingly and lay down to rest before leaving. The other women did likewise. Some of the candles flickered and went out. The coals in the brazier burned low, and soon there was nothing to be heard in the third cave but gentle snores.

Ko shouted loudly through the curtain. Nurse Wang raised her head and returned the shout. She grunted and rose. "Time to go!" she cried, and busied herself tying up the rugs. The other women gathered their belongings and, wrapped to the eyes in cloaks, filed out, through the darkened stables and into the darker night, gasping at the first breath of the bitter air. The ground about them was white with snow, and the black sky above sparkled with myriad stars. No fog, no wind. Clear. They were exhilarated.

Ko was waiting to hustle them into the sledges. He tucked Jao and the abbess into the first one, and handed Jao a package while drawing the cover over their heads. She gave a muffled shriek of joy and thrust the package into the saddlebag at her feet.

"He did it! He did it!" she cried exultantly, and snuggled deeper into her seat while listening intently for sounds that might indicate the approach of her brothers. She heard their distant voices, heard the crack of whips and some shouting. Then the sledge bumped forward and she hugged herself in glee while the caravan got under way. The abbess observed all this in silence. This beautiful, reckless child, how she attracted people. She would not forget the girl's helpfulness.

There seemed to be no road, just a way over the river ice. The sledges bounced along, tilting against the ridges, bumping over hummocks and occasionally capsizing. When the sledge containing Wang and the novice turned over, their screams stopped the caravan for the brief time that it took the drivers to right it and toss the women back into place.

Jao held her breath when Elder Brother rode past to investigate, but the caravan was already on its way again by the time he reached the place of the accident, so the secret of the nun's presence was kept. The sledges bucketed along for a long time after that without incident.

"Are you asleep?" Jao asked.

"Not really," the nun replied drowsily.

"I just love travel! Exploring and new places. This is my first long trip," Jao confided.

"Mmm. Where you are going, there won't be much travel, you know," the abbess said. "There will be lovely gardens, however, and a lot of beauty around you in the palaces, and birds singing everywhere. There will be peace of a kind. I, on the other hand, instead of being immured as I would like, must travel constantly to visit the nunneries under my supervision, many in the south, far away."

"In the far south? In the mountains of the aborigines?" Jao asked, excitedly latching on to the nun's casual remark. "The most mysterious place in the world! I have heard that the emperor sends his most experienced archers and the toughest mountaineers there to subdue the Miaos and the Yaos and the rest who raid Chinese villages. Do you have nunneries in those mountains?"

The abbess laughed. "Hardly. Even in the frontier villages there are no nuns. The aborigines kidnap Chinese women and they are never seen again. A nun would not be exempt."

"The way of the White Monkey," Jao said sagely.

"What's that?" the nun asked, giving up on her nap.

"Don't you know? Everyone has heard about him, even as far north as Taiyuan. He lives in a secret plateau hidden behind a waterfall, and carries off girls from the villages. About six feet tall, long arms, very strong, white hair all over."

"Oh, he's a man, then."

"Yes, a white one, and he trades with the villagers—salt for furs and knives. He's honest, but if anyone cheats him, he'll be found the next day with an arrow in his back. The villagers like the white monkey anyway, they say, even if they lose a spare female once in a while."

"Some monkey," the abbess breathed.

"The monkey is really a man, like I said. Aren't you listening? You are not hearing me because your mind is full of something else."

In the dark Jao could not see the nun's expression. She was smiling. "Yes," she said meekly.

The caravan came to a halt. After a long wait it moved ahead again and came to another halt. "Stop for watering the animals and feeding. Everyone descend," Ko yelled. He lifted the canvas from Jao's sledge and conducted her and the abbess to a back courtyard, where they found Madame Sun presiding over a brazier with a pot of freshly cooked millet porridge simmering on it. "Come, eat while you can," she invited.

Wang was the last to come in. She busied herself unrolling bedding and noisily spooning up her porridge. Jao noticed her nurse's activities while settling herself on her pallet to watch the shadows dancing on the walls. "Wang, go to bed," she said drowsily, and then saw the tears streaming down her nurse's cheeks.

"What's wrong?" she asked at once.

The nurse squatted by her pallet. "Ko has received orders to split the caravan as soon as we are inside the city gate tomorrow. You and Elder Brother will go directly to the palace, and the rest of us will go to his home, with all the baggage."

"That can't be true. You are my maid and must come with me. You promised my mother to stay with me for life."

"I am ordered to go to Elder Brother's family. He has six or seven children and he needs a good nurse. I explained about my promise, and he said that Lady Yang had no authority to arrange any such thing. 'I make the decisions in this family. You will do what I tell you,' he said. I don't know what is to happen to me. . . . I wish that I had never been born!" Wang wailed, so near hysteria that Madame Sun and the abbess got out of their bedrolls to help calm her.

Jao pulled out a small purse of silver from her waistband and tucked it into Wang's coat. "There," she said. "You will have to go with Elder Brother for the present, but you will still remain loyal to me, I hope."

"How can you doubt it! Why do you ask? I shall remain devoted to you until my hair is white! And if this is your money, I won't take it," Wang stammered, wiping away her tears with the back of her hand.

"Yes, you will, my treasure. If you are loyal, you will do what I ask and go patiently to Elder Brother's home. When I am established and promoted, I shall send for you."

Wang, much struck by this morsel of comfort, ceased crying. "I won't take your money . . . I have a little of my own."

Jao pushed the purse farther into the old lady's pocket. "My mother would insist, and so do I. Take it and hide it."

Wang dried her face with her sash. "I'll sleep with it inside my clothes, and in the daytime I'll tie it over my belly," she declared fiercely. Somewhat reconciled to her fate, she pulled her bedding around herself and fell asleep before any of the others.

"Well done," the abbess whispered, and Jao, hearing her, felt a small glow of satisfaction and pride, which slightly diminished her heartache at losing her nurse. Exhausted, she dozed off at once.

Ko wasted no time the next morning in getting his caravan mobilized for their last day on the road. He was handing Jao and the abbess into the sledge when the Wu brothers loomed up out of the darkness.

"Who is that?" Elder Brother demanded, pointing at the abbess with his whip.

"Reverend Lady, may I introduce a member of my family, Wu Yuanshuang," Jao said quickly. "Elder brother, this honorable—"

Elder Brother interrupted. "I forbade you to bring her."

"We are now at Changan and this good lady will leave us soon. She will be on time for the convent's New Year's rituals, which are very important to her."

Elder Brother's face grew red. "How dare you defy me? You, a girl, second daughter of a second wife! Worthless female that you are! You need a lesson that you won't forget." He pulled her out of her seat and slapped her face so hard on both cheeks that she fell against the sledge and would have fallen had Ko not caught her.

"Sir," Ko said urgently. "We must leave at once if we are to get into the city before the gates close!"

Elder Brother looked irresolute, and Jao seized her chance to stuff herself down into the sledge while Ko hastily tied the cover over the top. He then nudged the Wu brothers onto their mounts and gave the signal for the caravan to move.

In the darkness under the cover, Jao held her cold hands against her fiery cheeks until, realizing that the caravan was actually on its way, she let her breath out in a long sigh. Humiliated, she turned to the abbess. "I hope that you are not embarrassed because of what I did about giving you this uncomfortable ride."

Alarmed at the sound of choking coming from her guest, Jao put her hand on the nun's. The choking sounds became gurgles and then peals of laughter. At first in relieved giggles, and then more loudly, Jao joined in. If Ko heard the sounds of hilarity coming from under the canvas, he took no notice.

"Well done, little one!" the abbess exclaimed when she caught her breath. "I am truly obliged to you. I would still be sitting in that damp cave if you had not rescued me, and for that I am grateful. Now I will rub your face with a cactus lotion that I have in my bag, and the marks on your face will disappear by the time you get to the palace."

"*Wanfu!*" Jao murmured while the nun, carefully and methodically, rubbed the medication on her cheeks.

Soothed, Jao fell asleep and did not wake until Ko pulled the cover off the sledge at daylight. "We are on the last leg of our trek, and you no longer need to be covered," Ko said with a flourish. They had crested a small rise, and there below them lay the great city. The river Wei, a ribbon of ice along which they had been traveling, curved in a silver thread through the valley and up to the city walls, where it disappeared through a water gate. The sky, pearly with dawn, lit the earth, revealing its farmlands in their winter colors of grays and blacks. The sun, an orange ball above the horizon, colored the distant towers of Changan a luminous pink, and outlined the lacy treetops of the imperial park in gold. Guards pacing the battlements appeared as moving specks in the motionless landscape. And faintly heard in the windless air, came the sounds of distant temple bells. Jao caught her breath in excitement.

"We must move," Ko cried after the short pause. The caravan started up again for the city. Other travelers began to overtake them. Turks with fur caps, leather trousers, and felt boots rode by, and Uighurs from beyond the Tienshan, the mountains to the west.

"We can tell who the Uighurs are by their Manichean headgear—those tall stiff hats," the abbess said. "And this group of horsemen coming up behind are Tokharians from the oasis country."

"What elegant mustaches!" Jao whispered, her voice low because the riders were within hearing distance. "And what beautiful horses they ride, western horses . . ."

"They are probably from Kucha. See how their musical instruments are wrapped so carefully. Greatest musicians in the world, those Kucheans."

Jao gazed curiously. "Their dress is different, their coats are tight-fitted and not flowing like ours, their swords are longer than most."

"They may be heading for the palace to take part in the New Year's festivities," the abbess offered as the group clattered past. "I hope that you will be able to hear them if that is the case—one of the benefits of palace life."

The traffic thickened as they approached the city, but Ko skillfully guided them through it, taking them rapidly past the execution grounds with its display of decapitated heads, only slowing when they entered the north-gate tunnel. Men and animals inside the gate were packed closely together in a crush of bodies, farm carts, and loaded animals. A camel nuzzled Jao's neck, and she had to push away his wet snout repeatedly while the abbess pressed against her other side to avoid the protruding branches of a load of firewood. They were still inside the tunnel when a bedlam of sound reverberating from the tunnel walls assaulted their ears.

"The West Market is opening," the abbess said laconically. "Three hundred drumbeats at midday and thousands of stalls inside open, ready for business."

The sledge emerged into pale sunshine, and Jao looked delightedly about her. She stared at the lanes of open-air cubicles with their gaudy banners floating above the displays. "Look, pheasants already dressed . . . and the cake makers . . . and potters . . . and silk sellers!" she pointed out, craning her neck. "Anything anyone could want from everywhere!" The abbess smiled and nodded, feeling invigorated at being back once more in her dynamic home city.

"This city," she told Jao in her learned way, "is the largest in the world. Here we have a million people inside the walls and a million outside. Changan has been a capital for many dynasties and has often been rebuilt. Right now it covers about thirty square miles, all surrounded by enormous walls. The palace city, over there, behind those high walls, is a mile square."

"How can a person find any single place in all this vastness?" Jao asked in a faint voice. "Ko, for instance, how does he know where to go?"

"The city is built on a grid." the nun replied. "It's marked off in square wards, dozens of them, all walled and locked at night. Twelve city gates, sunset curfews, and guards. People can sleep in safety," she said complacently.

Jao was speechless with wonder as she absorbed the sights, the movement of traffic, the cacophony of sounds, and the kaleidoscope of colors in the holiday crowds. Inside the high walls of the wards were lower ones around private compounds. Gates opened into the compounds, affording Jao glimpses of the homes and gardens. The wealthier residents whitewashed their walls and displayed elaborate tiled gates, but the poorer sections had patches of fallen plaster and unroofed gates. Cheerful crowds pushed and squeezed their way through the lanes to the main streets, which were all lined with canvas-covered stalls filled with eye-catching displays for the holidays.

Although the city contained mostly one-storied buildings, each ward also had monumental structures that rose high above the walls: slender pagodas, tile-roofed temples, and detached palaces. Their straight lines were in striking contrast to the freely curving shapes of trees, mostly firs and willows, which also towered over the ubiquitous walls. Above was the cloudless blue sky, vast and overarching. Jao was silent, moved with excitement beyond words.

Ko drew his caravan close to the palace wall, halted and separated the sledge from the main caravan, sending most of it, including three of Jao's trunks, amid loud cries of farewell, into a quiet lane in one of the western wards. Jao waved sadly as Nurse Wang's tearful face disappeared around the corner. Ko then started with Jao's sledge along the southern wall of the palace en route to the eastern gate where she was to be delivered.

They struggled through the crowds in front of the palace's largest gate, the Chuchiu-men with its five double doors and its southern exposure. Villagers from miles around were thronging the plaza or congregating along the boulevard which ran arrow-straight for five miles. Vendors of food and toys were erecting temporary stalls along both sides of the boulevard which, five hundred yards wide, easily accommodated the men, animals, and goods flooding into it.

"What is that?" Jao asked, pointing at a great tower looming above the palace walls.

"That is the Lingnan Tower honoring the twenty-four generals who helped establish the Tang dynasty twenty years ago. Some of these generals are still serving in the palace. You will doubtless see all of them at one time or another. It is one of the few new buildings within the palace grounds. Everything else has been constructed out of lumber from torn-down Sui halls. You will doubtless live in a renovated old hall. The emperor is a frugal man who does not want to put more levies on the people, who suffered so much during the wars. He even rejects luxuries that are gifts from abroad if he can see no use for them."

"Mmm," Jao responded, unenthusiastic. She counted the twenty-four colorful war flags flapping in the breeze at the top of the tower. Whether a building was constructed out of new lumber or used lumber was all one to her.

Ko made poor time through the plaza. Jao and the abbess now wore shawls over their heads because the crowds were close and curious. Strings of camels and small donkeys with large loads jostled them. Covered chairs with female passengers pushed them aside while their runners shouted "Make way for the great lady." Open carriages were driven heedlessly through the throng, causing people on foot to jump hastily out of the way. When Ko at last turned north to follow the wall on its east side, they were in a quieter area, rid of the crush. Large establishments lined the way, one of them the Pinggang Quarter, where most gates were open to show garden vistas. Only guards and delivery men were about, as the courtesans within the mansions slept in the daytime.

"I will be leaving you soon. My convent is not far ahead," the abbess said quietly, gathering up her belongings. "It has been a good trip, and both of us have been blessed by good fortune. You have gotten your lacquer box back, and I have gotten a ride to Changan. You are entering the palace at a lucky time, when everyone is in a festive mood and busy with holiday preparations. You should be able to slip into palace life almost unnoticed. It will give you time to get your bearings."

Jao nodded thoughtfully. "Will you come to visit in the palace soon? I think that I would like to have what my mama calls a 'lay connection' with your convent. Perhaps you could administer the Bodhisattva Precepts to me."

"I cannot administer the precepts and you cannot receive them, because we are female," the abbess responded shortly. "One day it may be possible for women to share fully in the Buddhist way of salvation. The Lotus Sutra of the Good Law indicates quite clearly that women are as entitled to salvation as men, and that is one reason why I live by this sutra. The Buddhist Way should work as well for a woman as for a man."

"I have been taught to believe that the Four Holy Truths were for all beings," Jao responded. "Why should truth be only for men?" She was in an unusually serious mood for one of her happy nature.

"Justice for all alike has not been the aim of Buddhist practice in the past. The aim has been individual salvation for the few who can persist in following the Way."

"W-e-ll, as for that, I am not going into a convent and I am going into a palace, so I aim to be happy—wherever I am—and enjoy all the good things there are!" Jao declared roundly.

The nun received this in silence. She herself had little belief in the possibility of happiness in an unhappy world. She said finally, "You can live in reasonable happiness if you keep free inwardly. If you can accept the world for what it is and can accept the fact that worldly values can only lead to disillusionment, all might go well with you. If you accept this reality, half your battle with life will be won."

Jao stirred restlessly, and the nun felt contrite. "I am drowning you with my advice, but I do it while I have the chance. There will be times when disaster strikes you, making you feel lost and alone. Then it will be a comfort to you to remember that the world is a dusty place at best, evil, and everywhere evil is the outcome. There is hope, though, in spite of the seeming hopelessness of the Wheel of Life. Suffering is not the whole of reality. There is something more, another dimension, though no human being can tell what it is because it is beyond human experience. We call it nirvana. Living means suffering, yes, and it is like a fire which consumes. Nirvana is when the fire is put out, not necessarily by death. But all this must seem bleak to you."

"Not really," Jao said sturdily. "I am listening, and I am grateful to you for trying to help me. But I don't take anything very seriously, or so I am told."

The abbess smiled but said nothing, and the two rode on a little farther in silent companionship, the nun and the radiant thirteen-year-old.

"Here!" the abbess cried. Ko stopped the sledge and then climbed down to help her dismount. As he handed the nun her gear, she gave him a small packet wrapped in red, which he received with a grin and a bob of thanks. Then he whistled for one of the ubiquitous small boys who frequented the streets in Changan to carry the nun's luggage to the convent's side door. Jao waved when the abbess turned at the door with her palms together in the *anjali* salute of farewell.

After a short ride, Ko drew up before the towering Chunming gate. Iron-studded and barred, the twin leaves of the doors were forbiddingly closed. A small side door was open, however, which Ko knocked upon with the butt of his whip. A gateman appeared at once, and Ko explained his errand. This servant, with a curious look at Jao, called a guard, who motioned for Yuanshuang and Jao to enter. Hesitantly, Elder Brother dismounted. The admittance was too casual to suit him, but he was in a hurry. Haughtily, he stepped over the high threshold with Jao close behind, clutching her saddlebag with its precious lacquer box inside. She bid a warm good-bye to Ko while handing him another packet of thank-you money, and then, with a scared look, turned and entered the Gate of No Return.

The Wus were ushered into a bare courtyard occupied only by guards standing over a fire. They eyed Jao, wondering whether she was a servant or a delivery girl. Her proud bearing, however, confused them. The guard stopped before a gate opening into an inside court and asked for credentials. Yuanshuang got out a large red card and proffered it, demanding that they be escorted to the chief eunuch without delay.

"Wu Yuanshuang, Chief Clerk Chancellory, Grade Eight–Lower," the guard read.

"What are you waiting for?" Yuanshuang asked, irritated. Slowly, the guard became aware that there would be no tip, so, shrugging, he opened the gate into a busy court lined with offices and filled with clerks hurrying across the icy yard. Even more slowly he ushered the guests into a waiting room where there were a few stools and a brazier of coals.

"Wait here," he said, banging the door as he went out. Elder Brother walked to the heater and warmed his hands, while Jao stayed where she was near the door.

"Come here," Elder Brother ordered. "I have something to say to you that I do not want overheard. Palace walls have ears."

Jao stayed where she was. "I'm listening," she said.

"Do as I say and come here," he ordered angrily, forgetting that once inside the palace grounds, Jao was no longer his to command. She, however, was very much aware of her new status.

"I have been told that I shall have to be standing at attention much of my time when I am an attendant," she said, "so I shall begin standing at attention now."

"Stand then, curse you, you hateful child. Now then, you must never forget the fact that your first duty is always to your family. You are our agent here, miserable female though you are. Never forget that. You must behave well and obey the authorities, especially the emperor, so that when you see him, you can speak to him on our behalf. I will let you know what you are to ask for."

"I thought that my first duty was to the Son of Heaven, not to you," Jao replied argumentatively while looking down at her wet boots.

Elder Brother surveyed her with exasperation. "You sound like a Buddhist . . . bow to the Buddha first and to your parents second. It is not up to you to question, it is up to you to obey your family first. But you don't say so in public, you stupid female. Of course you have to act as if your duty is to the emperor, that is only polite behavior. In this regard I fear also that you are lacking. I imagine that you will not behave and will bring disgrace upon us."

"Why did you put me in the palace, then?" Jao asked.

"I didn't," he said incautiously. "It was your mother."

"She said it was you," Jao answered.

"When the palace showed interest in you, we had to comply or be in trouble, since both Yuanching and I are in service here. But all that is done with. Now that you are here, you cannot behave as you did at home, arguing with everyone and disobeying your elders. Here you will be punished if you do. You will find your back striped with fifty lashes before you can wink if you offend your superiors with your impudence. You not only have to obey, but show willingness to obey!"

"I have heard all this before, but not from you. *You* have not bothered with me at all," Jao said.

"Well, I'm bothering now. I quote from the sacred Shih Ching: 'For disorder does not come from heaven but is brought about by women. Among those who cannot be trained or taught are women and eunuchs.' Even though you cannot be taught, you can obey because you fear punishment, which could be severe. You could have your hands cut off, or be killed and have your body thrown on the refuse heap."

Shaken by his vehemence but unwilling to believe that such things could happen to the innocent, Jao paled but said nothing. Elder Brother then lapsed into an uncomfortable silence which continued until the door opened and a young man in a black silk tunic and cap of office entered, the red card in his hand. He was tall and well-built, with a soldier's bearing and a handsome face. He bowed.

"I am Yang Chifan of the Inner Palace Management Bureau, in charge of the tsairen—the Elegants. I must tell you that it is inconvenient to admit this young lady so late today."

"We were ordered to get her here for the emperor's special events at New Year's time, and so at great expense and inconvenience to the family, we have obeyed," Yuanshuang protested. "First we are ordered to bring her when her moon flow began, and then when—"

"Yes, yes," Chi interrupted. "Never mind all that—but if you leave her today, she will not be well taken care of. All the servants are busy. You may leave her if you understand this. Where are her maid and baggage?"

"We were told that the palace supplies all needs including servants," Yuanshuang replied loftily. He had no intention of giving up such a good nurse as Wang or such treasure as Lady Yang had put into Jao's trunks. "As for baggage, I have had it all taken to my home to be delivered later. At my discretion."

"Indeed," Chi interrupted. "You cannot be serious. Did you expect to leave your sister here on New Year's Eve without a maid and with only the clothes she stands in!"

Elder Brother perceived that his own face was involved, and so paused to gather his wits. "She may have one trunk . . . I'll send it in," he said arrogantly. He had nothing but contempt for eunuchs.

"Better to take her away, if you please, and bring her back when you are ready," Chi returned as he started for the door. At this, Elder Brother flushed and moved to block the way. Chi shrugged and started again for the door, but still Elder Brother stood politely and obstinately in his way.

"Your family is troublesome. You are certainly not making the girl welcome here," Chi said in exasperation. Jao gasped with shock, and this made the eunuch look at her for the first time. And reconsider.

"She will find it hard to live here without a maid," Chi temporized when he saw Jao looking at him appealingly. "If you pay ten silver pieces for a palace slave, we will find one for her." He was conciliatory, but Yuanshuang was not responsive. He always acted according to formula. When confronted with money matters, his formula was to oppose any first offer and seem affronted.

"You are rude and unmannerly. I am an official and you only a eunuch, servant to women, at that, and here you are trying to get money out of me. For yourself no doubt. Intolerable." He glanced at the eunuch slyly while deciding what to say next.

Chi's face was red with anger. His castration has been the result of a war wound, and his position of trust at the palace was a reward for his services to the emperor in war. Proud, he had little use for bargaining.

"Take it or leave it," he said.

Yuanshuang recognized the tone, realized that his line of attack wouldn't work, and began fumbling in his clothes for a coin purse. He counted out, slowly and insolently, ten pieces of silver. Barely restraining himself, Chi accepted the money only because of the anguish in Jao's eyes. Then without another word, Elder Brother bowed and made for the exit.

"Send her trunks," Chi ordered to his retreating back.

Humiliated and downcast, Jao stood with hanging head, clutching her bag and watching the melting snow form a puddle around her feet. When she was bidden to follow Chi, she did so awkwardly, limping from a leg numb from long sitting. The eunuch led her through gates and courtyards busy with servants preparing for the holidays, their own as well as their masters'. Jao followed in silence through a park and into a maze of alleys lined by patched brick walls until they reached a red lacquer gate in the northern section. Chi pushed one leaf of the gate open and called loudly. A woman guard materialized at once.

"Here is the last of the tsairen. Put her in the room of Wildgoose, and put Wildgoose in with Toto for tonight until I can find a place for her," he ordered. "The maid and her trunks will come later. Tonight is bath night, so see that this one is washed and ready to be presented to Chief Eunuch Kao at the sunset drum. Understand?" He raised his voice as if she were deaf.

The woman looked down from her six and a half feet to his five and a half feet and said in an expressionless voice, "Ket understand."

She then gestured for Jao to enter. Jao obeyed but stumbled as she lifted her numb leg over the high threshold. Chi looked at his new tsairen sharply, expecting an hysterical outbreak at such a bad omen occurring at her entrance to her new home.

"My foot went to sleep in the sledge," she explained matter-of-factly, casting a shy look upward.

"Run around the courtyard five times and you will be fine." He answered out of his soldier's experience, and then thought that it was possible that she was unlike her brother, possible that she would not be a trouble to him after all. He then hurried off, harassed by his duties, harassed by the girls and their troubles, and bitter about every aspect of life in the city of women.

Jao called to his retreating back, "Thank you, I'll do that," but he did not hear. Then she met Ket's look and they both grinned. "I just need to . . . hop around a bit," she said as she hurried after the woman.

Concentrating on the tingling of circulation returning to her leg, she was not watching where she was going, and so bumped into Ket when she stopped at a back door.

"Excuse me," Jao said, panting. Her head was at about the level of the woman's armpit. She looked up into the broad, flat face and smiled. "I am Jao," she added, pointing to herself.

"Me, Ket," the woman answered, her blank eyes lighting up for an instant. She was a muscular woman dressed in a leather tunic, with leather pants strapped into heavy felt boots. Her grizzled hair hung in a braid down her back and was held in place on top by an embroidered cap. One breast bulged roundly under her tunic, while the other side was flat. She noticed Jao's puzzled glance at her chest and put her chapped hand on the flattened spot. "Cut off one side, Sarmation custom for shooting with bow and arrow. Long time past, tribal lands far away, but women guards continue when serving in many harems, many countries."

Jao stared, fascinated, and then looked up into the rough features and smiled. "Is it hard work being a guard in the emperor's service?" she asked, intrigued.

"Sometimes," was Ket's laconic answer. "You come now, we find room." She opened a gate leading into the back court, and they entered a paved yard with a row of outhouses, bathhouses, and washing facilities lining the walls. A gate in the back led into another court, where the servants were housed. A two-panel door in the front led into the main house. Ket herded Jao through this door and into a small hall. Then, lifting a curtain, she let her into the *kang* room. Long, narrow, and warm, it was lit by small windows that had been covered for winter with translucent paper imported from Korea, a luxury few could afford. The only furniture was a heated *kang* which ran along one wall. It was covered with fine mats and was long enough for all the girls to sleep on it comfortably. In spite of its stark looks, the light and warmth made the *kang* room the most inviting chamber in the tsairen quarters.

"You last tsairen, you sleep at cold end," she stated.

Jao walked down the length of the *kang* and laid her bag at the place indicated, kicked off her wet boots and doffed her damp cloak. The *kang* was warm even at her end, so she climbed up on it and arranged herself cross-legged to wait for what would come next. The warmth felt good.

Ket watched in silence. She frowned and then disappeared, to return almost immediately with a bundle in hand. "Bedding of dead tsairen," she said, tossing the bundle to Jao, who caught it as it unrolled. It was a fur in good condition, so Jao smiled and hugged the soft fur around herself to show appreciation. Ket's face split in a grin. Then she proceeded to strip off the rest of Jao's damp clothing and to wrap her in the fur.

"Come with Ket," she grunted, scooping up all the clothing that Jao had worn day and night for ten days. She then hustled Jao into the cold yard and, crossing it rapidly, propelled her into the bathhouse, a small room filled with steam from water heating in several large iron caldrons. Ket seized a pitcher, poured hot water into a bowl, and with a moss sponge soaped, scrubbed, and sluiced her charge until the girl was gasping and lobster-red. Then Ket washed Jao's hair, clapped the rug around her body and hustled her back into the *kang* room. It was all over in ten minutes. Jao felt aglow, clean and warm, but naked, her clothes abandoned on the floor of the bathhouse. She looked questioningly at Ket, whose face split again into a grin.

"Beat 'em to it," Ket growled with immense satisfaction when the sounds of other tsairen and other maids on their way to the bathhouse reached her ears. They were setting up a priority list for the bath.

"Beat 'em to it!" Ket repeated in her guttural voice. "No maid for Jao, so Ket do it plenty good. Now find clothes." She disappeared, and was gone longer this time, while Jao huddled in her fur. None of the other girls had yet entered the *kang* room when Ket returned. She slapped down a quilted silk suit.

"Dead tsairen's clothes?" Jao asked apprehensively. Ket shook her head.

"No, this from tsairen who has hundred suits, never miss one. You dress, all right. Guard deliver Jao one trunk. Here now, but only baby clothes and shoes."

"Oh!" Jao exclaimed, appalled. "My brother has sent the wrong box! I don't have any clothes at all!"

Ket regarded her in silence, her heavy face expressionless. Then she said, "No worry, come!" She pulled off the fur rug and slid Jao off her perch.

"Po po, I can't wear someone else's clothes," Jao began as Ket shoved her legs one after the other into white silk underpants. "From some girl's wardrobe, I don't know whose," she continued helplessly as the big woman thrust her into the elegant ruby-red suit. It flattered Jao with its long, pleated skirt and small, fitted jacket. Ket braided Jao's hair and stood back to admire her handiwork, then picked up Jao's bag.

"Ket show you room of Wildgoose now. Leave fur rug on seat here in *kang* room. Jao look good now for go see chief eunuch. Come."

Lifting the leather curtain, she ushered her charge into the covered hall that ran the length of the building and around the four sides of the square courtyard. Bare trees, their trunks wrapped in straw, thrust lacy branches above the rooftops, and a goldfish pond, iced over, lay under a rug of snow. Ten rooms opened into the corridors that bordered the court, four on each side, a reception room across the front and the *kang* room across the back.

"Eight rooms for nine tsairen, where am I to go?" Jao asked, but Ket only shook her head. "Wait see what Master Chi do." She left without another word.

Jao looked around her. The room seemed larger as soon as Ket was out of it, more her own. There was little furniture, a straw-filled mattress on a wooden frame, and a couple of stools. A fresh coat of whitewash brightened the brick walls, and a window over the bed covered by translucent paper let in light from the reddening sky, filling the room with a sense of space. Welcoming, Jao thought while dumping the contents of her saddlebag on the bed.

Conspicuous among the items was the lacquer box. Jao pounced on it with glee, unwrapped and unlocked it. She lifted the little Maitreya from its bed on top of a layer of red envelopes, and then found all the jewelry intact beneath. Opening one of the envelopes, she found a gold piece. "For me to give away as New Year's gifts and spend on a few clothes if I don't like what is given me," she exclaimed in relief. Her mother's idea was good, especially at New Year's, but she hoped to make friends without gifts.

Chapter Three

Jao was coiling her hair into a knot on top of her head, hoping to make herself look older, when she felt someone watching her. Turning, she saw a pair of brown eyes peeping at her from the doorway.

"I'm Mulberry," Brown Eyes said, stepping into the room. "I'm a tsairen. You must be the newest girl . . . or are you a maid for Jade?"

"I'm not a maid for Jade, whoever she is. I'm a tsairen too . . . Wu Jao," Jao responded, happy to be making contact with her first house-mate.

Mulberry smiled. "I heard you come in. Where are you from?"

"From Taiyuan," Jao said. "I'm Number Two Daughter of the Wu family."

"A northern family!" Mulberry said, with a slight change of tone. "I'm from the south . . . from the far, far south. . . . Wait a moment! Only an hour here and already bathed—a miracle!"

"Wh-What?" Jao said, feeling uncomfortable because she was wearing clothes from some unknown wardrobe.

"It is a big event here to get a hot bath," Mulberry replied, not noticing Jao's embarrassment. "And here you are, already through. Me, I'd wait rather than have a row with the Three."

"Oh," Jao answered politely, wondering who the Three might be. "Why do you have to wait for anyone . . . if you don't want to?"

"Everyone waits for the Three to do everything first. You'll find out soon enough. But you don't know who they are yet, do you? First there is Jade. She's a Tsui from the most aristocratic and exclusive family in the country. Then there is Phoenix, a Lu from another antique family. And Peony, a Li from Lolang. Since these families are 'pure Chinese,' they look down upon even imperial families of 'mixed blood,' Tartar and Chinese."

"Which I am myself," Jao interjected with spirit as she at last caught on to what the conversation was about. Mulberry looked interested. "If you are from Taiyuan, you are from Tang country . . . merit mark for you! Pearl and I are from the south, demerits for us! Our families don't seem to count for much here, even though Pearl is from a wealthy clan, the Chens from Yangchow on the Yangtze River. You can see from her clothes that she is well off, and as for me, I am from the rice and silk country far south of the Yangtze, a Hsin from Hangchow on the West Lake."

Mulberry paused to see if Jao had heard of the Hsins or even of Hangchow, but Jao's expression showed that she had not. Mulberry sighed and tossed her heavy black hair over her shoulder. Restless, she poised on the edge of the bed. Like a sparrow, Jao thought, with inquisitive sparrow eyes.

"Couldn't expect you to, I suppose," Mulberry said wistfully. "I just hoped I could talk to you about home . . . but no matter, we'll talk about the palace and the tsairen. The Three. Their families all live here in the capital and give them whatever they want when they want it. All the great landowners live here, although their lands are downriver on the rich plains. It seems strange to me that they don't live on their estates instead of on this windy, dusty plateau. Why should anyone live here when there are warm, leafy, lovely places like Hangchow?"

She shuddered and a lost look came into her eyes. "I hate this place. I hate the wind that is always howling around the house, rattling and banging the shutters . . . what was I talking about? Oh, the Three, nothing more to say, I have said it all, only . . . Jade is bossy, Phoenix shows off, and Peony can't talk about anything but clouds and rain."

"Clouds and rain?" Jao repeated.

Mulberry giggled. "Love and lust. Don't you know anything?"

Jao was not a giggler. When she was amused, she either kept her silence or erupted into hearty laughter. This time she kept silent but turned dancing eyes upon her housemate.

Mulberry, looking sheepish, smiled. "But to change the subject . . . how old are you? I'm seventeen."

"I'm thirteen. Is everyone else here older?"

"You look older than thirteen," Mulberry comforted. "With your hair on top of your head like that, you look old, as old as I am at least. And dressed in that red silk suit, you look much, much older than you are!

The five old-timers have more years than we do: Phoenix and Peony are around nineteen, Cloud is twenty-one, Jade twenty. You new ones are young: Toto fourteen, Wildgoose fifteen, Pearl sixteen. Pearl is shy and does what the Three tell her to do. So that's four on one side and four on the other. Which side will you be on?"

Jao's eyes fell. Here it was, then, what her mother had warned her about: "The most important thing for you to remember in the palace is to keep out of cliques." Lady Yang had been brought up at the Sui court and knew very well how courts operated. "Jealousies and rivalries, new and old, are constantly forming or dissolving. Be friendly, but not too friendly, because you never know when your 'friend' will be pulled down and you with her." At the time, Jao had hardly listened. She could see nothing terrible about getting into trouble along with her friends.

"I don't really belong anywhere," Jao told Mulberry, backing off. "Thanks for comforting me about my looks . . . my dress and all," she said in acute discomfort. "Have you ever seen it, er, or one like it, before—anywhere?"

Mulberry cocked her head. "It's the latest style, with that open jacket and the square neckline. You're lucky to be so well turned out when you first arrive, nothing gaudy, just right. The silk is the best there is, and that ruby color is especially good. The long-life design woven in it also makes it special. That silk doesn't crush either—I ought to know because I come from silk country. What family did you say you came from? One of those haughty Four Chinese?"

Jao smiled broadly, amused and relieved about her dress. "My family is not pure Chinese," she said. "We are part Tartar nomad: I am one part Tuku Hsienpi and three parts mixed Chinese. Most of the nobility in Shansi and Shensi where I am from is like that. That is why we are tall and good-looking!" she finished, her dimples showing, her eyes merry.

Mulberry stared. "Po po . . . good looks? Are you calling yourself good-looking?"

"Yes, of course! You are too! More than that—beautiful. Surely you know that. Maybe it's all that matters around here," Jao said lightly. "Who cares about old grandparents and parents and family and genealogy?"

"You had better watch what you say," Mulberry gasped. "Who you are is everything!" However, the scowl faded from her face. "Well, I have been told that I am beautiful and desirable! Of course, that's why I'm here." Surprised by herself, she stopped. "Oh! I like talking to you! You make me feel good. Come, let's get out of your cold room and talk in the *kang* room."

The two girls hurried down the cold gallery and into the commons room. It was empty and deliciously warm. The western sun was pouring in, making the whole room glow. Mulberry ran her hand over the smooth surface at the kitchen end, where it was warmest.

"Here is Jade's place and there is your place." She pointed to the other end. "I'm in the middle next to Cloud. We all sleep here on cold nights. Here, sit next to me until the new girls come in." She paused, shyly. "Tell me, will you be my friend? You won't think that because I am a southerner that I am a nobody from nowhere?"

Startled, Jao answered quickly, "Of course I am your friend! We have to live together, don't we? How can it be otherwise? I shall certainly have no such small thoughts about south and north," she added indignantly, hitching herself up onto the *kang*.

The house was coming alive with noises, the sound of running feet, the banging of shutters, voices raised excitedly, slaps for flustered servants. Lamps were being brought in. One was hung in the *kang* room by Ket, who looked appraisingly at Jao and then left abruptly, noisily dropping the leather curtain.

It was almost immediately raised again and, with a rustle of silk, a girl came in. Stunning and willowy, she made an entrance, her delicate features, slender body, and petal-white skin combining to make a striking picture. Mulberry and Jao watched her, fascinated, while she surveyed the room, her eyes fixed on the newcomer. What a beautiful person, Jao thought, awestruck.

"It's Jade," Mulberry whispered.

"You are new here," Jade said, looking at Jao. She ignored Mulberry. "I see that you have already found a friend."

"She is the first one I met, and you are the second," Jao said cheerfully.

"Mulberry, you are not in your right place and neither is your friend," Jade said, "but since you are leaving it does not matter. Phoenix and Peony are out of the bath, and Cloud is having hers now, so run along, it's your turn next." Mulberry, to Jao's amazement, instantly scrambled off the *kang* and, with only a flick of her hand in Jao's direction, disappeared.

Jade then turned to Jao and said in a flat, polite voice, "Jade here—a Tsui from Poling. You are Wu Jao, I am told. I welcome you to this house. I hope that you have been shown your quarters and have been told the regulations."

"Wu from Taiyuan," Jao said eagerly "I just came."

Jade nodded and then, feeling that she had done her duty, settled herself on the *kang* and clapped for her maid to come to lacquer her toenails. Jao opened her mouth to continue, but realizing that Jade had lost interest, shut it again.

The curtain lifted and two more tsairen came in. They were visions in white, about the same height, but otherwise unalike.

"I'm Pearl. From Yangchow," said the first girl softly as she seated herself next to Jao.

"Wu Jao, Taiyuan," Jao responded, and smiled. Pearl had on a quilted tunic in a smooth fabric with a glossy sheen. It must be that new cotton material, Jao thought, recalling that her mother had recently purchased a bolt like it from an Indian merchant.

Pearl's face was glowing from her bath. Her hair, a shining cap framing her small head, was gathered in a knot low on her neck, where it was held in a pearl-encrusted net. She smiled shyly and settled in her place, a fragile, fairylike creature. Jao smiled back, liking her at once.

The other girl in white climbed up on Jao's other side. She was dressed in a fluffy cashmere wool, and her hair, skewered into a topknot, was already escaping in tiny curls around her face. Her eyes, a lively brown, encountered Jao's.

"You are the new Elegant!" she exclaimed warmly. "We have been waiting for you. I'm glad you have arrived safely! Now we are nine, complete. I am Cloud, I'm a Sun from Szechuan, and you are . . . ?"

"A Wu from Taiyuan," Jao responded, dimpling. Cloud is like a kitten . . . playful, she thought. "What would you like to know about me?" she asked aloud.

"Everything," Cloud replied promptly. "Are you easy to get along with? Do you have nightmares? Do you like red pepper and garlic? You can't have secrets here!"

Jao's spirits lifted. "I am Jao and I have no secrets. I've only been here an hour and—"

"Long enough to get into trouble," Cloud bubbled. "Have you?"

"I may have." Jao smiled, thinking of her borrowed clothes, "I often seem to. . . ."

Cloud laughed. "Think nothing of it. I am the oldest here and I am always in trouble. Stupidity, I suppose. But I'm such good company that everyone forgives me."

At this, the other girls jeered amiably. Cloud grinned and turned back to Jao, "Seriously though, we are glad that you have joined us and we welcome you to our happy home. Well, I suppose it really isn't happy. It's cursed, you see."

Pearl gave a little gasp, and Jade said coldly, "You are being crude and untruthful. You are old enough to know better than to say such things."

Cloud's eyes sparkled. "Calm yourself, Jade. The sooner the new girls know the truth about this place, the better. But it is now New Year's Eve and the time to enjoy ourselves, so let us talk only about happy things tonight." She broke off to shout at two girls who were entering, "Come in quickly, you two, you are letting in cold air. Here is Wu Jao from Taiyuan," she continued. "She is another new tsairen." To Jao she said, "Phoenix is the tall one with the black eyebrows, and Peony here is always red-cheeked and good-natured."

Jao slid off the *kang* and greeted them with her hands in the *anjali* position. Their eyes widened at the exotic greeting.

"Lu of Kangtou," Phoenix said.

"Li of Lunghsi via Lolang," Peony said.

"And Toto!" exclaimed another girl as she bounced in, her felt skirt whirling above her boot tops, her straw-colored braids flying and her blue eyes alight. "Toto Anakuwen," she amended as she posed in the doorway. "Of Kucha!" she finished cheerily as she came down the room to stand in front of Jao.

"Wu Jao here. I've heard much of Kucha. Musicians and dancers, the best. Lion's dance. Sword dance . . . dozens of others, so many wonderful songs we all love here in China."

Toto's eyes sparkled. "Come to the end of the *kang* where we both belong, and we'll talk!" She took Jao's arm and nudged her along to their proper places on the *kang*.

"Rescued you!" she whispered, and then said in a normal voice, "You are right, Kucha is the music center of the world, but some of the girls here haven't even heard of it because it is so far away—in the desert at least two thousand miles from here. I was fourteen when I left home, and it took so many months to get here that I'm fifteen now. And lucky to get here at all. How old are you?"

She beamed at Jao, and Jao beamed back. "I'm thirteen, almost your age. You must have had a wonderful trip, I envy you. I heard all about the horrors of travel on the Silk Route from our caravan men. Wasn't it exciting?"

"Oh, it was a great adventure, looking back on it, but I would only want to do it again if I were going home. Sometimes we didn't even have water to drink. And sometimes there was a dust storm and we wouldn't know if we could ever breathe again. Then it was lovely in the hot oases when we slept outdoors under the stars . . . and listened to the wind in the tent ropes."

She turned her blue eyes on Jao and looked her up and down. "You are so pretty, with your shiny black hair and that velvet skin. I'm Circassian. We're mostly blond and redheaded with pale skins. I feel like a freak here among all of you black-haired people."

"Oh, no . . . you are like a tropical bird. You bring us something different, something special—you bring us luck!" Jao blurted. Toto understood what Jao was attempting to say, and hunkered down on her crossed legs with a contented sigh.

"But you see, I just got here and I'm really homesick . . . for the high, snowy mountains, for the meadows, for the mountain torrents, and for our horses. I feel shut in here. I can't eat—this whole week—although I usually have a big appetite no matter what happens." She broke off, self-conscious. She had been speaking in a low voice so that only Jao should hear her. But Cloud, sitting nearby, overheard.

"Everyone is homesick," Cloud said in her soft voice. "But there is so much happening and so many diverting people around that we get used to it. Toto, you'll get hungry again soon. Why don't you start to eat normally now? Tonight? There are all these New Year treats to attract you."

Toto flashed her a smile. "It does sound tempting. Maybe you're right and I will enjoy food tonight. But . . . may I ask you something that rather bothers me? What did you mean when you said that this place is cursed? What is wrong here? I don't like secrets or frightening happenings."

"You four new girls," Cloud answered after a silence, "are taking the places of four who have left us. No secret, but then no one likes to talk about it either, because they all had such bad luck. One girl lost her mind and had to be sent home. That was hard on all of us because no tsairen was sent to the Front Court for months afterward. Another—really the loveliest of us all—died in childbirth. Another fell ill, a strange fever, and died. And the fourth also died, I think."

"Is that all?" Jao exclaimed in relief. "All that sort of thing happens every day everywhere. No mystery, no evil spirits, no fox women, no house demons . . . or were there? Why don't you know whether the fourth girl died? Did she or didn't she?"

"I speak only about what I actually know: I think she died, I don't absolutely know. She just disappeared and so far has never been found. In the wells or anywhere. The authorities took weeks to investigate, but this is a busy palace and much goes on here daily. There has been confusion in the Inner Palace since the empress died two years ago—she kept things in order there. The emperor refuses to put anyone in her place. Now there is a head eunuch and we have our own house master, Chi. He's an ex-soldier who was wounded, so things are sure to be better for us. Yin is over and Yang is beginning."

She turned her head and spoke loudly for all to hear. "The new girls are bringing us luck! To celebrate we are having a feast tonight when the New Year begins at the hour of the rat. We are all going to have our favorite foods from our hometowns! Chi is seeing to it."

The girls clapped cheerfully, except for Jade, who stood up. "Cloud, you may be the oldest here, but it is not your business to give out instructions. I am the head of this house and it is my duty. Now, I must warn you all to be in your best clothes and on your best behavior tonight. Our eunuch, Yang Chifan, will be offering the toasts to the emperor, so you must be quiet and attentive. None of this constant joking. Understand?"

"Please do be head of house and give instructions," Cloud said hastily. "As for wearing our best clothes, I, for one, have nothing to wear."

Jade looked at Cloud with suspicion. "Is that true? Or are you making fun of me?"

Cloud smiled placatingly. "Making fun? Really, you must overlook anything I might say that might offend you. I am always talking nonsense, you know. You mentioned that I am the oldest. You might also add that I am at the bottom of the list in accomplishments. I can't dance, I can't write poetry or do calligraphy. I can sew a little and I can cook. I have been on the emperor's list six times but was called only once . . . and then nothing happened."

The girls who were listening in on this conversation broke into delighted laughter.

"You will have other chances, before you die—if you try harder," Peony gurgled.

"I am not the one who has to try harder," Cloud began amid more whoops of laughter. Jade looked down her nose in dispproval at such undignified talk. Phoenix looked nonplussed, but Peony radiated interest.

The silence that followed was broken by Pearl, who did not quite understand the conversation. She did realize that Cloud was being put down in some way. "But Cloud can sing! Her singing is exciting and happy and heavenly!"

"I can sing like an angel," Cloud agreed. "Songs that you all know and love. I can sing like two angels when I have had a sip of our Szechuan wine. And tonight, when the New Year arrives, I will sing for you, all your favorite songs."

"Sing now," Peony ordered. "Sing 'Watching the Moon in Brahma Land.' I'll keep time on the gong."

"Not now, but after we have eaten. Then I will sing many songs besides that one, when we all feel like joining in," Cloud promised, lightly changing the disharmonious mood of the group to one of festive anticipation.

Jao watched and listened with attentiveness. Nothing that Cloud said or did ever seemed to arouse the blacker moods of her housemates. She just made them feel good. There is no evil in her, Jao thought.

A rush of cold air announced Ket's arrival. "Sunset soon. You come," she shouted at Jao, who slid off the *kang* at once. Ket took her by the arm and hurried her out of the house and out of the compound, then through several courts. Chi was waiting for them in front of a brightly lit pavilion, and Ket vanished when she saw him. He, also abrupt, steered Jao inside to an alcove where a portly man of sixty with a pale face and pouches under his eyes was sitting before a loaded desk.

"Here is Wu Jao, the last tsairen," Chi said. "Her brother delivered her an hour or two ago." This was her introduction. Jao, panting slightly from her run with Ket, bowed and then looked timidly at the great man. He was regarding her with tired, hard eyes.

"I have received the report of your arrival and your pennilessness. I have had you registered and have ordered a servant for you. That is all we can do for you at this time. I hope that you won't be a further nuisance to us."

Jao flinched as if she had been struck. "No sir," she said. Chief Eunuch Kao scrutinized her closely, her clothing and her grooming, her proud bearing and her dignity.

"You are presentable, everything considered," he stated, relenting slightly. "How did you manage without maid or luggage?"

"Ket did it all. She found clothes of a former tsairen while my own were drying," Jao said simply, a blush of embarrassment reddening her face. "One box did come, but there were only baby clothes in it," she added.

A flash of amusement appeared in the man's eyes.

"Ket! She has never been known to lift a finger for any of the girls before. What happened to move her to . . . purloin clothes like these for you?"

Jao considered. "After the mud was washed from me and from my clothes, there was nothing for me to put on. She had to think of something, so she did." Jao stole a glance at the awesome man and found him smiling now.

"I am indeed happy to learn that she found something," he said, thinking that for the first time, Ket's light-fingered ways had proved useful. "That is all, then. You may go, Tsairen Jao."

"Thank you, *wanfu*!" Jao replied, delighted that the interview was over. She slipped into her graceful one-kneed bow while laying two red packets of gold pieces on the desk.

"New Year's greetings from the Wu family," she said with shy politeness.

The official, surprised, picked up the packets and opened them, a look of gratification coming into his eyes. "You managed to keep some of your possessions, then?" he asked.

"Under my coat and in my saddlebag," she replied matter-of-factly, and, bowing again, turned to follow Chi out.

Kao could not restrain another chuckle as he watched her making her exit. Well brought up and no fool. He would keep an eye on her.

Chi escorted Jao to the back gate of the tsairen house and, with a curt nod, turned to leave. As he did Jao bowed and offered a red packet to him also. "New Year's greetings from the Wu family," she murmured. For a moment Chi was flustered. He did not look upon himself as a servant fawning for tips. On the other hand, at the holiday season one accepted gifts.

"Thank you, Tsairen Wu Jao," he said formally, and then abruptly left. Jao smiled. She understood the brusqueness of men from the north, and knew that she had done the right thing. One up for Mama, she said to herself.

Darkness engulfed the yard by the time she returned, but a lantern had already been hung above the house entrance and she could see her way. Suddenly, a tempestuous figure emerged from the bathhouse on the far side. Dressed in close-fitting pants and a jacket of soft deerskin, the figure whirled in accelerating circles, filling the yard with movement, and then abruptly stood still, gazing into the last red streaks in the sky. Jao stared, struck by such swift motion followed by such absolute stillness, and by the taut strength of the slight body. The stranger took several deep breaths, then spun into one cartwheel after another, turning and turning in exuberance. Jao threw off her coat and, waiting for an opening, sprang into wheels of her own at the other's side. Finally, the two came to a standstill together.

On her feet again, with not a hair out of place and barely panting, the strange girl eyed Jao in astonishment.

"I didn't see you," she said, "or—"

"You might not have done what you just did," Jao answered, catching her breath. "Now I feel better about being in this strange place? Don't you? Besides, it's a good way to celebrate the new year."

The other girl looked at her searchingly and then burst into a hearty laugh. "We are tomboys really, not palace ladies. We shouldn't be here," she said.

"But we are," Jao said.

"And I still don't know what to do about it," the girl answered frankly. "I thought, in the dusk and with no one about, I'd take the chance to stretch myself and let go. Here! I don't know who you are and you don't know me. I am Wildgoose, and you are perhaps the last tsairen to arrive? I hope you are, and not a maid or somebody like that."

"Not a maid. What servant can do a cartwheel? They're too old and stiff. I'm Tsairen Wu Jao from Taiyuan. And you are from Shansi, too, I would guess. Tatung, perhaps? Were you chosen because you are so light on your feet?"

Wildgoose laughed, a cheerful outburst that prompted Jao to join her.

"I came from the grass country near Tatung, and I wasn't chosen for my abilities or looks. In fact no one asked anything about me. I was just bundled off. I'm not even Chinese. I am a Yuwen from the steppeland. My father is a Hsienpi chieftain from ten generations back, and I am the fifth daughter of a fifth wife, so I am considered lucky. I was delivered to the Son of Heaven because both Turks and Chinese want good luck in having peace with each other just now."

"Well then, we are two of a kind, the cream of Shansi girldom . . . or boydom, whatever!" Jao said cheerfully. "Should we go in now, though?" she added as she saw Ket advancing on them.

Ket said nothing, but when she'd heard girls laughing in the dark yard, she became suspicious. On New Year's Eve men might be about anywhere. She recognized the girls, however, and shooed them into the house. She sensed why they had been so riotous.

When the two tsairen entered the *kang* room, they found the others there, already dressed and waiting, so they slid self-consciously down the aisle to the last two places, which were theirs, and squeezed next to Toto. The others had completed their toilets and were ready for the evening.

Jade's pale face was made paler by the powder covering it, and she had painted a rosebud mouth on her lips. Her hair was arranged in great loops over the back and sides of her head, and she was clothed in gold brocade. "Out of style" Mulberry whispered, and was immediately hushed by Cloud. Phoenix was in silver brocade, her hair arranged in the same fashion as Jade's, while Peony wore a rose silk that billowed out around her plump figure, and her abundant hair was coiled around an elaborate pin.

Mulberry had on a maroon taffeta creation from her silk-producing hometown, gorgeous and the latest fashion, but it completely eclipsed her. The two girls in white had remained in the clothes they wore when they first came into the *kang* room. Only the three newcomers were plainly dressed, and looked like the strangers they were.

All were waiting in eagerness to welcome in the New Year at the hour of the rat, when the spirits, wherever they were, were thought to descend to earth to be greeted respectfully with fireworks, gongs, rattles, chopsticks struck against bowls, and noisemakers of every kind.

Jao and Wildgoose had barely seated themselves when Ket hit the gong vigorously and announced that the holiday dinners were to be served in the reception room immediately.

"In front room," she shouted. At this announcement, Jade quickly slid off the *kang* and followed Ket into the hall.

"Not there, the reception room is now my room," she said, having commandeered the room without Chi's knowledge. "You must have the trays served in the *kang* room."

Ket pointed down the hall toward the reception room in the front of the building. "Charcoal heaters already in there. Round table all set," she said. "Master Chi's orders."

"Then you can just take it all out," Jade said. "I won't have it. That is now my room and no one comes in there without my permission."

"Master Chi's orders," Ket repeated.

"I'll have you beaten if you do not do as I say," Jade cried viciously.

Ket merely stared at her, then walked down the hall to the reception room, her head barely clearing the rafters, her short sword banging against her thigh.

The girls filed into the hall and brushed by Jade on their way to the front of the house, chattering excitedly. Inside the front room, which was cheerfully lit by big red candles, the table was set for nine. At each place were silver bowls and goblets and ivory chopsticks. Ket ushered the girls to their places and then went to the door and whistled. The maids from the kitchen filed in, jostling their trays and filling the hall with excited giggles.

Following the maids, Chi entered through the back door, impressive in his finery. He stopped when he saw Jade standing alone in the hall. Noticing the strange, set expression on her face, he bowed and courteously waved her forward. She did not move, and he waited for some time. Finally, she went slowly down the hall and took her place in the seat of honor in silence, followed by Chi. He knew what she was thinking, and wondered what he was going to do about it.

The servants had been preparing food for days in preparation for the holidays. The trays set before the girls contained seasonal delicacies along with regional dishes. As they began to uncover their bowls, squeals erupted when each girl recognized a favorite food.

"Lamb and peppers and onions on skewers, Persian style," Toto cried shrilly, startling the Three, who were so diverted, however, by what was on their own trays—bowls of pork and leek dumplings, and vermicelli with pine nuts and lotus hearts—that they ignored her outburst and attended to their own food with dainty gusto. Cloud lifted her chopsticks with relish to dip into her spicy beans with rice and red-pepper-cabbage pickles. Mulberry and Pearl, highly pleased by their chicken with walnuts and rice, ate hungrily as did Wildgoose with her noodles, millet, kumiss, and mantou.

Toto, seated next to Jao, soon noticed that she had no tray, so in midbite she picked up a bowl cover and added food to it, passing it down the line until, when it got back to Jao, it was heaped with food of all kinds. "No maid yet, so no food for me either, I expect," Jao mumbled as she tackled the plateful, elated to be included in this generous way by her housemates, and glad to try everything on it.

Chi stood watching for a few moments while the girls settled and the room quieted. Then he stepped forward and offered a toast to the emperor. The girls scrambled to their feet, goblets in hand, and touched cups to lips while Chi offered the salute. Then he said, "This dinner has been sent to you from Chief Eunuch Kao and myself with our compliments. We welcome you to palace life, and extend New Year's greetings and wishes for a lucky new year to all nine of you."

The girls tasted their wine and chorused their enthusiastic thanks. Chi returned their toasts, bowed to them, and escaped. They then settled onto their cushions, relieved to be free of his presence and to be able to eat with unrestricted appetite. Food arrived in a constant stream, accompanied by a variety of wines.

Jade tasted every drink, and in time her face was flushed and her tongue loosened.

"Is that butter?" she asked, pointing with her chopsticks at the kumiss before Wildgoose. "What a smell! We don't have butter in our house even for the servants . . . or any other form of milk."

"You are missing a lot, then," Wildgoose replied, unabashed. "How do you feed your babies—with pork?"

Jade wrinkled her patrician nose. "Butter and kumiss are barbarian food," she countered.

"Barbarian!" Wildgoose and Toto exclaimed together, while Jao stared at the scene before her, her chopsticks halfway to her lips.

"My family," Wildgoose continued, "won't eat pork because they think that it is fit only for dogs. And pork seems to be a favorite food of your family. How strange!"

The excited talking in the room died abruptly when the other girls realized that something unpleasant was taking place. Jade was looking Wildgoose over from head to toe contemptuously. "You are such a wild one that you must have been recruited for bedding only—if you ever get the chance, that is."

Wildgoose just laughed. "You can't hurt my feelings," she said loudly. "Say whatever you like—but just don't put a finger on me." Someone gasped.

Cloud stood suddenly, upsetting her goblet. "Changing the subject," she said in her soft, hesitant voice. "It is time for everyone to make her New Year's wish. It is getting close to the hour of the rat. You must make your wishes—off with the old year and on with the new. It's time!" She fluttered her hands. "You must all write out your wishes and start off by stating one now. You first, Jade."

Jade was sitting ramrod straight, huffily facing the room, but this appeal to her authority as first person in the household succeeded in diverting her. She made her statement at once. "To have a son, of course," she said, and called to her maid to bring paper and ink stones for writing down her New Year's petition.

Order was restored. The storm had passed, and the girls eagerly concentrated upon brushing in their wishes on strips of paper to send to the spirits in smoke. Jade had no inkling of the fact that she had just made an implacable enemy of a fourteen-year-old tomboy from the steppes. She would only have shrugged indifferently if she had.

Pearl turned to Cloud when she saw her hesitating in front of her blank strip of paper. "We have all written down our wishes except you, and soon it will be time for the ceremony of burning. Don't you have any wish, or is it a secret?"

"My wish is like Jade's, I want to bear the emperor a child. Only I want a daughter."

"A daughter! A girl won't get you anywhere!" Pearl responded in amazement.

Cloud answered sadly and slowly. "A girl will be enough and more than enough to bring me security and peace. The enmity that a concubine gets when she has a possible heir to the throne makes me shudder to think about. No, I want a baby more than anything . . . if she is a girl."

Pearl did not hear her because firecrackers began to crackle as the new year started. No one heard her. Cloud was not much noticed by the other Elegants.

Before dawn, during the hour of the tiger, Ket came into the reception room where Cloud was leading the girls in singing. She circled around and tapped Jao on the shoulder. Jao jumped with fright.

"Not bad news," Ket hurried to say, "but you come now." She strode off to the *kang* room, where a coarsely dressed person was waiting, a tall girl with a presence in spite of her apparent slave status. Ket pointed at her. "Your servant, name of Mi. She stay with you now. In room I show you for tonight only. Then you have front room and Wildgoose have hers back. Chi says."

Having gotten Jao settled, Ket returned to her warm bed. Jao, animated from the hilarity and the wine, patted the *kang* beside her, inviting Mi to sit. Mi, however, shook her head and stood before the girl who was to be her mistress and who was younger than herself. She waited, unsmiling, and Jao studied her.

Mi was tawny, her hair a dusky brown, her eyes amber-flecked with gold, her skin flawless. Jao had never seen anyone so well-built and firmly muscled, and she was suddenly full of gratitude for her luck in accquiring such a good-looking companion. Mi was taller than Jao by a head, impressive in appearance, and her way of holding herself was the essence of pride and sense of worth, no matter how raggedly she was clothed.

"Mi? Where did that name come from?" Jao asked finally, trying to think how her mother interviewed servants.

"It is the same as Mei in Chinese and it means beautiful," she answered simply. "I come from Silla in southern Korea. I am sixteen. I have no last name because I belong to the royal family, of chingol descent. The ruler now is Queen Sondok, whose father is my grandfather."

Jao stared. "Po po," she said in amazement. "Why are you here as a slave, then, if you belong to royalty?"

"I was kidnapped," Mi said simply.

"Kidnapped!" Jao exclaimed. "How? Tell me!"

"We lived in palace buildings spread on terraces on the southwest side of sacred Mount Toham. It's the highest point in a chain facing the eastern sea, and overlooks the rich valley of Kyongju." She paused and cleared her throat. "The cherry trees in bloom dot the land, and the blossoming clouds above dot the sky, and you cannot tell where the land stops and the sky begins."

Mi stopped suddenly and lapsed into silence while Jao looked at her kindly. "How were you forced to leave?"

"My brother is the closest male to the throne now that the male line has died out and women inherit the throne. For this reason, he was given the best in training, in etiquette, in equipment, and since I am his twin, I shared his advantages. One day, late last fall, he and I were out hunting. We went further than we had ever gone before, when a storm came up and we took shelter in a cave. We were seen by a Chinese hunting team who were scouting for young people to kidnap for sale in China. Korean slaves bring the highest prices in the Chinese market. After dark set in, we were surrounded and easily taken because our attendants had lost track of us and could not find us at night. It has been a long journey for us, from there to this remote plateau in China."

Mi's voice ceased again and the silence lengthened. Jao got off the *kang* and took her hand. "Mi, I am lucky to have you here, and I will do my very best for you. Now, have you a blanket and do you know where to sleep?"

Mi nodded. Her dull eyes brightened and she produced a tentative smile in response to Jao's bright one.

Not five hundred yards away from the court of the tsairen lay the large compound of the emperor. Hanging in the trees lining the emperor's courtyard were lanterns that shed flickers of light on icy pavements and on hurrying figures of guests. Guards in full regalia moved along the front of the main pavilion, clanking their spears as they turned. The night was rapidly getting colder, and their breaths formed plumes of vapor above their heads.

The Son of Heaven was not concerned with duties of empire this evening, but was welcoming in the new year with his family and friends. Inside the great hall were more lanterns, delicate ones of silk and gauze, shedding subdued light. A half-dozen great braziers excuded heat. A low and inviting *kang* extended along a side wall, and on it were heaped the warmest and softest tiger skins to be found in the empire.

About sixty people were in the room, gathering in groups and greeting one another with hearty *hau-hau*'s of pleasure. All were male, and while some were ministers of high rank, most were princes of the House of Tang, fourteen of whom were sons of the emperor. These magnates did not meet often, because they lived in separate establishments far apart.

The emperor stood in the center of the hall in easy access to all. Erect in bearing, broad across the shoulders and chest, he dominated the room not by what he wore—his uncles and brothers were all more elaborately dressed than he—nor by what he represented, but by his air of authority. There was no white in his heavy mane of hair or in his thick eyebrows and formidable mustaches. At the age of thirty-eight he was in the prime of life.

Standing next to him, as if by right, was his brother-in-law, Changsun Wuji, whose white hair was neatly gathered into a topknot capped by the gold bands of an archduke. He was a man who was big all over, with the hooked nose and gray eyes of his steppe ancestors. Immensely wealthy because of his share in the confiscation of the estates of Sui loyalists, he had risen through martial skills. Committed to the Tang cause early in the struggle, he had achieved first rank as commander-in-chief of the armies and was first of the twenty-four knights.

Near Wuji stood the ten-year-old son of his sister, the empress. Jer looked enough like his uncle to be his son, with the same heavy frame and large head. The boy's black eyebrows and proud stance were like his father's, however.

A slave approached carrying a tray of goblets filled with a golden Turfan wine newly brought by camel caravan to Changan. "An exotic drink, cold from cave storage. See how you like it," Emperor Taitsung urged, waving the tray to Wuji, who helped himself with alacrity.

"Let me be the first to drink to your health and good fortune, brother-in-law," Wuji boomed, his voice better attuned to the barracks than the palace.

"I drink to you also, to your health and longevity, and wish you prosperity and many sons. How many do you have by now?" Taitsung asked as he savored his wine.

Changsun Wuji laughed self-consciously. "Too many, at least thirty. I am not really up to date. *Wanfu!*" he shouted cheerfully, touching his glass to Taitsung's. "Enlivening drink," he added appreciatively as he beckoned to the slave for a refill. "I hear that the old man Wei Cheng has been lecturing you lately on your frivolities."

Taitsung raised an eyebrow. "Frivolities? I console myself for the loss of my empress. It is not the new women in the harem that bother old Wei—after all, old as he is, he has a young concubine himself—it is the expense. He is a product of the Spartan years, and now he begrudges every string of cash spent on what he calls needless luxury in the palace. He will probably be shocked by the luxuries here tonight."

"In addition," Wuji continued lightly, "Wei fears he is losing the power that he feels entitled to in his role as a censor of your behavior. He hates it when his advice is not taken."

Taitsung did not reply immediately to this, but Wuji was too thick-skinned to notice. "The old man never gives up," the emperor said neutrally as he turned to greet his son Tai, suave and well-groomed in his midnight-blue tunic. Tai was a serious young man and looked older than his twenty-four years.

"Well now, Number Four Son, I haven't seen much of you lately. How are you doing?"

Tai bowed to his father, his smile warm and excited, his eyes wary. Tai was ambitious and deeply involved in faction-forming, a fact that he took pains to conceal from his father.

"It has been good hunting weather these last few days. I have been able to bag six pheasants," Tai said in a nonchalant manner—his attendants had shot five of the birds—"and I have sent three of the best to your kitchen."

"A welcome gift!" Taitsung said, pleased. He liked his sons to excel in the martial arts and to engage in manly activities. He was always concerned lest they be spoiled by the enervating palace life. "You must be practicing archery daily to be able to get a pheasant on the wing. We'll have to have a match one of these days, how about that?"

"Any time you say, sir," Tai replied warmly, although he was aghast at the thought of taking on his father, who had once been the most skilled archer in the kingdom.

"Me too!" piped up Taitsung's ten-year-old son, Jer, who had kept silent long enough. "I want to come too."

"You!" Taitsung exclaimed looking down at the boy with affection. "Certainly I will take you on . . . target at fifty paces? I shall have to watch my step in competing with my Number Nine Son!"

Jer punched his father with a small fist and the men laughed. "You are laughing at me! I would rather watch than shoot. Watching is what I want," Jer said.

"Do you always get what you want?" his father teased. Jer cocked his head thoughtfully. He usually took his time about answering any question put to him, and the habit had grown since his mother's death. It was important to have his father's approval of anything he did.

"Almost always I do," he said after he had considered. "May Bixon watch too? We do most things together."

At the mention of his favorite daughter's name, the emperor smiled, "I gather that you are often at Fang Fei's residence. Good! She is an excellent mother. Yes, Bixon may come too—it will be a fete. I'll see to it!"

Tai pinched his half brother's ear. "I'll be glad to have you watch me shoot. I'll teach you too."

Jer pulled back. "Don't muss my hair. I'm dressed up and I want to stay that way. Anyway, I like to watch better than to do anything myself. I don't want to be like brother Chengchien, who is at his sports all the time and at nothing else. He says he'd rather go three days without eating than three days without hunting. Not me."

At mention of the crown prince, the three men who had been smiling at Jer stiffened, searching the room with their eyes. The heir apparent was not there. Jer, always sensitive, noticed the silence. "Did I say something wrong?" he asked, faltering.

His father drew him closer. "No, you have not said anything out of the way, but in the future it would be better if you would not talk about Elder Brother's behavior at all, to anyone." Jer nodded, looking up in his serious way into the hard eyes of the three adults. What he saw in Tai's frightened him.

Wuji caught the eye of a stout relative, "There is Prince Yueh and his son Langyeh. I must speak to them and get it over with. Yueh is so long-winded. Positively soporific."

"What's soporific?" Jer asked, relieved that the men were smiling again.

"Dull, boring," his uncle replied.

"Oh, now I know who you are talking about—Wei Cheng," Jer answered, startled but also pleased at the crack of laughter that greeted his remark.

The doors opened and closed as several newcomers entered. Suddenly there was confusion outside. A tense order to halt was punctuated by angry talk as a guard lowered his spear across the entrance.

"You dog, what are you doing?" a voice shouted. "I'll have you given a hundred lashes for this. Stand out of my way."

At the first hint of altercation, the emperor himself moved to the door. "This impudent wretch wants to take my dagger," cried Crown Prince Chengchien when he saw his father. His face was flushed and angry.

"The guardsman is only doing his duty, although he is perhaps too zealous. There is no one inside who is armed," the emperor said in a mild voice. "Hand me the dagger and then come in where you are eagerly awaited."

The prince hesitated, his flush fading as he gave up the dagger. He turned to the guard and said viciously, "I will attend to you tomorrow."

"You will do nothing of the kind," Taitsung interposed, without heat. "This man is an Elite Guardsman and is not under your jurisdiction."

The prince aimed a menacing look at the guard, who shuddered but stood his ground. Chengchien then entered the hall with a swagger.

"Don't be anxious," the emperor said to the guard. "It is your duty to see that no weapon enters this place tonight, and that is the way it is to be. You will be rewarded tomorrow." Then the emperor turned away and took the crown prince by the arm. "Now," he said, "the feasting can begin."

Six round tables were carried in and placed around the hall. Servants in immaculate costume then set the tables with bowls, goblets, and chopsticks, all of gold, and put down platters of appetizers. When they withdrew, Taitsung invited everyone to sit wherever he liked without protocol. A mild rush to the tables ensued.

Taitsung looked around the room with satisfaction. He had fourteen grown sons, and all of them were able to give a good account of themselves, although they had needed close scrutiny during their rearing. Conditions in the Inner Palace had become chaotic two years before, when the firm hand of his empress had been withdrawn by her death. Only now, with the appointment of new eunuchs under the supervision of a vice-minister of the treasury, was order in the Inner City being restored.

Before Taitsung seated himself between his first son and his ninth, he proposed a toast to the three archdukes. He saluted Wuji, who raised both arms and clasped his hands in acknowledgment of the cheerful bravos. Li Chi, on whom he had bestowed the imperial Li name for his great record on the battlefield, was toasted next. A stalwart man in his late forties, Li Chi rose and bowed. The convivial acclaim Li Chi received was a fraction more spontaneous than that received by Changsun Wuji. The emperor then saluted his chief counselor, "My faithful Wei Cheng!" and after that his chief minister, Fang, "My longtime friend and loyal minister!"

This done, Taitsung sat down and, in a clatter of dishes and rising hilarity, the serious business of eating began.

New Year's morning dawned clear. The sun pushed its red rim above the horizon, sending spears of light across the frosted roofs of the city. A thin mantle of fresh white snow lay like rugs in the thousands of courtyards. Festoons of crystal icicles hung from the end tiles of countless houses and sparkled in the early sunshine. Street sweepers were out clearing the immense court before the main throne hall, which, mounted on a three-tiered platform, towered over all else in the city. It was opened only three times a year: New Year's, Emperor's Birthday, and Winter Solstice.

Inside the colonnaded hall, braziers filled with burning charcoal dissipated the cold. Hanging silk curtains screened the alcoves for the benefit of the women. The center of the hall was cleared for the men: officials, religious notables, foreign ambassadors, and heads of great families.

Outside, drums located in the corner tower were struck as soon as the red ball of the sun cleared the horizon, the signal for the gates to open. Throngs of sedan chairs and carriages were admitted. At the same time, gongs in the inner courts alerted the palace inmates that the ceremony was soon to begin.

Ministers of the nine grades were first to file into the grand hall. They took their places before the dais, the highest three ranks closest to the throne. The robes of the officials, made of the best heavy silk, ranged in color from the purples of Grade One through the reds and yellows to the blue–greens of the lower ranks. Finally, the 120 women of the Inner Palace took their places behind the gauze curtains on the right wall, while the wives of dignitaries were ushered to the left.

Chi sounded the gong in the tsairen house. Dressed in their colorful silks, the girls promptly assembled. They had not had much sleep, but they still looked fresh and clear-eyed. Each had a fur cape slung over her shoulders for the walk through the grounds of the Inner Palace. They were then led out through the Chengdien gate into the courts of the administrative palace's throne halls. They started to chatter in high-pitched voices as they entered this masculine territory, normally forbidden to them, but were peremptorily silenced by the eunuchs. When they reached the back door of the throne hall, they left their mantles and proceeded in single file to their allotted space along the right wall.

Exclamations of amazement and pleasure, quickly suppressed, escaped them at first sight of the fairyland that opened before them: the towering interlocking beams and brackets overhead, and the lavish display of color in the apparel of the three hundred people below. The dais alone, with its rich lacquer and bronze furnishings, remained empty of people. The tsairen quietly stamped their silk-shod feet to warm them after the walk over the cold paving stones, but kept their positions in line. Only their eyes moved excitedly over the scene before them.

All craned their necks with one accord when the central doors opened and a flourish of trumpets announced the arrival of the imperial family and the archdukes. An advance guard entered first. Its complement of musicians played while the richly dressed princes moved slowly to the front. The hall was silent except for the drums and woodwinds and the swish-swish of feet.

With a thudding of her heart in anticipation of seeing the Son of Heaven for the first time, Jao stood on her tiptoes to look. She could not identify him because of the tall honor guard surrounding him, handsome men all richly dressed. Arriving at the dais, the archdukes and great ministers arranged themselves behind the throne and the guards filed into position below. The crown prince, handsomely arrayed in ceremonial dress with his Turkish jeweled dagger and sword, stood to the left, and several younger princes stood to the right.

An imposing figure separated himself from the group, and the emperor stood revealed. He gazed for a long moment in greeting the packed assembly and then slowly seated himself upon the throne. A sigh arose as if the audience recognized the extraordinary quality of both the event and the emperor. They were for the most part aware that this occasion differed from any that had gone before.

Taitsung continued his survey of this court, savoring the moment. He was feeling free at last to celebrate the success of the twenty-year-old dynasty, free to launch innovations that would demonstrate the quality of his own rule. He could show respect for customary ritual and regalia, and still break precedent in introducing new features.

The robes he wore were traditional, embroidered with the twelve symbols of his rank. His flat hat was adorned with twelve strings of jewels, which hung in front of his eyes and kept people from seeing his face. Few in the audience hall had ever seen the old customs displayed so impressively, and the experience was exhilarating. The young tsairen were especially stirred.

Taitsung signaled for the ceremony to begin. A conch shell sounded, and the great officials, led by Archduke Changsun Wuji, approached the throne, were recognized, bowed and filed past, laying gifts upon tables placed in the aisles. An army of secretaries recorded and took charge of the offerings. After the chief ministers came the generals and foreign envoys of high rank, each one individually greeted by Taitsung.

The conch shell's deep note sounded twice, and the middle ranks of officials came forward in groups and bowed together, shortening the process of greeting. They, too, left their gifts on tables. The conch's third call brought up the lower ranks, grades seven to nine. Its fourth call summoned the ladies, a breathtaking innovation. Amid much craning of necks, the four Fei, matrons of the first rank, moved forward and bowed when their names and ranks were called out. They then disappeared into a side room where the reception for women guests was to take place. A trumpet sounded and the nine Chaoyi consorts came forth. They bowed in unison. An ocharina sounded its lone, vibrating note, and the ladies of the third rank, the Chiayu, moved forward, gorgeous in their robes of state. At the sound of a flute, the Meiren moved up, causing a sigh of appreciation for their beauty of face and figure.

Finally, castanets rapped out three beats and the nine youngest, the tsairen, spaced themselves self-consciously before the throne, bowed and went off stage in a somewhat ragged line. Jao brought up the rear, feeling that something more formal was required, so she slipped into her effortless gliding walk that produced no foot movement, a walk that had distinguished the princesses of the fallen Sui dynasty. She bowed once more at the end as she passed Taitsung, and seemed to float without hurry off the platform. The emperor watched her with interest.

The dismissal chimes resounded, and the doors to the dining areas were thrown open. The crowds flowed decorously but purposefully to the laden tables where food, drink, and individual gifts—sets of gold spoons and chopsticks for each—were laid out. A chorus of convivial conversation arose at once.

In the women's reception room, the Fei and consorts received, and the wives of the great filed past them. The clothes worn by the guests were most spectacular, equaling or outdoing those of the palace women, but the balance was restored by the superior sophistication of the harem ladies and their impeccable good manners. The Chiayu and Meiren circulated, seeing to it that the guests had seats, and the tsairen served them immediately with rare teas and wines. Each lady was presented with a gold hairpin.

Such lavish entertainment pleased everyone and accomplished its purpose: to let the aristocracy know that when the great emperor of the new Tang dynasty launched an occasion, he did it on a grand scale and with style.

The tsairen were the first to be quietly shepherded off the scene by the watchful Chi. The Three, who had expected to mingle freely with the great ones, complained loudly when they were back in their own dull quarters. Chi listened to them and then said abruptly before departing, "I could not trust you to behave as expected on an occasion like this."

Watching his retreating back, Jade came to a decision. "Girls," she called out, "in an hour's time we should be making New Year's calls, dressed formally. Phoenix, Peony, and I will call upon the Fei; Cloud and Pearl upon the Chaoyi; Mulberry and Toto on the Chiayu; and Wildgoose and Jao on the Meiren. Hurry."

Thus appealed to, the girls set about refreshing their makeup, smoothing their hair, sorting out the capes that had been left at the door, and departing in excited groups.

Jao and Wildgoose looked at each other. "Do you know any of the Meiren?" Jao asked. "Do we just barge in? Do we take gifts? Or do we stay home and play cards?"

Wildgoose shrugged. "I wouldn't know, I'm just a barbarian from the wilds, remember? You are the one who knows Chinese customs. You decide."

Jao was braiding her hair with red ribbons. She finished. "We'll go, then."

They followed the path to the Meiren house, which was twice the size of theirs. As they approached the ornate front door, they could hear sounds of gaiety inside. They knocked but no one answered. They knocked again. Finally they entered cautiously into a hall full of women, the nine vivacious Meiren—women in their twenties—and their female relatives and friends, all talking at once. The lady nearest the door came to greet them. Curious because they looked so young, she inquired at once who they were. She sympathized with their newcomer status and took them around the room, introducing them. The Meiren gave the girls only cursory looks, noting the northern dress of Wildgoose and the youthful braids of Jao, and greeted them in a polite but indifferent way.

By the time Jao and Wildgoose had made the rounds, they felt deflated and ready to leave. Meiren Fang, who had introduced them, had noticed the coolness of the reception they had received, so she bade them good-bye with warmth. "Would you like to meet my cousin, Fang Fei?" she asked. "She is one of the highest-ranking ladies in the court, and now that there is no empress, much responsibility for deciding priorities rests with her. Her house is always full of delightful callers, including the emperor himself, people that it might take you a long time to get to know unless you do so at New Year's time."

The girls flushed with pleasure and assented eagerly.

"I will make the arrangements, then, and let you know later," she said, and they departed, excited and pleased. But they were also very tired. They hurried through the two courtyards without meeting anyone, and by unspoken consent went straight to the *kang* room to sleep.

Chapter Four

In mid-afternoon on New Year's Day the Elegants were napping in the *kang* room. On the other side of the leather curtain the house was damply cold, and outdoors the icicles, which hung from the tile ends, were lengthening as the waning day froze the melt and frosted the paving stones. Palace noises were muted or stilled while both masters and servants drowsed. The creaking sound of the front gate opening and closing woke some of the girls, and they sat up yawning. Toto stretched enormously and nudged Jao, who was curled up in a ball against the wall at the end of the *kang*.

Jao opened her eyes and blinked, trying to recall where she was, and then smiled sheepishly when she remembered. After all, it had only been twenty-four hours since she had first entered the palace. "It seems months," she said drowsily.

"Months? What are you talking about?" Toto asked between yawns.

"I feel that I've been here months and months," Jao responded lazily. Heavy footsteps were hurrying down the hall, and she propped herself on an elbow to listen. At that moment the curtain was roughly pulled aside and Chi peered in. He was scowling.

"The orders are that you tsairen are to appear at the door of the emperor's quarters at the sound of the sunset drum tonight. Dressed in your best, orders from the head eunuch. *My* orders are that you had better be on your best behavior, or you will wish you had." His scowl deepened.

"All of us?" Peony asked in a sleepy voice.

"All nine of you," Chi repeated. "So bestir yourselves. You have only an hour."

"Why?" Toto asked, irrespressible.

Chi whipped around. "Who said that?" His voice was menacing.

There was dead silence before Toto said in a stutter, "I did."

Chi saw that it was only a newcomer, so he became milder. "You never use that word 'why'—none of you—understand? Listen, I'll say this only once, you never ask why around here. You never even *think* why. In fact you don't think. You obey."

Now that he had everyone's undivided attention, he added another warning. "The chief eunuch is anxious that you new ones are not ready yet. You don't know procedures or what is expected of you. If any one of you say or do anything to displease the emperor, the chief eunuch will be blamed. And I will be too, so take care."

Jade spoke up, having recovered her equanimity. "I'll lead, and the others need only watch what I do and they won't make mistakes. I know court etiquette better than . . . anyone else." She had started to say "than the chief eunuch," but thought better of it. Chi stared at her not too politely. New to the palace, he did not know much about court subtleties. He had his mind set on discipline.

He said crossly to Jade. "Just the sight of you looking so superior may be the exact thing that will irritate the emperor. He is in a bad mood this afternoon because he has this gala event on his hands, which is becoming more than he bargained for. All his attendants are on their toes. Now . . . I'm leaving to put on my court clothes, and then I'll be back for you. Be ready!"

The silence in the room after he left was prolonged. It was finally broken by someone whispering, "Be ready . . ." followed by someone else's barely audible "Why?" There was an outbreak of muffled shrieks of laughter while the girls scrambled from the *kang* and ran nervously down the hall, yelling for their maids.

The three hundred drumbeats that marked the closing of the city gates and markets were throbbing through the cold air of twilight when Chief Eunuch Kao, bundled to the nose in furs, queued the girls up before the entrance to Taitsung's private quarters. Tall, rigidly erect guards flanked the doors, their spears crossed. They looked stonily over the heads of the tsairen until a chamberlain came to summon the shivering girls indoors. The guards then ceremoniously lifted their spears and stamped their feet as they let the girls pass. Jade went first with mincing steps, and the others followed sedately, for once not crowding each other.

Jao was last, which befitted a person only twenty-four hours in the palace. She had hardly passed by when the guards clashed their spears together again, actually brushing her shoulder. She looked up indignantly, meeting the sly, amused look of the guard nearest her. Jao was not one to let an attack, however small, pass. She moved forward demurely, but not before she had brought her tiny leather boot down hard on the guard's instep. Chi, who was anxiously bringing up the rear on her other side, saw nothing. He failed to hear the tiny grunt of pain from the surprised guard and the choke of laughter from his mate.

The room inside the doors was brightly lit with festive red candles. It was spacious, and hung on all sides with magnificent embroideries. Tables were covered with silk cloths and held dishes of tangerines. The ranking women from the harem were seated in comfortable chairs, while attendants stood along the walls ready with trays of drinks and sesame candy. Jao gave a small gasp of surprise as she entered the room, and then stood inconspicuously behind the older concubines while the other tsairen drifted aimlessly into the throng.

The emperor stood at ease before a huge brazier, his padded silk vest hanging loose from his shoulders. He greeted the newcomers with courtesy but no smiles, and ran a speculative eye over each one as she bowed before him. He also acknowledged the elaborate salutations of the chief eunuch before he negligently dismissed him.

"You girls will please line up so that I can see all of you at once," he ordered in a businesslike tone. Jade stepped forward and steered each girl into place, impatiently twitching Wildgoose, who jerked back at her touch. Then Jade pushed roughly at Jao, who was already in line at the end. The emperor's eyes slid over her as she did this, but they were without expression while he surveyed the young concubines that his officials had collected for him. He did not seem very enthusiastic at what he saw, and the chief eunuch's heart sank.

"I am planning a grand finale to terminate the holidays. All the members of my household will participate—it will be a special entertainment for the court," the emperor stated flatly. "You have been called here because I am settling the women's events now. First, I want two polo teams: the princesses against my concubines. Two of my older daughters who were born and raised in camp, and learned to ride before they walked, and three of my half sisters will make up one team. My sisters are expert horsewomen who served as scouts and messengers during the war years."

He paused and glanced at his sisters, who were now into their forties. They were laughing deprecatingly.

"We are really all out of practice, Shihmin," protested Shih, the sister nearest him in age, "except Shihhua who rides astride every day to keep her weight down." Here they all broke into laughter and comment, Shihhua among them. Taitsung, unamused, waited for quiet. It came immediately when they saw that he was in a sullen mood.

"Well then, you'd better start practicing now. You've got thirteen days. Now the problem is the opposing team. All the girls who have ever ridden or played polo are in this room now, and from your indifferent expressions, it looks as if none of you wants to form a team. Granted, you would have to practice a bit, but still, why not?" He paused in frustration and disapproval.

"My empress, who could ride as well as any man, has been in the Yellow Springs these two years, and the four Fei are not athletic and never have been. I have one here from Grade Two, the Chaoyi, who is willing to try." All heads turned to smile at Luminous Demeanor, who was tall and slim. She returned the smiles in a halfhearted way.

"From the Chiayu, I have five who are skilled in embroidery, three in music, and, again, only one who can ride," continued the emperor-general. Everyone looked at Suling Chiayu, who blushed and kept her eyes downcast. She was plump and rosy and adorable, but did not look as if she could keep her seat in a polo match for five minutes. It was possible that the emperor also thought so, because he continued hurriedly, "Grade Four, the Meiren, offer me two who might do."

He paused and glared at the nine tsairen. "You Grade Five girls are young and strong and ought to know how to ride a horse without falling off. How many of you do?"

Nine hands went up, and the emperor smiled for the first time that evening. "Well now, this is more like it. However, I need to see how well you can perform. Your skills listed on the eunuch's list sound passive. What I want is vigor and dash, maybe something even rough and risky, something that takes spirit. The whole court, officials, guards, and foreign guests will be watching, and they will expect the best from the palace."

He studied the handsome girls, beautifully dressed and politely attentive, with discontent. "You all look too timid. We shall have to put you on palace ponies." He scowled. "How many of you can ride bareback?" Three hands went up, from the youngest, Wildgoose, Toto, and Jao.

The emperor looked at them doubtfully and consulted his paper. "You are all from border-area families. Did you learn to ride western horses as well as the small steppe horses?" The three girls nodded shyly, but the emperor still seemed unimpressed.

"Well, we'll see. I'll have to watch you on the palace race course." He looked at the chief eunuch, who was perspiring. "Have them out there at sunrise tomorrow," he ordered. The eunuch surreptitiously wiped his bald head and bowed.

The emperor continued, "The selection of the polo team will have to wait until I see for myself what you can do. In the meantime I will use some of you for an obstacle race. You will have to jump on and off your horses without help. Can you do that? I would like to pit you against boy cadets—of your same age. That ought to be lively enough to entertain the spectators, even if none of you are very adept. You will all be riding horses strange to you. Are you up to it? Or are you too timid?"

There was a slight stir among the older women and an almost inaudible "po po po" of distress from one of them. The girls appeared very young and helpless, and the emperor seemed to be in a reckless, even harsh mood. No one had anything to say.

"Speak up, speak up," he said in exasperation.

Wildgoose spoke for the three, "We can try the big western horses."

He turned to his assistants. "Arrange for practice for them. Now then, how many of you are archers?"

Four hands went up, from girls who were brought up in the Kwannei area around the capital.

"Is that all?" Taitsung asked disgustedly. "We'll arrange matches in spite of there being so few of you. Are you getting this all down?" he asked his scribe, who was kneeling before his writing table with a busy brush. The scribe nodded, and the emperor continued.

"One last event," he said, "and that will be the best. This event is designed to show off the riding and archery skills of my special guards. I want one of you girls, from the tsairen, perhaps, to stand in the middle of a ring, balancing a lighted candle on her head, while the guardsmen ride around to see who can shoot out the flame. They will be far enough apart so they will not shoot each other. That's their skill. This event would make a splendid finale."

The silence in the room was absolute, broken finally by the quietly protesting "po po" from the same high-ranking Fei. Taitsung walked over to his stool and flung himself down.

"Women!" he muttered as he surveyed his wives and concubines. "Here I have the best women in the country, the most skilled and highest-ranking and best taught, and not one of you will volunteer to do what I want. Why? Must I be obliged to order one of you?"

There was a stir among the women, and a hand went up and then another. Soon all hands were up. The emperor's scowl deepened. "There you go, like sheep. You have to be chivied. No sense of sportsmanship. I will quote one of the ancient odes to you about women. You won't recognize the classic, of course, but you're going to listen to it now. It's about how a king lives.

"Here will he live, here will he sit,
Here will he laugh, here will he talk,
Sons shall be born to him,
They will be put to sleep on couches,
They will be clothed in robes,
They will have scepters to play with,
Their cry will be loud . . .
The future princes of the land.
Daughters shall be born to him,
They will be put to sleep on the ground . . ."

He stopped and looked challengingly around the room. Every eye was fixed on him and no one made a sound. No one knew what his meaning was, only that he was in a dangerous mood.

The emperor thought irritably, they all raised their hands to obey because that is all they could think of—to obey, dumbly to obey. My empress would have smiled broadly, her eyes bright and full of fun, and her spirit would have caught fire from mine and she would have agreed to do the thing I wanted, not out of duty, but because she wanted to. That was the way it was then, but not the way it is now.

Looking like a thundercloud, he quoted a bit more from the same ode.

"They will be clothed with wrappers,
They will have tiles to play with."

Jao raised her eyes, which had been politely fixed on her shoe tips, and shot a comprehending look at the absent-eyed emperor. I recognize that, she said to herself. It's only a bit of poetry about an ideal prince's home. All the old tutors make the boys learn it. It's easy because it lilts, and it's attractive to them because it puts women on the floor with all the other trash. She was thinking of her half brothers.

"They will have tiles to play with . . .
Only about spirits and food
Will they have to think . . ."

Jao found herself saying these words aloud. Heads turned in astonishment toward her, and she closed her lips in fright and shot an anguished look at the emperor, awaiting his wrath. He, however, did not seem to notice, and went on with a capping verse.

"For disorder does not come from Heaven
But is brought about by women."

Jao stole a glance at her housemates. They were all standing rigidly, their eyes downcast. The chief eunuch's head was now covered with sweat and he was watching the emperor in panic. Jao gazed directly at the emperor, her eyes wide, and when she discovered that he was looking at her in an interested way, she dropped into her graceful one-kneed bow and said,

"I will, Your Majesty."

He nodded, his black mood gone, and stood up. "Now we have our exhibition made up. This tsairen will stand in the center of the ring when my flying horse corps perform, and that will be the finale. It will be a good show. You are all dismissed now and may resume your holiday activities."

He watched in silence as the women dispersed, chatting lightly in relief while they glanced curiously at the small new Elegant. The Fei exchanged amused glances at the naiveté of the country girl. The Chaoyi, Chiayu, and Meiren were silent, offended, but the youngest were delighted at Jao's outburst.

Once back in the *kang* room and divested of their cloaks, the tsairen shrieked as they gathered around Jao, all talking at once in their excitement over her audacity. "However did you dare?" Peony asked, giggling good-naturedly. Toto and Wildgoose patted Jao's back in approval. Cloud just smiled, her eyes alight with admiration, and Pearl stared round-eyed and speechless. Jade looked disdainful but could think of nothing to say because, after all, Tsairen Jao had been quoting classical poetry.

Jao backed up onto the *kang* to warm herself. "Well, Peony, I never thought of daring or not daring, it was just that I did it before I could think. I opened my mouth and—"

"Your big mouth," Phoenix said on behalf of those who disapproved of Jao's behavior.

"My big mouth," Jao agreed at once. "I'll just have to learn to shut it!" At this they all laughed, even Jade.

Early on the second day of the holidays, Chief Eunuch Kao himself, much the worse for wear, bundled his shivering girls onto the field where their skills with horses were to be demonstrated. One corral contained the steppe horses, and another the big western horses. Grooms were busy saddling and bringing the mounts forward. The rumor went around that the emperor was among the judges, but he could not be identified in the gloom before sunup.

The trials began promptly, and after a good deal of head shaking, the girls for the polo team were finally selected. Wildgoose proved herself to be more at home on any horse given her to ride, whether western or steppe, than the other girls. However, she did not know the intricacies of the polo game and was eliminated while Phoenix, a lesser horsewoman, got the coveted place. Finally, Peony was added, while Jade was kept in reserve in a second team otherwise made up of Meiren. Jao performed creditably but, not being trained in palace polo, both she and Wildgoose were given other assignments for the show and were ordered to practice under the chaperonage of Chi, who was also to supervise Toto.

"You are to perform a solo sword dance, Toto," Chi told her.

"I'm not good enough," she protested. "With all these professional dancers from Kucha in town, I'd just make a fool of myself! I couldn't!"

Chi interrupted her. "You are not going to be seen by the public, this is a private show here in the palace put on by palace people, all of whom are amateurs. You have your orders. Practice as hard as you can."

Toto nodded, panic-stricken.

About mid-morning the trials for the archery events began, and although both Wildgoose and Jao wanted to participate, they were not allowed to. Their practice time was to be entirely focused on horsemanship. The only two tsairen to emerge as competitors in archery were Phoenix and Mulberry, who had both demonstrated admirable ability to put their arrows in the bull's-eye. The coaches looked at the small sparrow of a girl with surprised respect when Mulberry was chosen.

Chi now had five contenders with conspicuous roles, and he was worried. He had not expected any. It put him under unwelcome pressure to see not only that they did well, but also that they did not disgrace themselves. It was well into the week before the girls were allowed any leisure time at all.

Late one afternoon a maid from the Meiren house appeared with an invitation for Wildgoose and Jao to visit Fang Fei that day. As Jao was alone, she dressed hurriedly and went next door to walk with Fang Meiren to the compound of the four Fei.

"My cousin is the youngest of the four older consorts, the Fei," Fang Meiren remarked while they were taking off their clogs in the entry so as not to muddy the woollen carpets. They entered the reception room, where there were about a dozen women. One of them, a beautiful lady in her mid-thirties, looked up as they entered. About the age of my mother, Jao thought as she slid to her knee in a graceful bow, her knuckles barely touching the carpet.

"Rise, rise," Fang Fei greeted. "Come, sit near me and tell me about yourself." She patted the place beside her, and Jao took the seat, smiling shyly. "I recognize the graceful bow you just made. Where did you learn the subtleties of that particular style?" she asked curiously.

"From my mother," Jao politely returned.

"And your mother is . . . ?"

"Lady Yang. Wife of Wu Shihhuo of Taiyuan," Jao answered.

"Yang? I can guess where her beautiful training came from, and yours too—the Sui court. Of course we don't mention the name much anymore. I myself had such training once and I recognize it," she added warmly. "Now tell me, when did you come here and how old are you? You look very young . . . those braids, I suppose."

"I have eaten thirteen springs," Jao said, using the formal expression, "and I have been in the palace seven days. Is there something wrong with my hair?" She patted her head anxiously.

"No, no," the matron soothed, "but it is not done in a palace fashion. Here, I will twist your braids into a figure eight on the back of your head, so, and put in a pin to hold it." She called to a maid to bring one, and then thrust it into the shining knot.

"Tsairen *kuniang* looks elegant!" offered the maid, standing back, admiring.

"*Tsai tsai?* Elegant Elegant!" Jao quipped to the maid, and both women laughed.

"You do look more a palace girl now, less out of place," Fang Fei responded. "Just keep your eyes open and see what is worn by whom. If you are ever at a loss, come here and my good woman Fu will help, or I will."

"Thank you, you are kind, most kind." Jao was elated.

"You might give away the clothes you brought, and secure some new ones through the eunuchs, who can buy for you," Fang Fei suggested.

"I am being dressed in castoffs just now until my boxes come," Jao ventured forthrightly.

"Good heavens!" Madame Fang exclaimed. "Well, we'll just have to wait and see what turns up in the way of clothes. Be sure to spend enough, though, and put your hair up after this, do! Also you must meet the other Fei sometime and give them your special court bows. They will love it. Now, I want you to meet my daughter. Bixon, will you come here please?"

At the sound of her name, a delicate ten-year-old child left what she was doing and came forward. Jao met her with a formal *anjali* salute. This pleased the little girl, and her eyes shone with delight as she imitated it herself. They both smiled, and the women around chuckled approvingly. They were all Buddhists and understood the gracious meaning of the gesture.

After an interval during which tea and sesame-seed cakes were served, Bixon brought up a subject that was occupying her thoughts to the exclusion of everything else.

"My father, the emperor, is planning to end the lantern festival with a special show, and I am to sit beside him and Jer is too, so we can see everything. I have never been on the dais before." Her eyes were sparkling and her whole figure was taut with eagerness. "All the best horsemen in the flying horse cavalry and Elite Guards are in the show, and even my father and half brother, and the best women athletes. It will be the most marvelous thing! Will you watch it all too?" she added politely.

"I'll not only watch it, but be in it," Jao returned.

Bixon clapped her hands. "What are you going to do?" she demanded excitedly.

"They are trying me for several things. Watch for me, and when I see you I will wave." Jao was happy to have captured the interest of this lively child.

Fang Meiren stood up, signifying that the first call was over. Jao rose gracefully and left with her in a flurry of cordial good-byes, forgetting that she still had the costly gold pin in her hair.

As they passed the other three houses in the compound, Fang Meiren pointed them out to her. "This is the house of Number Three Fei, Pei Huade. She goes to everything, she is seen everywhere, and she is always dressed in the height of fashion. She has no children and is not ambitious for any higher rank than she already has. You must become known to her, but do not expect her to go out of her way for you. She doesn't for anyone.

"This next house," she said as they passed a charming pavilion set in its own formal garden, "belongs to the oldest woman in the palace. Liang Fei is forty if she is a day. She is seldom seen because she has few interests other than her garden and her books. She is an authority on Lady Pang's book on etiquette, which we follow here at court. Most of the palace women steer clear of her, even the eunuchs, although they say the emperor still visits her. She is never called to visit him, you understand."

They came to the last house. "This one is occupied by the Number One Fei. She's beautiful, but a bit matronly. She's also the mother of one of Taitsung's sons, Tai. She is greatly respected, although she may be a bit slow in her understanding. Nobody minds that. You must, by all means, bow to her and become known to her. As a member of the great Chang family of Changan, she has influence."

Jao listened carefully, nodding her head in attention, saying nothing. When they arrived at the entrance to the Meiren compound, Jao thanked her with a deep bow and a warm *wanfu*. She then went on to her own quarters.

Jade accosted her in the doorway as Jao entered her room. "Your hair looks different, you have a gold pin in it. How did that happen?"

"Fang Fei arranged my hair for me and put in the pin," Jao answered in a pleased voice. "She did me great honor. How kind she is!"

Jade and Phoenix, who had joined her, exchanged glances. Quickly, Jade followed Jao into her room and deftly plucked the pin out of her hair.

"Here," Jao cried, outraged. "What are you doing? That is not my pin, I have to return it to Fang Fei. Give it back."

Mi, who was standing beside Jao, ready to take her damp mantle, plucked the pin from Jade's loose grasp and stood back. At this interference from a slave, Jade's avarice turned into rage. She snatched her silk whip from her girdle and twice lashed it across Mi's face, leaving huge welts. She was raising her whip to strike again when Jao caught its end and gave it a quick jerk that sent Jade spinning. Equally nimble, Mi leaped to pick Jade up, but lost the pin in the scuffle, and it rolled into a corner.

"Pick up that pin!" Jade shouted to Jao, raising her whip on Jao this time.

"Stop!" ordered a heavy voice. They all turned at once toward Ket, who had noiselessly entered the room. When Mi saw her, she darted to the corner, picked up the pin and handed it to Ket.

"Whose pin?" Ket asked.

"Mine," Jao and Jade cried at the same time.

Jade put her hand out peremptorily and adroitly removed the hair ornament from Ket's grasp, then pointed with fury at Mi. "That slave struck me. A criminal act for a slave! You must punish her. By law, a slave who strikes a superior must have her arms broken. Do it now, I will have justice this instant. Or I will see to it that you yourself receive the punishment." Jade was angered that she had fallen and lost face.

This was big trouble in the tsairen house. Ket was slow but not stupid. She knew that Tsairen Tsui Jade was a very important lady, and that she, Ket, was accountable for peace in the house. Before anyone could move, she grasped Mi's lower arm and twisted it sharply. There was a loud crack and a scream. The scream was not from Mi, who paled but remained silent. It came from a horrified Jao, who could not believe her eyes.

Within seconds the room emptied and Jao and Mi were alone. Jao gently supported Mi to the bed and set her down, then pulled out her trunk to find a cloth to use as a bandage.

"What has happened?" Wildgoose had entered without knocking, as was her custom. Jao started to answer, when she saw Ket standing in the doorway and cried out in alarm. Ket paid no attention to Jao, but spoke directly to Wildgoose in her own tongue. She then disappeared as silently as she had come while Wildgoose explained what Ket had told her.

"Ket says that she had to punish your slave for striking a palace lady because that's the rule, but she also knows who was to blame. That's why she broke only one arm—for discipline. Now she has gone for splints. She really wants to help you."

Jao just stared while she tried to think. She was frightened to be in such trouble so soon. She said to Mi, "Are you willing to let Ket bind you up?"

Mi tried to ease her dangling arm with her free one, and fainted with the effort. Ket, who had come back with her supplies, nodded when she saw Mi go limp. "Good, now she be quiet for me to set." Ket grasped the affected arm, and feeling for the broken ends, quickly snapped them together. Mi moaned but did not regain consciousness. After greasing the arm with an aloe salve, Ket wrapped a band tightly around the arm and splints. She grunted in satisfaction, appropriated a shawl to hold the arm in place, and vanished.

Wildgoose and Jao looked at the unconscious slave and then at each other, thoroughly overcome by it all. "What a mess this is," Jao said at last. "It's a good thing that you understood what Ket said, and it's a good thing that she saw it all, but now Jade and Phoenix will hate me and I have lost Fang Fei's pin. What am I going to do?"

Wildgoose went to the door, looked out to see if anyone was listening, then said to Jao, "We are new here so we have to keep quiet and make no trouble. I won't say anything, you won't say anything, and it will all blow over."

"I have to get that pin back. I have to," Jao said. "I am going into Jade's room now and ask her for it."

"Do you want me to come with you?" Wildgoose asked.

"No, no, but *wanfu* anyway! You must not get into trouble on my account. You stay out of it."

Wildgoose looked unconvinced, and waited in the hall while Jao went to Jade's door and entered it unannounced. One maid was polishing Jade's fingernails, another her toenails.

"What do you want?" Jade asked. "If you came to get my pin, you are wasting your time."

"It is not your pin. It belongs to Fang Fei and must be returned," Jao said in a shaking voice.

"Who is going to believe you?" Jade replied coolly. "If you make the mistake of carrying tales to Fang Fei, she will just think that you are keeping the pin for yourself and lying about it. You will soon be known around here as a low character, a talebearer, a troublemaker, and no one will speak to you."

Jade did not like to have her housemates make contacts that she herself did not have, and she was especially against newcomers who got out of line. Jao's socializing must stop.

Jao clutched at the door frame. "What do I have to do to get the pin back?" she asked.

Jade thought a moment. "Wait upon me for a month as my servant," she retorted.

"But I have to practice for the emperor's show," Jao protested.

"Then you will have to do something else. Stand at my door for twenty-four hours and do not eat or drink or speak. Then I will let you have it. Start now."

Jao's chin went up and she took her position at the door at once. Jade smiled with malice. Even if she lasts that long, and she won't, I won't let her have it, she thought.

Jade dressed in formal clothes and then left Jao to be watched by her maids while she herself went out on her New Year's calls. Her last call was on Chief Eunuch Kao, to whom, with great delicacy and docility, she handed a silk-wrapped package. Attached to the package was a card with good wishes written on it and the value of the contents, ten gold ingots. He looked at her, his face creased in smiles. "And I wish you the same," he said suavely, and she bowed her way out.

Kao knew that Jade wanted him to put her on the next list to see the emperor. He could take names off, but not always put them on. This mistress Jade was called a year ago, the eunuch thought, but it seems the emperor has forgotten her.

Jade returned as dusk fell and lamps were being lit. She stamped the snow off her feet and brushed by the exhausted Jao when she entered her room.

"Has she been obeying my orders?" she asked the maids.

"Yes indeed," they chorused, "but she shifts from one foot to the other."

"You are not to do that, do you hear?" Jade shouted at Jao while the maids looked on with pleasure. A tsairen in trouble was an amusing sight to the kind of women whom Jade employed. Suddenly, the gong in the back hall sounded, and Jade looked startled. "Now what's that?" she cried. "Go see," she ordered a maid.

In a moment she was back. "It is the master Chi, and he wants everyone in the *kang* room," she said.

Jade scowled. "Master Chi! Master Chi interfering again! Well, I shall see that Master Chi is transferred one of these days!" She stamped her feet angrily as she went down the hall to the *kang* room to see what was wanted. All the other girls, except for Jao, were already there.

"The new girl, Jao," Chi said, "does she know that she must answer the gong? Where is her maid?" He called loudly, and Mi, looking pale, lurched down the hall.

"Jao's not in," she said.

"Where is she then? Speak up!"

"She's in Mistress Jade's room," Mi answered.

"Why hasn't she come?" Chi asked impatiently.

Jade, remembering the size of the gift that she had just given to Chief Eunuch Kao, said coolly, "Jao is being punished and has to stay there."

In exasperation, Chi said, "This meeting is important. Get her."

Jade didn't move.

"Get her!" he thundered, looking so menacing that Jade forgot that he was nothing but a eunuch and signaled to her maid to fetch Jao.

The minutes dragged by, Chi growing angrier by the minute. He had had a long, hard day, and the knowledge that he was responsible for everything the tsairen did worried him.

Jao entered at last, pale and barely able to stand. Chi stared at her. "Sit down," he ordered.

"She has to stand," Jade said pleasantly. The silence that fell upon the room was electric.

"Sit down!" Chi roared, his eyes angry slits in his face. He saw himself as a military man enforcing orders, not a lowly eunuch. Jao sat down.

"Now you listen to me, all of you. The emperor is putting on this show himself, with the most talented women as performers, and he expects the best from everyone. Surely that must be clear even to the tiniest brain. Your very best. Nothing is to interfere. Nothing! I am here now to review your schedules and to inform you when your rehearsals will take place. The majordomo will coordinate. Now listen."

Chi briefed the girls for a half an hour and then dismissed all except Jade. Nonetheless, she started to leave, pausing insolently at the door when Chi spoke.

"You are to leave Jao alone. You are not to interfere with her practice for the emperor's show, and you are to keep out of her way altogether. Understand?"

"And what if I don't?" she asked. "What can you do about it?"

"Plenty," he said. "For one thing, I can see that a red card never, never reaches you."

Her eyes dropped. It was her one desire above all things, to receive a red card. Chi had found her one vulnerability. She did not reply, but turned her back on him and withdrew. No doubt about it, Chi will have to go, she thought.

Chi watched her leave and then stamped out of the house to the kitchen. The night guard was there, listening attentively to what Ket was telling her about the fray over the pin. At Chi's orders, Ket repeated the story to him.

"I am going to get that pin from Jade myself. Now," he said.

Ket reached under her coat and pulled it out. "Have got," she said shortly.

"How?" Chi asked, startled.

"While you talk tsairen in *kang* room, I start dogfight in front court, and all maids run to watch. Then I take."

"Give it over," Chi demanded, grinning. "I'll deliver it to Fang Fei myself. Let Jao know it is safe. It is indeed a costly thing." He studied the gold ball at the end of the pin and the filigree and inlay, and shook his head while carefully stowing it away under his robe. Then he left and the house subsided into quiet.

The day of the fete dawned cold but windless, and the sun shone in a cloudless sky. The largest athletic field in the palace park had been swept, and straw ropes looped around the perimeter to keep the crowds contained. Clusters of pine branches were placed along the rope in the center of each scallop as symbols of a green and flourishing new year. Five hundred soldiers in polished hide and brass armor stood at intervals around the field, each with a spear crossing his neighbor's.

The triple doors of the Hsuanwu gate were open, even the central one usually reserved for the emperor. It had been opened at his orders for his high-ranking guests. The pennants of the emperor and the crown prince flew from the tower. Tents, erected around the field for the comfort of the guests, were furnished with tables, benches, food, and a bronze container of charcoal embers to take off the chill.

The stand for the imperial family was at one end of the field, while at the other, the performers assembled behind the red and white stripes of a canvas barricade. With a flourish of trumpets the emperor and crown prince rode in to take their places on the platform. Two children accompanied them, causing some speculation about who they were. They had barely seated themselves when the drums, sounding a rapid ratatatat, signaled the opening of the meet. A stir of excitement ran through the crowd. Every member of the court who had the strength to rise from his bed was present. There had never been such a spectacle before in any man's memory, and no one wanted to miss it.

The first event was an exhibition of a maneuver by Taitsung's foot soldiers, who filled the field and delighted the eyes with the convolutions of their marching, a spectacular display of sinuous rhythm, accompanied at every turn by the beats of their battle drums and the thud of simultaneously placed felt boots. Shouts of approval arose when the drums suddenly fell silent and the lineup of officers before the emperor's stand presented arms in unison as a final flourish. The emperor acknowledged this with his fists clasped overhead, while the men streamed off the field to become spectators in the area reserved for them.

A dress performance of the palace guardsmen in their colorful uniforms and their variety of headgear came next. Handsomely groomed, they were the cream of Taitsung's own guards. After they too left the field, an elite cavalry unit, the Flying Horse Corps, performed a breathtaking display of skilled horsemanship on the tall western horses, receiving loud and prolonged cheers.

Then the regular cavalry, on their shaggy steppe ponies, rode in bareback, hidden on the sides of their mounts so that the horses appeared to be moving riderless. They formed concentric circles, one moving in one direction and the other in the opposite, the two wheels stopping suddenly as their officers reached the stand. Loud stamping of feet and cheers greeted this performance, as most of the audience had more knowledge of steppe horsemanship than of the showmanship of the elite corps.

After a recess of an hour, a roll of drums and a fanfare of trumpets signaled the opening of the afternoon events. The spectators streamed back to their places, a throng now effervescent from generous servings of imperial wines. The tumult died down, however, when the attention of the crowd was caught by the appearance of six magnificent warhorses from the emperor's stables. One after the other, fully caparisoned with their manes and tails braided and bunched as if for combat, they entered the arena, riderless and proud, with arched necks and prancing side steps.

The emperor descended from the stage and leapt into the saddle of the lead horse. He sat easily, demonstrating a horsemanship that almost all present had heard about but never seen. The second riderless charger passed the stage, and the crown prince mounted with a sinuous leap. He too showed himself superb in the saddle. Senior princes Li Yuanguei, Li

Yuanjia, and Li Jencheng took the next three mounts, all proving themselves at home on war-horses.

Last of all, a small figure in blue tied tightly at the waist with a crimson sash, ran out into the field along the sixth horse, her head even with the horse's back, her body suddenly, without apparent effort, in the saddle. Her horse was perfectly attuned to the movements of the other horses. This unknown rider was a surprise. No one could understand why she was there until she showed a grace in the saddle unusual in a female. No one knew who she was except the emperor, who had chosen her, and Chi, who had supervised her. Ragged cheers and halloos of appreciation were heard on all sides, increasing in enthusiasm while the six riders put these personal horses of the emperor through their intricate paces.

The audience seemed to feel that this event was the culmination of the show, and some were preparing to leave when they realized that the emperor himself was preparing to appear in an archery contest with the crown prince. The target was set at a hundred paces, and when the crowd was quiet, Taitsung stepped forward, his horn bow in hand.

Taking his time, testing the wind and his bowstrings, fitting his whistling-head arrow, he pointed to the ground and drew until he felt the tension was right, then looked at his target a long moment, breathed deeply, lifted and loosed the arrow all in one movement. It soared for breathtaking seconds and then dived gracefully into the target.

The twenty-year-old crown prince followed his father, his style more mannered, but he too put his arrow into the straw target next to his father's. The crowd roared. The arrows were removed and the target set at two hundred paces. The performance was repeated this time with an allowance of two arrows apiece. Both men again hit the straw. The target was then put at three hundred paces, and this time three arrows were allowed.

A sighing sound went through the assembly. Prince Chengchien shot first, and two arrows hit the target, one missed. The crowd literally held its breath when the emperor lifted his bow. Two arrows, one after the other, split the former arrows, then one missed. Laughter welled up and cries of approval and "Well done!" echoed through the park. Neither contender had won, neither had lost, and the emperor remained unbeaten.

Any event after this would have precipitated a feeling of anticlimax had not the women's polo match begun at once. This was a rare spectacle, and no one wanted to miss it. To see the emperor's ladies in action! Who had ever heard of such a thing? People who had left the field crowded back. Imperial family women against the emperor's ladies, a great sight! The game was short and spirited, well-played and dramatic. Nor was it without some rough entanglements, during which two women were thrown. The spectators shouted with delight when the two who had fallen rolled skillfully out of the way of the horses' hooves and limped off the field in smiling disarray.

Two tsairen, Phoenix and Peony, were on one of the teams, and Phoenix turned out to be the star player, making the final goal that won them the game. The emperor took note—his tsairen were performing better than expected, and he felt a warm desire to reward them well.

When the women rode off the field, straw targets were placed for the archery contest. The archers included both the princesses and members from the first five grades of consorts, mostly older women, but Phoenix and Mulberry of the tsairen held their own against them. In the final bout, five targets were placed at a hundred paces and the five highest-scoring contenders were given the signal to shoot at the same time. Each had two tries. Phoenix got two arrows barely on target, and the third missed altogether. Wang Chaoyi first hit the bull's-eye and then placed her second arrow on target. Mulberry placed both arrows so close to the center that no one knew the outcome until the officials determined the winner. It was Mulberry.

The events that closed the entertainment included the acrobatics of Wildgoose on horseback, synchronized with the movements of a boy of fourteen from the cadets. The crowd shouted with amusement at the somersaults and handsprings performed on the trotting horses. Then they watched with pleasure while an exuberant Toto twirled through the sword dance of Kucha while the arena was being cleared for the finale.

The moment the dance was over, a number of the best marksmen and horsemen of the Flying Horse Corps trotted into the ring. People craned their necks for this last event. A small, familiar figure in blue ran to the center of the ring and a lighted candle was placed on her head. Excitement mounted as the audience caught on to what was happening. It increased as the riding and shooting went faster and faster and the spectators realized that they themselves were a part of the exercise when spent arrows flew over their tent tops. The flame suddenly went out when one of the arrows doused it, and the show was over.

With much stamping of feet and yells of gratitude, the crowd began to disperse.

The tsairen had done well and were excited. Their day had ended in high style when they were called forward to receive congratulations from the emperor himself. After they returned to the house and doffed their blue suits, they met in Jao's room, which most easily held them all. Mulberry was shrill with excitement, and Phoenix, who had lost to her, far from sulking, was paying her thoughtful attention. Mulberry kept saying, "It was so close, it was a tie really, they should have announced a tie."

Jade, who had been appointed to the second polo team, had not been called upon to play. She was, nevertheless, basking in tsairen popularity, which she appropriated as her right, since she considered herself head of household. She invited relatives to visit in her room after the show, and they were happy to come. For a couple of hours she was fully occupied with them and did not participate in the general merriment in Jao's room.

After they left, she joined her housemates. When she entered the room, the first thing that met her eye was Phoenix laughingly massaging Mulberry's hand for a strained muscle. The two girls were obviously enjoying themselves, discussing the fine points of archery and making plans to continue practice when it could be arranged.

Jade roughly grasped Phoenix by the arm. "You should have won!" she burst out, a vein throbbing in her forehead. "I saw where the arrows went. One of yours was in the bull's-eye and the other close!"

Phoenix turned to answer Jade peaceably. She was still holding Mulberry's hand. Jade went pale and slapped her hand away. "You are the real winner," she cried.

Mulberry, tired and self-conscious, started to cry at these harsh words, and the girls who were still in the room gathered around to comfort her. This exasperated Jade beyond reason, and she pushed Mulberry aside as she herded Phoenix and Peony out of the room.

Cloud quickly suggested that they all have tea. "Mulberry, I am going to brew some tea over the brazier in here. Would you like some? It is a special kind known for its fragrance and its flavor—Dragon Well tea from our farm near Suchow."

Mulberry turned to leave. "Thank you—good of you—but I don't believe that I can eat anything or drink anything just now," she replied in her confusion. "I think that I will just go to bed, if you will excuse me."

At this point Chi, who had made his report to the chief and had hurried to the tsairen house to congratulate the girls, entered the house. He felt that his own position in the palace hierarchy and his chances for promotion were enhanced by the efforts of his charges, so he was cheerful.

What he found was Mulberry crying, Cloud shouting at a maid to bring tea quickly, Phoenix standing defiantly beside her new friend, Jade rigid with some kind of strong emotion, and the other girls in various states of astonishment and fatigue. They all vanished into their rooms as soon as they saw him, and he was left without anyone to congratulate.

"Strange!" he ejaculated. "Strange! Girls! Will I ever understand them?"

He was suddenly aware of his own state of fatigue. He stood in the hall thinking about how he might spend his evening when a loud banging on the front door drew his attention. He heard someone answer and footsteps retreating, then Ket came in with an envelope of red silk.

"This is red card," she said. Chi jumped. "A summons for one of my tsairen!" he exclaimed. Cloud, Wildgoose, and Toto flashed across his mind as possibilities.

"For whom?" he asked. By this time heads were appearing around all doorjambs.

"For Mulberry," Ket said.

Shriek after shriek sounded from Mulberry's room. "I am ordered to the Purple Chamber, me! I can't believe that I am the one honored." She dashed into the hall to confirm matters with Chi, while the gallery filled with interested tsairen.

"I don't think that you are the one," Jade said. "There must be some mistake." She snatched the red silk envelope from Mulberry's hand and opened it. "See, no name! I am sure it is for me," she announced as a slip of paper fell to the floor.

Chi stared at her unbelieving and reached for the envelope in Jade's hand. She jerked back.

"Are you mad?" he said. "You cannot mean this. Let me see the card." He continued to hold out his hand, and at length she surrendered the card. The eunuch read it. "This summons is for three nights hence. The emperor is occupied tonight, and tomorrow he is going on a three-day hunt." He picked up the piece of paper that had dropped out. "The name on this is clearly Tsairen Hsin, not Tsairen Tsui," he said, surveying his tense audience. Mulberry looked as if anything could trigger her into hysterics.

Jade, with a strange, obsessed look on her pale face, tore the slip of paper out of Chi's hand. Her will had never in her life been thwarted for long, and she did not intend to be overborne now.

"You read the characters wrong, Tsui and Hsin are much alike, you read them wrong," she said as she went into her room.

Jao had been standing with downcast eyes, but raised them when Jade left. She encountered Wildgoose's blank stare, and recognized it as a strong signal that retreat was the best tactic. Toto was also edging away. She craved a bath, her dinner, a game of cards, and curling up on a warm *kang* for sleep. All this was apparent in the one glance she gave Jao, so Jao too turned to go, ashamed at abandoning Mulberry, but glad to escape.

Chi watched them all leave, then took his own departure without the slip with the name on it. In a few minutes he stood in front of Eunuch Kao, handed over the red card and reported the incident. Kao folded his hands over his stomach and listened. "We will provide another slip with the name of Hsin on it," he said, "easily done, but you will have to deal with Jade yourself. I suggest a hot bath and a roll in the snow afterward. Mulberry's family has sent a cartload of gifts in recognition of the honor paid to their unknown but wealthy clan."

"Gifts? To you? What for?" Chi returned sourly. Kao's face creased in a knowing smile.

"It is all very well for you to be disdainful, but you will be in my position someday, and then you will realize that if you do not solicit and receive gifts while you can, you will have nothing for your old age. I am happy to make life a little easier for Tsairen Mulberry."

"Harder, you mean. She is in real trouble now, and so am I," Chi retorted.

CHAPTER FIVE

The next morning the palace seemed very quiet, as normal life gradually resumed after the New Year's festivities. The tsairen dispersed to the various houses of the more senior concubines, where duties awaited them. Jao was pleased that she had been requested by Fang Fei to assist her. Setting out after breakfast into the cold blasts of an oncoming storm, Jao was chilled by the time she reached the Fei compound. She was glad to get into Fang's living room, which was warmer than the tsairen house ever was. She bowed to Fang Fei, who was seated on the fur-covered day bed, with Bixon kneeling against her, having her hair brushed. Bixon tended to reject services from the maids if she could get them from her mother.

A strikingly handsome woman was seated beside Fang Fei, and Jao bowed to her also. It was Princess Li Wencheng. The princess smiled at her, and Jao bowed again to hide her surprise. The princess looked so much like the emperor that, were she seen at a distance in his clothes, she could be taken for him. She chuckled when she saw Jao's expression.

"Strangers always wonder at my looks," she reassured Jao, and, turning to Fang Fei, added lightly, "I really should have been a boy because I have never liked girls' activities. Now here I am, embedded in a woman's world in this palace, with more and more restrictions every day. What I really like is what Shihmin does: hunting and riding, conducting court life, and having the power to order important people about!"

She paused because Fang Fei appeared shocked. "Nothing wrong in wishing, is there?" she asked. "Or do you disapprove of my use of Shihmin's name since the Shih part is taboo?"

When Fang Fei only nodded, Wencheng laughed.

"I am not defying the taboo. Shihmin told the family recently that he has given his brothers and sisters—thirty of us—permission to use his family name freely, as we always have. An honor for us but for no one else. Probably this concession is being worried over in the Secretariat, and so you have not heard. Those scholar-officials, they are like burrs under one's saddle—you can't do this, it's not good for the manners of the people; you can't do that, it's not good for the morals of the people! It irritates the emperor more and more these days. Like having a snake drop from the rafters into your lap when you are having a peaceful sit-down. It quite ruins one's comfort—"

She broke off when she noticed that three pairs of eyes were fixed too solemnly on her.

"How I do run on. I don't mean half I say!"

Fang Fei impulsively put her hand on the other's arm. "I love to listen to you. I especially like to hear the emperor's name because I can't say it myself . . . so say it often!"

"I'm sure to oblige because I talk about him so often! He is always doing something challenging. Living, for Shihmin, is to take risks, the bigger the better, and to live fully his own way. He can't bear to be hedged about with restrictions. The same with me." Wencheng smiled in her disarming way and reached for her shawl.

"Oh, don't go, you are my favorite aunt!" Bixon cried. "Stay and have lunch with us and talk. I love it when you're here." She reached out a small hand and stroked Wencheng's smooth cheek. "You look like my father but you don't feel like him."

The ladies laughed knowingly. "Shihmin does feel like a porcupine, at least to those who get that close to him . . . those bristling red mustaches that one could hang a bow on!" The princess chuckled. "I don't see how you can bear it, Fang, my friend."

Fang Fei shrugged. "I don't mind looking at it."

"But not feeling it," teased the princess.

Fang Fei shrugged and blushed, and then she sighed. "It is so good to have you around, my princess. I would surely wither away without you to laugh with. I don't like to be boxed in either, and I don't know what to do about it. You cope by just making fun of it all. There are so many things that I can't laugh at . . . this new trouble for instance. Please sit down again and let me tell you."

Wencheng hesitated, but returned to her seat while Fang Fei braided a ribbon into Bixon's hair. "There, you look neat. Now, please go play your new pachisi game with Tsairen Jao."

Bixon looked inquiringly at Jao, "Will you?" Jao took her hand and they withdrew to the alcove. She didn't mind, for she enjoyed being with the child and realized that Fang Fei wished to tell the princess something in private.

"It's about Jer," Fang Fei said at once. "Taitsung's household chamberlain told me that it is best to remain silent about the whole affair, but I feel that I should discuss it with someone who has Jer's best interests at heart."

She paused, and Wencheng said quickly, "If it is about Jer, I want to know. He's been unhappy ever since his mother died, and I am concerned for him. You know that I don't spread stories around the palace. That way of passing time is for the empty heads." The princess frowned, remembering. "I had heard that Shihmin sent the boy home from the royal hunt two days early because he was ill. There is no scandal behind that, surely."

"He is not just ill," Fang Fei said. "He had a bad shock. For two days now he hasn't eaten, and he does nothing but sit—not sulking, not difficult, just staring at the wall. The chamberlain brought Jer to me to see if Bixon could help, but he only answers her questions politely and goes back to his silence. He is here now. Taitsung has not returned yet from the hunt."

"What happened?" Wencheng asked.

"During the hunt, Jer was tagging along with Chengchien in his usual 'me-too' way, riding his pony as close to his brother as he could and enjoying himself like a normal boy. One of the emperor's guards was keeping an eye on him, and all went well the first day. The second day Chengchien shot quite badly, so he returned to his tent in the afternoon and started drinking."

"That Chengchien! He's an easygoing fellow, but so stupid," his aunt exclaimed impatiently. "Only the empress could do anything with him. I think it's his lameness that makes him so mulish."

"Well . . . yes," Fang Fei continued. "Once he was drunk he asked his Turkish friends to stage one of their favorite shooting games where they ride in a circle, with a dog inside, and take shots at the frantic animal until it is done for. The fellows agreed at once, pouring out of their tents while the horses were brought up and they were all mounted. There were lots of hunting dogs around, and Chengchien was about to point one out when he noticed Jer's pet dog. He grabbed it by the fur of its neck and tossed it into the circle. He ignored Jer's screams. Tutor Chu tried to intervene, but Chengchien just yelled, 'Out of my way, old man,' and gave the signal to start.

"When the dog started crying, Jer darted into the circle to get his dog. Fortunately, one of the riders grabbed him by his belt and tossed him to a guard. And so, Jer watched his pet die in terrible agony; the sight made him vomit. Then the servants hurried him into his brother's tent to clean him up, but he just lay on his stomach, shaking and refusing to get on with the hunt. Since he would have nothing to do with Chengchien, the emperor was fetched, and when Taitsung asked him what was bothering him, Jer said he wanted to go home."

The princess frowned at this. "How did Shihmin handle the boy's tantrum?" she asked.

Fang Fei shook her head. "You can't brush it off as a tantrum. Taitsung tried that but it didn't work. He told the boy that the best of the hunt was ahead and that he shouldn't let a little thing spoil the hunt for him, that it wasn't manly."

"What then?" the princess asked quickly.

"Well, Jer rounded on his father shouting, 'A little thing? A little thing! How can you say that? Would you like to have Chengchien's barbarians surround your best war-horse and torture him till he died? Would you? Would you?'

"They say Taitsung was properly stung. If there is anything under heaven, human or animal, that commands the emperor's devotion, it is his own personal horse. 'I'd kill them,' he said, and Jer answered. 'That's what I'm going to do.' That's when Taitsung sent the boy home," Fang Fei finished.

Wencheng frowned with thought. "Shihmin was so upset because he dreads the possibility that his sons will someday fall out and fight each other to the death . . . which happened when Shihmin killed his two brothers. That has shadowed his life ever since."

The two women fell silent, troubled. Then Wencheng jumped up, scattering the furs. "Jer is a spunky little devil and I know how he feels. The trouble is, I know how his brother feels as well. Both of them have got to learn to cope with things as they are, not as they stubbornly and childishly want them to be. I won't try to talk to Jer. It would do no good because I come on too strongly and people never listen when I'm like that. But don't let him brood. Get him in here with Bixon and Jao and have him just sit here with them awhile."

She squeezed Fang Fei's inert hand and, in a flurry of cold air, was gone.

Fang Fei stayed where she was, quietly listening to her daughter's happy giggles. Finally, she called Bixon to her. "Go to Jer, please. Don't say anything—just take his hand and bring him here."

In a short time, to the surprise of the serving women, Bixon appeared in the living room with Jer in tow.

"Sit down here beside, me," Bixon said coaxingly to the boy, "and watch me play. It's a new game that I've learned."

Jao patted the seat beside her, and Jer obediently sat, but he did so mechanically and without interest. Then the warm friendliness in her eyes and her expression of sympathy touched him in his loneliness. As he watched the plays, Jao explained the patterns on the board and the purpose of the game. He began to finger the counters and to notice strategies. When a maid brought in three bowls of soup, he took the bowl offered to him and absentmindedly drank it. Soon, he had joined in the play.

At this, the women in the room, who had been inconspicuously watching, sighed with relief. A bit later Bixon yawned and abandoned the game to climb upon the *kang* where she soon fell asleep. Once more Jer, without prompting, did the same, and fell immediately into a doze. He jerked and moaned but he did sleep. The women exchanged satisfied looks.

In a whisper Lady Fang beckoned Jao to a quiet corner. "I want to thank you for returning the pin," she said. "In such a nice way too, with Chi thanking me. He spoke highly of your good character."

Jao blinked and smiled with relief. She had not heard about the return of the pin. "Your ladyship has been very kind to me. I shall never forget! All my life I shall remember these kindnesses." Her body tightened in her effort to express her feelings.

Fang Fei smiled at her earnestness but was touched. "Please come here often. Come to see the children when you need someone to talk to about the way things are done in the palace. For instance, you really should appear with your hair up. I have a little pin—to give to you this time—and I will put it in now."

She twirled Jao's braids into a figure eight and thrust the pin into place. It was a plain amber piece that looked less expensive than it was. "There," she said, "it glows in your black hair and makes you look *tsai Tsai*!"

The homely pun put Jao at her ease at once, and they both laughed. Fang Fei glanced at the sleeping children and sighed. "You must go now, little one."

Jao glanced at the quiet room where attendants were sewing and the children were sleeping with their pets, and she rose feeling greatly comforted that she had indeed found friends.

"You have been a great help to me," Fang Fei said, "and the children obviously like you. I will send for you to visit again soon."

Jao gave her *anjali* salute and left at once. She easily found her way back to the tsairen house. The others were already in the *kang* room. They were sleepy and had dismissed their maids for the night. Phoenix and Peony changed places so that Phoenix could continue her archery conversations with Mulberry. Peony had gone to sleep at once in her usual relaxed fashion, but Jade, stony-faced, sat bolt-upright in her special corner. Jao climbed on the *kang* and settled herself, yawning contentedly. It had been a good day. While dozing off she heard Mulberry say, "I'll just go to my room now so that I can sleep late . . . " Jao's last conscious thought was that Mulberry would rather sleep in a cold room than endure Jade's silent displeasure.

It seemed to her that she had turned over only once before it was daylight. She went down the hall to her room and saw that a mantle of snow had covered the front yard during the night. When she went to the washroom, the same untrodden cover of snow was on the backyard too. It felt good to be the first one up, she thought while stretching. She returned to her room and took her time dressing and experimenting with her hair, trying out the best way to wear her amber pin. Mi came in and set about her morning chores, doing everything with her one good arm. Morning noises began as maids and mistresses stirred.

Suddenly, a piercing shriek came from the room next to the *kang*. Ket, who had just relieved the night watchwoman, hurried to investigate. Jao looked out into the hall and saw Mi and several others hurrying to the door of Mulberry's room. In a few seconds Mi rejoined Jao.

"It's Mulberry . . . she's lying there warmly covered but she doesn't move."

"There is nothing to get excited about, then. She said she wanted to sleep late," Jao replied crossly.

"She's dead," Mi said.

Jao gave a little scream. "What! Wh-What happened? Go find out!"

Mi returned to the crowd in Mulberry's room. Ket had covered the dead girl's face and was permitting no one to touch anything while she waited for Chi to come. He, in turn, summoned the head guard and a medical official. Jade, standing beside Ket, spoke in a hard voice with the officials. "Taking charge," Wildgoose said derisively, when she slipped into Jao's room.

"This time I am glad she is," Jao answered, shivering while she closed her door firmly behind Wildgoose. The house was filled with the sounds of heavy footsteps. People were stamping off the snow, officials were filling the halls interviewing the terrified servants, and guards were scrutinizing Mulberry's room after the body had been removed.

One by one, the girls gathered in Jao's room for comfort, but Jade lingered with the officials. She had remained in Mulberry's room even when curtly ordered out. Pearl and Toto sat down to play cards, hoping to calm their nerves. Peony had brought her embroidery and was trying to look appropriately sad, but Phoenix just sat with folded hands, staring into space. "This has all happened before," Cloud said. The new girls, startled, looked at her. "In a year and a half, one suicide, one going insane—with the emperor very angry about it—one dying of fever. Now this. The house is cursed." She subsided. No one else had anything to say. They were too frightened.

"Is anyone hungry?" Mi ventured, and when her suggestion met with sounds of approval, she went off to the kitchen. She soon returned with bowls of steamed millet and jugs of hot barley water. "This is all there was," she said with a diffident shrug. "The kitchen is in an uproar."

The sun climbed the sky and melted the snow, which had been muddied by hundreds of tracks. Icicles began to drop from the tile ends. The officials took themselves off, and gradually order was restored in the household. Jade buttonholed Chi while he was sealing the door to Mulberry's room.

"What is the verdict?" she demanded.

"She has been examined by both the medical and security people and the death certificate has been signed. It is all out of my hands now," Chi replied in frank relief.

"But what did she die of?" Jade persisted.

"She was upset yesterday, so the officials decided that the archery contest, followed by the call to the Front Court, was too much. Weakness in the heart . . ." He shrugged.

Jade nodded coldly, but Chi noticed that she seemed subtly pleased. He cursed the house and girls in general and left, banging the door behind him.

Wanting to keep the tsairen busy and get their minds off their fears, the eunuchs invited a courtesan to give them some lectures about good manners and bedroom behavior. At noon the next day, therefore, the eight tsairen settled on cushions in Jao's room, whispering nervously among themselves. The room fell silent when an elegantly groomed madam entered, followed by her servant, who carried several scrolls and lay figures.

She did not wait for the girls to come to attention. Fixing her eyes on the wall over their heads, she began her lecture in a high-pitched voice.

"You young ladies have all been carefully reared from birth for one purpose—to marry some youth of your own age and to raise children inside the protection of the family walls."

She paused, and Jao thought that she detected a hint of scorn in the woman's voice. "You expected an easy life, protected by your family and your many walls, an easy life until one day your husband introduces a younger woman into the household. Then it is no longer so easy because now there is jealousy and faction. But the position of the Number One Wife is not much threatened and she can live in peace in her old age, while the second wife and her children are at risk."

Like me, Jao thought. Second Daughter of Second Wife, even though my mother was never a concubine.

"Here in the palace it is very different," the courtesan continued. "You are all lesser wives here. You are not protected from jealousy and rivalry, and your position is never secure. You do not have the easy task of pleasing a young husband, but the hard task of pleasing an emperor who is, to say the least, not easy to please."

There was no chattering among the girls now. They were all seriously attentive. The courtesan continued, "Also, if you are successful in pleasing the emperor, even if you become a favorite, you may be—probably will be—exposed to the jealousies of all the other concubines. That is a great problem in the palace. Today I have come to give you tsairen special counseling because there has been so much trouble in this house. Your guardians think there is too much jealousy and inability to get along. Quarreling and such. The emperor is not pleased, and the chief eunuch is determined that such trouble must stop. The excuse for all your mistakes is that you are young. But you really cannot rely on such an excuse for long."

There was deep silence in the room now. Even Jade was listening.

"You are not by any chance blaming us for that southern girl's weaknesses and death, are you?" Jade asked coldly.

The courtesan stared. "What has being southern got to do with her death?"

"Everything," Jade retorted. "Everyone knows southerners are weak—their climate."

"What you have just said is an example of what is wrong with this household," the courtesan replied stiffly. She was from the Yangtze delta herself. "South or north, Chinese or non-Chinese we are all one now under Tang Taitsung. We are all of us men of Tang," she added proudly, "and you young ones must stop being stupid about petty loyalties to hometowns. You imperial women especially. To teach you correct behavior in the harem, I will start with the idea of attitude. Everyone must have the right attitude or there is no success. I repeat, the right attitude . . . what did you say?" She looked sharply at Jao.

"That is the way the Buddhists start their list of the eight roads to salvation: the right attitude," Jao said brightly. Several of the girls giggled.

"Yes . . . well . . . I don't know about that," the courtesan continued repressively. "But I can say this—that it is the most important step to your salvation in this palace. Now, what in your minds is the correct attitude in relation to the emperor?"

The silence in the room deepened, and the girls avoided each other's eyes.

The woman pointed at Jao. "You answer," she ordered.

"When you are called to the emperor's bedside . . . what is the best attitude?" Jao repeated, trying to think of something to say. "First to ask what he wants . . ." Jao was thinking of her stepbrothers. "Then to make sure that he is not asleep or drunk . . ."

Here tittering broke out and Jade interrupted. "Please overlook the bad manners of these childish new tsairen. They have not been raised in the best families and they do not know either correct manners or correct attitudes. You have asked us a serious question, and I will answer it seriously. Any consort called to the bedchamber should come prepared to take the initiative with the emperor. He is not young, and will expect not to make love to us, but for us to make love to him. And he will be annoyed by . . . silliness . . . or giggles."

The woman nodded, slightly taken aback. She pointed at Peony.

"The correct approach is to wait for the emperor's commands and to be ready to follow his lead in . . . anything and . . . *not* to take the initiative—that might displease him," offered Peony, who did not agree with Jade in everything. She felt that there was not much about clouds and rain that she did not know.

The woman nodded again and pointed at shy Pearl, who was surprisingly ready with her answer.

"To present oneself as attractively as possible, with flawless grooming and appeal, to look flowerlike. That will soothe him and capture his attention," she said.

"Well, to start with, yes," the courtesan responded. "You," she said, pointing at Cloud.

"The most important thing," Cloud said dreamily, "is to perceive how the emperor is feeling, to observe everything about him as you approach him, to convey to him that you share his feelings, whatever they are, that you are a part of him. Then mutual passions ignite—"

"I'm not sure about that mutual part," interrupted the madam. "Feelings and igniting and such. I suppose it works sometimes, when the emperor is young. You," she said, pointing to Wildgoose, who jumped when the anonymity with which she surrounded herself was breeched.

"Correct attitude? Well . . . to stand with downcast eyes and folded hands until one is spoken to," she offered.

The courtesan looked at her suspiciously, wondering whether Wildgoose was making fun of her. "Did you memorize that from Lady Pang's etiquette book? A respectable book, yes indeed, very clear about the dos and don'ts for normal life, but useless here."

This caused a stir among the tsairen and several discreet coughs.

"Useless here," she repeated. "Lady Pang's instructions have probably been taught to you by your mothers, who sighed and thought that they had done their duty by you. These instructions are useful in a general way to help in one's approach to other people in the palace, the titled women above you in rank and so on, but the very existence of this inner court is to serve one man—one man who is the only person who counts. Now then, let us get to the main point here . . . how many of you have ever been called to his bed?"

Three hands went up.

"I assume that you three have been deflowered and know something about attitudes and . . . responses. Now then, explain what is a correct attitude according to your experience."

She pointed at Jade, who answered hesitantly but still with full confidence in her own infallibility. "We were called in a group one evening. There was a party, some of the Meiren were there and the Chiayu. There were eunuchs there."

"His face was red and his eyes were . . . bulging a little," Cloud broke in. "He did not smile, but waved at a slave to serve us. It was millet beer and tasted bad, but the emperor's head eunuch signaled to us to drink it, and there was much noise and singing . . . and it was confusing and unreal, like a dream."

"No, it was exciting and fun and full of laughter and singing," Peony said. "Gay. Exciting. The right approach, a party and beer and all that."

"The party was not the important thing," Cloud protested. "What happened afterward was. Before we knew what we were doing, the room emptied and only one lantern with swinging shadows was left. The eunuch had us strip, and took our clothes and vanished as he pushed us to the *kang* where the emperor was. He was beating time on a little drum while he sang. He swept us all into his great arms, and then one of us was deflowered, but perhaps all of us, really, and then he fell over sideways and went to sleep. As for attitudes—there was no opportunity to think about such things."

The courtesan listened and remained silent. Most of her own experience was on a one-to-one basis, with men who paid highly for her favors and were eager to show their own prowess. In her heart she knew that she was out of her depth as tutor to young girls faced with the imperial whims.

"It was as it should be!" Peony exclaimed loudly. "I was deflowered, and it was all so distracting and happening so fast and so excruciatingly pleasurable. Even if it was a bit rough."

At this, the courtesan nodded and smiled and her elegant manner fell away. She understood this one. "And were you called again soon?" she asked approvingly.

Three heads bowed in dejection. Surprised and not knowing how to comment, the courtesan decided to drop the subject of correct attitudes. Although attitude was all-important to the courtesans of the Willow Quarter, where entertainment was the focus, it did not seem to be a norm in the palace.

"Now we proceed to a study of the thirty-two positions," she announced. "You must be in good trim and very supple if you are to be skillful in all." She signaled to her servant to unroll a scroll which illustrated the first five positions. After demonstrating with her lay figures, she closed by saying that she would test them the next day on what she had just taught them.

"Too much! Too much!" Jao wailed to Mi after everyone left her room. In less than one month . . . too much!"

"Run hard in one place and then stand on your head," Mi said. "The blood will flow the other way and the bad thoughts will run out of you and you will feel better. And then I will rub your back and feet and you will wake feeling stronger."

"Is that what you do? How do you know all this? I am only thirteen and I don't know much, but at sixteen you are so far ahead of me. Will you tell me how you manage to be so . . . so . . . unhysterical when no one else is?"

"There is only one solution for us palace girls—to create an inner strength that no one can ever disturb for long. It is good that I have cultivated my own strength—I will need it greatly over the next few months."

"Why, because of Mulberry's death?"

Mi hesitated for a moment. "Because I will be having a baby."

Jao gasped. "What? When? Who is the father?"

"In about seven months. But to talk about the father—I just can't right now. Sometime I will tell you, but not just yet."

Jao looked perplexed but said she understood. A baby was a wonderful thing, and if Mi wanted to be private about some things,. well, she would restrain her curiosity.

The next day the courtesan did not come, and the tsairen were never examined on their lesson of the five positions. The memory of this lone lesson was retained among those who had a sense of humor. Merely raising a hand with its five fingers spread out was enough to cause mirth. For some time, however, the household was so full of terror that nothing seemed funny, nothing seemed comfortingly everyday normal. The house was invaded by a full complement of officials and subofficials from the Ministry of Justice, who busied themselves interrogating the tsairen and arresting the servants to obtain their full disclosure. And all this had to be done before the magistrates, for according to the penal code, all investigation of suspects was to be held in public. Even torture when it was applied had to be held in open court.

The new descent upon the household was caused by the discovery that Mulberry's death was not natural, but inflicted.

The authorities, out of defense for the palace, questioned the girls and their white-faced eunuchs in an informal tribunal set up in Jao's large room. Word had come from the wealthy Hsin family that Mulberry had been murdered. While her body was being washed and her hair dressed for the funeral, a nail was discovered in her skull, driven deep into the top of her head. Since the officials knew the hours during which the death had occurred, the search for the murderer focused upon the eight tsairen and the score or so of their attendants and guards who had had access to the house during those night hours.

The maids were taken first. They were made to kneel before a table that had been set before the judge. His assistants stood beside him, armed with whips. Jao could hear their terrified screams as the whip was laid lightly over the backs of those whom the judge deemed to be lying.

The case had assumed awesome dimensions, out of proportion to its importance. High-ranking families were involved not only in the case in hand, but also in the cases of the previous years, those unsolved deaths that had been hushed up.

"The emperor himself is angry," Jao whispered, round-eyed. Wildgoose nodded. Her head was close to Jao's as the two huddled on the *kang* to keep warm. Toto lay curled up next to them, nursing her bruises from the interrogation. Cloud sat cross-legged, humming quietly to herself, easing her whiplashed back, while Pearl dejectedly pecked away at her embroidery, trying to calm herself for the ordeal ahead of her.

"The magistrate will probably mete out the severest penalties he can to all of us," Wildgoose muttered. Nomad-bred, she was under no illusions as to the possibility of draconian punishments if an example had to be made.

The day was cold and blustery, with sand blowing from the loess country. The cold penetrated even to the *kang* room. The servants were upset, and no one was attending properly to the fires.

"The emperor is angry that his private affairs are being made public." Cloud always seemed to hear about everything. "This scandal of the tsairen house is no longer merely a palace problem. It involves ladies of the harem who are all from influential families. The repercussions are the last things the emperor ever wants to hear about." The depressed tsairen took this in and a hush fell on the room. Then the leather curtain was raised, letting in even more cold air. Jade, Phoenix, and Peony came in, wrapped in padded coats. Jade surveyed the drooping tsairen coldly.

"What cowards," she exclaimed. "All terrified out of their little wits!"

"No!" Jao said hotly.

"Look who's spoken!" Jade sneered. "The newest little wonder, with her big mouth and her little brain."

Jao stared in amazement and Wildgoose stirred menacingly.

"You are all terrified, spineless creatures," Jade continued, hitching herself onto the *kang*. "Cold," she said, "the *kang* is cold!" She clapped her hands loudly, and when a timid maid looked in, ordered her to see to the *kang* fire. "And if you don't know how, you idiot, get someone who does. Move!"

She returned to her survey of her housemates. "Five tsairen have died in the last few months." There was a hint of gratification in her voice that made Cloud narrow her eyes. "Someone has to take responsibility. Someone has to be punished," she continued, this time with open relish.

"Some have already been punished,'" Cloud ventured. "As you must know. The medical officials were fined and demoted because they failed to discover the nail in Mulberry's skull. Ket and Ti, our guards, Chi and Kao, our eunuchs, have all been punished. Ti, the night guard, was given fifty lashes and banished. Ket was let off because she could prove that she was not even inside the palace grounds at the time, but she was chastised for poor service and reassigned. Poor Ket now grieves in her heart because she prided herself on her record of keeping the peace."

"How you gush," Jade interrupted. "You are sad because Kao Kuliang was reassigned in disgrace and Chi—" She stopped and looked around accusingly. "Chi, who is a number-one suspect, I suppose you will defend."

"Of course I will defend him," Cloud shouted amid a chorus of approval from the others. "He was good to us. How can you be so heartless!"

"Cloud, you are being more stupid than usual," Jade countered coldly. "Chi is guilty. He is the only one strong enough to drive the nail in and keep the victim quiet at the same time, the only one who had access. I will testify that it was Chi . . . I'm sure I saw him. He will be executed . . . you'll see!"

Aroused by the venom in her voice, the girls sat up, staring at her in consternation.

"Jade!" Cloud exclaimed. "All the evidence against Chi is circumstantial and you know it! What is the matter with you? You sound as if you want him to be executed!"

"I do," Jade said. "He richly deserves death. He went against me."

"She's a bad one, that Jade," Wildgoose whispered viciously.

"Chi is a good man. What is she trying to do to him?" Jao looked angrily at Jade.

"Enough of that kind of talk," Jade said, raising her voice. She grimly pressed her thin lips together.

Not wanting to continue the harsh discussion, they fell into an unhappy silence, broken when a tribunal official stamped down the hall to call Pearl to the stand. Trembling violently, the frightened girl followed him to the trial room. Ten minutes later she was returned unconscious, for her comrades to resuscitate, and Phoenix was called. Jade looked uneasy at this, and Phoenix, at last realizing her predicament, looked terrified. Soon her screams of anguish filled the house and even Jade seemed daunted.

"They suspect her because Mulberry beat her in archery," Jade muttered to Peony.

"Y-Yes," Peony stuttered in panic. Everyone knew how jealous she had been when Mulberry received the red card and she hadn't.

The interrogation of Phoenix went on and on and only stopped when the judge ordered a noon break. Phoenix was not brought back to the *kang* room, but was ordered to remain in her own room until the trial resumed in the afternoon. In mid-afternoon she was finally dismissed and taken to her room to recover. Jade quickly volunteered to go before the magistrate. She made a good impression on both him and the assistants. She had been assiduous in helping them from the very beginning and in diverting suspicion to others. Her very high rank encouraged leniency toward her as well. She was dismissed in twenty minutes and Jao was called.

Jao found that her legs were wobbly as she walked down the hall. She entered her own room, which had been made into a tribunal, and looked around cautiously. A red cloth had been thrown over a table and an empty scroll placed on it, with brushes, ink slab, and ink stick beside it. Three assistants stood at attention, but the judge's bench was empty. Behind the table was a panel with two large characters painted on it: REVERENCE and SILENCE. She noticed that there were bloodstains on the mat and shuddered.

"Bare your back and kneel!" the sergeant commanded. Jao was shocked but obeyed, folding her arms across her bare breasts.

"Lower your head farther!" the sergeant shouted.

Jao hung her head until her forehead touched the floor. She held the position for many minutes and she was going numb when the judge strode in and seated himself.

"Confess to the crime!" he shouted.

"What crime?" Jao asked in confusion.

"The murder of Tsairen Mulberry, you fool," the judge returned. "Why did you hate her?"

"She was my friend. I didn't hate her and I would never murder anyone, especially a friend," Jao stammered.

A whiplash flicked across her back and she winced.

"Don't tell lies," the judge continued. "Why did you drive that nail into her head?"

"I didn't drive a nail into her," Jao wailed. "I had never even heard of such a crime until I heard about this. I am not guilty, sir!"

"Do not talk back, you arrogant girl. Tell the truth, what made you do such a thing?" The whip came down on her back again.

"Please . . . I am innocent . . ." Jao was barely able to keep hysteria down while she was lashed again.

"You are guilty," the judge droned. "And you will be executed tomorrow at dawn."

"No!" Jao shrieked. "Your Honor is father and mother to the people. Your Honor would never condone such an injustice!" The whip struck her several times and she felt herself falling in a faint. She felt hands lifting her and the judge's voice far away, saying "Take her away," and then the relief of blacking out completely.

When she came to, she was back in the *kang* room, being revived by Mi bathing her and putting balm on her back with her one free hand.

"What is happening?" she asked, flinching as Mi touched a raw spot. "Where is Wildgoose?"

"Wildgoose is in there now. She's been there more than an hour. How are you feeling?" Mi asked anxiously.

"Not so bad," Jao returned as she struggled to sit up. She managed a smile. "It's all over now and that's good. But no one is in the tribunal now. It's all silent. Where is Wildgoose, then?"

"She is there," Mi said grimly. "They say it is bad for her. The judge thinks she is defiant. She has been there longer than anyone else but you hear nothing because Wildgoose won't cry out. Her torture is worse than anyone else's too, but she is the last one."

"Oh, poor, dear Wildgoose, my friend," Jao sobbed uncontrollably while Mi comforted her as well as she could. Mi herself had not been ill-treated. Her broken arm was her alibi.

In time, Wildgoose was brought to the *kang* room and dumped on the floor. Jao gasped and jumped off the *kang*, forgetting her own wounds in attending to Wildgoose. In great pain, neither girl slept that night, but by morning the opium that Mi administered was taking effect and they were able to lie down on their stomachs and sleep.

The officials packed up their gear and left the house. Their guards also left, and a new eunuch, a bland man named Liang, came to take charge.

They were all in the *kang* room the next day when he came in to tell them what the sentence was.

"There will be six months of house arrest for you all. The Hsin family have conducted the funeral and buried their kinswoman. They are satisfied that justice is being done because of the rigorous punishments. Now all that needs to be done is for you eight girls to live out your six months of isolation and for Chi to be executed if no other suspect is found."

"You can't be right!" Jade protested. "Surely *I* am not expected to be kept in house arrest, not I!"

Liang wiped his forehead and said apologetically, "You too, good lady."

The next six months were thoroughly unpleasant and tedious for them all. Frightened by the murder, the tsairen discussed it endlessly among themselves and then ceased talking about it at all. Jao listened but said nothing, distancing herself. She spoke cautiously to Mi about her suspicions and occasionally to Ket, who, lonesome for the company of other servants, was the only outsider to visit the quarantined house. The girls were allowed to sleep in the *kang* room but forbidden to converse except in passing in the halls. The Three began to encroach on the new girls until Jao and her friends could no longer remain neutral. They had to do the bidding of the Three or Jade would punish them with a swipe of her leather belt.

Fortunately, the heaps of dirty snow and ice in the courtyards melted early and the real spring followed hard on the heels of the false spring. Jao longed so persistently for an escape that she obtained permission to walk in the empty courtyards of the palace, the largest of which had once been occupied by the empress. Jao gravitated to this place more and more frequently, and stayed longer as the days turned warmer. One day she found a small, negligible-looking young man working in the front garden.

"Are you a palace eunuch?" she asked. He sat back on his heels and looked her over severely.

"No, no eunuch . . . are you worried by my presence? Don't be. My father was the head gardener of the empress, and even though I am so young, I am allowed the run of the palace. I do this garden and the gardens of the Fei. There is no one better than I . . . and I keep out of the way of the women." He waved his pruning knife. "No one bothers about me . . . no one even sees me anymore. My name is An. And who are you?"

As she talked, Jao gazed at the spacious court, the empty flower beds, the stacked pots and the tied-up trees. "It is so dismal here with no one living in the place. Why do you come here?"

"Because the best garden in the palace is here but no one knows it . . . the most expensive bulbs and perennials, beautiful peonies and cherry trees, gorgeous wisteria. Fang Fei is moving here in May because her daughter suffers from the heat and this compound is the coolest in the palace. Bixon is the only one whom the emperor would permit to live here." He unwound a wisteria trunk, one end of the straw rope in his teeth. Jao watched him.

"You are sweating," she said. "Would you like something to drink? Millet beer? I can get you some."

He brightened and spat out the rope. "That's what the empress always gave me," he said wistfully. Jao brought him some at once, cheered by this small contact with a world outside the tsairen house.

After this, she spent much of each day in the empress's compound while An pulled old weeds, loosened the soil around the budding trees, and placed great pots of azaleas and lilies along the galleries. He pointed out a giant wisteria and its overhanging branches, which he was carefully tying up and cutting back.

"Nothing," he said, "will stop a wisteria once it takes hold, but you have to take care that its blossoms hang in place like lanterns." He waved at the peonies. "Wisteria is easy but peonies are hard. They have to be nursed along every season, pruned and wrapped in winter, watered and watched for destructive pests in summer, weeded all the time . . . but they are worth it—that is, *mine* are worth it. I have moved the best new plants to this garden, and now they are my beauties!" He looked around him proudly, as he did every time Jao came. "This compound is all mine. I even have some plants from the beds of that cocky man in charge of the emperor's gardens, and he has no idea. Come summer, no one will have a better place than this." An looked up as he heard voices along the path. "Now you will have to go, or hide in the pavilion," he told her. "I have a gang coming to erect the summer arbors over these courts."

Jao nodded and retreated into the nearest hall to watch. They were quick and skillful in erecting the twenty-foot frames of bamboo which were to provide cool, dappled shade for the courts during the hot summer months. She stayed, intrigued, until they left.

The chance to be outdoors during the long spring days was a godsend to Jao because it seemed that her existence had been forgotten by everyone. No word had come from Fang Fei or even from the kind Princess Wencheng. No one seemed to want to have anything to do with the disgraced tsairen. Then one morning in May, a message came from Fang Fei requesting Jao's assistance in spring cleaning. Jao obeyed with alacrity. Even housecleaning was attractive.

She helped with every task that came up, although her major job was to keep Bixon happy. Winter bedding was unpicked, aired, and washed, and the silk floss linings sent off to be recarded. Winter clothes were packed in rank tobacco leaves, and woollen rugs were folded and stored in cedar chests. Fresh grass mats were laid down in the new quarters. Lady Fang's lacquer and ivory matrimonial bed and all her other handsome furniture was set in place, and then there was nothing left for them to do but leave the old house and walk down the path to the new.

Lady Fang, Bixon, and Jao stepped through the open gate into the well-swept courtyards of the empress's compound, now festooned with clouds of blossoms. "How did all this happen?" Fang Fei cried in delight. Bixon shrieked with joy when she saw the large goldfish pond.

"Gardener An arranged it," Jao said.

Fang Fei knew all about An. "That An, he's a magician," she said. "He has furnished my courtyards with flowers every season year after year, but this is beyond anything! We are going to have a happy summer, aren't we, Bixon my love? I shall have to do something for An."

"Give him millet beer," Jao said. "That will be enough." Jao knew that An had achieved perfection by wanting to outdo the other gardeners. Lady Fang never knew that her garden had been favored. No one else knew either, not even the rival gardeners. Some of the palace ladies were jealous of Fang Fei's striking displays, wondering why all her flowers flourished when theirs drooped, but they put it down to the vagaries of nature.

Jao returned to her house refreshed and more reluctant than ever to reenter the prison of the tsairen compound. She longed for the house arrest to end. Slowly she walked down the hall to her room, and her spirits rose when she met an excited Mi at the door. She was obviously pregnant now, but she still performed all of her duties. "I've something to tell you," Mi whispered, her eyes shining.

"Come in and tell, then." Jao shut the door carefully. "I'm so glad I was allowed to keep you when most of the other maids were transferred."

"You're lucky! Lucky I had a broken arm!" Mi laughed. "Now, listen. Almost all the other maids are in different compounds now, but they often visit in the kitchen. Ket too. But I must begin at the beginning—this morning some of us were putting away the furs in tobacco for summer storage and ripping apart the padded coats to recard the floss. Then we found a black padded coat. . . ."

Jao stared. "Only an old coat?"

"A very important coat!" Mi cried. "Not Jade's coat, but among her clothes! Also there was a gold lace scarf from India among Jade's things that didn't belong to her but to Ma Tsairen—the girl who went crazy. Ma's maid was helping us and recognized it right away!"

Jao frowned. "I don't see—"

"Wait!" Mi interrupted. "You'll see. About Jade—we have proof that she was the one behind other murders too!"

"Not proof, gossip," Jao said, disappointed.

Mi shook Jao's arm impatiently. "Listen, just listen! Her maid told us that Ma Tsairen was a tiny girl, delicate like a dream fairy, and nervous. Any little thing made her jumpy: small noises, mosquitoes, wasps, ordinary centipedes falling off the beams, everything alarmed her. Naturally, the mean tsairen teased her unmercifully. Then she was called to the emperor's bed. She was tormented horribly before she went to him. The maids say that Jade was like a panther on the trail of a doe . . . Jade followed the girl the whole day telling her that deflowering was an unbearable agony. Jade said she knew from experience, but of course she lied—everyone knew that Jade had never been deflowered, everyone but poor Ma Tsairen. She believed anything."

"That sounds like Jade. What happened?"

"That night she was dressed and perfumed and sent to the emperor, but she never came back. She was never seen again. The story soon leaked out . . . she had gone mad. The eunuchs had to tie her up and send for her family to take her away."

"Cloud mentioned poor Ma, but it's all past, so why are the maids discussing it now?" Jao returned thoughtfully.

"Because the servants think that our big trouble is not all in the past but is here now, ready to cause more trouble. Soon! Ma's maid shouted that the other tsairen who fell in the well was also the victim of the she-devil, the high-ranking tsairen who hits with her belt, the fox-woman who kills! Everyone knows she means Jade, everyone is afraid and quickly shuts her mouth. Then there's no more talk in the kitchen."

Mi distractedly folded towels and sorted them, exercising her bad arm to ease its stiffness.

"Well," Jao commented finally, "you've done all you can, listening in the kitchen . . . but we are no closer to proving who the murderer is."

"We are closer. I know. And I can prove it."

Jao stopped in mid-yawn. "Wh-What?"

Mi looked somberly at Jao. "The black coat. It was Mulberry's, and Jade took it. Two or three nights ago, one of the maids had to go through the front courtyard when it was dark and she heard noises under the lilac bushes. She thought it was just a wall guard making love to some slave, and so she stayed quiet and waited for them to go. When they did, she saw the light from the lantern over the house gate fall on a tall girl—a tsairen—in a black coat. The maid laughed like she was scared. She warned me not to tell because it would be bad trouble for a tsairen to have a small side affair with some bold guard." Mi's voice tapered off. "The coat was worn by Jade."

"Not possible," Jao answered. "Jade is a horrid woman and I hate her, but she would never do such a thing. She knows what would happen to a concubine caught having an affair—she would lose her head before the day was over! The laws are strict and the magistrate even more so. You are wrong."

Mi shook her head slowly while she picked up Jao's discarded clothes. She said slowly, "Laws are one thing, men are something else. Women too, even concubines."

"Well, there still is no proof that she killed anybody," Jao said. "I'm afraid the gossip about the tsairen of the past has nothing to do with Jade now. Anyway, Jade is not strong enough to have committed the murder of Mulberry. To drive a nail into someone's head needs three or four hands."

"She did it. She's not an ordinary murderer—she's a fox-woman, she's an animal in disguise." Mi straightened her shoulders. She appeared very tall and stern as she spoke. "Proof will come! The gold scarf came from Ma, the coat from Mulberry, and they were both among Jade's things. One of the tsairen does have the strength to pound a nail into a head, but no one can catch her except in the act. No fox-woman can be caught except in the act. . . . It was Jade. We wait."

Jao shook her head in despair. "What *do* we do now?" she asked. "Living here this way with a fox-woman?"

"What fox-woman?" Wildgoose asked, slipping into the room and closing the door.

Jao and Mi jumped at her quiet entry and did not answer.

"You may tell me. I am safe, especially since I already know what your secret is," Wildgoose said quietly.

"And so what do you think it is?" Jao asked, scowling at Wildgoose, who was leaning in a relaxed way against the wall. She knew that Wildgoose was tight-lipped and aloof, and that the nomad girl was a strong and reliable friend, but she was unwilling to share dangerous secrets with anyone.

"You know who the murderer is, don't you?" Wildgoose continued.

"Guessing," Jao said. "But no proof."

"Officials wait for proof, but for us, for now, we must take care of ourselves because we have a fox living with us. I feel it too." Wildgoose was somber.

Jao shuddered. "Someday we may be free of this thing that keeps us afraid all the time. For now, though, I'm not going to let Jade step all over me—or over Mi—while I wait for fate to do something to save us."

One hot day in August, the ban on the tsairen was lifted and normal life was eagerly resumed. Jao's joy at being released left her unaware of the heat, and when an invitation from Fang Fei came a few hours after the ban was lifted, she was even more ecstatic. The invitation was for a picnic in the large courtyard for the early evening and the entertainment was to be a puppet show. Jao chose a cool cotton dress made from cloth woven by Jewish weavers living in Changan, a special piece that Mi had found in the market. Jao spent more time than usual on her grooming, and then went happily down the familiar paths to Fang Fei's compound.

The trees, full-leaved and shady, arched overhead. Everything else had grown riotously since she had last been to Fang Fei's quarters. Locusts shrilled in the mulberry trees, excited sparrows were rowdy in their settling for the night, while magpies teased them by swooping into their midst and scattering them.

As she stepped inside the gate of the goldfish courtyard, she was greeted warmly by her hostess. Jao glowed and smiled in return. Fang Fei's magnolialike skin was slightly mottled with the heat, but she looked as plump and tranquil as ever. Bixon was thinner and Jer had grown in the past six months. He seemed older, more sure of himself.

Maids brought out trays of cold foods and a basket of golden peaches from Samarkand, rarest of rare delicacies. The children clapped their hands when the fruit was presented, and the eyes of the adults shone when they saw that there were enough peaches for each person to have his own.

The evening was perfect, neither hot nor cold. The sky overhead was rich with sunset afterglow, a large rising moon, and a few shy stars. Jao felt light-headed and lighthearted, as if she had been transported to the Western Queen Mother's paradise. The long twilight passed slowly as they sat in front of the little stage to watch the puppets perform. The children absorbed the dramatic wonders with bated breath, while the elders watched with relaxed contentment.

Just before the end of the play, a message came for Lady Fang. Disconcerted, she immediately consulted Princess Wencheng. Then she dispatched a servant and turned to the group.

"The emperor has sent for you children to take you on a boat ride under the full moon. It is just right tonight. He has also given permission for two tsairen to come and watch out for you."

The children jumped to their feet in excitement and went off at once with the escort the emperor had sent. Fang Fei turned anxiously to Jao. "Will you go with Bixon? She really should not stay up. You might hold her if she falls asleep. I have sent for another tsairen, anyone. You must go at once, but I depend on you to take good care of Bixon. It will take tact because the emperor does not understand frailty. Bixon does not do well in the summer heat, so we have to be strict . . . she gets so excited when she is with the emperor. My Bixon, I'm afraid, has a number-one spirit and a number-ten body."

Jao promised eagerly to do her best and hurried off to catch up with the others. When they reached the dock, they found that the emperor was already seated among the cushions of the sumptuous boat. Lanterns were hung alongside, and boatmen in neat black pants and jackets were ready with their poles and paddles. The head eunuch stood beside the gangplank to usher them aboard. Bixon gave a flying leap into her father's arms and squealed with delight. She was the only human being in the entire empire able to treat the great man with such abandon and be so wholly welcome. Jer was not far behind, and his father reached for him too.

Jao stepped cautiously aboard while the sailor steadied the boat. Then two tsairen came hurrying up, Peony and Jade. The head eunuch greeted them politely. "Only two tsairen invited," he said.

"There are two of us," Jade said sharply.

"One is already on board. Which one of you is going? The emperor cannot be kept waiting."

Jade looked at Jao and said, "That one has no rank in our house, she was the last to enter. I will go and Peony will go and that one will get off."

The eunuch said coldly, "She stays where she is, but one of you get aboard now."

Jade took her skirts in hand, ready to step aboard. Taitsung, only six feet away, suddenly pointed at Peony and said, "You . . ." Peony quickly and happily jumped aboard, making the boat tilt in her eagerness.

"Jao shall pay for this," Jade murmured as she turned away. No one heard her, but Jao saw her malignant look.

Jao soon forgot the incident in her enjoyment of the evening, in the flute music, the warm companionship, the perfection of the night, the moon reflected in the water, the pale glow of the August lotus in full bloom, the soft swish of the water along the sides of the boat. Everyone wanted to stay out as long as possible, so it was well into the hour of the ox before the boat returned to the dock. Jao guided the sleepy Bixon to her mother and then returned to her own house, filled with the magic and beauty of the evening.

A few weeks later, as soon as she was awake, Jao went to look for Chi. She finally tracked him down, weeding some peony plants in a neglected courtyard.

"May I talk to you?" she asked politely, noticing how gaunt he had become. He has a haunted look in his eyes, she thought uneasily.

"I believe I can still trust you," she stated directly. "Your mother was a Yang of the same clan as my mother, and I have a favor to ask because of that and because you were a good manager of our house."

He straightened his back to look speculatively at her. "Why are you here? It is unseemly."

"I just told you. When I first came to the palace, you told me to come to you if there was any trouble. There is . . . and you are the only one in the palace who can help."

"I had some power when I said that," he responded bitterly. "Now I am suspected of murder and can help no one."

"You have been accused unjustly. Jade has testified falsely about you, and nothing is being done. You are not the murderer."

Chi jerked his hoe angrily. "I suppose that a mere girl of fourteen knows more than the magistrates," he said sarcastically.

"Yes, I do," she responded.

He looked at her sternly. "Impudence."

His eyes are a soldier's eyes, not eunuch's eyes, Jao thought. They show his true character. So, for the first time, she told all she knew to someone else. She expressed all her thoughts about the case while he continued to hoe around the plants—he would seem to be busy at his job if there were any onlooker spying on him.

"It is dangerous for you to listen to such stories, and even more so to talk about them. And to be here at all, you little fool," he said.

"You are the fool, not I, if you don't believe me," she responded. "You must know that the murderer was someone within our house, someone who is still there. We are all frightened out of our skulls by this fox-woman. It is not some outside killer, or you would not be telling me what danger I am in. There is some clue that I cannot pin down—I feel that I may know something that would provide the proof that is needed for the tribunal to clear your name." Her voice trailed off in a frustrated sigh.

Chi looked thoughtful. "I keep thinking of those tsairen who met misfortune last year," he said. "There is someone who knows about drugs in that house and how to use them, because the court physician who was called after Mulberry's death told Eunuch Kao that he suspected she had taken a heavy dose of sedative that night. Apparently, the smell of it was still about her when she was discovered." He paused and shook his head. "You must leave me now. And talk about these things to no one."

Jao blurted out angrily, "Do you think that I am such a fool as to talk? Some people quote the ignorant, saying that no one can trust women and eunuchs. Those people *would* repeat such stupidities because they have nothing in their heads. You are trustworthy and I am trustworthy. And so, will you help me?"

"What do you want me to do? And why just now?" he asked.

"There is an urgency. Some weeks ago the emperor took two of his children and two tsairen for a moonlight boat ride. The emperor rejected Jade publicly while choosing Peony and me. Jade now hates me worse than anyone else in the house and has started to get revenge by punishing Mi in more and more dangerous ways. She doesn't care that Mi is pregnant, and gave her another lash across her face this morning.

We have taken turns sleeping and other precautions, but now that Mi is close to giving birth, I fear that Jade will do worse things and Mi will die if she is not removed. Can you get her away?"

Jao took out her scarf and unwrapped it enough to show ten gold pieces. Chi recoiled. "I am not bribable," he said.

"Of course not," Jao said impatiently. "This is not for you. It is for arranging Mi's delivery so that she can be out of Jade's reach, starting now. She's at the gate over there, watching that we will not be disturbed, so for the present she is safe."

Chi looked out the gate and then took the scarf and bundled it into his waistband. "Not a problem," he said.

"Thank you!" Jao cried. "I knew that you could do it! Just because you are here doing garden work does not mean that you have lost your wits!"

Chi chuckled wryly.

"And also," Jao continued hesitantly, looking around and lowering her voice still further. "If you receive another ten ingots, can you arrange for my being put on the list to be sent to the bedside? I have not been because the six-month house arrest was imposed just after I arrived, but now I think the emperor might favor me . . . and listen to me if I tell him what I just told you. Maybe he can do something. If I have the chance to talk to him, that is."

Chi looked at her in disbelief. "There is assuredly no fool like an ignorant fool. To blunder blindly into a situation such as you propose would make the bravest man shudder. To complain to the emperor is suicidal."

"But it is the only thing I can do to save both you and me," Jao said in despair. "After the boat ride it will only be a matter of time before I am drowned in the well like that other one."

Chi was silent. "I suppose you are right," he said. "And I will use the money you have given me for the necessary gifts. It may be enough. Now leave me before you think of something more . . . although you couldn't possibly think of anything worse than you already have."

Jao and Mi hurried back through the deserted courtyards. Storm clouds were gathering and branches of trees were blowing about in the rising wind. When they reached their own court, Jao said, "Mi, invite the guard to come to our room to gamble. There is a storm coming and she will want to shelter inside. Then we will not be alone."

Sure enough, Jade's servants kept coming to Jao's room, but each time they saw the guard, they left without saying what they had come for. The guard said nothing, but carefully made certain that her back was never to the door.

Late in the day, a rain-soaked errand boy came from the eunuch's office with an order for Mi to report to the apothecary's office without delay. Mi gathered her things into a shawl and started to leave when her way was obstructed by Jade and her servants. "You are not to leave the premises," Jade ordered. At this the guard stood up, astounded. She swept the maids against the wall with one arm and Mi vanished out the door.

"Orders," the guard said sternly, then went back to her game. She ignored Jade's shrill commands to get back to her station, and merely parried the blow when Jade's belt whipped at her neck. She stood up again and took the belt away from Jade, being careful not to harm her in any way.

"You will get your hide stripped from your back for this," Jade cried passionately, but the guard only looked stolidly at her. She had been told what to do if any of the tsairen got out of hand.

That night, the first snowstorm of winter took place, and when Jao awoke at daybreak, she saw the white cover on the courtyards. She suddenly remembered that a similar sight had greeted her on the morning after Mulberry's death. There had been no footprints in the snow then either. There were none now. Someone inside must have done it, and this was the proof. She had to see Chi. Here was the proof that he did not come back to the house that night. He had *never* been inside the house that night. This would free him!

Before Jao was able to proceed with her new insights, a messenger arrived with a red card of summons to the emperor's bedroom for Jao. "You must be mistaken," Jade cried to the messenger. "This card is for me. I am first in this house, and it is my turn anyway. I am the highest in rank."

Somewhat timidly, the young eunuch shook his head. "No mistake. This is Wu Jao's name on the envelope."

Nevertheless, Jade took possession of the card and went to her room. Jao also retreated to her room, hastily bathed and dressed before Jade could do so, and went with the harassed eunuch to the emperor's hall without the card.

Chapter Six

Jao was left waiting in an antechamber for an hour or more. Finally the eunuch in charge appeared. "You may wait inside," he said, holding open a heavy leather curtain. The guards posted in front of it moved noiselessly to one side. The bedchamber she entered was dim with shadows of the evening. A great lantern in the center of the room shed light on an enormous red and purple oasis rug, and glowing coals gave off heat from a brazier. It was placed in front of a great *kang* that spilled its tiger and bear skins in disarray. Curtains lined the walls; beneath one the feet of the attendant eunuch could be seen.

Jao, panicky, her confidence gone after her long wait, managed a not very graceful bow at the figure on the *kang*. Then, after a prolonged silence, she stole another look. The Son of Heaven was asleep. Relief washed over her. Reprieve, if only temporary. She looked at the feet under the curtain. They had shifted, so she knew that the figure was now squatting. He is making himself comfortable, she thought. Lazy so-and-so. I myself will stand and wait properly. She was grateful that Mi had taught her how to stand gracefully for long hours by commanding her muscles to relax and her lungs to breathe in a measured way.

The silence was relieved only by the sound of faint snores from two different corners, and once by the quiet clanking of arms when the guards changed outside the leather curtain.

"Have you been waiting long?" broke the drowsy quiet. Startled, Jao fell abruptly into her one-knee obeisance.

"Not too long, Your Majesty," she replied in a small voice, overcome by shyness and uncertainty.

"What is too long?" came the response from the awesome mound on the *kang*.

"From sunrise to sunset," she replied without hesitation.

The mound chuckled. "Come here where I can see you," was the next command, and Jao advanced, watching her feet to be sure that she was doing the formal glide properly. She stopped when she saw the fur-draped edge of the *kang* with the great bare knees of the emperor just above.

"You are Wu Jao, Second Daughter of my official Wu Shihhuo? The little tsairen who stood in the circle for my elite corps?" came the voice.

"Second Daughter of Second Wife, not a very important person," she replied in her truthful way.

Another chuckle. "You are refreshing," he said. "And right, of course—you are not very important. But you have made some very important friends since coming to the palace."

At this, she raised her downcast eyes in surprise. She could not think of any important person except Lady Fang. Her friends, Chi and Mi and Wildgoose—and Ket, of course—were small people at best.

"My son Jer, and my daughter Chinyang, the little girl you know as Bixon," he prompted.

"They are my friends? I'd like to think that! They are such lovable children. Nothing would please me more than to be their friend, but it is not possible. Because of rank and all that," she exclaimed, her whole personality alive as she looked directly and unself-consciously into the eyes of the enigmatic man in front of her. He was seated, but their eyes were on the same level. Jao, thinking about the children and not about the father, had lost her feeling of insecurity.

"You have no other friends that you can trust?" he persisted. She hesitated, afraid to mention Chi or Wildgoose for fear of bringing suspicion on them in the murder case. She remained silent.

"You are like me, then," he said lightly. "I would like to have even one friend whom I could trust absolutely."

"Me," Jao blurted before she could stop herself.

The emperor, surprised, regarded her with humor, wanting to laugh but also more than a little touched. "I believe that you mean that. Who knows, little one, I may keep you to your promise one of these days. You must pride yourself on being a trustworthy person, to have answered so quickly. But now, tell me about the people in your house. Do you have any friends there? Or anywhere in the Inner Palace?"

Jao considered. "There is Fang Fei and Princess Wencheng and my slave Mi from the royal house of Silla, and Wildgoose and—" She paused, "—the two eunuchs who were in charge of us." When the emperor showed surprise at this, she said hastily, "Who used to be in charge."

"Now what is this?" he said sharply. "Are those the same scoundrels who mismanaged the tsairen house last year?"

"An injustice," she whispered, her heart thudding against her ribs. "Eunuch Chi will be executed soon if the real murderer is not found, because he is the chief suspect. He did not do it . . . nor did any hired assassin do it."

Taitsung's expression was stony. Few were allowed to speak to the emperor in the heat of impassioned emotions. There was an army of experienced officials to handle such things so that the emperor was free from the harsher aspects of public contacts.

"Your Majesty must not be troubled by such things, forgive your slave." Jao fell on her knees in penitence and shock at hearing her own audacious words.

"The magistrates have been thorough. How can the word of one tsairen be measured against the findings of the tribunal?"

"They can't know all the facts. It is impossible for them to find out everything. That is why I am . . . why I have spoken," she quavered.

There was silence as Jao's head sank on her chest in her despair. But the emperor, instead of feeling irritated, found himself entertained. He was often annoyed by the pomposity and incompetence of some of his administrators—it seemed the higher the rank, the greater the self-importance and often the greater the incompetence.

"Now, miss, explain to me how you know that the eunuch did not do the murder for some reason of his own, or arrange to have it done—that would be like a eunuch, to avoid spilling blood himself."

"It had to be someone in the house that night," Jao replied.

"Explain."

"It snowed the night of the murder. No one from outside came into our residence after the snow began to fall, and that was long before the murder took place. I saw the courtyards early in the morning, and the snow cover lay smooth with no new footprints. And it had stopped snowing before I went to sleep."

"Hm, I see. Well . . . who, then?"

"Not one of the slaves, they have all been carefully examined. One of the tsairen, and not one of us new girls either. There is only one tsairen who has been making all the trouble, and no one dares report it. She is the cause of all the . . . mishaps before we came. Not Peony or Phoenix. And not Cloud. She does not have the psychology of a murderer. . . ."

The emperor suppressed a laugh. "So what does an experienced investigator fourteen years old know about the psychology of a murderer?"

She flushed. "I learned enough from my half brothers," she said at once, and halted, much ashamed. The emperor let out a burst of laughter.

"Let it pass, let it pass, but continue, you have not yet given me anything but a finger pointing at a so-called murderer. Who is it? Whom at least do *you* think is the murderer? And did the magistrates neglect this testimony of yours about the snow?"

"They don't know it. I only recalled the fact this morning."

"Hm . . ." the emperor murmured, interested. "Now what I want to know is why you risk yourself, little one, in this lost cause?"

"Because I am the one who will be murdered next," she said bleakly. "And because I have a solution."

He pulled her up onto his knee and settled her.

"Tell me."

"Take away our guard and leave me unprotected. You will soon see—the murderer will reveal herself."

"You are offering yourself as bait?" he exclaimed. One surprise followed another.

"Yes, yes, what else is there to do? The real culprit comes from such an important family and has concealed herself so well from the authorities that she will never be suspected unless she is caught in the act of killing," Jao replied. She trembled, not only because she was over her depth in this crusade of hers, but also because her body was disconcertingly close to the emperor. She had never been so near to any man before.

The emperor thought for a minute. "You may act as bait if that is your wish, but I will send along my best female agent. She can mingle with the other servants and keep an eye on you. Then we shall see. It may come as a surprise to you, but I am just as much interested in justice as you are, my wise one!"

He pulled her closer. In his bearlike arms, Jao found herself relaxing slightly against him, feeling his strength. Her thoughts were focused on the outcome of her venture. It now seemed as if it would be successful, and she was suffused with joy.

The emperor's voice changed. "Now that you are a woman and of my household, you should be deflowered. Shall I set about it now?" He held her close.

Jao fell out of her rosy glow into the reality of the moment, hesitating only a second.

"As you will . . . Your Majesty," she murmured shyly.

He ran his finger lightly over her delicate cheek and down her throat to her rounded breast and to the small, soft nipples. Her skin was satin to the touch and she was warm against him. He was pleased with her and gave her a great reassuring hug. Then, gently, he pushed her away.

"Not now, little one. Not yet. First I will expose you to a murderer, as you ask, and when that is all over, I will let you ripen. I will savor your presence and your personality and your mind on many occasions, and when you are ready, then I will take you."

Jao was escorted back through the empty palace courtyards to the tsairen house by the emperor's servants, one of whom, a strange female, stayed all night in the house, sleeping in the corridor outside the *kang* room while Jao stayed inside with the others.

It was a long time, however, before she could sleep. The tsairens' curiosity about the details of her night with the emperor had to be satisfied. To the questions of her deflowering and the pain that may have accompanied it, Jao gave no answer, frustrating them with a small, secret smile.

On the third day after Jao's visit to the emperor, she was awakened by a slave from the lying-in hospice with the message that Mi was dying and had asked to see her mistress. Jao hastily donned her padded clothes and hurried after the slave to the chilly pavilion where Mi was lying exhausted from her labor. Her eyes were glazed and her forehead beaded with sweat. The midwife, a fat and unkempt woman in her late forties, looked at Jao in unconcern.

"She has been in labor three days and the child will not come. It is turned wrongly. She will die," the woman said indifferently.

Jao wiped the sweat off Mi's brow with her sash and leaned down to hear her faint whisper. "If I kneel and midwife turns baby with hands Silla way," she gasped, "baby will come—" Her words were cut off as she arched in agony.

Jao turned to the midwife. "Why don't you do as she says?"

The woman's lips curled. "Why should I obey a slave? She will die anyway after this long a labor."

Jao looked helplessly at the assistant midwife, who was silently putting a great pad of clean bast under Mi.

"You!" she cried to the assistant. "Can you do as my slave has asked? Do you understand what she is asking?"

"Only second midwife here. Know how to turn baby. Have done it many times."

Jao turned to the first woman. "Will you retire to the kitchen and refresh yourself with special food that I will pay for while your second finishes this labor?"

The woman shrugged. "As you wish. You take the blame, then." She left with alacrity, and Jao turned to help the other midwife, who had already heaved Mi into the right position for delivery. Supporting Mi, Jao encouraged her to push when commanded. Labor went on and on, and Mi seemed spent beyond recovery. The midwife had small hands and she used them adroitly to compress the child's buttocks as she firmly turned it.

"There!" she shouted. "Push on stomach and he slip out." She eased the tiny head, and then, in a burst, the body followed.

She started to chew off the cord but was stopped by Jao, who remembered that the talkative midwife, in one of her long conversations with the abbess, had said that a baby's cord should not be cut for an hour after birth. "His lungs need to inflate slowly," Jao said.

The midwife shrugged, cleaned the baby's mouth and laid him against Mi's legs to wait. "A boy, strong boy . . . manager here be pleased!" she cried, proud of her accomplishment. Mi still looked like one dead.

"What is wrong?" Jao asked, alarmed. The midwife was feeling the pulses in Mi's ankle, wrist, and throat.

"She be all right soon," the midwife said, grinning broadly. She was exhilarated to have been able to succeed where her superior had failed.

Jao smiled weakly in response. "Now what?" said Jao. She was damp with sweat herself and her clothes were spattered.

"Cut cord, clean baby, give cumshaw," the midwife said simply. "Give cumshaw to first midwife."

"Why should I? Why should I give anything to that no-good palace servant who doesn't do her job?" Jao replied crossly. "This is my slave and I didn't want her to die. I will give you a big present, never fear, but nothing except her snack to first midwife."

When the baby was wrapped warmly and had stopped squalling, Jao put a silver piece in the midwife's hand. The woman waited, so Jao added another bit to it. "To pay for the care of Mi and her baby. Will this do?"

The woman nodded but said, "Same same for Number One Midwife . . . yes please, must do." Jao scowled, but finally, when the first woman returned to the room, all smiles, she agreed to their demands.

After Mi revived and asked for the baby, Jao realized that her friend was going to live after all, as the midwife had said. So, with some hesitation, she left the lying-in room. She paused in the door as she went out, giving a stern backward glance at the midwives. She was unhappy at having to leave Mi at their mercy. Jao did not yet know the techniques of servant management, but she had caught the spirit of her mother's gentle approach, which masked an iron will, and her manner showed it. The servants understood and were wary.

Jao returned at dusk and spoke cautiously to the new guard. The fierce woman indicated that she would sit up all night behind the curtain in the back entry and would listen carefully for any disturbance during the night. Jao could sleep in her own room. No one was as yet suspicious of the woman being more than an ordinary guard.

Jao stuck her head into Wildgoose's room. Her mouth watered when she saw her friend eating. Waving Jao to a seat, Wildgoose handed her a bowl of meatballs and noodles. "Extra food I prepared for you while Mi is gone," she said with her mouth full.

Jao ate hungrily. "Mi is all right now. This business of having babies—dying one minute and gurgling at an infant the next—I'm exhausted."

Wildgoose jeered. "It was Mi who had the baby, not you!"

"It took four hours after I got there before that child came, and it was hard work," Jao said indignantly. "You try it sometime, either helping or having."

"Maybe I'll try the having," Wildgoose answered airily.

"Sure, aren't you, that you'll be called to the big bed?" Jao answered with a yawn.

"Well, if I do have a child and it isn't an imperial one, then I'd just have to disappear, wouldn't I?" Wildgoose said as she licked her chopsticks. "And have the offspring somewhere outside the palace, in order to keep my head on my body."

Jao looked nervously around the room. "Sometimes I think that you are crazy the way you talk. There are at least three impossibilities in what you just said, and the last one is the most impossible of all. No one escapes out of here; it can't be done, especially by a tsairen."

Wildgoose smiled in a superior way. "Not impossible by us steppe people. There are many of us in the guards, patrolling the walls, caring for horses, serving as night watchmen. I know a number of them . . . some were brought up with me in the same encampment."

"Well, that may be so, but they are no good to you in the tsairen encampment," Jao said crossly. She yawned and took a bedtime drink that a servant offered her. "I'm off to bed now. Thanks for the food. I am glad that you are here and not in some yurt in the grasslands. I couldn't do without you, wild one that you are."

"Mmm," Wildgoose responded as Jao put down her drink and left for bed.

It seemed to Jao that she had barely closed her eyes when she felt herself struggling in a nightmare. She was suffocating, and tried to scream to wake up and save herself. Thrashing violently on her pallet, she finally came to her senses in time to realize that it was not a dream but reality, and that she was actually being smothered. She jerked off the bed, and, exerting all her strength, dislodged the weight on her face. A shadowy figure slipped out the door and she screamed.

"I can't breathe," Jao gulped while the guard helped her sit up. Gradually she calmed while the guard picked up a sheepskin from the floor.

"Is this yours?" she asked.

"No," Jao said, shuddering. "That must have been what was over my face."

The guard looked distraught. "Someone was trying to kill you, and almost did. I have failed to protect you. I will be punished!"

By this time all the girls had wakened and some were crowding into Jao's room. Wildgoose and Jade were in front.

"What happened?" Wildgoose hugged Jao tightly.

"Someone was smothering me, but did not succeed because of my good guard here," Jao said, panting from her exertions.

The guard let out her breath gustily in her relief. "All you tsairens go along to bed," she ordered. "I will sit here in Jao's room tonight and watch all night. Tomorrow we'll find out who the bad woman is here."

"You are the bad woman," Jade cried with venom. "You are new. Who sent you? Go away. We don't want such a bad guard here."

No one listened to her, and after a while she and the other girls disappeared. Jao exchanged a look with Wildgoose. "She has escaped again, this fox-woman," Wildgoose muttered, white with anger.

"Nothing to be done tonight," Jao said shakily, "so I'll go back to bed. The fox won't attack again, with the guard sitting right here."

"All the same, I'm leaving my door open, guard or no guard," Wildgoose whispered passionately. "This place is dangerous tonight. Foxes can never be caught, they're too smart. They can only be destroyed if they are caught in the act of killing, when they are off guard. In the act."

Jao lay in the dark, hour after hour. She heard the night watchman calling the hours—the hours of the rat, the hours of the ox, the hours of the tiger and her eyes stayed wide open. Sometime before dawn, during the hours of the tiger, the guard got up silently and went outside to relieve herself. Jao saw out of the corner of her eye a shadowy movement, and then a great weight settled on her head, and this time in spite of her violent efforts to remove it, she failed. She was losing consciousness when the weight was suddenly lifted and she was able to fling it to the floor. She gasped for air.

Two people were in the room, fighting viciously. There were running footsteps, and then the guard burst into the room. She set her small lantern on the floor and pulled out her dagger, but could not distinguish between the two fighters. Then one of them thrust a dagger deep into the other's chest, and the wounded girl fell with an agonized shriek. The other figure was putting away her dagger when the guard attacked and overpowered her.

Jao, sitting up now, screamed when she saw Jade's body on the floor and Wildgoose being trussed up.

"You killed her," the guard cried in a menacing tone, jerking the strap tighter around Wildgoose's hands. "You killed her, the high-class tsairen—"

"The fox-woman," Wildgoose panted. "I was lucky to get her . . . not a woman, a beast!"

The guard paused and looked at Jao uncertainly. She was very superstitious and confused, and became more so when Jao got up and put a trembling arm around Wildgoose.

"You two stay here," the guard ordered. "I'll get the captain. Give me the dagger," she said to Wildgoose, who handed it over.

When the guard left, Wildgoose said urgently, "Untie me—I must run."

"No!" Jao wailed as she freed Wildgoose.

"I have to escape before the guards come to arrest me," Wildgoose whispered, and she slipped speedily out of the room. In a few moments she was back in her outdoor garb with her saddlebag over her shoulder. "I will leave by the front door, and you must bolt it after I am gone," she said to Jao in a low voice, not wanting to arouse the others, who were staying in their beds on this second occasion.

"I have a lover to whom I was promised—long ago, before I was packed off to the palace. He followed me here and was taken on as a guard. I was with him that night under the lilac bush when the maid saw me in the black coat. He has told me just what to do if I were ever in trouble, so I have been packed and ready for some time. Do not grieve for me—I do not belong here, and so I would have escaped soon anyway. It is time for me to go."

She hugged Jao fiercely, then disappeared down the granite steps of the front entrance and melted into the night mist. When Jao could see Wildgoose no more, she shut and bolted the door, tears streaming down her face.

Loud noises in the back courtyard heralded the approach of the law to remove the body and to arrest the girl who did the stabbing. Jao was quizzed roughly at first, until it was established that she was the victim, not the killer, and then the officials paid no more attention to her in their search for Wildgoose. Jao took refuge with Toto, to keep out of the way and to escape being interrogated about Wildgoose. Soon the whole house had been roused and the other tsairen were being questioned, while Jao, twice a victim in one night, was allowed to sleep.

The next day, the palace was in a mild uproar as the grounds and buildings were searched for the missing girl. The wells were probed and the woodpiles tumbled. Wildgoose seemed to have vanished.

The winter days slipped tranquilly by. Wildgoose never was found. No shameful accusations came to light against Jade, and the Tsui family accepted the fact of her death and the promise of brutal revenge if Wildgoose were ever caught. Jao managed to escape suspicion. The tsairen house was cursed no longer—once Jade's presence was removed, the household could function normally, especially now that Chi was back in charge. There were six tsairen left, and the house was at last at peace.

Mi had been told that she could keep her baby for as long as he needed breast feeding, so she brought him back to the house. He never cried, and soon became the pet of the tsairen. One day, while they were all preparing for the baby's month-birthday party in Silla style, a message came from Fang Fei for Jao.

"She wants me to come to a party for Jer tonight which they have just put together," Jao said to Mi, highly pleased. "Jer's party today, your son's party tomorrow."

"My son is born in the same moon as Prince Jer, moon of dragon, auspicious for both," Mi said proudly. The social importance that Mi ascribed to the infant was now shared by the household. That he was not just a slave child was accepted by all, even by Phoenix, who was respectful of Mi's royal lineage, though it was foreign.

Jao hurried along the paths now strewn with the last leaves of fall. In the great hall she found Fang Fei, Princess Wencheng, and, to her amazement, the emperor sitting cross-legged on the floor playing finger games with his two young children.

"Here is Jao!" Bixon cried. "Now we can play parchisi and beat Father!" Taitsung pretended to look worried, and this delighted the children. The board was brought out and Jao, showing her dimples, shyly explained the moves to the emperor, who had never heard of the game. He was intrigued, and the time passed pleasantly amid childish crows of victory and the murmur of women's voices as they watched and chatted.

The evening was a thoroughly enjoyable family occasion, which sometimes happens even to royalty. When bedtime arrived, the party broke up with contented yawns. The emperor was first to leave.

"I'll have one of my guards take you home," Taitsung said to Jao as he stretched. He had noticed with amusement her attempts not to beat him at parchisi.

She nodded her thanks and followed him at a respectful distance, guards clanking ahead and behind. She soon saw that they were not going to her home, but she was afraid to remind the emperor of his error. When they reached his hall, he saw her and chuckled. "Since you are here, you might as well come in. I want to talk to you anyway, about what happened in the tsairen house."

He threw off his fur and sat down with a satisfied grunt. "Those two children of mine—out of the thirty or so that they say I have—are the ones I enjoy the most. They will grow up to comfort my old age! And now, little murderer-bait, I congratulate you upon escaping alive and helping to settle the troubles in your house."

Jao's eyes flew to his face in consternation. "You know . . . about everything?"

"Of course. I kept in close touch with your case, and you may be sure that my officials hurried to hush the scandal and set things right in that accursed house. Two deaths and an escapee, what a den of wickedness!"

"You know about Wildgoose, then?" she ventured fearfully.

"And about you, who gambled upon the chance that your emperor would take you seriously."

Jao lost her look of dismay and dimpled, her eyes shining, a look the emperor had seen before. This time it was more a delight to him than ever.

"It was an adventure to deal with a fox-woman," Jao answered thoughtfully. "Scary, and nearly the end of me. I knew who the fox was because my Silla attendant told me. Being sure made it something that we could cope with instead of a dreadful mystery making us all live in constant panic."

"Is that all you feel now that it is over—that it was an adventure?"

She pondered. "Up here," she pointed to her head, "I was determined to follow all the clues to a successful end to the affair. Down here," she pointed at her plexus, "I was afraid all the time. And but for Wi—for the guard, I mean, I surely would have perished. The fox-woman kept us all half-witted the entire time she was living with us. How could a fox get into this safe palace?"

"All sorts of fox-people get in past the guards," the emperor said soberly. "But," he added with a twinkle when he saw the alarm in her small, intent face, "we chase them out again." He laughed aloud as he watched her confusion melt under her sense of fun. Her small fist flashed out to hit him lightly before she could stop herself, and he laughed again, to see her panic at her affrontery.

"Come here and tell me how you used to live in the high country and what kind of people you grew up with . . . what kind of people you punched when they laughed at you."

Jao rose obediently and arranged her slight self on his great knee matter-of-factly while she thought of what to tell him.

"The Dees," she said, "our neighbors in Taiyuan. . . . Dee Jenjer is younger than I am, but he is sharp so I enjoy his company."

"The son of Magistrate Dee?" the emperor interrupted. "One of my brightest officials, loyal to Tang. He is a rare man, a man of integrity as well as a man of benevolence."

"Jenjer isn't benevolent to me because he says it isn't necessary to be benevolent to a girl, only to do one's duty."

"Proper Confucian, that one. How old?"

"Nine, going on ten. Everyone treats him as if he were a child, but he really isn't. He's grown-up already," Jao replied.

"Then I'll recruit him for my bureaucracy now. Most of my officials have the minds of boys of twelve. But tell me more. Where did you learn how to ride? Do you know much about horses?"

A happy smile lit Jao's features and she launched into an animated account of the Wu stables, every horse in it and every problem in the care, breeding, and breaking in of colts. The emperor listened, thoroughly interested. That world was his favorite place, and he missed having time to spend there.

The sounds of night reached their ears—guards changing, gates closing, and the squawking of starlings and crows as they settled in the great trees of the palace grounds. Inside, the coals glowed and fell against each other, and the room became quiet as the conversation died down. The emperor brushed his chin across her cheek and tightened his arm around her.

"Do you want me to love you now?" he asked.

Her eyes lifted to his. "If you like," she answered softly, beginning to pull off the sash around her waist. He watched her and then took the sash and tied it firmly back on.

"Not tonight, perhaps not even this month or year. You are a delight to me and a rarity among my harem flowers: too good to pick till ready."

He lifted her up and ran his hands down the length of her lean little thighs. "I will wait," he said. "In their eagerness to please me after my empress died, my officials bring me girls younger and younger. Ah well, some of them are more than ready at twelve, that big-breasted flirt in your house, for instance."

"Peony," Jao murmured helpfully.

"I suppose so. Ought I to know her name? But never mind that now. I want to say something more to you. I want you with me daily without arousing jealousies, nothing that will make life more difficult for you than it is now. You have had enough for a while. Do you understand, little one? I will appoint you to some low-level post that brings you here but keeps you safe."

Jao threw her arms around his barrel chest and laid her small head under his chin. He felt the muscles in her slender arms embrace him in a powerful grip, and she held it longer than he expected. Then she released him and slid to her graceful one-knee bow.

"That is a wonderful idea," she said, deeply content.

"You may leave now, but don't worry, you'll be invited here later to help me drive away my own fox-enemies."

The winter passed rapidly, and Jao was soon celebrating her first year in the palace. She was in and out of most of the homes of the other women, readily accepted because she did not appear to be a threat to anyone. She found her life full, with plenty to do. All was tranquility in the tsairen house, because the six girls wanted it that way.

Mi's baby remained at the house through the winter. The time came, however, when he could stay no longer and Mi was obliged to look for a foster home outside the palace. Technically, the boy was owned by the imperial household, but in view of his relationship to the royal house of Silla, the authorities let him go to the Sillan enclave in Changan for rearing. Mi went to make arrangements for her son's care and came back all aglow.

"A kind Silla lady who speaks the high court language agreed to take Chinpyong," she told Jao. "The headman of the ward helps because I am related to Queen Sondok. He also helped Yupyong, my twin who was kidnapped with me. The good news is that Yupyong is alive and well and . . . sold to the palace. However, he was also castrated to bring a high price."

Jao listened in sympathy, her eyes shining. She had never before seen her friend so animated. Mi continued, "Headman Chang sent a message to the palace, and Yupyong came to recognize me and make my words true. We laughed and cried so much when we met. He was good to my baby, even though he thinks Chinpyong is half Chinese."

Jao looked questioningly at Mi. "Is the baby really half and half?"

Mi returned her look steadily and proudly, "Chinpyong is not half and half. He is fully of the Silla royal house. I can prove it. . . . Sometime when he returns to Silla, he will have a big welcome."

Jao hesitated. "Is the baby's father Yupyong?" The ancient custom of sibling marriage was now frowned upon in China, but still practiced in Silla. Jao pressed Mi's hand between two of hers.

Mi looked down at their intertwined fingers and nodded.

"Your son is a very important person, I take it. Yupyong castrated can have no more heirs, and Queen Sondok has no son. I see what you mean about his return having a 'big welcome.' In Silla, lineage is everything, isn't it?"

Mi raised her eyes, and Jao saw fierce pride in them and that indestructible assurance bestowed only by high birth.

"Does Yupyong know? Does anyone know?" Jao asked in awe.

"Not yet," Mi said. "Someday when the time is right . . ."

Winter gave way to spring in spurts. The months passed. Summer faded to winter and then summer again. Jao frequented the Fang home more and more in order to comfort Fang Fei. Bixon, never strong, was growing weaker and weaker. Her illness seemed incurable, and the entire palace population was aroused by the child's condition because she was such a favorite. Taitsung called for daily reports and spared no effort on her behalf. Bixon revived from time to time and hope sprang up, only to fade again.

One rainy night, as Fang Fei sat at the child's bedside and Jao fanned the little girl, Bixon cried out in her sleep and then ceased to breathe. No one could believe that she had gone until the court physicians shook their heads mournfully and left to call the morticians to remove the little body.

The emperor, to the surprise of his hardened military, refused food for several days, rejected his usual pastimes, and could not be comforted. Lady Fang took to her bed and went into a decline from which she eventually recovered. Her looks, however, were gone.

Cool weather and the news from the frontiers announcing the conquest of the rich oasis kingdom of Turfan raised Taitsung's spirits, and he embarked upon plans for a victory parade with some of his former enthusiasm. At the same time, an envoy from Tibet arrived to ask for a Chinese princess for their young king. Taitsung was interested—such a marriage could go far in establishing better relations between the two countries, and could, he hoped, reduce the raids that Tibetans were constantly making into Chinese territory. It came as no surprise to anyone that Princess Wencheng was chosen to go.

"Aren't you terrified?" her friends asked, shuddering at the very thought. Not one of them could imagine taking her place. "Those frightful mountains and those savage people . . ." Fang Fei faltered, trying to face up to the loss of her friend.

"What? Terrifying? Nonsense!" was Wencheng's reply to all who commented. "It is just what I have always wanted—to be a ruler. I'm all for it." To Fang Fei she explained, "You know how I feel. Don't grieve! You know that what I want most is to run my own court my own way and build a little kingdom of my own. You know that I smother in a court of women and should have been a man among men. It is my good luck that I have this chance!"

Jao, listening, was impressed and thoughtful. The future was truly negotiable if you had a strong stomach. Even for a woman . . . She watched Wencheng assemble the tons of goods that she was taking with her, saw how enthusiastically Wencheng went about it, and admired everything the princess did. Finally the day of departure was upon them. The weather was favorable, cold and clear. Wencheng and her chosen entourage rode out through the palace gates, out through the city gates, and onto the great road leading west, the recipients of all the honors that a grateful sovereign could bestow. An expression of exuberance remained on Wencheng's face during all her good-byes, although she left many inconsolable behind her, especially Fang Fei and Crown Prince Chengchien. Jao, however, was left strengthened by her example.

Wencheng's caravan had scarcely disappeared over the horizon when the generals who had conquered Turfan rode in with all their loot and their hordes of prisoners, which included the king in chains. Scores of skilled musicians played their exotic instruments as they marched into the city. They so delighted the Changan crowds that the foreigners did their best. Even as prisoners, they appeared excited to be in the famous capital.

The parade itself was one of the grandest ever staged by Taitsung. Riding at the head of the procession, splendid in his gold armor, the emperor was followed by the magnificently clothed princes and by the generals in their impressive parade uniforms, helmets, and battle swords. Jao caught sight of Jer several times from her position with the other women in the south gate tower. She had not seen him since Bixon's death. He had grown, and it showed—he looked much older. Now fourteen, he had acquired a wife, a certain Lady Wang chosen by his father and the ministers. Jao, watching him, thought that he had attained a new sense of dignity.

The next few seasons followed one another in peaceful sequence. In Jao's world, little happened. In Taitsung's world, disaster built up. Taitsung was sensitive about bad blood between his sons because of his own past deeds of violence against his brothers. He noticed the secret growth of a faction supporting Tai rather than Crown Prince Chengchien. He was chagrined at the deliberate misconduct of both young men in encouraging this factionalism when such behavior had been outlawed from his court.

Minister Wei began to fail in health, but still came regularly to court to handle the trouble the princes were causing. One day he did not appear, and Taitsung learned it was unlikely that his indispensable minister would return. Saddened, he visited Wei's home to honor his faithful servant. Wei had his servants dress him in his usual court clothes, so strict was he about proper behavior, and thus he was able to receive his emperor with dignity. Before the visit was over, however, his life went out of him. A grieving Taitsung closed the palace and all offices for the unusually long period of five days in Wei's honor, and ordered an elaborate state funeral.

With Wei's restraining hand removed, palace politics took a turn for the worse. The activities of both Chengchien and Tai passed all limits of toleration, forcing Taitsung to demote both and promote fifteen-year-old Jer to be crown prince.

Taitsung slipped into a depression from which he seemed unable to recover. Disasters involving four of his most important sons, following upon the deaths of Bixon and his empress within a few years, left the emperor without trusted intimates. He resolved to pay close attention to the instruction of Jer and to take more young people into his daily life and train them over a period of time. Jao was therefore called to regular duty at the court so that he could have her by him throughout the day. She was seventeen now and a fully accredited court lady whose only remnant of childish impulsiveness lay in her merry eyes.

The emperor realized that his Jao was now a full-blown beauty. The promise of her childhood had been strikingly fulfilled in her teens. He realized that she would be attractive to any man who saw her, regardless of his age or state of senility. Exposing her to the sight of the few men admitted to his inner quarters would certainly arouse them. The thought of their discomfort amused him. Let them envy him! It would be good for his aggressive ministers to know that there were some things they couldn't have. Taitsung was unconcerned about Jer's regular presence in his chambers. His son was far too immature and far too devoted to his father to dream of making advances to one of his harem. And as for Jao, the emperor was certain she was loyal to him in every breath she took, Nevertheless, he chose to test her.

Jao was summoned. "Your new duties here will not be very exciting," Taitsung told her. "They entail long hours of standing about in attendance. I want someone within call with whom I can talk, someone trustworthy. Do you remember offering yourself for a service like this? The time has come, but I will have to make it possible for you to take on this service without subjecting you to the usual palace jealousies that follow any conspicuous promotion. So, I will give you a low rank and an unimportant task. I will ask my chamberlain to put you in charge of my linens, to provide clean towels whenever I need them. To be in my presence, tiring though it might be, is the only honor. How does it all strike you? Are you secretly disappointed or unwilling? Or perhaps you are unperceptive of what this job really means?" He watched her closely.

Jao had been wondering when he would get to the point of his proposal, so when he did, she was ready without an instant of hesitation. It was not the custom to raise one's eyes to a man, especially not to an emperor, but Jao looked directly into his. "If Your Majesty is asking whether this humble person would be willing to accept the lack of the symbols of honor in exchange for the real thing, the answer is a breathless yes! With a sky full of willingness and with an ocean full of devotion! Perhaps perceptiveness too—" She cut herself off after her short speech and dropped her eyes only when she saw the flash of satisfaction in his.

She was dismissed, and the next day she began her duties. There were some lifted eyebrows and some snickers but otherwise not a ripple on the surface of palace politics as Jao entered into the vortex where real power was exercised.

The crown prince was formally installed in April, in a ceremony that was held in the refurbished Hall of Supreme Virtue, the most important of all the throne rooms. The entire court attended. Jao, the other palace women, and the wives of high officials were present behind gauze curtains. The emperor has at last gotten the right son in place as his successor, Jao thought as she watched, the right choice if one is considering courage and character. Jer is not strong in manipulation, but he knows what he wants, she mused as father and son swung through the rituals, both in full dress, both wearing the flat hat of supreme status. They need each other, she reflected contentedly.

One day when Jao reported for duty, Taitsung greeted her with a new plan for her time. She was to study with Chu Suiliang, the chief historian, along with Jer in order to stimulate Jer to greater efforts and to make her a more interesting conversationalist for himself.

"Conversationalist?" she repeated uncertainly.

He chuckled. "Don't be frightened. I want an educated person to listen to me, to *listen* rather than to make me listen to him. I have more than enough of listening to my ministers. Apart from Jer, who is younger than you, I want someone to talk to when I need to mull over something aloud, someone who will *not* offer advice, *not* offer help, *not* belittle me in any way. I used to talk freely to the empress, but now that she has gone to the Yellow Springs, and with so many women established in my household, I have become wary of talking to anyone at all. Especially about politics, which I need to think about aloud most of all. That someone could be you."

He reached for his well-worn volume of Sun Tzu's *Art of Warfare*, and read, " 'inward spying means making use of the officials of the enemy . . . favorite concubines who are greedy for gold.'

"That is the sort of possibility that I have to guard against—such traitorous concubines greedy for gold."

Jao studied the emperor in consternation. Her five years in the palace had matured her. Now she was able to listen in silence before speaking or acting, and always her goal was to stay well away from intrigue and intriguers. "How can I be of use in the matter of spies? I have no experience for a task so vital to the welfare of the Son of Heaven. Surely the most astute of trained men are the ones that are needed."

He looked at her sternly. "I have all the trained men I need. But they are all essentially self-serving, they would be no good if they were not. No, what I want is an educated person who is without self-interest and whose ambition is to further my interests, not his own. That person might be you.

"I have loyal men in service to use against others—I do not need you to spy for that purpose. I need your help against the spies whose loyalty is to others. That requires an ability to detect what is good and bad in the people around me. Nothing strenuous! Just that! Now let me ask you this: Do you have any one in your life whom you can trust implicitly?"

"Mi," Jao said immediately.

The emperor looked taken aback. "She is only a slave. You can never trust a slave in the way I mean," Taitsung said.

"If you mean someone who has character, is educated, has had years of courageous service, and is totally loyal, she is that person. Her slavery is not her fault. She was kidnapped from the household of Queen Sondok of Silla. I know Mi. I would trust my life to her, and she can say the same of me."

Taitsung looked at Jao standing rigidly before him, and took note of the spark in her eye.

"You seem to know how to recognize worth when you see it, and that is all I ask of you," he replied thoughtfully, taking her chin in his hand. "Now be off with you and get started on your new studies."

Jao soon found herself seated for an hour each week before the august Chu, receiving what he thought were appropriate assignments. The following week she was quizzed on her assignment. Chu refused to see Jer and Jao together because he felt it unseemly. So, without his knowledge, they met in Taitsung's hall to study, Jao with her towels handy, and Jer sitting cross-legged on his father's *kang*, his hair becoming ruffled five minutes after he settled to his books because he pulled it so compulsively.

"Here is something," Jer said aggrievedly one day after Chu had gone. "Chu made me memorize it: Mo Tzu said, 'Nowadays all rulers wish their domains to be wealthy, their people to be numerous, and their administration to produce order. But in fact they obtain not wealth, but poverty, not populousness, but paucity of population, not order, but chaos—thus they lose what they want and get what they abhor. What is the reason?' "

Jer paused. "Chu wants me to be able to rattle off the reason . . . as if it were important. All that happened centuries ago. What has it got to do with today?"

"Everything!" said Taitsung, who was fondling the ears of his dog while he listened. "Mo Tzu is talking about good government anytime, anywhere. Consider the reason that Mo Tzu gives for the conditions that he describes. Jao, you answer."

"Mo Tzu said, 'It is because the rulers are unable to exalt the virtuous or to cause the capable to administer their governments. When virtuous officers are numerous in a state, it is well-governed. When they are few, it is governed badly. Therefore it is the business of the rulers merely to cause the virtuous to be numerous. By what method can this be done?' " Jao parroted self-consciously.

"Jer, answer that one," his father directed.

Jer had begun to take an interest. "I'll read it because I haven't memorized it yet. Here it is: 'Suppose, for example, that one wishes to cause good archers and charioteers to be numerous. In this case one will certainly enrich them, give them rank, respect them, and laud them. . . .' " Jer paused again, "I think the most important thing to do is to enrich them."

"Respect them," Jao said.

"Give them rank," Taitsung said. They laughed in chorus and broke up for the evening, but Jer's lesson had sunk in, and he became somewhat less resistant to his tutor.

Jao was in attendance at the morning meal a few days later. Her duties were menial—beneath the dignity of eunuchs, whose ranks were so exalted that they could only undertake service directly connected with the emperor. Her lowly service did not ruffle Jao's calm. It kept her within earshot of important happenings at court and allowed her to be, for all practical purposes, invisible.

The emperor and Jer were having an early breakfast before they left on a long day's ride. The two finished their meals, and when the emperor rose from the table, he glanced speculatively at Jao.

"You ride, don't you?" he asked.

"We tsairen play polo a great deal, and some of us ride every morning. Not lately for me," she answered.

"Would you like to go with us today?" he asked, and chuckled at her instant look of joy.

"Good old Jao," Jer exclaimed, rising. "We'll have a race or two like we used to . . . wait a minute, I'll be right with you." He disappeared around a curtain to relieve himself, and in a moment returned. "It will be a good day. We are trying out a couple of new stallions that just came in from Ferghana. Apparently they are quite a handful for our grooms."

Jao proffered him a towel and the usual bowl of water in her customary, courteous way. He splashed her face playfully.

"Now I have marred your makeup," he teased, splashing her again. "But you don't need powder and paint today, so clean up and come along."

Jao made a face. "Dew has conferred grace upon me," she retorted, and they both burst out laughing when they saw the disapproval on the face of the chief eunuch. Taitsung, amused, smiled at their outburst.

"You are quick with your jokes," Jer remarked cheerfully as he shrugged into his jacket. "You always were. We had so much fun together when Bixon and Wencheng were around. . . ."

Changan was vulnerable to the loess dust storms of the steppes, as well as to all the extremes of heat and cold typical of highland weather. Occasionally, however, the city enjoyed a special dispensation when all at once the day was a jewel of beauty. May was especially lovely, with its spring foliage, clear light, open skies, and windless warmth.

It was just such a day when the emperor and his party of five mounted their thoroughbreds and cantered into the extensive imperial parks to the north of the city. Taitsung had with him his head grooms, veterans from his wars, whom he had chosen to supervise the training farms that stabled the new horses.

At noon they rested their horses at a small stream near the first farm and ate their lunches. Not far away was a barn and corral for yearlings. There, they leaned on the rails, watching the Asian grooms exercise the colts. Jer was in his element when he was with animals, and when he had his father as companion, he was blissful.

The head groom in charge of the colts arrived at Taitsung's elbow to explain what was happening and to answer questions. "These yearlings are all broken to ride," he said, "and now we watch to see which ones are best for hunting, for racing, for polo, and so on. But one colt just cannot be trained. His name is Bad Luck."

Taitsung raised his eyebrows. "What is wrong with the colt? Point him out—better still, bring him to me," he ordered.

Bad Luck was watching the men closely, his ears cocked forward and his tail idly switching. He was a superb animal, coal-black, sleek and full of energy. A ripple of admiring grunts ran through the onlookers while they watched the colt sidle closer, bouncing challengingly.

Taitsung whistled. "He is a champion, no doubt about it. Even though he is now a bit long in his forelegs, he will grow out of that. He is a racer with a future. What's the problem with him?"

"He runs under tent ropes or low branches, anything to rid himself of his rider. He is so wily that no one can guess what he is going to do, or how fast, or when. He suddenly throws a rider, often hurting him severely, then is gentle like a baby. He's a devil. We have been doing our best to train him, but without results."

"He is superb," Taitsung said. "A pity if he can't be broken."

"May I ride him?" asked Jao suddenly. The men gaped at her as if the horse himself had spoken.

"Do you know what you are proposing?" Taitsung asked coldly. "Bad Luck is not for a woman, not even for his trainers, as you have just heard."

"Don't be a show-off, Jao, really," Jer broke in.

"Please let me try," Jao repeated. "I like that horse, and I think I could teach him. I was raised in horse country, and I recognize Bad Luck's makeup. What a conceited animal he is . . . look at him!"

All eyes swiveled to the prancing horse. "Sure," the head groom said sourly.

Taitsung came to a decision. "Let her try," he said.

Jer gasped. "No, really," he protested. "Jao's always got something to say no matter what, but half the time she is only joking. I don't think that she should be allowed to be so stupid!"

Taitsung considered another moment. "Let her try," he repeated soberly.

Silence descended upon all who were present. With great difficulty, Bad Luck was caught and saddled, the stirrups placed high on his haunches.

"Do you have an iron rod anywhere?" Jao inquired. While a bludgeon was being found, Taitsung asked her why she wanted it. She told him, "I will not be able to control him without it. If a tricky horse doesn't learn with that, an iron mace will be needed. If that doesn't work, he is indeed a killer and an iron dagger should be used to dispose of him . . . that was the opinion of my father's head groom."

The heavy rod was brought and passed from hand to hand until it reached her. She quickly hid it in her boot, preventing the horse from seeing it.

"Ready," she said. Bad Luck was brought sidling up to her by several grooms. She walked to the colt's head and grasped his muzzle with both hands, taking her time patting and talking to him. He stood still, curiosity mastering him.

"Throw me," she commanded, and was at once lifted to the saddle. The gate was opened for her and she trotted out. Then she was off, over the plain in a gallop which seemed, to the men who were watching, to go on and on until the horse could not be seen—only a cloud of dust.

Jao's light weight puzzled the horse and helped him decide that here was a good opportunity to assert himself. He looked for a convenient tree but there were none in view. Answering to a command to turn back, he then saw the tents beside the corral. A silent group of men watched him approach camp at great speed, apparently obedient to every command. Suddenly, he lunged toward the guy rope of the first tent. Shouts of alarm rose as the colt darted viciously under a rope, sure of being able to scrape off his rider. Jao had her leg tucked against the saddle horn, ready to slip sideways. One hand grasped the mane, while the other held her iron rod. As they went under, she slid down the colt's side and the tent rope only jerked across the horn, while she lashed cruelly into the colt's soft belly with the iron rod.

Neighing in surprise and pain, Bad Luck reared and bucked while slowly losing steam. He finally halted, blowing and sweating, for the moment a very confused animal. Grooms hastened to catch his reins and walk him while he cooled off.

Jao slid to the ground, trembling. The head groom ran to catch her in case she collapsed. When she did not, but instead occupied herself in dusting off her riding trousers, the men broke into surprised guffaws among themselves. Straightening up, she risked a direct look at the group, and saw to her relief that there was an expression of delight on the emperor's face. Jer looked dumbfounded.

"Well," the emperor said. "Well."

Jao grinned and wiped her grimy face. "He may be cured of the back-scraping stunt," she said. "If he isn't . . . one would have to use that mace, don't you think? A heavier weapon. If that wouldn't work, he would be useless, not even good for stud. What would you say?"

At this the groom, forgetting his manners, spoke up before the emperor could answer. "We have tried the whip on him but he does not learn."

Jao responded diffidently. "We had a bad horse like this once at Wenshui. He was a perfect animal in most respects and my father did not wish to have him butchered; so the head groom did not allow anyone to attempt to ride him but himself. He finally succeeded in breaking him because he knew what the horse was thinking."

"And how do horses think, young one?" the emperor put in.

"Oh that . . ." she replied, "the trick is to keep the horse from connecting his pain with the man on his back and let him think it was something else that hurt him."

"But Bad Luck is sure to think he got the iron blow from you," the emperor remarked, restraining his desire to laugh.

"No, I think not, because I hid the rod and he never saw it," she said.

"What will he think hurt him, then?" Taitsung asked.

"The tent rope," she replied.

By this time most of the grooms on the farm had collected to listen and were chuckling. "We haven't run into this kind of problem before," the head groom said stiffly.

"Do what you can with Bad Luck, then, and let me know how he shapes up," Taitsung said while turning away to whistle to his horse. "We will be moving on now. Thank you for your help."

"Anytime," the head groom stuttered, "but the help was mostly from the *kuniang*." His face was red with humiliation.

"Not to worry," the emperor responded. "I didn't know that one about training either, and I thought I knew all about horses."

The groom bowed in gratitude, and Taitsung saluted with his whip while moving off. The other four followed close behind.

The rest of the day was pure bliss for Jao. Neither Taitsung nor Jer mentioned Bad Luck, treating the incident as a part of the day's outing in a way that put her at ease. The afternoon wore on in long hours in the saddle as they followed new trails and visited new training centers. Reluctant to turn back, they spoke little, each one savoring the day in his own way. At sunset they stopped for a meal cooked over a bonfire. It was all the more enjoyable for being out-of-doors.

Jao felt herself enveloped in a haze of approval. Even the grooms oozed respect. She thought that she had never wholly achieved the emperor's regard before, but now she had, quite accidentally, obtained it. He was himself a man of so many skills that he was hard to match and therefore hard to satisfy. Jao pondered this as daylight waned. She now understood her own urge to excel in order to be worthy of him. She was also grateful for Jer's good-natured acceptance of the fact that she had outstripped him, a fact made worse by having his father present to see. Jer, however, was proud of her and let her know it. Nothing, therefore, seemed to have changed in her relationship with the two men because of the day's adventures . . . but everything had. Her status had risen considerably.

After eating, the three rode back to the city in a dusk enlivened by the croaking of myriad frogs in the marshes and rice paddies. It was dark, however, when they finally rode through the gates of the palace.

Jer turned his horse to go to the detached palace east of the main grounds. "Farewell, my wild one, I shall dream of you tonight," he said lightly to Jao.

"Dreams?" she called back. "Do you mean nightmares?"

He laughed and raised his reins.

"Come along with me and have a drink," his father suggested. Jer happily dropped his reins again and let the horse follow the other two.

An hour later they were all together still. They were in a sleepy, mellow mood, comfortably seated in a corner of Taitsung's great hall. Jer was listening to a harangue from his father, and Jao was surprised to see Taitsung looking at her in a different way, speculative and knowing; to her embarrassment, she flushed. She felt a tingling all over her body and realized almost at once what had happened to her. So this is what it means to be ready for a man, she thought as she shyly retreated as far as possible into the shadows.

The rain began in a sudden torrent. Far away, the sound of a single flute reached them across the wet rooftops. A eunuch quietly sopped up the puddle from a new leak in the hall, and a moth fluttered into the candle on the table. The two men talked on and Jao dreamed, buried in her own thoughts. So without warning had this mood of desiring love come upon her that she was at a loss. She recalled a recent conversation she'd had with Chi.

"I have been in this palace for five years, and I have not yet been called to the emperor's bed," she had told him.

"You are a late bloomer," he had said to comfort her. "You have so many other delights in your makeup that a man can wait for the sexual one, or do without it and still enjoy you. I know, because even I relish your company more than anyone else's." He had cut himself off, embarrassed.

Jao had not been comforted. "I am seventeen and I am not yet a complete woman," she said. "It is not very rewarding to know that there are several of me all there for several people to enjoy. I want only one—the Son of Heaven—and none other."

Chi had smiled bitterly. "Such crosscurrents happen," he said.

Jao recalled herself to the present when she became aware of the silence in the hall. Jer had taken himself off and the emperor was looking at her; looking in a way that sent a shock through her.

"You may leave," he said, not to Jao, but to the eunuch. He put out his hand to Jao. "Come, my untamed one. It is time."

She flew to him and put her arms around his neck in an eager embrace.

"My little one!" Taitsung murmured, grasping her tightly in passion.

She trembled as she pressed into his arms, while waves of feeling swept over her. She moved shyly as he began to explore her body with an experienced hand. After that, time no longer existed for her, as he gauged his lovemaking so that she hardly noticed the pain when he at last entered her. All she was aware of was unspeakable pleasure. Even after they had both sunk back into the furs, sated, he still lightly stroked her eyes, neck, and shoulders. She finally slipped into sleep closely cuddled into his arms.

Late that night Jao splashed through the puddles on her way back to the tsairen house, unaware of the wet. She was too much aware of herself and her newfound joy.

CHAPTER SEVEN

Taitsung stepped out onto his terrace with an eye to the weather, a habit of his at daybreak. He nodded at the two guards who had raised their lances when they heard his light footsteps. Low clouds were scudding overhead and there was a chill in the air. Good hunting weather, he thought, inhaling with pleasure. The air was redolent with the scents of pine needles, of fall flowers and of burning leaves which drifted across the walls from courtyards where the gardeners were already at work.

"Best time of the year, first frost," he remarked to the guards. "The time to be out on the steppes on a good horse and nothing to stop you." Their eyes lit up when he saluted them in a comradely way, and followed him as he strode on through the park to his stables. Being with his horses helped Taitsung clear his mind in a way that nothing else did, and he had serious thinking to do: Should he take to the field again? He was feeling vigorous and fit in spite of his forty-five years.

A campaign, he thought. That was what he wanted—a tough campaign against a tough foe. He was still young, and wanted once more to be in the saddle, to sit over campfires with his chiefs, planning strategy, coordinating moves, participating in battles, testing his wits, testing his will, parleying with tribal chiefs, dispatching spies, feeling the excitement of winning. . . .

Inspired by his thoughts, he returned to his residence determined to present his ideas to his ministers at once.

"Take a message to Commander-in-Chief Changsun," Taitsung said to his officer of the day. "Ask him to call a war council. I want all my top men there: Generals Li Chi, Yujer Chingde, and Chin Shubao. And my three ministers: Chu Suiliang, Hsiao Yu, and Fang Hsuanling. Also, I want my warrior cousin, Prince Jencheng, to be there. At the hour of the horse. All of them—at once!" The officer bowed, walked backward to the door and left hurriedly.

When the drums sounded the hour of the horse, Taitsung seated himself on the throne in the council chamber and looked over the men assembled before him. They were veterans, experienced in both warfare and statecraft, all men in their prime except for the elderly ministers Fang and Hsiao.

"Seat yourselves. You do not have to stand humbly in my presence. There are stools for your ease," he said. They took their seats wondering why he had called them. Taitsung wasted no time in enlightening them.

"The Korean question is the most important foreign policy concern of our empire, just as it was thirty years ago during the Sui dynasty, when China lost three hundred thousand men in those three Korean wars. It is time that we settled it. Now, the recent palace revolution in the north of the Korean peninsula, in Koguryo, was serious. Our vassal king Konmu was murdered by one of his servants, and now the kingdom is being ruled by this man under the title of Moliju. We may have to wage a major campaign, first against Koguryo, then probably against its neighbor, Paekche. With success, we would eventually be in control of the whole peninsula and at last have peace on that troubled border. I would take charge of such a campaign myself."

There was a heavy silence in the room as the generals thought this over. The well-groomed Minister Fang, the financier, studied his boot tips; and Minister Chu, nervously plucking at the few hairs on his chin, sat erect, his rigid pose radiating disapproval. As usual, Changsun Wuji, the emperor's brother-in-law, was the first to speak.

"Why you, yourself? Why should the greatest military strategist in the world deign to conduct a small war himself?"

"Because it will not be a small war. Or a short one," Taitsung replied. "It could be our hardest foreign war yet, and I am the only one who could win it—whatever great generals do or don't do, my friend."

"Why start it, then?" Changsun Wuji said lightly, exchanging glances with his good friend, Minister Chu. "Your generals have subdued the Western Turks and the oasis kingdom of Turfan, and the marauding Tibetans have been restrained by your gift of the princess Wencheng. The west is now secure and the trade routes open. I agree that military action *should* take place on our eastern border against this 'five-sword' usurper Moliju, but it would, and should, be a minor expedition, not calling for a military genius like yourself to expose himself. A great general doesn't have to take risks like that."

"No military measures at all against those eastern barbarians would be better," broke in Chu, who never failed to support Changsun. "Too expensive just now."

Minister Fang, an experienced politician, cut in smoothly. "Not too costly if the campaign is short. The Koguryan kingdom is partly located in eastern Liaotung. I presume Chinese troops would be invading there with the purpose of inquiring about what had happened to King Konmu. Such a campaign is not much to risk and not beyond our means. And Liaotung has good farmland which our Shantung farmers could develop. They are vulnerable to Yellow River floods and need additional land," he said as he rhythmically stroked his thin beard.

Chu shook his head stubbornly. "All three Korean kingdoms are unreliable and their people treacherous. Paekche is an ally of Japan, and Silla is ruled by a female king. What can you expect from a woman in wartime? She would be unable to furnish us with adequate assistance if we needed to mount a two-front war."

"I should think that the female king who rules Silla could provide more than enough assistance if we needed it," Taitsung replied mildly. "Silla always was, and still is, the most stable of the three kingdoms. Queen Sondok has now been ruling not as a regent, but in her own right, for twelve years. She has sent a stream of students to Changan, she has reorganized her armies, she has created Hualang, a ten-year training school for officers, her generals in the field are loyal and able, and she has faithfully declared loyalty to me year after year, sending tribute in every mission."

"Small gifts, I have no doubt," Changsun said, again exchanging glances with the obsequious Chu. The others in the chamber pricked up their ears. No one knew much about the remote kingdom of Silla, and it was apparent that the emperor did. In a court where everyone supposedly knew all about anything of significance, Jao and Mi nevertheless succeeded in keeping their knowledge about events in Silla to themselves. No one was better informed than they, and what they knew was quickly passed on to the emperor.

"Small gifts, yes indeed, but small with a flair," Taitsung said dryly. He studied his officials in silence and then decided to spark their interest by giving them more facts than they needed for military decisions.

"First there was a rainbow-hued silk rug, which delighted the empress so much that it is still on my bedroom floor; then there were some tiny horses, which the royal children still ride daily; and a rare hunting bird, which I used as long as it lived because it never missed its prey. A fur mantle of sea leopard for my personal use was quite a welcome gift. A couple of peacocks arrived and were the sensation of the day for the women and the children. There were food items also, and the best ginseng obtainable, which I now use exclusively."

He paused as a burst of laughter broke up his monologue. "Ginseng? Well, I need it in my battles . . ." Another laugh, louder and more ribald this time. He stood, grinning, knowing that he had accomplished what he had set out to do—get his powerful men interested.

"Small gifts," Changsun Wuji repeated, looking around with a condescending smile. "A great ruler should accept only large gifts."

"Small? Perhaps," Taitsung returned coolly. "With the distinction that they never failed to please. If that was what the queen intended, she succeeded. Only an experienced and intelligent ruler would think of such things, much less send them so that they would arrive safely. Why do I remember these trivial matters of tribute when I normally forget gifts as soon as I see them? Because they never arrived damaged. Because they showed timing, precision, and a consistency never shown by the other kingdoms, who usually sent too much or too little or sent what they thought was treasure and I thought was trash.

"Personal gifts are only a part of the Silla shipments, however. Every mission brings to China narwhal and walrus ivory, gold and silver, our best bells, and hundreds of bales of brocades. The Sillans are experts with armor and weapons, especially fine swords. My best sword, famous for its magic quality, comes from Silla and is a great treasure of mine."

Minister Fang was nodding, gently stroking his beard. He was aware of the Korean products and that their value was greater than all of the trade from the west combined. However, he failed to see what bearing they had on the subject at hand. Taitsung noticed the skeptical looks and decided to bring the meeting to a close.

"You all know your Sun Tzu, that we must first secure allies before we commit our own men. Silla has what we need."

At the mention of the revered military authority, every eye focused on the emperor. "He must be serious," Changsun murmured to Chu, "I can't believe it. He is an established emperor with a settled empire, a great reputation, none higher, and he plans to risk everything for a whim. . . . I can't believe it." Chu nodded sourly but kept his silence. Taitsung had begun speaking again and was looking at them with irritation.

"First, I can assign major expenses of this campaign to our most distant province, Szechuan. That will relieve our coastal provinces. Second, I can send out proclamations to all prefects whose districts lie between the city of Loyang and northern Korea, that they are to spend no money entertaining me or my officers when we pass through their territories, that all levies we may raise will be only for military purposes, and that we shall not send a great horde of soldiers through their district at one time. We can send a continuous flow of men, a line two hundred miles long, so that there will only be a few men at any one given place at a single time.

"The route taken will be down the Yellow River by barge and then north by land to Tingchow. It's close enough to the Korean border to serve as our base. Prince Jer would be left in charge to give him experience. I would then split the armies, about forty thousand to sail across the Yellow Sea and about sixty thousand to go by land around the coastal passes."

"We don't have enough ships on the whole China coast to transport four thousand men at one time, much less forty thousand," Changsun said.

Taitsung looked at him with a glint in his eye and said smoothly, "Szechuan province is far from the sea in the mountains of the southwest. It is rich and untouched by the recent wars. That is where our great forests are, as well as our best mines and wheat fields. I shall have them build four or five hundred ships this winter, which will travel down the Long River, then by sea to the Shantung peninsula. They can assemble there at the port of Laichow and their crews can take on Silla pilots to get the soldiers across the sea. As you know, Silla has control of traffic on the Yellow Sea."

Dead silence greeted this speech, a silence that Taitsung prolonged as he studied each face. No one had anything to say. Szechuan was a remote area out of the range of their experiences, and naval expeditions were outside of their interests. Their ignorance not only of naval strategy but also of the internal politics of the Korean kingdoms caught them all at a disadvantage.

"Has anyone anything to say at this time?" Taitsung asked finally, and, when no quick response came, said, "Then I shall ask for a formal vote. Who is for this campaign against Koguryo?"

One hand went up. It belonged to the indomitable Li Chi, the greatest warrior of them all. Taitsung glanced at him warmly and rose to dismiss the meeting.

"That is all, gentlemen. The campaign is on. We go."

A few months later Taitsung left Changan with his elite troops. He took Crown Prince Jer with him and the hardiest of his palace ladies and servants. Among these were Chi, Toto, Cloud, and Jao. The crown prince brought his concubine Hsiao, but left his difficult wife, Lady Wang, at home. Prime Minister Fang was put in charge of the government in Changan, and most of the officials remained with him. A skeleton staff went with Taitsung to Loyang to spend the winter there recruiting and training soldiers before launching the campaign the following summer.

Changan City gave the emperor an enthusiastic send-off. People took to the streets, cheering, whistling, and waving banners as the imperial train left the palace. Martial music and a close-file column made a parade of the departure. The column left by the great south gate, turned eastward along the palace walls, then northward to the east gate. There the palace civilians joined it.

Along the entire route the drumbeats of the soldiers thumped in time to the tramp of their felt boots. Street sellers called out loudly, donkeys brayed harshly, and the excitable metropolitan populace outdid itself in its noisy farewells. The emperor was never a loser, and no one doubted that once again he would bring home a victory. Every citizen over thirty knew of the three hundred thousand Chinese lost in the Sui wars with the eastern barbarians of Korea. Most families had lost someone, so the crowds were generally in favor of a campaign to blot out the stain and to get revenge. Taitsung was satisfied that his campaign was going to be a popular one.

Jao rode one of Taitsung's hunters, her face veiled under an oversized hat. She felt that she would burst with happiness at her release from palace confinement. Her eyes roved over the crowds, missing nothing. It all looked different from the last time she had ridden in the streets seven years before. The trees now towered over the crenellated city walls, and the walls themselves were higher as well, now forty feet above her head.

After several hours of slow travel through traffic, the column reached the famous Restaurant of Smiles and Tears, named for the fact that many meetings and partings took place there. The emperor and his immediate entourage paused for refreshment and to bid farewell to the dignitaries lined up to see him off. The cavalcade then settled into a steady progress eastward, until at nightfall they embarked on barges for the trip downriver.

The tedium of long hours in the saddle and crowded quarters in the barges did not bother the travelers. They made good time and were able to enter the gates of Loyang in ten days, unfatigued and, for some, actually refreshed. Jao was one of the refreshed ones. The opportunity to visit with many people during the informalities of travel was a great delight to her.

The welcome that the cavalcade received in Loyang was hearty enough, but as that city was one-tenth the size of Changan, it seemed tame to the visitors and provoked a good deal of joking about backward Loyang. More joking was to come as soon as they saw their lodgings in the half-ruined palace. The travelers found themselves in near-empty rooms full of cobwebs. Servants and local authorities quickly scurried about to round up the necessities of life.

Taitsung himself had comfortable, even gracious, quarters because years before, during his battles in and around Loyang, he had disobeyed his father's order to burn all the Sui palaces. He had refurbished his own courtyards but had neglected the rest. His staff, undaunted, found that their camping-out conditions were invigorating.

As spring advanced, Jao found pleasure in repeating what she had done during her first spring in Changan: exploring run-down courtyards, empty halls, and vast, weed-covered gardens and parks. Warm weather brought out the blooms of the famous peonies. Despite their neglect, hundreds had survived and were unfolding their flamboyant, satiny petals in all the courtyards. Jao discovered that the layouts of the old palaces had been well-planned, with spacious gardens, canals and lakes, attractive perspectives through well-placed gates, and terraces overlooking the courses of three rivers. The palaces were scattered but connected by paved walkways. Everything seemed exotic and open to the sky after the closed-in walls of the fortresslike palaces of Changan.

Cloud, Toto, and Jao had a large courtyard to themselves. They had little to do but enjoy life. The palace ladies whom they had been serving were all in Changan, and the men were fully occupied in campaign preparations. Toto gravitated to the stables, where she helped train the colts and rode daily. Cloud, one of the emperor's favorites, became an assistant in the clinic.

Jao assumed housekeeping duties in order to see that special foods and wines were obtained for Taitsung and Prince Jer, who were spending their days with the troops, organizing, training, testing weapons, and reshaping combat units. They were ravenously hungry when they came home at night. Their evenings, spent with their women, were brief, as they began their days at sunrise.

The emperor called no one to him but Jao during his entire stay in Loyang. He felt free from the restraints of court life and the need to care for his harem, and did just as he chose. Every evening they sat in his courtyard listening to the night noises, the noisy frogs, the birds going to roost, occasional splashes from a fish in the river below, and the distant sound of flutes. They were able to relish each other's company as never before, and to retire for long nights of love and sleep. Jao was radiant with happiness, and even the emperor reached new heights of well-being. It soon became apparent to all that Taitsung had formed an important alliance that looked to be permanent. He exuded energy and zest that spread to everyone around him.

Enthusiasm for the campaign increased daily. However, for a time Taitsung was obliged to cease work on war preparations long enough to receive a famous man of peace. The Buddhist monk Hsuantsang had left China illegally some sixteen years before. He had recently requested that the emperor allow him to return to his homeland from an oasis in Sinjiang, and Taitsung had granted his petition.

When the monk arrived in Loyang, Taitsung met him on the outskirts of the city. In several audiences with the emperor, Hsuantsang, who had walked most of the way across the continent to India and back again, told an intrigued Taitsung about his experiences. The emperor was so impressed with his daring accomplishments, and so pleased with his reports of Tang's great fame abroad, that he offered the humble monk an ambassadorship. This was politely refused, but the offer of a research pagoda (staffed with scholars to assist in translation of the sutras he had brought back from his travels) was gratefully accepted.

Shortly after the meetings with Hsuantsang, Taitsung left Loyang in the charge of his minister Hsiao Yu, sent the women back to Changan, and moved his campaign headquarters a hundred miles north, to Tingchow. There he established his forward base, putting it under Jer's command, and left for the front lines himself.

The rainy season came and went, and as the hot month of August was drying the earth, Taitsung and his commanders conducted scores of forays against the smaller Koguryan forts, subduing many. Finally, by taking advantage of a great wind, the Tang forces set fire to the main fortress of the border town of Liaoyang, and took it in a fierce battle. The conquest of Liaoyang was a major triumph, in spite of the high death toll and the large number of wounded. Taitsung was so pleased that he declared an amnesty for the civilian citizens, and forwarded only military prisoners to Changan. In his message to his son in Tingchow, he gave way to his feeling of elation by writing, "When I conduct a campaign . . . what else could you expect?"

With renewed energy Taitsung moved on to lay siege to Ansi Fort, a key stronghold commanding the main route to the crossings of the Yalu River. The entrance to the fort lay above a long apron of scree and up a stairway carved out of the structure's granite foundation. The steps then disappeared into a thick gate surrounded by high walls of granite boulders that towered overhead. Taitsung surveyed the tranquil scene and shook his head soberly. Koguryo resistance was not yet destroyed, and would not be, Taitsung felt, until this particular fort was annihilated. But taking the fort would not be easy.

He began the siege. The days passed, hotter and hotter as the summer heat reached its climax, and then the first hint of autumn arrived to warn the Chinese that time was of the essence. By mid-August, Taitsung had exhausted all the sophisticated military tactics known as well as some of his own devising, but the fort remained untaken. His most recent scheme had been to build a rampart of earth just outside the Korean walls, for the purpose of introducing an avalanche of invading soldiers over the walls. The task was enormous, accomplished only after much effort and the labor of hundreds of commandeered civilians, Chinese engineers, and Malgal prisoners. Finally, the day of the Tang attack arrived; it failed, and the Koreans succeeded in driving the Chinese off. Then, undaunted, the Ko chiefs seized the rampart and used it in their own defense.

At the first appearance of frost, Taitsung called in his officers. "Here we are, back where we were a month ago, and this cursed fort has not yielded. It is a small and poverty-stricken fort and hardly worth taking, but the defending Kos are fierce fighters and pigheaded."

"Besides, it is costing a fortune," Changsun put in sourly. "The best generals consider the cost."

Taitsung ignored his brother-in-law. "Up until now you have all been enjoying this campaign. You like being here in this invigorating, unspoiled country . . . as long as there have been no cold winds. But now we are obliged to bring the campaign to a close, and we are far from being in a position to bring the Koguryans to their knees. You may recall the error of my predecessor, Sui Yang Kwang, in letting winter overtake him. Fatal. We won't walk into that trap. Tomorrow we mount our final attack and put everything we have into it."

The commanders sobered and, without further discussion, dispersed to make their preparations. The next morning all seemed well—the Tang managed to breach the outer wall. Taitsung then insisted upon being in the lead and began scaling an inner wall. Suddenly, an arrow, launched by an archer who had not once removed his eye from the emperor, whizzed by Taitsung's cheek, grazing his forehead and an eyelid, and nicking his ear. A scratch, he thought, but the bleeding blinded him. The silent archer in the tower shot again, and, had Taitsung not lowered his head to shake the blood out of his eyes, it would have pierced his skull.

His companions saw this and were appalled. General Chingde, ahead, looked down and immediately dropped back, seizing Taitsung in an iron grip and easing him to the ground. Meanwhile, the imperial archers launched a fierce protective barrage under which Taitsung was swiftly passed down the line and moved to safety. He resisted but was hampered by his blindness. The Tang attack inside the outer walls of the fort wavered in the face of a ferocious counterattack. General Changsun gave the order to retreat.

Taitsung's wounds were washed, a swab placed over the torn eyelid, and the whole bound tightly. "I can now see as well with one eye as I used to with two," he joked while returning to the field. He was there in time to meet the last of the retreat. Standing on the battleground just out of arrow range, he concealed his bitter disappointment. We had victory in our hands this time, we were in there farther than we have ever been before, he thought as he surveyed the scene, and now a ridiculous scratch in my eyelid and a general who countermanded my orders have ruined everything.

Koguryan heads began to line the ramparts above, and then, incredibly, there floated down to his ears the lonely notes of a flute. Taitsung shook his head in bafflement, but also felt more lighthearted. This fort was indeed a miserable one. It was located in the heart of nowhere-land, it was undeniably barbarian, but the foe was worthy!

In spite of the coolness he displayed, his officers and men were dejected beyond reason to see their emperor wounded. The generals gathered before his tent without being summoned, still sweating from the fray. Some of the great men squatted on the ground in disarray, others stood leaning on their swords. Taitsung surveyed them through his bandage.

"Want to try again tomorrow?" he asked. No one spoke, until finally Prince Jencheng said lightly, "Of course, if you so command, but we will not let you do any hand-to-hand fighting yourself."

Taitsung gave a crack of laughter. "You dare to give orders to your illustrious commander?"

His laughter eased the tension, and the feeling of confrontation dissipated.

"The wise thing to do now would be to withdraw for the winter," he said reluctantly, and stopped, amazed at the strong shout of approval. He had not realized how much his generals detested the prospect of a siege where no loot would be forthcoming, nor how much they wanted to disengage from the poverty of the Manchurian countryside and from the implacable enemy. Only General Li Chi and Prince Jencheng understood Taitsung's attitude and what the campaign had meant to him.

Taitsung shrugged. "Those of you who feel that it is better to withdraw now and mount another campaign in the spring, raise your fists."

Another shout of approval arose as if from one throat, and all fists, it seemed, were thrust into the air—even Li Chi's. The emperor gazed at his men out of his one eye and his smile was crooked. He gave a short laugh and unstrapped his sword. "Next spring it is, then. In the spring, we return. I repeat—in the spring we return."

"When shall we start for home?" asked the commander in charge of transport. He was extremely anxious about the weather. Fodder was nearly exhausted and Manchurian weather unpredictable.

"Now," Taitsung said.

By the time the sun had reached its zenith, the tents had all been struck, the small native horses loaded, and the downward and westward trek begun. Koguryans who had geared themselves for a fight to the death stayed on the ramparts to watch the withdrawal, unable to believe their eyes. Some of them began to cheer weakly. Taitsung's tent was the last to be packed because he was busy with dispatches to Minister Hsiao in Loyang, Fang in Changan, and his son in Tingchow.

He said nothing about his wound, and no one was allowed to refer to it.

The journey home set a record. The weather was crisp and clear, the roads hard, supply wagons empty, and spirits especially high because the crossing of the Liao River had been accomplished without incident. Men felt closer to their homes once they were in Chinese territory. The officers rationalized that the campaign had been mainly successful, with Chinese objectives partially obtained, and they looked forward to celebrating the conquest of the important city of Liaoyang. However, a great misfortune in the shape of a blizzard roaring down from the north caught the Tang forces by surprise and many perished. The lot of the prisoners was terrible; those sturdy male prisoners who survived were ordered by Taitsung to be assigned to the Chinese widows who had lost husbands in the campaign.

In Tingchow, Taitsung joined up with his son. The two of them proceeded on to Changan, where they quickly settled back into the comforts of palace life.

The night before the arrival of the imperial pair, Jao could hardly sleep from excitement. It had been a long, hot summer for her in her old tsairen quarters after she came back from Loyang. She, Toto, and Cloud had had a hard time adjusting to the heat and sultriness of their Changan quarters after the vast gardens and roomy halls of their Loyang residence, but they were young and in high spirits and the days passed quickly. Jao was twenty. Taitsung was forty-five. The future looked bright and full of promise to her.

Tutor Chu was living in cool quarters, so Jao renewed her lessons with him during the hot months. She asked him to let her read Sun Tzu's *Art of War* while the emperor was on campaign. He refused. "Not a subject for women," he said shortly. Jao was surprised because she had not really been much interested—it sounded dull—but she had thought to be closer to Taitsung by having a look at the famous military manual. She remembered the refusual, and one day when Chu was in a good mood, asked again. He refused without an explanation.

"It is not the subject matter that I am interested in . . . it is that I want an appropriate quotation for the scroll of calligraphy that I am preparing for the emperor," she said coaxingly. "Please choose an appropriate text."

"Calligraphy?" the old man repeated. "Are you supposed to be practicing that? And am I supposed to be judging it?"

"The emperor ordered me to learn to write well," she answered.

"That is a different thing . . . how long will it take you to copy out your quotation?"

Jao considered. "An evening perhaps . . ."

He snapped his fingers to call his servant to bring the manual, then sat for an hour fussily leafing through it for a suitable quotation. The afternoon shadows were lengthening and he was tired.

"Here, I have put this ivory book marker in the right place—beginning here to the bottom of the page. Take the book, copy this out, and bring both book and calligraphy back tomorrow."

Jao bowed politely and left, delighted to have the book overnight. It was not especially long, and she was able to copy the whole by staying up and by using Mi to finish the last section in the morning as she dressed to go to her lesson. Jao took with her the selection that she had painstakingly copied and returned the book. The old man asked no questions. He read the scroll that Jao had written and shrugged contentedly. This particular quotation reflected his own views on economizing the costs of war; not exactly what Taitsung might like to see, but what Chu thought he ought to see.

Back in her room once more, Jao took time to read the text, and during the next few days did the calligraphy on silk instead of paper, in her most elegant style. She chose sandalwood rollers for top and bottom and silk cord for ties. The scroll was ready to give to Taitsung as a welcoming gift.

On the morning after the arrival of the emperor and the crown prince, a reception for the ladies was arranged. Jao took great pains over her dress, her fingers trembling while she applied her makeup. She put a ruby fleurette in her hair to match her oxblood coat and skirt, and carried her gift hidden in a fold of her dress, certain that she would be asked to remain after the others had left. She had never been closer to anyone than she had been to Taitsung during those spring days in Loyang. He had been full of youthful enthusiasm then, feeling especially fit, and the campaign plans had invigorated him.

Exultantly, Jao was aware that it was she who had been responsible for his soaring well-being. She had been on fire with joy then, and was still radiant with her memories. It had all happened only a few short months before. Surely he would meet her again with delight after their long separation.

Jao arrived at the hall in the Inner Palace to find that the highest-ranking women were already going into it, so she joined the tsairen and took her turn. Each lady passed before the emperor and received a gift and a polite smile from him. When Jao went by, she received her gift with the customary polite holding of her sleeve with one hand while her other was free to accept the offering. She cast an ardent look upward and gave an involuntary gasp when she saw the bandage over his eye. The emperor's face was expressionless. Numbed, she passed on mechanically, and assuming that her duties were to be resumed, she stayed in attendance braced against the back wall, stiffly holding her towels with the scroll underneath.

Once the formal reception of his ladies was over, Taitsung called in his close friends, Fang and Hsiao, whom he had left in charge of the two capitals while he was away, and they settled down to talk. His face brightened when his friends agreed to stay for a meal. The animated talk went on as the twilight waned and night set in. Taitsung loudly dominated the conversation while recounting in detail everything about his martial adventures.

Jao waited until the men left, her scroll still concealed in her skirt. She had furnished a towel once, but the emperor had not looked at her. By then she realized that something was very wrong. She had never seen him in such a mood. She waited until the head eunuch ushered in Peony and signaled for her, Jao, to leave; and then she had to go.

Back in her room, Jao threw the scroll into the corner and lay on her bed, refusing even to let Mi massage her feet, as she usually did when Jao had stood for hours without relief. Jao could not sleep. In the darkness of the tiger hours she got up, found the scroll, and read it by the dim glow of her night candle. One section of the passage horrified her:

> If victory is long in coming, the men's weapons will grow dull and their ardor will be dampened. If you lay siege to a town, you will exhaust your strength, and if the campaign is protracted, the resources of the state will not be equal to the strain. Never forget . . . supreme excellence consists in breaking the enemy's resistance without fighting . . . And the worst policy of all is to besiege walled cities . . . which will take up to three months; and the piling up of mounds over against the walls will take three months more.

Jao put her head down and wept. Worse than being ignored by the emperor for Peony, much worse, was the knowledge that he, the champion of the world, had failed. Neither she nor Chu had known the details of the campaign, but Jao had heard about them as she stood against the wall. Taitsung had not only failed in the "supreme excellence," but also in committing the "worst policy of all" by besieging a walled fortress and piling up mounds. Jao tore up her scroll and lay awake the rest of the night, unable to escape her own deep sense of defeat.

CHAPTER EIGHT

Autumn passed into winter, and Taitsung remained restless, remote to many of his former close friends. He hardly noticed Jao's existence. Toto, who had always been a favorite, was not called in to dance or to enliven any gathering. Cloud, the peerless, was not called. The only one who was sent for, night after night, was the brainless, blowzy Peony. She boasted long and loud about her successes, which her roommates tolerated. She was so often under the influence of opium that they pitied her.

Two days before the celebration of the winter solstice, Jao was standing in attendance as usual when the emperor spoke to her as in the past, and invited her to come talk to him. From then on her relationship to him stabilized, not as a lover, but as a trusted confidante. As the situation became clearer to her, Jao began to suffer another sort of despair. Eventually she went for counsel to her old friend Chi. He remained silent until she was through talking.

"I think you might look upon your present position as one of honor and respect—and be grateful for the confidence that the emperor obviously has in you. The eunuchs in positions of trust are all worried these days. The emperor's health is not what it was. His eye does not heal, but keeps having one infection after the other. The best physicians are secretly called in, but none of their prescriptions has done much good. Now the emperor has sent to India for a famous doctor.

"The girls he wants are those like Peony, who are good for only one thing and can be abused. And they are, let me tell you. Peony's servants tell me that she is covered with bruises much of the time. What is it that you want, then? Of him? Of your life here? We all know that our emperor has lost his happiness in some way, as well as his health. What can you do for him now?"

Jao listened thoughtfully, her feelings of hurt and rejection easing. "I see how I must act. You give me hope that I can still be of use in important ways." She grasped Chi's hand gratefully. "You are wise . . . you look into hearts and minds and see further than the rest of us."

"Perhaps," he said soberly, "it is because I myself have suffered first."

Jao looked at him in silence. "Yes," she said finally, and put her other hand on top of his.

Jao began at once to take a greater interest in the problems brought daily to the emperor's attention. She also took careful note of the food and medicines served to him. One evening a new vegetable from Nepal "for releasing the poisons of wine" was served to him. It was cooked in chicken broth.

"What is this? What is *this*?" he asked, stirring some large green leaves round and round in his bowl. "Cow food?"

The majordomo said hastily, "It is a gift from the king of Tibet, forwarded by Queen Wencheng." The food had passed all the tasters, but one could never be sure about poison. The majordomo added anxiously, "This spinach has been planted here and has been grown successfully. It is highly recommended for good health."

Taitsung tasted it cautiously. A small giggle escaped Jao.

"Good for your health, is it?" he exclaimed, looking at her, extending his bowl. "Here it is then . . . you eat it."

The emperor's attendants gradually concentrated on doing whatever was possible to restore his good spirits, but it was hard to get him to do anything pressed on him. He acts like a child, Jao thought dispassionately. She was getting used to her new role and was now able to tolerate clay feet in her idol.

One thing was sure to claim his attention at any time, however, and that was the progress of Tang arms, Tang expansion, and Tang control of the border areas. He had always been alerted to the affairs of nomadic tribes on the Chinese frontiers. It had been necessary in order to preserve the unity of the new China under Tang rule, but now the emperor was obsessed by it.

Lately the emperor had been concerned about Kucha, so Jao thought to quiz Toto about her oasis country.

They were sunning themselves beside a pool when Jao idly said, "Kucha never seems to have trouble with invading nomads like the other oasis kingdoms, does it?"

"No, our army is so good that the nomads think twice about attacking us," Toto said proudly.

"What about the Chinese armies?"

"Well, the king always stays on friendly terms with Tang China—*that* he certainly does." Toto flashed a quick glance around the pool to see if there were any listeners.

Jao sat up and looked at her. "You sound serious."

"I am. My brother is high in the hierarchy and close to the king, so I knew even as a child that our freedom depended on constant alertness. There is a small garrison of Chinese troops in our capital city, and there is nothing that its commander hates worse than any hint of collusion between us and the nomads. So we keep our dealings with the tribes secret. And that's why I'm here! A gesture to keep our king and the emperor on good terms! Valuable me!"

They laughed and fell silent. Then Toto said, "I am concerned about my country, though. Just before I left to come here, a huge number of western tribes consolidated under the khan of the Western Turks. He was trying to take over all of eastern Persia. We were worried because if he had succeeded, he would then have become the strongest power in Asia and our country would have been swallowed up along with all of central Asia."

Jao stared. "Surely not. There was Tang China—"

"Entirely preoccupied with the Eastern Turks. Taitsung had just come to the throne, and if either the Eastern or Western Turks had prevailed, Tang expansion would have stopped then and there." Jao looked surprised, but Toto continued. "It worked out all right in the end—someone assassinated the Great Khan, and his coalition split up into dozens of subtribes. My father was so relieved."

"Did someone from Kucha assassinate the khan?" Jao asked curiously.

Toto looked horrified. "Never! But I wouldn't put it past Taitsung to undertake such a . . . convenient circumstance."

Jao nodded. "Well, that fits what I know about his urge to break up any kind of tribal alliance. It's a sort of mania with him since his unhappy Korean experience. All the oasis towns have had, as you admit, some kind of tie with the Turks. He's interfered whenever he thought Chinese interests were threatened."

"What kind of interests are you implying?" Toto's tone was cool.

Jao glanced at her in surprise. "I'm not implying anything. It's only the silk trade I'm thinking of."

"China has conquered twenty-five oasis kingdoms in the last few years. Kucha is still free, but I am terribly afraid we are next. And China has now managed to detach another tribe—the Uighurs—into an alliance with Tang. Now the enemies we fear are no longer nomads, but Chinese. . . ."

Jao looked soberly at her friend's wooden face. "Toto, you can't go on this way, not knowing and dreading the future. If it does happen that Taitsung takes over Kucha, nothing much will change, I'm sure. Life will go on as usual, and Kucha will enjoy the protection of Great Tang Peace! Listen, the other day I was there when the emperor's agent from Kucha arrived and reported that your country is in league with the Turks—to obtain a greater share of the trade with India and Persia. . . . I really shouldn't tell you this, but you are my dearest friend and I can't have you suffering like this."

Toto remained rigid, her face turned away. Finally she said in a muffled voice, "When the agent reported this, what did the emperor say?"

"That as long as Kucha is a faithful ally, nothing will happen to her."

"And if Kucha continues to ally herself with the nomads?"

Jao dropped her eyes and said nothing.

Toto seized her friend and shook her. "You must tell me. It means everything to me!"

"He said . . . that if Kucha interferes with Chinese trade, she will be crushed . . . that his general Ashena is in the area and can at any time chastise Kucha. Oh Toto, you mustn't mind so much! None of this has happened yet—we're only guessing!"

Toto shuddered and dropped her face in her hand. Jao embraced her tightly, upset by her friend's anguish and angry with herself for breaking her rule of silence about what was said in the emperor's chambers. "There's nothing to be afraid of—"

"There's everything to be afraid of!" Shivering violently in her despair, Toto allowed Jao to take her back to the tsairen house.

Jao, now late to attend the emperor, was hurrying into the imperial headquarters through the back entrance when she bumped into Chi, immaculate in a new silk gown and with a wide grin on his usually dour face.

"Chi!" she exclaimed, catching her breath. "What are you doing here?"

"Waiting on the emperor," he declared exuberantly.

"Promoted? How wonderful! Tell me—" Jao stopped in mid-sentence when Chi gestured for silence.

"The emperor is still napping," he whispered.

"Good. Then he won't know I'm late. I've been with Toto," she added.

Chi nodded sadly. He knew why.

One morning when Jao was entering Taitsung's quarters, she was met by a pale Chi. "Have you heard the news?" he asked.

Jao stared. "No, I haven't heard anything . . . what's happened?"

"General Ashena has attacked Kucha and destroyed its army."

Jao tried to collect her thoughts. "Toto probably doesn't know yet. But if someone unfriendly to her lets her know, she could be reported to the emperor as an enemy," Jao said. "I can't go myself. . . ."

"Don't worry. I'll send a message to Eunuch Chao to tell her, and see that she does not betray herself," Chi replied. "He can give her a sedative to help."

When Jao returned to the tsairen house late that night, she found that Toto was asleep under sedation, and went thankfully to bed herself. The next day, the news was that part of the Kuchean army escaped, taking refuge in a small satellite oasis. In the fighting, a Tang general had been killed.

Days went by without any news from the front. Then, one morning at dawn, Jao was called into the tsairen courtyard to speak to Chi. "Bad news." His face was bleak. "The satellite town harboring the Kuchean army has been destroyed by General Ashena. To punish the Kucheans for the killing of a Tang general, five cities have been entirely destroyed, eleven thousand heads of fighting men have been taken, and tens of thousands of Kucheans have been slaughtered."

Jao put her hand to her mouth and shrank back. "How can I tell Toto?" she wailed.

"You can't. Just don't. Eunuch Chao will keep her away from court duties until the news of these details has died down. I've never known Chinese troops to behave in this extreme way against women and children of a friendly kingdom. Ashena is a Turk—he must be mad!"

"You have been a soldier yourself. You ought to know! How can Tang fame for just rule flourish when such things happen!" she protested bitterly.

"You'll have to conceal your feelings! But when you can, do anything to help Toto." Chi's expression was grim as he turned on his heel and left.

It was a year or more before the campaign ended. News trickled in, most of which Jao or Chi heard in the emperor's chambers. The emperor seemed deaf to the sordid details, and only heard what he wanted to hear concerning the victorious engagements and the rise of Tang supremacy in all of central Asia. Cities were razed, miles of underground conduits were destroyed, groves were cut down, and tons of treasure carted off.

"I'll call Ashena in now and we'll stage a great victory parade!" Taitsung exulted when the final report arrived, saying that the goal had been accomplished.

The same caravan that brought the official reports also brought private news to the Kuchean population in Changan. Toto soon learned that all but one of her family—a monk in the high mountains—had been killed. Of her former spacious home, not one stone was left upon the other. When Jao returned to the tsairen house that night, she found Toto sitting rigidly against a wall.

"Toto!" Jao said. "Come to bed."

Toto did not stir. She did not even turn her head to look at Jao. Finally she keened, "One man, one inhuman beast of a man, has done this, and no one has stopped him! When I look at the sky, it is dark because this man now fills it . . . this monster Ashena blackens the earth with his savageries. And now there is a parade to honor him. How can I bear it? How can I bear it?"

Jao was horrified. She tried to hug Toto close to her but was shaken off. Toto began to pound the wall with her fists, gasping over and over, "The worst evil, the worst, the worst . . ."

Eunuch Chao arrived and once more administered sedation and quiet sympathy. But afterward, Toto changed. She became silent and seemed half alive. Jao had little hope for her friend.

The triumphal parade formed outside the east gate on the appointed day. It was led by the victorious general Ashena, wearing the gorgeous costume of his Turkish forebears. He rode alone on a white charger, followed by his horsemen and foot soldiers in full panoply. The route of march, from inside the gate, was lined by palace guards drawn up in formal array. They were to control the many Changan citizens who had squeezed into the streets and the palace city, which had been opened up for the occasion.

In the procession were two military bands playing flutes, clarinets, oboes, drums, and bells, and, when called upon at the proper times, a specially trained chorus sang four triumphal odes. The army units marched past, dragging the train of living trophies, the prisoners, after them. The cavalcade proceeded inside the palace to the gates of the Li family shrine. There the musicians dismounted and waited in respect while the emperor went inside to announce his victory to the shades of his deceased ancestors.

The procession moved on to the tower, where the Son of Heaven, hurriedly transported from his family shrine, listened to the triumphal odes and received the captives, who were then informed of their fates. The king of Kucha received clemency and was awarded a position in the palace guards, whereupon his chains were struck off.

A few days after the parade, Taitsung gave a banquet for the general and invited his top staff to honor the occasion. When they had eaten and were relaxed and flushed with wine, Toto was called in to do the famous Kucha sword dance. She arrived, dressed in her Tokharian native costume—a pale blue jacket with red lapels and white skirt. Ashena looked startled when he saw her attire and darted a look at Taitsung, which the emperor failed to notice. He took Toto by the hand and introduced her to his guest of honor.

"Here is my tsairen, Toto, who has been with me for ten years. She is the most skillful dancer of the desert sword dance that we have in the palace. She will now perform in your honor."

Toto, excessively pale, bowed deeply in formal obeisance and took her two silk-wrapped swords from an attendant.

"Here!" Taitsung quipped. "Those swords look real. . . . Aren't you afraid to wave them around in such a whirlwind dance?"

"Not at all," she replied gently. "I am not afraid! I take this occasion to speak of my profound devotion to the Son of Heaven, my master for all these happy years, and I also take this occasion to appease the spirits of my warrior ancestors!"

Before he could answer, she signaled to her musicians and slipped into her dance, moving in slow patterns at first and then with increasing speed and frenzy, until all eyes were focused on her. There was absolute silence. Everyone sensed that something unusual was taking place.

Ashena watched her intently, and he was not smiling as he watched. The dance grew swifter and more violent as it portrayed the sweep and implacability of battle. Suddenly a sword seemed to leap into the general's breast, and the guests saw his blood gushing out over his brocade coat. Taitsung sprang up with a cry.

Toto abruptly ceased her dance, and then, bowing deeply before her emperor and holding the tip of her second sword to her breast, fell upon it.

Taitsung rushed to the side of his sprawled general to stem the flow of blood, but there was nothing he could do. Jao, without an instant's hesitation, ran to Toto. She lay so still on the floor, her life gradually ebbing away. In anguish, Jao started to pull out the sword, but Toto, still alive, looked up into Jao's face and smiled. "Better this way . . . dear . . . dear friend," she gasped, and choked as she died. Jao rocked back on her heels, torn with wracking sobs. She was not aware of the hands that pulled her away, nor the removal of the pitiful remains of the little tsairen. Thunderstruck, Taitsung stood in the middle of the hall while the confusion around him died down and the bodies of his general and his concubine were discreetly removed. His face, at first red with rage, became introspective as he watched Jao being escorted away.

I've lost two irreplaceable people now, he thought. It should not have happened . . . it should never have happened. . . . I feel to blame somehow, but how could I be?

In June, before the summer rains began, the court moved to the Chungnan Hills south of Changan. It was cooler there, and the emperor wanted to move to summer quarters early in the season. The compound was small and the accommodations spare and vacation-style, but all the top officials were obliged to leave their comfortable homes in the city and put up with discomfort as gracefully as possible.

In addition to the court, there was a contingent of eminent physicians in residence for the summer. The Confucian college was represented by five masters under the supervision of the chief physician. Each master had an area of specialty: medical herbs, general medicines, acupuncture, healing massage, and the psychology of the supernatural and magic.

The two chiefs of pharmacy stood between the emperor and the physicians. They bore the heavy responsibility of diagnosis, prescription, and compounding. Every medicine administered to the emperor had to contain three elements: one "superior" drug to lengthen life, three "middle" drugs to strengthen the patient, and nine "inferior" drugs to cure the disease. All compounding took place in the sickroom before the highest councillors of state and the commander of the palace guards. When ready, the medicine had to be tasted by the chief pharmacist, the chief chamberlain, and the crown prince. All this ceremony required the emperor to make a great effort to preserve his dignity before them. Most mornings, after they had all gone, the emperor lay back exhausted, finally drifting into sleep.

Late in June, a Taoist by the name of Sun Miao, brother to Madame Sun, arrived. He had refused to serve the Sui emperors but came at Taitsung's call. Sun was the author of the best-known work on medicine in China, a collection of 300 scrolls of prescriptions; his arrival was greeted with enthusiasm.

He was taken to the emperor's bedside within an hour of his arrival. Entering the sickroom quietly, he stood watching the horde of authorities in the room. He did not interfere, and spent his time in small talk with the emperor and his medical men. He brought with him only one medical assistant, and used no medicines. He confined himself to reducing the sizes of the doses whenever he could and drastically restricting the number of people in the room at any one time. In this way he got rid of the confusion of random comings and goings of officious bureaucrats. The emperor began to rest more easily, and the other doctors began to accept Sun Miao with courtesy and relief when they saw that he shared their responsibility.

Jao spent most of her time in the sickroom, leaving only occasionally to sleep. She was tolerated because of her self-effacing way. And, of course, no one else wanted her menial duties. She was watchful when the medicines were being mixed, observing every move with anxiety. After Sun arrived, she was less worried. The two soon became very much aware of one another, each recognizing the other as indispensable in the sickroom.

The treatments brought some relief. Dysentery was checked by the use of a local drug, and insomnia was treated by a theriacal pill composed of opium, hemp, and myrrh. Although Sun did nothing to change the treatments, he did not leave the premises. He ordered his bedding brought into the next room so that he could appear in the sickroom at any hour, day or night. After a while he was hardly noticed.

Crown Prince Jer at first spent his days with his father, but when the monsoon rains began, he started to attend at night instead. The days were long and, filled with the rushing sounds of rain, faded imperceptibly into night. Jer soon lost track of time. For the first time in four years, Jao was thrown into close contact with him. She felt his eyes upon her frequently, and whenever she risked a look at him, she encountered his stare, one that she now recognized.

He has always had women thrust upon him and never in his life has he gone on a girl-hunt of his own. And it shows, she thought. He likes me, he always has. Of course, now he's confused. I am a woman he cannot have. As for me . . . he is a man that I cannot have either. Oh, but I feel drawn to him, I feel it strongly. How very strange. . . . But perhaps it is not strange after all—he is young and very handsome and knows his own mind.

Jao was assigned to night duty by the chamberlain because she was so effective in soothing the emperor after one of his nightmares. Under the influence of powerful drugs, his sleep was interrupted nearly every night by dreams that made him start up from his bed shouting and reach for his sword, which he kept by him. His "magic" sword, he insisted, must be laid beside him on the bed.

The hours of the rat were the worst. After that, in the early morning hours, he became wakeful. Sun, observing the nightmares a few times, disposed of about half of the night potions. Then the bad dreams were less violent.

The first time Taitsung noticed that his son was with him at the midnight hour, he became animated and wanted to talk. "I may be laid by my heels in this bed, but I still have one more battle to fight." he said to Jer, who was sitting on a stool close to him.

"Battle?" Jer repeated, thinking that his father was hallucinating. Taitsung chuckled.

"The battle that I have in mind is a word-battle on your behalf, to destroy everything that you have been told about ruling! No one but I really knows how to do it! I had expected to have twenty years to teach you, but Heaven has willed otherwise."

Jer did not understand. "Don't upset yourself . . . I am being taught."

Taitsung slammed his fist into the bed. "A lot of empty, pretentious rhetoric most likely! What you are taught by your tutors is not the truth about ruling, but what they want the truth to be—starting with how they want the emperor to behave, a political interference that none of them would tolerate for long in their own lives!"

Jer grinned, although he still did not know what his father meant. Jao did, and looked alert. Taitsung continued.

"The Confucians teach you that regicide is the worst sin there is and that the orderly succession from father to son is the only way to keep the peace. They teach that the usual way—usurpation—is taboo. And they are right, but only partially. What I want to get across to you is the truth—that the ruler has to keep those Confucians and their ideas at a certain distance, that one has to keep a balance between them and their theories and the practical day-to-day handling of men as they are. Am I confusing you?"

Jer shook his head and made an effort to dredge up an answer that might please his father. "You are saying that my tutors are not teaching me the real secrets of how to rule, but their own theories. What am I supposed to think? Not to follow theory? But practice—"

"Both are necessary . . . I will explain. Ever since the downfall of the Han dynasty four centuries ago, every new dynasty that came into being was short-lived because another one was usually established by someone from within the government, by usurpation. Even today. Our Tang dynasty was founded by your grandfather by usurpation, taken over by myself, away from my brothers, the same way. This practice must stop with you or Tang will fall apart the way all the other dynasties have done. The tribes outside of China have an even greater difficulty with this succession trouble. Assassination of the ruler has been the greatest weakness of the nomads as well as of the settled kingdoms—worse because their culture condones it and ours doesn't. So they have no continuity, whereas we Chinese have at least some."

Taitsung, tiring, drifted into sleep but continued to have lucid intervals in the nights that followed. Sun Miao watched from the shadows and quietly laid on work for the doctors in massage and acupuncture, while continuing to reduce some of the heavier doses of drugs. He now knew that there would be no recovery, and mainly was concerned to ease pain and prevent pneumonia. These thoughts he kept to himself.

When Taitsung next had a lucid spell, he groped for his son's hand and continued where he had left off. He had the subject of usurpation on his mind. "All the dynasties just before us were founded by usurpers. Now Tang will have to give up this method and revert to the model of the Han."

Jer shifted on his stool. "That far back?" he muttered. "Four hundred years back . . . the dead past. It doesn't make sense. . . ."

Taitsung heard him. "Not so dead that it can't come to life. Han had the recipe for success in handling a great empire, which is a much more complicated job than running a small family kingdom. What I am saying is that you, like the Han, must rule alone, by balancing the various groups in government. If you let your relatives, or the army, or the great clans, or even your servants in the bureaucracy run things for you, someone from among them will surely try to usurp. Let no one get too much power, that's the trick! Balance your rule with officials from all groups, and get an educated corps of officers paid by you to attend to the machinery of government. The key to the Son of Heaven way of rule is balancing all the little tyrants . . . that'll stop usurpation!"

Taitsung's voice trailed off, and Jer, very thoughtful, stole a look at Jao. She was looking sober too, but smiled at him comfortingly. That girl knows what it's all about but no one seems to realize that . . . except me, he thought. I've got to hang on to her somehow. He rose and stretched and then returned to his stool to wait.

The next evening, when the emperor became lucid once more, he started in again as soon as he saw Jer back on his stool.

"You there, son? Good! Now then, I'm not finished. I want you to know how tiresome your salaried officials can be, your own henchmen whom you appoint, nobodies without your help, but . . . it is either put up with them or let the throne slip from your grasp. You can't keep the throne without the ministers, but you don't need to let them order you about either! It has always been a great problem for me, a warrior, to balance my officials, those who wield the sword against those who wield the pen."

Jer grunted. "I see—a ruler needs both."

"Yes. Without the warriors, you are feeble, without the scholar-officials, the great flood of taxes will not flow through the Purple Gate. When usurpers try to rule through their generals and families, it doesn't work—the money flows out, not in! I was a usurper myself, and I at first ruled through my generals and ministers from the great families, but I changed things. Now I govern by the Son of Heaven way."

"Are you comparing the tribal methods with the Son of Heaven method?" Jer asked, his attention caught.

"Exactly! Take the nomad Toba Wei as an example of tribal rule that had continuity. The Wei rulers did not divide up the rich farmlands that they conquered from the Chinese and distribute them among the tribesmen according to nomad custom. Instead, the Wei nomad conquerors borrowed the Chinese Son of Heaven way of rule."

"Which is . . . ?" Jer asked anxiously.

"Don't you know?" Taitsung wheezed, startled.

"Yes, but what you think it is . . . please say." Jer's expression was earnest.

Taitsung lay back, pleased. "You are with me, my son. . . . Now I know that you can pick out what is important from what is less so. Instead of their own ignorant warriors, the Wei used educated Chinese of integrity and loyalty to administer, relegating the tribesmen solely to military positions. That's the most important thing they did. The other important thing they did . . ." He paused, breathing heavily.

The room was silent but for the relentless hiss of the rain. Buoyed by what he felt he was accomplishing, Taitsung continued. "Maybe equal in importance was the ordering of intermarriage of nomads with Chinese and the adoption of Chinese dress. Even the aristocrats had to obey, and how the tribesmen hated this! But in the end it saved their empire for another hundred years."

Jer frowned. "The Wei were barbarians. Nothing to do with our Li family and the Tang dynasty."

Taitsung's chest heaved and he gave a snort of laughter as he sat up. "Your tutors tell you that? It's everything to do with us! We Lis have descended in a short, direct line from those early mixed marriages. We were ennobled by rulers who were themselves the results of mixed marriages. I'll give you three names of such families: Yuwen, who were mostly Tartar; Yang, who were half Chinese; and now us, Li, who are three-quarters Chinese. All of them seized supreme power by usurpation. First the Yuwen helped split up the old Wei empire, and then proceeded to conquer all of north China. Then the Yang usurped and conquered all of China with their Sui dynasty. Then our family usurped from Yang, and we are now lords of the greatest empire China has ever seen."

Taitsung fell back on his pillows, his eyes bulging exultantly while he fought for breath. He was tiring fast, but he still had something to do. He sat up again and marshaled his strength. "Wei . . . down . . . to us—we all used the same Son of Heaven way . . . based on keeping powers balanced between military and civilian officials. And using them to keep a steady tax flow. Now, the nomads succeeded because they adopted the Chinese way. They succeeded better than the Chinese aristocrats who fled south, abandoning their own system. You see? The system is what counts, not the people who use it, or even the customs of individual usurpers."

Taitsung stopped because his point was made. He settled back and into a doze, intending to take up the subject again when he felt better, an opportunity that never came.

"The emperor has been rambling," Jer commented sociably when Sun came in to feel the sick man's pulses.

"He has not been rambling," Sun said sternly. "He had this one more task to do, and he did it. I have kept him alive to do it."

Jer looked stricken. "Yes," he said humbly.

Jao pulled a cover over the sleeping emperor. I must write all this down for Jer, she thought. It is the emperor's last testament.

At the end of the first week in July, the emperor was sinking so fast that he knew his hours were numbered. He called in his chief ministers, Changsun, Chu, and Han, to meet with his son and Lady Wang. He asked his children to kneel, and, gasping for breath, had the three ministers swear to administer his will on behalf of his heir. They swore with fervor and in trembling earnestness to obey the emperor's instructions. Then, exhausted by their bumbling attempts to soothe him, he dismissed them all, except Jer.

"I want to talk to you about Changsun and Chu . . . they are running the government under my directions now but soon . . . under yours. Lately Changsun has simultaneously held the top posts in all three departments—and Chu had them for a year before that. I have not promoted any new men . . . since getting sick." Taitsung paused, and Jao wiped his forehead. "Whenever you promote someone, he will always think he is more powerful than he should be . . . Be careful about any promotions above Grade Three. Mostly I have had loyal men around me who speak their opinions freely but aren't united in factions against me . . . but I am never completely sure about them. I am not sure about my generals, either . . . Most of my best generals have died since my last campaign. Archduke Li Chi is now the most powerful. He is close to me and certainly devoted to me personally." He paused to rest for a moment. "I don't know whether he would render you the same devotion. He could usurp . . . and that is why I speak like this. Your uncle, Changsun, is also powerful, and I don't know whether he plans to eliminate Li Chi and govern the empire through you. I just don't know. You need them both. How would you go about keeping them both?"

"The way I would my women," replied Jer without hesitation. "Separate them."

Taitsung rested and breathed deeply. "Agreed. If two people are about to tangle, separate them. So, I will send one of them to a border area far away to test him. If he delays I will know that he is thinking of taking over, and I will have to order his execution. Yes . . . the cost of keeping your throne means the execution, sometimes, of the ones you like the best. If he goes at once, I will know that he is loyal to the throne. Then you can call him back and reestablish his rank and honors, and his loyalty will be transferred to you. Now, which man am I talking about?"

"Li Chi," Jer returned promptly. "You could hardly send away a relative."

Taitsung smiled grimly. "Li Chi it is. I hope that you will never have to exile someone you love the way I did your brother Chengchien."

A day later Chu came in to report the day's important business, especially the astonishing news about the departure of Li Chi for Hainan Island. Taitsung fell back on his pillows with a sigh. He looks pleased! thought the honest old minister in amazement. I thought Li Chi was one of his most trusted friends . . . strange!

Although busy during the daytime in subdued activities, the palace was quiet at night. In the early evening the courtiers played their endless card games and cautiously expressed their worries about the coming death and about their own futures. Even the servants moved around silently. Outdoors the rain continued its monotonous drip. Sun and Jao kept watch.

Toward evening on the ninth of the month a heavy storm rolled over the area. Black clouds darkened the afternoon. Lanterns were lit. Hangings billowed and shutters banged. Attendants busied themselves with the leaks which sprang up everywhere when tiles blew off. Wielding mops and setting out bowls to catch the drips, the servants refrained from their usual jokes, working in subdued silence. Slanting rain blew under the eaves, and although all the shutters were tightly closed, the air inside became so humid that clothes and bedding became damp and mildew quickly spread.

Jao woke to the hissing of the rain on the thatch of her bungalow and rose at once to help Mi secure the flapping bamboo curtains. Then, dressing quickly and responding to a feeling of uneasiness, she skipped her meal to come early to the sickroom. She found the three chief physicians standing at the foot of the bed, worry creasing their brows. They nodded to her as she wiped the perspiration from the emperor's forehead. She then changed the pillows, which had been specially prepared with cardamon seed to relieve the congestion in his lungs.

Shadows flickered on walls and rafters grew tall and merged. Suddenly the hall echoed with screams from the sick man as he wildly waved his sword and tried to get out of bed. The doctors hurried to soothe him but could not get his sword from him until several eunuchs, shivering in their night clothes, rushed in to help. A goblet of a safe potion was poured and offered to him, but he dashed it away, spilling the contents over the bed. His face, bristling with a new growth of beard, was gray, his eyes bulging from the shock of nightmare. Too weak to cope with the shock, he collapsed, unconscious.

Jer hurried in, alarmed by his father's cries, but the emperor was not aware of his presence. At midnight the storm slackened and the shutters ceased to rattle. The attendants, worn out, took to their pallets when they were told to do so by the crown prince, who remained to stand vigil. He watched while Jao bathed and wiped the emperor's head, her sleeves caught in a figure-eight strap to keep them out of the way, her hair coiled in a knot on top of her head. Her composed face was intent upon her task, as if she were willing her young strength into the dying man.

Taitsung was inhaling laboriously, his great chest heaving with every breath. When the hour of the tiger was sounded, Jao took a moment to stretch her arms and straighten her back.

How devoted she is, Jer thought enviously. None of his women would do for him what she was doing for his father. Wang was too spoiled and wouldn't think of it anyway, and Hsiao wouldn't know how. She would only flutter and make him nervous. The others would cover their lack of concern with polite words.

Jao caught his somber glance and smiled sadly. He continued to watch her. Suddenly, he saw her stiffen and bend over the emperor. Then she darted to the physician, who was dozing in his chair, and roused him. He came at once, but the labored breathing had stopped. Jer and Jao stood frozen in silence while Sun straightened and spoke softly to the prince.

"Your father has left . . . his spirit has gone to the Yellow Springs. If you wish, you may now call the ministers."

Jer nodded as tears rolled down his cheeks, tears he did not bother to wipe away. Jao put her face into her hands and moaned while great sobs convulsed her body. Han, Changsun, and Chu hurried in, their headdresses askew and their eyes blind with sleep. Then the room rapidly filled with other high officials and palace servants. Frightened attendants brought lanterns. The physicians withdrew inconspicuously and their assistants began the duties of the last rites.

The room was packed with people, all shocked and loudly lamenting. The sounds of their grief carried throughout the palace and were soon joined by wails from the women's quarters. Changsun and Chu recovered their equilibrium first, taking command with orders concerning procedures to be followed at once.

They retired, and then, dressed in formal robes, returned to the hall for the important ritual of conferring the new title. Jer was still there, leaning against the wall, overcome by the shock of death and by fatigue. Taking him by his arms, they led him to the bedside and had him kneel while they swore him in as the legitimate successor to the throne. They were formal and somber, already feeling the heavy responsibility that had fallen upon them. Soon they would issue a proclamation announcing the news of the death of the emperor along with the name of his successor.

All faces were turned toward the informal inauguration scene except Jao's. She was the only one looking at the emperor's still face. "I have just lost the greatest man I have ever known or ever expect to know," she murmured in farewell while being jostled out of the way. She picked up her damp towels and moved to the door.

There was now nothing left for Wu Jao, Tsairen Fifth Grade, to do, nothing more. She realized that her life was, in effect, finished—along with the lives of all the other ladies of the harem.

By the time that daylight penetrated the hall, the body had been washed and clothed in ceremonial dress and was lying in state. Large white candles were placed at the emperor's head and feet, casting spasmodic shadows on the silk-draped walls. Incense burners of gilt bronze and jade were filled with costly sandalwood from Champa and aloes from Cambodia, and clouds of their heavy scent filled the air.

Abbots from the great monasteries arrived to perform ceremonies for the welfare of the dead. Hsuantsang of the Fahsiang faith came, although the weather had not cleared and his cassock was drenched. Shantao of the Pure Land Sect brought his chanters to guide the spirit on its flight to the Western Paradise of Amida. Taoist dignitaries whom Taitsung had honored came with their banners and cymbals. The intoning of prayers began and continued all day and the next night.

Courtiers in mourning garb filed past the bier one by one before departing for their homes in the capital. They had all been living in discomfort in the outlying buildings of the palace, as required by law in times of emergency. Quarters had been cramped, mosquitoes had abounded, and the heat and rain—and waiting—had been nearly unbearable. Relief was apparent on many faces under the conventional expressions of grief.

The rain increased in violence that day, as if in keeping with the mourning. Broken branches were strewed across the ground, and puddles and mud made the roads impassable. By late afternoon, however, the storm was over and the clouds began to break up. Bits of blue sky peeked out for the first time in two weeks, and a light breeze began to dry out the landscape.

"Good omen!" the fortune-tellers said. "Good omen for the new era" was the cry that spread among the people.

Jer, now Emperor Kaotsung, had slept in the morning, his first sleep in three days. By afternoon he had wakened, refreshed and ready to keep vigil by his father's casket. When he entered the hall dressed in his mourning white, attendant courtiers looked at him curiously, the priests with compassion and the eunuchs with worried speculation.

The cool breeze blew through the hall where Taitsung lay. It made the candles flicker, but the sweltering mourners were grateful. Guards of honor stood at the four corners of the casket. The low sounds of chanting were joined by the soft, rustling sounds of mourners coming and going.

Before midnight the room was free of people. Only the sound of the chanting coming from the antechamber reached Jer. At last he was free to give way to his emotions. Although drooping with fatigue, he was an imposing figure, already looking like the emperor he now was. He knelt with his head on the silk cover of the casket, feeling more alone and desolate than he had ever felt before, feeling that he had no friend on whom to rely, no one at all.

He was beginning to get numb from kneeling too long when a small hand pulled his sleeve and he looked up. Jao was handing him a steaming cup of soup. He shook his head in revulsion. He could not swallow, how could anyone expect him to swallow? She did not go away, so he stood up and bowed his thanks while refusing. Jao just stood there smiling sadly, the soup on a tray. Finally he took a token sip, and the sip was so welcome that he took another until the bowl was empty. She took it on her tray and disappeared.

She looked pale and washed out, almost like a spirit herself in her white mourning clothes, Jer thought sadly, his feeling of loneliness suddenly assuaged. But a beautiful spirit, he realized, despite his sorrow. Jao's small gesture, which no one else had thought to do, had reached him at a crucial moment.

At daybreak Jer left the hall to prepare for the leave-taking. The day was cloudless, much to the relief of the officials in charge of the funeral procession that would escort the emperor's body back to the palace. The procession was already forming in the cool of the morning. After about an hour's rest, Jer took his place behind the casket. Four thousand soldiers lined the main road which had dried considerably during the night. Behind the soldiers, thousands of people gathered to watch their beloved emperor go by in his open casket.

The sun was not yet at its zenith when the procession reached the five-tunnel south gate of the city. The central gate through which none but the emperor could enter was thrown wide, and the bearers, with heads bowed, passed silently through. As the casket cleared the tunnel, both gates were closed and white banners of mourning hung over them. The great emperor Taitsung had passed through for the last time.

The bedraggled tsairen passed silently through an eastern gate of the palace, and a half hour later drifted through the gate to their own compound. They scattered to their private rooms, and once inside a familiar place, their restraint was gone. A cacophony of cries began, along with the thumps of clothing being discarded and contradictory orders screamed at the maids.

Jao stepped into her room and wrinkled her nose at the smell of mildew on the walls and of a musty odor from stagnant rainwater in a low corner. Mi greeted her with her usual smile and then went on laying out the mourning clothes. Jao stripped off her damp garments and dropped them on the floor, looking around vaguely. The room seemed strange and inhospitable now that she was about to leave it, alien and unfamiliar in spite of the many years that she had lived in it. She wandered aimlessly through the house, feeling more and more empty, as if she were being stripped of her identity. Slowly the emptiness within her began to fill with anger against her fate. She returned to her own room and beat her head against the wall and screamed in slow, heavy gasps. Each concubine had known for some time that the fate of retiring to a convent awaited her when the emperor died, and a few had already accepted it stoically. Most had not. Although Jao was suffering the lethargy of grief, it had not drained her completely, and her resentment and anger began to take over. Mi dropped her sorting and folding and, without a word, embraced Jao so tightly that Jao's arms were imprisoned and her flailings gradually ceased. Mi held her until her panting cries calmed and then led an exhausted Jao to her bed.

In the rest of the building there was still as much confusion as before. It echoed with the sounds of clatter and shouts as the tsairen wandered aimlessly from room to room seeking companionship and comfort. Cries of vexation arose when the women began to scatter their possessions about in their efforts to decide what to do with them. This state of confusion got worse as the day wore on, but gradually some order began to emerge as the maids, who weren't deeply touched by the turn of events, gradually finished the sorting and packing, and the bundles began to pile up in the hall. Most maids went about barely able to conceal their glee because their mistresses, utterly distracted, were giving away their most valuable possessions.

Before they blew out the candles at bedtime, Jao made her selection of what would go into the bundle that she would take with her. Mi spread a square of silk on the bed. Jao went around the room putting things on the silk. She began with her small Maitreya. It had never been out of her possession since her mother had given it to her on her departure from home. Then she added her ink slab, her fox-hair brushes, several blank silk scrolls, a pile of warm cashmere mantles that Wencheng had sent her from Tibet, and several paintings that had been given to her by the court artists, Yen Lipen and Yen Lite, which she rolled into tight scrolls. Finally she added her purses of silver and gold and tied the corners over it all with a jerk.

"That's it," she said tonelessly. Taking Mi's small hands between her own, she said, "The rest is yours, including a bag of gold pieces to use in educating your boy in the Korean Quarter. Take it and do the best you can with it. I'll never be able to repay you for what you have done for me—never—but one thing is certain: we are friends forever, no matter what happens to us."

Mi was silent. She just nodded her head. Jao studied her with a ravaged expression on her face, finally voicing some of her pent-up emotions. "You are so calm, have you no sorrow at parting? Have you no feelings at all?"

In her surprise Mi dropped the purse that she was holding, and for the first time in the twelve years that she had been with Jao, tears spilled down her face. "Not my way . . ." she said finally as she blew her nose with a near-violent gesture. "All day yesterday and all day today I felt torn up, torn up, torn up . . . but it would be so weak, wouldn't it, to show it?" She took a deep breath.

Jao stared. "I'm sorry," she stammered.

"Yes," Mi said simply. But her heavy breathing revealed what she was concealing, and Jao, in her turn, sprang up to take Mi in her embrace until she felt her friend relaxing, comforted.

Afterward, both of them felt better, and, realizing that they were hungry, they wound white cloths of mourning around their heads and went to the kitchen for their first meal in twenty-four hours. The day closed with more rain and an early bedtime. Exhaustion brought sleep, even to Jao.

The same kind of turmoil that was troubling the tsairen house was going on throughout the palace. The emperor's body had been installed in the antechamber of the family ancestral shrine, and a solemn vigil established there, to last for a proscribed time while the embalming and wrapping could take place and the official funeral scheduled for an auspicious day. The mausoleum site had already been designated by Taitsung himself—on a hillside, so that an expensive tumulus would not have to be built.

The new emperor, Kaotsung, had gone to his old quarters in the eastern palace outside the imperial city in order to eat a meal and change garments before the night's vigil. His servants were already clearing his rooms as well as the deceased emperor's apartments, in spite of the disapproving stares of the old eunuchs. Cleaning was to go on all night. Lady Wang, with the prospect of being made full empress, had given orders for the move from the old palace to the new to be done at once, rain or no rain, timely or not, unseemly or not.

Kaotsung did not notice that his old rooms were looking bare, he knew nothing of his Lady Wang's plans, and returned to his duty at the ancestral shrine unaware of the changes that were going on in his household.

The next morning dawned gray and cloudy but without rain. The palace cooks had been ordered to provide simple food for the inmates of the palace and to keep hot dishes ready for the chief mourners, so there was a bustle in the kitchens at an early hour. Later on in the day the usually busy offices were emptied and the normal flow of people in the courtyards stopped. The guards stood at ease, the doves circled in lazy flocks overhead, and an unnatural silence prevailed over all in the imperial city.

Long lines of porters, however, carried goods from Kaotsung's detached palace into the emperor's halls, where they were put down in the recently emptied and cleaned rooms. Kaotsung's sleeping room was the first to be settled, so that he, who would certainly stumble away from his night's watch half dead from lack of sleep, could fall into bed at once. Lady Wang was everywhere, excitedly supervising everything, ignoring the distress of the old chamberlains. She was noticeably more haughty now that she was to be elevated in status. Her family was also immediately in evidence in the imperial quarters. Lady Wang's mother, Lady Liu, was especially imperious.

When Kaotsung came to bed at dawn, he went where he was led, unaware of where he was. Waking in the late afternoon, the first person he saw was his mother-in-law sitting by the door, and he realized immediately what had happened. He frowned and looked around him, stretched, thanked the Lady Liu and asked her to summon his valet. She hesitated, then went out, suggesting as she left that a new appointee for the position of the valet was now in order.

"I don't care about that," Kaotsung said irritably. "I want my old Cho and I want him now. If you please." In the days to come he was to confide occasionally to his head eunuch. "Can't seem to go from bed to table in this palace now," he grumbled, "without stumbling over my mother-in-law."

In the tsairen hall, supplies ceased to come on the third day after the return from the Chungnan Hills. Eunuchs were in and out, collecting hampers of clothes and overseeing the gangs of women laborers who were cleaning and repairing. Chi, now on imperial duty, returned to the tsairen house for a final responsibility. He called the five tsairen together to inform them that they were to leave for the convent immediately. They could take with them what they could carry, but no servants could go with them. Later on, the wealthy families could make special arrangements with the abbess about servants for the members living in the convent, but that would not involve the palace. The imperial slaves had to stay in the palace. That included Mi.

When he said that, Jao's eyes flew to Mi and they exchanged glances that said their loyalty to each other was not at an end and never would be. When Chi finished his speech, his tsairen were in tears. All were aware of what was to befall them, but knowing did not prevent them from feeling shock when the time came for their expulsion. They were to go to the convent, Kanyeh-ssu, which was dedicated to the doctrines of Huayen, a new sect founded early in the century. The new perceptions of Huayen expanded the role of the monk or nun to include secular service to the community as well as religious teaching, making it possible for the convent to take the palace women.

Chi was smiling as he counted his charges. "The sun shines! A good omen for your good future!" he said, trying to cheer them up. He bowed in the Chinese way of offering condolence, and laughed his polite, shallow laugh, which concealed all expression of feeling, and then led his five tsairen to the gate. Jao and Mi were at the head of the line. When Chi paused inside the gate, Jao took both his hands in hers in the usual formal salute. Suddenly, she broke down and threw her arms around his neck in her anguish. He started back but did not protest—he himself was distressed. He wiped the tears off her cheeks with his sash and gently propelled her out the exit door.

Mi went out with Jao, intending to hand her into her carrying chair. Choosing the last chair in line, they stood together until it was Jao's turn to leave. Jao's voice shook when she finally said good-bye, but that was all. She had come of age in three days.

Chapter Nine

When Jao was deposited in the forecourt of the convent, she was met with a bedlam of sound rising from the seventy women already there. At the gate, a eunuch was calling off the names of the women in his charge as they entered, and the prioress was checking them off her list. He called out the names of the tsairen and then thankfully took himself off.

Jao stood just inside the gate and surveyed the scene. Looking for the abbess, she saw her standing on the terrace before the open doors of the main building, surrounded by a flock of gray-clad nuns. The abbess was directing them into the milling crowd to locate their assigned charges and to show them to their shelters. Jao pushed her way slowly through the throng until she was in front of the abbess.

"Welcome to your new home," the abbess said simply. "I greet you with joy. It has been a long time since our New Year's Eve ride together."

"It has indeed," Jao returned, smiling sadly as she performed the *anjali* salute and sank into a deep bow. "I return your greetings with devotion."

The abbess was now fifty years of age, but had few wrinkles or other signs of aging to show. She presented a well-groomed appearance, her linen robe was immaculate, and her rosary was intricately carved and costly. On her bald head, however, a mist of perspiration had gathered, and for a moment her eyes showed her pain as she looked into Jao's face.

"I join you in grieving for the passing of a great man," she said with composure. "We shall not see the likes of him again in our lifetime." She lapsed into silence. Jao inclined her head and also remained silent. Overhead the doves circled, the whistles attached to their legs making music that swelled and faded. From the women in the yard came voices that were heavy with lament and the sense of estrangement, voices frightened and querulous as well.

The silence between the abbess and Jao lengthened. Neither spoke, but stood regarding the courtyard with its throng of shocked women. The abbess then looked at Jao, noting her pallor and signs of strain.

"I have been hoping for your assistance here with the settling in. You could be invaluable to me if you only would," she said.

Jao remembered, in sudden surprise, that the abbess had as good a reason to mourn as she or any of the other palace women; yet in spite of her private grief, the abbess had summoned the strength to cope with the disastrous situation that had been thrust upon her. "Of course," Jao stammered, "of course. You must instruct me as to when . . . and so on . . . tomorrow?"

"I mean now," the abbess replied, studying her.

Jao's eyes flew to meet the nun's. "What do you want me to do?" she asked.

The abbess was pleased. She gestured at the crowded courtyard. The last of the highest-ranking ladies had just been delivered, and their eunuchs were leaving, abandoning without a backward glance the personages whom they had been obsequiously serving for years. The convent gates were then closed and locked by the prioress.

The abbess nodded when she saw this. "The four Fei have just come in. Neither they nor any of the other ladies realize yet how poor the lodging here will be. Nor are they aware how great a shock it is to us to be inundated like this. Many are not going to conduct themselves well when they find out. Your duty—if you are willing to show compassion—will be to cushion the shocks whenever and wherever you see them in evidence."

The abbess gave Jao a penetrating look and then handed Jao's bundle to an acolyte.

"Jao, you will be billeted in a small room off the pharmacy, and when you are done with your duties today—whenever you feel like it—you will go there."

The abbess turned to the women in the courtyard and smiled encouragingly. She announced that all rules of convent life were suspended for the time being and that the usual routines would not begin until the newcomers were ready for them. "Not all at once either," she added soothingly. A vegetarian meal would be ready at sundown, and the women would be served in shifts.

The abbess turned again to Jao. "Now, I would like you to come with me."

Together they went on to the main hall, where most of the women were now billeted. Mats were placed in rows upon the highly polished floor below the platform, which held three magnificent Buddhist images. Candles and incense in front of them were being lit in readiness for the evening service, which had been delayed because the disturbance in the hall was so great. A ululation of grief echoed through the big room. Some women were tearing their hair and clothes in abandonment, and others were giving way to mass hysteria.

When Jao saw what was going on, she understood why she, along with the experienced nuns, had been summoned.

She was needed. She straightened her shoulders unconsciously and waited for instructions. The abbess signaled to a group of singers to begin a soft chanting in the rear of the hall. The nuns spread out among the women, one nun to every woman, soothing and touching and bringing order into the assembly. The abbess waved to Jao to do likewise, so Jao chose a girl who looked like Toto. As Jao sat down beside her and tried to comfort her, she recalled the warmth and love she had felt for the brave Kucha dancer. The girl relaxed gratefully.

It was not long before all the other women began to respond to their helpers. Most of the palace ladies were ardent Buddhists, and when the nuns put rosaries into their hands, they slipped easily into the quiet worship that was expected of them.

When a semblance of order had been restored, a group of nuns with bowls of hot soup and steamed bread came in and distributed the food. Each nun sat by her own charge until the woman had taken her food, even when it was at first refused. The low chanting continued while the food was being served. Nightfall darkened the room and candles were lit. Rain began again. The floor was hard and the mats thin, and some of the women still wept softly.

When it was time to begin the evening service, the nuns conducted it as usual, going quietly through their chants and prayers. Not long after the service was over, the palace women lay down on their mats and gave themselves up to sleep. The abbess settled herself for the night in the center of the room, and other nuns did the same, each lying beside her charge. Presently the weeping ceased, and then the silence was interrupted by only a few sounds of distress from the women and the occasional scamper of mice in the walls.

The abbess beckoned to Jao. "There are a few tsairen there in front of the altar who don't seem to be responding," she whispered. "Do you feel you can cope with them?" Jao looked at her four housemates who had settled themselves in a row at the far end of the altar. She nodded. "Take this acolyte with you . . . give compassion," the abbess said, her eyes full of warm encouragement.

Jao made her way among the mats to where her friends were crouching. She spoke to Pearl, who was shivering so violently she hardly recognized Jao, and felt her forehead. It was hot. "Please fetch a quilt," Jao said to her helper, who hesitated and then went to find one. When the acolyte returned with the quilt, Jao wrapped Pearl in it. Pearl sighed at the comfort it brought, and Jao directed the acolyte to massage her friend's hands and feet.

She turned to Peony, who was hiccuping and laughing in low spurts and rocking back and forth on her heels. Jao put her arms around the girl and gradually her jerks stopped. It took her a long time to coax Peony to lie down on her mat, and when she did, Peony obeyed only mechanically.

I cannot give compassion, thought Jao in her fatigue. If Kuanyin would bestow some on me, perhaps I could make it flow to others. "Do you feel compassion?" she whispered to the novice.

The girl looked up. "I have not enough merit," she said humbly. "Besides, the misery of these people comes from their misdeeds."

"No!" Jao said angrily. "There are no bad characters here, no—"

"Then they must have behaved badly in previous lives to have such misery now," persisted the nun stubbornly. Jao tucked the quilt around Pearl's shoulders.

"Poor, exquisite sister Pearl with her shining beauty—and with nothing else to sustain her. Because of your words, I find myself feeling compassion," she said indignantly to the young nun. "Pearl is now no use to her rich relatives in Yangchow, who seem to have abandoned her. Even I have neglected her because she is so quiet and good and I am the opposite. Right now I don't think she cares what happens to her."

"Then we should let her die in peace," the novice said.

"No," Jao said indignantly again. "Why should she die? She is a beautiful person, a treasure. She has at least forty years of life ahead of her. She is not ready for death yet!"

At this, the other girls looked up attentively from their mats. Peony seemed especially alert.

"What is it to you?" Peony asked belligerently.

"A lot," Jao answered, whispering in a low voice as she saw the women nearby stirring restlessly. "Pearl is my housemate, as she is yours. I want to help her live."

"Do you feel the same about me?" Peony demanded.

Jao nodded impatiently. "Do I want you to live instead of die? Of course, you fool. There is so much happiness ahead of you . . . do you want to give up just because you have to live in a different way? You are acting like a baby. Pearl has a lot of good life ahead of her, and you do too."

At this Cloud sat up abruptly. She and Phoenix had been lying side by side, staring up at the rafters.

"What you are saying is that we are all in need of a box on the ears to remind us of our good fortune. . . ."

"Good fortune!" Phoenix hissed. She had only just settled quietly on her mat after hours of hysterical weeping. "Good fortune! In this awful place, wearing these rough, scratchy clothes, eating this disgusting food, seeing nobody but bald pates who tell us what to do. This is the worst that could happen to us . . . and you call it good fortune!" She began to cry hysterically again, and Jao shot an embarrassed glance at the abbess, realizing she was not doing so well with her charges.

Then Cloud and Peony attempted to soothe Phoenix, while Jao massaged her feet. Slowly, Phoenix relaxed. Then one by one they all dozed off. Jao, too, was emotionally spent, but remained awake. When the bell tolled the hour of the rat, she rose and slipped out into the shadows of the courtyard, where she stood for a while looking into the night sky. She could see the clouds scudding across the face of the moon and hear the breezes sighing through the trees in the courtyards. Suddenly she felt soothed and more at home in her new surroundings. She thought of Kaotsung in his lonely vigil beside the casket. "I wish I could help him by taking him some soup now," she said softly. "I wish I could comfort him as I have always been able to do in the past." Would he ever think of her? she wondered. Would he ever do anything to help her out of this convent? Walking softly, she made her way through the corridors to the room adjoining the pharmacy, which had been assigned to her. As she stepped over the sill, she was met with a welcome mingle of aromas, and, with a heavy sigh, she lay down on her pallet.

She pondered her own condition, wondering what her escape from deadly boredom could be. Try out everything, find out what best suits me and what I just can't tolerate. Discover the kind of life that lets me sleep at night, she thought dolefully. In this place there was nothing . . . nothing . . . nothing. It was so quiet here. So far from real life. What could she do with herself? To keep her mind going? There was nothing good to eat and nothing to do. How could she bear it? All she wanted to do at that moment was to lie on her pallet and give up.

The next two days passed slowly. The new women went on as they had, with no moves, no orders to follow, no changes. Most of them gradually explored their surroundings, to discover where the latrines were, where the well and kitchen gardens were located, where the washing was done, and wondered about the possibilities for a bearable life in the convent. Already used to life in a small space, that aspect of convent life was familiar to them. Personal servants from the various families were also filtering in, and this was a great relief to the nuns as well as to the palace women.

On the third morning, the rising bell sounded at the hour of the rabbit. The women assembled in the main hall, where the sleeping mats had been rolled up and stacked for the day behind the altar. There they sleepily arranged themselves in rows for morning devotions. Afterward they took the air in the courtyards, and were assisted by an adept in the performance of some of the simpler motions of t'ai chi. The rain had stopped and the sun was rising in a clear sky. They all sniffed the fresh air, and some even began to look around them and comment on the flocks of swallows circling overhead or feeding their young in the nests under the eaves.

Most had slept badly again, but many had been refreshed enough to take an interest in things. The soothing quiet of the temple grounds was broken only by the muted sounds of convent life: the creaking of the well wheel, the twittering sparrows, the padding of feet along the covered passageways, the chanting in the chapel. When they again assembled in the main hall at the hour of the dragon, they were a different set of women from the mob they'd been when they arrived. They were still depressed, but now quiet. Settled in the hall, they learned that they would all be received into religious life that day by an initiation ceremony of tonsure and the donning of convent garb. A ripple of shock passed through the assembly but no one became hysterical.

Jao was asked to go to the pharmacy, although she had not yet met the nun in charge. They must need me for a hysterical palace woman, she thought as she obeyed. She knew that the Buddhists did not separate the ills of the body from the ills of the mind, but treated them both together, that their idea of religion was to focus on healing mind and body. And in convents hysteria was thought to be a sickness, too.

When Jao entered the pharmacy, Nun Hsu greeted her with an absentminded gesture. The nun's crystal glasses had slipped to the end of her nose while she worked at the sorting table. She pushed them up and scrutinized the newcomer, while Jao took in not only the desiccated look of the nun's little body, but the intense alertness of her eyes. Nun Hsu continued in her unhurried way to finish her task of stripping the dry leaves off a hemp plant, then she motioned Jao to a stool to join in the work. When the basket was full of crushed hemp leaves, she brushed off her hands and turned to Jao.

"Do you know anything about diseases?" she asked.

"Reverend Mother, I know about the ordinary illnesses of women after living with them for twelve years," Jao began with hesitation.

"Not good enough. I will teach you while we do our work here. But now I must test you before assigning you to specific tasks."

"As you will," Jao replied.

"Very well," Nun Hsu said. "First we walk around the room, and you will tell me what you see."

Jao came to attention. This was interesting. There were numerous bins lined up against two walls. Several locked cabinets with shelves above took up a third wall. The fourth had a window and a door. Beneath the window was the long worktable under which were piles of baskets full of dried plants. The nun pointed at the first bin. "What is in that one?"

"*Tsingling* . . . onions. And there are braided strings of garlic hanging from the ceiling above."

The nun nodded with a small amused grin. "The next bin?" she continued.

Jao picked up an unfamiliar bean and shook her head.

"You are familiar enough with its oil," the nun said. "The castor bean—used to clean the intestines and bowels, as you must know."

"Oh," Jao said. "Well, I know what is in the next basket: seaweed. It's called kelp by the diving women of Chejudo, in Silla, who gather it. It's tasty to eat with rice, but expensive."

The nun looked sharply at Jao. "How do you know all this about kelp?"

"Oh, it's a favorite food of mine. You heat the dried leaves slightly until they turn from black to green, and wrap each leaf around a fresh-cooked rice ball. Delicious—crisp and salty, and smells of the sea!" She sighed. "No use to think of such luxury food in a convent," she added apologetically.

"Not at all," the nun returned briskly. "Just the opposite. This convent has a reputation for good cooking—food and drugs go so closely together. We often entertain high-ranking ecclesiasticals, lay patrons, royalty. We make a point of offering them the best food while we have them here. We need to, ahem, give our guests a good impression of our capacities," she finished piously.

Jao bit off her laughter. "Life in a convent is not so simple as I thought," she murmured, and pointed to the bin next to the seaweed. "That is ginseng, also from Silla. We used a lot of it in the palace in various recipes."

"What kind of recipes? What for?" the nun asked quickly.

"Aphrodisiacs and tonics," Jao replied.

"We don't use them quite that way here," Nun Hsu responded dryly. "We use them only for the treatment of severe indigestion caused by nervous upsets."

"Yes, well, I have a lot to learn," Jao said. "In the next bins I see what look like pepper pods, lotus root, and black vanilla beans. Hanging above—strings of red pepper, rosehips . . . for infusions? And those other herbs, I don't recognize. The last bins in the front row contain something used for demon possession—human hair and the kidney of the sea otter—in Silla they call it olnul."

"How used?" the nun interrupted, now much interested in the new acolyte.

"The hair? Burn it and mix the ashes with wine to stop bleeding. The olnul? Burn and mix with the hair ashes to drive off demons. . . ."

Nun Hsu nodded, pleased, and, fumbling with her keys, opened the locked cabinets. Inside were rows of small labeled drawers.

"In here we keep the expensive drugs. They are mostly imports. You will have to memorize their names, and hundreds of names of other products as well. That is central to our business—to know all there is to know about herbs and all other ingredients used in healing. And eating too, for that matter. What is safe and what is poisonous. The scholars who call themselves physicians do not bother to learn what *we* do about prescriptions, recipes, remedies, and side effects."

She pointed at the rows of drawers. "These small drawers contain the drugs of cloves, myrrh, nutmeg, powdered sandalwood, aloes, cardamons, and realgar. You must study each one, smell it and memorize its names and uses. The rarest and most expensive, reserved usually for royalty, are rhinoceros horns and resins like asafetida—that's an antidemoniac mixture—and citragandha—it stops hemorrhages. There are also three Roman theriacal pills."

"What are those?" said Jao.

"Well, it's an all-purpose pill. It has as many as six hundred ingredients. Now, I may tell you, they are exceedingly expensive as they are compounded of the most powerful drugs there are. In this second cabinet here are epsom salts and various materials to make up into cough remedies and other potions."

Jao paid close attention. She was familiar with costly medicines from her recent experiences in the emperor's sickroom. She said nothing about this, but stood silently, feeling slightly ill and waiting for the nun to give her further instructions or to dismiss her.

To her surprise, the nun did neither. Instead of continuing instruction or issuing a dismissal, she studied Jao intently, from head to foot. Then, making up her mind, she seated Jao on the stool and proceeded to examine her thoroughly. She counted Jao's pulses in both wrists, in her armpits, in her ankles. She examined her eyes, nose, mouth, tongue, taking her time. Then she asked Jao to take off her shift and to lie on the sorting table, whereupon she palpated the abdomen, her sensitive fingers reaching for every organ as far as possible, commenting on her findings as she went along.

"Mostly healthy," she said. "No signs of infectious diseases, no pregnancies. One mild bout with a lung ailment which seems to have left scar tissue. Lie still and relax all your muscles while I talk. You *are* suffering from something, however, suffering intensely. Tell me about it."

Jao stared at the ceiling. "Why do you think that I am suffering? How can you know when there are no visible signs?"

The nun just shrugged, as if Jao should know better than to ask such a question. "It is my business to know," she said, not unkindly.

Jao knew that she had suffered traumatic shocks in the past—Wildgoose's disappearance, Toto's suicide, the emperor's painful death, the loss of Chi and Mi. But that was all past and gone.

"Tell me," the nun said.

"There's nothing to tell," Jao said stubbornly. "Nothing. That is, I am fine, really, *now* I mean, but . . ." Her gaze met the nun's steady look, and tears sprang into her eyes. She dropped her head into her hands and there came a thundering in her ears. From far off she could hear her own sobs tearing out of her. The nun laid one hand gently over her navel, the other on the pulses in her neck. Jao shuddered, her misery abject, and uncontrollable once the floodgates had opened.

Time passed in the little room with its aromatic odors. The nun remained still while Jao's spasms gradually ceased and she began, shamefaced, to wipe her eyes.

"A thousand apologies, Reverend Mother," she began, but was cut off by the nun handing her some soft moss to wipe her nose.

"Nothing to apologize for. Stupid to think you have to apologize. Your groans and your tears were exactly what I wanted to draw out of you. Like pus . . . now you are clean and you will not have to suffer so. You have been in shock as much as, if not more so, those others out there who are lying on their mats venting their rage in weeping or drumming up quarrels because of the tonsure ahead."

"Rage?"

"What else?" the nun replied matter-of-factly.

"No rage in me. I don't feel anything like that," protested Jao.

"Then you should. What were you feeling just now when you denied rage? I saw a healthy flash of anger in your eyes. Express it in some suitable way when you feel anger. You must control it rather than let it control you. You have not once let go since you arrived. You are as rigid as a post."

"The abbess gave me some duties, and they took my mind off myself."

"Yes, the abbess had to take those measures with you because you are strong in your preconceptions, but, of course, they are not enough to save you from tearing yourself apart. Only your mind has been healing, not your body, which is being even more drained of strength by what you are enduring now. You like to think that you are superior to others because you do not give way. The very idea that you may be vulnerable like everyone else enrages you."

Jao stiffened, and the nun looked gratified.

"There are two ways to repair oneself after shock: to vent one's emotions by anger or by laughter . . . yes, laughter, the better way by far. Basic to survival. I do not agree with the monk Fahsiang, who denies the realities of the way our bodies work by saying that suffering is illusion, that all life is illusion. Saying that suffering doesn't exist solves nothing. Some realities must be met with remedies such as you and I are going to be dealing with. Now then, you must sleep for a while until I call you in order to give you a further shock."

Jao rubbed her hands together uncertainly. "A further shock?" she repeated with apprehension.

"I will see you through it. I will administer the rite of tonsure personally. It symbolizes the loss of your past life along with the loss of your hair. Donning the nun's garb symbolizes the start of a new existence. Both are painful for everyone, no exceptions. Afterwards, if you are willing, you can assist me in the tonsure of others. Do you feel compassion enough to help this way?"

Jao passed her hand over her thick mane of hair. "Willing? I suppose so. I am prepared . . . at least I have no objections. But I regret to say that I feel no compassion."

"None for any of the tsairen?" the nun asked shrewdly.

"Some for Pearl, yes . . . and Cloud . . ."

"Enough. Even just one living being, enough to begin with." The nun fell silent while arranging Jao's feet so that she could massage them, concentrating on her arches. Jao soon felt warmth in her abdomen and became drowsy. When the nun was through, she left the room and Jao slept.

An hour later the nun returned with an acolyte carrying a brazier of hot coals. The helper poured water into a kettle and placed it on the coals to heat, while the nun selected a handful of crushed herbs for tea. She dismissed the acolyte and took the lotus position in front of Jao, asking her to sit that way as well. The nun poured two cups of tea and offered one to Jao. She suddenly seemed formal and very far away to Jao, although the nun was suiting her breathing to Jao's and looking into her eyes while taking the tea. Jao followed her attitudes willingly while noting with surprise her own acquiescence.

She must be helping me to forget my body, to empty my mind, to forget myself, Jao thought. I feel as if I were participating in a meaningful activity, not a dead gesture.

The nun rose and lay a folded robe on the table and a length of cotton over it. "Now go to the bathhouse and wash your hair. The Fei may be there too, but refrain from talking to them. I will wait for you here."

Relaxed and free of anxiety, Jao did as she was bid, and returned with her hair partly dry, shining, and falling free. The nun asked her to kneel, her palms pressed together. She then combed and parted the hair, chanting passages of renunciation from Huayen's Avatama sutra.

"I am divesting you of your former identity with the shearing away of this hair," the nun intoned. "When it is done, you will no longer be a tsairen of the Inner Palace but a Buddhist acolyte." She picked up the first strand and cut it off. She laid it on a square of silk and then picked up the next strand. Incense was burning somewhere in the room, and its cloud soon enveloped both women with its fragrance. When there was nothing left but a cap of fuzz on Jao's head, the nun dipped her razor into hot water and removed the last of her hair until Jao was completely shorn.

"Rise and remove your clothes," the nun instructed, and Jao obeyed, feeling in her nudity utterly helpless—as if life itself were ending. Nun Hsu, however, was dressing her cheerfully, first in her undergarments, and then in the monastic robe. "Please kneel now and accept my blessing and my congratulatory gift," she invited.

Jao knelt, and the small nun slipped an aromatic rosary around her palms and lifted her to her feet. "You now have this rosary for life, to use on all occasions; before the altar, to count the beads when you are worshiping, or for comfort, when you are alone in your cell or are in trouble."

Jao was moved. She looked at the expensive rosary—a beautiful gift that she vowed to keep the rest of her life. She felt humble, perhaps for the first time in her life, certainly more so than she had ever felt in the palace, where she was supposed to feel humble all the time. Why, in this convent where any aberration of human conduct neither surprises nor upsets these unworldly women, where there is little social pressure to reduce one's self respect, she mused, why do I suddenly feel real humility and not just pretense?

Nun Hsu folded Jao's hair into the square of silk and handed it to her. Wisps of incense drifted past the tiers of medicines into the rafters, and there was an impish glint in the nun's eyes when she spoke in her normal voice. "I bestow on you the title of Assistant Pharmacist with my blessing—and with the hope that you will not kill instead of cure the patients!"

Lost in her dreamworld, Jao could not believe her ears. "Wh-What? Kill the patients?" she stammered. Then she saw the twinkle in the nun's eyes. "Oh," she said. "Oh . . ."

"The ceremony for the other women is beginning now and will take some time. There may be some disorder. Most of the Fei and the Chaoyi are now being shorn. Because they are more stable than the others, they will assist the thirty regular nuns in administering the rites. You will assist also."

Jao ran her hands tentatively over her bald head, not knowing whether to cry or laugh.

"Laugh!" Nun Hsu said with so solemn an expression that Jao had to laugh.

"Bald," Jao said. "Bald as an egg!"

"You are beautiful," the nun said, still solemn-faced. "Your head is a beautiful shape without the distraction of your hairstyle. Now that your pride in your appearance is diminished, you will find out what kind of a person you are." She stepped nimbly over the threshold.

Jao, following her, considered this thoughtfully.

Just before they entered the main hall, the nun turned to Jao. "Today and the next two days will be hard because we have to deal with the demons of depression that will attack everyone at the same time. Today we have enough to do in shearing and solacing these poor women. Tomorrow we will prepare herbal drinks and other comforts for everyone until they all get used to coarse robes, coarse food, and hard beds. Many will behave badly—not always the young ones either—but in time they may come voluntarily into a state of renunciation and even contentment."

They stepped into the hall, where a hundred women were already seated, waiting apprehensively for the ceremony to begin. The hall was noisy with their whispers and stirrings while latecomers took their seats. One nun was seated beside each lady who had been selected for the first round of shearing. It was her duty to carry out all the steps of the ritual.

The ceremony began.

When the first set of women were shorn, the nuns, helped now by the Fei and Chaoyi, took the second group. As hair fell, the room filled with the sounds of muffled cries. The women who were already practicing Buddhists tended to take their loss in stoic silence. The others wailed, and still others fainted or erupted in anger. Jao soon found plenty to do in helping the ones who were in the most trouble.

The women returned to their quarters when their turns were over. Without their silks and jewels, and without their elaborate hairstyles, they looked so changed that they were hardly recognizable to their colleagues. This was perhaps the worst shock of all.

When the turn of the tsairen came, Jao joined her mates. Pearl looked pale and ill but did not resist. Jao moved to support her but was not allowed to do so, and Pearl was left to go through the ceremony alone. Her eyes sought Jao's in appeal. Jao put her heart into her look of spiritual comfort so that Pearl was reassured and even smiled briefly when her hair fell.

If the feeling I have for Pearl is compassion, then I am not so hopeless after all, Jao thought.

Discordant noises increased as the day wore on, but the background of quiet chanting, designed to soothe and restrain, did have a partial effect. Several times quarrels broke out, but the abbess did not even turn her head to look. Brawny female sergeants-at-arms soon quelled the combatants, calmly and without anger. They merely picked up the fighters and carried them out of the hall until they cooled down.

The ceremony was completed by sundown when the last women were dismissed to go to their own places. Jao received the signal to leave, and lost no time scurrying to her cupboard of a room, thankful to have it for herself. It was warm and clean, and her unrolled pallet looked inviting. She sighed and lay down to rest. If I close off my memories, if I work with these healing plants and learn what these nuns know about endurance and compassion—it just might be interesting, she told herself. It could be . . . and Kaotsung could do something, or would that be impossible? What could he do? And why? Fatigued, she was soon asleep.

The long summer days passed slowly, and the convent gradually settled into a pattern of duties, meditation, ritual, and sleep. The ranking Fei, looking more alike now than ever in their baldness and similar robes, continued unchanged in their palace personalities, now exaggerated by convent conditions. Fang Fei, still grieving for both her child and her emperor, continued to lose weight, and before the year was out, gently and without struggle, died. The Fei called "Pure" and "Virtuous" found that they could continue to pursue their interests, one in the gardens, and one in the library. The Fei named Noble—accomplished in palace intrigue—saw her chance with the unworldly nuns to volunteer for services that allowed her to manipulate money and goods into her own hands. The abbess, who was by no means ignorant of the corrupt ways of the world, was nevertheless a generous-minded person, and it was some time before she caught on to what Noble was doing. When she did, she expelled the lady in spite of the uproar it caused.

"Morale is better now," she remarked to the prioress after Noble Fei left, "so the turmoil was worth it. And the lesson has been taken by the other women. In general, the further down a woman is in rank, the more obliging and willing is her behavior . . . or so it seems." She sighed.

By the coming of first frost Jao had learned the preparation and application of the simpler potions. Cherry bark and licorice were in demand for coughs and colds; marigold petals and comfrey root were used on open wounds; wild cabbage reduced festering; and datura relieved pain. She also memorized the names of hundreds of herbs and minerals. The nun refused to teach her about poisons, however. Nun Hsu was the only one in the convent entitled to release anything from the poison cabinet, and she had been given control of it only after she possessed enough religious discipline to be beyond temptation. Jao was disappointed, but accepted the good sense of this rule. And she had enough to do, as chief assistant, in trying to investigate the hundreds of new remedies being brought into Changan every year from India.

"They are being peddled by ignorant Taoists," the nun grumbled, "doing more harm than good. We have to be very careful and try them out ourselves before we dare use them. The women of the palace depend on us, and so do many others. The Taoists deceive the ignorant, but we Buddhists never do!" Jao had to smile at the intensity of Nun Hsu's competitive feelings.

As for practicing her newly learned skills, her superiors found that Jao adapted more quickly in the preparation room than in the sickroom. She accompanied the healing nun on her visits to the sick and learned something about diagnosing, but was inclined to render snap judgments.

"Watch yourself!" the old lady scolded. "A little knowledge is worse than no knowledge. You must stick to getting information about the patient: to detect the intensity of fever, to take pulses, to understand pain. That's all. Don't attempt to prescribe at this stage of your training—never. You'll kill people, not heal them!"

Jao listened and dutifully took pulses and made the sick more comfortable, but all this took more out of her than memorizing new material. She had to struggle to overcome her dislike of touching sick people as well as her revulsion at the sight of blood.

With the frost, the roads hardened and annual travel to central Asian markets was renewed. In addition, activities in anticipation of cold weather were undertaken. The gardens required attention to ready the annuals for cold weather. The convent gardens were especially vulnerable, and Jao was assigned to help move costly herbs into the greenhouse and to wrap up all the fruit trees and flowering bushes in straw. She became acquainted with crusty Mother Lin, the head gardener, who worked her unmercifully, both in the greenhouse and outside.

The old nun was an enigmatic character, good at her work, but a puzzle to the city-bred nuns who ran the convent. She had come from Szechuan originally and was at bottom more of a shamanist medicine woman than a Buddhist. For all that, she knew her garden better than anyone else the convent had ever had. She was a match for any bad character who tried to steal from her or palm off spurious products on her, so she was entrusted with heavy responsibility which she shouldered lightly. A hardy fifty years old, she was stocky and muscular and as strong as most men her age. Her features were prominent in a face bronzed with outdoor living and crisscrossed with good-natured wrinkles. Jao found herself drawn to her. There couldn't be a greater difference between two women, Jao thought wryly, than between shriveled, enigmatic, wispy Nun Hsu and loud, earthy Nun Lin. But she liked them both. It must be me, she concluded. I myself must be two people!

Because she could not write, Nun Lin kept Jao busy by candlelight compiling lists of seeds, seedlings, and imports needed by the convent, and in reorganizing a chaotic reference system.

"Where do you go to buy these things?" Jao asked one morning. "The West Market?"

"No, no, of course not. Much of what I want is not available in Changan markets, or only at prices I won't pay," the nun said shortly. "Tunhuang is the best place for the greatest variety and the cheapest prices. If I can't make it that far when I go on my fall buying trip, I'll stop at the markets in Lanchow. That's where the products of Szechuan come in, as well as some of the western countries, even India."

She stopped to give Jao a speculative look. "I have never had an assistant before who was not more trouble than she was worth. But I don't have to give instructions to you more than once. And you don't plague me with chatter. I need someone to go with me on my travels who is smart and knows how to take hardship. . . . Would you like to come?"

Jao took a deep breath. "I just might like to," she replied, hiding her excitement. The mere thought of a trip like that was enough to raise her spirits sky-high.

The nun looked at her shrewdly. "I'll talk to the abbess about it when I get the chance," she said.

Days went by and Jao stayed close to Nun Lin, helping her with her preparations for departure, hanging on her every word, but nothing more was said about Jao's going with her. She began to think that she had misunderstood or that she had imagined that she had been asked. However, she overhauled her sheepskin winter coats and wool underclothes and petitioned to go to market to buy heavy boots, just in case.

Two days before she was scheduled to leave with an outgoing caravan, Mother Lin stepped into the pharmacy and said in an offhand way to Jao, "The abbess has thought it over and has found the travel money for you."

Jao let out a shriek that scared the convent doves into wild flight and startled Nun Hsu into dropping her work basket.

"Did you hear?" Jao demanded of Nun Hsu. "I am to go to the western markets with Mother Lin!" She stopped what she was doing to clap ecstatically in glee.

"I heard and of course I knew," the pharmacist responded noncommittally. "I had to give my permission, didn't I? Better finish that batch of cough remedy because it is needed at once. You are not starting your trip this minute," she finished somewhat crossly.

Mother Lin listened to this exchange in silence, then turned to go. She said over her shoulder to Jao, "Meet me in an hour at the toolshed, then. There is much to do."

When Jao arrived in the back garden, she found the nun already there.

"Around to the rear," the nun said, pointing with her chin, her hands hidden in her sleeves. In the back, between the shed and the high wall, was an empty space of hard-packed ground. The nun took off her heavy robe and gestured for Jao to do the same.

"Now, I am going to teach you some simple body movements that will help you escape from anyone trying to hold you or take something from you. I am an adept in the Shaolin Buddhist system of the martial arts—kung fu—and I have permission from the abbess to teach you something about defense."

Jao grinned in surprise, greatly diverted. She had heard of the Shaolin exercises, which originated in the monks' need to stretch muscles after long hours in meditation.

Nun Lin took two small bags filled with gravel from her sleeves and showed them to Jao. "Carry these in your sleeves at all times. You can hit an unexpected assailant with your sleeve and stun him and thus escape." Jao eyed the bags and hefted them.

"Hmm," she murmured, impressed.

"First, sink them in the corners of your sleeves. Now, I'll show you how to use them. . . . Attack me from behind and try to knock this pouch out of my hand."

Jao obeyed, gently springing on the nun while aiming for the pouch. To her surprise, she found herself lying on her back. She scrambled up to try again. The nun was all business, and Jao soon put her mind to the matter, all jokes aside. After an hour, and after receiving some handsome bruises, she was dismissed.

"Come back at the hour of the monkey and we practice again," the nun said, wiping the sweat from her bald head and donning her coat. Jao nodded and, grinning to herself, dried her own head before returning to the pharmacy.

Before dawn two days later, Jao and Nun Lin were let out of the back gate by a sleepy night watchman. The gate was locked behind them as they mounted their donkeys for the ride to the grounds of the inn, where they were to meet up with their traveling caravan. Their heads were covered by padded hoods, with flaps tied under their chins. Jao's face was hidden by a scarf so that only her eyes showed.

"To keep people from seeing your pretty face and bothering you," the nun said. "After one look at mine, they don't try," she added wryly. Jao laughed. She was thrilled to the core to be out in the open, outside of walls, seeing new faces, having new experiences, free again as she had been on that glorious trip to Loyang four years before.

The two women were assigned their places in the caravan. Only minutes after the morning drums signaled the opening of the city gates, the caravan began to move. From that moment on, everything was an enthralling adventure to Jao. The travel, the jostling in marketplaces and inns, the haggling over purchases, the packing and loading and guarding of precious goods—all these put adrenaline in her blood and made every day one of absorbing interest. The only disappointment came after they arrived in Lanchow, where they discovered that they had missed the connecting caravan for Tunhuang and that the next would not start for a month or more.

"We cannot sit around here a month," Nun Lin fumed. "We'll just have to shop around in the markets for whatever bargains we can find here. And I am going to obtain guaranteed passage back to Changan today."

"Let me go with you to find the caravan directors," Jao said eagerly. "I want to see how you do it."

Nun Lin looked at Jao speculatively. "If you learn well, I can trust you to make the buying trips without me. I hate to be gone from my gardens for long, even in winter. Someone is always interfering with my arrangements. Come, then, but draw your scarf over your face."

The two women went out. There was a cold wind blowing from the

Gobi desert, and it was whirling dustclouds over the housetops and through the alleys. The women pulled their headcloths over their mouths and walked briskly past the stalls of the great market, a few of which were still open in the afternoon, and went into the caravansary at the end of the market plaza. Stables and inn were under one sheltering roof. The two women entered the forecourt, which was crowded with the camels of a recently arrived train, and made their way cautiously among the animals to the main reception center fronting the yard. Inside they found a score of drovers standing around several braziers.

Nun Lin stopped just inside the door and shouted out that she wished to speak to the headman of the next caravan going south. All heads turned toward her and two men detached themselves to find out what she wanted.

"Ko!" Jao shrieked, letting her hood fall as she dashed forward to greet one of the two men. He was older now, and grizzled, but still Ko. He stopped in surprise because he saw only a bald-headed nun whom he did not recognize at all. Jao took Lin's hand and pulled her forward.

"Mother Lin, this is Ko, our caravan leader from the old days," she said excitedly. Everyone in the room was watching now, their curiosity aroused. Jao grasped Ko's gnarled hand in both of hers, but he still did not recognize her.

"Ko! I am Wu Jao—the girl you took from Taiyuan to the palace twelve years ago! You saved my treasure box for me . . . and took care of the abbess too, and were so very kind!" She paused for breath, and Ko looked searchingly into her face.

"Yes," he said wonderingly. "You are that one. I remember now. I thought she had a great future, that one. Whatever has happened that you are so changed? And why are you here of all places?"

She chuckled. "You are shocked by my bald pate. Don't be! I am the same Wu Jao underneath. When the emperor died, we harem ladies had to go into a convent. That's the whole story. I am here on a buying mission for the convent."

Comprehension dawned in Ko's eyes. He nodded slowly. "I heard about the old emperor's death, but never thought how it might affect you. . . . Well, well . . ."

"We want to buy passage back to Changan," the nun said, speaking up because she wished to put an end to talk in such a public place. It was attracting too much attention.

Ko understood at once what was bothering the nun and quickly introduced his companion. "My son, Turk," he said with pride. "He will be leading the next caravan south."

The women gave the son an *anjali* salute, eyeing him with interest. He was a replica of his father, even in dress.

"You look just like Ko did when I first saw him!" Jao remarked, and Ko smiled ruefully.

"No longer young!" he said amiably as he glanced at the onlookers. "I can send my son with you to make the arrangements. There are a hundred inns in this place, so perhaps he can go with you now in order to make sure of the right place." He eyed Nun Lin to see if that was what she wanted.

She did. "Thank you," she said crisply. "Let us go, then." She glared at the crowding onlookers and hustled Jao out ahead of her. Jao had fully exposed her face while greeting Ko, and the nun had noticed the attention she was receiving from one dark, hulking fellow whose black eyes stared with unusual intensity. At the door she turned and gave him a quelling look to warn him off. She wanted no one following them.

The next morning the two set out for the market earlier than usual. The old nun was jubilant. "Now we can get our business done and be out of here in five days, that is, if we find our bargains in the meantime. Winter weather is upon us earlier than usual, and so a long stay would be foolish, to say the least."

They spent the entire day in the stalls but could find nothing but picked-over stock, and when they went back to their inn, they had obtained nothing but a sack of realgar. The nun had bought it at a higher price than she wanted to pay—it was a sovereign antidote for all forms of poison and was high on the wanted list. "Thieves and worse," the nun mumbled, hastening back to the warmth of the inn after the long hours in unheated souks.

"But it's yours now and well worth having," Jao said, sprinting to keep up.

The nun turned to answer and stopped short. "That man," she cried.

"What? What man?" Jao shouted above the wind. Turning to look, she caught a glimpse of a retreating back.

"The one in the caravansary, the one who was staring," Lin answered. They stood and looked but the man had disappeared into an alley. "Don't like it," Lin muttered, turning into the next alley in her search for a roundabout way to their lodgings. "Must lose him so he can't follow us anymore. Looks like a highwayman to me."

Jao shrugged. To be followed was no great matter, she thought. Normal for a pretty woman.

The next two days repeated the first. On their last day in Lanchow, the nun decided to try the best shop in town, the one she had avoided because it was the most expensive and the most resistant to barter. It was, however, her last resort, and she still had most of her orders to fill.

They started out early, and when they entered the shop they saw that they were the first customers. They were greeted with a speculative but courteous welcome from the owner. The shop was the only one in the market with an imported glass window and a door, and the only one in town to have a glowing brazier to keep the chill off. Nun Lin grunted when she saw the ample display of tree bark, roots, charms, and potions. Everything that one could possibly need or want, Jao thought enthusiastically. The big room was ablaze with color and the air was heavy with the scent of spices and aromatics. Baskets of red pepper, paprika, yellow saffron, and cumin lined the walls. There were tubs of flourishing green comfrey, mint and parsley growing under the window, as well as dried fruits, seeds, and nuts. And, most wonderful of all, an extravagant array of the most popular drugs.

"Ah," Mother Lin sighed. "Ah . . ." She began to wander around the room, selecting in her mind what she wanted, oblivious of anything else. The merchant watched her with a humorous twinkle in his eye. He expected two things from her: a large purchase and a spirited battle. He was prepared to furnish her with both.

After about an hour of studying the store's offerings, Nun Lin turned to the proprietor. "Please come," she said. He was remaining annoyingly close to the fire and not making any effort to sell. "I want to find out how much everything costs." He came, and then obligingly stayed at her elbow while she took her time. She would point and he would tell her the price. Jao watched carefully, but the process was long and drawn out and her attention wandered. No other customer came in, although there was a constant press of people looking in through the dusty window. Jao found the flow of faces past the window entertaining until she caught sight of the staring black eyes of the mysterious man who seemed to be following them. She pretended that she hadn't recognized him, and he disappeared. Jao shrugged, wondering lightly what the man could possibly want from two nuns.

By this time Mother Lin had begun to pile the merchandise that she wanted on the plank used as a counter. She had not bothered to bargain when the prices of each individual item were quoted by the merchant.

"How much is all that?" she asked, lumping it all together. The merchant calculated on his abacus and named a price. Lin gave a snort and walked to the door.

Now what? Jao thought, following her in disappointment.

When Mother Lin reached the door, the merchant named another sum, slightly lower.

Lin came back. "Half the first price," she said. This time the merchant turned away, and the nun said, "Two more silver pieces."

The merchant paused and was silent. "All right, then, you add ten more silver pieces and I will throw in that valuable theriacal pill that itself costs twelve pieces—it's the only Roman pill I have, and I saw you eyeing it. . . ."

"I did not," she cut in. "I don't want that dreadful pill at all."

"Yes, well, you may have it all the same, at ten more silver pieces . . . ten."

Lin had kept track of all the figures in her head. "Done," she said quickly, astonishing both Jao and the merchant, who had intended to withdraw the bait of the theriacal pill and to lower his overall price only a little.

Nun Lin watched closely as the merchant wrapped each item in rough yellow paper and packed it all away in her bag. It bulged to capacity when he finished. She hefted it. It was heavy, so she handed it to Jao to carry. Finally, she reached under her many skirts and brought out a pouch, which she emptied on the counter. "Just enough," she said, scooping up everything but ten silver pieces.

By this time the store was filling up with other customers, so the owner's farewell was polite but brief and the women escaped without further words. Outside in the street, Jao stole a look at the expression on the nun's face in order to find out what had happened, whether it had been good or bad for them. The old nun was smiling to herself, looking much too smug. "Foxed him good over that expensive pill, I did!" she yelled above the din of wind and traffic. "If it is worth twelve pieces here—and it surely is—it's worth fifty in Changan!" Jao gave a crack of laughter and her eyes lit up in pleasure. How diverting this trip was turning out to be!

The traffic was thick. They were often separated by pedestrians, donkeys, or carts going both ways in the narrow street. Jao was half running in order not to lose her partner in the crowd. Skirting around a cart of high-piled brushwood, she finally lost sight of her companion. Suddenly she was stunned by a severe blow to her head, bringing her to a dizzy halt. A strong arm propelled her into an adjacent alley. She started to shriek but her scream was cut off by a rug into which she was tightly and expertly rolled. In a matter of only a few more seconds, she was thrown over the back of a donkey, her head and feet dangling. Someone gave the animal a sharp slap and it started moving at a vigorous trot, bouncing his load viciously. Jao choked in pain and lost consciousness.

A ray of late sunshine played across her face when she recovered. Her head ached abominably and she felt dizzy. Her first thought was to feel herself for anything broken or bleeding but all she could find was a large lump on her head. Once she regained her bearings, she saw that she had been thrown into a dusty and airless storeroom full of crates and baskets. Sitting up too quickly, Jao was overcome by dizziness for the next few minutes. The rug had been thrown loosely over her. She threw it off and began to shiver with cold without her padded jacket, which was gone. The bag was gone too.

"How awful!" she moaned. "How very disastrously awful!" She pressed her hand against her aching forehead. "Nun Lin has lost everything she came to get. The first time she has ever lost anything—and it's all my fault!"

The sun's ray disappeared. The room grew colder. Frightened and feeling helpless, Jao slumped over a pile of sacks and drew the rug to her chin, trying to think of a way to escape. The wooden bolt to the door shot open, and she jumped with fright. The dark face of her abductor appeared. "Get up, you, and come out here where you can be useful," he ordered briefly.

She got to her feet and, staggering a little, went out into the room. Several unshaven men were standing around a fire, and at her entrance looked at her curiously. One came over to her at once, laying his paw roughly on her shoulder. Jao shrank back.

"Clear off, you," the first man exclaimed, giving him a shove. "She's not for the likes of you."

"Think you can keep her for yourself after all we done to help you get her?" the highwayman replied angrily, his hand still on Jao's shoulder.

"I'm selling her. She'll bring us a big price . . . a former palace concubine! Good value! One of these wealthy countryman will pay fancy for her. So just leave her alone, you clod. I don't want her mauled!"

The second man hesitated, then dropped his hand. "All right, all right, for now that is. . . ." He shrugged and strutted back to the fire, where the others laughed at him.

The dark man turned to Jao. "We're hungry. Get to work to fix us a meal. There is food in those baskets—go at it."

Jao looked around dazedly. Rabbits and onions were hanging from the rafters and a blackened pot lay in a clay stove. Her head was clearing and her dizziness was leaving her. She was getting back her wits.

"You'll have to get a shovelful of coals to start the stove going, then," she said.

"Do it yourself. There's the shovel," he snapped, scowling.

Jao understood her predicament, that unless she moved to placate these edgy men, she was in deeper trouble than ever. She immediately set about building up a fire in the clay stove, then unhooked a rabbit and picked up a cleaver. She shot a look at the dark man, who was monitoring her every move. "No," he said. "You won't want to use that on us. There are too many of us and your punishment would be—severe. Starting with Hoong over there, who is drooling over you."

Jao's eyes fell. She laid the rabbit on the plank table and studied it. "How do I tackle this?" she muttered. She'd never prepared rabbit before. Hmm, perhaps cutting up the meat, making a stew . . . She started, first frying the chunks of meat, then adding garlic, peppers, and quantities of onions, tasting at every step of the way. The men became restless. The dark man began to come to the stove to see what she was doing and to scowl at her. The enticing aroma rising from the pot was her only salvation.

"It's almost ready," she told her kidnapper when he did not return to the others. He stood beside the stove with his arms impatiently akimbo.

"Do you have anything to drink with this?" Jao asked innocently. Without a word he went to the storeroom and brought back a barrel of beer which he broached. Filling drinking cups and two large jugs with the strong brew, she set them on the table along with steaming bowls of stew. The men converged at once on the loaded table.

Jao watched them as they gulped their food ravenously and sighed with relief. Remarkably, her cooking had not turned out badly. She noticed that the dark man was wolfing his food even faster than the others but was not drinking much. What he did drink was making his face fiery red and his eyes bloodshot. Probably hasn't had much sleep lately, Jao thought. She looked around cautiously to see if she could find a way to escape. There was only one door and it was heavily barred. She had no coat, and the weather outside was freezing. She shuddered. The end of the room was piled high with loot of all kinds, and the floor near the door was covered with the men's sheepskin coats.

Then Jao caught her breath. Her bag was there among the coats, intact. Her eyes swiveled to the dark man. He was watching her with his cruel black eyes. When he saw her glancing around the room, he shook his head savagely, as if to tell her not to try anything. Jao dropped her eyes again. What a devil he was. He seemed to read her every thought.

The evening wore on, and one by one the men, even the dark one, overcome by fatigue, beer, and the poor air, dropped their heads on the table and slept. Their snores were soon the only sounds to be heard.

Jao stood watching, and then, inch by inch, crept to the door. She had her hand on the bar and was gently pulling it out when the dark man raised his head, saw what she was doing, and sprang toward her. Jao swung around, grasping her sleeves just above her gravel bags, and lashed out, aiming at one side of his head and then the other. Her stones cracked against his temples and stunned him. Quickly, Jao delivered the kick that she had learned in her karate lessons. To her amazement, he went down at once, unconscious. Heads lifted blearily at the sound of the thud. All they saw, however, was the dark man lying quietly on the floor, apparently asleep, and Jao leaning against the wall with her eyes closed. One by one they dropped sleepily to the table again.

Jao waited until the snores began, then finished unbolting the door, grabbed her bag in one hand and a coat in the other, and with infinite care to prevent the squeaking of hinges, opened the heavy door just enough to squeeze through. Once outside, she took the same care in closing the door, then raced like a lunatic down the alley into the maze of narrow streets.

Sustained by the euphoria of escape, Jao sped from one alley to another, trying to find a way out. Eventually realizing she was lost, she slowed down. To prevent herself from going in circles, she followed a canal, but even then it took her a couple of hours to find a landmark that she recognized. From there it was easy to find the right inn. It took an age to rouse the gatekeeper and another one to wake Nun Lin, who was sunk in sleep. The gatekeeper grumblingly went back to bed, and the nun sat up complaining and rubbing her eyes.

"Jao!" she shrieked when she was fully awake. "Jao! What happened? Where have you been? It's been a nightmare trying to find you!"

"It's been an even worse nightmare trying to get back to you!" Jao retorted, grinning. She peeled off the large sheepskin coat and pushed the bag forward.

"My bag! My drugs! You wonderful girl!" the nun shrieked again, this time rousing the entire household. The landlord rushed into the room in alarm, followed by most of the other guests. Since everyone knew already about Jao's disappearance and the loss of the bag, the story had to be told to all. Heads were shaken in sympathy, and only then, with smiles all around, did everyone withdraw to his bed.

The two excited women stayed awake talking until Nun Lin insisted that Jao get what sleep she could during the few remaining hours before their caravan was to leave. Jao agreed to humor the old lady and dutifully stretched out, sure that she could not unwind enough to sleep. However, as soon as her head touched the pillow and her eyes closed, she dozed off.

Mother Lin waited until the last minute to rouse Jao, but when the drums announcing the opening of the gates sounded, the old woman woke her up and hastily helped her don her coat. They rushed out, the old nun clutching Jao with one hand and her precious bag with the other, afraid of losing either one. The caravan was waiting for them, with Ko himself at its head. He had heard about Jao's adventure with the kidnappers and had decided to lead the train himself, with his son as armed guard.

On the way, Ko saw to it that no one and nothing was lost. It was a leisurely trip, the weather bright and invigorating, and the two enjoyed the small adventures that each day brought. By the time they reached the convent, Jao, having for the first time in her life mingled freely with the common people, felt enriched by her experiences.

The winter passed rapidly for Jao after her return to the convent. The cold was bitter and the sickrooms were filled with serious cases of pneumonia as well as with the lighter afflictions of colds and fevers. Several of the weaker palace women, as well as the strong ones who remained unreconciled to their fate, died of their illnesses. Jao was kept busy from dawn to dusk every day.

The abbess never hesitated to enter the sickrooms, to attend the worst cases and to give comfort to the dying. Jao watched her. She is a pillar of strength because she thinks little of death, Jao concluded. "Why fear death?" the abbess would ask in her matter-of-fact way when attending a frightened woman who was dying. "Why resist death when there are rebirths ahead? Why, when one can be rid of this old, sick body and have a fresh new one to enjoy in the next life?"

Jao observed the abbess, and after a bit began to feel the same way herself. She lost her fear of death even though she lived in constant risk of contagion and disease. She realized this, but also knew that her courage did not stem from the hope of a better life in the future. She recognized that she wanted her better life very much in the present, and that meant, first and foremost, peace of mind—a peace to be found in no small measure in interesting work.

There were several births to take care of as well. The abbess handled this problem with tact, setting up a convent nursury to care for the palace babies, although not believing for a moment that nine months previously the sickly emperor had fathered them. She acted as if everything were normal, thus saving both mothers and infants from the cruel fates that would have overtaken them had they remained in the palace.

It was late spring. The gardens had been planted, there was a lull before the rainy season, and Jao was asked by Nun Lin, again to her surprise, to go on another collecting trip. This time they would go to the seacoast to buy southern products and exotica from the tropics, which were yearly becoming more popular in China.

Nun Lin rented a small barge on which she loaded local products. She would use these to barter for the cuttings and other items to be acquired in Yangchow. A deal was struck with the master of an empty rice barge heading downstream, to allow her to hitch her small boat to the large one.

"If there is any trouble, we will cast you off," warned the barge master.

"Yes, yes," the nun replied. "If you give us a tow, you will have no trouble. We will chant our mantras and all will go well." Nun Lin had been deeply influenced by the new spells being practiced in neighboring Tibet, and used the phraseology without knowing precisely what it meant. The words were magic in themselves and never failed to impress.

"Hmm . . . that is to be seen." Although he was taken with the idea, the boatman hesitated. When he had agreed, they brought their boat up to the stern of the barge and he supervised attaching the tow rope. Then the two boats poled out into the current and started on their long drift downstream.

The women spent the first afternoon in erecting a small tent in the stern of their boat, where they also did their cooking on a charcoal burner. During the fine weather, they led an idle and idyllic life. They sat on coils of rope and watched the days roll by, spending a little time on the duties of cooking and devotions and the rest of the time observing the busy rural scenes that they were gliding through. When the rain fell, their miseries were legion, but the storms quickly passed, bringing relief along with the sun.

The journey downstream proved to be relatively speedy and disaster-free. "For which we are thankful to Maitreya and all the river goddesses," Nun Lin said, making sure that she placated the water spirits in her invocations, never omitting a daily appeal for protection to the powerful Dragon King who was master of all waters, whether stream or ocean. They had traveled down the Yellow River to Loyang, the second capital, and then on past into the Pien tributary as far as Kaifeng. After this great port, they took the Kuo River to the Huai and from it into the Grand Canal, which wound through rich farmlands a hundred miles to the Yangtze delta.

Each day there was something new to see as they slipped along through a constantly changing landscape—from the red loess terraces of the high country to the green lowlands. They sailed as if by magic through the wheat fields into the lush waterland of mulberry trees, rice and tea. Well within the month they tied up to a dock near Yangchow on the Yangtze River, where they parted with the rice barge. Nun Lin wanted her own mooring near the farm nurseries.

"We are picking up a load of warehouse rice to take back to Changan," the barge master shouted as the women rowed away. "If you would like a tow then . . . ?"

Nun Lin shouted back, "You mean that you had no trouble coming down and want none going back?"

"Something like that," he yelled.

The nun had had plenty of time to observe his habits and the way he neglected his leaky barge. "Thank you, thank you, but no . . . no plans yet." Easygoing in all his habits, the barge master accepted this and they parted company cheerfully.

"I'll look for a small, swift silk boat with an alert crew," Nun Lin said as soon as they were out of earshot. "I don't have time to waste with haulers who are likely to get stranded. We will have to pay to go upstream, but I have to get back as soon as possible. The gardens will be growing greatly while I am gone, and I don't trust my assistants to keep the weeds down. Today, as soon as we are tied up, I will inquire along the waterfront for a silk boat and I will send you to the market to do some bartering on your own. Would you like that?"

"Just start me in the right direction!" Jao exclaimed enthusiastically.

"Watch out, though, for kidnappers," Lin twitted, rolling her eyes.

"Never fear—not a second time." Jao jumped into a karate readiness pose, making the boat rock and Lin laugh. Jao was much rested from this easy trip, which was quite different from their strenuous fall excursion on the windy mountain roads. She found herself enjoying every moment of the comfortable travel. This second trip had brought her into the green and thriving delta area, where she at least would have the opportunity to test her skills in identifying the products they sought. The prospect made her exuberantly happy.

Marketing and negotiating for a tow back to Changan were accomplished with satisfying ease and took less time than they expected, so in ten days they were already on their way back. The going was slower this time. The only way to get upstream against the current was to sail or to scull upriver. When sculling was involved, the two women had to row their own boat.

The days passed pleasantly, however. There was enough breeze to fill the sails much of the time, breezes that were playful and laden with the many scents of summer. Jao and the nun spent much of the time in silence, watching the water ripple along the sides of their craft, listening to the sounds of people living on either bank and on other boats, to the creaking of the waterwheels, to the cries of children, to the flurries of birds in the thatches of farmhouses, and to roosters in the farmyards before dawn. The monsoon had not yet begun, so rainfall was of short duration and there were no delays or accidents. When Nun Lin and Jao stepped over the side of their boat onto the landing near Changan, they were sorry that the trip was over. Jao had never felt so free and happy.

For the short passage from boat to convent, Nun Lin and Jao remained in their mood of peaceful leisure. When they reached the convent, however, the atmosphere was filled with tense expectation. An elaborate memorial service on the first anniversary of the death of Emperor Taitsung was to be held there, and Kaotsung would arrive in only two days.

CHAPTER TEN

In preparation for the memorial service, the abbess herself was training the musicians, the chanters, and the bell and drum people, as well as supervising the rituals. Kaotsung, assisted by senior clerics, was to perform the main sacrifices and recite the major prayer. The kitchen was in an uproar, and the nuns and servants were everywhere in the nine courtyards, tidying, polishing, raking, and decorating.

Nun Lin took instant refuge in her gardens, but soon went in search of the abbess, to report. She finally located her in the main hall of worship, superintending its cleaning.

"Was the trip successful?" the abbess asked absentmindedly while running her finger along the great altar, inspecting for dust.

"Very," Nun Lin returned shortly.

"Well then . . . I'm glad that you are back safely," the abbess added as Nun Lin started to retreat. "How did Jao do?"

Lin smiled her rare smile. "She is almost as good as I am," she said.

The abbess grunted. "She can't possibly be within miles of you. In what way is she good? Knowing how to buy? Wielding her loaded sleeves? Saving you trouble?"

"In every way as far as learning quickly whatever I teach her," the nun retorted. "She could improve in attention to her devotions, however."

"That will come later. Give her time," the abbess replied, pleased. She did not realize that Lin was referring to spells for placating a variety of local animistic spirits as well as every possible water spirit.

Jao went directly to the pharmacy. She had barely rid herself of her coat before being loaded with work.

"I need another pair of hands, and yours have arrived just in time," Nun Hsu said, greeting her. "Here, you can prepare the incense and aromatics for the altar—the same recipes we used at harvest festival time. We'll use another kind for the ancestor worship service in which Emperor Kaotsung takes part—a special mixture that I will prepare myself, using the fresh aromatics that you no doubt have just brought." She sounded pleased, the first indication that she was happy to see Jao.

"In time for what?" Jao asked, startled. "Is the abbess planning to hold the memorial service here?"

"Of course . . . A service is also being held at the Li family shrine inside the palace grounds, as well as one at the Hungfu Temple that Emperor Taitsung established in memory of his mother. We want the ceremony that will be held here to be outstanding. I am quite pleased that the incense will be special. . . ." Her voice trailed off.

"The incense will be special because the ingredients will be fresh?" Despite the unsettling news, Jao found herself interested.

"Only partially. The mixture is the key—our secret," Hsu said, busily unwrapping the new drugs.

"Secret?" Jao pursued. "Why does a convent have secrets?"

Hsu bristled. "We have to be very, very careful of our secrets. The monks are jealous of their prerogatives and keep encroaching on us. This pharmacy, for example—they would have taken it over years ago if we had let them. And we have trouble with the Confucian bureaucracy. Their scholars study medical lore as part of their training, and so they like to think that any practice outside of their control is pernicious. They are all amateurs! The Buddhist practitioners can at least heal their patients, not kill them!" Again her voice trailed off as she turned to her work.

Jao could not concentrate on what the nun was saying. Her mind was in a whirl from discovering that the emperor would be visiting the convent himself. It has been a year, she thought. I hope that I can see him without his seeing me . . . with the way I look now . . . my bald head and my faded robe. I can't bear the thought of his seeing me this way.

A heavy monsoon rain was falling on the day of the ceremony, darkening the halls and filling the courts with puddles. "The better for our candlelit ceremony," the abbess said to the prioress while they stood in the open doorway waiting to receive the imperial party. "Our altars and ancestral tablets will seem all the brighter and the tone of our offering more somber—in keeping with the day." She glanced at the spirit tablet that had been placed in its shrine on a high table before the Huayen central image of Vairocana. Fresh flowers of the summer season, wild tiger lilies, bluebells, lotus, had been arranged early that morning along the front of the altar. The tantalizing aroma of incense was already spiraling into the dimness of the rafters. The candles were being lit with tapers, and their small flames flickered in hundreds of moving fingers over the silent images, over the flowers, over Taitsung's tablet and over the attentive faces of the former palace ladies and the regular nuns. The women were seated in the side aisles, waiting for the service to begin.

The nuns were still and silent, but the former palace ladies were restless, rustling in their seats in their eagerness to see the emperor and his entourage, wanting to feel for a moment that they were a part of palace life again. They did not have long to wait. With much stamping and shaking off of wet clothes, the imperial party entered and was welcomed by the abbess. Kaotsung, accompanied by the renowned monk Hsuantsang and several of the chief clerics of the nation's Buddhist world, swept through the doors and formally moved forward at the sound of the wooden clapper signaling the beginning of the rites. Confucian and Taoist leaders were also present, all surreptitiously aiming for positions near Kaotsung.

The emperor started first with a bow before the spirit shrine. The chanting began at the signal of the head Huayen abbot. Prayers were intoned by guest clerics, special passages from the Lotus sutra were read by a Pure Land bishop, and, at appropriate intervals, a Taoist notable struck the musical triangle and stone chimes. Jao, who was seated among the tsairen in the second row not ten feet away from the emperor, noticed with a smile in her eyes that Kaotsung made a small indignant jerk away from those who were trying to assist him to his feet after each kowtow.

Soon, however, along with the whole audience, Jao became immersed in the solemn ritual of lament that was being performed. The chanting was low, slow, and funereal, and as the minutes passed, a wave of loss and sadness filled the hall and subdued every person present. When the chanting suddenly ceased, marking the end of the ceremony, it left an emotion-laden silence in the great hall. The only sounds that could be heard were the distant patter of rain and the soft hissing of the emperor's silk shoes as he initiated the withdrawal from the altar and from the hall.

Just before leaving the hall, the emperor paused and looked over the seated audience, seeing all the conventional downturned faces. Jao's head, however, was lifted enough so that he could look into her eyes. She encountered the same opaque look that had set her blood pounding the year before. She hurriedly cast down her eyes, conscious of the crowd in the hall, conscious of her temerity, conscious of a feeling of gratitude for his acknowledgment. A flush spread over her face. My bald pate and all . . . she thought. Now I'm revealed, he's seen me as I am.

The abbess followed the emperor after a respectful interval. She felt the ceremony had been a success. It had been imbued with a moving spirit of remembering and mourning. "No one can doubt that Taitsung's spirit was present in the hall today," she exulted, "and that he was pleased with our offerings."

In leaving the hall, she gestured to Hsuantsung and to the abbot of Huayen to precede her. The Taoist, emboldened by Taitsung's decree that Taoists should precede Buddhists, felt that he should be the foremost attendant, and quickly stepped in front of the abbess. She, however, was not to be maneuvered on her own ground. The Taoist did not get by. Once outside the sanctuary, the abbess stood aside and let her guests file past on their way to her elegant tea room, where they were to receive refreshments in the company of the young emperor. The abbess gracefully included the Taoist visitor with the other high officials in the selected group.

An hour passed, and the guests, having had refreshment, were waiting to leave. Servants were trooping noisily onto the veranda, collecting rain gear and calling for palanquins. The nuns in the hall were dismissed, the candles quenched, and the doors of the sanctuary closed. Jao returned to the pharmacy and was getting into her faded work tunic when she was summoned by the abbess. She hurriedly restored her formal robe and followed the messenger, wondering how the abbess had freed herself of her guests so soon. When she knocked, the familiar voice bade her enter. Obeying, Jao found herself in a room still full of notables, unable to retire before the emperor did.

"Wu Jao," the nun said. "The emperor admires our incense. I would like you to make some fresh and bring it here at once."

Jao glanced swiftly at the emperor. She bowed and presented her *anjali* salute as she backed out of his presence. "Most certainly . . . at once . . ." she said in a small voice. He watched her with that unsmiling stare of his, surely aware of the fact that all the eyes in the room were upon him.

Back in the pharmacy, Nun Hsu stopped what she was doing and hastened to prepare the new mixture. With Jao handing her the ingredients, it was not long before the preparation was made up and Jao was able to return with the incense. The guests had long since finished their tea, and were noticeably anxious to leave. Jao handed the box to the abbess with a low bow, one hand offering the box, the other touching her sleeve. The abbess then wrapped the box in a piece of yellow silk and placed it with a graceful bow in the emperor's hand. He in turn gave it to an attendant. The visitation was over. He thanked the abbess formally and turned to Jao.

"I thank you, as well," he said formally. "You were always so helpful to my family when you were in the palace, and I see that you have not lost your skills. Your year here has done you no harm, indeed your appearance shows good health and good spirits. Your future will undoubtedly be bright."

The hated flush spread over her head, and Jao lowered her eyes quickly. All the people in the room were staring. "Thank you for your consideration," she murmured, and, bowing her way out backward again, fled.

A few days later Empress Wang sent a letter by her head eunuch, inviting Wu Jao to grow her hair and to return to the palace and into service there. The letter was left at the gate, and before the imperial envelope reached Jao, everyone in the convent knew of it, with the exception of the abbess, who was above the normal flow of gossip, and Jao herself.

Jao was sorting mint leaves when the silk-wrapped letter eventually arrived at her door. She washed her hands and disappeared into her own cubicle to read it in privacy. Her blood pounded in her ears as she took in its meaning.

"A summons back to the palace! The emperor must have had a hand in it somehow!" she exulted. She stood transfixed for a long time, collecting her thoughts and calming herself. Then she poured cold water into a bowl and slapped it on her face, dried herself and went back to her work to await an interrogation from Nun Hsu. When none came, she offered her the letter to read.

Nun Hsu took time to study it, then looked up appraisingly. "What did you do to deserve this honor?" she asked coldly. Jao was stunned by her attitude.

"I know nothing about the actions of the empress, nothing about her reasons. I have had no contact at all with the palace except to make up remedies which you send regularly," Jao answered, a red flush on her cheeks.

The nun noticed this and spoke more gently. "You must take this letter to the abbess at once. An imperial summons takes precedence over everything else." Nun Hsu was stiff with disappointment. She did not wish to lose Jao.

When Jao met the abbess a little later, she looked into the older woman's penetrating eyes and bravely held her own. Nevertheless, she reddened.

"What is behind this?" the abbess asked sternly.

"I don't know," Jao answered.

"You don't know or you aren't saying?" the abbess persisted.

"I can only guess. . . ." Jao replied, trembling with strain.

"The emperor surprised us the other day by honoring you above the other palace ladies—by speaking to you so flatteringly in front of all the guests. He made you conspicuous. Why?"

"I don't know," Jao returned, in such a low voice that she could hardly be heard.

The nun looked at her speculatively. "You don't know, I accept that," she said at last, "but you can tell me what you think about it and whether his attention made you feel good or bad."

"I didn't want him to recognize me—the way I look now, the way I am now. And I was shocked. But I was thrilled too. I am sorry that I am such a bad nun to be thrilled, but . . . there it is."

"Thank you for being frank. Now tell me what your relationship was with him before—when you were Taitsung's concubine."

Jao's eyes flew to the nun's face. "There was nothing improper. I knew him when he was a little boy, when he missed his mother. I helped Fang Fei take care of both Jer and Bixon. And he was often in his father's sickroom when I was in attendance."

"At any time, did you fall in love with him?" the older nun asked bluntly.

Jao looked directly into her eyes. "No," she said briefly, and there was something in her tone that convinced the abbess that there had been no incestuous relationship.

The abbess sighed. "But he must hold you in high regard one way or another, that's obvious. It is not a good thing. You are older than he and will be blamed for seducing him if it gets to be known that there is something between you two. How much older?"

Jao paused. "I'm not sure."

"He is now in his twenty-second year," the nun said.

"And I am in my twenty-fifth," Jao answered. "Have you ever heard of emperors taking concubines as old as I am? I am past it—even if I were not a nun! And even if I were still beautiful with all my hair," Jao cried heatedly.

The abbess looked at her thoughtfully. "Why are you so upset? Do you have regrets about being in a convent, about being one of us? You have settled in well and are respected here, you know. Do you want to leave?"

Jao hesitated. "No, I don't want to leave you. Or Nun Hsu. Or Nun Lin. Or this quiet, lovely place. But I still miss the excitement of the palace, and the companionship of others there, and the feeling of being in the midst of imperial activities outside of my own petty life!"

"You are thinking of worldly affairs and the shallow lives of palace people. The life of the spirit is not to be found in the palace."

"I know," Jao responded, feeling torn. "I know, really I do. I'm not a young girl anymore and I know what life is. I have found that I am like Nun Lin, practical and a bit rowdy. I am like Nun Hsu, careful, precise, reliable, and also that I am intelligent like her. I am a little like you too—ambitious for the role of leader and willing to accept the discipline required to take on that role."

The abbess was startled. "You know yourself? Tell me then where you think your duty lies, where you feel you could lead the best life."

Jao remained silent a long time. The sounds of women at the well came in from a distance. The incense in the abbess's room drifted upward. The nun remained still, her eyes closed, waiting quietly.

"I am useful here and I like the demands of the pharmacy. I am learning something new every day and I am respected more and more. I confess it. I feel satisfied in my yearning to be somebody. I feel fulfilled, I feel needed."

"Would the thought that you might one day take my place as abbess tempt you to stay with us?" the abbess asked, her eyes hooded.

It was Jao's turn to be startled. "To be truthful, I think it would."

The abbess looked at the letter in her hand. "You can politely refuse this invitation, you know," she said. The silence that fell between them when she said this was heavy with their thoughts. At last it was broken by the abbess. "I want you to meditate on this matter all night tonight. Sit in the lotus position for clear perception. See me again in the morning. Will you?"

Jao bowed humbly and withdrew. She did what was asked of her.

When she reported again in the morning, heavy-eyed and limp with exhaustion, she said at once, "I will stay. I feel safe here."

"I'd like you to wait three days before you reply to the empress. I will make inquiries about what the situation is in the palace and then I will call you in again."

Jao bowed and left her presence.

The abbess had many friends among the middle officials in the court, men who carried the real weight of administration. What she found out from them made her thoughtful. She was unusually serious, even troubled, when she confronted Jao again.

"Things are very much awry at court. A clique of powerful old ministers are taking things into their own hands and making a puppet of Kaotsung. This would not be so bad, since they are old and the emperor is learning his job—if it were not for the interference of the empress and her powerful Liu family. There is also friction between the empress and the favorite concubine, Hsiao. Hsiao is apparently both likable and beautiful, and is also mother of several of Kaotsung's children. Opinion is that the empress heard about Kaotsung's attention to you the other day and has leaped at the chance to bring you into her court and reduce Hsiao's influence."

Jao's eyes leapt to the abbess's face. The nun's expression told nothing. "How does all this affect me?" she hazarded.

"I have thought matters over long and carefully," the nun answered. "I know what my conclusion is, but I cannot steer you in any direction at this point because whatever you do is going to cost you much suffering as well as achievement—because you cannot help but achieve. You must meditate until you know within yourself what you must do."

"But I already said that I would stay here," Jao said.

"You said that you would stay here because you felt safe and because you felt fulfilled at being needed," the nun corrected. "Now that you know the needs of the palace, you must give me your considered answer again. I do not want a nun here who has deeply divided loyalties."

Jao looked troubled. There seemed to be nothing more to be said, so she withdrew. After several sessions with her superiors, she faced the abbess again.

"I will be plain," she said. "I am probably one of the few people in China who is close enough to Kaotsung to help him privately." She paused, hesitant to continue. The abbess only nodded, and did not interrupt.

"I know that," Jao continued. "And I know that I could possibly succeed and . . . and . . . change things at court. You have called my attention to my craving for leading roles—for power perhaps—and my ambition for roles where my skills are needed. Finally, my wanting to be safe in a convent may not be very admirable. I don't know. All I know is that I have thought about this until I can think no more. All I can now say is that I am willing to go. If my superiors agree."

The nun's face was carefully expressionless. "This peaceful empire of ours, this House of Tang, this harmonious government, these are worth more than you or I or a thousand like us," she said enigmatically. "You will always have my friendship—and the friendship of all of us—whatever you do."

Jao bowed humbly and withdrew. She carefully penned her reply to Empress Wang: she would return after her hair had grown three inches, six months hence, at the time of the winter solstice.

The closed sedan chair waited in the middle of the convent forecourt with its bearers squatting beside it. The eunuch in charge of the escort waited at a distance in his own chair. Cries of hawkers from over the wall penetrated the temple precincts, informing householders of hot food for sale. A side door opened with a squeak of unoiled hinges and a group of nuns crowded through, followed by the abbess silently steering Jao before her. Some of Jao's former housemates were there as well. Peony was scowling, but Cloud was radiant. The abbess stopped by the sedan chair and pressed her palms together in farewell. Chief of pharmacy Hsu and head of the gardens Lin, their faces stern, did likewise. The other nuns, bunching together, made the *anjali* salute of farewell, some with tears in their eyes.

The abbess stepped back, and the eunuch Ho seated Jao inside her chair, fastening the curtain to close her in. The bearers hitched into their harnesses. The chair lifted and paused as Eunuch Ho went ahead through the central gate, now open especially for them. Then Jao felt her chair move forward and heard the doors close behind her. I'm leaving for the last time, she told herself. No more freedom to come and go as a humble person . . .

She settled cross-legged on her cushion. She was saddened to leave the nuns and the work she had loved, and wondered if she had made the right decision. Her fate was to live in turmoil rather than in tranquility, she thought somberly. It was now her karma to live out her life within palace walls. Imprisoned? Or free to grasp the best that life could possibly offer a woman? I am now yin, she told herself. I could move into yang, a very, very exhilarating possibility.

A series of jolts told Jao that her chair was in the midst of the holiday crowds in the main street. She peered through the side curtain to watch, and her depression gradually lifted. Everywhere the street signs, the lanterns, the booths, the passersby dressed in their best clothes—so close that she could touch them—advertised the season with all its diversions. The vitality of the city excited her, and she bounced awkwardly as she strained to see. The bearers grunted while steadying the chair, making Jao laugh. Soon their hearty guffaws joined her chuckles.

The winter sun lowered in the western sky, and the day closed in early, bringing a cold wind and the promise of frost. People began to hurry, even the bearers, to get under shelter. This was like her first trip through Changan. The same cold weather, same destination, same big changes ahead of her, same nervous excitement—and the same me, she thought, only thirteen years older. I'm less frightened in one way, more frightened in another. Frightened—terrified really—of only one thing, other women. How will I manage both an empress and the favorite concubine? Jao thrust her cold fingers under her arms to warm them. If she just listened, nodded her head and remained silent . . . if she just said little and smiled a lot . . . if, if, if . . .

They halted at the northeast gate of the palace, and Eunuch Ho's chairman thumped on it. A shivering guard whose mates were gathered around a bonfire in the middle of the court tugged one panel open just wide enough to let them through. Ho directed the chairs across the yard, through the adjoining courts and narrow passageways and past the compound of the four chief concubines. Jao threw aside her curtain when her chair passed the former residence of Fang Fei, where so many hours of her first years in the harem had been spent: with Bixon who had died so young; with young Jer, now emperor; with Princess Wencheng now empress in Tibet; with plump, adorable Fang Fei who had herself died too soon.

Fang Fei didn't want to live, Jao thought, realizing that she herself could have easily let go had it not been for the abrasive way the abbess dealt with her. Jao shrugged when she recalled how heartless she had thought the abbess at the time, and how shallow she herself had been. Now she was able to work, and to receive consolation from it. She was no longer vulnerable to every wind that blew.

Her chair was set down with a jolt. She was in the compound of the empress. Taking out her bronze mirror, she patted her three-inch locks into place. Hands reached in to pull her out of her cushions. The cold wind swept through the courtyard, and Jao shivered as she waited impatiently behind the eunuch to be admitted. After a prolonged delay, a harried-looking maid ushered them into a small lobby and scratched on another door, which opened at once. They then stepped into a hot room brightly lit by a dozen lanterns. It was filled with palace ladies, and in their midst, Empress Wang stood waiting expectantly, her pale face round with a smile.

"Your Majesty," the eunuch greeted, kowtowing. "We are here."

"Empress Wang, my lady!" Jao murmured, kneeling, her hands hidden respectfully in her sleeves. The empress was tall for a Chinese woman, tall and thin and angular. Her head was too small for her body, and her face wore a discontented look. She gave the impression of being unfinished as a mature person. No presence, Jao thought.

"You are welcome to my court, to be sure," the empress chirped. "The emperor and I are delighted to have you back in the palace and in our household. Despite your age, you still look young and have your looks. This pleases me. Come closer to the fire, you are cold. Your nose is red and I see that your hair has grown out enough so that you can face the palace without, er . . . embarrassment. Well, it's enough, I should hope, to please the one and only man of our lives!"

She giggled coyly, causing both Jao and Ho to drop their eyes. Unaware of any gaucherie, the empress turned to Ho. "You may go now. Have Jao's baggage put into the end room of the last court—the storeroom, which has been vacated for her."

"There is no baggage," Ho said austerely.

Dear me, Jao thought, painfully aware of her change in status from nun to palace lady. "Empress Wang," she said quickly, bowing her head. "I have been wearing only nun's clothes these past years, and I have left them all behind. I have no palace clothes yet."

The empress giggled again, because the situation was beyond her. "Of course! It would look strange for me to have an attendant dressed like a nun! Of course it would not do. By tomorrow we shall dress you with everyone's castoffs . . . at least at first! It really will be fun, won't it? Ho! Why are you still here? You may go!"

The eunuch, disconcerted by the curt dismissal and by the nonappearance of the customary red envelope of thanks, backed out of her presence. He noted, however, Jao's grateful look.

There was a rustle from the attendants when he left, and an uncomfortable silence while the empress collected her wits.

"Well," she said, trying to cover the awkwardness of having an important addition to her household with nothing but the rough garments in which she stood. "That's that."

Jao could not suppress a smile. "This is all exactly the way it was when I first entered the palace. I had nothing to wear then—I was thirteen years old—because my baggage did not arrive when I did. That time it was worse."

The ladies-in-waiting, who were impeccably dressed, pricked up their ears. Even Empress Wang looked interested. "What did you do?" she asked.

"It was New Year's Eve, and all of us tsairen were obliged to appear in our best clothes, so our warden, a giant of a woman, stole some beautiful things for me, and no one seemed to be the wiser." A ripple of laughter greeted this.

"Tell us more," the empress commanded, happy to be diverted.

Jao did as she was bid, feeling that she was being accepted by her new colleagues as well as by the empress. She means well, but is abrupt, Jao consoled herself. She chattered on with funny stories from the past, dispelling tension as best as she could. It was hard adapting to the trivialities of palace life after the convent.

She recognized two of the women. They had been in the palace a long time in minor capacities. She had spoken to them cordially, and they had responded cautiously. Everytime she encountered their eyes, they were looking with frowning absorption at her telltale hair. Finding me unacceptable, I suppose, Jao thought dispiritedly. The younger women, on the other hand, after a few whispers and giggles, seemed to forget her peculiarity and on the whole accepted Jao as the empress had—a welcome if undistinguished addition to their group.

The empress had had the long *kang* torn out and replaced with a newly fashionable high matrimonial bed. There were also many new western-style chairs lined up in pairs against the wall. She pointed to them and raised her voice, recovering the ladies' attention.

"Now I want you all to try these new chairs. See how you like to be up off the floor. I will take this central chair, which is a throne." She hitched herself up into an armchair slightly higher than the others. With much giggling, the ladies cautiously edged onto their seats, feet dangling.

Suddenly the empress clapped her hands in consternation. "These chairs were made for men. They don't belong in a woman's apartment. I am embarrassed. Someone has made a mistake. I will have to chastise the chief eunuch."

"Is he the one in charge of furnishings?" one of the ladies asked, curling her feet up under her on the wide seat. "There, that feels better." The other ladies followed her example amid grunts and laughter. "You'll have to appoint one of us to find out who is responsible for these male chairs," she ventured, and was greeted with good-natured laughs.

"Yes," the empress said. "Jao is the last one to join us, so she must."

Amused and curious about what the newcomer would do, everyone looked at Jao. She was about to demur on the grounds of ignorance about the whole business, as she would have in the convent, but thought better of it. She said lightly, "A pleasure. It gives me an auspicious beginning." Frantically, she cast about in her mind to recall how such things were cared for in the past and how to find out who was in charge now.

"Time for small food," Empress Wang said, bringing the attention back to herself again. She hit her gong and the first drinks and snacks of the evening were brought in. The ladies paired off so that those who wanted to be together could share a wall table between their two chairs. Jao chose a young woman with an appealing sparkle in her eye and a flouncing way of settling down.

"I am Yang Hua." She smiled. "I am glad you are here, it makes a change to have someone like you to enliven things. It's pretty dismal sometimes."

Jao glanced at her in surprise.

"I don't mind telling you. Lady Liu, the mother, keeps us all jumping. You will have to be very careful not to displease her."

"Thank you for your advice." Yang Hua reminded Jao of Mulberry, so she found it easy to plunge into talk with the friendly girl, just as she had once done with the lonely tsairen.

Conversing in a relaxed way, she surveyed her surroundings. The hall itself was familiar from the days that Fang Fei had occupied it. It had been sparsely furnished then, with only the low *kang*, a few low tables, some stoneware stools, and one large, colorful carpet. It had been a restful room and a gracious one. Now it was crammed with cabinets full of painted lacquerware and gold-inlaid silverware. The walls were hung with embroidered hangings, with paintings of various protecting gods of the house, and with the new mountain-water landscapes. Altars to Kuanyin and the house gods dominated one area. Chairs and tables were abundant, and on the floor, a multitude of small rugs were scattered. Jao liked it better before.

The evening dragged on. Jao listened to the chatter, meeting the glances cast in her direction with smiling eyes and nods. She felt herself relaxing slightly. The ladies were amiable but, fatigued, were falling silent. Lady Wang began to dismiss them one by one. Jao waited for permission to retire also, but it did not come. She remembered the abbess's advice on the empress—that the best tactic for her was to make no requests and no complaints—so she did not ask to be allowed to go. Finally, there was no one else in the room. The empress took up her embroidery, took a few stitches, and put it down again.

"I lived in the eastern palace of the crown prince for eight years before he became emperor," she said. "During those years, you were in the entourage of Emperor Taitsung, and I heard about you, how good an attendant you were, standing against the wall for many hours daily, holding towels, always ready for toilet service. That will be your role here. Officially you are only a Grade Five tsairen still, but your role as first-class attendant entitles you to respect in spite of your low rank. You will be happy here."

She smirked. Jao's face remained expressionless while her world seemed to her to be crashing around her feet. Did the empress imagine that mindless service of this kind in the household of a mere empress was in any way comparable to the role that she, Jao, had played in the great emperor's court? Or that this role equaled in any way the responsibilities she had carried in the convent?

She froze in silence. Embers fell in the charcoal brazier at the empress's feet, lovebirds cheeped sleepily under their covers, and the minutes stole slowly by.

"The hour of the beginning of the day of winter solstice is here," the empress remarked, "so it is time for me to retire."

She was yawning delicately when the door was flung open and a woman muffled in furs surged in, surrounded by attendants. The empress sprang up.

"Mother!" she exclaimed. "What are you doing here? At this hour? In this weather!"

Lady Liu ignored this while her ladies were divesting her of her wraps. The mother was twice as wide as her daughter, and her facial expression doubly hard. They were alike, however, in almost every other particular.

"I came to look over your new lady-in-waiting from the convent," she said. "The old emperor's girl who is supposed to be better-looking than Hsiao Fei."

"Oh," Empress Wang said. "She is here. Wu Jao . . ."

Jao bowed politely while Lady Liu shrugged off her last shawl, looking Jao up and down as she did so.

"Your hair," Lady Liu said finally, "is quite impossible. For tomorrow's events you will have to wear a cap or turban until it is long enough to dress properly."

"I have a circlet that the emperor Taitsung gave me—" Jao began.

"No," Lady Liu said.

"No?" Jao asked doubtfully, and looked at Empress Wang for guidance.

"No. Too forward for a nobody. You should wear only a widow's band under a simple headdress," Lady Liu said.

"I will take care of that tomorrow," the empress put in hastily, "when I can get together a wardrobe for her. She has nothing now."

Lady Liu was diverted. She stared.

"Indeed," she said. Then she turned away, dismissing Jao. She had satisfied herself that the woman was of little account. "Well, I have more important things to do. I am meeting with the chief of palace ceremonies to give instructions about tomorrow's festivities. Here you," she called to her servants, "bring my cloaks and open the door."

"I hope that Mother did not give offense to the chief of ceremonies," the empress murmured when the door closed behind her parent. She was finding it difficult to fulfill her duties as empress, and was developing a tic as a result. It had been so much easier when Kaotsung was only a crown prince.

After Lady Liu had gone, silence fell upon the room while the empress collected her wits.

"Wu Jao," she began, clearing her throat, "the emperor will not come tonight. He is fasting for tomorrow's ceremony . . . and keeping away from women as required," she added, simpering. "But tomorrow night he will be free, and we are having a gathering which you will be expected to attend. Hsiao Fei will be here also." The empress made a face. "Oh, and tomorrow morning we must all go to the throne hall in our best clothes . . . and just when will I have time to get clothes for you? What a nuisance."

"Yes," Jao said. "I beg your pardon for the trouble I am causing."

Lady Wang scrutinized her. "Yes," she repeated. "Yes, it is a nuisance, but we can find something secondhand. Not mine, of course, mine are too elaborate."

"I've done that before too. I mean I've worn secondhand clothes before. Anything that your ladies have that you think is suitable, I'll wear. With thanks."

Lady Wang's face cleared. "That's all right, then. I'll have someone look through the discarded garments that would have been given away to the maids." She hit her gong. When a tired-looking servitor appeared, the empress gave him her orders. He looked Jao over with disfavor but thawed when his eyes met her appealing look.

"At once," he said, and left.

Jao waited, expecting to be dismissed.

"Wait here until he comes back," the empress ordered, yawning widely while calling her maids to put her to bed. "Just wait here," she repeated as she drifted out of the room.

The first watch was calling the hour when the eunuch returned with some garments hanging over his arm. His eyes were dead with fatigue, but he brightened when Jao jumped up eagerly to meet him. He handed the clothes to her.

"I don't know—" he began uncertainly, but Jao cut him off with a little shriek of delight.

"Ruby red! Of the finest Suchow silk! A repeat of the red outfit I wore at New Year's when I first came. It will suit me perfectly!" She held out the tunic and the pleated skirt to match, plain and tailored and soft, the fine silk falling into shape without ironing.

"It has no embroidery or hand-painted panels," the eunuch began, "but it was the only unsoiled garment in the heap."

"Thank you! It could not be better," Jao exclaimed cheerfully as she handed him a small red-wrapped gift of money. She had about a dozen such packets in a pocket in her skirt, put there before she left the convent. The eunuch looked amazed, his fatigue gone.

"Th-Thank you, my lady," he murmured, embarrassed but pleased.

"And now, can you advise me about something?" Jao asked. "The empress never dismissed me. Am I supposed to stay here all night?"

He paused on his way to the door. "I should just retire to my room if I were you," he said.

"I don't know where it is," she answered.

The eunuch halted abruptly and a flash of understanding passed through his eyes. "Then she probably means for you to wait here. It's not so bad here, and it is warm. I'll bring you a quilt."

The next morning Empress Wang sent a maid to conduct Jao to her room in a distant hall. The former storeroom was small, unheated, and unlighted. It was clean, however, with a bed in one corner supplied with quilt and sand pillow.

"I am to stay with you and dress you in whatever was found and see that you are presentable," said the maid shyly. "But first, I'll order in a brazier to warm you. My name is Meimei."

Jao nodded cheerfully. She had been much refreshed by her sleep on the floor of the hall and not at all daunted by the slight that was intended. She was confident that her new clothes were adequate to the occasion and that she was also. When the gong sounded for assembly, she was ready.

"You look just lovely," Meimei said, surveying her speculatively. "No jewelry, no adornment, just this luminous silk and your black eyebrows and your red mouth. Oh, and the way you stand—like a princess. You don't need anything more, you really don't. Your hair and your uncovered head won't do, though. I must find something. . . ."

She dashed out of the room, and in a short time reappeared with a gold-starred gauze cap which she fixed on Jao's head, clucking and nodding as she worked.

"Now go," she said finally, giving Jao a little push. "You are the equal of Hsiao Fei in spite of all her jewelry."

"But," Jao said, resisting, "the cap, whose is it?"

The maid laughed somewhat nervously. "It belongs to the empress, but she doesn't know it."

"Then I can't—" Jao began.

"Yes, you can. The cap is exactly right, a perfect match, and she'll never know. Besides, I was ordered to make you look as beautiful as Hsiao Fei, even though I was given nothing to do it with. Lucky for me that you look so perfect anyway."

Jao's smile lit her face. "Thank you," she said simply. "This is a little something for you," she added, and slipped another red-wrapped packet into the girl's hand. Again it was the right gesture. The maid was surprised and immoderately pleased. Not many small rewards around this palace, Jao said to herself thoughtfully while the maid leaped to help her put on her outdoor mantle from the convent.

An hour later Jao stood with the empress's ladies behind the screens in the throne hall, watching the notables take their places by rank on the dais. She remembered the great celebration that Emperor Taitsung had organized thirteen years before, realizing that this was a poor show in comparison. The top officials, all elderly men, were grandly dressed, but they shuffled to their places to the sound of slow and muted music. The Elite Guard marched in great array but without fanfare, and then to the sound of conches and woodwinds came the slender and youthful Kaotsung, overshadowed by the bulky figure of his uncle, Archduke Changsun Wuji, in his gorgeous robes. The other great ministers, all in full dress, came next: anxious, obsequious Chu; silent, wily Yu; and uncompromising Han. They formed a central knot on the platform, closely clustered around the young emperor.

After an interval came Archduke Li Chi, also in full regalia, paced by a martial drumbeat that began the moment he entered the hall. Heads immediately began to turn. He stood to one side on the dais and gazed out over the heads of the assembled court. As if he were looking for some special person, realizing that a Taitsung would never again enrich any gathering, Jao thought. Li Chi had been Taitsung's most reliable officer, possibly the most loyal that the great man had ever had. Jao felt drawn to him.

She turned her attention to the emperor. He was eclipsed by those powerful men around him, she realized, appalled. He wore his robe and his emperor's hat with dignity, but looked like a nonentity. Deeply concerned, Jao saw him going through his ritual moves without hesitation and without prompting. He was doing his best, but it didn't show, she decided, feeling both pride and depression.

Once the ceremony was over, the hall emptied quickly. It was no longer heated as it had been in Taitsung's day. Jao dutifully followed the empress into her warm establishment, where she stood over the braziers with the others. Lady Liu and her brother, the prime minister, were already there directing the servants. Empress Wang gave a quick glance at the four large tables in the reception hall and drew her mother and uncle into a small adjoining study.

"Four tables! Forty places? Why?"

"Yes," Lady Liu responded, "there are more guests than you expected, but your uncle felt that some of the loyal lower-ranking officials who agree with his policies should be included."

"Exactly how many?" the empress asked. "The emperor did not tell me about this."

"He doesn't know. It is not his concern. It is a private family party, not state business."

The empress frowned. "Then who is coming here tonight?" she asked sharply. "I have plans for the evening. For you Elders, singers to entertain you. We younger ones will use the next room and we will have the dancers. That will take care of everyone satisfactorily."

"It won't do," Lady Liu said. "The Elders will feel slighted if the young ones enjoy themselves elsewhere. No. Besides, we require the presence of the emperor. Did you expect to take him off with you 'younger ones'?"

"The emperor is the center of our group, the main attraction. He needs to be with us young ones too. How can you plan something for him that will spoil his evening?" exclaimed the empress angrily. Her tic flared up and her head shook.

"Temper!" Lady Liu exclaimed coldly. "You forget yourself. This is a state occasion. It is his duty. He must make more of an effort to be sociable and agreeable—especially to the Elders who govern the country. Your uncle, who is in a position to enforce his will, expects him to do better, and insists on your being on your best behavior as well."

"But this is a family night, not a state occasion, as you just pointed out," the empress protested. Her cheeks were flaming. "The emperor has been fasting, unlike the Elders, and he is eager to put off his ceremonial robes, now that the period of abstinence is over, and enjoy himself. Privately. With us . . ."

"Daughter!" Lady Liu exclaimed sharply. "You and the emperor are young and willful and self-centered. Like children. You forget that you are an empress now, no longer a concubine. You forget that you cannot just play when you feel like it. Your first duty is to set an example of docility for the people."

The empress stamped her foot. "How did the people get into this? The emperor and I are the only rulers in this palace, no one else!"

"Mind your manners!" her uncle shouted, entering from the banquet hall. "This is an important occasion. The whole privy council will be here tonight, all of Taitsung's best men who are still living, even Archduke Li Chi, and the really powerful ministers. It is your duty as empress to be attentive to them, every one of them! Do you hear me? You must show good manners, now of all times. You are vulnerable, you know."

She did not hear his last words. "Attentive to a lot of old men?" she stormed, now thoroughly aroused. "I am the empress here. I am above them all!"

Lady Liu looked around hastily. There was no one in the room but two stony-faced attendant ladies and Jao, who did not count.

"Listen to your uncle!" she shouted.

"You have only been empress eighteen months," her uncle said fiercely. "And before that you were his number-one concubine for eight years, but to what avail? You still have no son, no heir to the throne!"

The empress flushed a fiery red and her shoulders sagged. Her tic had flared again. She exchanged a long look with her mother. A thrush chirped sleepily in its jeweled cage. Chopsticks of gold clicked upon their holders as the servants finished setting the tables in the next room. No one spoke. Suddenly, a nervous servant entered to report the arrival of the first guest, and stumbled against the empress.

Empress Wang swung on the servant. "Clumsy slave!" she said hoarsely. "Leave. Get out, you idiot!" she continued, kicking the cowering maid. Her mother and uncle stood watching, and the two attendants flattened themselves against the wall, pretending not to notice. Jao sprang forward as the empress kicked the girl in the stomach.

"Here, let me get her out of your sight," Jao cried, seizing the girl's arms and hastily pulling her out of the room through a back entrance.

From the next room came sounds of entering guests stamping the snow off their feet and shedding their cloaks. After handing the unfortunate maid to a eunuch, Jao returned to her duties in the banquet room. There she found the empress standing rigidly in front of the door, flanked by her mother and uncle, bowing formally and greeting guests as if nothing unusual had taken place. The empress saw Jao enter and gestured for her to come forward.

"You will be in attendance tonight," she ordered. "There are eight of my ladies here, two of you for each table. You are to stand behind the tables and personally see to it that everyone is served whatever he wants throughout the evening. This is the order of my uncle, the prime minister."

The ladies-in-waiting bowed, their faces expressionless while they took their places. Jao glanced at the chief steward, and he pointed to a table in the northeast corner. She had taken a position behind it when the emperor entered and was shown to that table by the head steward himself, who came forward to serve him. The young emperor smiled his thanks, and Jao kept her eyes lowered, pretending not to notice Lady Liu's hand waving to her to move. Jao was well-satisfied to be so near

Kaotsung and to be able to look him over at leisure. He seemed much older, thinner, and without presence, she thought in dismay.

Cries of greeting filled the room while the guests were being seated, nine at each table, with the Lius and the empress and emperor separated and distributed to each of the four tables. Changsun Wuji was seated at the northwest table so that he was looking south, a seat of honor normally reserved for the emperor. To his left were Prime Minister Liu and the two vice-ministers of the prestigious Department of State Affairs. The archduke, Li Chi, had an honorable seat at the southeast table. He was a handsome man in his prime, finely dressed, high-ranking, but all the same it was clear that he was not one of the palace inner circle. Women took to him on sight, however, and Madame Liu was no exception. She had arranged to sit next to him, and proceeded to make the most of it. In general, seating arrangements were pleasing to the rest of the guests as well, and the banquet continued well beyond the usual retiring hour.

Twelve courses followed one another in an unhurried way. Then the toasts began. By this time the merriment drowned out the toasts. Kaotsung touched his lips to his goblet in acknowledging all of them, but drank little. Suddenly, Jao met his gaze. Kaotsung looked around deliberately, and when he saw that he was unobserved, raised his glass forehead high. He touched it to his lips in a toast to her alone, keeping his eyes fixed on hers.

In their inebriated state and preoccupied with each other, the guests revealed their disregard for their emperor. Kaotsung's salute directed at Jao was personal and passionate, bold and meaningful. It went unnoticed by all. Kaotsung held his look for a long moment, staring steadily over the rim of his cup.

Jao felt herself flushing and her breathing became shallow. How daring, that he had singled her out under the noses of the empress and all the great ones of the court! How audacious and defiant! It was exhilarating and superb. Just as deliberately as he had done, Jao picked up a goblet from the table in front of her and touched her lips to its rim, then raised it to her eyes in return.

The party ground to a halt when the guests realized that they had reached their limits and needed their beds. Changsun stood up to leave, not waiting for a signal from the emperor as he should have done. Hurriedly Minister Liu stood also, spilling his wine in his haste. Li Chi was one of the few who looked as if he were far from finished, but he rose with the rest. His red mustaches were still fiercely in place and his whiskers jutted jauntily in well-groomed style as he pushed his way to the emperor's table to take his leave. He bowed in his usual formal way, in stark contrast to the others, who had merely slapped Kaotsung on the back in bidding him good night.

Kaotsung put out his hand and caught Li Chi's. "I am glad you saw fit to attend this party," he said cryptically.

A twinkle appeared in Li Chi's eyes, revealing his understanding. "Pleasure. A privilege and a pleasure," he said. "You look so much like your father that it has done me good to see you. You are getting more like him every day."

Kaotsung flushed. Nothing could have pleased him more. He kept Li Chi's great paw in his and impulsively turned and left the hall with him.

The room cleared rapidly after that. Even the Lius left without a backward glance, taking the empress with them. Jao emerged from her daze long enough to inquire of her companion, "What do we do now?"

"Just go," the other said. "I for one will fall on my face if I have to stay on my feet another moment."

Jao nodded her thanks. The servants were whisking the tables away, extinguishing the candles and clearing the remains of the party. She hurried out with them, and once outside, ran rapidly through the mists in the silent courtyards, into the comfort and privacy of her own cubbyhole.

CHAPTER ELEVEN

The next day the empress rose at noon and immediately summoned her attendants to help her dress for her afternoon reception. At intervals during the brief afternoon, the four Fei arrived with their royal children. Each group was welcomed vivaciously by the empress, even Hsiao Fei, who was the last to come. The empress greeted her with a little shriek of welcome and beckoned to Jao.

"Come, Wu Jao, I want to present you to an important lady, Hsiao Liangdi. And to the other three Fei: Hsu Fei, Hsueh Fei, and Tsui Fei." Jao gave each an elaborate, graceful bow. Stealing a curious look at Hsiao Fei, she saw a charming and attractive woman, little and plump and rosy, exuding her enjoyment of life. There could hardly be a greater contrast to the empress, so much so that it was comic. Few in the palace, however, dared to joke about it.

"Wu Jao is a Grade Five tsairen, as she was in Taitsung's day," the empress explained. "I have persuaded her to come out of . . . retirement to join my entourage and serve me. Naturally, she is grateful and happy to be here."

The eyes of all four Fei swept to Jao in patronizing curiosity.

I'm a freak, Jao thought, with my hair like this and my convent life. Nevertheless, she smiled brightly, and at least three of the Fei decided that she was harmless, an older woman past her prime and a bit stupid perhaps.

The empress lost no time in reclaiming attention. "The emperor will soon join us, and then we'll all be cozy," she warbled, and all heads turned back toward her. They were aware of the excitement in her voice, and the artificiality, and wondered what she was planning. Jao's eyes met

Hsiao's and both women smiled politely. Hsiao does not know why Wang has brought me here, Jao thought, and I'm not entirely sure either. She read a similar message in Hsiao's large, slightly protuberant eyes and saw her wary look.

The children jostled one another while the maids were seating them, and this drew Hsiao's attention. Her expression changed to a fond smile as she patted her son. "Sujay," she cooed, stroking his handsome black head. He was a plump boy of seven, aware of his status as a possible crown prince and of his rights as a male. He pulled away and her two small daughters instantly cuddled up to her.

"I Yang and Kao An, my babies," she cooed, hugging them to her as her eyes challenged the childless empress.

"Come here, Chung, and let me put this new belt on you," the empress ordered, rising to the challenge. An older boy, Kaotsung's first son, came forward to bow to her, followed by two smaller boys who were nudged on by their nurses. The smaller boys' mothers were not present, as they were low-ranking concubines. The empress fastened a jeweled belt on Chung. She was adopting the boy as her son, who would thus be eligible to be crown prince. She then waved all the children to the low table, which had been set with sesame cakes, barley candy, and individual gifts.

"Four sons of the emperor," Hsiao Fei whispered in Jao's ear, "and only my son Sujay is high enough in rank to be the crown prince. The empress has no son," she added pointedly while she stroked her boy's hair. He again dodged away.

Jao did not know how to reply. She could not say, "Yes, it is a problem for the succession because the empress has no son," or "No, it is not a problem because you have a son." She just smiled and quickly moved to the children's table to help there.

Kaotsung entered so quietly that she did not realize he was there until the empress raised her voice in excited greeting. The children scrambled to their feet to bow, their mouths full and their teeth stuck together with taffy. Kaotsung, amused, joined them at their table and made them all laugh by seating himself on one of their low chairs. He put on a bib, and this evoked more giggles.

The empress monitored the scene, and as soon as the young ones had finished eating, called a eunuch to usher them out. The emperor wished to have them with him for a while longer, but the empress wanted to keep to her schedule, so the emperor's children were all obliged to leave. After the last child had been gathered up and wrapped against the cold, the servants lit the lamps and brought in trays of refreshments for the adults. Kaotsung, meanwhile, joined his ladies, and the room filled with their laughter and delighted sallies as they gathered around him. He was enjoying himself greatly.

The empress soon put a stop to the bantering, which she was not good at herself. She struck her gong and announced that she planned to bring in entertainers for their amusement, then signaled for the musicians to enter and begin to play. When the program was over, she indicated to her guests that the party was over. She was being every inch an empress, according to her ideas of the role, but she frustrated others at each turn.

The Fei, bored now, but still polite, bowed and departed, except for Hsiao, who readied herself to leave with the emperor.

Jao stood uncertainly beside the door, observing the graceless behavior of the empress and the emperor's strained impatience. Jao was dressed in the same red gown that had now seen three palace functions, and she no longer felt beautiful in it. Kaotsung had not looked in her direction once during the party, and this had shaken her. He playfully tweaked Hsiao's ear while his furs were draped over him by his attendant, bowed to the empress, and made for the door.

"You will escort the emperor with a light, Wu Jao," the empress directed in a loud voice.

Jao jumped nervously. Kaotsung turned to look at her, then nodded agreeably before he went out. A muffled gasp escaped Hsiao. Jao looked inquiringly at Empress Wang, who had a doltish look of satisfaction on her face as she stared at the humiliated Hsiao. The maid Meimei wrapped a shawl around Jao's shoulders and ushered her through the door after the emperor. All were aware that something momentous in harem life had occurred, but no one offered a word or made a sound.

The night was windless and bitingly cold. There was no moon, but the dark sky was sparkling with its millions of stars. Guards with flares gathered around the emperor and Jao, escorting them through the intricate passageways. Except for the hollow thuds of footsteps and the clinking of metal weapons, the silence was unbroken. At the entrance to the emperor's residence, the guards halted, leaving Jao and the emperor to enter the imperial hall alone.

Once inside, Kaotsung threw off his furs and turned to Jao, picking up a lock of her three-inch hair between thumb and forefinger. He then pretended to scrutinize it.

"New style?" he asked. "Boyish—like a half-grown lad. To see you at a distance, no one would know that you were a girl. Becoming, though, b-becoming." He stuttered in his excitement. Jao's heart was pounding. Here was the moment that she had dreamt about, although she would not openly acknowledge feelings that were so violently forbidden by the society in which she had been living. Neither she nor the abbess had spoken about this possible reason for her return to the palace, and yet it was, at bottom, the most potent of her mixed motives.

Kaotsung flung off his heavy belt and tunic and threw himself on the *kang*. Jao stood stiffly before him, more uncertain than ever of what was expected of her. The conduct of both empress and emperor was confusing her. Nobody is in charge of this court, as in Taitsung's day, she thought in dismay as she watched Kaotsung seat himself. He patted the place beside him and motioned to Jao to join him.

"Sit down, will you! Don't just stand there," he said in his former youthful way.

"Yes," Jao said, edging onto the *kang*.

"Yes," he mimicked. "All I've seen you do is stand around and say yes. Like you did last night at that damnable party for the Elders."

"Yes," she said again, sadly.

He stopped grinning to look at her closely. "Is something wrong?" he asked. "You are no longer having to hold towels as you did in my father's court."

"The same as," Jao replied.

"That doesn't make sense," he said.

"To Empress Wang it does. She expects me to serve her in the same way I served Emperor Taitsung. She does not see that there is any difference."

Kaotsung stared at her incredulously. "I don't know how Wang's dear little mind works. I never did and I never shall. Nor do I know what the Lius are up to or what they want. It's always something," he said.

"Yes," she said again, and then laughed uncertainly.

Kaotsung, relieved, joined her. "Don't use that word 'yes' to me again," he said, pulling her down beside him. "Just act yes and I will be satisfied. And don't let me talk about anything serious. I get enough of that in the daytime. I don't need it at night too!" He put his arm around her and tightened his hold.

"Happy to oblige," she said breathlessly. "See, I didn't say yes!"

A tingling sensation spread over Jao as his body pressed against hers. Slowly, she felt herself soften to his touch. It had been years since she had been so close to a man. She found that she had to concentrate to relax into his embrace. It was a delicious feeling, gradually reaching into every breath she took, breaths that became more and more shallow as she curled herself against his chest and shoulder, preparing for more ardent lovemaking to come.

Kaotsung was content to hold her close for the moment. He remembered the party he had just left and the empress's quick substitution of Jao for Hsiao and chuckled. "Wang was fast that time!" he whispered into Jao's ear, and then rubbed his cheek against hers. "I love having you here with me, having you to myself for a change. Do you realize that this is the first time we have ever been alone together?"

Jao nodded, and he tilted her chin and brushed his lips lightly over hers, then pulled her more tightly against his body and sighed. She could feel the hardness of his muscles, how rigid they were, and could sense a slight slackening in his ardor. Gently she stroked his arms and then began to dig into his muscles with searching fingers.

He breathed contentedly, then hesitated. "I care for you deeply, you know that?"

Surprised by this turn in conversation, Jao was silent. He loosened his embrace to allow her room to move.

"I care about you, too," she murmured shyly. "But I can't be certain of your feelings. There are . . . the others. I have been hoping to find some place in your heart just for me."

He turned quickly to look down at her.

How handsome he is! she thought. How much like Taitsung, only younger, younger, younger. How much I care . . . if only I can show him. If only I can find a way to please him.

Kaotsung remained silent, gazing at her steadily, his eyes full of deep emotion. His arms were so tight around her that she could scarcely breathe. She relished his mood, a mixture of adoration, lust, and contentment, but worried about how tense he was.

She blurted out, "I would like to relax the muscles in your shoulders for a little while, if you will allow me."

"My shoulders?" he asked diffidently. "That would be very pleasant, but is it so important just now?"

Jao put her fingers gently on his lips. "I understand, and yes, it is important just now." She felt sure of herself at last. He had said that he cared for her, and the words rang gloriously in her head. But her medical training told her that something must be done about his extreme tension before anything else could happen. He so obviously needed the Buddhist massage techniques that she had mastered, used for the alleviation of illness. "You would benefit just now from Nun Hsu's mild kind of massage, if you will allow me."

He sighed and gripped her again in a fierce embrace. "Well, then. I'd love it . . . I really would."

Jao giggled, unperturbed by the change in mood. It actually relieved her—they both needed time to renew their complicated relationship.

Kaotsung seemed content to hold her for a long moment, then sighed. "You have a point, go ahead, then, with your relaxing rubs. There is plenty of time for everything. We'll try your way."

They sat close, silently watching the glowing embers in the brazier at their feet while Jao gently located the sore spots and worked on them with perceptive fingers, perplexed at finding so many.

"This is the first time I have felt . . . comfortable since my father died. When he and you and Fang Fei and my own familiar servants were suddenly taken away, I was bereft. I have been alone ever since, without anybody I liked just to talk to."

He slipped out his words so softly that she barely heard them, and he leaned more heavily on her. She punched pillows around him and then continued slowly and soothingly to work on his shoulders, arms, back. No area of his body seemed to be relaxed. It's like that time in Fang Fei's house after his dog was killed, something like that anyway, Jao thought as she worked, gradually causing his tensions to lessen and his twitching to cease.

"Are you always like this? Unrelaxed?" she whispered.

"No, what do you mean? I'm more comfortable than usual. I've just been to a party with the children, and I have you back. I'm perfectly fine," he answered, every muscle tight and hard.

"Maybe," she responded. "But I can make you more so."

He continued to talk while she continued to rub. He did not seem able to stop his flow of words, but went on and on about the happy experiences of his childhood, about his mother, about Bixon, and about his horses. He then switched into an account of the gratifying days in Loyang when he and his father worked together organizing the Korean campaign, then about his heady experiences in Tingchow when he was left in charge of the campaign base.

The fires in the braziers were burning low by the time his words began to come more slowly. Finally his voice ceased and he slumped over in sleep. Jao's hands ached from her hours of massage. She drew a silk-lined fur over him and lay down beside him, her back comfortingly pushed against his. She lay quietly awake as the minutes dragged on, waiting for him to wake, waiting to discover what he needed from her next; but he never stirred. Instead, he sank deeper and deeper into sleep, and so, in time, did she.

She woke when he threw off his robe and sat up bright-eyed and rested, shouting for his valet and morning hot water. The sun lay in a streak across Taitsung's beautiful Persian rug, and Jao looked at it in amazement, realizing that she too had slept. Many hours had passed and she also felt refreshed. Kaotsung suddenly saw her and burst out laughing.

"You here? How did we manage this! Your boy's hair is standing straight up like a peacock's tail and your dress is rumpled and you look like a bundle of washing!" He swept her elatedly into his arms. "And surely more beautiful this way than ever!" He quickly set her down when his startled valet came in with the hot water.

"Eunuch Kang, my good man, please hurry with breakfast. For two. We are very hungry. And order a chair for the lady and my riding clothes. I am going hunting today. I can see that it is perfect hunting weather. Order my head groom to come at once, and send notices to my cousins, Jencheng and Jenyang, asking them to come with me."

Jao's chair arrived before the breakfast did, so she parted from the emperor with promises to come back at night, and then left, glad to escape. She had been surprised at her own shyness the night before, but excused herself on the grounds that she had been in a convent many months and needed time to adapt to a man. After all, it has been only forty-eight hours since I set foot in the palace, she reflected, her dimples flashing delightedly as she recalled his toast and the situation that she was now in because of her night of deep sleep with the emperor.

When her chair was set down beside her door, she jumped out briskly. She wanted to get to the privacy of her room before anyone could see her disheveled appearance. She was intercepted, however, by a servant of the empress informing her that she must report at once.

Jao opened her door. "I will come as soon as I am dressed," she said pleasantly.

"You are to come now," the servant insisted. "Without delay."

Jao stood with her hand on the door handle. "What is your name?" she asked.

The maid lowered her eyes. "Meilan," she mumbled.

"Thank you for your message, Meilan," Jao returned. "I will come soon, so you won't be in trouble, do you hear? But I will wash and change first."

Startled, the maid looked down at her hands. "Yes, my lady," she said.

When Jao entered the empress's living room, Wang looked up eagerly, dismissing her attendants. "All of you!" she said impatiently when two of the highest-ranking attendants did not move.

"Now, you, Wu Jao," she said when only Jao remained in the room. "How did it go? Did you please him? Do you think that he likes you as well as Hsiao Fei, enough so that he will stop seeing her? How is it going to turn out? Will the emperor cease to have any more sons by her?"

"Oh," Jao responded, suddenly enlightened as to the empress's true motives. *This* was the purpose for which she had been brought back. To prevent the births of any more boy babies to a high-ranking concubine, boys who could be in line for the throne. She stood twisting the end of her sash, repelled by the use being made of her body.

"Well?" Lady Wang cried sharply. "Speak up!"

"Your Highness," Jao began, at her wit's end about what to say. "The emperor seems well this morning. He slept well and has gone off for a day of hunting."

"Pooh," the lady interrupted. "You are quibbling. Did you please him? Answer!"

"I can't say. I think I did but I can't say. Why do you not ask him yourself?" Jao could not see herself telling the empress about Kaotsung's snores. And about the whole unromantic night. Now that she knew the full extent of what was expected of her, she did not dare expose herself as already so unsuccessful.

"I will! I will! That is the best way!" Wang exclaimed, cracking her knuckles. "You should have seen Hsiao's face when I dismissed her last night and sent you with the emperor instead! She was so shocked!"

Wang laughed immoderately, her tic activated, and Jao lowered her eyes. "Now," the empress continued when her laughs subsided. "I want you to massage my feet and hands. I have heard that is one of your convent skills. Massaging will be a part of your duties here."

Jao looked up quickly. Had the empress learned about her night with the emperor from someone? Who? But she soon realized that no one had reported because no one knew anything. The empress was merely putting another duty upon her while still seeming to be a magnanimous patron. Jao shrugged, and was secretly relieved that she had had such a good rest and was now prepared for whatever the day might bring.

She was kept busy all day. She saw Hsiao Fei from a distance and bowed, but Hsiao looked past her as if she did not exist. Jao raised her eyebrows thoughtfully—she now had a formidable enemy.

It was late before she was dismissed. She had barely gotten to bed when a summons came from the emperor. He had returned from his day of hunting and wanted her. How fortunate I am, she thought wryly, to be shuttled between their majesties. She struggled into her red gown and got into the chair that had been sent for her.

Kaotsung greeted her with a joyful cry. "I shot three pheasants myself and had a go at a leopard. I had a tremendous day! Come here, sit beside me, use your talented hands on my back . . . there, that's wonderful. Yes, I had a good day. I noticed this time that my hunting partners, several of the princes, my cousins and nephews, the ones who are sports-minded, treated me . . . well, respectfully, the way they ought. As if I had earned a right to their goodwill, if you know what I mean. I was outdoors with them all day, pelting across the steppes on fast horses and bringing down the birds with fast arrows. They seemed surprised when I did as well as they did, and it was just marvelous. It has been a long time since I have had a chance to be with people *I* choose to be with!"

"Haven't you been associating closely with the princes all along?" she asked incredulously.

"Not really. I've been kept so busy being taught how to rule—while others do the real ruling—that I haven't had much of a chance to go hunting, or rather, I should say, I haven't wanted to go. Today I did things my way. Today, all day, I did things my way!"

Kaotsung's laugh is happy, Jao thought, listening to him talk as she rubbed his sore muscles. Eventually she succumbed to sleep when he did.

The night passed as the one before had, in deep sleep for both. The next night was the same, and by week's end the emperor was not only more relaxed, but less irritable, and his well-being was obvious to all. The eunuchs exchanged knowing looks and decided that it was all because of this change in his love life. "She must have a magic way with him," they assured each other confidently. Jao, guessing at what they were thinking, privately chuckled and kept her embarrassing secret to herself.

"Tomorrow," Kaotsung said to her when they sat side by side on his *kang* eating their breakfasts one morning. "I have to go back to the privy council meetings, which I have been shirking. I hate those meetings with the Elders, but tomorrow they are going to get a surprise."

"What do you mean?" Jao interjected. "What kind of a surprise?"

"I am going to have my way about my hunting lodge. And Changsun and Liu are going to let me."

"Do you want a hunting lodge in some dangerous place that they are opposing?" Jao hazarded.

"Yes and no. It's a place that I wish to refurbish for my own use—an old lodge of my father's in the high country. Safe enough. But not to hunt birds. It's for hunting large animals."

"What kind of large animal?"

Kaotsung hesitated. "Tigers. My uncle says that he can't approve it for me, although he himself has hunted there many times with my father. As if I were a child. I won't have it. I am going after tigers in the next few weeks while their winter fur is at its best. It is great sport, and I can handle it!" His eyes shone and he threw his head back in a gesture very much like Taitsung's.

All at once he seemed like a different person, not at all a browbeaten victim of an aggressive family. Jao stared at him, so confident and handsome, and thought, I love him, but the only words that came to her lips were, "Tomorrow morning, then, I'll wake you in plenty of time!" She rose and pulled on her outdoor mantle in a daze of self-revelation.

"What is your hurry?" Kaotsung asked. "Why are you in this rush to get back to the empress?"

"It is not wise to be late," she replied, and Kaotsung's face flushed.

"We will see about that," he said ominously.

On the evening of her tenth day in the palace, Jao was too tired to wash or prepare for bed. She had spent a long day coping with temper tantrums on the parts of both the empress and her mother. They had been planning New Year's wardrobes. They had had dozens of rolls of silks and brocades unrolled before them, but nothing seemed to suit them. They had finally had the silks taken away. Jao thought longingly of one rich fabric she coveted but put the thought out of her head. She lay quietly, staring at the polished rafter overhead while the maid Meimei laid out her secondhand clothes—she was still waiting for the seamstresses to finish her new ones—and idly mused about her situation. By the time her summons came, she was rested enough to don one of the garments that Eunuch Ho had found for her, and got into her chair.

She found Kaotsung sitting pensively before a pachisi board.

"I have had to wait for you!" he greeted her. "What took you so long? I have heard about lovers who deliberately keep their partners waiting in order to increase their ardor. Is that what you are doing to me?"

Jao had her eye on the game, which she had almost forgotten how to play. "Do you need a lover for pachisi?" she exclaimed, seating herself cross-legged before the board.

"To make it doubly interesting, yes," he answered. "I win, you pay a forfeit. You win, I pay."

"Agreed, agreed!" she answered. "I seem to recall that I am better at the game than you are, and so I am already thinking of some monstrous penalty for you to pay!"

He flashed a challenging and already passionate smile and made a first move. She countered with a move of her own, with half her mind trying to think of some way to avoid being so tired all the time. Life was better in the convent, she mused as they played. Everything was so mixed up here, with no one person in command. If only Kaotsung were totally in command. She would let him win this game, to please him, she thought. No, she couldn't do that, he would know and somehow that would be a mistake.

It took a long time to play out. It soon became apparent that the favorite game of their youthful days was to be a contest of wills as well as of chance. When Kaotsung threw down his winning piece, he was exultant.

"I win," he shouted, leaping up, spilling board and counters over the floor. "Now I have you—you must do what I say. You have never kissed me. You always reserve yourself. Now do it. Kiss me without holding back!"

He stood still, arms akimbo, waiting. Jao, on tiptoes, gave him a peck on his chin.

"Oh no you don't," he said, lifting her so that he had her off the floor, his mouth on hers. Then he took her wrist and pulled her around the room, dousing candles and booting out the dogs who usually slept at the foot of his bed. "No jealous yapping dogs needed," he said into her ear. "And get out, you," he shouted at a night-duty eunuch who was discreetly hidden behind the curtain.

When the room was empty, dark, and still, and lit with only a few flickers from the charcoal embers, he spoke into her ear. "Now, it is your turn, it's up to you. . . ."

She could feel him trembling, and put her arms around his neck. His embrace tightened with a convulsive strength and a passion that she had not encountered before. Taitsung had always been gentle and leisurely.

She buried her head in his shoulder, then lifted her lips to his with abandon. This was what he wanted. He responded joyfully, and that night they had little sleep.

Jao was wakeful all night, savoring her satisfaction, radiant with contentment, heady with a sense of victory. I suppose this is what I really came back to the palace for, she mused. Nothing can ever take away from me what I have had tonight! Kaotsung feels for me something that he feels for none of the others. Surely something positive would come of this.

Just as she was dozing off, the predawn drum sounded with its prolonged ratatatat, rousing them both. Kaotsung opened his eyes and smiled when he saw Jao. "So it wasn't a dream," he murmured.

She flushed. "I hope not."

He stretched out an arm to hold her tightly, then sighed. "Do you know what I think? I think that the successful ruler is one who can sleep whenever and as long as he likes."

"Can't you manage naps while the ministers are droning on?' Jao responded, stretching cautiously. Kaotsung grinned and rubbed his cheek against hers.

"I do that too," he said. "But these dawn sessions are too much. I must go to them right now, however. There is one petition that is coming up soon that I will have to watch carefully."

Jao yawned. "The tiger hunting?"

"More dangerous. It's a petition that hasn't been drawn up yet; in fact, no one has yet thought to do so. It's about recommending Wu Jao for the post of Chaoyi."

Jao gave a little shriek and jumped to her feet, her eyes as round as moons. "But that is in Grade Two, the consorts, just below the Fei and empress. Impossible! I am only Grade Five now. It can't be done!"

"We shall see," Kaotsung said unsmilingly while his servants draped his court robe over his head and hurried him off to take his place on his throne just as the sun cleared the horizon.

Minister Liu had a long petition to offer. "All it needs," he said, rolling it up, "is your signature—a formality—and Chancellory can send it out as edict from the emperor immediately."

"I don't know what I think about it. I have not yet heard it discussed," Kaotsung said. All the ministers jerked to attention. What was the young man up to? He had never queried anything before.

The emperor's uncle, Changsun Wuji, stirred irritably. "This matter has already been thoroughly discussed and has been approved by the heads of the three departments. There is no need for delay at this point."

"But I don't know whether I approve or not," Kaotsung returned.

This annoyed Changsun even further. "You don't know what to think because you are ignorant of procedure and you have been neglecting the dawn meetings."

"I admit that I have been at fault there," Kaotsung said, "but I intend to come to every meeting after this. And I intend to make all my own decisions."

Minister Chu exchanged a sharp look with the archduke, who shrugged. "You are trying to hunt tigers with a small bow and to interfere in government matters blindfolded. Is it because of that woman?"

The way he said "that woman" was a mistake. Kaotsung flushed a fiery red.

"You are quite right, my uncle, to remind me of how shamefully I have been neglecting my duties as emperor. I will now make up for my past neglect by studying the measure that Minister Liu has just presented and by returning my opinion in a day or two for discussion, before the black seal is stamped on it. I also want to take up the other matter, about the lodge. I must order repairs at once if the place is to be ready for me in the upcoming hunting season."

Kaotsung knew that he was talking too hurriedly and too loudly. He paused. There was a strained silence in the room, every face closed and forbidding except one. Historian Hsu, who had been Kaotsung's tutor at one time, was in attendance pro tem to present a petition concerning a departmental problem. He was looking keenly interested. One friendly face at least, Kaotsung thought.

"No," Changsun said flatly.

"Who is emperor here, then? Who is entitled to say yes or no?" Kaotsung retorted unwisely. Chu sat up sternly, looking like a chipmunk defending its young while Changsun responded.

"Now then, do not raise your voice like a child of four. Your father left it to me to watch over affairs of state while you are young. That is what I am doing."

"Repairs to my father's lodge—my lodge now—what has that got to do with affairs of state? It is not your business to interfere with my tiger hunting. In fact you are not invited to join the hunts."

Chu gasped. "You are speaking to your uncle. Don't be impudent!"

Kaotsung turned to him with a mulish look on his face. "What is it to you, old man?" he said, forgetting to be courteous in his drive to assert himself.

Changsun stepped in again. "You are not going tiger hunting. It is too dangerous. I forbid it."

Kaotsung surveyed them in silence. "I am twenty-three years old and full-grown. You and my father were only eighteen when you fought a cruel war to establish this dynasty. You were not fighting tigers. You were fighting far more dangerous animals—men. So do not push me. As for this business of the lodge: you need not decide today. Tomorrow will do. So let us get on with further business now."

Changsun shook his head, causing his horsehair cap to slide over one ear. "No use to study it, my boy, just put the matter out of your head. I am not about to let you endanger yourself, and that is final."

When the meeting was over, Kaotsung strode to his quarters without his usual courteous acknowledgment of his guards' salutes. He was seething with a resentment readily apparent to his curious attendants. He trod heavily into his study, threw his fur on the floor and sent for Hsu. When that surprised official arrived, disheveled in his haste, the emperor greeted him cordially. Attendants hovered avidly within earshot, but Kaotsung briskly cleared them out while he waited for Hsu to complete his kowtows.

"Rise, rise. Sit comfortably near me on this stool. There, that is fine," Kaotsung began. "When I saw you in council meeting this morning, I was reminded of your years of service to my father and how highly he regarded you. I remembered also the time I wanted to know the history of Changan and you were the only one at court who knew anything. I imagine there are still only the two of us in the court who know anything about Changan!"

Both men laughed and immediately felt more comfortable with each other. Hsu stole a quick look at the young man. He was more adept than he expected. Gossip had it that he was stupid and weak. Hsu wondered who was putting out that sort of talk.

"I have called you here to consult you on a small matter which should be easy. Unfortunately, I don't know how to go about it. I am determined not to fail in the attempt, however."

"Like the hunting lodge fiasco?" the older man asked with a chuckle.

"Not so ridiculous, but possibly as frustrating," Kaotsung retorted cheerfully. "First, am I right in assuming that you are friendly to me? I don't just mean in a general way, I mean are you willing to risk displeasure from certain other officials by supporting my decisions?"

Hsu flashed him a wary look, but was quick enough to grasp the political possibilities of aligning himself with an emperor who was obviously not stupid and probably not weak either. He assured Kaotsung of his discretion and willingness to serve him in any way he could. He was beginning to grasp the motives behind the gossip. He knew the Elders were getting old and that the emperor was young. This opportunity to help the emperor could promote changes in the power structure which would be greatly to his own advantage.

"Do you know the Lady Wu, who has been recently released from Kanyeh Convent in order to enter the service of my empress?"

"I have heard of her," Hsu replied, pricking up his ears, "and because I had heard good things from Abbess Li, I entered her name in my file of notables as one with a future either as a metropolitan nun or as a palace lady."

"Have you, now," Kaotsung exclaimed, gratified. "Well, I'll get to the point at once then. I want her promoted. What can be done about it? Lady Wu is still enrolled in Grade Five as a tsairen. She is entitled to a higher rank."

"I shall be glad to inquire what openings there are among the women in Grades Three and Four—" Hsu began.

Kaotsung interrupted. "There is an opening in Grade Two among the Chaoyi consorts," he said bluntly.

Hsu lowered his eyes. "A promotion of three grades all at once," he said softly, "might arouse severe opposition from the current power holders."

"The Chaoyi vacancy has not yet been filled, as far as I know," the emperor answered, "although there seem to be several ambitious families inquiring about it. We should be able to deal with them."

Hsu shook his head. "No, the power holders are the archdukes and top ministers of state. The Chaoyi is a high grade, just below the empress and the Fei. The Elders are quite touchy about the position of the empress, which is understandable considering Minister Liu's stake in it. I could inquire at the correct offices to find out what the situation is. Then it would take a petition from some minister of the third grade or above, and that would have to be accepted by the privy council in order to assign the post to Lady Wu. On the other hand, you could just order it by edict."

Hsu watched the emperor while he pondered. "I have reasons for preferring the first way," Kaotsung said, wanting to avoid the subject of his own lack of power.

"I understand," Hsu said, not understanding at all. He did not know that the Elders met in private, excluding the emperor from their secret sessions. A long silence ensued.

"I called you here because I feel that you are the right one to present the petition. No one else has the reputation and standing that you have, in case any official tries to block the appointment. Believe me, you will not be doing this for nothing. I will see to it that you are generously rewarded!' Kaotsung said, springing up to pace the floor.

At this Hsu ceased to consider the disadvantages of the project and decided to sponsor it. Hsu was a famous scholar, but was known to be avaricious as well.

He bowed deeply. "I will do my best," he said. "However, I shall have to investigate Wu Jao's standing in court. How she is regarded by the other ladies, by the servants and eunuchs . . ."

"Go right ahead," Kaotsung said. He had listened to so many compliments from his empress and her ladies about Jao's good nature and helpfulness that he had no qualms of this nature. "Right now they are all singing her praises. But avoid Hsiao Fei, if you please."

"Certainly, Your Majesty, I am highly honored to be chosen to render this service, highly honored indeed," Hsu said, bowing to the floor as he backed out of the room.

The days passed. New Year's festivities came and went. Kaotsung dutifully occupied his throne during those twice monthly dawn sessions attended by all nine grades of officials. He was also punctual in showing up at the smaller privy council meetings of only the highest ministers. He decided to drop the hunting lodge request before he lost face by being forced to give it up. Consoling himself by going tiger hunting on the sly in the company of several of the more daredevil princes, he enjoyed some hair-raising experiences and acquired some fine pelts.

The spring solstice was approaching when Hsu presented the petition regarding the Wu Jao promotion. He had waited until she had been long enough in court to acquire a certain popularity not only with the titled ladies, but also with the army of servants. Hsu felt that the moment was right to introduce his recommendation. He was astute enough not to risk failure by poor timing.

He arranged to have himself scheduled to attend a privy council meeting on matters concerning his own department. At the end of this business, he planned to present the petition. When he finally spoke, the

Elders were all half asleep, but when Changsun heard the memorial, he started up, scowling. Chu instantly protested with vigor any such promotion which elevated a lady from the former emperor's harem to a ranking post in the current emperor's household. It was bad enough, he pontificated, to have her back in the palace at all.

At this point the empress's uncle, Liu, cut Chu off so firmly that Changsun shrugged, deciding to let the matter pass if the empress's family wanted it. Chu immediately reconsidered and gave his reluctant approval. Kaotsung was looking absently around the room, paying no attention. In fact, he seemed more bored than usual. Seeing this, each official deemed that the business was no affair of his but concerned only the Liu family's attempt to reduce the influence of Hsiao Fei and her claims for her son, Sujay.

That evening the empress was settling down for a foot rub when the emperor sent for Jao. This was the first time that Kaotsung's wishes conflicted with the empress's as far as Tsairen Jao was concerned. The empress frowned and fidgeted. "Start rubbing," she cried angrily, and Jao, showing reluctance, complied. In a few minute the empress, more and more upset, shouted, "Go then, but return to finish here as soon as he dismisses you!"

Somewhat puzzled, and secretly daunted by the emperor's long silence in regard to his promise of a higher rank for her, Jao had been unusually depressed. She found Kaotsung sitting imposingly in his raised chair, waiting stiffly to receive her. This depressed her further. She bowed in a formal way in greeting.

"Enter and accept my felicitations, Consort Chaoyi Wu—Lustrous Demeanor," he said.

Jao stopped as if frozen. "Your Majesty . . ." she began uncertainly.

"Don't you like the title?" he asked, pretending nonchalance. "It goes with the rank."

Jao threw herself into a rapturous kowtow. The attendants smiled. They had long guessed at the true state of affairs between the emperor and the concubine they all liked so much. Kaotsung waved at them.

"You may all leave now," he ordered, unable to conceal his excitement any longer.

When the room was empty, Jao rose, her eyes full of stars. "Your Majesty . . . my friend Jer . . . my patron . . . Your Honor!" she cried incoherently. "It has happened. You made it happen?"

"It is real, all right," he answered, abandoning his formality and reaching hungrily for her.

"A miracle, an enchantment, a dream come true!" Jao gurgled from somewhere among the robes on his chest.

"Not at all, it was easy," he lied. "It just took time, that's all. Who do you think has the say around here? Who do you think has the power to make your dreams come true? I am the emperor, am I not!"

He could not resist boasting. He so enjoyed saying such things to Jao, and when he saw admiration and gratitude leap into her eyes, he felt lifted in his self-esteem. I feel the way I ought to feel as a man, as an emperor, he said to himself. He pulled Jao to him so tightly that she had to struggle to breathe.

It was late when Jao finally mumbled something about duty to the empress before she retired.

"No, indeed," Kaotsung said. "She can't order you around like a menial now that you are a consort!"

Jao's spirits expanded with lightning speed while she absorbed the implications of her new status. "What if she goes into her holding-towels-for-Taitsung act?" she responded somewhat breathlessly.

"Tell her to hold her own towels," Kaotsung suggested.

"Oh!" Jao exploded mirthfully, delighted with him. He seemed somehow enhanced, fully aware of himself as a man in control. She felt herself increase in stature too. Suddenly, she saw that she might have a future in the palace, after all.

The announcement of Jao's promotion was received by the inmates of the Inner City without much notice, good or bad. No one of importance opposed it, and whatever jealousies it aroused soon died down. More crucial for Jao than her elevation in rank was the sponsorship of the powerful Lius. When she moved into her spacious new quarters, she was gratified to find that the eunuchs were exerting themselves to furnish the residence handsomely and to make available a new wardrobe.

Empress Wang was not sure at first that she liked the promotion. However, since there was no change in Jao's behavior or services, with the exception of shorter hours and the introduction of a skillful blind nun to do the massaging, the empress allowed herself to be gracious. Jao also arranged the hours of her attendance so that they never again conflicted with the hours demanded by the emperor. Jao reveled in the glorious knowledge that she was first in Kaotsung's eyes. This elated and sustained her through the long days of complicated duties to both emperor and empress. She realized that, first of all, she had to please the Lius or plunge herself and Kaotsung into deep trouble. The empress was soothed for the moment, now that Hsiao Fei was conspicuously out of favor with the emperor.

Jao watched with enormous secret satisfaction as Kaotsung blossomed in his conduct of both his public and his private life. He had begun to gain respectful attention, not just in her eyes, but in the eyes of more and more officials, especially the younger ones. He arranged administrative schedules to suit himself—privy council meetings were now held every other day. The Elders did not object, as they continued to meet privately to make decisions before attending the official sessions.

Spring was early and summer was hot and dry. The farmers and even the officials began to worry about their harvests. On the night of the seventh day of the seventh moon, the skies filled with clouds and the rain began to pour. It was a great disappointment to those romantically inclined not to be able to see the Milky Way and the one-night meeting of the Weaving Damsel and the Herd Boy. The rain, however, did more than spoil a starry night. It continued for ten days, and by then it had reached flood proportions. The rainmakers had been called in, but they were hurriedly dismissed and other shamans were soon engaged to stop the rain. Both groups were lucky when clear skies arrived in time to dry up the earth and save most of the crops.

All the public furor over the weather and the successful escapes from both disasters redounded to the credit of the young Son of Heaven. People nodded sagely to one another, "he is in tune with Heaven, and that is the main thing," they said while pounding the tabletops in the tea shops to accompany new songs in his honor.

One morning before Jao left, the emperor stopped her. "It is time that you are free in the daytime to ride with me or to do whatever I want you to do with me," he told her.

"I can't. It would not be wise to offend the empress or her mother at this stage of my life here. It has only been six months since I came, and I am still responsible for keeping things balanced in the empress's court."

"You never go with me on any of my expeditions into the country. You make so many excuses," he continued, as if he had not heard her.

Jao looked at him reproachfully and did not reply. Was it possible that he did not know the full extent of what the empress required? The long hours of standing, the constant call upon her to soothe, comfort, and deflect the many temper tantrums that mother and daughter indulged in whenever they were together. Did Kaotsung think for a moment that, once an idea had got into the empress's head, she would ever let go of it?

Empress Wang had reached the conclusion that Jao's reputation for pleasing the awesome Taitsung was the result of her being on call at all times to render smiling services whenever needed, without collapsing from exhaustion or becoming surly. She thought Jao was a treasure of a servant, harmless, an inferior. She conveniently forgot that Jao had rank now and should receive better treatment.

Jao, as a result, was getting thinner, and her looks had lost some of their luster. Every day drew her deeper into a situation from which there was no escape. She saw clearly that not even the emperor could rescue her from it.

"You go on your long ride. It is—you are right—such an ideal day. Tell me all about it when I see you tonight," she urged wearily, careless of what he might think.

He finally agreed, but looked sullen. He too was beginning to look careworn again. He sagged. No one knew the reason for the disappearance of his usual good nature, although some believed it was because of his continual clashes with the Elders.

That evening he did not send for Jao. Gradually he tapered off sending for her at all. The heat of the summer was at its August height, and everyone's temper was frayed, so Jao did not worry too much at first. She was too grateful for her desperately needed nights of sleep.

During the daytime, the tensions within the empress's court increased along with Lady Liu's more prominent presence in the palace. The old lady thought that her daughter's courtyards were cooler than her own, and so she imposed on the empress, her servants, and her attendants. She was becoming the real mistress of the empress's court, as her brother, Liu Shih, had become the real decision-maker in the government.

Arrogant, horrible woman, Jao thought one afternoon when the old crone lashed out at a maid who had dropped a slippery teapot. Seizing a bronze vase, Lady Liu hit the girl in the back, sending her sprawling. Jao leaped forward to stop another swipe aimed at the girl's head and received a bruising hit on her own shoulder. The old lady, enraged at Jao's interference, aimed another blow, this time at Jao. She missed her head but cracked her collarbone. Eunuchs sprang into the fray, took away the bronze vase, and seated the heavily breathing dowager with soothing hands and voices. The empress at last broke out of her stupor to administer aid and comfort to her mother. A guard summoned by Jao hastily removed the hysterical maid.

"Is your honorable mother going to be all right now?" Jao asked when peace had been restored. She was holding one hand to her collarbone in an effort to relieve the pain.

She spoke too soon. Lady Liu was far from pacified. She spat at Jao. "How dare you, a nobody like you—and a woman without morals at that—how dare you interfere with me when I am disciplining a servant? A servant yourself! Leave at once!"

"Honorable parent," Wang began in a small voice. "I beg of you—"

Lady Liu brushed her daughter aside, aiming at Jao's obviously injured shoulder with her cane. Jao stepped nimbly out of the way, and a vigilant eunuch captured the old lady's hand in a caressing gesture. Jao bowed to the empress, who stammered permission for her to depart, and Jao swiftly left the room.

"Go to the pharmacy at once and have your shoulder looked to," whispered Head Eunuch Ho, holding the door open.

CHAPTER TWELVE

Jao had paid a courtesy call on the chief pharmacist soon after her arrival in the palace, so she was kindly received in his clinic. Her collarbone was set with little chirps of solicitude from the chief himself, her shoulder bound tightly, and her arm supported in a sling. She was sent on her way with cheerful assurances that she would soon be all right.

Once on her pallet, she dozed off into such a heavy sleep that she did not wake until the next day when a woman from the pharmacy brought her a bowl of nourishing broth. She obediently drank it and then immediately fell asleep again. When she woke the second time, she realized that no one from either empress or emperor had called on her and that no one was attending her. She was abandoned. It looked as if she now had no support at all. In the old days when she was a tsairen, she at least had Chi behind her as well as his superior, the chief eunuch.

I don't think I can survive the enmity of the powerful Lady Liu in addition to the malice of Hsiao Fei, Jao thought. And I certainly can't survive the withdrawal of Kaotsung. He seemed to think that she was more concerned about the welfare of the empress than about him. The best she could hope for, Jao decided, was to be dismissed. She could not go back to her mother in Taiyuan, because of the hostility of her brothers. The abbess just might have compassion and receive her back in the convent, but she would be forever discredited, and Jao wasn't certain that the abbess would have her. Jao's thoughts went round and round, but she could perceive no comforting outcome anywhere.

Her calculations omitted one element that was in her favor—the silent goodwill of an army of servants. Some of these she had treated politely, and others had never seen her but had heard of her helpful conduct on behalf of the two maids who had been hurt by the Lius. One of these servants investigated Jao's condition and brought food while she healed and rested.

The weather broke and the chill of autumn settled over the capital. Lady Liu returned to her own home outside the palace, and the empress sent for Jao the minute her mother was out of the way. Jao's depression lifted a little after she slipped back into her duties. In time, a summons from the emperor also arrived and her spirits took another rise. She hurriedly donned a new tunic that had just come from the seamstress and presented herself at the imperial pavilion.

Kaotsung was standing in the center of the room waiting for her when she was ushered in. She slid into her usual graceful bow at once, her heart thumping.

"First, I want to tell you that I have arranged with Eunuch Kang to transfer your former tsairen manager, Chi, into my service," Kaotsung told her. "He will be assigned the duty of caring for you. I want someone who has your interests in mind to keep an eye on you. I also want to tell you that I have just heard from Kang—who had it directly from the empress's eunuch, Ho—a report of what you have had to endure. I now understand why you insisted on placating the empress instead of yielding to my wishes when I asked you to ride out with me," he said stiffly.

She kept her head bowed and did not answer, but hope and elation took possession of her, banishing her ability to think at all. He did not wait for her to rise, but swept her up.

"How could I treat you this way, how could I doubt your loyalty, how could I be jealous of your duty to the empress? What a fool I have been," he stammered bitterly. "When you are the only one left who has been truly loyal . . . But that is what I did, that is what I did. By Heaven, I'll never be fool enough to do so again."

He pulled her close, roughly and clumsily, taking her breath away while he clung savagely to her, as if she were his lifeline in a tumbling sea. Her confusion left her and for the first time in their relationship she responded without reserve. Kaotsung was feeling something new in his love life, the surge of deep emotion and elation from achieving a woman whom he had been obliged to work for.

"You must help me, you must put up with me, you must put up with anything I do," he whispered, caressing her with increasing passion, her face, her breasts, her thighs. "I want you all the time. Never leave me again. I can't let you go."

"Yes . . ." Jao murmured breathlessly, entwining her arms with his. "There is nothing more that I want, either. If only Heaven will permit." She was more aroused than she had thought possible, responding not with art but with lust.

The night hours passed with nothing to spoil their time together. They reveled in making new discoveries about each other. At dawn, when they could bring themselves to part, Kaotsung pulled her chin up, searching her face. "This is the best thing that has ever happened to me. I did not even know that I could feel this way about any woman," he said simply. "Now! What must be done so that nothing can come between us again?"

"It is the same with me," Jao whispered, so softly that he could barely hear her. "The same. Nothing like this has happened to me before—to be a part of someone else as if the two of us were one. It makes me afraid."

"I know. But we must not be afraid. If we do not hide things from each other, we can find the strength to deal with whatever happens. The most important thing just now is that everything has changed. We are one now and nothing can come between us if we don't let it. Knowing this will bring us the strength we need.

"The first problem is the matter of your status here: I see that I, personally, must see to it that your life is easier. I know that you are being drained somehow. You don't tell me everything . . . and that's why we must not hide things from each other. Right now I suspect that you are denying me your presence during the day because you don't want to stir up the empress or her family against me. We must change that. Sooner or later I shall take care of all three of the Lius, I swear. But it will take time. Shall I start helping you by seeing that Mi is restored to you? She is somewhere in palace service. Would you like that?"

"Would I like it!" Jao repeated, stunned, tears of joy filling her eyes. "Above all things! More than anyone else, I need Mi! She will make all the difference in my ability to find a way out of these palace struggles. She is the best one there is to help me help you!"

A few evenings later, not called to the emperor's bed, Jao was able to fall on her pallet early in the evening. She slept heavily, hardly moving from sunset to sunrise. It refreshed her so much that she was slow to rouse herself when morning came. A hand seemed to be tugging at her wrist, a voice seemed to be saying, "Here is hot morning tea. Wake up, my lady!"

Jao opened one eye, then sat up with a jerk. "Mi?" she whispered. "Mi! Is it really you?"

Mi was standing by the bed, smiling in her joy as she put down a cup of tea from which a thin spiral of heat was curling invitingly. "In your service once again!" Her voice shook slightly.

Jao jumped up, grasping Mi in her strong young arms, tears welling into her eyes and splashing on her cheeks. "I can't believe it . . . after all this time!" She pushed her friend away and looked into her face. "How did this happen?"

"Chief Eunuch Kang arranged it. I received my orders, and lost no time, you may be sure, gathering my things and getting here."

Jao squeezed Mi's slim arms spasmodically. "You must tell me everything that's happened to you. I know you couldn't have been allowed to see me before, so don't leave my sight now! Did you know Chi is now in the emperor's service? It's been such a comfort to see him occasionally, but to have you here! I can't say it in words. With you here, I can cope with anything."

Mi patted Jao's back, her smile of happiness softening her usually stern features. "Well, I am here to stay this time. Shall I start by rubbing your feet to calm you down?"

Jao laughed. "Certainly not! Just hand me that tea!"

During the days that followed, Jao went about her duties in a daze, daydreaming about the night before and about the night to come. She had craved the emperor's love for a long time without allowing herself to expect it. The implications for them both if a permanent liaison were to come about opened up all sorts of possibilities for her. In her vaulting hope she nevertheless realized that there was an element of desperation in Kaotsung's lovemaking that puzzled her. She understood her own despair: it resulted from her dangerous position between the empress and Hsiao Fei, and now the hostility of Lady Liu. She had a premonition that in the end it would be up to her to find some way out on her own. The people who had power over her looked upon her as a remnant from the previous emperor's harem. She knew she would somehow have to change that. Right now, nothing she did by way of willing and courteous service was accomplishing anything for her. I am still expendable for them, she thought in one of her despairing moments, if not for the emperor. In fact, I am now worse off than before.

It would be up to her to strengthen the emperor. There was something else troubling him, besides his power struggles, that he wouldn't or couldn't tell her. I shall have to wait and see, she thought.

Kaotsung's thoughts, while he sat through a dreary three-hour session, were also on his situation with Jao. He anticipated the night ahead, but these ardent thoughts were mixed with small misgivings. Jao will be truthful with me someday, he told himself. She simply smiles now and still makes excuses whenever I ask her to be with me in the daytime. He wondered if Wang really did torment her. Jao probably felt obligated for being released from the convent. Perhaps she regretted leaving the convent for the palace, he thought. Now that he felt certain of her love, he could wait for the truth.

Autumn that year was brighter than usual, the skies clearer, the turning leaves more vivid. The moonlit nights—the harvest moon was large and brilliant—shone on the cheerful outdoor crowds as they celebrated. Kaotsung and Jao continued to be absorbed by each other during the festival nights, enjoying a hitherto almost unheard-of period of freedom from palace interferences, a miraculous period of privacy and peace.

A month after the harvest moon, chill winds from Siberia finally brought an end to good weather and an end to Jao's felicity. Despite her happiness and outward lightheartedness, persistent stomach trouble caused her to lose weight. At first this did not bother her. The lack of fresh food made upsets like that frequent among all the palace inmates.

Kaotsung, on the other hand, felt expansive, striking out on new ventures with enthusiasm and handling familiar routines with greater ease. He made mistakes, however, and one of them was his neglect of Hsiao Fei. He callously omitted his visits to her and rarely troubled to call upon his increasingly fretful empress. Hsiao Fei lost her aplomb and became restive, unlike her former self. Both women began to behave in spiteful ways, embarrassing their attendants. The empress was shrill in causing trouble in one dispute after another and Hsiao Fei also began to engage in frequent controversy with everyone about her.

When Jao's intestinal troubles made her late in her attendance on the empress, Lady Wang vented her rage upon Jao. The second time that this occurred, Madame Liu and her brother happened to be calling, and Minister Liu stared hostilely at Jao all the time he was there. This worried her so much that she eventually told Mi about it.

"You should be reducing your service to the empress since every night you are in attendance on the emperor. And you should be resting in the daytime and eating better now that you're pregnant," Mi said bluntly.

"What!" Jao ejaculated. "What did you say?"

Mi looked at her mistress in astonishment. "I said that you should eat better because of your pregnancy. It's nothing to be alarmed over."

Jao gradually closed her mouth and took time to think things over. "Of course, with my pharmacy experience, I should have known, but lately I have been so nervous about so many things that I was paying no attention to such inconveniences. Mi, where did you hear this story, that I am pregnant? Who is spreading it?"

"Many know about it, especially Lady Liu's servants, who have been spying on your every move. I, of course, observed your symptoms as soon as they began. I assumed that you didn't want to discuss it yet."

Jao swallowed. "So that is what Prime Minister Liu thinks. That is why he has turned on me. His position here depends on the empress, and hers on whether she has a son to succeed."

"It is true, my mistress. But the news of your pregnancy is not just palace gossip, not something to anger you, it is an honor and should be openly acknowledged. I thought that you were not admitting your condition because the Lius are worried. Everyone is talking about how the empress adopted Chung to make him the crown prince, and about how the Lius are pushing it through with no more delay. Didn't you know?" Jao shook her head. "Your pregnancy has stirred all this up."

"Well . . . well . . . but for now, hurry and dress me. I am late in attendance again, and the empress will pile duties on me to punish me."

Mi looked searchingly at her mistress while clothing her. Jao stood rigidly, her expression unreadable as she let Mi ready her for court. An anxious frown pulled Jao's black eyebrows together in an ugly line. "I'm afraid, Mi, I'm afraid," she whispered as she walked to the door.

"You, afraid?" Mi exclaimed. "Never. Not you, my lady. You couldn't possibly be with such good news at this! So auspicious, such good luck!"

But Jao did not hear her. She had gone.

"Jao!" Empress Wang exclaimed impatiently when Jao made her morning bow. "You have kept me waiting. My ankles are swollen and the nun is not here and I must have you massage me at once." She had little need to be kind to Jao now that Hsiao Fei had been denigrated. "I must be able to stand comfortably at the reception ceremony this afternoon for Crown Prince Chung, my son," she said. She was at her haughtiest now that she felt herself secure at last in her role as empress. Jao listened silently and complied.

That evening Kaotsung also greeted Jao with unusual impatience. "I did not see you at the celebration today," he said at once. "I expected you. This whole matter of Chung has been foisted on me so suddenly that I have barely had time to adjust. It is too hastily done—after being crown prince myself for eight years, and now only on the throne two years, I am being given a crown prince of my own. The Lius attended the celebration today in force, along with my uncle, Changsun Wuji, and all the ministers above Grade Three."

"What happened?" Jao asked with restraint.

"Minister Liu inaugurated it and the Elders endorsed it to a man. Liu kept harping on the fact it was a danger to the dynasty not to have a settled successor, and other such nonsense. Everyone knew why he was so insistent, of course—he wants his niece to have added status as mother of the successor and thus ensure his own standing in court."

"Did you back Chung's adoption and his elevation to being crown prince?" she asked, her face carefully still without expression.

"I did not, but then I don't care one way or another. I have fifty more years of life. I am only twenty-three, so why should I care what they do? The Elders pushed it through as usual," he said unguardedly.

Jao glanced worriedly at him, noticing suddenly how dejected he was. She was getting a glimpse of the truth that he tried to conceal from her. It was so important to him that she see him only as a winner, never as a loser. Realizing this, Jao exerted herself to congratulate him and to tell him that he had done everything just as he ought. He revived after that.

"Why weren't you there?" he asked again.

"I wasn't invited," she returned.

He stared, warding off knowledge of what Jao was concealing from him, the extent of her isolation and helplessness in the hands of the empress.

"The Lius?" he asked. "They have always been your supporters. It could not be trouble from that quarter?"

"But it could," Jao responded, her lips trembling. "Because I am now about to give you a son myself."

"What!" he said swiftly, his eyes alight. "Serious?"

"Yes," she said.

"Well!" he exploded, letting his voice out in a joyful bellow. "Well

. . . such good news! This changes things . . . well, well! I can support you more openly now that you, a ranking consort, are giving me a son!"

He pulled her gently into his arms as if he were afraid that she would fall apart if handled too roughly. This made Jao laugh, and she suddenly felt free of her fears. "It happens, you know. It happens to everyone! It's nothing to worry about and I'm so happy that I have been blessed this way. It is good fortune for both of us, surely."

Kaotsung placed his hands with their long, sensitive fingers around her tiny waist and stared at her. Jao laughed again and felt a surge of pride. "You won't be able to span my waist with your two hands six months from now." She chuckled.

He grinned with delight. "I will enjoy seeing you thicken. At last I will have a prince whose mother I love!"

"What if it's a girl?"

"Not this time," Kaotsung retorted decisively. "Next time!"

The emperor's vigorous sponsorship only increased Jao's troubles. The Lius were openly hostile, and Jao was run off her feet by a now jealous empress who conspired more and more with Hsiao Fei against her. Hsiao indulged in small harassments: Jao's bed was often found drenched after water had been dumped on it, her clothes dragged in the mud, and dead animals left on her floor. Jao reported none of this to Kaotsung.

One evening he noticed her haggard look. "Here," he said, "you look awful."

"I know," she replied, crossing her arms over her extended stomach.

"Not that," he said hastily, "that is our son! I mean you look sick. Are you? Do you want to be moved completely out of the empress's court? That might be managed, but I don't know whether that might do you more harm than good."

"If you could have the grand eunuch invite the Taoist Madame Sun to take charge of my pregnancy, you could rest your mind about both me and your son," she said lightly. "If Sun were in charge, the empress would have to let go, wouldn't she? What could she do about it?"

"Done!" he said in great relief.

That evening the midwife arrived. The meeting took place in a side pavilion of the emperor's suite. He himself insisted on being present, with only his trusted eunuch, Kang, in attendance. Madame Sun found herself warmly welcomed and was gratified. Jao took Sun's tiny hands in her own and pressed them. Her voice trembled when she reminded the midwife of their days in the cave thirteen years before. Madame Sun beamed and then took hold of Jao's wrists, feeling her pulses as she talked. Her eyes strayed to Jao's swollen legs and feet, and, still talking soothingly about the welcome change in weather, she guided Jao to a chair and propped up her legs on a stool to feel the pulses in her ankles.

Kaotsung watched with curiosity, the more because he was supposed to stay well away from such female matters. Sun felt around Jao's abdomen in a leisurely way while they all chatted. Then she stood up and bowed.

"I will arrange for some helpful medicinal draughts for her to take during the three months ahead but there is nothing more that I can do unless she stays off her feet most of the time."

"But—" Jao began.

"I will see to it," Kaotsung said, his lips set grimly. He turned to Kang. "Send orders to the head of the palace midwives to put herself under Madame Sun's direction for the next three months, and send one of your most reliable staff members to supervise so that it is under your control and there is no slip-up."

Eunuch Kang bowed and lowered his eyes. He had heard palace gossip about a certain conversation regarding Jao that had been overheard taking place between Minister Liu and the empress. Liu had supposedly told the empress to keep Jao in attendance all day without rest until the minute she was to report to the emperor. When the empress told him she already did that, Liu suggested withholding food as well, thus contributing to a poor condition that would encourage Jao's natural death in childbirth.

Eunuch Kang exchanged a knowing look with Madame Sun. He bowed. "I shall take care of it," he said soberly. He knew that many palace servants had seen the treatment given to Jao and disapproved. "She is pregnant," they said, "and even commoners know better than to mistreat a pregnant woman."

"And you," Kaotsung said to Madame Sun, "you will move to the palace yourself when the time comes?" She too bowed low. "And I myself will speak to Empress Wang," he continued, and turned briskly to Jao. "That should do it!" he exclaimed cheerfully.

But it didn't.

When Madame Sun visited Jao again in two weeks, she was appalled. "What are you doing?" she asked. "Look at your ankles—regular puff balls. Are you keeping you feet up?"

"No," Jao said.

"Why?" Sun asked, just as briefly.

"The emperor has spoken to the empress, but she is ignoring his orders. My hours are longer than ever. Even the attendants are noticing."

"Someone must report this to the emperor. You are in a dangerous condition."

"No," Jao exclaimed. "I don't mean to contradict you, I just mean that the emperor is extremely sensitive to any flouting of his authority, and this, because it stems from the powerful Lius, would precipitate a conflict from which Kaotsung could only emerge as a loser. I am at my wit's end as to what to do. So I do nothing."

Madame Sun's eyes narrowed. She was infuriated but she had much experience with spoiled women like the empress. Her face was expressionless. "I will petition the emperor to send the usual chair for you at a different time, a different place, and with a different escort," she said at length. "The chair will go to the front steps of the empress's main pavilion in the morning immediately after her levee, the escort to be Head Eunuch Kang himself and a contingent of the emperor's own guards."

"All the empress has to do is to say no and dismiss the chair," Jao said gloomily. "Or for Madame Liu to do it. Or Minister Liu—"

"All the same," Madame Sun interrupted. "I shall petition the emperor."

The next morning the chair and escort appeared for Jao in the forecourt of the empress's establishment. The empress scowled and with a wave of her hand ordered her lowest ranking attendant to dismiss it. Her mother went out on the gallery to see that the order was carried out. Eunuch Kang, who had his own chair, was polite but insistent about carrying out his orders. The empress forbade Jao to leave, Jao obediently complied, but the chairs remained waiting and more guards appeared. The empress, at length, in spite of her mother, let Jao go.

"This once," Lady Liu shouted. She had never forgotten nor forgiven Jao's actions in interfering with her beating of the maid. The following day, however, the chair came again, this time with an enhanced guard and the entrance of Eunuch Kang into the formal waiting room. The empress could do nothing but allow Jao to go.

Minister Liu was called upon to handle the situation. He tried to see the emperor informally and browbeat him, but instead he was asked to bring his concerns to the next council meeting. This the minister would not do. He could not risk the loss of face that interference with a pregnant concubine would bring upon him. In the end, the empress dismissed Jao from her court "in disgrace" because the daily uproar was causing too much attention and covert ridicule.

Jao benefited at once from being relieved of the mounting harassments of court attendance. Madame Sun ordered strengthening broths and infusions of the traditional prescription for pregnant women of three boiled turnip roots with thirty chrysanthemum buds and one handful of roasted sesame seeds every four hours. Jao felt better at once. Everything being done for her was soothing and helpful, especially after Madame Sun herself moved into the palace.

By four in the afternoon of the same day, the sky had darkened and Jao had sent for lamps. She was sitting languidly on the warm *kang* listening to Madame Sun's cheerful anecdotes. Mi was folding small lengths of bast inside cotton squares. She was very much interested in everything the old lady had to say.

Jao's feet were propped on a stool. She shifted frequently, trying in vain to find a comfortable position. She was small and the infant large enough that it pressed on her in all directions. She could not even breathe properly.

"How long is this going to last?" she asked irritably. Both of her companions looked at her attentively. "This is worse than I expected and probably is going to get even more so," she added gloomily, and they both nodded in sympathy.

Madame Sun smiled benignly, but her look changed when she saw Jao clutch at her stomach. "What is the matter?" she asked at once.

"Nothing," Jao snapped. "Something I ate, I suppose . . . added to everything else," she said bitterly.

"Well," Madame Sun replied. "Maybe not tonight, but soon!" She listened to Jao's heartbeat and that of the baby. She looked speculatively at Jao. "When did you eat last? I seem to remember that you have refused everything since breakfast, and that was only barley gruel." Jao nodded. "Satisfactory," the midwife said. "And now we must give you a hand wash and prepare the silk ropes for you to pull."

When this was done, Madame Sun arose. "It will be a long time before you really need me, so I'll go into the next room and have a bit of sleep now while I can. I'll call in the palace head of midwives to take care of you while I nap. She'll make sure that you are comfortable."

"Of course, do have a nap—but not too long!" Jao was still bright-eyed and excited.

Madame Sun returned after midnight to find Jao disheveled and tiring. "You should doze off between bouts," she told her. Jao flashed her a hostile look.

The midwife drifted in and out of Jao's room all night, checking that the braziers kept the room warm and the water steaming, while the palace midwives wiped Jao's face and steadied her during her pangs.

Snow was still falling when dawn broke and Madame Sun returned wearing a new, clean tunic over her other clothes. She was much refreshed and ready to resume her duties.

Kaotsung kept coming to inquire, but became so distressed that Jao and Madame Sun requested that he stay away until it was over. The day waned and night again set in, but the baby still would not come. When she was conscious, Jao screamed in an almost unbroken keening. The attendants were beginning to look distraught, but Madame Sun only looked grave, and continued to do everything possible to assist a normal delivery. At daylight she turned to the fatigued palace midwife and said, "It is as I thought; the child is turned and is caught. He cannot come, so we will have to resort to manipulation to turn and ease. Let me see your hands."

Midwife Pak showed her hands. They were tiny with long fingernails. "Will you allow me to cut your nails and oil your hands?" Madame Sun asked. Another agonized scream reverberated through the crowded room. The woman nodded with curiosity, and Sun prepared her hands.

"Now," she said. "Everybody out of here except Mi. Let us have some quiet and some room to breathe. Out!" Firecrackers were being exploded to scare away the evil spirits, and there were many onlookers sliding in to watch. When the room was cleared, Madame Sun said to the palace midwife, "You know your business, so I am going to trust you to deliver the baby. No, don't interrupt. You are to turn the baby if you can while I hold Jao in my lap. Now . . ."

Madame Sun was a strong woman. She arranged herself on the *kang* with Jao in her lap, her knees up, and with Midwife Pak kneeling in front. She whispered instructions in Jao's ear. "You are fighting the birth and the baby cannot come. . . . Give up fighting and let me do it. Give up . . . give up . . . let the Tao have its way . . . breathe and push when you feel me breathe and push . . . let me do it for you. . . ."

Jao gradually obeyed the rhythms set up by the woman holding her. Madame Sun controlled her breathing while massaging the child into a better position, and the other midwife, with her strong, small hands, eased the head under the pelvic bone. Toward noon, the child was born.

"A boy." Jao heard the blessed words and slipped into a restful unconsciousness.

Kaotsung came to inspect the boy and to heap gifts upon his beloved concubine when she revived. He had declared a holiday for the entire palace. The baby was named Hung, and twenty-four hours after his birth the storm clouds cleared off, the sun shone on a dazzling white world, and notices about his birth, both formal and informal, were sent out.

Madame Liu was an early riser, and received her notice with her morning tea. Agitated, she slammed down her cup, called for her chief eunuch, quizzed him for details, ordered her chair, and left for the palace.

The empress was not yet up. She was not even awake when her mother burst into her bedroom. She sat up in fright. "What is the matter?" she stammered as her furious parent swept across the room to her bedside.

"That woman has given birth to a live son, that's the matter," Madame Liu cried. Attendants crowded in behind her to close the doors against the cold and to divest her of her wraps. Wang stared at all these people who had no business in her bedroom and pulled the bedclothes to her chin.

"What of it?" she replied sullenly.

"What of it!" her mother repeated incredulously. "How can you sit there, you fool, and refuse to see what a disaster it is!"

"Yes, yes, it is a disaster, but—all you people, please wait outside . . . outside now, if you please." Reluctantly, the onlookers were shown out by the two authorized attendants, and Wang turned to her mother. "Now Mother, do sit down. You make me nervous pacing about."

"I want to stand!" Madame Liu shouted. "Listen here, you little fool. That Wu Jao has a son, and Kaotsung will want him as crown prince!"

"But Chung is crown prince now. Kaotsung would never depose him."

"Yes, of course he would," Liu stormed. "My brother's plan, to see to it that the baby would never be born and for that woman to die, has failed."

Wang stared dumbly, at her wit's end for any solution.

Her mother looked grim. "We must dissolve that family. There is only one recourse now. We must call in a powerful sorcerer and have him lay a spell on Wu Jao and her child."

The Lius, by offering a large fee, obtained the services of the most notable of the Black Shamans of Changan. They came with incantations, clouds of smoky incense, awesome robes, and spell-binding invocations carried on in solemn ritual. As they performed spastically with frothy spittle and bulging eyes, they terrified everyone within seeing or hearing distance.

When at last their torches were extinguished after their withdrawal, an effigy stuck with knives was found under the emperor's bed. The palace drew conclusions about the meaning of it all. To many it was clearly an assault upon the emperor himself.

An office of White Shamans was maintained in the palace to protect the court. They exorcised evil spirits and acted for the good of all, not for the harm of anyone. This respected body of shamans heard about the spells cast by the outsiders. They were so affronted that their chief called upon Jao—by way of getting to the emperor—to accuse the Lius of fomenting serious trouble by employing the Black Shamans. Sorcery was a serious crime if invoked for inflicting death, especially if directed against the throne itself.

Kaotsung confronted the privy council with the accusation. Minister Liu listened to him with sweating palms and attempted to dismiss the fiasco out of hand. The others listened with poker faces. Finally one of the Elders said, "Minister Liu is your father-in-law, nothing can be done."

Kaotsung had privately decided that this was the time for his showdown with the Elders. His voice, when he replied, was harsh and menacing. "Nothing can be done? Oh yes, it can, something can indeed be done. Or do you all condone an attack upon the throne? Do some of you wish to join Minister Liu in exile? Because that is what is going to happen to him. At the very least."

There was a prolonged silence.

"What are you going to do about it?" Kaotsung demanded at last.

"Investigate," Changsun Wuji said reluctantly.

The Elders made inquiries, interrogated attendants, probed into the world of the shaman, and tortured servants. The Lius were found guilty, Madame Liu in particular, but they could not be convicted because of their palace connections.

"Have you heard any of the details about the verdict on the Lius?" Eunuch Kang patted his lips delicately and set his soup bowl down. Eunuch Ho raised his eyebrows judiciously and tried to look decently downcast. After all, the Lius were the parent and uncle of his mistress.

"Some, not all," he answered. "What have you heard?"

"It seems that they were very—unwise," Kang returned unctuously. He had privately deprecated the interference of the two Lius in palace affairs. They had made trouble for him personally a number of times. "It was lacking in common sense to invoke the shamans to solve their political problems. To be candid, I don't think that Minister Liu had a hand in the reprehensible death-dealing fetish they found under the emperor's bed. That was not the minister's way, to begin with. Too dangerous. He knew that sorcery is one of the Ten Abominations and is punishable by death, even if the women didn't."

Ho looked at Kang questioningly.

"Oh yes," Kang said carefully as he looked around for possible listeners. "Your women have everything to lose if Wu Jao's son ever becomes crown prince. It would oust them completely from power."

"I know nothing about their doings," Ho said hastily.

"Come, my friend, you know all that is to be known about their affairs. You know, for example, that if the plot against the emperor had worked and if he had died, then the empress and her relatives and even Hsiao Fei had everything to gain. Wang's adopted son is the first in the line of succession and Hsiao's son is second."

Ho's eyes fell. "Pity."

Kang was surprised. "What do you mean?"

"It's too bad the Lius have had to take the blame for the Black Shamans. Even the Palace Office of Shamans is up in arms against their act in bringing in the cursed outsiders. I'm sorry for the old man, but not for Lady Liu."

Kang smiled cynically. "It is indeed a pity," he commented ambiguously.

The month-feast to celebrate the new infant's healthy survival was held in Kaotsung's private quarters and was attended by all the high-ranking ladies of the court. Informal and low-key, it was a thoroughly enjoyable occasion. Hsiao Fei stayed away, but the empress, realizing that Jao and Jao's child were far more of a threat to her than flighty Hsiao had ever been, came to salvage what she could.

When the short tea party was over and the infant carried off—he had slept through all the noise of celebration—Kaotsung detained Jao.

"I have scarcely seen you for this whole month, ever since the baby's birth," he complained. "Stay now and talk to me."

Jao hesitated for a second. Kaotsung did not notice. "Yes, of course," she answered warmly.

He did not notice, either, how slow she was to respond, and later, nestled under furs in the dark, he confessed with satisfaction that he had not made love to anyone else in four months. "When the matron advised against intercourse in the last month of your pregnancy," he hesitatingly told her. "I discovered that other concubines failed to appeal, and I was embarrassed. . . ."

Suddenly Jao understood Kaotsung's secret, which he would not reveal to her. She cradled him lovingly.

"Does it bother you that you are impotent sometimes?" she asked.

He started. "How did you find out?" he asked in agitation.

She drew him closer. "I didn't 'find out,' as you put it, because there is nothing to find out. This is something that happens to all men."

"All?" Kaotsung repeated.

"Every male has problems of that kind occasionally. The courtesans informed us when we were tsairen."

"What! What a thing to talk about to the tsairen," Kaotsung sputtered and Jao laughed gaily.

"Why ever not?" She giggled. "We were told what to do because Emperor Taitsung was not so young anymore."

Kaotsung grunted, then laughed sheepishly. "It has been humiliating for me, especially after I became emperor and acquired all those new women in the harem. Most of my children, I got while I was still crown prince and couldn't care less." He suddenly realized that he was in the middle of confessing his secret to Jao and that she did not take it seriously. All at once, it did not seem so bad to him either. He sighed.

"I always seem good to you. I stand tall to you no matter what happens. Except for you, I have not been able to make love very often since I became emperor, and I don't know why. Well, I didn't want to be with some of those women . . . especially Wang who was foisted on me by my father. I was doing fine with Hsiao Fei, but after I became emperor, I have been impotent much of the time . . ."

He continued talking. Jao was tired and far from recovery, but she began to listen with increasing interest.

"When do you feel most powerless? What are the times that you lose your . . . your peace of mind?" She felt him move restlessly.

"Always the same thing hitting me at the same time of day. Headaches and tension until you came. I am not so bad now."

"But you are still nervous. I want to rid you of what makes you nervous," Jao said finally. "What is 'that same thing hitting you at the same time'?"

He grunted. "Don't you know yet? You must have guessed."

"Is it your uncle?" Jao asked.

"I just can't . . . I just can't . . . cope with him. He rolls over everyone. Nothing can stand in his way. I feel small after most privy council meetings, and even with you here, I still do. Nothing of importance is ever brought up for serious discussion in my presence, and all the important decisions seem to be made behind my back. I never even hear about some of the new policies. Nothing of importance seems to be going on in the empire in any of the reports made to me. I go round and round in a fog, and the three thousand officials I have in this palace do not look to me for orders. They do what they like. Not the way it was in my father's day."

His voice was shaking with the bitterness that was spewing out of him. Jao was transfixed. She felt her cheeks becoming hot with anger.

"Who are 'they'?" she ventured at last.

"Sometimes I feel strangled, so that it is hard to breathe. Who are 'they'? I'll tell you: the people closest to me. Wuji, Chu, and Han."

Jao put her arms around his barrel chest, her face against it, soaking him in a storm of angry tears. He began to relax as she once again demonstrated the genuineness and extent of her feelings for him.

"And a third thing," he murmured drowsily. "I cannot function well when I feel that you spurn me."

"Spurn you?" Jao gasped. "This is a nightmare. Any action of mine, or all of them, that might be construed as putting a distance between you and me has been, always, *always*, to throw dust in the eyes of my enemies. I rely on you to know that. What do you mean by 'spurn'?"

Kaotsung sat up suddenly. "You never have spurned me? I am afraid of something that does not exist? And what is real is your . . . your affection? All I want to hear is that you love me. It's all I have ever wanted to hear and will keep on wanting to hear."

"Jer," said Jao, hesitantly touching the skin on his chest. "You are a devil to frighten me so."

"I must know how you really feel about me. Can you . . . respect me whatever happens?"

Jao suddenly knew that he feared that he did not measure up to his father in her heart. She said, looking deep into his eyes so that he could see the truth in them, "Jer, listen to me . . . I loved Taitsung romantically and idealistically and most of the time at a distance, but I am really in love now, with my very own Jer, totally, with a love that is like fire and just as consuming."

"Jao," he said, and this time the drop of water that splashed on her arm was not from her eyes. "Jao, you can't know what you have just given me—you have given me life. I already feel stronger in the face of 'them.' "

"Down with 'them,' " she said, and they both began to chuckle and then to laugh outright.

During the unusually cold days that winter brought upon them, Jao and her baby son were made comfortable in a side pavilion of the imperial quarters so that Kaotsung could be in close touch with them. Kaotsung returned to his normal good-natured habits, and life in the Inner City picked up in general good spirits. Jao began to receive lovely gifts delivered at least once a month in recognition of her status as mother of a son of the emperor. Such handsome gifts caused a flurry in her new household, and Jao enjoyed it. She sorted them out and gave most of them away to those around her. Service with Jao became the most desirable position in the inner palace. There were even some officials who became aware of Jao's influence and approved heartily, in spite of the fact that the older, entrenched officials were becoming more and more intolerant of her presence.

It became apparent that the relief of ridding the court of the Lius was not especially successful in bringing real peace to the Inner City. Kaotsung visited the empress, formally requesting her to keep better control of the harem and to reduce her contacts with Hsiao Fei. The two of them had now become notoriously destructive.

"Do you see her daily?" he asked.

"Of course," she said sullenly.

"I am told that you discuss nothing but ways to embarrass Wu Jao. I want that to cease," he told her. Naively, he expected her to comply.

The empress said nothing, and the emperor, after a long silence, took his leave in an uneasy frame of mind. The empress was a stupid woman, and Kaotsung feared her because of it. He was beginning to understand that stupidity in persons of rank was always dangerous.

Jao had become pregnant again and was quite ill. Madame Sun was called. Secretly dismayed by Jao's bad health, she set up a routine with the palace midwives that was strictly enforced. She was rewarded by handsome gifts that were periodically delivered at her door. Jao was bored, but grateful for the chance to be idle. This did not mean that she reduced her attentions to the emperor. It was now more important than ever to keep up his morale, and to keep alive his attachment to her.

With her second pregnancy so difficult, Jao began to long for her mother. Her elevation in rank and her secure status made her feel she could send for Lady Yang at last. Kaotsung was pleased by the idea, and Jao was wild with excitement.

It was a month before her mother could come, so Jao secured a comfortable house just outside the east wall and arranged servants and every comfort. Jao spent the day that Lady Yang was to arrive in the new house, waiting for her. When her mother's chair was lowered in the courtyard, Jao rushed out to greet her, and Lady Yang burst into tears. She's aged, Jao thought, taking her mother into her arms. That was to be expected after twelve years—but not this much.

Hours later, when some of the excitement began to die down, Jao observed her mother's fatigue. "I'll leave now," she told Lady Yang contritely, "and let you rest. We have plenty more time to talk—all the rest of your life." At this, Lady Yang gave her daughter a dazzling smile, and Jao realized with a pang how dear her mother was to her. "You are too thin . . . let us change all that," she said in parting as she wiped an unaccustomed tear from her eye.

Not long after Jao's mother arrived, Jao offered to have her now-widowed sister come to the palace as well. Holan, overwhelmed by Jao's new status, quickly accepted. Jao was grateful to have her around, and Holan showed little of her former jealousy toward her sister. She had changed in the years they had been apart. Now, whenever Jao was too sick to attend Kaotsung, which was often in her difficult pregnancy, Holan was willing to go in her place. Jao did not want Kaotsung to relapse into impotency, but neither did she want him to slip into profligacy. Lively Holan was good company and a good solution. And when she became pregnant, the breach between the emperor and Hsiao Fei widened even further.

If Jao and Kaotsung now felt that the worst was over as far as Jao's position in the harem was concerned, they were sadly mistaken. As her second pregnancy advanced, Wang and Hsiao were more than ever in an alliance of hatred, not only against Jao, but even more virulently against her rapidly growing son. Jao, with watchful Mi to help her, took great care to supervise the care of Hung and the people who were allowed near him, but Kaotsung exacerbated the situation by his continued neglect of his proud, high-ranking ladies.

The new baby was born before its full time: it was a girl and weak. Madame Sun had difficulties in inducing it to breathe, and when she finally laid the child beside Jao on the bed, she looked at the little crumpled face with its small rosebud mouth and shook her head worriedly.

"Poor wee mite," Jao said, "a girl, just a girl this time."

"Well, she is here safely, and now you may rest. Take this special drink and then sleep. Nothing else is more important for you now than sleep. I shall tell the attendants you are not to be disturbed for anything. I myself am going to retire, but I am leaving the two most responsible palace midwives in charge here. Just close your eyes, that is the best thing for you now."

The palace midwives were drowsily gossiping with Mi when the empress made a surprise visit to see the infant. They stood at attention as she swept into the room and approached the bed. She called out, but Jao was too sound asleep to hear her. Turning back the cover, she picked up the baby. She cuddled it for a few seconds and hastily returned the bundle to the bed. She left as abruptly as she had come.

When Kaotsung arrived some time later, Mi came forward and woke Jao to receive him. He was all smiles.

"I came to see my new child," he said eagerly.

"It's a . . . daughter," Jao answered diffidently.

"Let me see my daughter, then," Kaotsung said, bending to lift the little bundle into his great arms. He stood quietly for a minute or two, then his expression changed from a fatuous grin to one of shock.

"Madame Sun, where are you? Come quickly. This baby is not breathing!"

"Wh-What!" Jao exclaimed weakly. "What are you saying!"

Madame Sun was found and brought hastily, while Mi held her severely shocked mistress in her arms. Kaotsung paced the room while Madame Sun examined the baby. Sadly, she pronounced it dead.

"This baby was alive when I left and Jao was asleep. I gave orders that they were not to be disturbed," Madame Sun stated grimly.

Kaotsung confronted the frightened attendants. "Who has touched this child?" he asked sternly. There was silence, then Mi said quietly. "No one here touched her. Only the empress who came by."

He turned to Jao. "Was she here?"

"I didn't see her. I was asleep," Jao replied faintly.

The emperor asked each woman separately about the baby and about the people who had handled it. All agreed that no one but the empress had been near the infant. Kaotsung's face was flushed and an artery pulsed in his neck. All his pent-up distaste for the empress flared up. "The empress has murdered my daughter!" he exclaimed, while Jao in her weakness cried bitterly.

"My poor little mite," she kept saying over and over again.

Kaotsung, at a loss about how to comfort Jao, stamped around the room. "Before this, the empress was jealous of Pure Concubine Hsiao and did everything possible to destroy her, and now she has done this deed," he said. This he continued to believe, although the midwives and imperial physicians came to the conclusion, in an effort to smooth things over, that the baby was born too early and had been too weak to survive. Others privately believed as Kaotsung did.

August was hot and dry again after a shorter than usual rainy season. Holan was extremely uncomfortable in the airless rooms of her mother's house in the eastern section of the city, and was relieved when she gave birth to a boy the last day of the month. He was named Hsien and Jao took him to raise as her second son.

Kaotsung began to feel that he should raise Jao's rank because both the empress and Hsiao Fei were higher in rank than she, but he could not do so because the four positions of Fei and the one of Empress were already filled. He proposed in privy council that a new post be created, higher than the Fei, just under Empress.

Grand Secretary Li Ifu, a fervent supporter of both the emperor and Jao, was present on special business, much to the annoyance of Changsun, who did not give even one look in his direction.

Kaotsung did not beat about the bush. "I propose to establish a new position for a lady in my establishment to be above the four Fei and below the empress. Owing to her services to Empress Wang and for giving me two sons, I wish to elevate Consort Luminous Demeanor Wu Jao to the position as soon as it is created."

"She has not performed useful services to the state," Chu said in an offhand way, as if that disposed of the matter.

Kaotsung flushed. "She has been in attendance upon the empress for nearly three years, and the empress has praised her inordinately. She has given me three children and has faithfully served me, your emperor. I wish to promote her. What have you to say?"

Before Chu or anyone else could answer, Changsun spoke up in a fatherly way, "Put the idea out of your head. The proposal should not even be discussed. It is not suitable. She is not suitable."

Li Ifu said in a perplexed manner, "The emperor is serious. Why shouldn't this proposal be discussed?"

Changsun turned on him. "What business is it of yours? Why are you here anyway?"

"I was ordered to take official notes of the proceedings for my superior."

Changsun pointed to the door. "There will be no need for notes today. This matter is not for the record."

"Why not?" Kaotsung interrupted in a loud voice.

Changsun glared at the unruly young emperor but kept his manner fatherly. "Your judgment is faulty, that is why, my dear boy." Then he turned and in his general's voice commanded Li Ifu, "Leave!"

After this, every official who had any other business hurried to transact it, and the session ended without discussion of Kaotsung's proposal.

Kaotsung and Jao discussed the matter that night. They were both in good health for the first time in months, and their days were pleasantly full of receptions for foreign envoys, inspection of foreign tribute, and delightful sessions with their little boys. They were not inclined to be discouraged. Kaotsung was in a mood to let his proposal go in favor of another idea that had occurred to him several times since the death of his daughter.

Kaotsung cleared his throat importantly. This was a sign that he wanted her full attention. Jao turned to him and waited expectantly.

"Jao, listen carefully: I would like to drop all these measures to promote you to some super rank among the consorts. . . ."

Jao gasped in consternation but remained silent.

He continued. "I want to make you empress instead!"

Jao's heart turned over. She stuttered, "But you have an empress . . ."

"I will when Wang is dismissed. Then I will have you!"

"But, but—"

"Now don't interrupt me. We have to begin our plans. Obviously, I must persuade my uncle privately to support me in this. Perhaps he feels that I have not paid enough attention to him. After all, he is my mother's brother and very important to me. I will call on him this week and you shall go with me."

Jao listened skeptically. "As you say," she agreed.

Archduke Changsun lived in a mansion covering a vast acreage in the northeast section of the city. He had thirty or forty children living in separate courts with their mothers, and about three thousand servants to take care of them. When the emperor and Jao called on Changsun, he, his chief wife, his sons, and his newest adolescent concubine met them graciously. They were entertained in the formal reception hall with refreshments of wine and sesame biscuits. As the afternoon wore on, they became convivial, slipping out of formal manners and into informal ones. The women sat together, soon exchanging highly personal stories about babies, food, and illnesses.

"It is a great honor that the emperor is conferring upon his uncle by visiting him in person," ventured the worn-looking first wife to Jao.

"Good Aunt," Jao responded, realizing that the lady was ignorant of court gossip and knew little of their purpose in coming. "The emperor is very fond of his mother's brother. He relies on his uncle for guidance, as you must know. It has been five years now since the death of the former emperor, and Changsun Wuji has been untiring up till now in his attention to affairs of state. Up till now."

"Yes, I know," the lady agreed with composure. "He comes home daily very much fatigued because he carries the burden of the empire on his shoulders."

"Changsun carries the burden of empire?" Jao repeated, thunderstruck.

"Who else?" the noble lady answered, innocent of the enormity of her remark. Jao could find no words with which to reply.

The afternoon faded, and still Kaotsung stayed on, in spite of Jao's frequent glances in his direction for the signal to leave. Changsun dodged any discussion dealing with either the empress or the concubine Jao. He did, however, invite the couple to stay to dinner, a stay that turned out to be even more convivial than the afternoon had been. Two grown sons were sent for, and Kaotsung conferred special honors upon them. He distributed costly jewels among the ladies, which aroused delighted squeals from the young and approving nods from the elderly.

"Now, Uncle," Kaotsung began, finally at the end of his patience. "You have seen Wu Jao for yourself, her manners, her beauty, her devotion to myself. Please consider seriously my wish to elevate her. Surely you must have changed your mind now that you have seen her. Come, answer me!"

Changsun rose, cup in hand. "This is to drink to the good health and long life of my dear nephew and to thank him for his visit. I am sure that all of you feel as I do." His voice was drowned in the swell of assenting voices cheerfully uttering their approval with *"hau-hau"* and *"hsi-hsi."*

"Wanfu!" Kaotsung responded. "But now I ask you to speak your mind about Wu Jao."

"I understand, but now is the time to drink a second toast to you in thanks for your generosity to my sons and daughters and to my concubines. Let us all drink to this." There was a bustle while the company rose and sipped in farewell. Kaotsung and Jao, caught up in the ceremony, found themselves bowed out. Kaotsung especially was dismayed, shocked, and angry.

Back at the palace, he exploded. "We must not give up on just one try," Jao said comfortingly. "Tomorrow we can send more gifts."

Kaotsung brightened. "Really handsome ones, then he can't refuse to listen to me. He can't be that hard. Mother was never harsh when she knew all sides of a situation, and neither was my father. Changsun will be like them, I feel sure. Fairness is fairness."

The next day he sent Chief Eunuch Kang to the Changsun mansion in an imperial chair followed by ten cartloads of gifts, silks, jewelry, gold. Only a few gifts were accepted; the rest were sent back. Then Kaotsung had Jao send Lady Yang to call on Lady Changsun with more gifts. She made several visits and was well-received. The ladies of the household understood that Jao wanted support and were sympathetic. Changsun, however, resisted every effort.

Kaotsung set his jaw at the affronts and decided that the time had come to push for deposing the empress for the crimes of murder and sorcery.

If feminine pressure did not work, Kaotsung decided, then pressure from a respected colleague in the ministry would. He sent Minister Hsu of the silver tongue to talk to his uncle. Hsu was made to wait quite a while before being admitted to the archduke's presence. He did his best but failed, as the others had before him. Changsun Wuji was inflexible. Hsu not only failed, but received the rough edge of Wuji's tongue in the process.

All the pressure annoyed the old general, and he began to retaliate. He set in motion a system of transfers to remote posts of any official who supported Kaotsung. Li Ifu was the first, finding his title lowered and his pay reduced. Li lost no time in calling on a colleague for help in his crisis. His coworker was also a Grand Secretary and a nephew of Minister Hsu. He was, therefore, well-briefed on the affair. He told Li Ifu cynically, "You will knock your head against a stone wall if you oppose the powerful archduke. You will bring down great trouble upon yourself if you try. However, it is my opinion that if you can think of a way to please the emperor by promoting the interests of Wu Jao, you can change your bad luck into good luck and your career will be made."

Li Ifu thanked his friend fulsomely and thought over what had been said. Then, being a man who could deal with only one idea at a time, he requested an audience with the emperor to discuss urgent and important business. His request was granted and he soon found himself in the imperial presence. He had barely risen from his kowtow when he boldly launched his petition that Empress Wang be deposed and that Lady Wu Jao be made empress in her place, in order to satisfy the wishes of the Chinese people. Kaotsung was taken by surprise, but was not displeased to receive such a petition coming voluntarily from an official, and a younger one at that. He moved to have Li's transfer canceled and confirmed him in his current position. This was done through the Secretariat and was obeyed without question as an administrative move too small to be carried to the privy council. The emperor also sent Li a reward and recommended that he be promoted.

In addition Jao sent a secret word of thanks to Li, which was electrifying to him and to his uncle Hsu. Almost at once, a party of support for Wu Jao sprang up around Hsu and Li. These men were younger officials from the hardworking middle ranks, men who had expertise but little power.

The tide had turned.

CHAPTER THIRTEEN

The tide may have turned, but it did little except infuriate the great officials who viewed the movement in support of the emperor as aimed to break their hold on the government. "That woman," Changsun said, "I knew she would cause trouble. We must get rid of her. She encourages Kaotsung to take the bit into his teeth."

There seemed no easy way to get at Jao while she lived in the imperial compound with her babies, and so the year wore on in deadlock. The young couple sometimes slipped into a depressed mood, but not often. They relished to the full their life with all its luxurious enhancements.

"Would you like to attend the privy council meetings regularly, Jao?" Kaotsung asked one morning while dressing for the dawn session of the council.

"Is it possible?" she asked eagerly, even though only half awake. "Would a female be allowed?"

"It's customary for royal women of rank to attend once in a while. No one cares as long as they observe the proprieties by staying behind a curtain and are neither seen nor heard."

"Like children," Jao mumbled.

"What?" Kaotsung asked in a muffled voice while his robe was being lowered over his head.

"Nothing," she answered quickly. "I would love to go. When?"

"Tomorrow we will be discussing the new appointments for ten or more magistrates. Your old friend Dee Something is among them. He is being transferred from an upcountry post, and the debate will be about where to send him. He is such a clever one that he always gets posted to trouble spots. This time, Penglai on the coast perhaps."

Jao's eyes shone with interest. "That's Jenjer, for you! Always reliable. . . . How I'd love to hear about him again!"

"I'll have Eunuch Kang escort you, then," Kaotsung replied, pleased that he had thought of the diversion.

"That will be perfect. I'll come gladly, and I'll be quiet as a mouse."

Jao was bright-eyed with excitement when she took her place. Through holes in the curtain, she could see all the officials. Changsun Wuji looked huge, his legs spread and his stance radiating authority. Chu was small and wiry. With his beady eyes, busy mouth, and invisible chin, he resembled nothing so much as a squirrel. And although Yu had a mole from which depended several hairs, he was always elegantly dressed, every fold and buckle in place.

Jao soon found that she enjoyed hearing the debates, acrimonious though they were. She never failed to return from a session without having her understanding broadened as to Kaotsung's problems, as to how the government worked and how power politics at the highest level was practiced. She had not been attending the meetings very long, however, before tension began to increase during them, especially in connection with matters concerning her. As time went on, there was no improvement in the obstructionist attitudes of the ministers over the question of deposing the empress and elevating her.

It was toward the end of the year, therefore, at a time of his own choosing, that Kaotsung requested a special session with the powerful officials in order to force a confrontation. They suspected what was coming. General Li Chi stayed away on a pretext. The others all appeared punctiliously, and Jao seated herself behind her curtain. While waiting in the lobby, Chu approached Changsun.

"You are above everyone else in the empire." Chu said. "You are the most important pillar of the state, so your decisions must be final. I am sure that the matter of deposing the empress will come up today. His majesty's mind is made up, and this time those who oppose him will receive punishment by exile or worse. He must never risk the infamy of exiling his own uncle. I, however, came from a thatched cottage and a humble family. I have fought in no wars and am therefore no hero, but Taitsung entrusted his will to me. Let me take the brunt of the dispute."

Changsun pretended to reject the offer but finally nodded agreement. As soon as the ministers were arranged before him, Kaotsung spoke his mind without preamble.

"Empress Wang has no sons. The Chaoyi Wu has. I propose to make the Chaoyi the next empress."

"Quite impossible," Chu said, flushing with the heat of his feelings. "The empress Wang comes from a great family and was married to Your Majesty by order of the emperor, your father. On his deathbed the emperor took my hand and said, 'I entrust my son and daughter-in-law to you.' Your Majesty heard him. Now, since the empress has committed no crime, how can she be set aside? I cannot comply."

"No crime? What about her attempts to kill me through the Black Shamans? What about her murder of my daughter? How can the Chief of the Secretariat be so ignorant?" Kaotsung replied, flushing.

Chu spoke again, even more forcefully. "If Your Majesty insists on a new empress, I request you to choose someone from the highest-ranking families. Why the Lady Wu? Why her? Why someone who has been demeaned by being in the harem of your father? Everyone knows this. You cannot hide that fact from the eyes and ears of the world. Thousands of years hence, posterity will ask why Your Majesty did this. You must think about your proposal again and yet again and reconsider."

"So it is not the will you are worried about, it is Wu Jao," Kaotsung said slowly. "What kind of a person do you think she is?"

Chu looked up, his crafty face set in mulish lines "Everyone knows . . ." he began.

"What does everyone know?" Kaotsung asked dangerously, but Chu was silent. "What does everyone know?" Kaotsung repeated. "Wu Jao performed outstanding service for my kinswoman, Abbess Li at Kanyeh Convent, then, in the palace, she earned unlimited praise for her services and kindness to Empress Wang. Now she serves me with the utmost faithfulness. What do you mean when you say 'everyone knows'?"

Chu knocked his head on the floor in a passion. "Your Majesty is blind—she is a woman of no account, and—"

"How did such a worm as you get into high position in my father's service?" Kaotsung thundered. "I myself have never heard of anything that you have ever done that entitles you to such high office."

Chu cast discretion aside and knocked his head again and again on the floor until the blood came, so great was his fury. "Your Majesty does not know my worth because you never came to the meetings. . . ."

"What meetings?" Kaotsung asked menacingly. Suddenly the room was very still. "So, it is not the will. It is not Wu Jao. It is you. And your colleagues who make important decisions in those precious secret meetings of yours. It is not the problem of the sorcery practiced against me, nor the conduct of the empress in the murder of my daughter, which agitates you. It is your determination to sweep out of your way the one person in this whole court who entirely supports me, so that you may continue to hold the reins of power."

Kaotsung's voice ceased and he surveyed the shocked officials before him. He saw that they were goggled-eyed, and their eyes—before they could lower them—openly showed their hostility. He saw determination to overrule him, he saw inflexibility, and he shuddered.

Chu, beyond reason now, continued to knock his head on the floor. He lay his ivory tablet of office on the steps of the throne. "Take back this badge of office," he shouted, and stripped off his cap. "I am through here, having offended an emperor who, although he is wrong, has the power to punish. I will retire to my farm—"

"You will not retire!" Kaotsung said, aghast at the open defiance.

Chu paid no attention, did not listen, and continued his diatribe until he lay unconscious on the steps.

"Take him away," Kaotsung said, breathing heavily. He signaled to his four guards, who were standing at attention against the wall.

Jao, white to the lips behind the curtain, muttered, "How can this be? An official speaking to the emperor like this? Rebuking, disobeying, insulting. He deserves death."

Changsun Wuji, offended by Kaotsung's outburst, finally spoke up. "Here now, here now, what does the emperor mean by willfully rejecting Chu's advice? What is it intended to accomplish? Here is the eminent Minister Chu defending Emperor Taitsung's will as he should, and Your Majesty foolishly refuses to listen. He may be a bit indiscreet, but he cannot be punished."

Kaotsung turned to his uncle, and for the first time the two looked into each other's eyes as enemies.

"You, too," Kaotsung said sadly, all anger gone, "This dispute is not over Wu Jao at all. She is just a scapegoat. You are after me, not her."

Changsun flushed a fiery red, the veins in his temples standing out alarmingly. "This is shameful. You are not yourself, the good, amenable person you used to be. It is her fault." He turned and, ignoring protocol, stalked out.

That night, neither Kaotsung nor Jao could sleep. On the following nights they could get only snatches of rest while they tried to think of a way out of their trouble. All those who had acquired position and promotion under the five years of the rule of the Elders bombarded

Kaotsung with petitioning memorials, and sought audiences to persuade him to let well enough alone.

Han Yuan, Chief of Chancellory, was almost as bad as Chu of the Secretariat, weeping as he tried to convince Kaotsung of the unwisdom of deposing the empress. Kaotsung ordered him to leave the council room; but in the days to follow, Han refused to take no for an answer. He sent in more memorials, pointing out, as if to a half-wit, that even among commoners marriage ties were unbreakable. He referred to empresses of the past, reiterating that the prosperity and peace of the nation depended on their good conduct; he cited the example of the Yellow Emperor of legend whose wife was ugly but of enormous help to him in controlling the empire.

"What nonsense is this?" Kaotsung said to Jao that night. "You are a greater help to me than all the other women of the palace combined, and you are not ugly, thank heaven."

"So much trouble just because of me?" Jao responded in a small voice. "What about Li Chi? Is he also berating you because of me?" she added, her voice trembling.

"The others have sent in similar petitions, but I have not heard from Li Chi at all. Perhaps I should ask him to report," Kaotsung said. "In addition to his commanding position in the military, he has the title of Ssu Kung—Controller of Works. That is the highest honorary title in the country. He is greater than Changsun in his influence . . . greater in judgment too."

Jao was thoughtful as she absorbed this. Kaotsung scowled, wondering how he could get Li Chi to attend the sessions again. In the course of the court's normal routine, however, Li Chi appeared in audience one morning without being asked. He was his usual urbane self. He presented his survey of the military establishments on the frontiers; he recommended the desirability of strengthening coast guard centers in Shantung; he praised the new defenses built for the navy at Penglai. The Korean question, he said, was still the most important item of foreign policy in the empire. Kaotsung's spirits rose. It was stimulating to have something vital to discuss with a responsible and hardworking official. He sighed with satisfaction.

Li Chi looked intently at the strained face of the young emperor. He put out his hand in an involuntary gesture of empathy. Kaotsung responded by abruptly bringing up his problem of the empress.

"I wish to make the Chaoyi Wu the new empress, but Minister Chu and the others fiercely oppose it," he blurted out.

Li Chi showed no surprise. He remained thoughtful for a time, then said, "This is a family matter, it is a private decision of Your Majesty. There is no need for outsiders to discuss it."

He bowed and took his departure, leaving Kaotsung breathless with excitement. He immediately sent for Jao and told her Li Chi's thoughts. She caught the implications in a flash.

"He means that it is up to us to rally our support among the younger officials ourselves, and to act," she exclaimed excitedly. "I suppose that is what he meant. Perhaps we can sidestep the deadlock in council by going after the support of younger, friendlier officials."

Kaotsung stood still, looking at her. "We could," he said. "But you may not like what will happen. Do you really want to be empress? Tell me. It might prove to be more trouble than it's worth."

"Do I want to be empress? Do I? Do I?" Jao cried, facing him, her whole body taut with emotion. "More than anything else in the world I want to be empress!" Her eyes flashing, she walked swiftly back and forth before him. "To be your empress, equal to the one I care for more than anything else in the world, living such an awesomely meaningful life with you. How could anything be better . . . ever?" She stopped pacing and threw herself into his arms. He caught her, and, feeling her exultation, swung her wildly off her feet.

"It is yours, then—to have as long as we both live—if that is what Your Majesty desires!"

"Oh you! You generous, exciting, wonderful man," she cried against his chest. "All right—let's get to work."

In a few days Kaotsung started on a program of seeking out some of the more amenable officials and engaging in frank talks with them. Minister Hsu was the first to take up cudgels on behalf of Kaotsung by speaking forcefully in the next meeting of the council. He took the line of ridicule. "Even peasants when they have a good harvest take a new wife. How much more the emperor should have the same right without everyone meddling and starting trouble!"

Hsu was also useful in energetically launching some of the most necessary actions to aid Kaotsung in reaching his goals. Changsun, enraged, withdrew to his country home for a time. Minister Chu was punished lightly by downgrading him to a provincial office. The ladies, Wang and Hsiao, were reduced to the status of commoners and put under house arrest, their relatives exiled to Kwantung in the tropical south. The two women had tried for high stakes—had Kaotsung died after the death spell was laid on him, they would have been regents for the boys Chung and Sujay. They seemingly met their punishments with fortitude.

Six days after the verdict against Wang and Hsiao, Hsu, supported by a strong group of young officials, presented a petition to Kaotsung, requesting in glowing terms that a new empress be appointed. Kaotsung solemnly accepted it. Jao was behind the screen and heard the edict being formulated. Feeling that she would burst with excitement, she dashed to the emperor's hall to talk it over with him. The moment that he was free, Kaotsung strode to his chambers to speak to his new empress.

"Did you hear it all?" he asked in high spirits.

"Every word, every single, glorious word," she bubbled.

"We've made the miracle happen . . . we've made it, we really have! Now I'll have to get a bigger throne so that you can sit on it, too!'"

"Crazy . . . !"

"Of course. And you, how are you feeling?"

Jao flung off her court cloak and spun around and around him, her arms out like wings. "Like this and like this, and this!"

Kaotsung finally captured her hands and sat her down beside him. "Breathe deeply and calm down long enough to think about the installation ceremony. You'd better get started right away, so that we can have it without any more delay," he said.

"Do you want me to plan it myself?" she asked excitedly.

"Why not?" he replied lightly.

"Why not indeed!" she repeated with enthusiasm. "I helped with gala events in the old days. I like the preparation, the excitement—I like a good show! I want to start off my life as your empress in style. To make you proud of me!"

"What a speech! Get going, then," Kaotsung replied, laughing. "You are like a hummingbird beating your wings to get at the nectar!"

"I remember Emperor Taitsung's New Year's festivities and the effect all the shows had on the people. The shows gave them good entertainment and the chance to be inside the palace," Jao said happily. "Result? Delighted acceptance of Taitsung as a great monarch!"

Kaotsung laughed, "Beat Taitsung, then."

By dawn of the first day of the eleventh month, all was ready. The weather was clear, windless, and cold. The ceremony was to take place at noon, but already at dawn the sweepers were cleaning the snow and frost from the three great courtyards fronting the main halls. Doorkeepers were opening all five gates of the main south tower, including the central gate usually reserved for the emperor alone. This time it, too, was opened for the two archdukes and highest princes in recognition of their services to the state during Taitsung's rule.

Hundreds of honor guards assembled early, clad in their best regalia, carrying their parade weapons. Banners flying, they formed up to the slow beat of the drums. Everyone in the palace, servants included, dressed in their best for the occasion.

Jao prepared herself in her Chaoyi quarters, attended by her newly appointed wardrobe mistress. She had been bathed and perfumed with attar of roses from Persia and clothed with soft white silk undergarments. The dresser covered these with a tunic of stiff brocade, a traditional ceremonial garment worn by queens on high occasions. On top of this was placed an overgarment of dark blue satin painted with flying phoenixes in rainbow colors. Falling from neck to hem was a broad red satin band on which were embroidered the imperial symbols amid stylized clouds in gold thread. Her small satin slippers and wide belt were embroidered in gold as well. Last of all, a shimmering headdress in gold filigree was pinned to Jao's chignon by Mi, who would allow no one else to touch it. It had been a gift from the Changan Korean community, and both it and the matching earrings had come from Silla.

The maids clapped their hands when Jao's costuming was complete. She seemed to have changed before their eyes, from court lady to empress. Suddenly, she was a person apart. Even Mi responded to this phenomenon by bowing, as they all did, while Jao silently walked out of her rooms to the waiting carriage.

The vehicle began to move as soon as she was in it. It was new, painted a dark blue to match Jao's tunic, and decorated with the same gold symbols. Its wheels and top had been made bright vermilion. Purple curtains hung at each of the eight small windows. Pheasant plumes fluttered from the horses' heads and harnesses, which were themselves enhanced by gold buckles, studs, and straps. Handsome horse guards rode in front of the carriage, following a colorful escort of insignia bearers. They moved forward in an orderly procession, reaching the throne hall promptly.

There was more of a crowd than had been expected. Curiosity about the new empress was great. Most of the two hundred Tang princes were there, and all nine grades of officials fully decked out in formal court robes: purple with gold and jade belts for the top three grades; two shades of lavender with gold belts for the fourth and fifth grades; two shades of green for the sixth and seventh; and two of blue for the eighth and ninth.

There was much rustling of silks and craning of necks when Jao entered on the stroke of the opening bell. The guards lining the center aisle crossed lances along each side and stood motionlessly at attention as she walked alone between them to the foot of the dais. Waiting there were three men. The emperor stood in the center, majestically alone, impressive in his imperial robes, which had been newly made for the occasion. In the position of honor on his left stood handsome Li Chi, his gray topknot covered by a full-dress military cap and his large figure by armor, intricately decorated with the insignia of his status. On the other side stood Minister Yu Cherning, impeccable in dress as usual, the highest eligible official after Li Chi. Owing to the fact that never in Yu's entire professional life had he made himself conspicuous by taking sides in a controversy, Kaotsung felt comfortable using him in the ceremony despite his former status as one of the inner group of privy council ministers.

Wu Jao halted at the steps leading to the dais and waited while her attendants, two Fei and eight Chaoyi, grouped behind her. Minister Yu read the mandate, and she mounted the steps, her long train flowing behind her. Li Chi handed her a box of glowing jewel-jade containing her seal of office. She bowed gracefully, her sleeves covering her hands to denote her humility. One of the women gathered up her train, and the archduke seated her on the queen's throne while the emperor was enthroned by Minister Yu.

Congratulatory poems in four-word lines were read by Minister Hsu in ringing tones which reverberated to the rafters. The poems were long, but Hsu knew how to abbreviate them so that the closing lines came to an end when the chimes signaling the close of the ceremony began to sound. Bells, oboes, flutes, and drums combined to make even the departure of the audience a lively part of the ceremony.

Kaotsung and Jao stood to receive their guests: the foreign envoys, the civilian and military officials, and the dignitaries of the city. The two ministers stood beside them. This innovation seemed to please most of the guests, although it obviously distressed a few. The line passed slowly, and when it descended from the dais, each guest was escorted by a well-groomed guard to the refreshment hall. Later in the afternoon the guests were entertained by singers and dancers, the best in Changan. The short winter day was ending by the time the last guest left and the chamberlains closed the doors.

After warmly thanking Archduke Li Chi and Minister Yu, Kaotsung and Jao took fast sedan chairs to their quarters, where they shed their formal clothing, left it on the floor, and fell exhausted but exuberant into bed.

The coronation turned out to have been a stunning success, inducing at one stroke acknowledgment and approval for the young couple from the people who counted in Tang society. The public also indicated approval by crowding the streets to watch any palace activity and to cheer the emperor and his new empress whenever their carriages appeared. There were, however, a number of people who remained hostile, and in time they proved to be a very dangerous group. The emperor's uncle and the new empress's brothers belonged to this second category.

Life at court fell into slow tempo, a relief after the frenetic events preceding the coronation. Jao understood the role of empress and played it with vigor and aplomb. She sensed that she had most of the palace servants on her side and a growing acceptance from an officialdom that had been more than ready for a change. She began to feel that she was destined to be empress and was going to do justice to the position. Kaotsung, too, perceived that he had established himself more firmly on the throne and was more popular than before. He had finally demonstrated his ability not only to inherit power, but also to exercise it.

Jao installed her mother and sister in a nearby pavilion where she could see them daily. It was a great boon to them all. Jao had thought to ask Kaotsung to give Holan a high rank in the harem, but Holan refused. She did not want to be confined in the palace. As for her son Hsien, after Jao had taken him, she rarely saw him. "You are more than welcome to him," she had told Jao. "I am glad that he is in good hands, that he is in line for the throne . . . and that I don't have to take care of him!" Lady Yang had looked shocked but had said nothing, and Jao had laughed with Holan.

"I want you to be content here and do as you like."

"What I like are those handsome Elite Guardsmen on leave!"

"She doesn't mean that," Lady Yang said hastily. "She likes to shock people—especially your brothers."

At this Jao looked up and spoke sharply, "Do they come here?" Surprisingly, they had not bothered her in years.

"Often. They are continually making off with whatever they see around that they like."

"What!" Jao shouted. "What right have they to come at all! I hope that they are courteous. . . ." At this, Holan snorted. "You hope! They treat Mother worse than ever, take away maids, villify you, behave exactly like the scoundrels they are."

"I'll see to that," Jao cried, her face dark with anger.

She sent for her brothers at once. They came speedily, as both worked close by in the administrative part of the palace. They did not bow when they came in, and Jao did not ask them to sit. She let them stand until they became uneasy.

"Did you have something important to say to call us away from work?" Yuanshuang blustered.

"Yes. I am going to transfer you, one of you to Hainan Island in the south and one to the border country near Tibet." Both brothers went pale with shock.

"You can't do that. We don't want to move, even it if is a promotion. Thank you but no, we don't go. We'd rather have money."

"You are in disgrace, do you understand?" Jao said sternly. "Disgrace. The guards are going to take you out of here in chains!"

Yuanshuang took a threatening step toward her, his face purple with rage. "You worthless slut," he bellowed. "You—" He did not get to finish. The sergeant at arms hurried him out of her presence along with the sweating Yuanching. Jao herself was pale, and beads of moisture had burst out on her forehead.

The next morning she petitioned Kaotsung formally to assign her brothers to posts in the provinces well away from the capital. This he did. Only in the privacy of their bed did he comment that his dear spouse had a tough side to her.

"Do you mind?" she had asked. "My brothers were disrespectful and cruel to my mother after my father died and are still imposing on her here. I am ashamed. They belong in the country," she added bitterly, remembering her youth. "Their families can accompany them, but—lucky, lucky—I get Nurse Wang back for our two!"

The move against the emperor's in-laws pleased the Confucian bureaucrats, causing many of them to eye the new empress with approval. She was behaving as she ought. It was not difficult for them then to accept the demotion of Chung as crown prince and the appointment of Jao's son, three-year-old Hung, instead.

Kaotsung, in his newfound buoyant frame of mind, began to entertain various young members of his court and some of his cousins, something that he had never done before. The Tang princes as individuals or in groups, young men from the great families and officials from the middle grades, were entertained by Kaotsung with new games and popular entertainers, singers, shadow players, performing monkeys and dogs, and most amusing of all, dancing horses.

Jao also was in good physical and mental trim. In addition to all her new interests and new duties, she found time to cultivate seasonal flowers, a hobby that she kept up no matter what else was happening to her. She had dozens of pots of Chinese lilies sprouting in dark corners, and when they bloomed in time for New Year's, they were put out in all the halls. She studied the life of Lady Pang of Han, and her famous book of etiquette for women, and wrote an up-to-date treatise herself for use among her women. She got the busy Hsu to help her with the research, and entitled the result, *On the Conduct of Women at Home*. Nun Hsu would like it, Jao thought merrily, but I don't know about the abbess. I think she would only look at me and ask if I were joking.

After three months of undiluted well-being as empress, Jao found that she was pregnant again, and her enjoyment of good health abruptly ceased. She sent in haste for Madame Sun, and was gratified when that good lady turned up at once, unchanged except for a few more gray hairs.

Jao greeted her with affection.

"What now, Your Majesty?" Madame Sun asked. "Is there another imperial prince on the way? I hope that you will have better luck this time."

A shadow passed over Jao's face at the thought of her tiny daughter who never lived, a memory that often returned to sadden her.

After Madame Sun, in consultation with the palace midwives, examined her, she and Mi put Jao on a strengthening diet and encouraged her to relax but remain active.

So, on the first balmy day after Madame Sun's visit, Jao ordered her chair for a visit with her mother to tell her about the coming of the new baby. The day was cheerful with budding foliage, and Jao found herself free, for once, of morning sickness. She went off in a lighthearted mood.

Kaotsung, whose tour with his officials had been short, was also attracted by the day to stay outdoors. He toured his familiar palace grounds, examining the azaleas, watching the goldfish in the ponds, listening to the swallows as they built their nests in the painted eaves of the halls, and loitering with pleasure in the warm sun. His wanderings led him into a remote part of the grounds where he observed a servant passing a tray of food through a hole in the wall.

"What is that for?" he asked. Before the servant could answer, loud wails and familiar voices erupted from inside.

"Great heaven," he said in surprised recognition. "Is that you, Lady Wang?"

"Indeed, indeed," she sobbed while Hsiao Fei also raised her voice.

Shocked, the emperor replied, "Tell me how you are."

They cried louder than ever. "We poor concubines are here for our crimes, why address us by our former titles? Please call our prison the Court of Remembrance."

In great distress, he promised to do so. He did not care that once this title became known, it would be perceived by the court as a reversal of the charges against the women and as a slap in the face to Jao.

Hurrying away, he stumbled through the weedy courtyards of the deserted back gardens, trembling with shock. He lost his way, spending long minutes wandering among buildings with falling plaster and roof tiles littering their yards.

He muttered to himself, " 'The Court of Remembrance' . . . indeed I do remember. I do understand what they were saying . . . those poor, poor women! And Hsiao especially, dear Hsiao . . . House arrest is one thing. Making them live without comforts is another. I shall most certainly do something."

He stood by the well a long time, gradually calming himself as he made plans for the relief of the two. While he stood there, his frightened attendants discovered him. His elbow was tugged by a discreet hand and he allowed himself to be urged back to his own quarters.

When Jao returned from the day at her mother's house, she felt relaxed. She stopped in her forecourt to look at the newly unfurled iris and breathed deeply in contentment. Mi brought out a shawl and draped it over her shoulders, then quietly told her the news of the day and of Kaotsung's visit to the ladies Wang and Hsiao.

"What!" Jao screamed, going white to the lips. She staggered as if struck. In alarm, Mi supported her inside and put her to bed, piling quilts over her rigid form to stop her shivering.

"What is the matter?" Mi ventured when she had done all she could to ease her mistress. Jao seemed not to hear. She stared at the ceiling, her sense of security vanishing as if it had never been.

All night she remained open-eyed and unhearing. Mi remained at her bedside offering sips of water from time to time, gradually understanding Jao's fears.

In the morning, Jao sent for Head Eunuch Kang and asked him to set up a screen around her bed, and to see that the Chief of Security Office, Li Iyang, reported personally to her.

"It is an emergency," she said. Li Iyang—Li Ifu's brother—arrived out of breath in his haste. She began by thanking him for his courtesy. Wasting no more time in preliminaries, she said, "Did you know that the emperor has visited the two condemned ladies?"

"Yes, Your Majesty," he answered warily.

"And did you know that they maneuvered a concession out of him within seconds?"

"We know that," he returned uneasily.

"Do you know that this won't do? Something must be done. The emperor is a kindly man and does not like to see punishments applied—even to our two boys when they deserve it. I have called you because this is not a family affair, it is state business, Talishe business, and thus your responsibility."

Li Iyang's long face grew longer. "Difficult," he murmured, "and dangerous, if I understand you."

Jao was sitting up, her face flushed, her voice high. "They were given only a light sentence. What does the Tang code have to say about punishment for the crime of sorcery against the throne, and traitors who do their best to harm the Son of Heaven?"

Li Iyang was on firmer ground now. "The penalty is death," he said. "Important cases like this are handled jointly by the Censor's Office and the first-class secretaries of Chancellory and Secretariat. If execution is involved, ratification by the emperor is required. In the cases of Wang and Hsiao, the punishment was mitigated. As long as they cause no more trouble, they are deemed harmless."

Jao broke in with jerky sentences. "The emperor wants no more trouble. He wants passionately to have no more trouble. Now he sees two helpless women as no kind of threat. He wants to ease their lot. He doesn't see that there are still factions in court who are opposed to him. Many of the older princes fared well under Changsun Wuji's rule. A solid group in the bureaucracy are just waiting for a chance to rally around the deposed empress. When and if she is free to be approached."

"I see Your Majesty's point," the Talishe chief said, suddenly more alert. "You fear that these malcontents will act?"

"They are sure to. And I will taste bitterness again," she said. An expression of such agonized hardness appeared on her face that Mi became thoroughly alarmed.

"Don't," Mi said. "You are ill and must not be so upset."

Jao paid no attention. "What do you suggest?" she asked the chief.

"A formal and lawful execution would take care of the situation," he responded coolly.

"Lawful?" Jao asked. "It must be lawful. . . ."

"I will consult with the authorities," he said, "and I will find out what can be done."

Spring's balmy beginning rapidly changed with sandstorms from the Gobi desert. They blanketed the whole of North China with a penetrating red dust. Even in the palace, life was brought to a standstill when the first storm broke. Shutters banged and flowerpots rolled around in the courtyards while servants with cloths over their mouths struggled to keep the sand—as fine as flour—at bay. The food was especially vulnerable. The days were dark even at noon, and traffic in the streets ceased until the storm should end.

In the midst of it, Jao was alerted by Mi that Talishe Li Iyang waited to see her. She rose at once and hastily took a place behind the living room screen, as was customary.

"It has been done," he said.

Jao swallowed. "How? And when?" she asked uncertainly.

"An hour ago. Only the executioner and I—by law I have to be present—were there. It was all done quickly. The women did not know what was happening when they were taken out of their prison, and had no fear. They only realized what was to befall them when they saw the executioner's ax. The empress, who was first, had to be helped to kneel. 'I see that death is my lot,' is all she said."

"What about the other one? Please report," Jao asked, dry-lipped.

Li Iyang paused. "As you will, Your Majesty. Hsiao Fei was hysterical. She watched the knife fall on the empress and then exploded in fright and anger, screaming and struggling. She shouted—pardon, Your Majesty—'Ah, Wu is a fox who has done this thing. In my future lives I will return as a cat and she will be a mouse and I will tear her throat out!' Then her head was severed and all was over. Only a few minutes, Your Majesty . . ."

Jao said nothing. She was trying to control her churning stomach.

Li Iyang continued. "My brother, Li Ifu, and my uncle, Minister Hsu, worked it out with the Censorate. They agreed that the Elders could well seize upon any leniency toward the empress as a golden opportunity to reinstall her. They need a pipeline into the palace again."

"Your actions have been correct," Jao mumbled as she paused to wipe the red dust out of her eyes. "How did the privy council decide on this . . . this action?"

"At the appointed time we presented to the privy council the accumulated list of crimes requiring execution—about a dozen from the whole empire for the winter—and the emperor reluctantly, as always on such occasions, ratified it along with their punishments."

"Did he recognize the names of Wang and Hsiao on the list?' Jao asked.

"I read out the list of the crimes they committed—murder, treason, sorcery, all from the Ten Abominations—and then separately read the list of names."

"Did you do that so that he would accept the petition without hesitation, not realizing what he was doing?" Jao returned after a short pause. Li Iyang did not reply to her question, and, after a pause, she concluded the interview.

"Thank you for your report, then. I am grateful. The emperor will be grateful—in time—when he fully comprehends the danger to his rule in this case. Accept our thanks. As soon as the wind dies and transport is available, there will be five cartloads of gifts delivered to your door."

That night, Jao refused her food, refused to see her sons, and begged for a night away from the marital bed on the grounds of illness. She could not sleep, but finally, in the early morning hours, she drifted into a doze from which she awoke screaming. Apparitions appeared by her bedside—two headless women, disheveled and bloody. She had heard them shrieking in their agony. She covered her ears and crouched in a corner to get away from the sight and sound.

"My lady!" Mi cried, grasping Jao's flailing hands. "Wake up! You are having a nightmare!"

Mi gathered Jao into her arms and rocked her until she gradually recovered. Confused and ashamed, Jao put her hands over her eyes and breathed deeply, while Mi pulled the quilt around her, clucking in dismay.

"Now stay warm and I will bring a drink of barley water and that good sedative from Silla which will calm you," Mi said. When she returned and Jao had taken the medicine, Mi settled herself on a mat beside the bed, as she had in the days when Jao was a tsairen afraid of being murdered.

"Now you sleep, Mi is here and will not leave for any reason," she murmured in soothing tones.

"Th-Thank you, Mi, I'm all right," Jao gasped, stretching out on her *kang* bed and pulling more quilts around her. She was so cold.

No sooner had she fallen asleep, however, than the apparitions appeared again, and this time a monster cat was with them. The cat sprang at her throat and she screamed so loudly that she could be heard throughout the compound. It was a long while before Mi could quiet her the second time. The servants gathered half dressed and alarmed, until Jao, thoroughly awakened, dismissed them, half laughing and half shuddering in panic. She did not try to sleep again that night, and the next morning lost no time in issuing an order that all cats in all six palaces were to be disposed of at once.

The following night she could not sleep at all. Mi administered more powerful drugs, but they seemed only to confuse her and prevent sleep. Mi was thoughtful. "In Silla," she told Jao, "we believe so strongly in the magic power of names that our kings and queens and all their families are given Buddhist names for protection. Other names, ominous names, can also be effective, but against one's enemies."

"Tell me," Jao said.

"If the empress Wang could be renamed, it would determine the nature of her rebirth. Call her 'mang'—snake—and she could never get near you because every man's hand is against snakes and none are ever loose in the palace. Wang-mang, easy to repeat in an incantation. The magic name of Hsiao could be shiao—vulture. Hsiao-shiao, Wang-mang, Hsiao-shiao . . . say them over and over. Wang and Hsiao will be reborn snake and vulture, and so will their descendants. Do this and then you will sleep. Wang-mang, Hsiao-shiao . . ."

Jao was aware of the shadowland she was entering, where only the shamans should venture, but she followed where she was led. Mi was a shamaness in her own country, adept in the mysteries . . . The magic of the words was hypnotizing and Jao was comforted.

Soothing Jao's temples, rubbing her feet, and chanting the monotonous spells, Mi finally got Jao to doze. She woke again in an hour, but had not had a nightmare. Believing that the magic had taken effect, she easily slipped into sleep again.

This surcease was short. The ghosts appeared to her so frequently that she felt she must do something drastic or go mad. She sent for a well-known Taoist exorcist to rid the palace of evil spirits. He arrived with an army of assistants. They brought out their most powerful sorcerers and performed their most efficacious rites, using incantations with accompanying drums and rattles, performing live sacrifice with animals, and burning clouds of incense. The noise reached Kaotsung's ears, and when he heard that the sorcerers had come at Empress Wu's bidding, he lost no time in calling her to account.

"It is dangerous to have these people invade us like this," he said. "We have enemies, no one knows that better than you, and some of them are sure to twist things, accuse you. . . ."

"Of what?" Jao asked, blunt and frightened.

"Of black magic, not white magic."

Jao looked sick. "These sorcerers I hired are ridding the palace of ghosts and evil spirits. The palace shamans—who never practice black magic and never even learn about such criminal activities—are working with the city shamans. They will surely rid us of the evil spirits that are all around us now. Please, have patience."

Kaotsung listened attentively. "Nevertheless, I'd rather not have the city sorcerers here. Their chanting the same thing over and over again for hours, all this smoke of burning feathers, burning flesh, burning incense—get them out."

"Of course," Jao replied, nervous and on edge. "I'll arrange it immediately."

The nightmares continued sporadically. Jao became worn and so ill that she could not leave her bed. Kaotsung, believing that her condition was due to her pregnancy, did not worry. His own sleep, however, was being severely disturbed, and this soon worried him more. Every night the rats came out, ran about in the rafters, had fights, and created a constant scurrying over the ceilings. There seemed to be hordes of them nightly.

"The rats racket about without fear," he complained to Eunuch Kang. "Order the Household Office to do something about it."

Eunuch Kang cleared his throat. "There are no cats in the palace city anymore, and the rats have multiplied beyond control. They are now so bold that they attack infants in their cribs."

"Then bring in all the cats you can catch and have done with the matter! Bring in an army of cats and that will be the end of it," Kaotsung returned, both irritated and amused.

"Yes sir," Kang agreed, "but impossible, Your Majesty. Empress Wu has outlawed cats from all the palaces."

"What!" Kaotsung exclaimed. "Whatever for? Well, never mind, then I shall ask her about this . . . and also how she manages with the rats."

When he visited Jao that evening, he brought up the subject at once. She told him the story of her nightmares, not without shudders and pauses and nervous choking fits. She did not, however, reveal the source of her dreams. Kaotsung was taken aback.

Jao, trembling in her misery, said finally, "I'll get Chi to round up some cats, lean and starving, and they'll rid your quarters of rats immediately." She watched him closely while he sat in silence, then said, "It is more than just cats and rats. This place, this palace city, is old and on low ground and is water-stained from leaks and full of rats and scorpions and fleas and lice and mildew, and it has been thirty years since Taitsung had this place patched together out of the old Sui palaces."

She had Kaotsung's complete attention. "What are you trying to say?" he asked.

"The Taminggung, the old firebird summer palace in the imperial park north of the city . . ."

"What about it?" he asked warily.

"It is on much higher ground, and it is free of the bad spirits of this palace. It was newly built by Taitsung as a retreat, a vacation home. It would be lovely to move into it. A change is just what you need."

"I'm all right here, where I have been all along—comfortable and close to the government."

"Too close," she muttered so softly that he did not hear. "You will be more comfortable in the Taminggung than you have ever been before," she continued desperately.

"Are you defying me?" he joked to lighten the conversation, while eyeing her speculatively.

Pulling his sleeve, she sat him down next to her sand tray. She drew a picture of the buildings of the Taminggung in the sand with her finger. "There! Let us think about how to fix this unused palace to suit ourselves. We'll draw up some plans together tonight. The babies do not thrive as they ought here, and neither do I. Nor do you, if you only knew it. In the firebird palace on the hills you could see over the city and enjoy the cool summer breezes. . . ." She stopped and peered at him anxiously.

Kaotsung looked at the tray, looked out at the courtyard darkening in the early evening, and said thoughtfully, "We might try it. Let's see how it works."

Jao hid her face in her hands in relief. "You'll see," she mumbled. "We can make it a delightful home. This palace is haunted. I hate it, I hate it!"

Kaotsung said in consternation, "I'll give the orders for the renovations tomorrow."

New and spacious quarters in Taminggung were prepared for occupancy within the month. They were whitewashed, hung with colorful curtains, and outfitted sparsely with freshly constructed bamboo furniture. The rooms appeared uncluttered and cool. Kaotsung walked through his suite, beaming with satisfaction.

"Very good, excellent, I congratulate you," he said to the director of works, Yen Lifu. "We will move in at once. You have thought of everything!" Yen bowed. He was pleased. It had been a challenge at such short notice, but he had willingly accepted the assignment. He was a master builder, the best in the empire, and felt obliged to do as good a job for the third emperor of Tang as he had done for the second.

The move into the new palace by the imperial family was carried out smoothly on the one bright day between two rainstorms. Guards and servants were obliged to camp out in unfinished outbuildings, but they joked about the innovations that they were obviously enjoying.

"You won't have to sit up all night any longer because of evil spirits or because of my nightmares," Jao whispered to Mi as she draped gauze mosquito curtains over the boys' beds. "We can enjoy a peaceful summer here, and I can eat and rest and behave myself for the benefit of the new baby."

"Yes, Your Majesty," Mi agreed, looking around her with approval. The boys accepted the change excitedly. Hung, age three, and Hsien, two, romped through the new rooms, shouting. Corralled by their nurses, they were shown their own room and prepared for bed. There was a full-sized new bamboo bed for Hung and a cot for Hsien. When their nightclothes had been pulled over their heads, Hsien ran for the large bed and settled on it with a challenging thump. Hung watched him in silence. He was leaning against Jao, who had come in for the customary hug at bedtime.

"Which bed to you want?" she asked him. Hung pointed to the smaller one, which was adorned by a new tiger pillow.

"Hung wants the tiger," he answered and dived for the stuffed animal pillow with its glowing amber eyes sitting on the cot. Thereupon Hsien set up a howl. "My pillow! Mine!" he yelled, dashing to grab hold of one furry ear. Hung quickly let go of the tiger, and Hsien lost his balance and toppled. When everyone burst out laughing, he immediately stopped yelling and began to laugh too. Mi scooped him up, tossed him to the rafters, and cuddled him into his own cot.

Hung, in the meantime, looked up at his mother, his eyes dancing.

"I don't like tiger pillows. That's why nurse didn't put one on my bed," he whispered.

"You little devil!" she cried, hugging him with approval at this display of diplomacy. Hung glowed. Her approval was hard to get.

The summer evening had darkened into night when the nursery finally settled and Jao could go to Kaotsung. She was jubilant. "We are going to be happy here," she announced. "You'll see!"

Chapter Fourteen

Kaotsung stepped over the threshold, scowling. It was four in the morning of a cold day in November, and he was late for the bimonthly plenum of his ministers, a session that still gave him butterflies in his stomach.

Jao shot a puzzled glance at Mi when the door closed behind him. Arranging a seat near the glowing brazier, Mi missed the look entirely. "Here, my lady, sit down and rest your feet on this stool."

"Thank you," Jao replied. "The emperor is cross much of the time these days, and it worries me. Nor is he paying much attention to me."

Mi paused in arranging Jao comfortably in her seat and gazed perceptively at her. "He will pay attention soon—when he gets this new son. This baby will be his first boy whose mother has high enough rank to entitle him to be crown prince at birth. He is very keen on that. And don't worry, you'll get more than enough attention as soon as he can get Your Majesty in bed again."

"Mi!" Jao scolded. "How can you joke about such a thing! How dare you!" They both laughed gaily. Jao felt better at once, although she was uncomfortably heavy, and tired of waiting. She watched Mi move gracefully around the room unpacking baskets of supplies for the midwives and arranging them in convenient piles on the *kang*.

"You look so well this morning. Your skin is glowing, your cheeks are rosy, your hair is shiny. I envy you!" Jao said slowly.

Mi stopped in her tracks and stared, her slight figure motionless under her hand-loomed woolen tunic. "Me? For heaven's sake!" She chuckled. "Your jealousy won't last long, I assure you. Your figure will soon be more slender than mine and your skin more satiny and your smiles more radiant—right now you are not at your best, true enough. You're too pale. You aren't worrying again, are you?"

Jao pulled at her shawl and frowned. "Just a hair's breadth," she sighed, "just that much separates me from disaster—that's all."

"Whatever do you mean?" Mi protested. "What nonsense! Here you are, already a year on the throne as empress, on top of the world with all under heaven below you, and best of all, your new son is expected. How can you say such things!"

"All the same, that is the way I feel! I may be on top of the world, but I could topple at any moment! Just one push too much against Kaotsung and I am gone. He is the only one between me and total disaster. More than ever before. All those powerful men leaning on Kaotsung—Changsun and Chu and the rest."

"Now you know Chu was sent away, exiled, to a far province last year when he so openly and violently opposed your marriage and elevation to the throne."

"I know. But Chu was sent as a military governor and has charge of troops. He could secretly bring them to Changan to aid Uncle Changsun in toppling Kaotsung."

"Mistress!" Mi interrupted. "That is preposterous. You are not well . . . the baby."

Jao's eyes fell. "The baby, yes, of course. I hope he will come soon—now! I hope that he will be another boy to strengthen my position here. And it would please Kaotsung and strengthen *his* position. But still, I don't know . . ." Jao rose abruptly and started to pace restlessly up and down the hall. "The Elders are growing stronger day by day, while we enjoy ourselves in this new palace. I am isolated while I am having this baby, and the emperor is—well—passive, while they are active. They're now planning to put Kaotsung aside and elevate Prince Chung to the throne, I hear."

"Prince Chung! The forgotten adopted son of ex-Empress Wang, what a nightmarish idea! Impossible! Chung is no longer crown prince and is not in line for the throne, Hung is!" Mi exclaimed.

"That is just why I worry. If they push Kaotsung out, I am out, Hung is out, all of us are out!"

"No way to talk!" Mi protested, frowning while Jao stalked about the room.

"It's snowing," Jao said after a few minutes of prowling.

"So it is. That may be why Madame Sun has moved into the palace. For fear, perhaps, that we would be snowbound as we were when Hung was born. It's a good thing too. The way you are walking, I think you are close to delivery."

"Do you think so?" Jao brightened. "I so want to have this baby for Kaotsung. He has done so much for me. He has never weakened in opposing all those formidable Elders for my sake. I would do anything to repay him."

Mi chuckled. "You do more than enough for him already," she said lightly.

Jao grimaced. "Yes indeed, just now I am remarkably attractive, winsome, and indeed peerless!" she said cynically.

Jao was not in a better mood at dusk, when a draft of cold air swept in as Kaotsung entered, snowflakes still on his tunic. He was in good humor.

"I had a wonderful day chasing rabbits and birds," he said. "I got a brace of pheasants. How about you?"

"Nothing to boast about," Jao said, her spirits rising now that he was back.

Kaotsung's damp mantle fell on the floor. Eunuch Kang, who had come in behind him, picked it up. Kaotsung dropped down on the *kang* beside Jao. "I'm hungry," he announced.

"The kitchen is ready with your dinner," Kang offered. "They know you are back, and are bringing a meal now." A rattle of dishes could be heard as the serving cart was wheeled along the terrace.

"Good," Kaotsung replied absentmindedly as he scrutinized Jao while the food was being laid out on a trestle table. He sat down.

Jao found that she was able to eat for the first time in the day. Her cheeks grew red and her eyes bright. She began to look happy and lighthearted. Kaotsung responded with admiring glances, raising her spirits still higher.

When the dishes were removed and the attendants dismissed, Kaotsung leaned back on the *kang* and sighed. "Tasty food after a fine day hunting, I feel good. And you . . . you too?"

"Good enough!" Jao returned judiciously. "I've been trying not to think of . . . worrying things."

"Right!" he said forcefully. "I am too. In fact, I'm greatly encouraged about life in general. Li Chi is back of me—in his own mysteriously successful way—and most of the new officials are reasonable men, so perhaps we are in for some peaceful times ahead."

Jao looked at him sharply. "All the old problems fading out and no new ones yet? That seems unlikely."

"There is one—and it seems silly—but it's still real. The great families have hundreds of sons who want positions in the government."

Jao looked surprised. "What do you mean? Why is it your problem?"

Kaotsung picked up the tongs and shifted a coal. "The clan families have had years to enhance their great estates. Their wealth from the plains keeps pouring in. Every year these families grow more affluent."

"What's wrong with that?" Jao replied in astonishment.

"Nothing—except that each one of the numerous sons of all these notables is aiming for service in our government, and lifelong luxurious support furnished by the state. The families of the Tang princes number in scores. The great families number in the hundreds. New men from the provinces cannot find positions because the powerful families seek posts day and night for their own."

"What has all this got to do with you? Why are you concerned at all?" Jao was still mystified.

"Because every day, the Elders and their friends among the princes and the clans are putting their own men into the central government and manipulating the officials who support me into rural posts."

"Oh," Jao said. "Yes, I see. Our palaces are surrounded by mansions, newer and more splendid than our pieced-together buildings . . . each one with at least twenty children, dozens of concubines, and of course, thousands of servants. Changsun Wuji must have about thirty sons, not counting daughters, and so far all his adult sons are in government positions in Changan."

Kaotsung nodded. "You see as I do. What else?"

"Well, about rural candidates for high office . . . I hear about the Dee family through my mother. Jenjer is brilliant but is continually being assigned to rural posts and never appointed to the central government. There's no place for him here in the capital, and his family is discouraged."

"That's why I aim to change things," Kaotsung said. "With my man Hsu in Chancellory and my man Li Ifu in the Secretariat, we are well set to control appointments in the future."

"With Han still second in Chancellory and Lai in Secretariat, the Elders are still in position to make trouble," Jao objected.

"Hsu and Li will stop the manipulation," Kaotsung returned. "They know that it will become a huge problem unless dealt with now."

"That's good to hear—" Jao stopped abruptly, aware of sudden inner turmoil. "Oh dear!" she gasped.

"What?" Kaotsung began. "Shall I send for Madame Sun?"

"Right away would be best," Jao suggested.

Madame Sun entered, looking pleased. "So," she greeted Jao, "You have decided that you need me after all."

Jao smiled excitedly. "No one is more welcome than you!"

"That is right, I endorse Jao's greeting a hundredfold," Kaotsung exclaimed fervently as he tried to appear nonchalant. He only succeeded in looking daunted and upsetting Jao.

Madame Sun bowed formally and then directed an expectant look at the emperor. "Your Majesty is leaving us now?"

"Well, yes, I suppose I was on the way out," Kaotsung said. He took both Jao's hands in his, pressed them hard, and stumbled as he stepped over the threshold, red-faced and beginning to perspire. Eunuch Kang held the door for him.

Flustered, Jao watched him leave. "He's not used to being dismissed," she said uncertainly.

Madame Sun patted her back. "It is time for you to forget him and think about yourself. It's time. Warm in here, very warm. Good."

Madame Sun did not leave the hall all night, but stayed close to Jao, talking to her calmly and giving her encouraging instructions. All was normal. The infant was in a good position, and Jao did not not fight her instructions. She pulled on her silk ropes when told to, rested when told to, and strained when told to. At dawn the baby arrived without incident.

"Wh-What is it? Tell me quickly," Jao stammered.

"Male," was the reply, and Jao had enough strength left to give a shriek of joy.

"A son!" Kaotsung shouted when he came into the hall an hour later.

"Are you pleased?" Jao whispered, her cheeks wet with tears of weakness.

"I'll name him Chung—Chungtsung," Kaotsung said, rubbing his hands. "The empress has given me another son, and now I have three. *Hau, hau.* Good, good. We shall celebrate, not only in the palace but also in the whole country! Kang—set off the palace firecrackers now and have the gate-tower drums beaten!"

Jao burst into tears, unable to speak.

The days passed, heavy and dark, with leaden skies and cold winds. Every day Jao ventured out briefly into the near courtyards for fresh air, quickly retreating indoors again. She moved into a room near the nursery and, on her first day there, selected a wet nurse, a red-cheeked woman from a nearby village. In the days that followed, in spite of good care, the infant was slow to gain weight, and slow in other ways as well. Jao kept a watchful eye on him, but meanwhile expanded her own activities until she was back into her normal schedule of court duties.

One evening, after a day of one misfortune after another, she lost her temper. The children had been fretful and at the end of the day would not go to bed—tractable Hung as well as intractable Hsien. Baby Chung was restless and refused to come to his father, crying in fright for his nurse. Even Kaotsung was surly after all the wrangles with his ministers.

"It's all too much," Jao muttered. She spoke sternly to the children. Hung looked startled and Hsien put his thumb in his mouth. "You may all leave now, nurses and all," she said in such a harsh tone that Kaotsung looked at her in surprise. The nurses hastily departed.

"What's wrong?" he asked.

"It's no use. Nothing will ever work out for us here. Here in this drafty palace, here in this windy city of Changan, here in this isolated plateau country. This poor palace is outshone by too many great estates."

"Well, if that's what is bothering you, I can build you a new palace—" Kaotsung began.

"A new palace won't solve the problem! We'd still be surrounded by these supercilious people. We are entrapped by them!"

Kaotsung nodded grimly. "My father was free of them, of course. And of all their pressures."

"How can we escape?" Jao paused, suddenly breathing heavily in her excitement. "Let us flee!"

"Flee?" he repeated in amazement.

"Yes . . . flee this wretched city. And go to Loyang. It is our second capital and logical for us. It's located in the rich lowlands near three great rivers and the Grand Canal—it's more the real center of the empire than Changan. You could set up your own court and live in peace. You have said before that the administration is in good hands here."

Kaostung was silent, but a speculative look had come into his eyes. "Let us talk about it," he said. They remained in the dark, wrapped in furs, talking until late. Their voices were low and their fingers locked while they sat closely together, making the decisions. Jao was enchanted. She had Kaotsung's full attention again and his interest. He was won over.

They started for Loyang in the third week of the new year. Baby Chungstung was two months old and deemed old enough to travel. Everyone took to the journey with a sense of adventure. Kaotsung had with him only a skeleton staff, having left the major politicians behind with all the great families. Taitsung's former Loyang palace had been refurbished and enlarged enough to house everyone comfortably, even his royal highness, Baby Chung.

The young emperor and his empress soon found that Loyang suited them very well. For a while they enjoyed a second honeymoon, learning to love Loyang better than any of the other places they had lived.

A few weeks after their arrival winter ended and spring began. The neglected palace gardens came to life with flowers and trees blossoming riotously in all the courtyards. Hung and Hsien took avidly to their new freedom to run about, to climb trees and to play in the ponds. Inevitably, this caused their servants endless trouble, but cheered them as well. There were open courts, open skies, streams and canals everywhere, and the chance to explore. It was an enormous contrast to the cramped palaces of Changan. Even the baby, scrawny from birth, gained weight and strength while he lay naked in the warm air.

Rural magistrates and generals learned very quickly to dispatch their reports directly to Loyang, bypassing the upper bureaucracy in the main capital.

Kaotsung was more than satisfied by his new position of control over middle-level bureaucracy. "I am in direct receipt of information from all over the country in a way that I never was before," he told Jao one spring evening when they were sitting in the garden, enjoying the long twilight. "Not only because of the lesser bureaucracy, but, with all the canals and rivers, communication is faster here in Loyang. That's not the only reason I like it better than Changan—it's warmer, it has all these lovely gardens, and none of the wealthy families would dream of living here."

Jao laughed. "Is that why I feel nothing hanging over my head here as I did in Changan? Whatever the reason, I love this place. I wish we could stay here forever!"

Kaotsung shook his head. "Someday we may move the capital here permanently, but not yet," he said gloomily. "I'm doing well here, but the fact is that I am only doing half my job. We have to go back to Changan soon. This place may be better for local affairs of administration, but it doesn't work at all for foreign affairs or high politics."

Jao looked rebellious but was afraid to anger Kaotsung by arguing. He knew very well how she felt. She set about readying the family to return to Changan in late spring.

"We have now run away to Loyang five times in thirty months," said Jao one evening in March as she picked up her embroidery. It was more than two years later and they were still officially domiciled inside Changan's palace city. She cast a speculative glance at Kaotsung. "We have lived in Loyang as many months as in Changan. We are always much healthier there, especially Baby Chung." He was two and a half now and finally sturdy.

"Yes," Kaotsung said. "I enjoy Loyang too, but I have to stay on top of things here. The foreign representatives and their enclaves are all here, and right now the Koguryans are crossing our borders. I have sent our best general, Su, to the frontier to stop them."

Jao watched Kaotsung closely. She was feeling her way with him. "People think that we are wildly frivolous to be traveling so much, with three babies at that. Of course, they're blaming it all on me," she added. She gave a tiny shrug and stole another wary glance at her husband, but Kaotsung ignored her comment.

"Let me tell you about this matter with Li Ifu . . . humorous really," Kaotsung said. "I can't do without him, but he is always stirring up something."

"What has he done now?" Jao asked in a bored voice. "Has he created trouble? You wanted him to do that—against the right people, of course. He is just a talented opportunist, it seems to me. Good-looking, but greedy and sly."

"He is all that and more," Kaotsung agreed. "Sometimes he doesn't show any more sense than a four-year-old. This last escapade of his was a storm in a teacup, but the censors have been aroused and blown it out of all proportion. Apparently, Li took a fancy to a woman prisoner and winkled her out of jail. A censor eager for promotion heard about it and pounced."

"What have a female convict and a petty official got to do with anything important enough to reach the privy council?" Jao asked, mystified.

"The same old thing," Kaotsung answered, "raising its ugly head again. The Elders are behind it. In this case they are after Li because he is a mainstay of mine. The accusation is that Li used his high office to murder an official."

"Murder!" Jao exclaimed sharply, her attention caught.

"The jailkeeper committed suicide, thus removing himself from having to testify. They say that Li drove him to suicide."

"Guesswork. Specious," Jao answered disapprovingly.

"I agree. Han and Lai, the Elders' strongest men, have been after Li a long time. Now Hsu also interests them because he's our main supporter, but they are more afraid of him. I had thought that these two pairs of men—Hsu and Lai, Li and Han—would balance each other and keep the government stable. Instead it has been like putting a mongoose in a cage with a cobra. The case was dropped, but another censor is after Li now. After the Elders failed in their outrageous attempt to reinstate Chu, they are trying this censor tactic. So far I have foiled them. I aim to be respected."

"As you should be!" Jao broke in.

"Also respected by my empress," he added.

"That seems fair," Jao said.

"All will be well then!" Kaotsung returned lightly. "And as for my uncle Changsun, as long as he works on the history of the first two emperors of this dynasty and stays out of my business, all will continue to go my way."

But all was not well. In a few days Kaotsung sought out Jao to warn her that they could not go to Loyang at any time in the near future. "So don't ask! Someday we may permanently move the capital to Loyang, but not yet. My men have not been able to withstand the pressure of the Elders. This time they have plotted a new conspiracy. They are now rallying around Wang's adopted son, to establish him as the new emperor if I prove to be unacceptable."

"What!" Jao cried. "Unacceptable! How do they dare think that they can remove you! How do they dare?"

"Well, they do," Kaotsung answered patiently. "After all, my uncle Changsun was one of the principals in removing the Sui dynasty and establishing the Tang dynasty. He was key in removing First Tang Emperor Kaotzu and establishing Second Emperor Taitsung. Why shouldn't he remove Third Emperor Kaotsung and establish ex-Crown Prince Chung? A neat move, leaving him yet again in a position of great power."

Jao jumped to her feet in agitation. "The situations in the past were very different from what we have now. You have been emperor for eight years and the country is peaceful, prosperous, and settled. You are a good emperor and are running a good empire! Yes, you are—don't interrupt—you are a good ruler. All this conspiring is despicable!"

"Don't worry. I'm exiling the worst of the Elders to the country—Han and Lai—as governors of outlying provinces. They will never to serve in the capital again. They learned nothing from Chu's having being sent away in disgrace, but petitioned to have him brought back, and stepped up their efforts to conspire against me. And I've made sure that Chu is exiled to a more isolated spot in the mountains. That will do it. The Elders are scattered now and can't make me any more trouble."

"I hope that you are right," Jao responded dubiously.

"Kaotsung laughed. "Don't be so pessimistic. It isn't like you to look on the dark side of things! I'm rid of all the Elders, the threatening ones at any rate. My headaches have ceased. I have favorable reports from General Su about his patrols of the borders of Koguryo. So it looks as if all my worst problems are being solved."

"Yes," Jao said with all the enthusiasm she could muster. "No one could have made better decisions or carried them out better. You have already achieved enough for history to declare you a good emperor, and you are only twenty-nine. In fact, you are now so well-established that the Elders will have to give up harassing you and begin to enjoy their old age in peace."

Kaotsung nodded in agreement and they smiled at each other. Surely the Elders, scattered now, would cease their conspiracies.

It was the first evening that was warm enough to sit out on the terrace. The twilight was accompanied by the sounds of migrating birds settling in for the night to the accompaniment of myriad croaking frogs in all the lotus ponds.

Kaotsung sighed heavily a number of times and moved restlessly in his seat. Jao became apprehensive.

"What is the matter—tell me at once!" Jao urged.

"My uncle," Kaotsung said grimly.

"Again? I thought he'd given up."

Kaotsung glanced down. "Far from it. There has now been a confrontation. It's all come to a head."

"What happened?" Jao quavered.

"Hsu brought up a case. It seemed minor—involving a low-ranking librarian on the staff of my son, Chung."

"Oh, no, not Chung again! I'm afraid to ask what his librarian has to do with your uncle."

"Hsu accused the man of forming an illegal opposition party. The poor wretch is a close friend of Changsun's Number One Son. Changsun is using the two to direct yet another movement to dethrone me and replace me with Chung."

Jao went pale. "Is this true?"

"Hsu says the coup is imminent. But it doesn't make sense. Why should my uncle conspire with a nonentity? I can't trust Hsu entirely. I have a bad headache . . . I don't want to talk anymore." He went inside abruptly.

Jao watched him leave and beckoned to Mi, who was waiting a respectful distance away. "Mi, listen to me carefully. A coup is about to be launched, and Kaotsung, if he is lucky, will be exiled. And I? If I'm lucky, I'll get to go with him. If not . . ." She looked at her friend in great agitation. "How can we escape? Perhaps to the convent, with Kaotsung disguised. . . ."

Mi was silent for a moment. "It hasn't happened yet," she said at length. "And you have everything on your side. But you have to fight back. Ruthlessly."

Jao nodded, her face set in hard lines.

The emperor did not call on his uncle and what was worse, his uncle did not call on him. Hsu, however, was upset at finding himself out of favor with Kaotsung. In despair, he sought out Wu Jao for a private interview. She received him in a small reception room where there was a convenient screen for her to sit behind. Hsu told her that the bureaucracy was totally demoralized and that neither he nor Li Ifu could control the dispersal of loyal officials out of the central government to rural posts. The strong support that Changsun enjoyed from the powerful families of Changan was far too deeply entrenched.

"The older officials maintain a front of authority and stern determination while Kaotsung has allowed the exiled ministers to agitate in the provinces. Now no one knows which side is going to win out."

Jao gulped. "Is this true—what you are saying? A crisis? How could Kaotsung have known that the Elders were going to continue to agitate after their exiles?"

"No one, of course," Hsu answered impatiently. "The trouble is that rulers have to consider all possibilities or they no longer rule. Something must be done to strike terror into these exiled old officials. To do this, I want to publicize the downfall of Empress Wang and give out the story of her execution. I will then proceed with further punishment for the exiled Elders who are actively hostile. Do I have your permission to exaggerate the fates of Wang and Hsiao and hint at worse to come for all conspirators?"

"I don't like this . . . I have no authority to interfere," Jao began in a frightened voice, terrified that her part in those executions would be revealed to Kaotsung in all its worst aspects.

"There is no alternative now! This faction, especially Changsun Wuji, must be wiped out or you are done for," Hsu said harshly. "We can't deal with these men on any other basis. It has been ten years since Emperor Taitsung's death, and still there is no peace."

Jao winced. "Kaotsung has been a good ruler all these years," she began. Then she recalled the efforts that she had made to placate and cooperate with Changsun, that her mother had made, that Kaotsung and Hsu and others had made, all to persuade him to let Kaotsung rule unhampered. All had failed. Hsu was right when he said that she was done for if Changsun's faction survived.

She said finally, her face as pale as his, "Very well."

Hsu bowed and left her presence.

In the next few days the privy council met in further stormy sessions. The court and city buzzed with frightened speculation. The story of the execution of the two ladies, Wang and Hsiao, was luridly retold. Supposedly, they had received a hundred lashes apiece, had their hands and feet cut off, were thrown into a brewing vat where they lived for several days before expiring, and then, finally, their corpses were cut into small pieces. Jao called Hsu to an audience when she learned about this propaganda through Chi.

"Why a hundred lashes?" she asked in consternation. "In their miserable conditions, such delicate women could not stand even ten. Why exaggerate when the decapitation alone was bad enough? No one but a fool will believe all this, a hundred lashes and the rest of it!"

"The world is made up of fools, madame," Hsu responded dourly.

At long last Kaotsung permitted his chop to be put to the decree that stripped the great Changsun of his rank and titles, and exiled his sons with him.

"My uncle is to be furnished with guards and given full honors in his exile," Kaotsung stipulated sternly when the fatal session ended. At the same meeting, edicts were prepared to recall the exiles, Han and Liu Shih, to answer new charges. The conduct of the treason trials was put into the hands of the most influential man to be found, General Li Chi himself.

Meanwhile, Jao requested that her friend Cloud be permanently released from the convent to take a position with her as her chief attendant. She was as much of a comfort as Mi in a protracted crisis. Cloud's kind empathy always helped reduce a problem to manageable size.

"I need you both!" Jao said as she hugged Cloud. "Mi is a treasure, a priceless treasure, but she never becomes emotional. I do. Especially now that my fate is tied so closely to Kaotsung's." Jao was close to panic in her anguish. "This is the worst thing, the very worst thing that could happen to Kaotsung—to have to preside over the trials of old family friends, supporters of his uncle, and be unable to soften their sentences because the least sign of sympathy makes him look weak and foolish to his own supporters."

Jao began to pace the floor angrily. "There are so many of them. Floods of them! And all of them, all of Changsun's faction, have to go in order to destroy their power base."

"Does Kaotsung appreciate that this purging will make him secure at last?" Cloud asked quietly. "And you too?"

"He knows, but how he feels is another thing. As for me, I can't stand this waiting, this endless waiting!"

Cloud greeted this with a nod. Waiting was what she did best.

The next morning the three women were sitting together in dilatory conversation when the news came that Changsun had hanged himself. Kaotsung burst into the women's parlor, speechless with shock. They hastily gathered around him to commiserate and soothe.

"He died like the great man he was," Kaotsung said bitterly, his eyes glittering with unshed tears.

"I agree, I agree," Jao cried in sympathy. Nonetheless, she felt that Changsun would have been a greater man had he retired in the normal way and died in his bed, thus sparing his family and friends untold suffering.

In November, winter settled on the highlands in earnest as one dark, windy day followed another. Kaotsung remained moody and depressed just when he should have been relieved and happy because of his victory. Jao was thrown into confusion, not knowing how to handle the new situation. She started her campaign to cheer Kaotsung by organizing a big double birthday party for him and three-year-old Chung. Since she disliked the old Changan palaces more than ever, she followed this with a project to move to Loyang. Now that the threat of usurpation was a thing of the past, she wanted a permanent residence there. Kaotsung gave no resistance, but was not enthusiastic either. The birthday celebrations fell flat and neither thirty-year-old Kaotsung nor three-year-old

Chung had a good time. Jao, disappointed, turned to organizing the move to Loyang.

Prince Hung, age six, was left as nominal regent in Changan, providing the symbol of the authority of the throne. He was to be under the personal protection of Lady Yang and under the official protection of a trusted staff headed by Archduke Li Chi. Fortunately for Hung, he liked this grandmother who gave him all her time and undivided attention, and so he did not miss his parents overmuch.

In a short space of time the new court was again established in the dispersed palace buildings of Loyang. To the surprise of all the naysayers, it functioned satisfactorily, more efficiently than anyone thought possible after all the chaos. Kaotsung grew more cheerful, though he remained unsettled in his mind. He was well aware that he was regarded as a weakling by many because of his reluctance to deal with his uncle and the other Elders. This depressed him immeasurably. He also stopped sleeping with Jao, who was shocked into considering other and better means to lift Kaotsung's depression.

She tried encouraging conversation. "Really, isn't it much better here in Loyang? Don't you feel so much freer?"

Kaotsung turned and stared at her. "I've merely exchanged the old power-hungry people for new ones just as bad."

"The new officials aren't just as bad," Jao protested. "You yourself appointed them—unlike the old ones appointed by someone else." Kaotsung seemed not to hear. "You're not listening," she said huffily.

"Manipulators all," he said. "The new ones include many old ones who happened to support me—whoever appointed them."

Jao narrowed her eyes. "By 'old ones' do you mean Hsu—and me?"

"Perhaps." He turned and left the room. Jao stared after him, dejected. If she lost Kaotsung's support, she lost everything. His indifference was frightening.

That evening when Chi was leaving the imperial residence, he paused at Jao's door. After bowing to her, he shot her such a penetrating look that she became alert at once.

"What is it, Chi?" she asked. "Do you have something you wish to discuss?"

"I do, Your Majesty, I do but it is not something that I can talk about."

"Why not? You have nothing to hide—at least from me."

"It is not about me, it is about you," Chi said bleakly.

Jao looked frightened for a moment before dropping her eyes. She reached for a seat. "Sit down, Chi, there is no one about just now. Tell me. *I* have nothing to hide from you. From everyone else, perhaps, but not from you."

Chi smiled briefly. "You yourself do not know why you are feeling as you are at present. I know why, but I am afraid to tell you."

"You afraid? I've never seen you afraid, Chi. Tell me, what is wrong with me?"

"I did not say that . . . you said something is wrong, so you must be feeling concerned."

"Nothing is wrong," Jao began stubbornly. "You are imagining things."

Chi bowed and turned to leave again.

"Wait!" Jao almost screamed the word. "How could anything be wrong, now that Kaotsung is at last free of the monstrous burden of the Elders, and I, after five years as empress, am now secure and my sons are secure? And Kaotsung is extraordinarily good to me. He does not use his harem, only me . . . at least I think so."

Chi looked sympathetic.

She lifted her chin and continued. "What woman is more lucky than I? What woman in the entire world is more favored than I? With all under heaven at my feet!"

"That does not mean all is well, madame," Chi said.

Jao looked at him and then glanced away. Finally she said in a small voice. "Kaotsung has withdrawn from me. He has withdrawn from everyone just when he should be ecstatic with victory and relief."

"That is what is bothering you, then. You expected to be perfectly satisfied once you had reached your goal. You and Kaotsung have been rulers for five years and have bought your happiness by ignoring some of the rules of how to exercise power. Only now are you faced with what it feels like to have to exercise real power and what it costs in human terms. This is not making either one of you happy."

"Kaotsung is young and strong," Jao began, her mouth dry, "and should have bounced back from his difficulties with Changsun."

Chi licked his lips. His mouth, too, was dry. "It is you who have made him strong," he said briefly.

"What are you implying? Kaotsung is not a weak man," Jao said hotly.

"All men are weak, don't you know that? All men—and I include myself," Chi replied.

"That is an empty remark," Jao said.

"It is true, though. Heaven has made men that way, so we must hide our weakness. We have discovered that Heaven has also decreed that it takes at least two to make a man strong in this lonely world. Add one male to one female and you have the strongest entity there is. A pair who need each other is a strong pair. Ironic, isn't it? Two weaks to make one strong. Even I have found my strength in cooperating with a female, my empress."

Jao did not reply. She was absorbing too much at once.

Chi continued, "Kaotsung and you make such a pair. It just does not often happen to rulers. They are usually rendered ineffectual by too many females in too large harems. You two are something special on the throne, as Taitsung and his empress were. The trouble comes when such a pair separates. Then each individual is weak again."

Jao gulped. "Is that what is wrong now? We have broken apart? Kaotsung is weak. I am weak. It spells ruin."

"This is why I have spoken," Chi said.

"I thought Kaotsung was so strong. I have had full confidence in his judgment. Now I see that all this trouble with the Elders dragged on for five years because Kaotsung was too weak to issue the decree to banish Changsun long ago. My entire world could collapse if Kaotsung continues to be weak."

"That is the way you were talking the night that Chung was born. I was in attendance in the anteroom and heard. You forgot those feelings afterward in the enjoyment of the good life you led for four years, your life with the children and an affectionate Kaotsung. You have become plump and cuddlesome—like Hsiao Fei—and complaisant."

Jao's eyes rounded and she flushed. "Chi, you are going too far!" she muttered.

"Not far enough," he returned. "That business with Hsu's propaganda to frighten off would-be opponents with stories about the brutalities inflicted on Wang and Hsiao—that was irresponsible of you. Kaotsung never knew your part in those executions. And now he must wonder. Along with his feelings of guilt about being a cause of Changsun's suicide. He is a miserable man just now. Has he come to you for relief and comfort?"

Jao lowered her eyes. Chi stood silently before her, his black eyes unreadable. He seemed to her a symbol of inexorable fate in his ink-black tunic, his heavy black eyebrows, his hair flat under his black cap of office.

"Say something," Jao cried at last.

"You're not yet an empress," he said. "You're just a wife."

Jao met his eyes. "What would you have me do to . . . qualify?" she asked quietly.

"Kaotsung is one of the best endowed men to come to the throne," Chi said. "He has his father's strength of will along with his mother's compassion. But in a ruler, any hint of compassion toward one's enemies is taken to mean weakness. Kaotsung's mercy to his uncle and associates only led them to step up their attacks. Ingrates, all of them."

"Is that what is troubling Kaotsung now? And making him withdraw from me?"

"No doubt about it. As to his withdrawal from you, please remember that you are one of the causes of his estrangement from Hsiao and Wang and from his uncle."

"But not the only one, and not the most important one," Jao returned stoutly. "But let us not quibble. What is important for me to do now?"

"Nothing. Nothing outwardly. Inwardly you must make a great change—from leaning on his strength, to supplying what he lacks in pragmatism yourself. Let *him* be sentimental, but never give way to it yourself. If you do this, you two will be the strongest entity in the nation, able to keep the throne and this empire prosperous and growing for many years to come."

Jao gave him a bitter glance. "Are you speaking of remote possibilities or probabilities?"

"Probabilities, madame. You have already demonstrated your ability to take decisive action—with respect to the political liabilities of Wang. You could do so again."

Jao felt a flicker of hope. "You may go now," she said finally. "In five minutes you have destroyed my world. I must think. Go now and let me cope with it. But do not leave regretting the recklessness of your words. I do appreciate them and . . . you are a greater treasure to me than ever before."

He left abruptly in order to hide the radiance that her words had brought to his expression. He thought exultantly. That last sentence of hers had given him more hope for her than anything else. She had understanding and timing. That was enough to start.

As soon as the door closed, Jao began to pace, jerkily and angrily. A new experiment in power politics, she was thinking. She couldn't . . . Kaotsung wouldn't share power, they couldn't rule together. But what a dangerous, challenging, alluring idea! Kaotsung and herself together in power! To manage the empire. To surpass even Taitsung. Kaotsung's reign could be—could just be—one of the greatest in Chinese history.

Jao's leaping thoughts took possession of her, and she remained alone in her room with her visions for the future. She spent the rest of the day and night there, refusing food, dismissing attendants, coming to grips with the realization that her future depended once more on herself alone. Is this what Chi meant by being empress, not wife? she mused, paralyzed at the risks involved, but tempted nonetheless.

Kaotsung, however, remained unapproachable, especially by her, Jao discovered. Although stability was being restored to his regime under the capable hand of a new man called Liu Jen, Kaotsung himself remained unresponsive.

Despairing, Jao chose to confront him. "What is the matter? Can't you tell me?"

He shrugged, determined not to be drawn out. There were many threads of white now showing in his black hair.

"Something is bothering you and it concerns me. Look how you avoid me during the day, in the evenings, even at night! Tell me, please!"

He shrugged again. "Since you insist—I hold you to blame for my uncle's ruin. I hold you partly to blame for Wang and Hsiao's downfall."

Jao froze. "You really mean this?" she asked at length.

He shifted his feet. "I suppose I do!"

"You suppose! When you know that your uncle was undermining you and I got in his way by supporting you? The fact is that I am your greatest asset!" Kaotsung's face was hard, but Jao could not stop her flow of words. "As for Wang and Hsiao—Wang brought me here to distract you from Hsiao. Was that my fault? When I bore our first son, they used treasonable sorcery—was I the criminal that time?" In her self-righteousness, Jao had become shrill.

Kaotsung looked at her in distaste. "You connived at their executions." Jao wilted in shock. The silence grew.

"You knew then?" she answered listlessly. "I tried so hard to protect you, because Changsun's faction would have restored them to power if you eased their sentences at all. And you were about to . . ."

Kaotsung stirred uneasily. "I don't want to discuss it." He turned to leave the room.

"Let us flee Loyang." Jao cried desperately.

A look of amazement swept across his face.

"We could take a long vacation from all court duties and go to our ancestral homes in Taiyuan. We can leave on the first warm day of spring, taking only a small guard. Let us go up into the mountains and smell the fragrance of the long grass of the steppes, putting every grievous happening of the past behind us, take our babies, and just go. . . ."

Kaotsung's eyes softened. "I'll think about it," he said.

In five days, miraculously, they were on their way. It took them two weeks, going by chair and ox cart. Once there, they settled comfortably into the Wu family home, now cared for by retired retainers. Their small staff was domiciled with neighbors like the Dees, who were delighted to have people from the palace as their guests. Lady Yang came up from Changan with Nurse Wang, now an energetic seventy-year-old. The slow pace of life in the old residence and the constant presence of the children at first irritated Kaotsung, but finally soothed him. The visits of Jao's childhood friends diverted him. Short visits, small banquets, and long days in the sunny courtyards began to take effect. Office work took only an hour a day. Jao began taking more part in policy-making, by preparing the drafts of Kaotsung's memoranda. Once the drafts were completed, she turned them over to his secretary, who never approached Kaotsung personally.

One morning they were sitting on the low porch in front of the main hall watching the children splash in the rain puddles. "Hung has grown in the few months since we left him in Changan," Kaotsung commented. "He has always been quiet, and now he seems confident as well as careful. Look at him now, rolling up his trousers to keep them dry. The other children are already soaking."

Jao was distracted by the sight of six-year-old Hsien slamming three-year-old Chungtsung into a puddle amid fierce sounds of battle. Both boys stopped at a piercing whistle from Nurse Wang, and little Chungtsung, seeing his chance, bolted into the safety of her endearments while Hsien charged around the courtyard splashing everyone else. Nurse Wang handed Chungtsung to his own maid to change his wet clothes, and Hsien made a beeline for her in order to receive his share of her endearments mixed with purring admonitions about his poor conduct. She gave him her undivided attention until he went off contentedly to change into dry clothes.

"Did you see that?" Jao exclaimed.

Kaotsung laughed. "Yes, I saw. Little brats. Both of them deserve whacking instead of all that cooing and cuddling from toothless old Wang."

"Your discipline would have them screaming around for an hour. With her way, we have peace in the house in less than five minutes," Jao countered.

"Sheer bribery!" Kaotsung cried. "And corruption!"

"Not really. Hsien got an earful of scolding along with the love words—which he did not deserve but which were all the sweeter for that. Who does not behave well when he gets a gift, if only of soothing words? The children don't see Wang as a toothless old hag, they see her as a warm, ministering angel."

"Angel or not, surely we don't need such old servants."

"Far from being too old, Nurse Wang is number one among all the nurses here. She makes the others look like amateurs. The boys have the others running around after them like demented hens. Wang justs sits there without moving and everyone runs to her. She always mixes hurt and heal without isolating anyone as a 'bad boy.' She doesn't incur resentment, and she doesn't encourage selfishness either."

Kaotsung listened in silence, and Jao watched him. I hope he is thinking of his new officials, and how he should go about controlling them.

Kaotsung took a sip of his strong tea and peeled an imported peach. "First a man learns how to govern his family, then a province, then an empire," he mused, "but I do it the other way around, with an empire first. Maybe I'll end up knowing how to manage just one woman." They looked at one another and laughed, reaching out to touch each other. Jao was elated beyond words. Kaotsung was coming back to her.

The rain clouds cleared away and the sun dried up the puddles. The family continued to sit and watch the little boats in the stream that wandered through the lower court. A visitor was announced. It was Dee Jenjer. Dee had matured into a very handsome man, with a confident air and a look of command. His eyes were bright under heavy brows, and his beard covered a strong chin.

"Judge Dee!" Jao exclaimed, her eyes sparkling.

Kaotsung, who had read the young magistrate's reports, smiled a warm welcome.

"How long has it been since we inspected Ko's camel?" Jao cried. "You were eight . . ."

"Now I am an old man of thirty," he said, shrugging. "With heavy responsibilities—a chief wife, three babies, and a cage of the singing thrushes of Taishan."

"Bring them," Jao said. "Not the thrushes—your women. I want to see you cuddling a baby the way Kaotsung does. I want to see what kind of wives you have—not bossy ones, I am sure. Bring them all."

"They have been sent to my chief wife's home for the summer while I visit my parents here. I am between assignments now. I'm going to Penglai on the Yellow Sea next."

Kaotsung perked up. "Penglai? I am glad to hear that an energetic magistrate like you is going to be in charge. It's key to our control of that area, and we are having trouble with the Koreans as usual. Ever since that Moliju usurped authority, he has been mobilizing the tribes in Manchuria and Korea, and is forever crossing the borders of our neighbors, causing trouble. You, no doubt, are aware of all that. Enough. About you now . . . I have read your reports. I confess that I go to sleep with most reports, but not yours. Your cases are so hair-raising that I stay with each one to its end!"

Magistrate Dee smiled deprecatingly, but he was pleased, especially when Kaotsung added, "I am all ears to hear more."

"Don't believe half of it," Dee responded, his sunburned face alight. "I am so far down the ladder of promotion that I must dramatize myself or I will never be noticed, and will be continually assigned to some forgotten nook of the empire!"

"But it is just those nooks that provide the exciting criminals that you hunt," Kaotsung said, "so of course the state affairs people must send you there. Penglai is no sinecure, with its large colony of Korean smugglers and racketeers. I will enjoy reading how you handle it all." Kaotsung's voice was animated.

Dee shook his head modestly, but his eyes sparkled. Jao gazed at him thoughtfully. She had kept up with him through the gossip between their mothers, and from what she knew about his assignments, it looked as if he had been purposely kept in the provinces. She beckoned to Mi to bring refreshments.

"What would you like to drink?" she asked Dee. "Hot or cold?" River ice was cut each winter and stored underground for the family to use in the summer.

"One of your famous iced drinks, if you please," he answered. Jao turned to Mi and ordered, using a Silla term. When Mi returned with the drinks, Dee looked at her carefully while taking his goblet, and thanked her in her own language. She was astonished, and Kaotsung and Jao looked inquiringly at him.

"I was assigned to a post in Tengchow once, and I have often visited the Silla inns there. I have picked up a few words of the language," he explained.

"You use the correct Silla breath," Mi returned approvingly.

He laughed. "I knew better than to use Korean words without the right enunciation or precise verb endings."

"Explain," Kaotsung ordered, interested.

"The way one pronounces and the way one uses the verbs establishes one's social position, and I am a snob," Dee answered amidst general laughter. He rose to leave, as the customary twenty minute audience was over.

"Come tomorrow for dinner," Jao said at once. "And bring your wife."

"She is in Chinchow," he started to say, with a faint touch of his old asperity.

"I mean your traveling wife," Jao replied.

"How did you know?" he began, joining the laughter at his expense.

"Knowing you and your ways," Jao retorted.

"My ways at eight years old? Hardly up to a wife, I seem to recall. . . ."

"Nevertheless, your attitudes toward women were set even then," she said, twinkling. "I am delighted to see you again and want to chat at leisure. Bring your little concubine to dinner and be your own outspoken self. You will be doing the emperor and me a favor."

Dee flashed her an appreciative look, bowed respectfully, and took his leave.

Jao watched Dee depart and smiled. She had succeeded in arousing his old interest in her, which he expressed with the same questioning manner of his childhood. She could tell he felt genuine admiration toward her, as well as an unconcealed pleasure at being in her company again.

The next evening, Dee Jenjer brought his rolypoly concubine Hua to dinner with the royal pair, as arranged. Jao turned to the little concubine who was daintily dressed in a fashionable summer cotton. "Where is your hometown?" she asked.

"Hangchow is my home," Hua replied shyly.

"One of the empire's famous beauty spots!" Jao commented politely.

"Actually, in the Chekiang mountains nearby, where some new monasteries are being built."

Jao looked interested. "The important new sects are locating in the mountains instead of in the cities, to be in closer touch with nature! Have you visited any of them yourself?"

Hua's eyes shone. "Most of them. My father is a builder. His last work was with a Chan sect newly located in the south." Hua snapped open her fan. "A Chan monk painted this breezy mountain scene. . . ." At the click of the fan everyone looked at her.

"What's that?" asked Kaotsung, amused by the novelty. Hua flushed. "A fan that folds . . . something new," she said shyly.

Kaotsung drew Dee aside in order to discuss foreign policy. "About Penglai now," he said. "The Koreans there are a mixture of merchants from the three kingdoms of Koguryo, Paekche, and Silla. The merchants are uneasy with one another because their homelands are constantly raiding each other's territory."

"Do you think that there will be trouble in Penglai this coming year?" Dee asked.

"Absolutely. Outbreaks here and there, small wars possibly," Kaotsung answered soberly. "I have been receiving reports from General Hsueh, who has been on the Liao delta area between China and Koguryo for five years now. He wins some encounters and loses others. Either way, never more than two thousand heads are lost. Last year, I also sent the redoubtable Su Tingfang there, but now I have recalled him. We have a stalemate on our hands. We are on our way to another defeat from those treacherous Koguryans perhaps. All our top officials and almost all of our generals are against stepping up the effort to subjugate the Koguryans once and for all. What are your thoughts?"

Dee was shaking his head. "I am thinking that Tang does not need any defeats like the Sui suffered," he offered without hesitation. "These are dangerous people, and any war against them is risky because of the long supply line, because of the treacherous climate, and because they would be fighting on their own terrain. Hopeless."

Kaotsung saw that Mi was listening, her face flushed as she directed an outraged look at Dee. "What are you thinking of, Mi?" he asked.

"Hopeless! A feeble word," said an unusually spirited Mi, surprising everyone. "Of course it is hopeless if one continues to repeat the same mistakes over and over again." She spoke with passion and authority, forgetting herself. Jao gazed at her in surprise.

"What do you mean?" Kaotsung's attention was caught.

"Why not a new approach?" she said. "A new approach that is not only not hopeless, but could not be anything but successful."

She had their full attention.

"It has been more than ten years since Emperor Taitsung ordered the court not to engage in any more wars with Koguryo," Kaotsung said thoughtfully. "Small defensive actions on our borders are all right, but not wars."

"Their Moliju knows this and laughs," Mi said. "And makes sweet talk with Paekche and the Manchurian tribes. They all build forts, more and more every year, so that Silla is surrounded, and they gradually steal our territory." Her voice ceased and she bowed apologetically.

"Well," Jao said. "Well . . ."

"What are you implying, Mi?" Kaotsung asked. "Are you saying that Silla needs help? And that China should give it to her? Isn't that a bit farfetched and impractical?"

Before Mi could answer, Dee spoke up. "Military adventures involving the Korean kingdoms are not for China. Emperor Taitsung was right in forbidding them. All three kingdoms are advanced states with high degrees of centralization. Besides, they are civilized and China-oriented in their customs. We must deal with them cautiously. I know from experience that we have to deal firmly and justly with these people or we have trouble on our hands. They are peaceful if well-treated, but otherwise an unruly lot."

Kaotsung frowned. "The Koguryans are constantly raiding Chinese territory. Our past policy of peaceful control of the borders through bestowal of titles and other honors to the tribes is breaking down now as the three kingdoms consolidate and grow more aggressive. China's policy, which has worked for seven hundred years, is out-of-date."

He looked around the room at the thoughtful faces before him. "Tell me, in three or four words, what you think should be China's policy, now! Dee?"

"New treaties and a brisker trade—seduce them with our silks!" Dee said, the Confucian pacifist.

They all laughed except Mi, who said under her breath, "We have silks too, the best there are. The Chinese can't seduce us with their silks as they do the nomads."

"Mi, you must speak up clearly, I can't hear you." Kaotsung turned toward her. "War or peace?"

With eyes downcast, Mi said, "Both, Your Majesty, both. An alliance with Silla and a victorious attack first on Paekche and then on Koguryo. It's the only way to get peace in this peninsula. Paekche shut off Silla's access to China when they cut the corridor we had in the middle of the peninsula. She deserves chastisement from China. After reducing Paekche, Chinese and Silla troops would occupy all of Southern Korea. Chinese troops could then attack Koguryo in the north, across the Liao River. They would move south at the same time that the southern forces move north, thus closing in on the Ko capital of Pyongyang, a mouse in the trap . . . a great victory for China."

"Hmm," Kaotsung grunted. "That's a tall order! Dee, what do you think?"

Dee, who was as fast as lightning in reaching new conclusions when presented with a credible argument, said, "She makes a good case—if she is correct in her facts."

"No one is in a better position to have all the facts. Mi is related to the Sillan royal family," Jao said, "and I have never heard her distort the truth."

"I believe you," Kaotsung said. "Your turn, Jao."

"You said that you wanted us to state our opinions with few words, so: attack! Send your best general with the best troops the shortest way against the weakest enemy!"

"Su Tingfang and his veterans, the best general," Kaotsung said, laughingly capping her generalities with specifics.

"The weakest enemy, Paekche," Mi put in.

"The shortest way, by sea to the Paekche coast in Chinese warships piloted by Korean sailors," Dee said lightly.

Kaotsung laughed, then said soberly, "Let us recall what Sun Tzu had to say about first steps in any campaign. Let's see . . . didn't he say that one must first line up one's allies, get their friendship, loyalty, and help? Silla seems to be the right ally. She could furnish us with warriors, spies, and guides who know the terrain and the languages of the other two kingdoms. Your ideas could work, Mi. They aren't bad at all."

Dee was looking thoughtful, and the women carefully watched every expression on the men's faces. No one spoke. Then Kaotsung rose and went to the gong. "Here," he said. "This is no time to discuss heavy matters. Let us enjoy ourselves this evening. Four of my Kucha musicians are here, and I am told that they have some new songs to celebrate the occasion. I'll call them in."

The next day, to Jao's inexpressible delight, Kaotsung returned to active life. He started by calling a plenary session of all officials who were currently stationed in Taiyuan to discuss the Korean problem. He announced a quick return to Changan to discuss the matter seriously there. He would take Dee with him.

In Changan there was much opposition from the bureaucrats to the idea of war, but in the end it was agreed that China should send a small punitive force against Paekche for its transgressions in interfering with the China trade. Jao drafted the orders that the emperor sent to the authorities in Szechuan. They were to build four hundred warships at once and move them downriver to Shantung by late fall. At the same time, the Shantung district magistrates were ordered to recruit Silla pilots and crews, and General Su was told to report to the emperor for instructions. When the orders went out, half the battle with the bureaucracy was won.

Miraculously, the plans, at first so tentative, blossomed into realities. Orders for equipment and supplies were filled. The weather was uniformly good. Ships and men collected at designated assemblage areas and were outfitted. General Su, after noisy ceremonies performed by the shamans for his troops' safety, sailed across the Yellow Sea to the Korean coast and then down to the mouth of the Kum River. Twice daily the fleet took shelter under the lee of some island to fish, eat, take on fresh water from springs, and maneuver above the thirty-foot tide. Su, traveling in the flagship, had on board pilots experienced with the sea lanes and the delta area of the Kum river, and in addition, all vessels had experienced Sillan crews on board. Consequently, the fleet successfully made port before the Kum fortress without losing a ship.

The Chinese debarked on the white beaches of Paekche and were divided into three groups. Most of the soldiers were highland men who had never seen the sea before, and many had been seasick, but a day's rest ashore and they were combat-ready. The job of taking the small local fort was child's play to such seasoned warriors, and the fort was soon reduced. Then General Su started off at once with the two groups he had told to proceed along the riverbanks, and he left the third group to go upstream by ship. His couriers kept the three forces in touch.

Kongju was defended only by its civilian inhabitants, who were not equal to the task of fending off Su's veterans. "Ten thousand killed," read the report that Kaotsung received. The subjugation of Kongju was quickly followed by other victories, until the Paekche king and most of his court surrendered. Paekche, with its population of four million and its lengthy west-coast territory extending from mid-peninsula to its tip, had been conquered in record time, a stunning victory.

When the news arrived in the two Chinese capitals, there were exuberant celebrations throughout the cities. Bells tolled all night and firecrackers went up from palace and city walls. The court was jubilant. This was the first major victory of Chinese arms in the notoriously difficult Korean peninsula for a generation, and the first major military success in Kaotsung's administration. The populace went wild with excitement.

For about a week the emperor and empress lived in a state of euphoria. The sudden release from the tensions caused by launching such an enterprise against expert advice brought them to heights of happy celebration expressed in palace banquets, public displays, and awards. They had never before been so thoroughly pleased with events, with their countrymen, and with themselves.

CHAPTER FIFTEEN

Kaotsung was meeting with his privy council. The meeting was an informal one concerned largely with a discussion of what had been gained by the campaign in Korea. He looked around the room. "Anything else?" he asked.

General Liu Jen coughed. "A small thing, but interesting," he said. "General Su found a large Buddhist pagoda in Paekche that had been built a hundred years ago. He has had a memorial celebrating our victory engraved upon it—as a reminder to the people so that they would not forget for ten thousand years!" The officials all smiled and nodded, except for one man who was Buddhist. He did not look pleased.

"Thank you, Liu. Now, if—" Kaotsung began, when his eyes suddenly glazed over and he became unhearing, unheeding. In great alarm the palace physicians were summoned and guards carried the emperor to his bedchamber. The physicians took his pulses, examined his eyes, fingers, and feet, probed his abdomen, and shook their heads. Setting up screens before the bed, they organized constant attendance and forbade all access to the patient, cautiously following the rules laid down in the manual for the care of an emperor. Since their own lives were at stake, they were understandably strict.

Distracted, Jao stood behind the screens, hearing the activity but forbidden to take part or even to come near Kaotsung. Growing more and more outraged at being removed from him in his helpless state, she began to view with suspicion the heavy hand of the medical authorities. When she finally demanded a report, the chief physician somewhat impatiently told her that "contrary to nature, the wind is rising in the body. If blood is let, the head will be cured."

Jao cried angrily, "Such talk merits death! How dare you propose to draw the emperor's blood!"

At this, the physicians prostrated themselves and Jao could hear their muffled voices beseeching clemency. Suddenly she heard Kaotsung's weak words, "My head aches intolerably. I shall let them do as they will."

"Very well," Jao agreed in a shaky voice. She stood rigidly listening to all the preparations that the doctors made. Fearful and trembling themselves, they bravely went about the business of drawing off the emperor's blood. Presently Kaotsung said, "My eyes are clearer . . . I feel a little better."

Jao bowed to the ground although she was alone behind the screens, crying in relief. "It is the will of Heaven that he has been helped, and I am grateful . . . the empire is grateful! Continue to do your best!" Then she called to Mi in a loud voice. "Nevertheless, we shall stay here and keep watch."

After the bloodletting and Kaotsung's subsequent relief, Jao took time to attend the next privy council meeting. She went to the council hall for the usual audience. She seated herself behind her embroidered curtain, but no one else arrived except the clerks from the State Affairs Department who brought the boxes of dispatches. It was difficult to keep her eyes open after only three hours of sleep, but she continued to wait. Eventually Hsu shuffled in, yawning. He ordered the boxes opened so that he could deal with the contents. He read in silence. The other ministers did not appear. Finally Hsu ordered the clerk to deliver any future boxes to the Chancellory and abruptly disappeared.

Jao was left alone behind her curtain. She was appalled at such casual treatment of state business of the highest importance. Returning to the antechamber, she called Eunuchs Kang and Chi and discussed the situation. They, too, were blocked from interfering by the medical rules and were as upset as she was.

Jao continued to sleep on a pallet in the anteroom, with only Mi in attendance, during the ten days it took for the physicians to decide that it was safe to withdraw. Not once during that time did they consult her or allow her to attend the patient, as she had been allowed to do for the desperately ill emperor Taitsung. The instant that Mi, who was watching the comings and goings, saw the back of the last apprentice taking away the last of the medical paraphernalia, she alerted Jao and they both hurried into the bedchamber. Kaotsung, hearing Jao's voice but unable to see her, felt for her hand and clung to it. It was a long time before he would allow her to leave him again.

Several weeks passed but Kaotsung did not improve. Jao began to worry whether the medical authorities were up to their jobs. They had achieved their positions through some kind of patronage, and, moreover, were too powerful. In the future, she thought, Kaotsung should retain in office only the best and most trustworthy. He should recruit new men, the best obtainable, even if he had to send to India as Taitsung had done. How easy it was for any bureau to surround the emperor—and control him—if the excuse were legal and plausible. How easy to prevent access to him by any but the neglible, anonymous servants, Jao reflected. The servants seemed to be the key. She sent for Chi.

"Sit down and be comfortable. I wish to discuss something with you."

Chi raised a quizzical eyebrow and seated himself carefully on a stool. "I am honored, Your Majesty,' he said respectfully.

"The emperor is in danger," Jao said flatly. "Not entirely from his illness, although that is major. It is his helplessness and how he feels about it. Some of his ambitious supporters may feel that, now that they have been successful in ousting the Elders, the way to the throne may be open to them. It is a temptation that several of them will not be able to resist."

She paused and saw Chi's eyes flash with understanding. No one in the army of caretakers knew palace politics better than Chi, she said to herself, considering how best to put her request.

"Here in Loyang," she said finally, "we have the military headquarters of the Korea campaign. I have heard that the troops are already coming back here to be reassigned or discharged. I want you to search among them for outstanding men who may have been castrated or wounded in some way that would make them eligible for service in the Inner Palace. Men like you with strong character, experience in combat, and worldly knowledge. Who are unspoiled by the soft life of most of our present staff of eunuchs."

She paused to search his face for any expression of misunderstanding. "Are you taking offense at that last remark?" she asked abruptly.

He grinned in the old way, "My own private opinion exactly," he said, and they both laughed.

"I want you to find six able men who have matured normally and are trainable for eunuch service in the palace, to be answerable only to the emperor. Six men who will serve in consecutive two-hour shifts as personal bodyguards, in lifetime service to him. These men must be willing to serve discreetly as servants. In reality, they will be superior attendants, of top quality in intelligence and loyalty. Impossible?"

Chi was silent, thinking. "It can probably be done, but will take time. If I may have a month's leave, I will go to the camp and find out whether such men are available. There should be a good choice because these troops were seasoned men to begin with. I will see what I can do. The idea of such concealed servant protection to the emperor is, if I may say so, a brilliant one."

"Thank you!" Jao cried, gratified. "I was such a servant myself once and was quite useful to Emperor Taitsung, as you well know. I am aware of how difficult this assignment is. If you succeed, I will see to it that you are promoted to whatever position in the palace most appeals to you. The emperor is sure to take to the idea, and will endorse your promotion." She watched Chi as he took in the implications of what she was offering and prostrated himself in gratitude.

"Rise, my friend," Jao said, elated. "I take it, then, that you think the plan is feasible and you are willing. Whether it works out depends entirely on you."

He shot her a look of such devotion and approval that Jao was vastly cheered, and remained so all day. That evening a deerskin pouch was delivered to Chi. It contained more than enough to pay his expenses.

That winter was just cold enough and just damp enough to keep the ground blanketed in light falls of snow. The tree branches were frosted much of the time and the tile roofs glistened. The straw-wrapped fruit trees and peony bushes in the gardens were gaunt forms in black and white, and they caught the eye in differing guises as the light shifted. Kaotsung could see well enough to be intrigued by the wintry scenes outside his window, and it helped ease the boredom of his long convalesence.

No reports of any kind reached him. There were callers, but they were received and turned away by the officials. Visitors, most of whom were other officials from service bureaus or en route to new country posts, were thanked for their courtesy and told that the emperor was grateful for their good wishes but could not see anyone personally.

"It is all supposed to be for your own good," Jao assured him without much conviction. "You are not supposed to be bothered by news of any kind, good or bad."

"That is just what I don't want—to be kept in the dark," Kaotsung cried one blustery day when he was feeling especially isolated. "Being put aside as if I were not emperor at all. How can I govern this empire if I am kept mewed up? How can I govern if my eyesight is not good? Will I ever sit on my throne again? Just when I was well into my stride and on top of things, as a ruler ought to be."

"No!" she said. "No to all of that. No! You are still the emperor and are rapidly recovering your health. You will soon sit on your throne as usual. There is nothing the matter with your ears, and it is ears that you need more than eyes. You can listen to the memorials and the petitions and the daily arguments. It is your ears that matter." She stopped to observe his reaction to her tirade. He was listening intently and he seemed cheered.

"I could, couldn't I?" he said simply. "This silence, this pretense that all is well in the empire and that it is running itself, irks me. No news is bad news to me. My present chief officials are practiced opportunists accustomed to riding to success on faction-forming. I feel that some of them are gathering like vultures, as they did when I first became emperor after my father died—but this is foolish of me. The Elders were highly experienced men, used to authority and strongly entrenched. The present officials are in their positions because I put them there, they are not entrenched. I put them in and I can take them out. Of course, I must attend the audiences again. I can certainly sit there and listen. Yes, I could do that."

"You have every right to feel up to such an activity," Jao answered soothingly. "It won't hurt your health to sit in meetings any more than it hurts your health to sit and look at the garden, if none of it lasts too long."

"In fact, I strongly wish to do so," Kaotsung returned. "Strange! When I used to hate sitting there, I now want to do just that, so I will know everything that is going on anywhere in this country. I want to get back to my duties and keep my ministers attending to theirs too, the blackguards! If only I could see better."

"That should not bother you, should it?" Jao replied. "I could sit behind the curtain and write everything down for you and be your private, your very private, secretary."

While he thought this out, the corners of Kaotsung's expressive mouth turned up in the old way he had of showing satisfaction. Jao observed this and felt much encouraged.

"I can watch their faces from behind the curtain. They think that you are blind—and we can see that they continue to think so. They will not conceal their true thoughts when they talk to you, and I will observe them." Jao frowned in concentration.

Kaotsung brightened. "You could do that and we could discuss it all afterward. But what if they want my opinion immediately, before we have had a chance to talk? These memorials are worded in cursed polite phrases that mean the opposite of what they say. I can't think fast enough to figure things out unless I have time to disentangle it all." He stirred restlessly, discouraged again.

"You are better off now than you were before," Jao exclaimed at once. "Much better off! You now have a weapon that you did not have before. You can tell your ministers that because of your illness you must have a day to consider before giving your opinion. No decision on the spot, no snap judgments. What could be better?"

"I could do that," Kaotsung replied slowly. "But what if I suddenly get dizzy or tired!"

"Abruptly say, as if you were displeased, 'You are dismissed for today.' Easy for you . . . irritating for them."

Kaotsung grinned. "Suppose the pushy ones push. Or bang their heads on the floor like Chu did?"

"Let them bang," Jao said.

At this Kaotsung burst into laughter—the first good laugh he had had since his seizure.

A month later Chi asked for an audience to introduce the six servitors whom he had recruited. Kaotsung had been greatly intrigued by the idea when Jao explained it to him, and was now eager to meet the men. They kowtowed when they first came in, then stood stiffly at attention so that he could inspect them. All were soldiers in their thirties, well-muscled, neatly dressed, self-contained. They had seen hard service in Paekche and were well-informed about most aspects of the war.

Kaotsung, already more keenly interested in the Korean war than in anything else, received them with enthusiasm, and their service started immediately. The eunuchs who had been waiting on him were overjoyed to be transferred to palace duties in Changan, and left at once. At the same time, the new men were adapting quickly to Kaotsung's needs and to palace routine, especially their leader, a strong, dark man named Lim. The emperor fell into long conversations with these servants, rekindling his interest in the whole problem of Paekche. Jao made good on her promise, and Chi was promoted to chief of the emperor's private attendants, putting the new men directly under his supervision. Both Jao and Kaotsung were highly pleased with the arrangement, with the new men, and most of all with Chi himself, who went around purring with satisfaction.

Kaotsung's reentry into palace life was the occasion for a change in the reign name to Lung Shuo—Dragon Inauguration. Kaotsung sat with folded hands in council meetings, looking sleepy, sometimes even with closed eyes. His ears, however, were alert, and when his decisions came, they were informed and well thought out, surprising the ministers. This approach was paying off. In addition, Chi's veterans were a source of stimulation in conversation as well as a mine of information about Paekche. Jao was elated. Things were going her way.

Soon after Kaotsung's resumption of duties, Hsu presented, in formal audience, a long list of appointees. Kaotsung refused to accept them without studying the list. At home he went over it with Jao, requiring biographies and records of education and degrees taken. When he finally presented a modified list of his own, Hsu objected strongly to the cancellations.

"Why do you object?" Kaotsung asked mildly.

Hsu broke into a long explanation to defend his candidates. Li tapped a long fingernail impatiently on his chair arm. The other ministers watched intently.

"None of those fellows is qualified." Kaotsung was beginning to lose patience. "Three failed their examinations, one never pays his bills, and one is a notorious philanderer. Their only assets have been their families' abilities to buy them privileges."

Jao, watching through the curtain, saw Hsu glare angrily, openly expressing defiance at the emphasis Kaotsung had put on the word "buy." Li exchanged a sarcastic glance with his assistant, making no attempt to show deference. The other ministers wore various expressions of support for Hsu and Li.

"Cancel the appointments of those five. I will put my chop on the recommendations for the others."

Hsu's scowl deepened. "But it is too late. They—"

Kaotsung interrupted. "You heard me. Cancel these five." Li went on tapping his fingernail.

"Stop it," Kaotsung said.

The ministers looked at one another in surprise and then at the emperor inquiringly.

"The tapping noise—stop it," Kaotsung repeated. The tapping stopped and Kaotsung heard what he was listening for . . . a tiny, suppressed giggle.

Kaotsung cleared his throat. "The new reign name is intended to bring luck to a new project. Dragon Inauguration expresses our situation exactly."

He now had their full attention. All eyes were fixed on him. Some showed wariness, others revealed apprehension. The smirks had disappeared.

Kaotsung continued. "We have just wound up a successful campaign subjugating all of southern Korea, but it is only the first step to a larger goal. Now we will do the same to northern Korea."

This was too much for Hsu. "Now is the time to rest on our laurels, not embark on another idiotic scheme—"

Kaotsung cut him off. "We must move ahead." Behind the curtain Jao saw that all the ministers were now scowling. Kaotsung continued blandly, "I plan to send Su north by sea and he can repeat the same strategy that brought him victory in Paekche. He will sail sixty miles up the Taedong River to the Koguryo capital, which he will then take. At the same time I'll have General Hsueh and that intrepid general Chibi Holi move down from the north to close the trap. We have never before taken their capital. Now we will!"

Jao saw the ministers move restlessly in their seats, but Kaotsung continued to insist that they make plans and send out preparatory orders without delay. Only after they had yielded to Kaotsung's plan did the meeting break up two hours later. "He is mad," Hsu muttered as he shuffled out behind the emperor.

Jao's face lit up with glee when she joined Kaotsung in their quarters later. "It was hilarious! They were all shaking with rage but didn't quite dare to overrule you in formal meeting. You came on like an avalanche!" She broke into laughter and Kaotsung somewhat ruefully joined her.

"Perhaps I am going too far in this idiotic scheme, but—"

"You wish to do it!" Jao supplied gleefully. "And that's important. Although I do have some doubts."

"What?" he demanded challengingly.

"Well, I don't even like to hear the word 'Koguryo' after the miserable troubles that Taitsung had with that unruly, barbarous, treacherous nation—"

"I know," Kaotsung cut in. "I know all that. My father was ill so he could not finish the job of pacifying them, and therefore they have become insolent. I am sending our best general to teach them a lesson."

"Li Chi?" Jao exclaimed hopefully.

"Not Li Chi—he's too old for the field and anyway, I need him here to counterbalance the malcontents. Also," he added, "when the ministers have a war to divert them, they have no time to hatch conspiracies."

"You sound smug," Jao said.

"I am, I am," he returned. "As long as everything goes my way." They joined in mirth, as they often did these days.

The send-off of the troops began at high noon; Kaotsung restored in health, stood on the balcony of Loyang's largest gate while his armies, marines, and sailors marched past in their new uniforms, banners flying, drums thudding, feet falling in near perfect syncopation. Kaotsung was bright-eyed with enjoyment. Musicians had composed special songs to kindle enthusiasm, and these lively new tunes were heard for the first time as the bands passed by the reviewing stand.

"We just might succeed where my father and grandfather, not to mention the Sui, have failed," he said in a low voice to Jao. "As a matter of fact, I am privately planning to go to Korea by sea. I'd like to take on the Supreme Command myself."

"Excellent!" Jao said, her eyes shining. She could see that her dreams of achieving success through Kaotsung's increased prestige were coming true. "Wonderful, wonderful!" she reiterated. "This is only the beginning of your fame overseas."

Kaotsung smiled at her enthusiasm and continued to talk about assuming command of the campaign himself. Jao listened but was suddenly quiet.

"Your Majesty," she began, and he pricked up his ears. When she addressed him formally, there was something important on her mind. "Your Majesty, it would indeed be a good thing for you to take command yourself. If, however, your generals run into the same old defeats and difficulties, they will take the blame, not you. You should wait for some victories, perhaps, before you risk involving yourself and the prestige of the throne."

"I thought of that too," Kaotsung agreed. "I must see what happens first, but I do want to plan on going soon. Because it is so important to prepare properly, taking command myself is still a thing of the future. It is not something I will do tomorrow morning. For now, however, let us put aside such talk and enjoy ourselves." He rested his hand on her hip and she flushed. She was only too happy to abandon her advice-giving when she realized that she had been throwing cold water on matters that excited Kaotsung in more ways than one. So she said no more.

A violent blizzard settled over North China, halting all traffic and forcing all living creatures to take shelter. It extended across the Yellow Sea to northern Korea. Kaotsung listened to the wind tearing off tree limbs and scattering roof tiles.

"Bad weather for our troops in Koguryo," he said gloomily.

Jao was tense. "Are you worried that this is exactly the kind of weather that was to blame for all those defeats for China in the past?" Pregnant again for the first time in six years, lately she was often ill and consequently nervous.

"It would be just terrible if we went down in ignominy also . . . and for the same reason. The country would never forgive me," Kaotsung replied anxiously. "General Su is a great soldier, but we still haven't heard from him. It should have been either a victory or a retreat. Either way, he should have been back to report long ago."

Jao felt ill as she remembered the bad news from southern Korea—a revolt in Paekche that erupted as soon as General Su sailed out of the area's waters. She responded critically.

"Your General Su wasn't so great if he didn't know better than to let his troops loose on the Paekche population to rape and kill as they chose. And his savaging the soldiers who had surrendered just goaded them to rebellion." Jao's voice was fierce, her eyes hard as she stared, arms akimbo, at Kaotsung. "Now peace is impossible in Paekche."

Kaotsung glared back at her. "You were the one who recommended General Liu Jen. He's responsible for what's happening in Paekche now, and is obviously failing to cope. He should be giving the Packcheans the benefit of good government under Tang rule, and there should be peace by now."

"Benefits of good government!" Jao ejaculated. "What benefits? When Tang troops are losing ground daily to that seven-foot Paekche giant? That ridiculous peasant with the equally ridiculous name! And now the ministers want to stop the war and recall everyone, including General Liu. What an abysmal mess!"

"What do you suggest?" Kaotsung asked coldly.

"Leave Liu there. If he sits tight, he'll win in the end," Jao cried impulsively.

Kaotsung eyed her silently. "I'd like to agree with you. We now have such a stalemate that only some supreme effort could break it. Perhaps Liu is capable of making the effort. If he does, I'll let him stay there and slug it out with that Korean giant. Ah! I've just remembered his name—it's Heijer Changjer—Black Teeth Long One."

Jao burst out laughing. "What's his name got to do with it! Except we'll hope to have Liu change it to No Teeth Short One! This is all so unbelievable . . . Great Tang to be vanquished by a peasant!"

"Calm down," Kaotsung said. "Calm down. And wait to see what happens. Wait."

The court waited in suspense for news from the various fronts, which came only slowly. General Chibi Holi had arrived on the banks of the Yalu, ready to cross and join Su at Pyongyang. All he needed was cold weather to freeze the river so that he could cross. The blizzard came, the Yalu River froze, and Chibi crossed, engaging the Koguryans in a major battle. It was a great victory in which the Korean Moliju was defeated. His death toll was staggering.

Not long after Chibi's news reached a jubilant court, Jao strode into her quarters, a look of rage and failure on her face.

Mi rushed over to her. "My lady, what troubles you?"

The empress was obviously distressed. "The blizzard that did so much good for Chibi seems to have completely overwhelmed General Su. He was supposed to have met Chibi, but instead he retreated, thinking he would lose his army. And he's had terrible losses—one of his commanders was killed with all twelve of his sons."

"What a disaster!"

"But there's worse news, Mi. No sooner did we get Su's report than we learned that General Liu has had to retreat as well."

Mi looked grave. "From Paekche? Where is he now?"

Jao paced across the room and sighed. "In Kongju, completely isolated. How could this happen! The court is in a complete uproar—everyone is shocked and no one now seems to remember Chibi's victory at all. They want to abandon the war at once—Chibi has been ordered to withdraw."

"But he's in striking distance of the capital."'

"It's senseless. And now ships are no longer to be built, and Liu has been ordered to retreat all the way to Silla," Jao cried in fierce disappointment. "This is a worse failure than all the other failures in the past. I just can't accept it. Kaotsung's officials are all cowards, even the famous General Su!"

"Not a failure at all." Mi was thoughtful. "Just a pause to regroup. We in Silla have been fighting this war for generations. We know all about temporary retreats."

"We need better communication if we continue, then," Jao mused, calming herself. "Carrier pigeons perhaps. No one here or on the field knew about Chibi Holi's great victory until it was too late. He might have ignored his orders to retreat had he been an established Chinese general. As a foreigner in Tang service, he did not dare disobey. So now a Chinese success has been frustrated, and those wretched Kos were saved by their weather again!"

Jao was discussing the Chibi Holi situation with Kaotsung a few days later when a report from General Liu came in. She grew more and more excited while reading it, finally stopping to cry, "He has done what Chibi didn't dare do! He defied the orders to retreat. Listen to this:

> All my officers are in favor of a retreat as ordered. However, I gave them my views of the aims and general strategy of this war. . . . Now that we hold the enemy's stronghold, a retreat would be ruinous and would spoil everything just when we could clean up this whole land. The army has had to retire from Pyongyang . . . but we should stand firm, wait and seize an opportunity to strike. These people are over-confident and already off their guard. I beg leave to continue as indicated above. Liu.

Jao jumped up in excitement. "You see!" she shouted. "That's just what I told you he should do! I was right!"

"Irrational, but doubtless right," Kaotsung agreed. "Perhaps we should do as he suggests?"

"It is your war, and you have to decide. You know how timid your officials are for fear of failure. Someone has to stand firm. When you have officers like Liu and that Chibi Holi, you can continue until you win. And as for myself, I agree with Mi—this is only a setback."

"I am going to harass the privy council tomorrow until they agree to what I want," Kaotsung said, setting his chin.

He got his way, and the court finally backed a minimal peacekeeping mission in Paekche that the council called a truce. When officials tried to raise new troops to send to Liu, however, the response was apathetic. He got only seven thousand recruits.

Little progress was made anywhere on any of the Korean fronts as the year dragged on. Jao and Mi kept close watch on developments through Chi and the servitors, and through Jao's attendance at the audiences. Jao, however, distracted by her pregnancy, lacked her usual enthusiastic interest.

Late one moonlit night, only Jao was stirring. She realized that her time had come. "Mi," she said. "You had better send for Madame Sun. Cloud too." Madame Sun was aging, but she was still an adept. She had retired from practice, keeping only the empress as her client. She came into Jao's chamber, which had been especially prepared for delivery and, joking constantly, took charge. She was famous for her running flow of conversation with her patients, which she maintained while concentrating on the mechanics of delivery. Partly because of her care and partly because of Jao's confidence in her, in only twenty-four hours of labor Jao was delivered of a fourth son, whom Kaotsung happily named Tan.

Tan was a lean baby, long and slim, and he slid into the world with an ease and lack of fuss that endeared him to Jao immediately. As the first months of his life rolled by, he daily showed some new skill which brought pleasure to his parents. They had time to spoil him, as they had not had with the others. He easily became the pet of all Jao's intimates. Lady Yang, Cloud, and even Mi, who was normally neutral in all her dealings, were utterly charmed by his antics and good temper.

Tan was over a year old before the issue of the war in Paekche was resolved. In October, General Liu Jen and his colleague, another Liu, along with King Munmu of Silla, sailed down the Kum River and surrounded the Japanese and Paekchean forces in their center on the delta. Four fierce encounters took place. They won all four. When the Paekche resistance failed, their king fled to Koguryo. He did not dare escape to Japan for fear of the wrath of the Japanese. Wu Jao read General Liu's report to Kaotsung, "Our forces burned more than four hundred Japanese ships. The smoke filled the sky and the sea ran red with blood. All the country is pacified except one small fort. Liu."

Jao threw her arms around the neck of an exultant Kaotsung.

"Total victory at last!" he cried, hugging her back.

They declared a three-day holiday with amnesty for prisoners and remission of taxes for a year for the province of Shantung which had supplied most of the troops and borne most of the burden of war. The lighted palaces and gate and the feasting in palace and city excitedly embarked upon were made especially enjoyable by the mild fall weather and a full moon. Rejoicing was in the air. Jao soon became pregnant again.

The next two months were busy for both the court and the Sillan community in the capital. Chinese relations with Silla had reached a new height. King Munmu's son duly arrived in Loyang on his goodwill mission, armed with instructions and with lavish gifts. Jao herself organized the festivities in his honor.

"Let us acknowledge Mi officially and honor her as she richly deserves," Jao proposed. Kaotsung agreed, so in an impressive ceremony, with the Silla envoy present, the emperor bestowed a title upon Mi and her son. The prince also was loaded with rich gifts and gratifying honors. He was impressed. He enjoyed talking with Mi in the aristocratic idiom of the ruling classes in Silla and treated her respectfully as a result.

When the prince left, the purely political alliance between Silla and China had been strengthened by a personal tie at the highest level.

After the departure of the Sillan prince the weather turned hot, and remained so throughout August. Masters and servants alike felt the stifling heat and were cross. Kaotsung, especially, felt irritable. His interest in the children waned when they became fretful and naughty. He turned, in order to relieve his boredom, to flirting with the ladies-in-waiting, keeping them excited. He sent Hsu off on a long holiday and left the day-to-day administration in the hands of the chief eunuchs and the minor ministers.

Jao could not rest well. She could neither lie down nor sit up comfortably. She blamed everyone's restlessness not only on the weather, but also on the evil spirits that she felt still inhabited the Changan palace. She was concerned enough to have Mi call in the shamans to exorcise the malignant influences.

Kaotsung summoned Jao. "I want to speak to you," he said sternly as he sniffed the incense-laden air. He scowled as he noted Jao's bloated appearance.

Jao looked into his hard eyes and stiffened. "Of course, please sit down, Your Majesty."

"I prefer to stand," he said bluntly. "It's about these sorcerers and their din. There have been serious complaints about the goings-on, and I don't like it. It must stop."

"These are white shamans, who are powerful enough to exorcise the palace of the evil spirits that are so plainly disrupting the palace these days. They are doing this at my order, for the good of all who live here," Jao replied civilly, hanging on to her temper.

"Whatever they are doing, stop them. I won't have it."

"What if I don't?" Jao returned, her face ghostly in its pallor.

"I will have your shamans thrown out," Kaotsung replied, turning to leave.

"You can throw me out with them." Jao stood up as she spoke.

Kaotsung heard her tone of voice and knew that she meant what she said. "I'll do just that," he said viciously, and left the room.

Jao sat quietly, feeling the baby kick her unmercifully. She struggled to get herself under control. She then went to visit the shamans, thanked them and gave them an hour more before they had to leave. The next morning, she did not attend the council meeting and did not take notes for Kaotsung.

Word of the sorcerers soon reached the bureaucracy, which was still staffed with many of the former adherents of the regime of the Elders. These officials had survived the purge but had not been promoted and had not been allowed to get coveted positions on the staff in Loyang. One of the disaffected, who had served ex-Crown Prince Chung, soon heard about the sorcerers in the inner palace and recklessly reported the accusation to the emperor. Soon he was emboldened by the emperor's willingness to listen to criticism of the empress, and petitioned for her deposition. It had happened before and it could happen again.

The meeting between Shanggwan I and Kaotsung was short, the emperor in a bad temper and the official silkily smooth in voicing his complaints about the exorcists. He implied that their activities as ordered by the empress might be treasonable, likening Wu Jao's behavior to that of Lady Liu and Empress Wang, malignant for the state and dangerous for the welfare of the court. This was a calamity to be ameliorated by the degradation of the empress without loss of time. Kaotsung listened, received the petition in silence, and dismissed Shanggwan I with an order to return the next day with his petition in writing.

The two servitors on duty at the time belonged to Chi's secret guard and they reported at once to him. Distressed, he strode quickly to Jao's quarters, where she was lethargically counting out a layette. He quickly detailed her situation.

"Please see that a formal audience with the emperor is arranged for me at once," was all she said as she pushed aside the small garments. She rose, thanked Chi, and disappeared into her dressing room. An hour later she reappeared, dressed in court robes that were well-calculated to conceal her pregnancy. Her face was carefully made up and her crown was new, another gold sequin and filigree gift from Silla.

Kaotsung awaited her arrival in surly impatience, noting in surprise her formal dress and her low kowtow before him. He heard her stifle a groan as she bent over, but failed to see that it resulted from her pregnancy.

"What's all this?" he cried peevishly. "This charade . . ."

She kept her head bowed. "May I speak, Your Majesty?" she asked. He could see a tear splash on her hand, and realized that the matter was serious, not just a family tiff. There had been many of those recently. He dropped his bullying tone.

"You may. Please proceed."

"Your humble spouse is questioning the report of an obscure bureaucrat regarding the exorcist rites that she has had performed in order to cleanse the palaces. This sweeping out of evil demons has been done in the interests of all who live in this palace and was in no way the concern of this bureaucrat.

"The next thing your humble wife is questioning is Your Majesty's view of her conduct. Has she failed as a wife at any time?"

Kaotsung remained silent.

"There have recently been an endless number of things to keep your humble wife busy—the repairs on this crumbling palace, transcription of the notes on the audiences, the organization of state banquets, the sorting of foreign tribute, and the supervision of the daily life of the palace women and children. Your wife lies awake at night thinking ahead, planning, making decisions, all to keep Your Majesty comfortable and free of worry. If anyone wishes to take the place of your humble wife, she is more than welcome. Your empress is ready to lay down the burden.

"But all this is of minor importance compared to that which concerns what we two, as emperor and empress, are doing to support and strengthen and enhance your reign. Your empress has one goal in life, and that is to help the emperor attain his desires. In this your empress has not spared herself and believes she has, up to now, been successful.

"Your Majesty is at this moment a great monarch. The Turkis, the Tibetans, the Khotanese, and many other states either are enjoying the benefits of Tang peace or are suing for it. And now for the first time in history, southern Korea is in the hands of Tang. Your Majesty has done all this together with your empress . . . and can go on doing it. Why should Your Majesty listen to a Changan bureaucrat?"

Kaotsung interrupted her to dismiss his confidential attendants.

"Now go on," he said, but she shook her head.

"There is no more to be said. I have said it all." As she tried to rise, she stumbled, and Kaotsung leapt up to help her. He pulled her into his arms and pressed his cheek against her pale face.

"I will not grant this petition. I will dismiss this—this Shanggwan I," he said awkwardly, "and I will call back Hsu from his vacation to deal with these people who are so persuasive and whose motives are hidden from me."

Jao, standing with her head bowed, said diffidently. "Please do not send for Hsu. He needs his summer rest. And please be patient about this matter of the exorcists. During this heat, perhaps the best thing to do is nothing. Do nothing for the present would be best, wouldn't it? That will set my mind at rest," she bowed quietly. "While I am absent from your service in giving birth to your son."

Kaotsung let his hands fall to his sides. He had forgotten. "You may leave now," he said awkwardly, and stood stroking his chin as she bowed and retired.

Who is there to trust if not my own officials? he asked himself in self-pity. Was there no one at all who was not after his throne or his favor? He stood silent, buried in cynical despair. Soon, however, he thought of the loyal Liu of Paekche, of the loyal Li Chi, of the loyal Hsu. They were all old men over sixty, but strong supporters nevertheless. And then there is Jao, he thought, "the most faithful of all." He felt ashamed.

It was not a son who was born a few days later on a hot afternoon so stifling that the midwives and Lady Yang were dripping with perspiration. It was a girl, small and easily delivered. She was welcomed with exclamations of relief from Madame Sun and the other women in attendance because she had arrived so much earlier than they had expected. Jao herself was pleased to have it all over with and did not seem to mind that she had borne only a girl. She whispered quietly, "A daughter! Just for me! After all those boys. Heaven has been kind!"

Kaotsung was notified and came at once to call on his empress, to the surprise of all. He had, after all, been warned that "it is only a girl." He smiled at Jao, wiped her hot face with the end of his linen belt, and assured her of his gratitude at being presented with a girl.

"A daughter is just what I wanted," he told her cheerfully. "She is sure to be my favorite person as soon as she can smile. I congratulate you!"

"She already knows how to smile," Mi declared.

"Smart girl," Kaotsung said taking another look at the small bundle. Carefully, he lifted the baby into the curve of his arm. He had never done this at the birth of his other children. He sat on the bed, studied the child's tiny features and investigated her hands and feet. Then a little hand curled round his thumb. "Amazing!" he mumbled. "She can already hang on. We must find a good name for her. Do you have a suggestion?"

Jao caressed the soft cheek with one finger. "She has arrived opportunely to make peace between her parents. Let us call her Taiping—Great Peace."

Kaotsung looked at Jao sheepishly. "Taiping it shall be," he said, and stood up. "Now I am going out to celebrate . . . the same as if she were a son." He grinned, and left amidst a ripple of pleased laughter from all the ladies in the room.

That night the heat broke, and the morning dawned with the first hint of autumn in the air. "A good omen," Jao remarked weakly as she looked into the big, unfocused eyes of her child. "She is smaller than the others."

Lady Yang said cheerfully. "A perfect child, though tiny, already eating and sleeping and breathing well. No problems."

"Good," Jao sniffled. Lady Yang looked at her in surprise and clucked in dismay.

"Don't take me seriously," Jao gasped, blowing her nose. "I am very happy, really . . . that she is a girl and that she has come at this time . . . and that the emperor is pleased and lets me name her Great Peace. That is what I need now, some peace. I seem to be tired, so very tired. And I don't want any more babies . . . ever."

When Hsu returned to Changan, Kaotsung sent for him at once, and, among other matters of urgent business, mentioned the Shanggwan I petition. Hsu's head snapped up and he looked, to Kaotsung's amused gaze, like a hunting dog being pointed for attack.

"What! An open attempt, disguised as a righteous petition by an official, to depose the empress herself! Using Wang's protégé Chung as a rallying point to gain power! By still another set of traitors! It is not Wu Jao they are after—it is Hung. An attack on the throne itself . . . outrageous!" Hsu spluttered indignantly, and Kaotsung had to smile in spite of the seriousness of the occasion.

"What do you recommend doing about it?" he asked mildly.

"Investigate! Hsu said hotly. "May I have permission to leave?"

Kaotsung granted the request, and Hsu strode off, his garments billowing in his haste to dig into the matter.

Shanggwan I soon realized with horror that he had been exposed by the emperor and that there was nothing now that could save him. In the eleventh month of the year, Hsu brought formal charges against him. He was imprisoned, his possessions confiscated, and his family enslaved. His downfall also brought down the wretched Prince Chung whom Kaotsung himself could not save as he had before, now that a new conspiracy had risen around him.

Soon after his success in defending the empress, Hsu petitioned that the status of the empress be raised in the eyes of the court and that henceforth the imperial pair should be entitled the "Two Holy Ones."

Jao responded from behind the curtain, "This humble person is honored to have her small services acknowledged. Such a move may achieve more honor and respect for the crown, but again it may not. The gesture seems to be negligible in comparison with the greater one of raising the effective status of the Crown. The prosperous condition of the empire warrants a recognition from the empire as well as from the world outside. The emperor deserves it. To raise the status of the empress is not what is needed.

"It has been sixteen years since Kaotsung mounted the throne. It has taken sixteen years for him to emerge as an able successor to his father and grandfather. He is worthy of special honor. It is time to celebrate in a style that will tell all under Heaven that Kaotsung is as successful a ruler as the two before him. He has pacified the border areas, conquered Paekche, and brought peace to all under Heaven."

This challenge from the empress came as a surprise to everyone in the hall, including a stunned Kaotsung. When she ceased speaking, the silence in the council chamber was so profound that the chirping of swallows under the eaves was the only sound to be heard.

Hsu was the first to recover. "We have had bumper crops this year, it is true, and we have achieved a truce in Korea, it is true, and we have new canals and roads, new markets and new forts, it is true, and the business of government is going forward prosperously, it is true. What does the empress have in mind?"

"The offering of the Feng and Shan sacrifices at next New Year's celebration, on the top of the mountain Taishan," she replied.

This time the silence was even more profound. Finally Hsu said in muted excitement, "A magnificent idea . . . tremendous. The Feng and Shan sacrifices symbolize a dynasty's achievements in acquiring a peaceful and contented population within the empire and in the border areas. It has been celebrated only rarely in all the centuries. Probably now, more than at any other time in Chinese history, the Great Tang Peace is a reality."

After a time of soul-searching by officialdom about the appropriateness of undertaking such an ambitious ceremony, and the usual agonizing over expenses, preparations began under the personal direction of the highest luminaries of the court, including Li Chi. Officialdom, aware that China was without doubt the greatest empire in the known world, pridefully authorized the expense.

"A lot of fuss," Kaotsung grumbled to Hsu. "The court on the move for six months. Tiring."

"Yes, Your Majesty," Hsu agreed fervently. He was in his sixties now, and wondering how he would manage.

"But traveling is amusing when the roads are dry," Kaotsung added. "And it is an escape from the everlasting dullness of meetings."

"And it raises Your Majesty's prestige to a new height," Hsu said, following the emperor's change of mood.

"I have come far in sixteen years, haven't I?" Kaotsung mused. "And this makes it all seem worthwhile."

"Best of all," Hsu said in the same mood, "the princely families, the nobles, and the monks are all taking fire. I've never seen anything like it!" He congratulated himself on his fine idea.

Jao flung herself into preparations for the sacrifices. Reviewing the ritual, she was disturbed to discover that there was no part assigned to any female. "Even though the ancient rites require it!" she said heatedly to Cloud. Cloud's eyebrows rose and she studied Jao in silence for a long moment. "Petition them!" she said thoughtfully. "The only thing to do."

Jao nodded slowly. The next day she petitioned the council in a formal audience.

"The sacred ceremony of Feng and Shan is a very ancient tradition," she reminded the officials gently. "The worship of Heaven is in keeping with that tradition, but the worship of Earth is not. The spirits of the previous empresses are supposed to receive offerings—from men. This, in the humble opinion of your empress is a mistake. The whole concept of Heaven and Earth is based on clear recognition of the two sexes in the altars: one is round for Heaven and is male; one is square for Earth and is female. The offerings to earth should be the duty of female members of the court, should they not? Perhaps the spirits of the empresses will not show themselves to males. Your humble empress should serve, perhaps as an example to future empresses."

No official could think of a way to overrule this petition. Jao was named First Assistant.

Chapter Sixteen

The imperial cortege turned off the narrow country road and slowly circled to its campsite at Taishan. There, at the foot of the mountain, it stopped in front of the terraces leading to the altar. Kaotsung's litter was set down on hurdles and his bearers straightened their backs in relief, bantering with each other in low voices. Lim and his men rode up and dismounted with a clatter of harnesses while the tent carriers, not far behind, shouted loudly to clear the way so that they could unload. Frost rimmed their fur caps and the bitter Siberian winds sweeping over the desolate plain reddened their faces. They all had one wish—to get their shelters up as quickly as possible.

Jao rode into the sacred site on her tall western horse and stopped. The horse sidled nervously, his sides heaving and his nostrils blowing spirals of steam into the freezing air. She looked eagerly around her. Empty land stretched in front and high cliffs rose behind. The ribbon of road snaking across the low foothills was filled to the horizon with moving specks of people and baggage in a queue thirty miles long. A wintry sky arched above, empty except for the westering sun. There was no village, no human habitation to be seen.

Jao's entourage rode up around her and noisily dismounted, joking together to help them face the appalling wilderness. This is a nightmare, Jao thought while waiting for her grooms. How blithely we embarked upon this ambitious undertaking, the risks we took! And now here we are. A bad storm, a whirlwind, a sudden freeze could halt everything and bring death, and disgrace to the throne. She shuddered.

Jao's grooms hurried up and she slid off her horse. She stretched and looked toward Kaotsung's litter, but he had not yet emerged. A roaring bonfire was lit and a caldron of hot soup was hung over it. Jao's women gathered around and she heard them laughing about their red noses and disheveled appearances. Cloud began to massage the frozen fingers of one of the princesses, and Mi supervised the unpacking of the imperial baggage. Taitsung's sister, Queen Wencheng, undaunted, calmly sipped her soup and idly watched the turmoil.

"You actually look as if you were enjoying this venture," Jao said as she joined the older woman. Wencheng greeted her cheerfully, shrugged her square shoulders and continued her study of the darkening sky. The evening stars were gradually appearing. "The omens are good," the Queen said.

Jao caught her breath and leaned against the older woman, hiding her face in Wencheng's shoulder. She dared not waver, and yet, because of her dread and her fasting, she felt very weak and in desperate need of reassurance. "The omens are all good," Wencheng repeated bracingly as she held the empress in a comforting embrace.

Chi and Lim extracted Kaotsung from the palanquin. In an effort to restore his circulation he stamped around the bonfire that was now burning hotly inside its windbreaks. Behind the fire, amid shouts and warning cries, the imperial tent went up. Once its guy ropes were securely fastened, servants dashed inside with rugs and braziers. Kaotsung was not far behind.

The caravans carrying foreign guests wheeled to their sites, directed by Chinese camp masters. More tents went up and dozens of new fires were lit. By the time the sun had sunk below the horizon, its red disk gleaming hugely through the mist, a hundred tents had been raised. They were all different. There were the leather and felt yurts of nomad khans; the cloth tents of turbanned visitors from India; the sheepskin roundels from the Tibetan guests; the woven bamboo and reed hutches of those from the south seas; and the hide shelters of the Koreans and Japanese.

Jao and Queen Wencheng joined Kaotsung inside the imperial tent while Wencheng's yurt was being prepared. Kaotsung greeted his favorite aunt with enthusiasm.

"It's good of you to come with us in this pilgrimage so far from your home," he said, covering his anxiety with a smile. "We would invite you to dine with us tonight, but we must fast instead. We'll celebrate later and all have a good time, you'll see." He frowned. "Those dark clouds in the east, let's hope they don't mean hail . . . or a blizzard." His laugh was forced.

Wencheng chuckled in her gusty way. "They might, and they might not. But with all the world here expecting Heaven's smiles, we should have—we must have!—the best that great Heaven can offer. You have boldly challenged Heaven. Now we shall see."

Kaotsung and Jao stared at her in acute dismay, but Wencheng was not trying to frighten them. She was studying the pole star, which was now clearly visible. "The omens are good," she said with conviction, and this time Jao believed her.

The cold increased, but already most of the participants of the trek were inside their tents. Each entourage formed its own little city with stables, guards, and armies of servants. The Tang military had hide barracks, now crowded to overflowing with warriors who had cheerfully come from the far corners of the empire to demonstrate their skills to both fellow Chinese and to foreigners. The opportunity to mingle with other soldiers was of keen interest to all, especially when they could fraternize with enemies like the Koguryans.

The sky darkened to a black canopy of stars that seemed to hang close and bright over a dark land. The wind died down, allowing cooking fires to be lit in a scattering of lights for miles around. The long queue of travelers was now gathered in encampments and at rest.

Jao and Kaotsung were at last in their cocoonlike beds. There were ten or more felt rugs beneath them, soft furs on top, and glowing braziers all around. Kaotsung had a pottery hot-water bottle at his feet and ermine on his head and hands. Occasionally there were rustlings behind the curtains where the attendants were settling.

"Are you asleep?" Kaotsung whispered at length.

"No, I'm not . . . I can't," Jao whispered in return.

"I'm cold," Kaotsung said.

"You can't be," Jao retorted. She herself had seen to the hot-water bottle, caps, and mitts.

"I'm cold," he repeated stubbornly.

"Come in with me, then," she said after a pause. She guessed his terror. She heard him struggle with his covers and gasp as the cold air hit him. She threw aside her own furs to help him roll in beside her.

"B-Better," he whispered, pressing against her. "Now I might sleep. But I'm so . . . what if . . ." He caught his breath, and Jao held him closer.

What had Wencheng said? "The omens are auspicious," she whispered back, "you'll see."

When Mi touched Jao on the shoulder to waken her, she found Jao wide-eyed. Mi was holding a candle that flickered wildly. Chi and Lim were rousing Kaotsung, who had slept well and was grumbling at being wakened.

"You didn't sleep?" Mi asked.

"No, not much," Jao said, still tense. "Tell me quickly—what kind of weather has Heaven bestowed?"

"Windless, cloudless, couldn't be better," Mi replied.

"Let us up, then!" Jao exclaimed in vaulting relief.

She scrambled to her feet, her strength returning despite her weakness from hunger. Mi quickly led Jao behind a curtain for ritual ablutions, while Kaotsung's servitors did the same for him. Dawn was only a few minutes away when emperor and empress, heavily wrapped in their imperial finery, emerged from the tent a short time later.

The altar of Heaven was dimly outlined by torches. Lanterns hung from poles at intervals to frighten off evil spirits that could not tolerate light. Banners of yellow silk fluttered from other poles. Nine concentric terraces rose in the center of the square, and on the top was the round blue altar symbolizing Heaven. In front of the altar was a stone table on which were placed three jade tablets. The middle one was inscribed in gold to the spirit of Heaven; the other two bore the names of Kaotsung's father and grandfather.

The rites master ascended to the altar and lit a sacred fire. When its aromatic smoke lifted skyward to invite the spirits of Heaven, the Mountain, and the imperial ancestors to be present, Kaotsung stepped forward. The ceremony had begun. Hidden singers chanted an invocation while the emperor slowly mounted the steps to the altar.

"What a striking figure! Regal!" Queen Wencheng murmured approvingly. She was in place beside Jao, who nodded proudly in response, overcome by emotion. The emperor's robes, though in traditional style, were new and heavily formal, embroidered in gold with the twelve symbols of rule. These shimmered as he moved, calling attention to them. The three symbols of supreme power that only the emperor could wear were conspicuous—the sun, moon, and stars.

Jao's eyes searched the sky for the fading moon and found it. Soon the sun will rise, she thought, her heart pounding in her chest. And then there will be all three: sun, moon, and stars, together at one time to show that Heaven above is blessing the Son of Heaven below. Her hands slid together in a beseeching gesture of worship.

The invocation grew louder as the emperor approached the top. At each step a different line of music was sung, and when he reached the altar, all sound stopped while he prostrated himself. Then he rose and faced the sun as its tip pushed above the horizon. "Perfect!" Jao breathed. She heard the other women stir around her and bowed her head in gratitude.

Kaotsung waited until the sun had cleared the horizon, then poured the libations and offered prayers which were written on silk. He then laid the silk in a jade box, sealed it, tied it with gold thread, and placed it within a cavity of the stone table. At this point a long line of dark-clad figures passed in front of the table, burying it with colored soil they carried in baskets. This happened so quickly that it seemed to the onlookers that the mound rose by itself. When the last of the basket carriers disappeared into the mist, Kaotsung descended briskly to the tune of lively music. He had barely reached his position at the foot of the stairs when a rapid beating of heavy drums announced the entrance of two groups of young dancers onto the open area in front of the audience. They performed two dances which symbolized the two aspects of the rule of the Son of Heaven, one the duty of providing peace and harmony for all under heaven, and the other the duty of military.

The opening ceremony was over and all had gone smoothly.

During the morning hours the emperor and his auxiliaries rested and refreshed themselves with only barley water. The sun dispelled the frost on cliffs and path. The wind remained in abeyance. The signs were favorable, so the distinguished group could begin the ascent of the mountain. The most important part of the rites was still ahead.

The sun was close to setting when the participants, all male again, reached the mountaintop. They waited there silently until dawn, when the invocation to the spirit of the Mountain began.

Dark figures gathered around the open-air altar, torches casting flickering shadows on stern faces. Light mists eddied among the peaks, blending with the smoke of sacrifice and drifting skyward. Kaotsung officiated, offering wine libations and prayers. He had just begun the concluding movements of the ceremony when the mist suddenly cleared away and the sun emerged. This was the best portent that could possibly happen, the most auspicious of omens! A ripple of excitement passed through the audience and expressions of elation appeared on every face.

"The Spirits are pleased with us," Kaotsung pronounced in high excitement and gave the signal for immediate descent.

There remained only the third-day sacrifice to the spirit of the Earth. Jao, the key figure in this part of the program, was on tenterhooks.

The altar to Earth was a mile away from the altar to Heaven. A little before dawn on the third day, Jao's bullock cart rolled into the sacred grounds. She descended with her attendants. Kaotsung waited at the top of a shallow flight of steps to greet her and pour the first libation. Jao poured the second, and the ranking princess of Taitsung's generation the third. A drum accented each movement, but the offerings to Kaotsung's mother and grandmother were made by Jao in a profound silence, punctuated only by strokes on bells and chimes. The ceremony was short and, to everyone's surprise, attended by a huge crowd of spectators. Moreover, only after it was over did the day become overcast and the wind rise.

The sacrifice to Earth marked the end of the Feng and Shan and inaugurated three days of entertainment and intermingling. Every evening, feasting took place in the tents. All participated, visitors, performers, serving men, everyone from the lowest bearer to the most prestigious guests. All the military services were represented, and during the day impressive maneuvers took place. Kaotsung had been at pains to assemble his most able veterans. Foreign visitors, many of whom had come for the one purpose of viewing Tang military might, were on hand at every display, showing keen interest.

The night before the final dispersal, Kaotsung entertained twenty guests at a sumptuous banquet. The ten Chinese included ranking princes, ministers, and generals. The other guests were foreign—the Byzantium ambassador, the son of the Persian emperor, two Turkish khans, two Tibetan chiefs, and, arousing much curiosity, four elegantly attired princes from across the eastern sea. One was from Yamato Japan and three were from the Korean kingdoms. They were young: the son of King Munmu of Silla; Fuyu Feng of Paekche, former king and now governor there; and Nansheng, eldest son of the Moliju.

An hour after the twenty guests had assembled in the imperial tent, Wu Jao joined the group. Dressed in an ethereal feathered cape from Lingnan, she seemed to float across the room. Her hair, still glossy and black, was elaborately arranged, and her eyes sparkled with pleasure. Her dazzling appearance commanded instant attention from every man present. With her were first attendants Cloud and Phoenix, dressed in gauzy silks—Jao's equal in beauty if not in presence. Phoenix held a decanter of Turfan wine and Cloud carried twenty small replicas of the mountain Taishan, all of jewel-jade of the deepest green. Jao spoke to each guest personally, asked knowledgeably about his family, served him wine and presented the jade memento. The three women then left as modestly as they had come.

No man in the room could ever forget Jao after this. They now saw her not only as a notable empress, but also as a beautiful woman of extraordinary grace. It was a major achievement to have been able to bring together the Far East and Far West in an environment of peaceful, exciting equality. It was the first time in history that such an event had taken place.

Kaotsung spent an hour the next day in formally concluding the last of his official business. He declared the celebration auspicious on all counts, and said that those who had participated shared in the good fortune bestowed by Heaven. He conferred titles and awards and announced promotions for the hardworking officials. Finally, he proclaimed a general amnesty and remission of taxes for those who lived in districts through which the caravans had traveled. It became obvious, as visitors took their leave, that Kaotsung had emerged with a new prestige that now reached beyond the boundaries of empire, and that Jao had acquired a new dignity and acceptance as a person of importance in her own right.

"The miracle," Jao said in bed that evening, "is that your health has stood up to all this. No dizziness, no headaches, no loss of vision. You were looking healthy and vital through it all!"

"Vital?" Kaotsung growled, pretending exhaustion. "I'm all in bits, all in bits!"

Jao giggled. "It's safe for both of us to give way at this point, now that the empire is declared to be the greatest on earth, and Heaven has safely smiled on its son."

"It's odd, but I don't want to give way. For the first time in six months, I want to be in the thick of things!"

"How lucky . . . how lucky it has all been," Jao said. "We had a wonderful harvest throughout the empire, we had a tremendous response from foreigners, we lived through the court's fierce opposition, and now we have showed the world."

"Emptied the treasury, impoverished the people," Kaotsung added.

"Loyang has been rebuilt and is no longer the run-down Sui dynasty survival that it was. Thanks to Yen Lipen being as great an official and fund-raiser as artist and architect, we have new gates, a new pagoda, and the largest throne hall that has ever been built. Tang has put on a great show!"

"Not just us," Kaotsung retorted. "The princes spent their own money on refurbishing their Loyang town houses, and the temples emptied their coffers in repainting rafters and eaves, retiling roofs and erecting new guest halls. And the shops, they put out colorful new signs and cleaned up the streets. Imperial funds did not do it all. No!"

Jao laughed. "But we triggered it. Without us there never would have been a Taishan. The officials are always so tight with the money for government enterprises, public buildings especially. Money spent that does not directly contribute to their own well-being is not well spent in their opinion. A big gesture was long past due. We had to whittle down the self-esteem of the aristocrats. We had to give the foreigners a taste of Tang splendor. And I'm so glad that we built the new throne hall, or we would have been outclassed. Don't you think?"

Kaotsung did not answer. In a few moments a snore told Jao why. He seemed profoundly happy and finally at peace, Jao thought contentedly, and she slipped into a deep sleep herself.

No sooner was the imperial family reestablished in the once-despised Changan palace than the emperor was confronted with a crisis. News had arrived that the Moliju was dead, and a great debate arose as to whether Tang should now attack Koguryo. Kaotsung, encouraged by his new status from the Taishan rites, sided with the war party. He assembled the generals and asked for opinions.

"We should make plans to complete Tang's subjugation of Korea," he told them. "I have chosen a new reign name to encourage you to act—Chienfang, Approved by Heaven. I have ordered Chibi Holi to Liaotung to be commander-in-chief, and I am requiring him to collect the information needed for a general attack—maps, roads, forts, that kind of thing. Then we can pounce."

Each general soon had a specific assignment in preparation for an all-out attack on Koguryo.

At the same time that the high-level meeting of the generals was going on, Jao was having a low-level conversation with Mi and Chi about the same subject.

"Chi," she said, "the Koguryans who were brought into palace service fifteen years ago after Taitsung's campaign—you made friends with them and learned their speech, didn't you? How many of them are here now?"

"About half a dozen, Your Majesty," Chi answered. "They were war casualties, and all came from the Ansisong area. They are good fellows."

"Mi, do you know these men? What do you think of them?"

"We are friendly, although they were enemies of Silla at one time. Now we are all servants of Tang. We understand each other's speech a little, but we prefer to speak Chinese. They are assuredly loyal to Tang by now—especially since none of their tribesmen would trust them if they returned to their homes in Koguryo."

"Chi, what do you think? Could we trust these men to act as spies?"

"I don't know. I will investigate immediately." Chi's interest was caught, and Mi was obviously excited. They both supported an all-out attack on Koguryo.

That evening, Jao persuaded Kaotsung to go for a walk in the main palace garden to admire the double cherry blossoms that arched overhead in billowing pink clouds. He appreciated the beauty but he also knew Jao.

"What have you got on your mind?" he asked.

She gave him an amused glance. "Not much. A small matter . . . but I have been thinking that, now that the Moliju has died, it would be a good idea to inform ourselves about conditions in Pyongyang. The Moliju had three sons who might share the new dictatorship, but perhaps they do not get along with each other. Would it not be to our advantage to find out?"

Kaitsung looked at her under his brows. "What are you thinking?" he asked warily.

"That we might see to it that the brothers don't get along. When I presented the jade gift to the oldest son, Nansheng, at Taishan, he seemed dazzled and ready to accept Tang friendship, however packaged. He could be induced to join us against his brothers perhaps. The younger brothers are anything but friendly toward us. We could send agents . . . this is just a thought."

"A small matter!" Kaotsung exclaimed later, as they were walking on a garden puta. "A mere trifle! Only that it is impossible. In the first place, we don't have the kind of agent needed—well-informed, well-trained, accustomed to court etiquette, and, most difficult of all, willing to undertake such a dangerous task. And if, by a miracle, we could recruit even one such man, he would be unmasked the moment he opened his mouth because he would not know the local language. But it was a good idea," he hastened to add.

"I know of six or seven suitable men," Jao said.

Kaotsung halted in the path and stared. Falling petals brushed his shoulders. Jao whisked them off. "Chi for one," Jao said in an offhand way.

"A palace slave? No—not possible."

"Why not? He is extremely intelligent. He is tight-mouthed. He is loyal—no one more so. And he once performed similar services for your father, did you know? Give him his permit and a secret assignment and send him to Koguryo. Why not?"

Kaotsung seemed rooted in his tracks as he absorbed Jao's proposal. "What about language?"

"Chi has been learning how to speak with these men in their own language for fifteen years."

"But the idea is so bizarre . . . the generals would never accept it."

"The generals should be the last persons to know about it. Few people know about your six secret guards—nine of us altogether, you, me, Chi, and the six—but it is a valuable service to us. This venture would succeed if Chi were in charge, and would be of equally valuable service to us. Listen, we'll have some fun with this: you set up a formal spy system through Chibi Holi, all according to Sun Tzu's manual, and I will set up this small enterprise, and the one of us who gets the most valuable information wins a prize. Agreed?"

Kaotsung grinned and resumed walking. "My humble empress with her small ideas! All right, I'll do it. What will be the prize?"

"Fifty gold ingots and a feast cooked by the chef of the Tientsin Bridge Inn."

Kaotsung chuckled. "Done!"

After formally celebrating the winter solstice in the palace square, Kaotsung and Jao retreated to their own quarters in the Changan palace to spend the rest of the day in the company of their children. Hung was nearly fourteen, Hsien twelve, Chungtsung nine, Tan four, and baby Taiping two. In the midst of a noisy game of hide and seek, a visitor came unobtrusively into the hall. He stood and watched for a time until Jao noticed him. "Chi!" she exclaimed.

"Uncle Chi!" the boys shouted as they rushed to greet him. He had been gone the entire autumn. "Where have you been? We missed you!" Hung shouted. The others pounded him on the back and yelled.

Kaotsung finally had a chance to ask Chi to seat himself and share refreshments with them. Chi, elated by his warm reception, was soon telling them about his adventures. The children settled down, wide-eyed, to listen to him, even Taiping, who sucked her thumb and fell asleep against Jao's knee.

When the children finally went off to bed, Jao said eagerly, "Now, tell us about your real mission. Did you accomplish anything?"

Chi grinned in gratification. "Successful beyond belief. First I sought out the Moliju's oldest son, Nansheng—whom you entertained at Taishan."

Jao nodded attentively. "Did you present the gifts? Did he like them? Tell me!"

"He was overwhelmed at being recognized so handsomely. Yes, he liked the gifts, but the one he treasured most was that jade Taishan you gave him. He carried it around the entire time that I was with him."

"What about the six Koguryan palace slaves that you took with you?" Kaotsung broke in. "Did they defect when they reached their homeland?"

"They didn't dare. They had all been wiped off the tribal rolls long before," Chi answered. "I sent them to investigate the Koguryan strongholds—as many of the hundred or so forts as they could get to—to see for themselves exactly what conditions were like in each. They went as charcoal sellers and woodcutters, and their hesitant speech was accepted as natural for men who live such isolated lives. They aroused no suspicion."

"They must have had bad moments," Jao remarked.

"Yes, but they are a quick-witted lot," Chi answered briefly. "And none were ever taken. They had close calls, which I will tell you about later. They had agreed beforehand how they felt about betraying their own people. They all felt that the tribes would be much better off if they could set up trade relations with China in a friendly atmosphere instead of being constantly drained for war. They really put their hearts into making a success of their search for information. They discovered, each one separately, that a little-known fort far up the Yalu River called Hsin Cheng is extremely important. It is located where the river crossing is narrow and the trails along the mountain ridges are ideal for contact with all parts of the kingdom. That fort is like the center of an enormous spiderweb."

"Why important if it is so remote and isolated?" Jao asked.

"It's not really isolated, because of all those mountain trails," Chi replied. "It is well-built and serves as a headquarters and supply center and is, by every standard, the strategic heart of the Ko military system. My men can all make sketch maps of the fortifications, main trails, bridges, and so on."

Jao caught her breath and glanced triumphantly at Kaotsung. He was looking delighted.

"This information is valuable beyond price, if it turns out to be true," he said happily. "Now I want to know more about what you yourself were up to."

"I caught up with Nansheng as soon as I entered his country, as I told you. I changed my clothes into formal ones, presented my letter from you and delivered the gifts. He welcomed me cordially, and as time went on, I suggested, when the occasion arose, that he should protect himself from his brothers—"

Kaotsung interrupted with a choke of laughter. "Incredible!" he said.

Chi grinned sheepishly and continued. "I then went to Pyongyang and made trouble there."

"So that is what caused Nansheng to turn to us," Jao cried. "I thought it had just naturally happened because of brotherly rivalry."

"Well," Chi said, "maybe so, but your humble servant spent time and thought on helping it happen."

Kaotsung slapped his knees in pleasure, and continued to ask questions until he felt he had every detail of what Chi could tell him. When Jao noticed that Chi was exhausted, she interrupted. "It is late," she said. "We are enchanted with you, your news, and your services. We will thank you properly soon. You may leave now, however. Good night, my friend."

"Yes, indeed, indeed we are grateful," Kaotsung said cordially.

Chi bowed and, and when he said good night, there were elated smiles on all three faces.

"Yes," Kaotsung said, turning to Jao when they were alone. "Yes, indeed!"

Jao dimpled. "I won! I won our wager! Now what about that dinner?"

"Yes," Kaotsung said for the third time. "I lost, I pay. Tomorrow we will have that meal! Now I want to know what to make of this news. What do you think? None of the generals has turned in any report about strategic Hsin Cheng, so we must alert Li Chi. Tactfully, of course. Let's consider the main war plan. The commanders that I have in place on the Korean borders are the best. They can now pounce—"

"Pounce?" Jao inquired, studying her hands. "Is that all?' Her mind raced. Here it was, here was her chance of attaining her dream. Here was the chance of accomplishing what none of the other Chinese military strategists had been able to do. Here was Kaotsung's chance to win fame, for China, for himself. And for me, she concluded wryly.

"Well, yes, of course, those Koguryans need chastisement after sixty years of raids and conquests of neighboring territory."

"If chastisement is all you have in mind, you might as well forget it. Those Koguryans know how to recover from chastisement in rapid order and to go on as before."

"Is it the problem of a three-front war that worries you?" he retorted. "With the old problems of noncommunication and bad weather?"

"Exactly, and the risk of an ignominious defeat like the ones the Sui and Tang Taitsung met, and what we have already suffered ourselves." She was still studying her hands.

"What is on your mind?" he asked bluntly.

"If you would only resist the traditional insistence on short, cheap wars such as is advocated in Sun's *Manual of War*, and launch instead a long-term, full-scale war, focusing the whole of Tang might in men, money, and matériel—like winter clothing and accurate local information—you would be sure to win. If you don't launch such a war, you might as well quit now, put Nansheng back in power, withdraw, and claim victory even though the enemy is still the enemy." She finally raised her eyes to his and read his expression.

"As usual, you want the moon. No one in the government will see it in black and white as you see it. Is Mi behind all this?"

"Half measures, this is what they will propose, and half measures will fail again. Yes, of course Mi is behind it. But good ideas are good ideas. I share them, and I think you do too."

Kaotsung said nothing, breathing heavily. Then he changed the subject.

The next morning when Kaotsung opened his audience, he faced a tense house. They were all aware that the war would be discussed, and each man intended to have his full say.

"We must prepare for a hard war in Korea," was Kaotsung's opening statement.

"Perhaps not so hard," said the leading statesman, Hsu. He was seventy-seven now and had less stomach for doubtful issues than he once had. "We have Nansheng in our control and can put him back in power."

"It won't do," Kaotsung said sternly.

"The Koguryans are only tribesmen, and nothing to fear," began General Kao, who was temporarily in the capital.

"I seem to have heard that you lost two engagements with those same tribesmen recently and had to be bailed out by other generals," Kaotsung remarked in a soft voice.

General Kao turned fiery red and subsided. A prolonged silence ensued.

Kaotsung then continued to address the ministers. "We have to choose our most able general and give him absolute command. We must get the people behind us—they are cynical now, from the thousands of Chinese lives lost already and the huge amounts of money disappearing into official pockets. Officials handling pay and supplies have been criminally corrupt. This must cease. We will then sponsor a sense of mission, have patriotic, martial songs written for the teahouses, and induce good men to volunteer."

"It is only one Korean state after all—impoverished at that—and we don't need the prestige," Hsu began again.

"Do you want to risk another humiliation at the hands of that encroaching, war-hardened kingdom, then? I want a full discussion." Kaotsung sat back to listen.

Two hours later Kaotsung was still keeping his silence and the officials were showing signs of fatigue.

Kaotsung cleared his throat. "What is your will, then? The same strategy, the same tactics, or a new, complete effort to restore Tang prestige—a war to the finish?"

To this no one had an answer. The silence was prolonged, speaking only too loudly. Finally Hsu coughed. "The man to put in charge should be our best, then. I suggest General Hsueh, despite his advanced age."

"Not good enough," Kaotsung said. "I want Li Chi."

Gasps were heard. "He is eighty," Hsu said, obviously amazed. "He surely won't accept."

"He will. I have asked what his conditions would be. If he is given total authority and the whole revenue of Hopei, the nearest province, he will manage."

"We will let him have authority over the war, of course, but we will manage the funds," said the minister in charge of taxes and expenditures.

Kaotsung looked at the minister coldly. "Did you hear what I just said? Li Chi should be given total authority over the revenue of this province—total authority."

The minister ventured another comment. "But that would put him outside the control of the . . . the civil government."

"Precisely," Kaotsung said.

In the end, Kaotsung's plan was accepted. It was savagely resented by military suppliers and officials who made a significant income from their army contracts. Li Chi started preparations immediately, and it took him all winter and summer to complete them; it was nine months later, in early autumn, before he was ready to start the campaign in the field. Before leaving Changan to take command, Li Chi had a final audience with the emperor and empress. He explained to them about preparations in Hopei and about strategy and tactics once Chinese armies left Chinese soil.

"When you begin the attacks, where will you start?" Kaotsung asked.

"Fortunately, we now hold Ansi Cheng," Li Chi began.

"Then what?" Kaotsung asked. "One fort after another all the way to the Yalu border, I presume. North to Puyu too."

Li Chi looked at him curiously, and Jao said with a nonchalant shrug, "That includes the Hsin Cheng fort, I suppose?"

Li Chi became suddenly alert, and Kaotsung chuckled. "A trivial piece of information has reached us about this one place, and we merely wanted to corroborate with you. . . ."

A month later, when Li Chi led his armies across the Liao River, he briefed his commanders: "We focus first on a fort called Hsin Cheng, which is far off the routes we took before. It is located a hundred miles southeast of Liaotung on an old trade route. This fort is the hub of Koguryan defense. Unless we take it, all the other forts, about a hundred, will not submit easily because they would always be supplied through this central depot.

"I have placed an agent, a very able man, inside Hsin Cheng to discover which officer is the weakest link and to subvert him into unlocking the gates. I shall diminish Koguryan morale further by encamping around the fort—outside of arrow fire, of course—for a month, doing nothing. This will confuse them because they all know all about Sun's advice on short, cheap wars and they won't understand the opposite, especially in the face of oncoming winter.

"After Hsin Cheng falls, I will fan you out in different directions to take key forts, and will arrange to meet naval forces just below the capital of Pyongyang when the time comes. In this way we foil their strategy of cutting our supply lines behind our backs. I will also induce a traitor within the walls of Pyongyang to open the gates. Otherwise they could hold out for months, as they have in the past."

Li Chi stood in the center of his command tent, his head of white hair still thick, his body still strong and his presence still keenly felt. To a man, his commanders were satisfied with his strategy, and signified their approval by raising their fists when he dismissed them. Regardless of personal rivalries, they all were proud to be included in Li Chi's last campaign. After dismissal, several of the commanders walked back to their tents together.

"What's this Hsin Cheng fort?" was the refrain after the meeting, but nobody knew.

A lull in government affairs set in after the army left for Koguryo. The slowdown persisted all winter, as if the Taishan pilgrimage followed by serious war preparations had exhausted the bureaucracy, as in truth it had. The emperor maintained control by perfecting his technique of sharing duties with Jao, but he had overstrained himself and no one was surprised when he had another stroke and was incapacitated again.

"You will just have to shoulder the whole burden now," Cloud said to Jao. "We will help you with all we have. We can take turns sleeping near you and keeping track of the complexities for you."

Jao grasped Cloud's hand and pressed it jerkily. "You are willing to do that?"

"Need you ask? Pheonix's sons are grown now and she is an able organizer. She could join us. There is Holan Kuochu, your niece, and Shanggwan I's daughter, who is now a palace slave but educated like a boy."

Jao thought a moment, then asked, "Do you mean that I should have a group of private secretaries? Literate women to serve me day and night?"

"Something like that," Cloud replied carefully.

"I'll think about it," Jao said.

At first she did not like the idea that anyone but herself should have access to government business and power politics of the devious variety that she was exercising so informally, but she soon found that Hsu and others expected her to carry on exactly as she and Kaotsung had been doing, so she began to rely on her trusted female assistants to help her with the many duties that now seemed to shower down upon her.

She had to spend much time with Kaotsung keeping him amused enough to get his assent to the more important business at hand. He was also helped in his convalescence by the keen interest he took in the progress of the war. He tired easily, however, and this was an ever-present anxiety.

It was well into November of the next year before news of the final days of the campaign arrived in the capital. A weak sun was shining through the bare branches of the northern park where Jao and the children were watching the gardeners beat the chestnuts out of the trees. The older boys were helping the gardeners and dodging the prickly burrs that were falling onto their heads. Other gardeners were in the persimmon trees, picking the fruit that hung like orange lanterns in the bare branches.

Kaotsung joined the family, a formal dispatch in his trembling fingers. His eyesight was still poor so he thrust the scroll at Jao.

"It is from Li Chi. If it is news about some disaster, I shall collapse, so please find me a place to sit."

"Here is a tree stump, sit here," Hung said. At sixteen, he was tall for his age, and keenly aware of anything agitating his parents. Jao undid the silk ties and opened the letter. She skipped the honorifics and started down the page.

> Tang armies have wintered successfully on Koguryan soil and have gradually taken all the strongest forts, including Hsin Cheng and the northern capital at Puyo. There have been many skirmishes and several great battles, one in which the enemy suffered thirty thousand dead. Three armies led by Hsueh, Kao Kan, and Chibi Holi, following different routes, made a juncture on the Yalu River. There, the Koguryan army made a final stand and we attacked with full, united strength, defeating it totally. We then pursued the fleeing fragments a hundred miles to the city of Pyongyang. After a month's siege of the city, King Kojong surrendered with ninety-eight officials. His son, Nanchien, held out, but was betrayed and the city turned over to us on October twenty-second, 668. We then burned it to the ground.

Jao gave a gasp and looked at Kaotsung, who was spellbound. She continued reading.

We are bringing to Changan King Kojong and his court, Second Son Nanchien, and thousands of males of military age. We have struck camp and are proceeding in groups downriver to make the sea crossing before the winter closes in. The omens are good and the winds are with us. This time we have defeated the Manchurian weather by careful timing, and now seek the favor of the gods for this last sea crossing. Li Chi.

Kaotsung snatched the dispatch from Jao's hand, and Hung tore off his military cap and threw it in the air in glee.

"Done it . . . done it, by heaven!" Kaotsung cried, finding it hard to breathe while Jao hugged him and wept tears of joy.

"No one else has ever been able to do it . . . they have all failed, but now you have done it!" she cried, her eyes incandescent with delight.

The other children and the gardeners who had been listening began to shout so loudly that everyone within earshot came running. Attendants, guards, children, and nurses crowded around, all bursting out clapping and shouting when they heard the news. Announcement of the victory then spread with lightning swiftness throughout the palace and city. It had been a long time since Tang arms had had a victory of this size, and the people were not slow in seizing the chance to celebrate.

The victory revived Kaotsung enough to enable him to supervise preparations for a giant parade to take place when Li Chi returned. Jao, who had learned the value of a political display of might at the Taishan rites, put aside all other considerations to help him organize.

"A lot of goodwill is generated by the excitement of pageants," she said to him after a meeting with the officials in charge. "We have to order up new imperial equipment, banners, staves, flags, insignia, uniforms, lanterns, musical instruments . . . everything new to gain new respect for the crown."

Kaotsung grimaced. "Respect is the last thing that these Changan people ever think of. I'll settle for smiles and cheers."

"Smiles and cheers, then," Jao agreed, laughing. "Let us stir everybody up, have new parade gear made, and create some new banners in your honor. I'll see to it myself."

Kaotsung grinned. "I'm certain of that," he said. "The palace gates are going to be crowded with your artisans going and coming, and no one will have any peace."

"Good," Jao returned. "That is the way I like it."

The auspicious day, January fourteenth, dawned cold and clear. All during the night workmen had been busy rigging poles with lanterns and festive pine branches along the route of the parade. Bearers, soldiers, and guards assembled in assigned places, where they warmed their hands over bonfires. By noon all was ready. The emperor and Li Chi mounted their groomed and caparisoned horses and took their places at the head of the column.

Jao had suggested open sedans, but Li Chi declined. "I have never ridden in a palanquin, and it is too late to start now. What a figure of fun I would be for my men," he told the official sent to discuss it with him. Jao had hastily agreed, although she wondered whether Kaotsung could stand the long ride.

"Good!" he had said, "I will ride my most handsome stallion—it will give the people a treat to see my horse!"

The two men were dressed in military costume with trousers and armor, as the usual ceremonial robes could not be worn on horseback. When Kaotsung and Li Chi rode up to the starting point, they received wave upon wave of spontaneous cheers from their men. Behind the two rode Kaotsung's four sons, who received their share of cheers. Six-year-old Tan's erect bearing garnered him extra attention. Jao in a palanquin aroused more applause. A long procession, it advanced slowly through the main streets to the sound of drums and other music.

Kaotsung and Li Chi outdid themselves in poise and presence and in conveying their innate goodwill to the people. The citizens responded, often cheering wildly, sometimes with a low ripple of clapping but always with a sense of pride.

Necks were stretched when the prisoners clanked past in their chains. The king and his nobles were ill clad and blue with cold. Later, when they were granted amnesty and the chains struck off, all they wanted to do was reach shelter and food. The ranking prisoners were awarded positions in the guards, and the king was given a title and quarters in the eastern park.

The day was drawing to a close when the procession ended. Li Chi, with his white hair and rich uniform, was conspicuous. Still erect, he finished his ride looking as fresh as at the beginning. Kaotsung, too, looked vigorous and in his prime, letter perfect in all that he did both during the parade and in the rites afterward. The day had grown colder, the paraders dispersed, and the people, stamping their feet and turning their faces away from the gusting winds, sought inns, shops, and homes, all feeling immense gratification for their country and its rulers, and feeling that they had had their money's worth that day.

Kaotsung and his sons rode into the palace grounds and dismounted at the gate of the emperor's residence, Jao's palanquin just behind. Riders and bearers were all shivering with cold. Kaotsung's chamberlains were waiting on the steps to help him inside, and Jao followed speedily to get into the warm quarters.

"We got through it," Kaotsung said, warming his hands over the brazier.

"In style!" Jao cried happily. "Your humble wife saw most of Taitsung's celebrations. Yours today was the equal of any of his. People won't forget today."

Kaotsung beamed and color began to return to his cheeks. He put out his hand to Jao and they sat comfortably together, sipping the hot soup that had been brought in when they appeared.

"Tastes good," he said, spooning out the last bit of meat in his third bowl.

"Hm," she murmured drowsily, wriggling her toes, which were warm at last. "Heaven has honored us, one good thing after another. Perhaps now Heaven will let us live in peace without the yin-yang pattern of our lives so far, success, failure, success."

"What did you say?" Kaotsung mumbled, dozing off.

"Nothing," Jao replied, "nothing, really. I was just thinking that we've made it! We've accomplished something big and we've done it together. Nothing can take away this success from us now. Your reign will go down in history as the third reign of strong emperors who united China and brought good times to the people. Also . . . we've proved that a couple working together can bring good luck to whatever they touch!"

But Kaotsung didn't hear, and Jao soon fell asleep. At forty-five, she was happier and more confident than she had ever been in her long life.

Heaven did not change the pattern of success-failure. Now that yang had peaked, yin set in. During the severe cold that settled on the land after the victory celebrations, word reached the palace that Li Chi was very ill and refused to see a physician. Jao sent Prince Hung to inquire, only to learn that the old war-horse had died during the night.

"His brother was with him," Hung reported. "He told me that Li Chi had died the way he had lived, bravely. His last words were instructions to his sons and grandsons to continue the same service to Tang that he himself had rendered for some sixty years. He also ordered his brother to thrash, to death if need be, any descendant who gave poor service or was even unworthy."

Jao looked gratified. "So like Li Chi . . . always big in whatever he did. There's just no one to take his place. Thank you, Hung, for performing this service for your father. We were sorry that he did not get to Li Chi's bedside in time."

Hung flushed with pleasure. "I like to do things like this. I like to help." He hesitated.

"Is there something more on your mind?" Kaotsung asked. He had been listening carefully to what his son had to say.

"When Li Chi said that his family should be punished if they failed in service, was he serious, do you think? Or was he just talking?" Hung asked carefully.

"People don't just talk on their deathbeds—they are serious," Kaotsung replied. "Was there something about this that bothers you?"

"Yes. I think that he was worried about his grandsons who are my age—Chingyeh and Chingyu."

"Why do you say that?" Kaotsung asked. Jao gave Hung a quick look of inquiry.

Hung shrugged, "It's just that they are so aloof whenever we meet."

"Louts," commented Chungtsung, who had been listening intently.

"Disrespectful?" Jao asked, ignoring Chungtsung's remark.

"No, not that. They know their manners. It's just their way, their sense of importance."

Kaotsung frowned. "You will find, when it's your turn to sit upon the throne, that most of your ministers are like that. My father told me on his deathbed to watch every official above the third rank very carefully. Just see to it when you are emperor that this Chingyeh never gets above third rank."

"Would that be just?" Hung asked.

"Maybe not, but you cannot neglect early signs of a self-importance so great that it is incapable of genuine loyalty to anyone or anything. People like that can never qualify for the highest positions for the simple reason that they cannot accept orders."

Hung smiled in understanding. "I really enjoy being crown prince, you know," he confided. "Because you and my mother are teaching me as we go along. Send me out on assignments often!"

"Not on any more courtesies connected with death, I hope," Jao said lightly.

Mi stood behind Jao on the gate tower as they watched the spectacular funeral column bearing Li Chi's body to his tomb. They stayed until the last banner bearer disappeared through the city gate, and then they turned together to leave. Jao was silent as they descended the many flights of steps, thinking sadly of her private loss now that Li Chi was no longer there to fall back upon in times of trouble. Once on the ground inside the palace, Mi, who was silent much of the time, seized her opportunity to say something to Jao in privacy.

"Your Majesty," she said. "The time has come."

Jao, recognizing the seriousness in Mi's voice, stopped in the path and looked into her eyes. "You will have to tell me what you mean because I don't want to guess," she said.

"The time has come for your humble servant to return to her homeland," Mi said, her eyes holding Jao's in an expression of deep sadness.

Jao was stunned. "I have thought that I would have you always—" She faltered.

"I know," Mi murmured, "and that has been my wish ever since I first knew you. To serve you till I die."

"Than what has changed?" Jao insisted, incredulous.

"Something bigger than I," Mi returned. "My country. To keep the new alliance between Tang and Silla in working order. That is something that will not happen by itself. There is too much ignorance . . . and . . . stubbornness, if the truth be known, in my country. I am needed to keep the alliance bright. To help my son."

"Your son?" Jao ejaculated. "What of him? I heard some six or seven years ago that he had disappeared. I didn't ask you about it because you showed no anxiety. I thought then that you knew where he was and would tell me when you were ready."

"It was as you say," Mi answered. "I was grateful for your silence because Chingpyong left illegally after Tang's final victory over Paekche. My son left in the night in the guise of a third porter in a trading group and was undetected. Eventually he arrived safely in Silla after several difficult voyages."

"I would have obtained exit and other permits for him," Jao said.

"That is the reason he left illegally. It would have been embarrassing for you and for everyone at the time. You were pregnant with Tan, and we did not wish to ask for such a great favor. We just could not!"

Jao listened with her head down. "It has been seven years. Why did he go when he did?"

"Tang had just conquered Paekche, and that radically changed the balance of power in Korea. Silla was left facing ambitious and warlike Koguryo. A confrontation of two states is more unstable than that of three, where there is the chance to play one off against another. My son was urgently needed in Silla for his knowledge and skills."

"Why didn't you go with him? Your skills are greater than his," Jao asked, struggling to understand.

"Because I could not leave you. Because you were pregnant. Because the emperor, if left on his own, could never have handled a major war with Koguryo. Because you did not know how to handle the ministers by yourself. Because of all those many things that you could not handle alone."

"And now I can?"

"Now you can."

Mi stopped and put out her hand blindly. Jao took it and pulled her friend into a close embrace, the two of them trying to conquer their tearing grief.

"You may be right," Jao murmured finally. "You always are." But she didn't have to like losing her other self, her Mi.

Although Jao had told Hung that she did not expect him to be sent on more visits of condolence after the one to Li Chi, Hung was sent out on many such errands in the months to come.

On the heels of the death of the supreme commander came another, the loss of the indefatigable Minister Hsu. He too was given a state funeral. Then on a windy day in March when the air was full of Gobi dust, Jao received word that loyal old Nurse Wang had died. "I mourn her, too," she said, and wrote a memorial for her servant. She copied it on a silk panel and gave Hung the task of presenting it to Wang's family, thus bringing them great honor.

Hung was sent only once to Lady Yang's bedside when she became ill because Jao herself went daily. "Mother," she said one day, "I hate to see you wasting away. Just tell me what I can do to help you get well. So far nothing has availed."

Lady Yang just smiled. "It is my time. Don't grieve. I'll be glad to go."

Jao buried her face in her mother's quilt. "Is it all the trouble you've had between the two sides of the family? You have suffered greatly, and I have failed to ease your life."

At this, Lady Yang roused herself. "Nonsense. You are the delight of my life and always have been. No, it is just that Heaven has willed that I must leave you soon." Jao buried her face still deeper in the quilt and gave way, for once in her adult life, to a storm of tears. Her mother kept patting her head. "There now, don't cry, don't cry," Lady Yang repeated weakly, as she had done so often when Jao was little.

When Lady Yang died, Jao was with her. Jao had insisted upon sleeping in the sickroom and serving her mother herself. In the end she was exhausted by these vigils and distracted by worries at every level of her life. The drought and famine in the country at large was especially trying. She nevertheless extended herself to organize a great funeral for her mother. "She deserves it! She always helped me to the best of her ability all her life," she said to Kaotsung. Privately he worried about the ostentation of such a funeral in times of hardship.

The funeral was held on a blistering hot day. The procession was a long one, assertive with its banners, bearers, mourners, great catafalque, and soldier guards. It wound its way through the shriveled fields to the elaborate tombsite. Jao herself was chief mourner, assisted by the wives of officials above Grade Three, whose attendance she required. The ceremonies were carried out in spite of the appalling weather. The amenities were observed and Jao was satisfied.

All was not well, however. A wave of criticism arose. Outrage was expressed that the empress had dared to flaunt her family in the face of a country suffering from famine. Jao for once was nonplussed. She did not have the support of those who used to help her before, and she was left to handle personal criticism as best she could. She apologized in court for the extravagant funeral and offered to abdicate as empress. The high officials, led by the astute Yen Lipen, Chief of Secretariat, refused to let her expiate in this way, and Kaotsung vigorously supported her, refusing to notice her petition at all, much less authorize it.

Surely, Jao felt, yang must begin again soon.

CHAPTER SEVENTEEN

After her humiliation in court, Jao wished to do something to restore the good name of her Wu family. Impulsively, she arranged for the sons of her stepbrothers to be brought to court and installed in the imperial household. Chengssu and Sanssu were the same age as Chungtsung. It was not long before the three had such a dynamic effect upon each other that their boisterousness and cheerfulness infected the whole palace.

Kaotsung, far from being annoyed, took an interest in the boys and enjoyed their antics. He often sat in the sun watching the boys race their ponies headlong, bareback, and at times sitting backward. He would laugh heartily when one of them took a tumble.

The boys were growing fast. Their lives were strictly supervised in a routine of study and athletics, where discipline was maintained by blows and kicks. Nevertheless, it all seemed to agree with them and they flourished. Occasional alleviations were arranged. Special dinners where wine was served were provided from time to time, enlivened by the presence of carefully recruited flower girls. Early sexual experience was part of the training.

One day Kaotsung called their tutor to him. "Come sit down here with me and tell me about these boys," he said. "How are they doing?"

"Lazy scholars," old Chang growled.

Kaotsung laughed. "No doubt! But are you able to polish them up a bit so that they know how to behave in polite society? What do you think of them now that they are almost through with their education?"

"Your son Chungtsung has grown as much as he is ever going to," the old man replied casually "He may be short, but he has filled out and is now a man—as you can see."

"No, I can't see very well. Tell me," Kaotsung said simply.

The old tutor flushed in embarrassment over his mistake. "Striking-looking lad, your son, with his heavy black eyebrows and a look of cheerful expectancy," the tutor said carefully. He was a gifted scholar soured by being saddled with adolescents.

"Yes, I like to hear his laugh. Cheerful is right. But what about other qualities? He is not scholarly, I know, and I don't care about that. But in leadership, has he any ability there?" Kaotsung queried hopefully.

Old Chang thought for a moment. "He takes the lead among the three boys, especially with young Sanssu, who is slow and a copycat."

"He is!" Kaotsung exclaimed amused. "An unusual Wu, then! They usually err the other way!"

"Sansuu grins, laughs, chuckles, gurgles, claps his hands, slaps his knees, wriggles ecstatically in his efforts to approve of everything Chungtsung says or does," Chang said sarcastically.

Kaotsung grinned and shrugged. "What about Chengssu?"

"Quite a different story," Chang said, with some reserve. "Chungtsung and Sanssu are extroverts, but Chengssu is an introvert. I never know what he is thinking. I'd say he was an idealist. He is slighter in build than the other two and has to outthink them to protect himself—which he does very well. Usually, he gets his own way, even against Chungtsung."

"Hm," Koatsung murmured. "Now tell me how I might use these boys in court in a year or two."

Chang frowned thoughtfully. "Chung is close to the throne and therefore should be exposed to problems in the control of men . . . of women too." He paused and looked at the emperor warily.

"Do you mean that he lets himself be put upon by females?" Kaotsung's voice had a critical edge to it.

"Not exactly. It's just that he thinks that all his females are as wholeheartedly devoted as they pretend to be."

"How can you teach children to recognize guile?" Kaotsung interrupted.

"If they don't get the knowledge by experience, especially in this court," the tutor replied humbly, "I just don't know. But to get back to their court positions: Chengssu is a born manipulator and influence-wielder and should be assigned to promotional schemes. He's a bulldog once he gets his teeth into the jugular of a desired goal. Sanssu, on the other hand, is a past master at avoiding commitment or collision. He's a joiner, a follower, and might be good at soothing injured feelings of colleagues."

"They're eighteen now," Kaotsung said. "When will you be finished with them?"

"Within the year," Chang replied, a small sigh of relief escaping him.

It was late in the afternoon when Kaotsung joined Jao. His face was lightly browned from his afternoon in the sun and he was relaxed. Jao was restless, having spent her afternoon going over reports from various Chinese headquarters in Korea. She didn't know what to think about Silla's recent actions against China. She talked shrilly about the matter, although Kaotsung did not want to listen.

"Nothing to worry about," Kaotsung said finally in a dismissive tone of voice. "Silla is firmly in our camp. Koguryo has been pacified these five years and—"

Jao interrupted. "Koguryo . . . peaceful? Hardly! We put their king in as governor of Liaotung to keep order. We put the crown prince of Paekche back into power as our agent. Now they are conspiring against us. Again!"

"Exile the kings to China and put in General Kao to quell the rebels. He'll do it fast enough." Kaotsung was impatient.

"No, it won't do. They are uniting against us—Silla too! When rebels in the north are chastised by our commanders, they flee to Silla, where they are welcomed. After all we have done for Silla!"

"Perhaps that report is rumor," Kaotsung soothed.

"No, it's a fact. King Munmu of Silla sent troops to aid Koguryo and Paekche against Tang, and he's even taken forts away from the Chinese for himself," Jao continued.

Kaotsung looked disconcerted. "All right, we issue orders in council deposing the king and sending his brother to be king in his place. We can also send troops with General Liu to discipline Silla."

Jao was furious. "Not enough! I am privately sending a messenger to Mi. I'll find out what is going on . . . and she had better have a good explanation."

Sailing conditions were favorable, and so, in two months, Jao received a highly conciliatory reply from Mi. Along with this was a gift of tribute gold from the king and the return of General Liu, who had quickly settled an agreement to keep the peace.

"Have you restored order?" Kaotsung asked sternly when Liu appeared before the imperial pair.

"I have used the same tactics with them that I used before with Paekche." Liu said deferentially. "There is no other choice if Your Majesties wish to bestow Tang Peace on those Korean kingdoms. Harsh treatment always provokes rebellion. Now Silla is suing for peace on favorable terms. They have acknowledged over and over again Silla's gratitude to Your Holy Majesties."

"What do you recommend?" Jao asked bluntly.

"Recall the king's brother and leave King Munmu on his throne."

"It seems clear that Silla wants peace," she said shortly, "but a peace on its own terms without Chinese troops or even our civil officials on their soil. What kind of a peace is that?"

"A cheap one," Liu replied instantly. "Silla has never been slow in acknowledging China's suzerainty or failed in proper obeisance or appropriate tribute. After all, this is what the emperor had indicated is our goal in Korea. Korea as a whole cannot be held indefinitely by Chinese troops."

Kaotsung hesitated. "Why do you think that?"

"Foreign troops quartered on a civilian population is bad enough in wartime, but it cannot work in peacetime. It is inevitable that Silla will contrive to be the only ruler in Korea, but only after the rule of Your Majesties. They are too devoted to you personally to try it in your lifetimes."

"We will think about it," Kaotsung said, dismissing Liu after seeing the stormy look in Jao's eyes.

"If we adopt this radical policy in Korea, we will have to make some reforms here too," Jao said flatly.

"For instance?" Kaotsung asked.

"Reform in the way our overseas and frontier troops are paid," she replied crisply.

"Not possible," Kaotsung said, shaking his head. "I forget just how they are paid in peacetime, but the system is entrenched, whatever it is."

"The custom is to pay the soldiers out of contributions exacted from the local populations, truly an archaic way of keeping the frontiers safe," Jao said critically. "As if the empire was so poor that special levies have to be made every time there is a crisis. Perhaps this was necessary in the past, but not now."

"What would you, a female, suggest, then?"

"As an ignorant, irrational female, I do have a suggestion," she replied silkily.

"I'm waiting," Kaotsung said, in order to end the argument.

"Abolish the old system and put in a new one—regular pay instead of irregular donations."

Kaotsung looked up sharply. "A good idea," he said finally. "I wonder why it hasn't been suggested before."

Jao, delighted at this shifting of ground, flung her arms around his neck. "Thank you for listening to me! Many thanks, many thanks . . . Do you know I adore you?"

Kaotsung flushed. Every so often Jao's exaggerations reached his heart.

"Seems to me," he murmured in her ear, which was now close to his mouth, "we should listen to some of your other ideas too, if we're going to do anything at all."

Jao said softly, her face buried in his chest, "Like beating down the overpowerful officials and giving the lower ranks some opportunity to advance?"

"Certainly! We might as well take on the biggest tigers while we are at it. Reform of any kind is liable to kill off the reformer . . . we might as well die for something big as for something small."

"I agree . . . I couldn't agree more!" Jao pulled away in her excitement. "But if, by good luck, we win with our reforms—and we are not 'killed off' by spiteful officialdom—could we retire to Loyang? Where we have always been so comfortable?"

Kaotsung pulled her roughly back into his arms. "You and your usual chorus—but, yes, Hung is twenty years old now, and he could be made regent in Changan. Then we could leave. It will give him experience and us some peace."

Jao smiled in triumph. Her vision to repress the overpowerful and aid the vulnerable was far-reaching, and her desire to move the main capital to Loyang serious. Reformation had begun.

"We're nobodies in this court," Chengssu complained after a grueling morning with irascible tutor Chang. "No one respects us."

"What do you mean? Everyone respects us!" Chungtsung was astonished by Chengssu's words.

"No, no, he doesn't mean you—us," Sanssu hastened to say.

"No, I'm including Chungtsung," Chengssu said. "If we were all recognized as being in line for the throne, we would be respected."

Chungtsung thought a moment. "Hung and Hsien are ahead of me and so I haven't a chance in my lifetime, is that what you mean?"

"Of course, you fool. And they haven't included Sanssu and me at all," Chengssu stated resentfully. "You have to be eligible to be emperor to get respect in this court when you're young, or else you're nothing. We should have stayed in our village where we were treated with respect."

Chengssu seemed to be criticizing Jao, and Chungtsung didn't like it. "Now you are being the foolish one," he said stoutly. "You're getting the best of everything here in the palace. So what if you are black and blue from beatings at times? So are we all. And we have the best there is in good times. Would you rather be a clod in a mud hut somewhere just to receive big respect? Fool!"

Chengssu flushed. "I mean what I said. I'm not so childishly satisfied with life as you two are. You're soft!"

"What are you boys up to now?" shouted their tutor, who had had overheard Chengssu's last remark. He swung a whip at Chengssu and missed. "Get back to your books, Master Wu! I'll teach you to be grateful for what you have, ingrate that you are."

Within the year the reforms asked for by the emperor and empress were instituted in a fiat of Twelve Decrees and they moved to Loyang. Hung functioned as regent in Changan. Hsien was given an appointment as a military governor, and Chungtsung—with his two Wu cousins—was absorbed into the Loyang bureaucracy.

Kaotsung missed seeing Hung daily, however, and when he thought that the separation had gone on long enough, he spoke to Jao about it. "How would it be to have Hung here for May? The cherry blossoms and wisteria will be lovely this year, I'm told, and Hung will surely enjoy them."

"I'll send an invitation to him today," she said at once.

"Thank you. Tell him that we won't take no for an answer." Kaotsung's eyes lit up when he said this. Our firstborn is his favorite, just as he is mine, Jao thought, and turned immediately to her writing table.

Never had parents and son been more relaxed or more at ease in one another's company. Jao had had to do the political disciplining and it had become a burden to her because Hung was idealistic and unperceptive about some of the realities of political power. Now, though, having experienced both independence and reality, Hung was much more understanding of his mother's opinions.

The first two weeks with Hung and his little wife Min were idyllic. Kaotsung and Jao put aside all other engagements in order to be with him. Jao saw that the food was what he liked, and Kaotsung supervised the entertainment. The days dawned one after the other, bright and warm, and the fruit trees blossomed in more and more bursts of blossom. The stones of the paths were soon carpeted with the lavender and pink petals of yesterday's blooms, while the canopy above expanded daily with fresh bursts of delicate clusters.

Hung glowed, put on weight, and spent long hours with his parents and friends. "It is not often that anyone has the full attention of both an emperor and empress," he joked happily.

Jao noticed one day that Hung was looking pale and wincing if anything touched his side. She asked him about it, and he looked at her as he used to when he did not understand something that troubled him. "Mama, there is a pain there and I can't get rid of it. It is getting worse. I have tried to put up with it without complaining, but . . ."

"Of course!" Jao cried, shocked. "We will consult your father's physicians. They are here on call. They will come at once."

But the physicians could do nothing, and the pains became excruciating. His parents took turns at his beside, unable to eat or rest very long when they realized that he was not going to get well. Kaotsung was with Hung in the early morning hours when his son went into a coma from which he never recovered. His wife never left the room, and threw herself on his body when she was told that he was gone, her high keening upsetting even the doctors. Jao rushed to help, but in her shock could not contain her own grief. Eventually, all Jao could do was to usher the stunned Kaotsung out of the sickroom, escort Hung's wife to her chambers, and turn over to the eunuchs the care of the dead.

Kaotsung could not bear the sudden loss of his son, and, shocked beyond endurance, became ill. It was again left to Jao to deal with the problems—and with the ministers, who wanted a new crown prince named immediately.

"The new crown prince will have to be our next son—Li Hsien," she said numbly to the prime minister without consulting Kaotsung. He would not even hear what she said. Liu nodded in agreement with her words, his face serious.

"Hsien is a generous, likable youth. Although impulsive and competitive," Jao added, "perhaps he will grow into a capable and responsible ruler if you take him under your wing."

Liu said nothing, only listened with careful attention and understanding.

"He isn't clever about people," Jao added painfully. "He makes bad judgments about them. We had to limit the people he saw when he was young and try to appoint intelligent attendants to guide him."

"I will undertake to set him up in the crown prince's palace in Changan and to see to it that he is well-served," Liu offered. "I will also take care of the arrangements for Hung's funeral, if that would relieve you."

"Please do. If you can help the emperor this way and allow me to be free to take care of him myself just now, our gratitude would be boundless."

General Liu bowed deeply. "It would be an honor," he said sympathetically, and meant it. He was a plain man, without guile. He had met many crises on the battlefield and in the council chamber, and was always able to take them in stride.

Hung's funeral was in keeping with his youth and the prestige of his position. A new feature was added to the customary imperial arrangements, a Buddhist participation in the rites. The emperor favored Taoism whenever possible, but for Hung's funeral he did not insist on exclusive Taoist practice. For once, he needed comforting Buddhist rites as well.

"I am almost fifty, and I'm through," Kaotsung remarked coolly as he lay unmoving when Jao tried to get him up the morning after the funeral. "I'm not going to audiences—beginning now."

Jao took a deep breath. She herself had not recovered from the shock of losing Hung. "It's plenary audience today. All the ministers will be there to offer condolences. I've never seen anything quite like it. People seem to be genuinely grieving."

"I can't do it," Kaotsung said.

"Not even for Hung's sake? Can't you make the effort this once—for his sake? There won't be any business, just the observances of mourning."

Kaotsung did not respond, but after a while he slowly pushed his way out of bed.

"This once, then," he said.

The audience that day was impressive. Astonishingly, Kaotsung dominated it as never before. The strength of his feeling for his lost son was apparent in every line of his body. Jao had never before seen so many people united in a deeply felt emotion, and she found herself deriving comfort from this outpouring of sympathy. Not only did it revive her, Kaotsung improved as well, and although he continued to be aloof after the audience was over, at least he did not lie motionless in his bed.

"Do you think that you could attend an important council meeting tomorrow?" she asked one evening when he was settling himself for sleep. He was silent for so long that Jao thought he had not heard her. Then he sat up suddenly.

"I was going to abdicate in Hung's favor and spend my last days in peace. That was what I was going to do before he died. I have been held responsible for so much . . . and now I am responsible for my son's death. I am to blame . . . you are to blame. We are being struck down by Heaven for raising ourselves too high. We call ourselves Celestial Rulers! What a farce!"

Jao felt numb and could only listen in acute dismay.

"Hung was poisoned," Kaotsung cried. "We let him die! I did . . . you did. You were responsible, and you failed!"

This was more than she could stand. She protested with passion. "The physicians said that there was a huge blockage. The physicians could feel it. A lump that grew in his right side . . . not a matter of poison . . . it was bothering him for days, a lengthy disease. Poison is fast."

Kaotsung was not listening, withdrawn into self-condemnation.

This is appalling, Jao thought in despair. I must do something about it or he will go mad. He kept his back turned towards her.

The next morning she sent for the abbot of a small Fenghsien monastery in Lungmen where the family had often picnicked. The monastery had intrigued Kaotsung once. The monk came at once and was shown into her private study.

"His majesty is cast down with grief. Have you any recommendation for the revival of his spirit?' Jao asked.

The old monk bowed his head in perplexity, but he had been with the imperial family many times in the past. "Perhaps a long stay with us would rest him," he ventured. "Our religion has many ways to comfort and heal."

"He may respond to anything done in Hung's name," Jao murmured.

"A memorial? Would he be interested in building something as a memorial in honor of his son?"

Jao brightened. "Could we not camp out on the banks of the river Li and look at the old Wei and Sui caves there . . . and see what happens?"

"We would welcome Your Majesties with all we have, and do our best to serve you," the abbot replied simply.

"Thank you, then. We will put ourselves in your hands. I will send our eunuch with supplies and we will follow in a few days if I can persuade his majesty to go."

Jao sought out Kaotsung at once. "Could we not go out to Lungmen and camp out in the temple courtyards and look at the old Buddhist cave temples? Perhaps we could do something for Hung . . . to help his spirit, something so superlative that it surpasses anything that has ever been done before as a memorial."

"Memorial?" Kaotsung repeated. "Nothing could be good enough."

"A great Vairocana, Buddha of Endless Light, the most splendid ever? To be carved out of the cliff for our beloved son?"

The words tumbled out of her mouth as she tried to interest him. Only gradually did the idea of doing something to aid Hung's spirit finally filter through to him. After that he revived. Within the hour after he agreed to go, they were on their way. Tan was thirteen, lengthening out and eagerly reaching for new experiences. Tai was eleven, the right age to welcome an adventure. It relieved both children and servants to escape the gloom of the palace, and the trip of twelve miles, although it took all day, was exciting. When they arrived, tents were already up and charcoal fires for cooking were lit. Even Kaotsung and Jao felt cheered and were glad they had come.

The summer weeks passed. The children grew tan and gained weight in outdoor living, and their parents gradually grew stronger as well. Jao allowed herself to wade in the river when the children were swimming but spent most of her time supervising government affairs through couriers, and sleeping. Kaotsung prowled through the ruins of the cave temples and, accompanied by the abbot, took numerous walks over the site of the old Fenghsien temple which had been built into the granite cliffs. They discussed the possibility of building a new monastery and creating new Buddhist images in the cliff surfaces. From this it was but a step to calling upon the best sculptors in the empire to work on the carvings.

A panorama of the Buddha of Endless Light and his satellites gradually took shape under Kaotsung's supervision. During the autumn months, he visited frequently, his presence bringing out the best in the sculptors. He enjoyed seeing the emerging human forms endowed with physical vigor and spiritual power. He returned home after each visit refreshed by the optimistic message that the artists were expressing.

One evening at a family dinner, after Kaotsung had returned from the site, Jao asked him about the project.

"Are you certain you want to hear?" Kaotsung said, eyeing his sophisticated sons skeptically. A chorus of good-natured assent greeted this. Kaotsung shrugged, saying, "Those artists understand what they are doing. They are aware of the religious ideas as well as the techniques of their trade. They have expressed their idealism in hard stone."

"Idealism? What's that?" Tan asked.

"Poetry, aspiration . . . reaching for the stars . . . the great dreams," Kaotsung replied, eyeing his family speculatively. "I am told that Indian idealism as stated in Buddhist Vairocana worship has been enlarged by Chinese Buddhist thinkers."

"Why is that so important?" Tan asked.

"Because our Vairocana in Lungmen is presented in company with two disciples. This follows the old Confucian model of the ideal balance in upper and lower relationships. Look at our Chinese symbol of yang and yin, where the ideal is also balance." Kaotsung stopped and regarded his family in amusement. "Over your head, son?" he asked Tan.

Tan looked him in the eye. "Balance? Any slow-wit understands that."

Kaotsung laughed and Jao glanced quickly at him—he so seldom did so. He patted Tan's shoulder. "Balance is something we Chinese understand. The Confucian teacher—or the Buddhist Vairocana, who incorporates all knowledge—is balanced by the presence of the learner, the disciple, as a symbol of every man's possibilities. Very Chinese, as is in our symbol of yang and yin and the intriguing notion that they constantly increase or diminish while remaining in balance."

Jao continued to stare at her spouse. She had never before heard him express his views to his family in such a way. Her own ideas were somewhat different, but she listened without interruption while he finished his train of thought.

"Our Buddhists are now applying this concept to religion, to offer the same salvation to all equally. This is different from the Indians, with their castes. What we are doing out there on the cliffs expresses this idea—it fills me with pride."

"It's not some disembodied ideal, Indian or Chinese," Jao interrupted vigorously, "but a down-to-earth expression of life here and now! The artists feel good about Tang rule!"

Kaotsung grunted satirically, and the rest of the family burst out laughing. "Mother is so serious about Great Tang," Tan cried.

"She needs to be because the emperor is not!" Kaotsung said wryly. "However, about that work out there, I am serious . . . it is going to surpass anything yet done in our great empire."

"In what way, may I ask?" Chengssu inquired, alert for information about any new fashion.

"The way the sculptors organize the proportions, combine strength and delicacy, and use high relief to show the strength of spiritual feeling."

"Oh." Chengssu said without much enthusiasm, and they all laughed again.

"Never mind, you may laugh and I may laugh, but this cliff temple is worthy of Hung. And he was worthy of it."

Forced to be serious for a moment, the family stared round-eyed at Kaotsung, even Jao. Dear old Kao, how he surprises me, she thought, how he constantly surprises me.

In the next few years, Kaotsung continued his patronage of Buddhism and his close association with his family as a way to keep his spirits up. He knew that he was not getting better. The shock of Hung's death was followed by the disgrace of Crown Prince Hsien, who had fallen in with a dissolute crowd and had to be degraded and exiled because of a conspiracy. It was too much for Kaotsung's low vitality. His depression was then exacerbated by Hsien's suicide. Jao herself recovered only gradually from the loss of her sons.

Floods followed years of drought, and the Yellow River burst its banks in many places, causing havoc in the plains downstream. Loyang was flooded, including the palaces, disrupting life for all. Jao decided to retreat to their summer place, the Palace of Nine Perfections in the highlands above Changan.

"This place is called the Nine Perfections so that no one would notice the imperfections," Tai said. She was now a personable, if irrepressible, young lady of sixteen. "Maybe there are nine perfections somewhere about, but I can't find them!"

"I suppose these floods and droughts," Kaotsung said, "even the leaks and the rot of this place, must be the fault of the Son of Heaven. People have to have someone to blame, and I'm it, I suppose."

"You're not to blame for anything!" Tai replied cheerfully. "You are the most blameless human being that ever was! Tan and I *like* imperfections, and we *love* this place because we don't have to take care of clothes or mud or manners!"

"Well, Tai," Kaotsung said sourly, "if you like this rough life, you may have it, with my blessing."

Tai directed a quick look at him to see if he was serious. She decided that there was a twinkle somewhere in his eyes and giggled.

"Never mind all that," Jao said. "What we need to do we are doing. Living here in these informal quarters, we are showing the empire that we are doing penance. Besides, this high plateau is good for everyone's health."

"Hmm," Kaotsung grunted, and Tai giggled again. "That is one way to look at it," he growled, by way of agreement. He did feel somewhat better among the scented pines of the uplands.

By the time they were all settled more or less comfortably in their palace of perfections, a distraction was provided. Tan was suddenly determined to marry.

"The girl is not exactly what I would have wished," Jao argued discontentedly in private to a patient Kaotsung. "She's beautiful, of course, and her family is good enough, though not rich, but . . ."

"But she has a mind of her own," Kaotsung commented idly as he watched Jao out of the corner of his eye.

"Just like Tan," Jao said crossly. "But she's not good for Tan. Now there will be two of them mooning around and creating problems."

Kaotsung's eyes went blank and he remained silent.

"Well . . . what are you thinking?" she asked sharply, and when he still did not answer, she went on. "Are you thinking that I'm too hard on the children and interfere too much? Only Hung and Tan seem to have had any feeling for politics. None of the rest do, and that is fatal in a family like ours. I have to interfere for their protection. Hung has gone to the Yellow Springs, and so has Hsien, and now Tan is second in line for the throne. I wish he were more practical. . . ." Jao frowned.

"I know, I know." Kaotsung could see that Jao was seriously upset. "Do you want to break it up, then?"

"Yes!" Jao exploded. "She's a bad influence on him. He's the smartest child we have, even more so than our Hung was. He takes in a wider range of knowledge, understanding, feeling, perceptions. He can always see two sides of everything. That makes him neutral, and unwilling to lead people and enterprises as he should. Passive and worse—a thinker! And she's just like him!"

Kaotsung looked at her under his brows, and she met his look, her breast heaving with emotion.

Kaotsung sighed. "Tan is like me in many ways. You won't put a name to it because the word is anathema to you, but there it is. It's in both our personalities, this humanity that politicians abhor because it confuses issues. The word that politicians apply to personalities like Tan's and mine, my dear one, is 'weak.' "

"No!" Jao protested again, more upset than ever.

Kaotsung took her hands in his. "The only way out of the dilemma is for men like us to have strong yin partners like you, my dear."

Jao felt her hands relax in his strong grasp, and she gradually began to breathe normally. He waited. "We know how Heaven has blessed us with our women, Tan and I."

At this, tears welled up in Jao's eyes and she angrily wiped them away. "I have my weak moments too. . . . It's lucky you and I are not weak at the same time!"

"There you have it, dear lady! Now, what are you going to do?" He held her to him.

Jao paused, rearranging her thoughts. "We can have their wedding here. The old Tientai temple has such a huge hall that it can accommodate the gathering, and its guest quarters are commodious enough for the girl's relations," Jao murmured from next to his chest.

"Good." Kaotsung still held her close, but a bleak look returned to his eyes. Jao must never know, he thought, how repelled I am by her harshness at times . . . although at the same time I am grateful.

Summer nights after Tan's wedding were spent in the garden. There were no mosquitoes at that altitude, and the light lasted until late in the evening. The emperor and empress and Taiping listened to music every night, but one evening Tai dressed up in the ceremonial garb of a military officer of medium rank. Wearing a turbanlike cap on her head, a purple tunic and a heavy belt, she moved gracefully through the cadences of a dance, keeping time on a hand drum. Her caricatures of the military officers soon had both parents laughing hilariously.

"Making fun of my generals, are you, you impudent girl." Her father chuckled. "Come here and sit on my knee and tell me how you learned to be such a good actress!"

"It's just me," she said, making a face.

"So what are you acting out now? Do you want one of these men you are making fun of—for yourself? Is that it?" he asked, tweaking her ear.

At this, Tai pointed to her costume and said, "If you should ever want a son-in-law, this should show you where to look." She slapped his cheek in fun, slid down off his lap and ran out of the room.

Kaotsung looked inquiringly at Jao. "Just what was all that about?" he asked.

Jao shrugged. "She wants a lover, no doubt, and wants him to be a military man. And I think she's lonely since Tan was married."

Kaotsung looked unhappy. Tai was his only daughter and his youngest child. He did not want to lose her.

Jao watched his face. "One way or another, she won't be denied. If we marry her to one of those good-looking foreign guards, she can live in the palace and you won't lose her."

The wrinkles smoothed out from Kaotsung's forehead. "Do you have any idea who might be eligible?"

"Not offhand, but I'll look around and do some investigating. Tai likely has someone in mind. There's a small town near here that is quite beautifully situated on a mountain stream, and there's a new, spacious temple there. We can use it for her wedding."

Kaotsung stopped her. "You take my breath away. . . ."

"If something seems inevitable, I want to get it over with as gracefully as possible," she said flippantly, but her eyes were sad.

Kaotsung's made no response. His expression was deeply thoughtful.

In two months' time, on August eleventh, 681, the wedding took place. Jao, the master showman, had again exerted herself. The ceremony took place out-of-doors on the wide terrace of the new Huayen temple, and, happily, the weather was perfect; cloudless, and cool with the first hint of fall in the air. The groom was a handsome guard named Hsueh Shao, from the oasis city of Turfan. His fellow guardsmen were present in full dress to stand in place of his family, who could not manage the journey from Turfan in time.

Taiping looked enchanting in a gauzy scarlet gown with flowing sleeves and scarves. Her black hair, lustrous and carefully coiled over her shapely head, was crowned with a stunning diadem in gold filigree. The audience gave an audible gasp when she appeared on the terrace followed by her attendants in gowns of shaded reds. Jao's face flushed and Kaotsung seemed stunned. She looked as Jao herself had at seventeen—a beauty beyond compare. The groom's eyes were filled with a delight that was plain for all to see.

The ceremony was simple, performed by the chief prelate of the temple. It took place at high noon and was soon over. The sun was still high in the sky when the young couple left the reception, riding away on horseback instead of in the traditional palanquin.

Guests lingered until twilight enjoying themselves. Kaotsung, although cheerful, was exhausted by the time the affair ended and had to be carried to his bed. His health was growing more precarious daily. Jao lay beside him and they talked over the happenings of the day, while outside the summer twilight faded into the blackness of starry night.

Finally Jao said sleepily, "How do you feel about things now?"

Kaotsung sighed. "Empty . . . a bit forlorn," he muttered. "You?"

"Yes," she answered. "But now we've got to compose ourselves and get through Chung's wedding."

"Not I," Kaotsung said. "I resign from any more of these dramatics. They're all yours."

Jao chuckled "I thought you enjoyed today. We'll see. . . ."

"Well, Chung, my friend, who would ever have thought it? Even a short while ago—I never imagined this," Chengssu began enviously. He and Sanssu were lodged in palace guest quarters prior to Chungtsung's wedding.

"What? My getting formally tied or my promotion?" Chung asked cheerfully as he slapped Chengssu on the back. "It's good to see you. What have you been doing with yourself?"

"Nothing much. A bore, my job. Your sudden rise to crown prince—how do you feel about your good luck?"

"No different. A bit of a fool perhaps, having to wear a lot of stiff dress-up robes and officiate at ceremonies. You think your job boring . . . mine is worse."

Sanssu laughed, but Chengssu didn't. "Your father had eight sons, and you're the seventh. You didn't have a chance," he persisted. "But now you are first in line."

"Oh that," Chungtsung returned, "fall of the dice. I'm really not very happy about it, you know, because of what happened to Hung and Hsien."

"You're twenty-four years old, and there are still half-brothers in line if anything happens to you and Tan. We're not on the list at all," Chengssu continued, frowning.

Chung shrugged. "Your good luck!" he said. "The others aren't eligible at all. And nothing is going to happen to me!"

When the flurries of the weddings were over, life at the Palace of Nine Perfections resumed its former slow pace. Emperor and empress continued to keep themselves insulated from the woes of the nation. Bad news from the frontiers did filter in, however. The drought on the steppes brought nomads in search of food raiding across Chinese frontiers. With Kaotsung far too ill to rule, Jao attended council meetings and had to deal with the problems. Her decisions were uniformly successful, particularly her decision to send the Korean general, Black Teeth Long One, now a loyal vassal of the emperor, to cope with the tough Tibetans. Using beacons, a Korean device, the general had improved communications on the frontier and was managing to keep the border peaceful.

The fall passed and the new year brought the end of drought, good harvests at last, and three new grandsons. Chungtsung's infant was named Chungjun and immediately listed as heir to the throne. The imperial house became stabilized, with Chungtsung functioning as regent in Changan, under General Liu as advisor. Jao and Kaotsung felt free to return to Loyang. Once there, Jao launched a program of extensive repair of a palace outside the city so that Kaotsung could spend his last days in comfort. He was sinking fast, and Jao had all she could do to care for him. The bureaucracy more or less ran itself, and the newly appointed prime minister, Pei Yen, was gradually growing more powerful.

On the morning of the winter solstice, Kaotsung demanded that his servants dress him in full regalia. Jao was hastily called.

"I have decided to conduct . . . the ceremonies of the winter soltice . . . myself," he announced.

"Unwise!" Jao protested. "Dangerous! It's very cold today and windy."

"Of course it . . . is . . . dangerous, but not unwise." Kaotsung was short of breath with the effort he was making to dress. "My farewell . . . from the Tzutien tower over the bridge . . . the plaza there is wide."

Jao felt herself grow faint with apprehension. She watched him being robed, and then, understanding that he was determined, ordered her own mantles and silently accompanied him as far as the throne hall. There, Kaotsung found that he was unable to climb to the tower to speak to the crowds already filling the plaza. Instead, he ordered that the gate to the palace grounds and the front doors of the audience chamber be opened so that the public could come to him. While the crowds watched in awed silence, he delivered his farewell words. Jao, having given up trying to protect him, stayed behind a screen to let him make his final gesture alone. He bore up until the ceremony was over and the throne hall empty once more, and then collapsed, unable and unwilling to move. He sent for Pei Yen to entrust him with his will.

"Why not our friend, General Liu?" Jao asked gently.

"Because . . . Liu is eighty and won't live . . . Pei is fifty-five and will last." Kaotsung concentrated on breathing and staying alive.

Pei hurried into the hall in half dress. Crown Prince Chungtsung also hurried in.

Kaotsung spoke in low tones between breaths, "Chungtsung, you are . . . the new emperor. You must—you hear?—you must refer important matters to your mother. That's the way . . . for thirty years the way it has been done . . . the way it should be."

Pei was deeply moved. He wrote out the short statement, then did not linger to trouble the imperial couple in their time of parting.

Kaotsung lay on cushions dragged from the throne to ease him. Candlelight from huge tapers that had been hastily assembled flickered across his face and his closed eyes.

Jao knelt beside him, wiping his brow. His hands plucked at the quilt that she had thrown over him. She waved the attendants back out of earshot and asked Chungtsung, who was too upset to control himself, to withdraw for a while.

"Go away and rest just for an hour," Jao told him. "I will watch, and then you can join us. He gets restless if I am not by him all the time. He seems to know even when he is asleep."

Hardly had Chungtsung gone when Kaotsung opened his eyes and smiled. "I'm going now dear. . . ." he whispered. "Come with me . . . help me in the spirit world. I need you . . . always." Jao bent over him, her eyes blind with tears, her hand on his chest to give him comfort. He coughed several times and was gone.

Jao remained bowed over him, her tears dropping on his still face. She slipped her amber betrothal ring off her finger and put it on one of his. Covering his face with her shawl, she waved back the army of officials who were converging. She kneeled by his side until Chungtsung joined her. He dropped on both knees beside the emperor's body and buried his face in his hands to hide his weeping. Jao patted his back comfortingly until she noticed his exhaustion. He was entirely worn out by the turmoil of his feelings, as she was herself, except that she had learned to cope with crises and he had not.

"Withdraw for now, my son," she said. "I will stay. His spirit is still hovering, and he would know if I deserted. Come back at dawn and keep vigil during the day while I rest." Chungtsung awkwardly got to his feet, bowed sleepily toward his father's body, and disappeared into the cavernous darkness of the dusty throne hall.

Jao bent over Kaotsung's still form. "I will spend the rest of the night at your side, my last night with you," she murmured. "I won't leave you while you find your way in the spirit world. Forty-five years together. Now to separate . . . unendurable, unendurable . . ." She rocked on her heels.

The doors of the hall were closed, but the drafts kept the candles flickering. Unseen attendants rustled and came and went, but Jao sat on, desolate, aching, and alone. Her feelings washed over her. Unable to part with the past, unable to face the future, she put her hand on her husband's chest a last time. To reassure him, she thought in desolation.

CHAPTER EIGHTEEN

Pei Yen blew on his fingers while he waited in the antechamber of the small Hall of Audience. He had a large head and a frail body, but he radiated an iron will and a sternness that made him seem to be a much larger and heavier man. "This will be an important meeting," he remarked to First Minister Liu, who was looking drawn and ill in the chill dawn hours a week after the death of the emperor.

"Everyone is here—no one is absent," Pei added calculatingly as he surveyed the room that had gradually filled up with dark figures who collected around the double doors of the throne room. Liu nodded, silently withdrawn. Pei shifted his feet. "Since you are leaving for your home in Changan now that you are retiring, I am moving my chancellory office into the corner suite that you have been occupying. If you have no objections."

Liu directed a quick look at Pei and then away. "As you will," he said.

The voice of Emperor Chungtsung was heard through the doors. Talking stopped and the gathered officials listened avidly, but all that came through was an impatient order to get things started. The doors were thrown open after that and the group hurried gratefully into the warm hall.

Chungtsung was seated on his father's throne, ill at ease, his knees spread in the classic pose of the military leader. He was dressed in white mourning clothes and wore no crown, only a white military turban. Behind the throne from ceiling beam to floor floated a gauzy purple curtain which screened Wu Jao, also in white clothes. At almost sixty, she was still beautiful, and showed her age not at all. A gong was struck and all ministers kowtowed, some with stifled groans of distress from age and stiff knees.

"Rise, rise!" commanded Chungtsung, who had been briefed on protocol just minutes before. He gazed uncertainly over the stern faces before him and pointed his ivory baton at Liu.

"You, sir. You are first minister on the left. Do you have anything to say?"

"Your Majesty," Liu said, catching his breath after the effort of rising. "This is a felicitous occasion. All of us are wishing you a long and successful reign and much good fortune."

"Yes, well . . . thank you. Anything else?" A silence ensued, which lengthened.

"The promotions and titles," Wu Jao prompted softly.

Chungtsung cleared his throat. "The first order of business today is the distribution, or rather the redistribution, of offices under my regime." He laughed jovially, but when no one joined him, he hastily returned to business. "Any suggestions?"

Pei Yen coughed. "Your Majesty, please consider me for the post of Chief of the Secretariat."

Chungtsung looked around the room for a hint of what to do next. "Why? You are already Chief of Chancellory," he said finally.

"It is so," Pei replied smoothly. "I have been trusted with the will of the late emperor, and for this reason I assume that I should combine the two offices in order to be more efficient in implementing this all-important document. I have it here now to read to the council so that all will know how I intend to proceed."

A whisper from Jao came from behind the curtain. "Call on General Liu."

"What?" Chungtsung exclaimed. "Oh, what is your opinion about this request?" He pointed his baton at the embarrassed Liu.

"My colleague Pei Yen is correct," he said easily. "Both with regard to reading the will and combining the functions of both Chancellory and Secretariat in implementing it. I suppose that you will eventually include the office of State Affairs too. Long enough to implement the will, that is."

Jao smiled grimly to herself. General Liu has indicated that the three offices should be under one head, only for a short time, only for implementing the will, she thought. How clever Pei was to insinuate himself into so powerful a position. They would have to watch him.

Chungtsung licked his lips. "Read it," he ordered.

Pei rose importantly. He brought out a purple-tied scroll from his sleeve and unrolled it. He had prepared the document himself from the notes he had taken at the bedside of the dying emperor, using the most elegant phraseology in composing it. After the formal salutations, he read: "The crown prince will ascend the throne at once. Let there be no delay in this for any reason, for obsequies or state funeral. Let him be declared emperor and let the lady Wei be declared empress. Let the dowager empress Wu continue to be consulted in all important matters, both civil and military. Let there be no extremes resorted to in any administrative matter, and let there be no period of chaos. Let there be peace and harmony in all the empire. This is my last wish for my people."

A chorus of approving "hau-haus" rose from the assembled minsters when Pei's heavy voice ceased and he rolled up his scroll. They were men who dreaded change of any sort. The terms of the will were soothingly vague, and many sighed with relief. Some, however, directed inquiring looks at the curtain, but there was no comment from that quarter either.

"Titles," Chungtsung said after a short silence. "There is the matter of conferring honorary titles as a . . . a benevolent gesture on the occasion of my inauguration. There are the surviving imperial princes, Yuan Chia and Yuan Kuei. There are the two highest posts of honor in the empire, Supreme Commander of the Armies, and Controller of Works. Li Chi held both titles before, but now Yuan Chia should be awarded the first title and the fief of Han, while Yuan Kuei should receive the second and the fief of Huo." Jao nodded behind the curtain. She had encouraged her son to send important princes away from the capital with work to do. "It saves the treasury immense sums," she had told him.

Pleased at his successful handling of the audience so far, he looked around him with satisfaction, noticing that there was a long petition in the hands of the Minister of the Board of Rites. He pointed. "You."

The minister bowed and proceeded to read off a long list of new names and new appointments. Everyone listened attentively. Chungtsung grew restive and was about to put an end to the session when Pei signaled that he had another petition to present. Chungtsung reluctantly gave permission.

"This is on behalf of Li Chi's two grandsons, Li Chingyeh and Li Chingyu. They plead for the customary amnesty issued on auspicious occasions like this."

"Explain, please. Why do they need amnesty? What did they do?"

Chungtsung asked, caught by the name of Li Chi and suddenly realizing that he had heard something unfavorable about the grandsons.

"They have been exiled to Yangchow with some of their colleagues. For corruption. They have repented and now want to have their positions back."

"What do you think?" Chungtsung asked.

"Reinstatement. On condition of good behavior."

"Well then, if you so wish, even though I don't think much of those two," Chungtsung responded grandly.

"One moment," came the voice from behind the curtain. "Could you not postpone this decision until after your inaugural ceremony? There is too much for you to take care of all at once."

Chungtsung looked vexed, then his face cleared as it always did when he was dealing with his mother. He nodded in agreement while Pei merely bowed and looked away, stony-faced. Pei disliked Jao as much as she disliked him. Here she was, interfering again.

"I've just remembered something," Chungtsung said. "I want two names added to the list of promotions. I have promised a position in the fifth grade to the son of my wet nurse as a reward for her services. Also there must be a position for Lady Wei's father as Chief of Chancellory. . . ." His voice trailed off.

"Out of the question," Pei said stiffly. "For both your nurse's son and Wei—he is only a provincial governor. He has had no experience at all in the central government. The position that you suggest is one of the four highest in the empire. This Wei does not qualify."

"He is as qualified as you are!" Chungtsung retorted, flushing. "You were a nobody yourself four or five years ago. You got your promotion into third grade by executing all those Turkish khans who had already submitted!"

Jao stirred uneasily behind her curtain, rustling her garments while ministers coughed or shuffled in their embarrassment. Pei's face turned a dull red.

"Your honorable father trusted me with his will," he said in a frozen manner.

Unaware of the disapproving atmosphere in the council chamber, Chungtsung continued. "My father turned to you in his extremity, but that does not mean he was endorsing you as his chief official. You are not eligible for that honor because you are not a cultured man. Your lodgings are poor and scantily furnished and your manners are at fault.

You have been so buried in your books, and in maneuvering incessantly for higher office, that you have not learned court etiquette."

Chungtsung was repeating only what he had heard in gossip, but Pei assumed Wu Jao was the source, and he chalked up this public insult against her. He flinched. Pei, though incorruptible, was Spartan and frugal in his habits, a self-made man but no courtier.

"Ten thousand apologies," Jao said at once, but Pei was too distraught to hear.

"Your humble servant," Pei was saying as he bowed, "has had a spotless record in serving the state. If Your Majesty will order that I be investigated, Your Majesty will find that this is so."

"If you are so spotless," Chungtsung interrupted, "why did you just ask for leniency for Li Chingyeh and Li Chingyu, who have been convicted of bribery and abuse of office?"

Pei let his feelings of outrage show. "They are the grandsons of one of the greatest servants of Tang that has ever lived. Why should we not show leniency to them at a time that an amnesty is being extended to all?"

Wu Jao cleared her throat. "This discussion is not forwarding the agenda. We are in a serious privy council meeting, not in a classroom. Let us proceed with business."

Once again her words were either not heard or ignored.

"I'll tell you why," Chungtsung said, his voice shaking. "I was in the room when my brother Hung told my father that Li Chi's last instructions to his brother were to flog, even to death, any descendant who failed in duty to the throne. I remember very well. This Chingyeh and Chingyu may deserve death at this moment, not leniency!"

A shocked hush fell upon the room. Chungtsung was not passing on gossip, he was stating facts that he knew about. Many minsters had not heard about Li Chi's last words, and they remained silent, absorbing the implications. Pei was silent as well.

Feeling that he had gained the upper hand in his role as emperor, Chungtsung continued. "The name of the son of my wet nurse is Yan Yanhu. It should be added to the list of inauguration appointments I have already ordered. Take note of it."

All heads swiveled toward Pei. It could not be done, this awarding of coveted rank and position to an illiterate. Pei, however, remained silent throughout the rest of the meeting and filed out silently with the others when dismissed. No one was aware that in his heart he had become an implacable enemy of the young emperor and of the dowager empress herself.

Chungtsung returned to his quarters. He was pleased with himself, and soon hastened to his mother's hall to receive her congratulations on his first formal audience. He also wanted to complain about the way his proposal about his father-in-law had been treated.

"Why did you insult the Chief of Chancellory as you did?" she greeted him as soon as he set foot inside the door.

Taken by surprise, he said, "Because I don't like him. I did not like him when he served me in Changan while I was regent for Father during his last illness, and I don't like him now."

"What does that have to do with the way you treat him as an official responsible for public affairs?" she asked bluntly. "He is a high official and must be listened to with respect when he is in privy council. Politely. Whatever you like or don't like has nothing to do with your management of public business as an emperor."

"Well, what I said was true, and as an emperor," he said stubbornly, "I can do what I like."

Chungtsung was so disappointed by his failure to impress his mother that he was careless in what he said. Jao sat in silence while she considered how best to teach him how to conduct himself in his new role. She realized that he had been overprotected in the palace. There, he did not need to be careful not to make enemies with his tongue. He had always been free to say what he thought—with relative impunity. Nor did he distinguish between Jao as his mother and Jao as Chief of State.

She said aloud. "Sit down comfortably and let me go over everything that happened in council today and show you what was wrong. First, a ruler must keep his government in balance, never letting either yang or yin go their length. In politics, resorting to extremes is anathema to the established government. Strict justice is not the aim of the emperor. When there are complaints to settle, one must redress matters by appearing to give each side something in an evenhanded way. Only later may you administer justice—inconspicuously."

"I don't know what you are talking about with yang and yin and all that," Chungtsung said crossly. "If I order something, I want to be obeyed."

"What if your best officials oppose you on good grounds?" Jao asked. "What then?"

"I'd discharge them. Get some new ones."

"Like the son of your wet nurse?" she retorted ominously.

Chungtsung looked sulky. "My officials must obey me or else," he countered.

"You sound like a military man," Jao said. "Off with their heads. You can't run an empire from the back of a horse."

Chungtsung recognized the quotation. "All right, teach me," he said.

Jao tried to teach her son to the best of her ability, but to her dismay, she discovered that this son just could not learn the art of politics. Hung and Tan had learned, and Taiping seemed to absorb diplomacy through her pores. Chungtsung simply lacked identification with others that was so necessary for an emperor, when throwing out his political net, to catch his fish. She taught him, but he did not learn. He continued to put forward, in every formal audience, his proposal for the appointment of his father-in-law, attempting to overrule the official opposition he received until, finally, he was confronted by open defiance.

"It is not possible," Pei said sternly. "Your Majesty should not bring up this matter again."

"If I wished to hand over the empire itself to my father-in-law, what is to stop me!" Chungtsung was enraged at being balked. He brought the session to an abrupt end and left the hall. "Do not come back until you are prepared to do as you are told," he shouted when he went out the door.

Shocked by his behavior, Jao forced herself out of her lethargy in order to have Chungtsung and his empress, Lady Wei, to dinner. She listened to the ardent arguments of the empress on behalf of her father, and heard her son support everything Lady Wei said. They refused to listen to her opposition. This business is the empress Wang and her uncle Liu all over again, Jao thought. Letting nothing stop them from burrowing to the source of power with every means at hand.

The dinner was not a success, and the young couple left early.

The next day Pei presented a petition to seat Tan, known also as Juitsung, as emperor and to demote Chungtsung by giving him the title of Prince Luling and a fief and removing him from court. Chungtsung was not present but Jao was, and felt sick with dismay when most of the ministers concurred. It was up to her to fight this move or to let it happen. She let it happen.

"You and the vice-chief of the Secretariat, the north gate scholar Liu Weijer, along with the palace guards, will have to handle this." she told Pei. "I will not deal with it directly."

Several days later, when Chungtsung condescended to preside over a plenary session of the court held in the Chienyuan audience hall, the commander of the palace guards led his men into the hall to deliver an order, signed by the empress, demoting Chungtsung. The general forced him to descend from the throne, and read the edict of demotion to him.

"Take me to the empress dowager," Chungtsung roared," and we will soon get to the bottom of this outrage."

Face-to-face with Jao, he read no forgiveness in her eyes and was shocked beyond measure. "What is my crime?" he demanded, white-faced.

"You still don't understand," she said sadly. "That is why you cannot continue as supreme decision-maker, dealing with all the complexities of the empire. You say that you have committed no crime and ask me to explain. You don't see what you have done to deserve this. As an emperor presiding in a serious council meeting, where every word you say goes into the record and affects the lives of thousands, you cannot threaten or even seem to threaten that you could 'give the empire away' as you see fit, especially to your wife's family. That is a notorious situation which is terrifying to every official who has ever studied Chinese history. Such a statement causes a furor and is taken seriously. Nothing you could possibly say to the ministers could shock them more . . . and you don't even perceive it."

Chungtsung wilted pathetically under her blast, and Tan, who was in the room, put out his hand in sympathy with his brother.

Jao softened. "You are a good man, Chung, forthright and direct," she said. "You have the capacity to enjoy your life in the right surroundings, far from the whirlpool of predatory politics. I will exile you to the country, sending you to the mountain area you love best, high in a valley that can be guarded. You will have your wife and children and your sports and music, and you can live the life you like without interference. Being emperor is a punishing job. Your father never liked it, but he had a strong sense of duty so he persisted. You do not have to be an emperor. Use this opportunity to escape."

Tai, who was playing with her dogs in a corner, clapped her hands. "Yes, Chung, that will be wonderful. It will be like paradise, and I'll visit you often."

Tan put out his arm again and laid it across his brother's shoulder, but Chungtsung flung it off and, flouting protocol, stormed out of his mother's presence.

"Come," Jao said, "sit close to me, you two. I wish to talk to you. How do you feel about all this?"

Tan shrugged. "Tai and I have discussed Chungtsung endlessly. We feel about him as we always did, despite his present disgrace. But you have made the only right decision."

Taiping broke in, "Chung has never been aware of how other people feel until it is explained to him, and even then he does not act accordingly. He is always so offended when his will is crossed because he always thinks he is right. And his wife Wei is just like him. They act as if they were at the same level in authority as you and our father, without considering your experience and prestige."

"Did you not expect too much of poor Chungtsung?" Tan asked lightly.

Jao looked at him inquiringly.

"You expected—from Father's will—that Chungtsung would take the place of father and then you and he would continue as a pair to rule the empire as you have been doing all these years, did you not? In consultation, the two of you. Probably Father thought so too, from the way his will is set up. But it couldn't work with Chungtsung. He can't share power. He has to be boss or follower. In our childhood games we either followed his directions or he followed ours—which he often did, in order to please us."

Tan was beginning to perspire in his emotion, triggering the stutter that occasionally bothered him. "S-S-Sharing opinions, s-s-solving puzzles together as you and Father did, is not his w-w-way."

"You are probably right," Jao said. "But now what? I want to protect my children from my enemies and their father's enemies. I want to and I will. But only as far as is possible. Do you want the position?" she asked Tan.

"Wh-Wh-What position?" he temporized, pretending not to know what she meant.

"Don't!" Tai exploded. "Don't make Tan sit on the throne! He is the opposite of Chungtsung, he knows exactly how to manage people, how to get his way, and is bored with himself—and the world—every time he does. He sees through people at a glance and thinks that being emperor is a poor way to spend one's life. Tan would be just no good sitting on a throne!"

Jao looked into two pairs of eyes staring into hers, all so exactly alike, and took a deep breath.

"Your children are such a disappointment to you, aren't they?" Tai continued, taking her mother's hand.

"None of you seem to have both the politics and the will," Jao began, "although you have had every chance to learn."

"Not every chance, not even the essential chance," Tan said. "There were t-t-two of you," he added, serious for a moment. "You don't seem to realize that you and Father together were an invincible t-t-team. Each one of you separately was a political cripple—Father because of his illness, you because you are female—but together you were un-unbeatable. How long did you work t-together? Thirty-three years? Successful, in the end, at whatever you undertook in spite of illness, childbirth, rebellions, t-treachery. We never knew where one of you left off and the other began."

"He means," Tai said, "that while other rulers dominated people or situations by means of all-power-absolutely at one end and all-obedience at the other, you two ruled jointly somehow, and no one ever knew who was in charge."

Inspired by the uniqueness of the opportunity to talk like this to Jao, Tan said. "N-n-neither one of you could ever have been successful without the other. The fact is that you'll never find anyone in all the empire who can take the place of the two of you. There is going to be trouble because dozens will t-try."

"He means," Tai cut in hastily, "Chungtsung can't rule your way and Tan won't try."

Jao's eyes rested on her son in sad speculation. He returned her look so searchingly that she became thoughtful. "What are you trying to tell me?" she asked.

"Wh-Who wants to fail?" he returned.

"Fail? Hardly . . . when I am always here to help," Jao replied.

"That's the t-trouble," Tan said, so mildly that Jao didn't take it in. Tai, for once, did not attempt to explain, knowing that if she did, she would be crossing the dangerous line between her mother's statecraft and her personal life.

"You could try," Jao said soberly. "You are the smartest of them all."

"That's even more trouble," he said again.

"What *do* you want, then?" Jao asked.

"Protection from people who want to use me to try for the throne themselves," he said. "Here is Chungtsung, two months on the throne, and already the chief minister is at his throat and so are most of the other officials. Everyone is gossiping about Chungtsung's downfall and hoping for the downfall of more—yours, mine, the whole imperial family perhaps." He shrugged flippantly.

"Nonsense, no such thing. What a defeatist you are!"

"It is up to you then," he said, "to save us all." This time he was not so flippant.

"I shall certainly do something to save us from the fiasco of Chungtsung's reign," Jao said finally, in a tone that made her children shiver. "But I need to know seriously what you young people are good for, what you want of me. . . ."

"The life I have been living has been good," Tan mused. "I like living in Loyang. I like these palaces and parks. They are home to me. Make me your emperor if you like, but only in name. You know how to rule and you are supremely good at it. You go on ruling and let me live as I have been living. I will assist when I can."

Jao turned to Tai. "And you?"

"Me too," she said.

Jao sat alone in the dark after her son and daughter left. She dismissed the servants bringing the lamps but allowed them to bring a brazier of freshly burning charcoal into the chilly room. She needed time alone to face the fact that none of her children were fit for ruling. Hung had been, but he was lost. Kaotsung's leniency had encouraged all the others to go their own ways and escape the call of duty. For the first time she clearly saw the realities, and her disappointment overwhelmed her. Juitsung was able but unwilling, and he had that ridiculous stutter when he was upset. It could be imitated in every teahouse in the country, undermining the prestige of the throne.

Jao's guards changed outside her door. Her attendants waited in the anteroom, and she remained unheeding. Eventually a low-pitched altercation at the door attracted her attention. Then someone entered and hurriedly dropped into a kowtow in front of her. It was Chengssu.

"Here," Jao said sharply. "What do you think you are doing? I gave orders that I wasn't to be disturbed!"

"Forgive me, Your Majesty!" Chengssu said abjectly, his nose in the carpet.

"Well?" Jao said irritably after a long pause.

"It is the right time for me to offer myself in Your Majesty's service," he quavered as he stole a calculating look. Her face was barely visible above him in the glow of the fire.

"You are already in her service," she said in a stern voice. "Even though you have a privileged position in the palace, you cannot burst in upon the empress this way. You must be insane to—"

"Burst in upon my empress?" he repeated. "No, no, not empress—but emperor," he murmured. His manner was meek.

Jao scowled. "You *are* insane! Heaven save me from the service of a relative who talks so dangerously."

"Emperor," Chengssu repeated doggedly. "Not empress." He had been watching the changes of crown princes with avid attention. Sanssu had helped him spy on the activities of the imperial children. He was well aware of Jao's problem with her sons, and was not about to miss his chance to promote himself.

"It is time to declare myself totally at your service, to declare my undying loyalty, to declare my offer to obedient service and my stand in favor of Your Majesty as emperor—there is no one else in the country who could possibly be better!"

Jao was shocked out of her lethargy. "Chengssu, you must not utter such dangerous thoughts . . . you must not even think them. I am a woman and a Wu and would be viciously opposed, if not assassinated at once, at a hint of such open assumption of power. It's unthinkable. I will overlook your error this once, but I warn you to seal your lips from now on. I appreciate your offer of yourself and will think about how you can serve me. Now leave."

Tan was duly enthroned as Emperor Juitsung, with Jao doing the actual ruling. She set about making the new situation effective by changing the names of all the central government offices. The division of State Affairs, being first in importance, she named Heaven, and the next in importance, the office of agriculture, she named Earth. The Secretariat became the Terrace of the Male Phoenix. Chancellory became the Terrace of the Female Phoenix. The Office of Rites became Spring, War became Summer, Justice became Autumn, and Public Works became Winter.

The dignified and conservative ministers were mortified to use such fanciful names for their offices. Worst of all, Jao canonized her ancestors and changed the name and location of the main capital. Loyang was renamed Shendu, Divine Capital, and Changan was reduced to second status. Facing down the enraged objections of the wealthy who were centered there, she realized that Changan was too important to be neglected. Her best minister was Liu Jen—she decided to appoint him viceroy. She was sure he would welcome such an assignment, since the mansion that Kaotsung gave him for services in Korea was in Changan.

Liu refused the appointment. He wrote that he was old and unwell, and reminded her of the disasters brought about by Empress Lu for her interference in court affairs. This rebuke angered Jao, but she needed him enough to persist. She wrote a confidential letter explaining her actions. Juitsung had a speech impediment, she said, so she had been forced to take over some of his functions to save the throne from vulgar ridicule. She begged him to withdraw his resignation, agreed with him about Empress Lu, and assured him that she would never imitate that empress. She then summoned Chengssu.

"You declared yourself willing to obey me in whatever I asked you to do. I want you to act as courier. To start with, I have a highly confidential letter to send to General Liu Jen. Along with the letter is a seal of office and a formal appointment. Will you undertake the assignment?"

Chengssu bowed deeply, joy expressed in every line of his body. "I am at your service, Your Majesty! With all my heart! And I will fulfill the assignment faster than anyone else. You will see!"

Jao smiled encouragingly. Her nephew bowed his way out backward. He knows his court manners, she thought.

The next weeks passed speedily for Jao, before Chengssu again presented himself. Jao read Liu's reply—the general had received her explanations and assurances and would accept the position. She rerolled the scroll and smiled.

"Well done, nephew," she said with satisfaction. "I am pleased and will reward you with an appointment in State Affairs. You will be sent out on other important jobs."

"I will work diligently!" Chengssu said excitedly. "I will support Your Majesty with every breath I take! And promote the Wu family in every way possible . . . Your Majesty first and foremost . . . who should be Huang, Emperor, not Huanghou, Empress."

"Stop right there! Not so fast—it's too shocking. A Wu dynasty cannot be tolerated during a Tang dynasty. Do not whisper such a thing, do not even think such a thing. You may, however, promote the interests of the Wu family, if you like."

"Yes, Your Majesty," Chengssu replied easily, her warning unheeded. He bowed deeply and left her presence.

Because it pleased her to promote her family, Jao followed through on her promises to Chengssu. He, at least, unlike her children, was both able and interested when it came to politics. She gave him scope to advance Wu prestige by putting him in charge of building an impressive new ancestral shrine. Nor did she interfere when he set about building a faction in support of a change of dynasty. She could not, however, take him very seriously.

"The opportunity is now! The omens are favorable!" he told her repeatedly.

"Yes, yes," Jao would agree, humoring him. "But we must bide our time until the opposition wilts a little. Let us not be so naive as to think that such a change could come about easily."

The anniversary of Kaotsung's death was observed in a memorial ceremony attended by all Jao's children and grandchildren and by eleven Wu relatives. The winter was short. An early spring ripened into a humid rainy season and brightened again into a hot August. A great comet appeared, trailing its immense tail across half the sky, and it stayed in position night after night. Jao found herself bewitched by this phenomenon. She spent hours every night contemplating its luminous sweep across the blackness of the skies. Gradually, she convinced herself that that this heavenly display was a sign that Heaven approved of her. Profoundly moved, she began to consider herself as the sole ruler and, significantly, she discarded the reign names of her sons.

On the tenth night of the comet's appearance, a group of about twenty young men gathered at a boat restaurant in Yangchow to celebrate. They were handsome men in their thirties, from wealthy families, restless and pleasure-seeking. They were also rebels. Their host, Li Chingyeh, grandson of Li Chi, looked around complacently. His brother, Li Chingyu, had his feet on the rail. With him were his cronies, Wei, Tang, Lo, and Hsueh. Most of them were exiles and new to the fabulous city of silk in the Yangtze delta.

The party had the upper deck of the restaurant to themselves, with its unobstructed view over the water of the twinkling lights across the river and the comet-lit sky above. Softly glowing lanterns lined the railings and cast shadows on the smooth surface of the water below. Above floated a harvest moon.

"Perfection," Tang murmured, cup in hand. "A paradise . . . how is it that a crowd of rascals like us deserve such a place of exile? Mysterious fate, delightful fate. . . ." He raised his cup and drank to the moon, as his mates laughed. "We could have been exiled to the hideous far south, Hainan or Vietnam. . . ."

Chingyeh frowned. "Tang, you are a soft fellow, content wherever you are if you are comfortable. The disgrace of exile and dismissal from office, and the boredom of nothing to do, have slid off your back as if they did not matter."

"They don't really, not much anyway. This suits me," Tang returned tipsily. "When I was shut up in those dingy offices in Changan, I did not know that paradise existed. Now I know. The authorities have done me a favor."

Chingyu laughed and drained his cup, but his brother's frown deepened. "Laugh, you idiot, but the fact is that our situation here is intolerable for men like us. You are simply too stupid to realize it."

"Not too stupid, just adaptable," Chingyu retorted, stung. "Are you so sour because you have fallen from the lofty height of renown as the heir of the great Li Chi?"

"Great in a turtle's belly," Chingyeh returned. "No, we are as capable as he was, potentially more so, because we are better educated and less willing to serve so blindly. We are just not bestirring ourselves as he did. I am serious. What kind of future do we have here? We are prevented from getting back to the capital or having our offices restored as long as that she-devil is in power. I have heard that some of her top officials are just waiting for their chance to get rid of her."

"You are right," cut in ex-Censor Wei.

"Of course I am right," Chingyeh cried. "That women has even robbed her own sons of the throne, and the ministers have supported her, including that wily Pei. Never a hope for us now that she has usurped the power."

"I don't know about that," Hsueh said. He still had his job as censor, but lack of promotion made him rebellious. "She is severely handicapped—there is no law or precedent for her conduct as long as she has a fully grown son in office. She has no claim at all. My very canny uncle Pei seems to support her, but he is actually isolating her."

Silence fell on the company. Water rippled along the sides of the barge. Distant sounds reached them in a muted way, the chink of dishes, the laughs of revelers.

"Your uncle?" Tang repeated, suddenly sober. "Pei Yen is your uncle? He is the most powerful minister ever to emerge. He combined the three most important branches of government under his own hand. What are you all doing sitting here in disgrace?"

Wei emptied his wine cup and threw it overboard. "Waiting," he said.

At this, everyone spoke at once, but Chingyeh was the loudest. "All of us are sitting around like puppies waiting to be drowned," he cried viciously. "Waiting for yin to turn into yang for us without doing anything to help it happen. The omens are good and Yangchow district is perfect for a start. A local rebellion for good fighters like ourselves should not be difficult."

Feet came down off the railings with resounding thuds.

"Let us meet here two days from now to plan strategy," Chingyeh continued, his color high. "We have enough experience and expertise. Tang here was a grand secretary, Lo an assistant treasurer. I was governor of a fief. Hsueh is still a censor of high rank. We can do it."

A chorus of sober yeas greeted his proposal and the party broke up, no longer in a mellow mood from the charm of the night.

Magistrate Dee looked at his water clock. It was not yet time to open court, so he stepped into his garden for a look at his flowers. The reds and yellows of zinnias and chrysanthemums were repeated in the fallen leaves carpeting the flagstone paths. The quiet in the garden was disturbed only by the muted cries of children at play in the family courtyard and the calls of passing street peddlers. Dee stretched restlessly. His assignment as district judge was not demanding. In fact, it taxed him not at all. Not what I need at this stage, not what I need at all, he mused.

The barking in the street increased, and he could hear the sounds of commotion in front of the yamen gate. He frowned and was checking with the water clock again when a clerk burst into the yard. "An imperial courier is here!" the clerk announced excitedly.

"What is his errand?" Dee asked. A number of possibilities, all negative, flashed through his mind.

"He is carrying an imperial edict that is most important, he says. He's impressive-looking—he wears the clothes and insignia of the State Affairs. He is very formal." The clerk was out of breath from his haste.

"Clear the tribunal and put a sign on the gate that court will be postponed today. Have the courier wait in the courtroom, seated in my chair. Tell the scribe to put the tall table against the north wall of the courtroom—facing south—and light an incense burner on it. I will come soon."

Judge Dee donned his formal robes and put on his cap with the wings of high office, and then entered the courtroom in his usual way from behind the unicorn screen. The courier stood up at once. He was holding a box wrapped in yellow silk. Though a small man, he held himself well, and Dee could sense his importance.

"Welcome to the yamen of Hangchow County," Dee said in greeting.

"Thank you, Your Honor," the young man said gravely. "I have come to deliver an important message from the empress. My name is Wu Chengssu."

"You are welcome, Wu Chengssu," Judge Dee replied, leading him to stand before the high table.

Wu ceremoniously raised his box to eye level and placed it on the table next to the incense burner, whereupon Dee added fresh incense to the burner and kowtowed nine times before it. He was wondering as he did so what could possibly be in the edict that prompted the special formality.

When he stood again, the messenger unwrapped the box, opened it, and took out a scroll mounted on yellow brocade. He added incense in his turn, stood back and said, "The edict will now be read."

Dee, his heart racing, carefully unrolled the scroll with both hands, holding it high so that the imperial seal would not be below his head, and read the contents aloud: "Whereas—respectfully following the illustrious example of our august ancestors in their policy of appointing officials of merit to those positions where their talents are employed to the fullest in duty to us on high and for the people below, and whereas—the Office of State Affairs has recommended Dee Jenjer of Taiyuan now magistrate of Hangchow County in Shantung who faithfully discharges his duties in redressing the wrongs of the oppressed and punishing wrong doers, thus setting our mind at rest and giving peace to our people . . ."

Dee paused to take a breath. Perspiration beaded his forehead and his heart thumped in anticipation. He read on. "Therefore it is our will that owing to pressing affairs of state leaving us no rest either day or night, we need to summon men of extraordinary talent to assist us, we now issue this edict appointing the said Dee to our Metropolitan Office of Censors, effective immediately. Tremble and obey!"

Dee concealed his elation behind a stern expression and carefully rerolled the scroll, rewrapped it and put it in its box. He then turned in the direction of the capital and kowtowed again in gratitude.

At sunset, while the comet palely trailed its train in the west and the sun set hugely red below it, Li Chingyeh and his fellow conspirators met again at the restaurant. No wine was served and only the plainest food was provided. Chingyeh did not stand on ceremony.

He rose to his feet while the others were still eating and read out his plans. "Wei's colleague, Hsueh here, is still in good standing, a high officer in the Censorate. He is not in disgrace like the rest of us."

"Hear, hear . . ." someone began amid grins and jeers. Chingyeh continued as if he had not heard, "Hsueh should arrive at Yangchow with a full complement of guards five days from now. He will be on duty as a censor from the central government. Meanwhile Wei, as an official also on active duty, will inform Hsueh that Yangchow's governor is a criminal plotting rebellion. One of us will arrive as a military governor with a forged decree entitling him to execute the governor and take charge of the imperial yamen, the armory, and the treasury. You, Hsueh, and you, Wei, do you hereby pledge yourselves to perform these assignments? For the sake of this revolt? For the greater good of all?"

Much moved, both men agreed. Chingyeh then nudged Chingyu.

"Ah . . ." Chingyu said. "Yes . . . there is now the important decision of who is to be in command. My brother is the only one who can bring it off. Chingyeh must take on the dangerous role of the military governor. He should be the one to make use of this decree and to launch—with strong hearts—our historic revolt."

"Not revolt—restoration!" Chingyeh cried amid shouts of approval. Excited voices rose noisily, and Chingyeh glanced hastily around the deserted deck to see if anyone was listening. The deck was empty except for a busboy busy juggling trays of dirty dishes. Chingyeh stood solemnly before them. He was a good-looking, muscular man—an ideal leader for what they had in mind.

He acknowledged their acclaim briefly and continued, "I've drafted a second document, a decree authorizing me to raise troops to crush a rebellion—in another province in order not to alarm the authorities here. I have both documents here tonight so that you can judge whether they are good enough to fool the officials. Lastly, I will start off this campaign with an inspiring announcement to the public here in Yangchow that this action of ours is a Restoration Movement to Reinstate the Sovereign. That will catch the eyes—and hearts—of the people."

The documents were passed around and quickly approved.

Chingyeh then pulled Lo forward. Lo Pinwang was a little man, plain and pale. He appeared so timid that no one could imagine him opposing anyone, even a wife.

"Lo here is quite a poet." Chingyeh said, hitting his bowl with his chopsticks to get attention, "quite a poet, quite a fierce one. He has outdone himself this time by writing some propaganda for us which shows how unpleasant he can be when he is unrestrained. Let him read it."

Everyone watched Lo curiously while he slowly rose to his feet.

"I have written an attack—in deathless words," Lo said diffidently. He unrolled a scroll with a flourish that brought on a laugh. "This is poem about a woman. Wait a minute, don't laugh, listen to me: 'The usurper woman Wu now occupying the throne by false pretenses is of low origin. She first entered the palace as a lowly maid under Taitsung, attending to his toilet needs. Behind Taitsung's back she courted the favors of his son and ensnared him with her wanton charms and fox's wiles. Her jealousy drove her to trample upon Empress Wang, leading our sovereign into the way of the incestuous deer. With the heart of a serpent and the savagery of the jungle beast, she has persecuted or driven away from court loyal ministers and surrounded herself with only the disreputable.' "

"Hear, hear," Hsueh interrupted, and Lo shot him an apologetic glance while continuing, "Sorry to insult your uncle Pei, but I have to be forceful with my lies. Now listen, the best is ahead: 'She killed her sister and butchered her stepbrothers; she assassinated the emperor and poisoned her mother. Now, with the sinister purpose of taking over the throne, she has imprisoned her sons and raised her thieving relatives to positions of power. Stirred by these events, and with the purpose of restoring the Tang to power, believing that this is the desire of the people, Li Chingyeh, whose family has received the highest honors from the emperor, hereby raises his banner to drive out the wicked tyrant. The war drum is sounded, the banner unfurled. Horses' hooves shall be heard from the plains of southern Yueh to the mountains and rivers of the far north. . . . The roar of soldiers shakes the mountains, battle cries tear the silence of the skies. The cause is just, its might irresistible. Rally to this cause. Victory is assured!' "

Lo made a business of rolling up the scroll. Cheers greeted him and clapping broke out. When the noise subsided, Chingyeh said, "Raise your fists if you approve of publishing this attack."

All fists rose at once. Chingyeh began to gather his papers. "That's all then. You, Tang, will be in charge of printing and posting this in as many towns as possible."

"Print? You mean copy this out in brushwork?" Wei, the perfectionist, corrected.

"Carve it on wood, roll it in ink, and print many copies," Chingyeh said impatiently. "Like the Buddhists do in distributing Buddha's sayings to the pilgrims."

Wei stared. "A new technique? Well, I suppose it's a good idea . . . saves time. Lo's sayings are at least as good as Buddha's."

A few grunts of amusement greeted this, and then the men rapidly dispersed.

Within ten days Chingyeh swept into Yangchow at the head of a dozen horsemen in his guise of military governor. All went as planned. He set up his headquarters in the yamen, he executed the imprisoned governor, emptied the prisons to enhance his army, and recruited about a hundred thousand troops. A neighboring governor came over to the rebels with his three districts north of the river. Several battles were won and only a small hilltown called Hsiu-i was successful in resisting. Exhilarated by his success, Chingyeh's objectives changed. He began to talk about splitting north and south China into two halves again, and putting himself as emperor on the southern throne at Nanking.

The bad news about the revolt reached Wu Jao after the first impressive victories had been won by the rebels. She listened to the reports at an emergency meeting of the first ministers.

"Is that all?" she asked finally.

"No, Your Majesty," a grand secretary said in a halting voice. "There is this poster that our agent tore down from a city gate. It is just propaganda, not important, not worth noticing, but it does show the extremes these renegrades will resort to. I feared to neglect to report it. . . ."

"Read it," she ordered.

"Aloud? Here?" he asked in a quavering voice. "Certainly, Your Majesty, if you order it . . . but, Your Majesty, I would rather not. . . ."

"Read it," she repeated.

When he finished Lo's diatribe, there was a stunned silence in the room. The official rolled up the poster with trembling hands and his colleagues bowed their heads in shock, waiting for the storm to break. Jao's shoulders were shaking as she suppressed her laughter. It was all so thunderous—like a boy of four having a tantrum. The absurdity of such half-baked invective, so full of falsehoods, was magnificently ludicrous. The facts of her life in the palace, known to all its three thousand inhabitants, gave the lie to every allegation.

Containing her amusement, she asked, "Who wrote this?"

"Lo Pinwang, an ex-clerk in the Treasury," the secretary mumbled.

"The ministers who handle promotions are to blame for overlooking such talent as this and for allowing this man Lo to remain obscure," she observed chattily. "Such elegant words, such rolling phrases, such poetry. . . ."

The ministers could not believe their ears, then someone gave a low, dry chuckle. Wu Jao laughed aloud and the room exploded in admiring guffaws and a smattering of applause. The ministers, heartened, quickly got down to the business of organizing defense and planning strategy.

The moment discussion ended, Jao called in the couriers, including Chengssu, who had returned from his errand to Dee's yamen, in order to send out directives. She realized that there was no time to be lost. Her first action was to promote the leaders of the small town of Hsiu-i to be town officials in charge of resistance. Then, after declaring a general amnesty for the citizens of Yangchow and all other towns coerced into rebellion, she put a price on the heads of Chingyeh and the others. At the same time she dispatched a Tang prince, Hsiao I, with an army of 300,000 to put down the rebellion. She preferred to use a civilian prince, not a military man, to handle these Chinese citizens.

After she had finished with all the urgent business, Jao retired, exhausted, to her own quarters, where she found Chi anxiously waiting for her.

"The court is doing something about those rascals in Yangchow," she commented, "but so far it is just words without action . . . only words as Chingyeh and the other demented revolters take town after town. I called you here to ask you to approach the Beggars' Guild secretly. To find out how widespread this thing is and what is being said in the teahouses and shops in Yangchow. In the yamen and barracks as well. Official information about this uprising was much too slow in reaching me. Dangerously, perhaps even fatally, slow."

She handed him a bag of silver pieces, which he received in sober silence. He had heard about the poster and took it more seriously than she did. He smiled encouragingly, however. Chi was getting older and his black thatch was grizzled with white, but his one-sided smile was as youthful as ever, and Jao brightened.

"You didn't mean that, surely," he said. "And yes, I will contact the head man of the Beggars' Guild at once."

"What didn't I mean?" Jao asked defensively. "I meant every word I said, and more. . . ."

"That word 'fatally,' you can't mean and mustn't mean it even for a second."

Jao was reminded of the tone of voice he had so often used with the tsairen. She smiled grimly. "Chi, I am uneasy . . . something is more wrong than a revolt in a distant province, and I can't put my finger on it."

Chi folded his hands in his sleeves and was silent. Finally he said, "Your feeling of dread is probably justified, but you will have to be patient. Right now Your Majesty is possibly one step ahead of your enemies. You could not have chosen a better way of finding out quickly how widespread the disaffection is and how, in general, the people of the Yangchow delta feel about this revolt. I'll get the guild chief to start the inquiries tonight. We should have answers in twenty-four hours."

Jao frowned. "Chi, my good fellow, I know that you wish to relieve my anxieties, but do not go to the extent of telling me a story like this. Twenty-four hours? Impossible! It can't be done!"

Chi remained composed. "Yangchow is a wealthy city, neglected by the bureaucracy because it is in the distrusted south. It is not neglected by the Beggars' Guild, however. The guild has a network there—all over the delta—and it is organized in a tough and disciplined way, I do assure you. What is important to Your Majesty is their intelligence system. The beggars have their own amusements and their most cherished is pigeon racing. Their pigeon fanciers are the best in the empire, and the leaders regularly communicate with one another by means of carrier pigeons which they keep out of sight in each center. They will cooperate with me now as they often have in the past because they need to know something of what goes on in the palace—nothing of a highly secret nature, I assure you," he added hastily when Jao's frown deepened, "but general news about the goings-on here. I trade information with them. They trust me because I don't, ah, gossip."

"Why haven't I been told of this before?" Jao asked irritably.

"Because there has been no need," Chi returned frankly, "and because strict secrecy is involved. The beggars kill anyone of their number who disobeys their crude rules. How can I tell secrets to my empress with stipulations that she must not repeat what I tell her!"

"Well, you have now," Jao returned, "and I will honor your stipulations. Very well, leave at once . . . and get me the news I need."

Her dimples showed when she gave Chi a wan smile.

The next morning her nephew Chengssu called on her in a state of nerves. Wearily she listened to him while he complained about the attitudes of some officials and some princes. "They are too sympathetic to the cause of the restoration," he cried. "Too dangerously interested . . . they are traitors. You will see."

Wu Jao listened and merely nodded her head until he was finished. She then dismissed him. He was greatly dissatisfied.

However, she brought up the subject of possible rebels in high circles in the privy council meeting. No minster wanted to risk an opinion except Pei, who defended the princes.

"They are not involved," he stated categorically.

Wu Jao dropped the subject, but like Chengssu, was dissatisfied and began to suspect her officials as well as the Tang princes.

In less than twenty-four hours Chi had brought the information that the Beggars' Guild had already ordered all their men off the streets for fear of the recruiting patrols who were kidnapping every male in sight.

"I regret this," Chi said, downcast. "The beggars cannot canvas opinion because they have all been called in. Those who have already been captured and are in the barracks will escape from the battlefields when they get the opportunity to bring news. However, the conclusion that their leaders have reached so far is that no one wants to join the revolt, no one of the common sort, that is, and all see no reason to fight the government. This is, in its way, the good news that you were hoping for. I also have a list of the names of the chief rebels. They were forwarded by a busboy of the restaurant where the plotting took place before he was forced into Chingyeh's army."

Jao thanked Chi and almost snatched the list of names from his hand.

After he left, she sat in contemplation for a long time. She had seldom felt so at her wit's end, so threatened. She did not quite know why. I can't decide how to act or which way to turn, she thought. I am behaving as Kaotsung did when Hung died. Defeated, the forbidden word, defeat. She felt surrounded by sinister forces working in the dark—how could she protect herself? I am so frightened, and feel I can't win this time. Is this what Chi sensed when he snapped at me?

Her attendants melted away when they saw that she wanted to be alone. She sat for hours trying to sort things out. She refused food and turned away visitors, even her beloved Taiping. This won't do, this wu-*wei* . . . this paralysis of fear, she told herself. I must do something about myself, retire to a retreat for a while, something. She walked to her gong and hit it harder than necessary. Her attendants came running.

"I desire to go to Lungmen for a few days," she told her eunuch on duty. "Please attend to the transport and entourage. Only a few persons, if you please. How soon can you be ready?"

The eunuch paused. "A day should be enough, Your Majesty. The imperial rest house there is always in good order, and the distance is not great, only twelve miles."

"Very good. We shall start at dawn the day after tomorrow," Jao answered, brightening a little. "Also see that Cloud comes to me as soon as possible." Cloud was the one person in the palace whom Jao turned to when she felt vulnerable and confused. Now white-haired, she was still the same perceptive and witty self that she had been in tsairen days. Cloud was soothing company whatever happened.

The eunuch departed with alacrity to carry out his orders. Among his errands was a special call at the office of First Minister Pei to report on the doings of the empress. He was paid generously for his daily information. He felt uneasy about it, but reflected that no harm could come from such unimportant reports on such trivial matters.

Pei received the news of the Lungmen expedition in silence and dismissed the eunuch. Now was the time, he decided, the moment for him to act and get rid of that woman. He could certainly arrange an ambush to annihilate such an inconspicuous caravan of pilgrims as Wu's train would appear. He could settle the problem of her interference in government once and for all. He decided to hire men from the Beggars' Guild.

The morning dawned in torrential rain. Jao heard the water pelting on the tiles above her head when she was wakened by her maid, and sleepily canceled her trip to Lungmen. Cloud was asleep on a pallet in Jao's room. She stirred when she heard Jao cancel the outing. Oh good, she thought sleepily, now we can stay inside and relax today. That's all Jao needs—just to relax.

When Jao appeared in the audience chamber for the day's meeting, Pei was furious at being thwarted. He took charge of the agenda and immediately attacked.

"This revolt in Yangchow is serious. It is growing like wildfire and surely expresses the will of the people. The Son of Heaven is now of age, yet does not sit on his throne. That is why a worthless dilettante like Li Chingyeh is able to raise such a storm. I herewith propose that the empress dowager return the government to the emperor. Then the rebellion will die of itself."

No one dared to open his mouth, and the silence lengthened.

"Which emperor. Chungtsung or Juitsung?" Jao asked sarcastically.

"You have put both into the positions they are now in. Which one will best suit your purpose in achieving supreme authority for yourself?"

Pei Yen remained aloofly silent. He had declared war and felt entirely justified in doing so. Jao was only a woman who was stepping out of line.

A senior official from the powerful Censorate finally spoke up. "Pei Yen has been entrusted with Kaotsung's will and is responsible for carrying out all its injunctions. Pei's authority is of the highest in the realm, and yet when he hears of rebellion, he does not want to suppress it. He suggests that the empress Wu should abdicate. He must have some dark design."

A chorus of shocked comment greeted this speech. Wu Jao said nothing but watched grimly while her ministers, already highly nervous over the revolt, lashed out at Pei. After hours of fierce discussion the decision was reached that Pei must be arrested for investigation. He was not allowed to withdraw to his office or to his home, but was taken at once into custody and handed over to a court of censors for interrogation.

During the next few days the issue of Pei's guilt took precedence over even the rebellion. Jao was more and more appalled. The significance of the delays was not lost on her. Were others as guilty as Pei? Her distress doubled when the Beggars' Guild informed her of Pei's aborted attempt on her life.

At a loss as to whom to trust, she called in the great scholar and vice-chief of the Secretariat, Liu Weijer.

"About Pei. Is he guilty of treason or not?" she asked.

Wei replied earnestly, "Your Majesty, Pei Yen is a great statesman, there is none better. He has served the throne with a whole heart. All the empire knows this. Pei is no traitor. Your humble servant knows this in his heart for certain."

"Then you had better ask your heart to think again," replied Jao. "Your Empress has proof of Pei Yen's treachery. Only you investigating officers do not know."

Undeterred, Weijer responded passionately, "If Pei Yen is a traitor because of his dissenting advice we are all traitors!"

Wu looked at him disillusioned. "Your Empress knows that Pei Yen is a traitor and she knows that you are not. You are dismissed."

She watched him bow himself out, subdued but unconvinced. Then she wearily called in the only courier available at the time. She wrote out his orders to leave at once for Changan, to spare no expense, to waste no time. She handed him a letter that she had written to General

Liu Jen the night before and told him to pick up his fast horse and leave immediately. "You have orders to obtain the best of the relay horses at every station. Now go."

He obeyed her orders in silence and left the palace immediately.

In the days that followed, Jao felt sick whenever she recalled General Liu's previous objections to her usurpation of authority. She waited in dread for the courier to return with Liu's answer, worrying. General Liu's warnings sounded much like Pei's to her. The only difference was that Liu had not tried to assassinate her . . . at least not yet.

In a minimum of time the courier was back. White-faced, Jao received the dispatch, dismissed the the man, and then retired to the sanctuary of her bedroom to read the fateful letter. The message was short: "When I asked your courier about Pei's case, he said that he had long known about it. This courier knew about Pei's treachery but did not report it."

Jao expelled her breath in a long sigh. "Thank heaven!" she cried loudly, and Cloud came running. Jao told her, practically crying in her relief. "I now know where Liu stands, and that is solidly behind me. I can rely on him! I am beginning to find people I can trust—and he is the greatest of all, my own Li Chi!"

"It's the first battle won in winning your personal war," Cloud commented thoughtfully.

Jao met her eyes in a knowledgeable look. Then she turned to her secretary, an educated palace slave named Shanggwan Waner, and issued the order for the execution of the courier. She exhibited General Liu's letter in privy council meeting and her action was endorsed. It had to be done as a warning to all would-be traitors. Deciding it was time to use the military, she dispatched to the disaffected area a commander who she felt was reliable because he had been a protégé of Liu's. Black Teeth Long One was sent with a large army of trained troops to the scene of the revolt, to attack from the south, while Tang Prince Li attacked from the north.

Differing ideas about strategy and tactics arose on both sides of the conflict. Chingyeh, victorious and confident, obsessed with creating a new dynasty in the south, decided not to march on the capital at Loyang but to entrench himself in the south. He chose to defend his territory by setting up strong forces at both ends of the major north to south route which ran along the length of Lake Hungtse. He sent his brother Chingyu to the north end of the lake and the rebel Wei to the south end, while he himself brought his best volunteers to Kao Yu, a village located on the Hsia-ah River which connected the system of lakes, the Grand Canal, and Yangchow.

On the imperial side, Prince Li wanted to contain the rebels but not to risk combat. His associate, Censor Wei, was all for fierce attack. He goaded Prince Li into assaults on Chingyeh's strongholds: on Chingyu's forces in the north and rebel Wei's in the south. Both capitulated, abandoned their troops, and fled northward to the Turks.

Chingyeh, undaunted, readied for a decisive battle by posting his worst troops, the old and tired, on the banks of the Hsia-ah River and placing his best troops in their rear.

Censor Wei sent out spies to bring him information about Chingyeh's troop disposition and about the all-important matter of the weather. When notified that the prevailing wind was now blowing from north to south, the censor hurriedly ordered fires set by the dry reeds on the southern bank of the Hsia-ah, where Chingyeh's weakest men were stationed. A roaring reed fire started and the imperial troops crossed the river in its wake. The wind whipped the flames into clouds of fire and smoke so dense that the troops on the bank broke at once. Nor could the elite troops stop the rout, and they suffered enormous casualties in their defeat.

Chingyeh, Tang, and Lo escaped to Yangchow where they collected their families and posted to the coast to take ship to Korea. But the winds defeated them and the ships could not sail. Their party fled into the coastal swamps, where they camped out waiting for a favorable wind. Before this happened, one of Chingyeh's rebel officers killed him for the reward. Tang, Lo, and twenty-five other leaders were hunted down, captured, and decapitated. Their heads were delivered to Loyang, where they were impaled on the city walls. The entire family of Li Chingyeh was destroyed, and even venerable Li Chi's tomb was desecrated and his remains scattered.

At the time of Chingyeh's defeat, the comet disappeared.

Wu Jao was relieved, enormously relieved, but still uneasy. She went at once to the new Altar to Heaven on Mount Sung near Loyang to give heartfelt thanks—for heavenly intervention on the occasions of the auspicious comet, the rain when Pei had planned to assassinate her, the right wind at the battle of Kao Yu, and for the wrong wind when the rebels were trying to escape. After taking care of formal thanksgiving to high heaven, she visited a shrine of the Western Queen Mother that she had built in the palace grounds and burned incense there as well. Women divinities helped women, she felt gratefully.

Later, in the darkest hours of a moonless night, she went to the pagoda housing the memorial to Li Chi, which had been erected in the year of his death. Accompanied only by Chi, she knelt and sacrificed to his spirit, letting rare tears fall upon the cold stones. "I am sorry," she murmured. "I am so very sorry."

The rebellion was over but the aftermath was not. The revolt had affected a small region and was over in two months but, as usual in civil conflict, the investigation of its causes took longer. Pei Yen was executed despite the numerous officials who still felt that he should have been spared no matter what his actions had been.

Jao said to Juitsung during one of the difficult days of allocating blame, "These learned scholars tell themselves that Pei was a loyal minister justly planning to restore an emperor to his throne. It cannot be loyalty to the throne to depose one emperor and then plot for the restoration of another, can it? Loyalty to whom? And loyalty to me to plan my death? These scholars escape so easily into their compartmentalized minds, laying all blame always on Heaven, or the Son of Heaven—whichever is handier."

Juitsung listened in silence, his eyes somber, his manner comforting. "You are upset. You should be elated." he said. "You have s-s-somehow managed, without indecisiveness, to cope with a powerful and traitorous prime minster surrounded by his fellow ministers, and have degraded or exiled his supporters. The execution of a famous and successful general for his support of Pei was accomplished without incidence, and it took place in an area far from Loyang among his own troops. You have overcome a serious rebellion in the vast southern province that has been a part of the empire less than fifty years. You have won out in every instance. Your spirits should be raised to the s-s-skies! Such accomplishments equal the performance, under such conditions, of any sovereign at any time. Heavens above—honorable parent—what more could anyone ask!"

Jao's eyes shone and she placed her hand on Juitsung's shoulder in gratitude. "I'm truly gratified to hear you say these things—I couldn't be more so! But I owe it to you, my son, to tell you that I am not satisfied. I can't accept congratulations when I am so disillusioned. Who can rule without reliable officials? I must call a full session of the court and confront them from the throne."

Jao could not rest until she had her confrontation. She spoke to her whole court, standing unconcealed below the throne in formal audience. She spoke from memory without notes.

"We have just passed safely through one of the greatest dangers that a state can face—rebellion on the part of discontented citizens. We have also passed safely through an even greater danger—treachery on the part of the highest officials of government. Who is the government? You men here today. And I, your empress, am I to blame for these rebellions? If so, what have I done to deserve such disloyalty? Those of you brave enough to oppose me are surely courageous enough to speak up now to accuse me of misrule or any other crime against the state. If you have a just cause, speak up! I will guarantee you amnesty as long as you do not bear arms against me unjustly!

"I assisted the late emperor for more than thirty years, wearying myself with the cares of the empire. Your ranks and your titles and your prosperity are all yours now, thanks to us. The peace and tranquility everywhere in the empire is the result of our care. When the late emperor died, he bequeathed his duty to maintain prosperity to me and my sons. I did not dare to think of myself only, but studied to benefit and cherish you.

"Now I find that the leaders of rebellion were all military and civilian officials of the government. Why?

"Among the statesmen who received the will, there were those who were treacherous and insubordinate, like Pei Yen. There was a scion of the great house of military men, Li Chingyeh. An old general skillful in war, Cheng Wuting. All these men were highly respected, but they were hostile to me, and it was up to me to find the strength to resist them. If any of you feel that you are more able than they and wish to continue in opposition to me, act accordingly and speak up now! You will be protected if you speak in open audience."

She stopped and faced the audience, searching the upturned faces with her eyes. When no one spoke, Wu Jao retired in unsmiling silence to her quarters, ushered out by silent but admiring bodyguards. They had never before been witness to anything so stirring in any of their dealings with lofty personages, and felt proud to be in the service of such a one. This was also the prevailing spirit that day with most of the younger officials who had listened to her.

Jao found the double doors of her hall open to the warm breezes of the mild day when she reached her living rooms. She found her eunuchs and waiting women and servants of all ranks lined up to receive her. Applause began as she descended from her chair. She stopped in surprise while her staff bowed or fell to their knees, still clapping. Moved, Jao had to blink rapidly to control herself. She clapped in return to greet and thank them.

Inside she found Juitsung and Taiping. Like their mother, they were dressed formally in light mourning.

"Well," she said, and sank with a rustle of skirts into her cushioned chair. "I threw down the gauntlet today, and now . . . we shall see."

"Brave of you," Juitsung said admiringly as he stood waiting to be asked to sit. Taiping did not stand upon such ceremony, but sank into a cushioned chair when Jao did.

"Sit . . . sit. Here, bring your chairs away from the wall and sit closer to the table of food where we can talk quietly. Heavens, my voice has failed!" she croaked, rubbing her throat.

"Strain," Tai said, and Juitsung nodded.

"I hear that you gave them no quarter," he said. "I admire you s-s-so very much for facing up to them."

"You were tremendous," Taiping chipped in vigorously while chewing on a date.

Jao watched her children help themselves to tidbits, but she herself was too distressed to eat.

"Why are you still so grim, after such a superlative performance?" Juitsung asked.

Jao did not answer at once, then said, "The whole court was there today, everybody. No one sent in an excuse because of illness. They all listened, and no one, not even one, raised his voice in either agreement or dissent—a most disturbing experience. After my long record of successful administration I have been rewarded with treachery and rebellion, and, what is worse, with no hint of gratitude for my services. I fear that I am dealing with a court of ingrates."

Taiping stared round-eyed at her mother and Juitsung put his hand over hers. He looked at her with an understanding far beyond his years.

She continued. "I deal with them openly. I lay the problems on the table before them so that together we can make effective decisions. I give them realty in increments small enough to cope with, but they flee from it."

"I know." Juitsung's voice was so emotional that Jao's eyes flew to his face.

"How?" she asked.

"I know about the w-w-way everyone escapes into silence and then reassembles in silence to attack you. The only way I can deal with life myself is face-to-face communication. I cannot deal with silences. I can only deal with give and take on both sides. I can't fight their way, so . . . I don't fight at all. They all operate the same way, those politicians. Most of them are honorable men according to the official d-d-definitions, or they would not last long in the central government, but they are used to the system of resolving conflict through their agents. They seldom solve things directly or in confrontation, as you did so beautifully today. Your way," his mouth twisted in a wry smile, "is the best way. But men are ingrates and often cowardly and become enemies of those who are neither. Such a life, always dealing with enemies, is not for me. I have t-t-to live a life of harmony, not incessant struggle. Nevertheless, your way is the better way."

Jao felt tension leaving her. "You are a comfort to me," she said.

"Not a thorn in your side?" he countered. "I am like your courtiers, I escape harsh reality by letting others take care of its worst aspects."

"By 'others' do you mean me?" Jao responded lightly, pretending to be occupied in divesting herself of her shawl.

Juitsung paused, the sickness he always felt when skirting dangerous subjects with his mother arising. "It was easiest to let you s-s-solve everything. We could never successfully deceive you. Of course, you overlooked our failings most of the time and protected us, but you always knew . . . and that defeated us. You always knew."

"Having two lives to live often presents one with difficult choices," Jao said simply. "I profoundly wish it weren't so, and hereby beg your pardon for any harm that has come to you through me."

Juitsung then did what he had not done since childhood. He knelt before her and put his head in her lap. "You take the high jumps for all of us."

Jao stroked his satiny hair, remembering the days when he was small and upset over something. Tai came and snuggled into her arms also, and Jao felt suddenly that her heart was full and that life did have its great moments after all.

CHAPTER NINETEEN

The winter was long and harsh. The days passed with dark skies and endless winds from the Gobi desert. Jao's depression did not lift. She felt the silent disapproval of many in her court regarding Pei's execution. The continuing cold caused the deaths of many of the elderly and the unwell, including the hardworking viceroy of Changan, General Liu.

"Oh no! It cannot be!" Jao was shocked when the news was brought to her. "I cannot take care of this empire without him," she said to herself. "There is no replacement for him, the closest is General Heijer Changjer, and he's not Chinese. The great men are all dying and only the parasites are left!"

Numbed by her loss, she set about the planning of a great state funeral for the general and when that was over sat idly in her rooms for hours each day, watching the tossing of the bare branches of trees in her park. No matter what she did to escape the feeling of vulnerability, it was still there, destroying her little by little. I feel bereft—I am bereft! she thought. There are still conspirators on all sides!

Jao felt herself at a standstill. None of her previous visions suited her present conditions, and new visions eluded her. She was forced to bide her time.

Her Wu family members, on the other hand, had no such problem. Wu Chengssu had encouraged many of his relatives to come to court, and they had their visions clearly in mind. They did not notice the cold or the gloom in their cheerful and even boisterous involvement in palace politics. They seemed to be everywhere, their ostentatious dress overwhelming their small bodies as they called attention to themselves and to their new importance.

Wu Chengssu in particular made himself conspicuous. He appeared daily in Wu Jao's quarters in his tireless pursuit of power. Undeterred by Jao's coldness and frequent refusals to see him, he relentlessly pushed forward his notions regarding a change of dynasty and a spectacular emergence into the supreme position of emperor for Jao herself.

In her effort to determine what she should do to survive, Jao considered her behavior in similar situations—the recruitment of the maids as informal spies when she was in Empress Wang's service, and the recruitment of the experienced veterans to be Kaotsung's special bodyguard. She needed to do something like that now, she told herself, employing a wide net of informers to catch potential rebels wherever they might be. Also, she needed to plan for the protection of her family, especially Chungtsung and Juitsung, who would be the storm centers of restoration movements. Chung will have to remain in exile, she thought, but Tan . . . I can protect him here in the palace.

She frowned as she considered her situation. The ministers had given Chungtsung total support at first. Then they decided that their best hope of keeping the government as it had been was to keep the team method that had worked in the past—when she did all the work and the nominal emperor got all the credit. Playing that role under a husband was bearable, but it was different to do under a son whose wife was empress while she herself was only dowager empress. She was in a trap again, and she could not escape . . . unless she changed the government and all the men running it. She knew it was naive to think that she could change things by giving the offices new names. She would have to move most of the big officials out, ostracize most of the Tang princes, and put new officials and new princes in . . . like her Wu relatives. That is, if she wanted to remain alive.

Business in the palace city began early. It had taken Dee several weeks to prepare for his move to the capital, and several more for him and his family to travel. The first morning after his arrival, he dressed carefully and presented himself at the doors of the hall of justice when they were first opened. He was accompanied by his sergeant, Liang. They entered the dark and cavernous hall, and a yawning clerk ushered them at once to the cubicle that had been allotted to him. "Always the least comfortable in the building for the newcomer," Dee murmured.

Liang grinned. "You won't be here long," he replied.

"You are right—the next move will be for the better. Or for the worse," Dee said dryly. He was aware of the political turmoil presently threatening the court.

On his desk Dee found his first order, an assignment to attend the audience of the day in lieu of the chief. His eyebrows rose as he read the order, but he shrugged and went to the reception desk to find the audience hall on the map of the palace buildings. He was studying the entrance screen painting of the city of Loyang when he was accosted by a stranger.

"You are Dee Jenjer, newly arrived, I take it? I am Lai Chunchen, also new here."

Dee turned to reply, his face expressionless, as was his custom in meeting unknown people. "Judge Dee—at your service," he said, examining Lai with interest.

Lai's smile was warm and his manner cordial, although his eyes seemed watchful. He was a handsome man with iron-gray hair and a high color, impeccably dressed. "I'm told that you are supposed to be attending audience this morning. I wonder whether you would like a companion. That is, if you don't plan to skip the assembly," he said.

"Delighted!" Dee said briefly. "And I don't plan to skip. Is that permissible around here?"

"Not advisable, but one never knows," Lai returned lightly. "Let us go."

The two men arrived at the audience hall just as the doors were closing. They squeezed into the packed room, where Emperor Juitsung was presiding. The emperor quickly covered the small business of the day, and then Empress Wu came to the front of the dais and waited for quiet.

"The most important part of the agenda today," she said, "is the matter of recruitment of new officials. I wish to introduce bold and enterprising men from all the different regions of the empire—not just from the central provinces. I want the magistrates to seek out new men of talent wherever they are to be found—new men whom I can trust not to betray me."

A stir of dismay swept through the hall. Dee felt Lai twitch uncomfortably at his side. Jao continued, "I want men whose chief loyalty is to me personally, rather than to the recruiting agents of the bureaucracy. In addition, those who are now in office and who prove to be unfit for their responsibilities will be dismissed, cashiered, or executed. If any magistrate is slow in supporting this effort of recruitment, I shall go over his head and, without regard to normal procedures of degrees and graduates and ranks and perquisites, I shall appoint men of no education who know how to get things done. The way I want them done. Tremble and obey. You are now dismissed."

The officials seemed too shocked to move, and disbursal began slowly in silence. Dee was more dismayed than anyone else. "A bit confusing, no?" he remarked noncommittedly to his companion when they were well out of earshot of the imperial minions.

Lai gave him an enigmatic look. "You could say that. I think she means exactly what she says, though."

"I can't believe my ears." In his dismay, Dee forgot to be cautious. "Does she mean to destroy the established system? It sounds wild and reckless to me."

"Wild and reckless!" Lai repeated, pleased with the phrase. "It just fits Wu Jao's rule! It is the way she will be toward anyone who opposes her, and that means anyone—especially the entrenched power wielders!"

Dee stole a glance at his perspiring companion and muttered, "One thing is certain—if her majesty actually does what she threatens do to, she will be making dangerous enemies at every turn."

"That she will! She will indeed, and it will be my business to cope. She has just appointed me to be chief of a new office of investigation." Lai halted in his excitement, and Dee stopped with him. "Incidentally, are you for her in these changes, or against her?" Lai asked.

"For her, of course," Dee returned instantly, recognizing a chasm opening at his feet.

"Safer that way," Lai mused, continuing his walk.

Dee was aware of his hint.

As the days passed, Jao issued detailed instructions to all magistrates to be alert for plots of rebellion in their areas. These instructions included provisions for funding transportation to the capital of any informer, with the assurance that he would be granted an audience with the empress the day he arrived.

This novel invitation provided not a trickle of informants, but a tidal wave. Jao was swamped with stories of disloyalty from honest louts who were ignorant of what constituted disloyalty in lofty circles. She was obliged to provide Lai's office of investigation with more money and more assistants. It was not long before the number of traitors who appeared before Jao was even greater than before, and consequently, the number of executions she had to order.

Depressed by this situation, Jao kept busy managing the other sweeping changes that she was bringing about. She reviewed the personnel and management of all offices, discharging men who had achieved sinecures, employing new men to take their places. The records office kept track of the new developments, and in the end they found her actions salutary. "The empress is not sparing in the bestowal of ranks and titles," was one entry. "Even a wild, reckless fellow can be made an official without regard to the normal order," was another entry, "and those unfit for their responsibilities are cashiered in large numbers. Her broad aim seems to be to select men of real talent."

Administration had gone slack during the last years of Kaotsung's reign. Officials had been free from imperial supervision and could come to work or stay at home as they pleased. Now, under Jao's energetic probing, there was no office so obscure that it escaped her scrutiny. During the daytime, therefore, Jao found relief from her feelings of depression in her work.

At night, however, she could not escape. Chengssu was always around, aching to be of service, impressing her each time he appeared with his devotion to her cause. He was, however, tiresome. Taiping and Princess Chienchen, on the other hand, were refreshing whenever they they appeared in her chambers. "I'd visit my mother more often," Tai said to the princess, "if she weren't so frightfully grim these days, and so unplayful. What is life for, I ask you, if not for enjoyment?"

"I've noticed those dark circles under her eyes and how she scowls at the high spirits of some of our companions," the princess mused. "However, I think that I know of a way to make her unbend."

"Well, I don't think it is possible," Tai returned.

The princess was a posthumous daughter of Kaotzu, venerable founder of the Tang dynasty. Witty and accommodating, she was more than fifty and was one of the few Tang princesses and princelings whom Jao and Tai really liked. "I'll bring in someone who cannot fail to amuse her!" she told Tai.

The next time Tai and Chienchen visited Jao, the princess smuggled in a tall, handsome man, about fifty years old, to meet her. His eyes sparkled with animation and intelligence, and his mouth was wide and generous.

"Here is Feng Huai-i," the princess said.

Jao regarded him with raised eyebrows. He bowed.

"Feng is the most unusual man in the empire," the princess began. Jao looked distant and unapproachable. The princess continued. "He is a peddler of medicines. He is a wrestler. He is an architect and builder. He is a Buddhist with great powers. He is the master of all trades. Anything that anyone wants done, he can do!"

"Amazing," Jao said, flatly.

"Yes, isn't it?" Huai-i said, looking so droll that the two younger women laughed and Jao unbent enough to give a small smile.

The man has presence of a kind, one must admit, she thought. He is totally at ease in our august company. Most people were so frozen that they could barely breathe.

The princess beamed. "You should see the pagoda that Huai-i has built for me, complete with lotus pond and pergola, a paradise filled with every delightful thing. I shall live out there in the hot months because Huai-i discovered where the prevailing breezes are likely to be and placed the summer house to catch them. Clever man!"

Jao stared in surprise at the normally dignified princess's girlish antics toward her guest, who smiled at all her sallies. His eyes, however, stayed upon Jao herself.

Impudence! Jao thought mildly.

Taiping helped herself to the Turkish confection on the tray and drank her wine, all the while keeping up a running chatter. She also seemed excited by the man whose presence mysteriously animated all in the room. Jao listened to the hubbub in a tolerant, absentminded way, finding herself increasingly diverted, increasingly aware of the big man's unblinking appraisal. She stirred restlessly. I am sixty years old, she thought. It is not possible that this . . . this person sees me not as an empress, but as a woman, and desirable at that. He is certainly a madman.

She turned to Chienchen. "How did you get an outside crew into the palace to build your pagoda, Chi Chi?" she asked when there was a break in the conversation.

"Oh!" the princess exclaimed in mock consternation. "Naughty of me, wasn't it? But it was all arranged in a proper way by alerting the guards to admit the workmen on certain days while notifying the resident women to keep out of sight. Of course, we could peek at the men but they couldn't peek at us. And as far as smuggling in guests at night is concerned, it is a matter of the proper gift."

She giggled and watched Jao out of the corner of her eye. "Have I offended you, August One? Please forgive? I am a reckless one, and cannot change at this late date. Everyone should be reckless once in a while!"

Jao had had her share of wine. "Why not?" she said. "Cautiously reckless, that is."

Feng spoke up. "By day I am in the palace to build the princess pagodas and gardens, and by night to provide her valuable potions and unguents. I would say that I am cautiously reckless myself."

Tai and Chienchen exclaimed in one voice, "Cautious? You!"

"You don't know the half of it!" he responded solemnly. They laughed again and started to tease, but Jao's interest was caught.

"Potions?" she asked. "What kind of potions?"

"Love draughts," he answered unabashedly.

"Effrontery," the princess cried in delight. Tai's color rose also, but Jao, who was pursuing her own line of thought, ignored their incipient lewdness.

"Is this your true business then? Selling medicaments to women on the sly? No one knowing what you sell or to whom?"

Feng gazed at her unsmilingly. "It is complicated, this business of mine. Each potion or unguent has to be prepared specially for each client. I may be a peddler, but I am a high-class peddler catering to those who can pay. These medicines are not for everyone. Many drugs come from foreign lands, not always easily or without danger."

Jao looked at him with sudden interest. She had been a handler of drugs herself. "What if I should ask you for a mild potion now? To make me sleep?" In surprise, Tai and Chienchen ceased to chatter and listened carefully.

"I have a phial in my belt that might work," he answered slowly, keeping his eyes on her. "But it is not really necessary."

"Is that your considered opinion?" Jao was intrigued. She heard soft steps behind her as Tai and the princess left the room.

"It is my reckless opinion. Because Your Majesty does not really need a sleeping potion," he replied.

"Perhaps," she answered, unaccountably dry-mouthed. "But the other . . . the other potion . . . What do you have?"

"Your Majesty does not need a love potion either," he said, and put his finger with a feather touch on a pulse at the base of her neck. She sat very still while he touched a dozen other places on her neck and shoulders so lightly that she would have hardly noticed what he was doing except that it made her breathless with pleasure. In time he loosened his belt and let it fall. His coat flew open, and she put her hand gently on his taut navel.

The night hours passed and were rung by the watchman, but Jao did not hear any of the sounds of the night. Toward dawn she began to awaken but was conscious only of acute euphoria, of being inflamed by an ecstasy that she had not experienced before and that she had not known existed. For a woman of sixty, impossible . . . a miracle! Or magic, she thought drowsily as she became more aware of her surroundings. The first light of day was shining faintly through the screens when the scrape of the door was enough to tell her that the big man was leaving. Then she fell into a deep sleep.

Early in Jao's social evening, Chengssu had come to her residence to discuss something he thought was urgent. It was raining too noisily for the guard at the outer gate to hear him, and he was at the door of her small, lighted living room before he was stopped. The talk and laughter of feminine voices mixed with a male voice was audible, and his curiosity had been aroused.

"Strict orders not to disturb her majesty tonight," said Lim, who was on duty at the time.

"Out of my way," Chengssu had ordered. Determined to join the party and discover what was going on, he had pushed ahead. He had disregarded orders before and gotten away with it. Another guard quickly appeared beside him.

"What's the matter?" the second guard had asked.

"The empress sent for me—I'm going in," Chengssu cried, moving forward sharply.

"You are mistaken, she did not send for anyone tonight—sorry!" Lim had taken him by one arm while Suh took the other, and before he knew what was happening, they had whisked him along to the outer gate, where they delivered him to the gateman.

"Here is an intruder who got past you." Lim had spoken sternly to the very frightened gateman.

"You imbeciles!" Chengssu had shouted at Lim's retreating back. "Tomorrow I shall make you suffer for this! And you too!" He had lunged past the gateman, but was stopped again, not too politely. After a few moments of ineffectual struggle, Chengssu had been obliged to give up his plan to visit the empress.

It was now morning, and Chengssu was the first to appear in the anteroom of the council hall where Jao began each day's session. The room filled up with sleepy ministers who slowly shuffled into the hall when the doors were opened. They waited for Jao to appear, and when she did not, the first minister conducted the routine session. Disappointed,

Chengssu started on his rounds to find Jao, but without success. He finally cornered a cleaning woman in an empty court.

"You! Come here, I want to ask you something."

She stared at him, frightened. "What does Your Highness wish? Who are you?" she stammered.

"I am the nephew of the empress and I am being denied access." He softened his tone. "I am worried. Can you tell me if she is ill? This is all so unusual." He pressed a coin into her hand.

She looked at the coin and then at the well-dressed gentleman and opened and closed her mouth. "Her majesty is not ill, far from it! She has never felt better, to be sure," she sniggered, nervously shifting her load of cleaning supplies from one hip to the other.

Chengssu grunted in surprise, rapidly jumping to conclusions. "So that's it," he cried with a leer. "Look here, my good woman, keep me informed—whether my aunt is well, I mean—and I'll pay you. Come to the kitchen entrance of my quarters—number one Wu residence in the east palace—early each morning. You will be well paid."

"How much, Your Highness?" the woman ventured, forgetting her timidity.

"A year's wages for one month's service. You will have to be alert and you will have to report accurately the comings and goings of a person of importance who calls on the empress at night. You understand what I mean? You understand?"

Greed showed in her eyes as she nodded with vigor.

Chengssu watched her appraisingly. "Secrecy and strict attention to orders are required—or severe punishment. Understand?" He drew his finger under her throat.

She bowed abjectly, bobbed her head, and scuttled out of his sight.

The rain had cleared and the morning was bright with sun when Jao awoke. "I've missed the morning audience," she cried in dismay. Sunbeams were slanting across her bed. "Hua!" she called, and her head maid came in hurriedly. "Why didn't you call me?" she chided.

"I was afraid to disturb you!" the maid replied, lowering her eyes.

"Oh, all right then . . . bring tea." Jao was embarrassed beyond measure as her memories of the night flooded over her. This was impossible! Last night was . . . impossible, never to be repeated, never. . . .

A flush spread over her face as she recalled details. Undignified at my age, she thought. What could I have been thinking of? Shaking her head as if to banish the memory, she quickly dressed, ate a hearty breakfast, and then threw herself into her bustling day. To her surprise, she discovered that she had more vigor than usual.

In the evening, Jao was reading one of the many reports that had resulted from all her reforms, when Taiping dropped by to say good night. She did not sit down. After chatting briefly about her day's doings, she turned to leave.

"I'm glad you enjoyed the entertainment last night," Taiping said.

"A nice trap you laid for me," Jao snapped coldly.

"Yes, of course, it was nice, wasn't it?" Taiping assented lightly. "We all meant well, though, and it worked, didn't it? Oh, I must tell you that Chengssu camped on my doorstep today complaining that he was roughly turned away by your guards. I told him plainly that it was totally against protocol for him to descend upon the empress unannounced—inexcusable. He only looked through me as if I didn't exist. I hate the little rat! You are a bit too lenient with him, aren't you, dear Mother?"

Jao frowned. "He's useful. I need him. Too bad that he's turned into such a small-minded creature. He's absorbed all the bad aspects of palace life. Pity."

"Useful?" Taiping echoed. "Maybe he's useful, but he's also dangerous."

"Nonsense! You're just jealous. I patronize all the other Wu cousins as well. He's just a small man. Small."

"He may be small, but not too small to have huge ambitions," Taiping said sulkily. She bowed formally and left the room as Jao watched her uneasily.

Jao took up a report to read as soon as Taiping left. She soon put it down again and restlessly rearranged her silken cushions. She found herself listening to every sound, her thoughts wandering. I'm actually hoping that he'll come, she reflected in dismay. An hour passed. She called her maid to prepare her for sleep. "And, Hua," she said. "Tell Lim to admit Taiping or Princess Chienchen or their escort Feng any evening, but not any of the Wu relatives without notification." She thought that sounded general enough.

"Certainly, Your Majesty," Hua said unctuously as she bowed and said good night.

Jao sat dozing against her pillows until the midnight drum. Then she pinched out her candle and lay down. Almost immediately she heard a soft swishing as the curtains of her bed were pushed aside. She felt a light touch on her shoulder exactly where the big man had placed his hand the night before. Sitting down beside her, he pulled gently on her earlobes and cupped her chin in his hands as he gave her time to accept his presence. His fingers explored her shoulders and lightly stoked the back of her neck.

Delicious, Jao thought. His hands, avoiding her breasts, slid down to her waist. There he encircled her with his gentle, massaging fingers, around and around her navel. He then pressed along her spine and she felt the tingle of relaxation throughout her nerves, muscles, heart, and lungs. He knows the taboo against touching an emperor's head, she thought, which I learned about when I was being prepared for Emperor Taitsung. He exerted pressures of arousal on the palms of her hands and the soles of her feet so slowly that she began to feel a refreshing release from mental tensions as well as physical ones.

What bliss, what bliss, she thought dreamily. His hands shifted to cup her thighs as he prepared her small body to receive his engorged member. Then he took his time, steadily pushing until she almost lost consciousness in her ecstasy. Afterward he cuddled her hips into his lap and soothingly chanted a lullaby until she fell asleep. An hour later he woke her with renewed lovemaking of greater intensity, which continued in a crescendo of a rippling, long-drawn-out, shuddering delight that she felt long after the spasm had relaxed. She fell back in exhaustion. "Dear man, dear man . . ." she murmured as he nestled her against him once more.

"Women like you are the best lovers in the world," he whispered. "Women of many talents who seldom fully experience love at first. They have to have many exposures to bring everything into focus. They have to build up slowly, repeatedly, uninterruptedly."

Jao buried her face in his chest. "How do you know all this?" she asked dreamily.

"I've had a lot of experience—not just experience, I've also experimented. Most importantly, I see to it that I have the right approach," Feng replied carefully.

Dawn was near and Jao was now fully awake. "How did you get here?" she asked gently. "Will there be trouble if you are caught?"

"Yes," he answered. "I am in some danger as I am officially trespassing in the Inner Palace. This time Princess Taiping bribed the guards. Do you want me to continue to come?"

Jao lay still, torn as to what to think, but finally said, "Yes, I do—but not this way, endangering your life if you are caught. Let me think, and if you can come a few more times with Taiping's help, we will arrange a better way."

Feng rose and noiselessly slipped on his robes. "I'll leave now, but tomorrow night I'll return." His bulk was a shadow against the screen, and then gone.

The compound at the Li Ching Gate—the Gate of Beautiful View—was now commonly known as the Gate of Legal Finality. There, Lai and his staff, So and Jo, organized fearful means of extortion and torture to terrorize their victims. It was the center of Lai's star chamber, known and feared all over the country, which worked outside the system of Tang justice.

Lai had created a hardened power base in little over a year. Hundreds had been drawn into his clutches. If a man was pardoned, he was secretly captured again. When Jao declared an amnesty, victims were killed before the amnesty could take effect, so that no one who could possibly testify against the perpetrators was left alive.

Inside these headquarters, Wu Chengssu faced Lai. The cold-faced man was seated at his desk in soundproofed quarters in the prison.

"A new development!" Chengssu exclaimed, arranging his robes tidily over his knees. The room was damp and cold.

"Yes?" Lai asked attentively. The world he lived in was an artificial one consisting of hearsay and allegations. Lai was a man who did not care about the truth at any time. He much preferred distortions and tale-bearing, the fuel that fired his career. He was also deeply in love with the career which provided him both power and excitement.

"The empress has a lover and does not appear in council meetings after a night with him," Chengssu blurted.

"Surely not! Nevertheless, interesting, interesting . . ." Lai began.

Chengssu interrupted. "This is a valuable opportunity. You could run the names of the accused through the morning privy council when the empress is not present and get the emperor's seal on the executions without her knowledge."

"So I can," Lai mused. "So I can. Let me know the next mornings she will be absent then. . . ."

Chengssu rubbed his hands together excitedly. "In return you will eliminate certain enemies of mine."

"Certainly," Lai said with his easy smile, his eyes hard as marbles.

"Start with Jao's two guards, Lim and Suh."

"No," Lai said. "They are insignificants whose disappearance would alarm the empress so much that she would pull down our roof over our heads. All this must be kept secret from her majesty while we move ahead speedily. Use your head, man, don't touch her guards!"

"I hear you," Chengssu said sulkily. "But sooner or later, I'll destroy anyone who crosses me. For now, then, I am targeting the Tang princes—two hundred families or so. They are opposed to Wu Jao's control of the throne and must go. . . ."

Lai looked at Chengssu curiously, enigmatically, but made no comment. The silence lengthened. Chengssu rose, bowed stiffly, and left.

Jao postponed the talk she had promised her lover until she was ready a few nights later. She lit her lamp as soon as he was safely in the door and patted the bed for him to sit. He blinked in the sudden light but jauntily complied.

"It's time to talk," Jao said seriously. "You've been lucky so far. Taiping must be paying heavily. Too chancy, though. We must change all that. I've inquired about you . . . relax, there's nothing too bad in your background, and much that is interesting. For one thing, you are Buddhist and it's said that you take it seriously. You belong to Huayen, I suppose. Everyone does these days."

Feng settled himself uneasily. "I was an orphan who grew up in a monastery. I was taught a trade and grew so handy with it that I reached the dizzy height of master builder. Then I was entrusted with Buddhist building—which has mushroomed lately, as Your Majesty knows. I was an ordained monk by the time I was twenty. But no, I am not Huayen. I avoid such fashionable trends. Besides, the complexities of Huayen, the avatars and ten heavens, and the many heads and many arms or heads of Kuanyin, all that complex symbolism is not for me. I like simplicity and reality, I suppose. Would you call it Life Strength? No matter, I'm sure it's too unrefined for Huayen. I am a follower of Maitreya, He Who Listens to the Common Man."

Jao's eyes glistened. "I too, from childhood . . . I was a nun for almost two years."

Feng was startled. "That explains why we are so attuned sexually."

"Why do you say that?" Jao asked, intrigued.

"Your being a nun and my being a monk explains our common sexuality, not because of the physical part of it, but because of our similar spiritual experiences and our awareness of all living things," he explained carefully.

Jao looked disbelieving. "But sexuality?" she protested. "Buddhism forbids it to the clergy."

"True enough, but what we have learned as Buddhists also teaches us to be greater lovers . . . if we get the chance," he said simply.

"You took the vows of poverty and chastity!" she chided.

"I observed them too. Poverty still," he said, and paused. Jao wanted to laugh when the pause lengthened, but restrained herself because he was serious. "Poverty, yes. Chastity no. I have been influenced by new religious thinking in India that claims that the best and surest way to true spirituality—and the attainment of compassion for all living things—is through the experience of sex. Sharing, joining, uniting with a woman, it teaches us how to love. A woman, after all, is the best creation in a world of marvels."

"Surely, that is not Buddhist teaching," Jao said cynically.

"No, that last thought was mine," he said, studying her.

"Are you implying that being unchaste is a way to attain compassion? And that being compassionate is the end goal of successful human experience?"

"Both concepts are true, I believe. Human beings are mulish and generally unteachable about sharing, about compassion, so an attractive way must be found. So—yes," he said.

"You really do believe these things, don't you?" she asked softly, making up her mind about what to say next.

"Something like that," he said diffidently.

"All right, then. Would you like to exercise your skills as a monk once more? As an abbot of an ancient and prestigious monastery where Maitreya is still worshiped?"

He looked at her quizzically. "You are teasing me, Your Majesty," he said. "It is cruel."

"I see that you like the idea. I think that you would like the ordered life, the worship, the brotherhood, the prestige, even though you appear to be a thoroughly untrammeled spirit, free of all constraints—that's a pose, isn't it?"

"Perhaps," he answered as he gave her a penetrating look. "Do I seem untrammeled to you? Free? Freedom is a dream. There is no freedom in the wild life of the forests or in the wild life of the streets. Constant alertness restrains all living beings—especially when any moment might be the last. That is the way some of us want to live, however, wild and reckless, the only way for some of us who keep trying to break out of restraints."

"Have you escaped your constraints long enough by now?" Jao persisted. "Would you like a more rewarding life?"

Feng lost his look of introspection and met Jao's keen eyes with alertness. "If you are asking whether I am ready to put what I have learned to better use than selling cosmetics, the answer is yes, of course. But such a dream is only a dream, nothing more."

"What if you were appointed abbot of White Horse Monastery here in Loyang?" Jao asked.

"The White Horse?" Feng repeated forcibly. "Clearly impossible for such a one as I. For one thing, the hierarchy would not permit it."

"I believe they might if one approached it in the right way," Jao said. "It would take time. You would have to reacquaint yourself with the monastic rules. You would have to use your personality to persuade the monks that you are one of them. You would have to put your extraordinary intelligence to work on something important for once in your life."

"Intellectual skills? Now then, my good lady—those I have not got, having spent much effort avoiding such learning," he said hastily.

"I am not talking about academic skill of the arid kind that can be acquired, even by stupid people, through study. I am talking about the intelligence that one may be born with, a gift of the gods. I am talking about a gift that makes one able to give. You have it, although you seem to be acting the fool for fear someone will find out. Do you think that anything that might raise you above the herd might destroy your camouflage? Could you bear to be the head of an organization, to manage a busy monastery, for example?"

Feng stiffened. "You mean this, don't you?"

"Fully. I can call in the White Horse officials who control sacristy, business, and guest accommodations, and find out their different needs. I could call in the other officers and find out their hopes and dreams. I could listen carefully and become a patron. After that, it would be no miracle if you receive an invitation to the highest honor in their means to award."

The big man stared at Jao as if he had never seen her before. Then he dropped to his knees to bury his face in her lap. "It would be beyond my wildest dreams," he murmured. "Do you know what monastic life was intended to be originally? When it first began? It was meant to create a model society for the world to see, so people would know that such a society could exist in peace in an otherwise warlike and strife-torn world. To me now, to me a man of fifty, an opportunity to create a utopia has to be the greatest gift of all time!"

Jao listened in surprise, in wonder, and in gratification. "I think I understand. You are a greater man than you seem, and this pleases me immensely. Would you share with me your thoughts and feelings?"

He hesitated. "If you wish . . ."

"And teach me how to feel?"

"That too," he replied simply, from a deep well of knowledge. "If Your Majesty wishes to learn." He then pulled her to him exploringly until she was ready to make love, this time with a tenderness absent before.

The next morning, Jao attended to her daily worship at the shrine in her room somewhat later than usual. She lit her incense before her little statue of Maitreya and stood quietly before it, her hands folded and her mind stilled. She wanted enlightenment as to how to help her talented, disreputable lover. "He needs to be divested of his past," she prayed. "His name means roystering and playing the fool. He needs another identity."

When she completed her worship, a thought flashed across her mind. Royalty could bestow a family name on a commoner in order to honor him, as in Li Chi's case. So perhaps . . . something like this for Feng. She pondered for a time, then called a servant to invite Taiping to her quarters.

When Tai arrived, Jao spoke about trivial matters at first. Finally, she made a direct request. "Taiping, please advise your husband, Hsueh Shao, that I would be much indebted if he would bestow his family name upon and adopt our friend Feng, who may be the new abbot of White Horse Monastery."

Tai narrowed her eyes. "Shao is too young to have a son fifty years old," she said shortly.

"I mean adopt him as his father," Jao returned. "Shao comes from Kaochang, a remote oasis in the west, and so it is unlikely that anyone would know whether it were true or not."

"Revered Mother," Tai said in exasperation, "everyone would guess. . . ."

"The man Feng, your good friend that you introduced to the palace and to me, is now in a position requiring another name, other than the demeaning one he has now. It would be a graceful gesture and quite easy to do," Jao continued levelly.

Tai scowled but said only that she would talk to her husband immediately. After she left, Jao waited impatiently for her return.

The news was not good. "Shao is stubborn," Tai muttered. "He does not want to do this thing. I tried to convince him that it would be an honor, not an indignity, but he would not listen."

"I will promote him, substantially," Jao interrupted, thinking angrily that after all she had done for her son-in-law, he was unwilling to do this thing for her. Ingrate that he was . . . as they all were! Cynically, she tapped her foot on the slate floor and waited.

Taiping looked at her mother from under her brows. "As you wish," she responded, and took her leave with her usual courtesy.

In a short time the name of Hsueh was legally bestowed upon the gratified Feng. He soon applied for, and received, admission to the White Horse Monastery, where he proceeded to exercise his talents in making himself indispensable.

At the same time, Jao exerted herself to discover what was most needed by the monastery. She quickly found that repairs were long overdue and that many buildings were actually in decay. In a formal meeting with craftsmen of many skills, she called in the architect Feng, now Hsueh, in the same manner that she had called in dozens of others and discussed monastery needs. She stayed behind her customary curtain.

"Can you take charge of the rebuilding of the White Horse establishment?" she asked. "Do you have any idea of its costs?"

"A clear understanding, Your Majesty," Hsueh answered.

"Then I will call in the abbot and his chief assistant and discuss the matter. Do they know enough about your architectural skills to call upon you?" Jao asked.

"It seems reasonable. I have already helped them in the mending of several leaks in the main chapel, and they are used to me," Hsueh replied politely.

"Then have plans drawn up and suppliers located at once. Please come to see me as soon as your architectural drawings are ready. I am very interested in the building of public halls and want to be included in your plans at every step. A favor to me," Jao said.

"I hear and obey," Hsueh said elatedly as he bowed out.

The remodeling of the White Horse Monastery took six months. No expense was spared, and a new and impressive complex appeared rapidly. The workmen were interested, the monks were enchanted, the laity stirred to enthusiasm, and the ceremonies accompanying the completion brilliantly carried out. The abbot accepted a transfer to a prestigious establishment in Changan, and Hsueh was rewarded by being installed as the new abbot. People nodded sagely. "He deserves the honor," they told each other. "We have never before had such an excellent temple in our district. Now we have this. This man has accumulated much merit!"

Hsueh's enhanced status became apparent also in the way he was treated at the palace. Now that he was an abbot, he could enter the palace openly. The Wu cousins often welcomed him at the empress's gate and escorted him when he left, holding his horse while he mounted. From being almost unnoticed, he was now only too conspicuous.

Jao and Hsueh had formed the habit of studying the day's construction plans for the monastery when he first appeared in the evening. Now they concentrated on monumental architecture, keeping specific new public buildings in mind. They spread out drawings and discussed details, deciding on the kinds of wood to use, the best tiles for the roofs, the landscaping and layouts. They spent a great deal of time in studying Buddhist structures of all kinds, including the great temples in India from sketches brought back by the monk Hsuantsang. They also pored over designs of the best Chinese buildings: the huge Huayen city temples, the southern mountain monasteries, the northern cave temples of Tatung, and the western cave temples of Tunhuang in the arid plateau country.

One evening when Jao's enthusiasm was at its height, she proposed a novel and ambitious plan. "The emperor Taitsung wished to build an imperial tower in the Changan palace to be called the Tien Tang—Temple of Heaven—and a grand Ming Tang—Tower of Illumination—beside it, but it was never done. A great empire needs a great central audience hall like the Ming Tang. Let us do it! I could get the north gate scholars to research the traditions, and you could draw up the plans. We could tear down the present audience hall, which I don't like anyway, and we could build on its site."

Overwhelmed, Hsueh was silent.

"Could you manage it? The tearing down, the obtaining of great logs from mountain trees, the construction?"

"As soon as Your Majesty obtains prescriptions from the scholars, I could draw up plans and start with the recruitment of workers—thousands of them—and then we shall see," was his laconic answer.

Her enthusiasm not at all dampened, Jao knew her Ming Tang would become a reality.

CHAPTER TWENTY

Jao began to regularize her life again. She worked with Hsueh and once more attended privy council meetings. At once she became aware of the flood of execution orders and set about questioning the censors. When she discovered that most of the accusations were coming from Lai's office, she summoned him and received him without a curtain. He bowed before her with the utmost deference, his usual cordial smile on his lips, his eyes discreetly lowered.

"Explain," she ordered coolly.

"Your Majesty," he answered sadly and patiently, "there are many conspirators out there. They are all intent on assassinating Your Majesty."

Jao stiffened. "What about the findings in the courts of justice that many of the men you list for execution are innocent?" she asked. "The prefect of Loyang himself, he who masterminded the strategy against the traitor Chingyeh, has been condemned by you. Why?"

"He has conspired," Lai stated firmly. "He signed a confession. He is now on the way to the execution grounds."

"Send a reprieve."

"I am afraid it is too late." His tone was sorrowful but reasonable.

"Yes, yes, I hear you. You may go now," Jao said.

She beckoned the sergeant of office guards as soon as Lai bowed himself out. "See that a reprieve pardoning Wei Yuanjung is taken in double-quick time to the execution grounds. Report back to me here."

The guard bowed and left in haste. In less than an hour he was back. "The man you wished to save was found just before execution."

"Were you able to stop proceedings and get him away from the jailers? What happened?"

"Your Majesty, we successfully fulfilled orders. He is now at home."

Jao saw a gleam of satisfaction in the guard's eyes. She gave a small smile, thanked him, and gave him a purse with a reward in it.

In the next few days Jao launched two measures to curb the excesses of her investigating officials. She set up an urn in the West Market in which information designed for her eyes alone was to be deposited. Anonymous complaints could be dropped into it by anyone who had any knowledge of a conspiracy, or had a grievance against government or against the empress herself. Her second measure was the declaration of amnesties as an official part of formal celebrations.

Chengssu was ushered into Lai's office. He had barely seated himself when he burst out, "Something must be done. The empress is spoiling our procedures."

"Not to worry, my friend," Lai said soothingly. "I have had the urn stuffed with complaints in illiterate handwriting, purporting to come from many sources against each individual I want condemned. Wu Jao trusts the evidence of the urn. Fortunately she believes in her own ideas!"

Chengssu burst out laughing and Lai smiled primly.

"Moreover, when I hear that she is about to proclaim one of those amnesties, I quickly have the men who are already condemned executed."

"What about the multitudes she releases?" Chengssu asked worriedly.

"I rearrest them," Lai said blandly, and Chengssu again gave a bark of laughter.

Jao spent each evening studying the plans on the drawing board for the building of the Ming Tang in preparation for her daily visits to the site of construction. The old hall had been torn down in rapid order and the site cleared. Giant trees were felled in remote forests and transported by ox teams and by water to the capital. There, the walls of the city and palace had to be breached temporarily in order to admit the logs. The bustle attendant upon the construction of the enormous throne hall captured the imagination of the population, so that every phase of building was attended by crowds of onlookers.

Jao, attended only by her guards Lim and Suh, visited daily for the twelve months it took to complete the hall. She watched each stage. She was also curious to see how Hsueh performed, and was somewhat taken aback when she found him so absorbed in his work and in his handling of the army of carpenters that he was often unaware of her presence.

Nobody else was unaware. She was a little disgruntled at discovering that she was not needed by Hsueh once his energies had been released in his work and he was free of dependence on her. To her amazement, this fact increased rather than diminished her infatuation.

The Ming Tang reached a height of nearly three hundred feet by the time it was completed in the last month of the year. It towered over the city and could be seen from the horizon for miles around, arousing admiration and awe in both local residents and foreign visitors. Abbot Hsueh was duly awarded the title of duke and given the rank of general in return for his services.

The opening of the great hall was an occasion for celebration and fanfare. The public was invited to view it amid a variety of entertainment. "It has been exactly five years since Kaotsung died almost on this spot," Jao remarked to Chi as they watched the crowds from a high balcony. "I hope his spirit is watching. He would enjoy all this. Maybe he wouldn't like what I've become, though. I'm a changed person."

"No," Chi countered. "You aren't, not much at any rate. You are the same at sixty-three as you were at sixteen now that you have met this Hsueh Huai-i. In spite of the hardships of your sons' deficiencies and the conspiracies against you, this Hsueh is keeping you sweet—yes, don't contradict. You are not growing hard and bitter. Nothing has changed much in your environment. There is still the same bureaucracy, the same community of princes, the same empire at large, and life goes on in the same prosperous and stable fashion. Owing to you—don't interrupt—you are holding it all together. Men are still unruly and ungrateful. You have changed how you view yourself, that is all."

"I don't know what you are suggesting," Jao retorted.

"Formerly your purpose in life was to spend all your energies reinforcing the five men in your family—Kaotsung and the sons who were crown prince or nearest in line for the throne. Now you have changed direction . . . as great a change as east is from west."

"What do you mean?" Jao still felt defensive.

"There is now nobody to reinforce—nobody important, that is. You are alone on the throne."

"Illegally!" she burst out. "I hate it. In the old days with Taitsung and Kaotsung, I had established and respected positions, and my life was real. Now I have all this heavy responsibility of rule, behind the fronts my sons provide, and I have to help that monkey Chengssu too, and my life is not real. It is all a sham and I hate it!"

Chi eyed her somberly. "It is a sham, true. Change it, then."

He bowed and before she could collect her wits, he pretended that he had permission to withdraw and backed away, then stopped and said one quiet sentence: "You and I have this in common: we can't escape. When you have a powerful position in the palace, whether eunuch or empress, it's a grim business of either up—or out."

Jao shuddered. She knew that he was referring to the throne and her reach for it.

Chi bowed himself out and passed Chengssu, who was entering.

"Illustrious Aunt," Chengssu began in greeting.

"Yes?" Jao said. "What now?"

Wu Chengssu decided that his moment had come to strike openly. "You are too vulnerable and unassuming in your present role as empress. You should become Huang, not Huanghou."

"And you should become the crown prince, I suppose!" she answered with an irony that passed over his head.

"Yes," he said, "we Wus have much in common."

"You mean that we have the throne in common?"

"Of course!" he agreed, and that surprised her so much that she ended the conversation abruptly, much to his mystification.

A wave of conspiracies mounted. Jao was appalled. More officials of higher and higher rank were brought into court for treason. "This is out of hand," she told Hsueh one evening. "Tell me what you know about it. You have never commented."

"I avoid that outfit," he said. "I never ride out of the White Horse compound without a bodyguard of armed monks. We sometimes get into brawls in the street, with various Taoists and censors and the like, but nothing to amount to anything, just street fights."

"What do you mean by 'that outfit'?"

"Lai and Jo and, er . . . Lai and Jo," he answered, carefully omitting reference to Wu Chengssu. Jao looked at him thoughtfully but decided not to question him further.

He is unwilling to criticize my nephew, she thought when he left her. She was beginning to suspect Chengssu, but, still needing him, she chose to give him the benefit of the doubt.

Nobody would tell her anything, but the implications were shattering enough, reflecting as they did upon her rule. She considered putting Juitsung on the throne with full powers, with herself as advisor only. She was in the middle of elaborate plans for a public restoration ceremony when Juitsung paid an unexpected visit. He looked strained and pale, but Jao was too distracted to notice. "This restoration will restore confidence and halt the conspiracies," she told her son.

"It won't w-w-work," Juitsung said. "It would only intensify the conspiracies boiling up in the three great centers of power—and in a dozen not-so-great ones. They all want the throne itself. Chengssu will only become more fiercely hostile to me as a rival. I can't accept your proposal because if I did, it would only t-t-trigger open war between two of the major power seekers—the Tang loyalists in the bureaucracy and the Wu forces. I am already a storm center. If I become emperor in truth, I would soon be assassinated. And I can't accept for that other reason—my impractical, apolitical nature."

Jao gazed at him thoughtfully. "You mentioned three groups of power seekers. Were you referring to the Tang princes as the third? The princes of Han and Yueh? There are six or seven brothers of Taitsung still alive and active, and more than three tens of others of princely rank."

"As far as I know, those old senior princes are peaceful graybeards. What discontent there might be is surely confined to their sons," Juitsung returned. "N-N-No, it's Lai and company."

Jao threw down her papers angrily. "Nonsense! He is just an underling at my beck and call. When I say stand, he stands. When I say kneel, he kneels!"

Juitsung looked at her enigmatically. Although a recluse, he kept a knowing finger on the pulse of political affairs.

"Why do you look at me like that?" she asked.

"Are you aware of how threatened most of us T-t-tang princes feel?" he asked mildly.

"Which princes?" she returned, instantly alert.

"There is Prince Han's son, Huang, who seems to be the center of discontent," Juitsung said in a tone of voice that captured Jao's whole attention at once.

"And there is Prince Juitsung, how does he come into it?" she asked sharply.

"He doesn't, but Prince Huang has issued a decree falsely claiming to have come from me in which he calls upon all princes to raise troops in their d-d-districts to move on Loyang in order to rescue me. The false decree has inspired another Tang prince, Langyeh, to issue a second one saying that the empress is trying to destroy the imperial family and raise up the Wu clan in its place."

He watched his mother as he said this, and put out his hand to her when she winced. "How does it happen that you know this and I don't?" she asked.

"The news is probably w-w-waiting for you in privy council at this moment. Everyone is afraid of telling you."

"But you are not?" Jao retorted, gaining time to think.

"Of course I am. I am right in the center of this. A close friend indirectly warned me that my name was being used."

Jao stood up, her expression grim. "Be careful, then, and just now refuse to see visitors of any sort, especially visitors from—anyone at all! I'll put a special guard around your residence. And, my son, thank you. . . ."

The princes' revolt collapsed a week after it had begun. "What a pathetic effort," Jao told Hsueh. "More feeble even than the rebellion of Li Chingyeh four years ago. A senior prince of the Tang imperial house tries to restore a legitimate emperor because of a possible usurpation by me, and what happens? I have the complete support of my army and can even count on the rebel princes themselves to run away at the first opportunity. Now I know that I have the goodwill of the people who count."

She felt exultant, but greatly hardened at the same time. "I know what to do about conspirators against me personally. If they want war, they shall have war!"

She immediately sent for Chengssu. "You must strengthen the Wu faction," she said. "We may be at war with the Tang loyalists, although the princes as a center of rebellion have been destroyed. Now we must deal with all the bureaucrats who are loyal only to Tang."

Chengssu's eyes glittered. "War it is, then. I will build new Wu ancestral shrines here in Loyang, leaving the Tang shrines in second place in Changan, and raise the Wu ancestors posthumously in rank. Tomorrow I will devise a plan to glorify Your Majesty in some unprecedented way to build up Wu prestige."

Jao nodded, her eyes hard. "Come back tomorrow and present your plan."

Chengssu followed through on his promise. His plan included the creation of an auspicious talisman to give luster to the launching of a new dynasty. Jao was impressed by his inventiveness and eagerly welcomed his work in discovering a miraculous stone in the Lo River. It bore the inscription, "Holy Mother comes to rule in perpetual prosperity." She publicized the so-called discovery by emphasizing the perpetual prosperity theme in a spectacle the likes of which had never before been seen in Tang times. She had a special altar built, and before it, in a great semicircle, she displayed state treasures never shown to the public, costly insignia, rare tribal gifts, and foreign birds and animals strange to China. The Lo stone was the centerpiece.

The New Year's ceremonies offered Jao an opportunity to conduct glamorous rites in the new Ming Tang, so she staged the festivities hinting at her rise to supreme power in three ceremonies. To celebrate New Year's Day itself, Jao wore the most sumptuous of her imperial robes and carried the jewel-jade kuei, which symbolized emperorhood. Juitsung, impeccable in appearance and behavior, acted as first assistant, while his son, the crown prince, served as second. Sacrifice to Heaven was first on the program, then sacrifices in honor of the founder of Tang, Kaotzu. Following this, to everyone's surprise, came an equal sacrifice to the spirit of Jao's father. There was a great stir in the audience as the meaning of this act was recognized, especially when Wu Chengssu was appointed head of Chancellory. The culminating accolade was Jao's assumption of the title Holy Mother Divine Imperial One.

"A mouthful, that title," Taiping said on their return from the ceremony. "I shall shorten it to Holy Mother—easier and just as polite. Your ceremony today was the most remarkable I have seen!"

"Chengssu arranged it all. He reminds me of myself when I was first appointed empress. I staged the grandest show ever at the time," Jao returned nostalgically.

"For whose sake was this show then, yours or his?" Taiping snapped inadvisedly.

"Mine, of course." Jao's tone was curt. "Don't exaggerate Cheng's powers. He is a busybody—no more."

"I am not so sure. He is both stupid and ambitious, and that is lethal. And now he is Chief of Chancellory," Taiping murmured, having the last word, as she often did. She was the only person in the palace who could. She bowed politely and left at once.

That evening Jao repeated her new title gleefully to Hsueh. "It sounds all-encompassing, does it not? Covering all bases . . ." She laughed, but he did not. She put her small hand over his great one. "Do you not like it?"

"It makes a mystery of you, making you even greater than a mere emperor, making you a goddess, even more powerful," he replied unhappily.

"Well?" she asked.

"Not my affair, but yours—you must do what you must do," he said finally.

At the same time that she was putting on these demonstrations of imperial prestige, Jao worked long hours reviewing the flood of confessions. Lai and his assistants were able to insert into the regular bureaucracy more of their own men. Still, they did not have complete control of the system of justice yet, and continued to hide their illegal seizures and the tortures that they were obliged to employ to get confessions.

Two courageous men were their chief obstacles: a magistrate named Hsu Yugung, and Dee Jenjer. The empress knew them both personally and admired their characters. Manufactured evidence against them or against their clients could not get by her. Dee and his colleague Hsu began to speak openly against the spy system. Even more infuriating to Lai and Chengssu was their defense of the accused in open court. Hsu had such an enviable record from his days as magistrate in provincial posts that he was known for fairness throughout the country. He was respected even more for his record of never having had a man flogged in order to obtain a confession. Teahouse gossip had it that anyone appearing before Lai was sure of death unless he was defended by Hsu. Hsu began to appear daily in the hall of audience, where he quietly defended the wrongly accused (both underlings and superiors) so well that he saved the lives of hundreds. Jao supported him, recognizing integrity when she saw it, and began to rely on his judgment. Many cases asking for clemency were also being presented by Judge Dee.

More stirring than any of the other demands on her time, thoughts, and emotions was a novel development from within the Buddhist establishment. A group of priests had been studying a sutra called the Great Cloud Classic, which dealt with an incarnation of Maitreya. They offered an opinion that caused a great sensation. Their interpretation was awesome: that the signs all pointed to the current existence of an incarnation in the empress herself. They argued that Maitreya had come to earth in the guise of the empress in order to bring the blessings of prosperity and good rule to all mankind.

The Abbot Hsueh was deeply involved with the movement. "I did not feel that an ancient animistic symbol like the Lo stone was very helpful," he told Jao one evening.

"Didn't you like my title of Holy Mother Divine Imperial One?" she teased.

"It's just Taoist superstition, bestowing on you attributes only just beyond the merely human," Hsueh said critically.

Jao stared. "Is that so insignificant?" she answered stiffly.

"Certainly not! But our Buddhist concept of the avatar of Maitreya is infinitely more encompassing and magnificent. And I believe it is valid," Hsueh returned slowly. "You are a being of such astounding abilities and such strong policies of reaching out to the poor, that I can well believe that you are an incarnation of Maitreya."

Jao was speechless. She put out her hand blindly. "Do you mean . . . do you really mean that?" she stammered.

He nodded, too profoundly moved to speak. She, too, was deeply stirred.

That evening they worshiped together in the new Great Cloud Chapel, sitting up all night in quiet meditation before opening the doors to others.

Living with the assurance that she indeed was an incarnation gradually became a reality to Jao and changed her. She began to believe that the miraculous events of her life and her own great successes could be explained in terms of an incarnation. She ordered a printing of the sutra and its wide distribution to the large Buddhist population of the country. In addition, she funded the building of a Great Cloud temple in every district.

Most significantly, Jao now felt that it was in her stars to be emperor in fact as well as in theory. The titles she held—Empress and Empress Dowager—did not confer supreme power. Moreover, an old prophecy had recently been brought to her attention. In Taitsung's day, the planet Venus had come into visibility several days in succession, and the astrologers had declared that it was a portent of the future ascendancy of a woman to supreme power. After three generations, the story went, a female sovereign named Wu Wang would control Tang as the martial king. Emperor Taitsung took offense and ordered all officials named Wu sent to distant areas. He consulted his grand astrologer and was told that the Wu in question was actually living in the palace as one of his harem, and that in forty years would rule the empire. The portents showed that this was inevitable. Taitsung replied, "Why not exterminate all possible suspects?" The reply was that Heaven's decree could not be set aside, but that in forty years time, the one fated to rule would be aging and growing more compassionate, and that if Taitsung slew her, Heaven would cause another to be born who would be worse. Taitsung accepted this, and Wu Jao continued to live as a tsairen unrecognized and in peace.

Now Jao resurrected this prophecy, and to her joy, the people, including some of the most conservative scholars, accepted it. Jao took her time, however, and her progress to the throne was not hurried.

Only in early September of 690 did Jao permit Chengssu to organize a petition calling for a change of dynasty, from Tang to Chou—which was the name of a thousand-year-old dynasty founded by a legendary Wu. A censor presented the petition and Jao rejected it, in accordance to Chinese practice. Another petition containing sixty thousand signatures was then presented. These names included all officials, the names of surviving Tang royal relatives, the important members of the Buddhist and Taoist establishments, the great rural families, and the tribal chiefs.

Jao did not accept this second petition either. A third effort headed by Juitsung, who also requested that his name be changed to Wu, was graciously accepted by Jao. She followed through by declaring a general amnesty and by holding a grand ceremony honoring the change of dynasty. Even then she did not ascend the throne herself. She waited three days for this.

Jao was so caught up in her excitement during these final days that she could not sleep. She floated through the days in euphoria while her army of servitors flawlessly carried out the prescribed rituals. Wu Jao was now the Son of Heaven, and she carried her family to the heights with her. Juitsung became imperial heir, and his son imperial grandson. Chengssu became Prince Wei, and Sanssu Prince Liang, while the entire Wu clan of twenty-three households was raised to princely rank. Jao held up vigorously, but when it was all over, she could barely stand upright and had to be assisted to her quarters.

Chengssu, also worn out with all his exertions to bring about this change, was in no condition to bear the shock of finding that a Tang prince was heir to the Wu throne after all. He withdrew to his home, seriously ill.

"Well, Mother, Holy and Divine Huang, I congratulate you!" Taiping bubbled after the inauguration, when the family gathered in Jao's rooms.

"My congratulations also," Juitsung said, echoing his sister in the easy way they had.

"You two, always teasing," scolded Jao, who was nevertheless sparkling with the effervescence of complete and total gratification.

Juitsung put a goblet of wine into her hand. It was a product of a famous vintage from Turfan. "To my mother, the Huang!" he said.

"To my mother, the Huang—*not* Huanghou!" Taiping said, and they all erupted into the easy laughter that privacy and the cynical understanding of court life gave them.

Almost immediately after the fanfare and excitement of the launching of the new dynasty died down, Wu Jao came into conflict with the star chamber. Lai and his assistant, Jo, had tried repeatedly to frame the intrepid Hsu and had failed. At last Jo had managed to have Hsu arrested for conspiring against the throne and ordered executed. Jao was informed. Angered, she stopped the execution and released Hsu, offering him a new post. He refused the appointment, and Jao called him to a personal interview to find out why.

When he appeared, he looked far from the calm and courageous defender of others who had confronted her so often in privy court. She was faced with a miserable man kneeling abjectly at her feet.

"Why?" she asked gently.

"Your humble servant is like the deer of the forest who is constantly hunted. Your servant is unable to fulfill his duties as a judge bound to uphold the laws, because he would be forced to connive at a monstrous perversion of Your Majesty's justice. If your servant refuses to connive, he would be killed. Your servant must refuse this appointment."

"Nevertheless, I insist," Jao said, steely voiced. "I shall have you guarded at all times and protected to the full extent of this ruler's authority." Hsu reluctantly accepted his assignment, and Wu Jao felt confident that this setback would be enough warning to Lai's investigations.

It was not. Pressured by the empress's nephew, Jo stepped up his program of victimizing Chengssu's private enemies. Among these new victims was the powerful General Chiu, who had served Jao in the princes' rebellion and other crises. He was summarily executed. Wu Jao immediately called in Lai and ordered him to investigate his colleague Jo. Lai did what he was told to do and used his most fearful methods of torture to obtain a full confession. Jao spared Jo's life, exiling him, but en route to his place of exile, the relatives of some of his victims caught up with him and the life of the notorious Jo came to a sudden end.

If Jao thought that Jo's demise and her own coldness to him would restrain Chengssu, she was mistaken again. Not long after Jo's death, the faithful censor Wei Yuan and Jao's good friend Dee were arrested and accused. Lai offered to spare their lives if confessions were obtained at the first interrogation. Wei refused. "If you want my head," he said to Lai, "why not cut it off? Why bother with confessions?" For this he was deprived of all amenities and treated harshly.

Dee, on the other hand, obliged with a statement that sounded like a confession: "Now that the Chou revolution has taken place, the old Tang officials are sure to be executed for loyalty to Tang." His treatment improved and some of his guards were even friendly. Realizing an opportunity, Dee loosened the winter lining of his robe, wrote a letter about his persecution to his son on a piece of the silk, and restored the lining.

"Now that the weather is turning warmer," he said to a guard, "will you have this coat sent to my home to have the lining removed?"

In hopes of a generous reward from the family, two of the guards agreed to deliver the coat. Dee's son, correctly interpreting the request as being more than it seemed, found the letter and immediately went to the empress. She received him, read the letter, and sent for Lai to explain. He denied any persecution and asked Jao to send someone to look at Dee for himself. The official Jao sent, terrified by having to enter the dreaded premises, took one look and returned almost at once to report that all was in order. Lai followed this report with a forged confession of Dee's guilt ending with a plea for execution as his last request.

Jao was puzzled by this and deeply troubled. Her loyal friend was accused by her loyal appointee, and now Dee was confessing that he had betrayed her. It made no sense. Jao ordered that Dee be brought before her.

"If you utter one word against me to the empress," Lai told Dee while personally escorting him to the palace, "I will kill all your family—after torture!"

Jao looked unsmilingly at the prisoner Dee when he was ushered into her presence heavily bound, as if he were the worst kind of criminal. Jao raised her eyebrows at this.

"Did you actually confess to conspiring against me?" she asked.

"Yes," Dee answered briefly when Lai dug the tip of a dagger into his back. Jao saw Dee wince.

"Leave," she told Lai peremptorily. Lai stood his ground.

"Did you hear me?" she asked ominously. At her tone, her own guards stepped forward. Protesting loudly, Lai took his time, glaring threateningly at Jao's guards. They did their duty in spite of his warning looks, and Lai was forced to leave the hall.

"Now," Jao said, "tell me the truth. Did you actually conspire?"

"I would never betray you," he said. "I would have died under torture eventually had I not obeyed Lai."

"You, too!" Jao exclaimed. "How dare these miserable officials mistreat my friends!" She stared at Dee in confusion, and he stared back, equally confused.

"You do not know about the extent of Lai's operations, then? About the tortures that your most loyal and innocent officials like Censor Wei are undergoing from these secret police?"

Jao listened carefully. "I shall expect you to report everything to me in writing—down to the last detail. In the meantime, I assume this is a forgery." She handed him the confession with his plea for execution. He read it.

"Let me prove its falseness," he said.

Jao sent for her scribe to bring paper and brush. Dee wrote something for her that made her chuckle: it was a quip at Lai's poor calligraphy. The forgery was in fact clumsily written in comparison with Dee's elegant script.

With profound apologies to Dee and Wei for the suffering they had undergone, she released them as was her custom, and, sent them both, heavily guarded, to posts in the country before recalling them almost at once for promotion.

It soon became clear to the court that the star chamber had lost ground in a serious way. It was also apparent that Wu Chengssu was not advancing. His hopes for the position of heir to the throne were lost at the time of the change of dynasty when Juitsung was named heir. Aware of his tenuous position, he felt it necessary to distance himself from the disgraced Lai and exert himself to regain influence. Seeing these efforts, the prime minister secretly warned the empress about giving Chengssu too much power.

"He is my nephew. Therefore I trust him as a confidant," Jao said.

"A nephew is not so close to an aunt as a son to his father, and yet there have been parricides. How much more likely to find such acts among nephews? Wu Chengssu is not only a nephew, but a prince and first minster of the Chancellory. His power is almost equal to your own. I fear that Your Majesty will not long peacefully possess the throne."

Having this possibility brought into the open forced Jao to do some thinking. Perhaps Chengssu was not the harmless busybody that she had always thought him. Weak people were often the most dangerous of all . . . she ought to have known this, she thought.

Two days later, Jao deprived Chengssu of his position but left him his princedom. She soothed him immediately, however, during the New Year's celebrations by using him as first assistant and Sanssu as second in another grand ceremony in the Ming Tang. On this occasion she left out Juitsung and his children, who were happy to watch the performance from screened alcoves.

Without warning, however, Juitsung's household was suddenly unsettled by an accusation of witchcraft. A slave girl swore she heard Juitsung's wife, Lady Liu, and his favorite concubine, Te Fei, casting spells against the empress. Informed of this, Jao had had both women to her quarters for a formal visit, feeling sure the witchcraft accusation was nonsense. After the visit, however, the two women completely disappeared. Juitsung was worried, and Jao, suspicious, did not know what to think. Everyone in high position suddenly seemed suspicious to her.

When, however, the same slave girl who had accused the women turned on Juitsung, Jao listened to her accusations with incredulity and surrendered the girl to the office of Criminal Affairs to be investigated. She was soon found guilty of treason by the dalishe and executed.

Immediately after her execution, two of Juitsung's closest friends were accused by Chengssu of conspiring against the empress. Lai had the two accused officials executed in front of the great south gate. Unknown to Jao, they were killed by a method long outdated in Chinese practice as excessively cruel—they were pulled apart by oxen. After this, a freeze settled on officials throughout the palace. No one dared open his mouth in criticism or have anything to do with Juitsung.

Jao was resting in her palace when a distant roar roused her. Curious, she called for her eunuch. There was some kind of torture going on in the palace, he said. More than that he did not know. The uproar sounded again and again, horrifying her. She sent for Chi.

When he arrived, she asked whether the eunuch's story was true.

"Yes, Your Majesty." For the first time in their long association, his voice was cold.

"Where? And by whose order?" she persisted, deeply distressed.

"In the kitchen court of your son Juitsung. They are flogging and racking his maids. As to who is doing this, I have no answer." He refused to meet her eyes.

"You may leave," Jao said angrily. Torture of Juitsung's servants? Impossible! And what was this story about Juitsung's friends being killed in the public square by a method banished by Taitsung? Such enormities happening in her reign, without her authorization or knowledge. . . . Full of wrath, Jao rose to her feet with a jerk and hurried for the scene of uproar herself.

As she approached Juitsung's quarters, she could hear the screams of the maids: "Yes, yes . . . it is true . . . the imperial heir is guilty of conspiring. . . ." She walked into the courtyard to see her old gardener An, who had taught her everything she knew about the raising of peonies, leap forward to confront Lai. He was screaming, "The imperial heir is innocent! Innocent of all wrongdoing! You are the guilty one! No one could be a more dutiful son than he. Cut out my heart as proof of this truth!"

An had his small, sharp pruning knife in his hand. He plunged it into his abdomen and fell at Lai's feet, his blood and intestines spattering the pavement. The interrogators stopped open-mouthed in the middle of operations to watch, and Lai stood dumbfounded over the fallen man. Suddenly, they noticed Jao's presence. A deathly silence fell on the crowd while they opened a path for her.

"Quickly—bring my physician," she ordered. She was beside herself with shock and anger at such an occurrence within her palace walls. She had seldom seen blood spilled, and when she slipped in An's blood, she paled and searched the court with angry eyes to find the ones responsible. Lai was unobtrusively slipping out of the gate. He pretended not to hear her and disappeared as if by magic, leaving his henchmen to face her wrath.

"Arrest these men!" she cried, waving at the bloodstained interrogators. Her guards, who were crowding into the court in increasing numbers, obeyed instantly.

"Help these wounded servants to their pallets and give them aid," she ordered her eunuchs, who were not far behind the guards.

"This man's life must be saved," she said to her doctor, who had arrived perspiring. "Save him," she repeated.

"If Heaven wills," muttered the great man as he threw off his robes and got down on his knees to see if the unconscious An was still breathing.

"If Heaven wills, yes, but more to the point just now—if your emperor wills," Jao retorted while she watched the doctor carefully pack the intestines back into place and stitch up the gaping wound with mulberry-bark fiber. He then applied chimney soot against infection, and bound his patient tightly before allowing him to be moved.

"Take him into my quarters," Jao said. "Will he live?"

"He may," the doctor replied, eyeing the empress curiously. "He looks tough. He must not be fed even water for three days."

"He is my faithful old gardener and I want him entirely restored," Jao said, her anger still roiling her. "I hold you responsible."

The crisis attended to, Jao demanded to be taken to her son. She found him in a remote garden on his hands and knees, weeding. He was pale but composed.

"What are you doing?" Jao demanded sharply. "Are you aware of what is going on in your household?"

He rose at once and brushed off his knees. "I am f-f-finishing the work that An was doing when he was taken," Juitsung said. "It is the least I could do . . . I heard him and s-s-saw what he did."

"You saw him?' Jao asked in surprise. "Where you were?"

"I was in the kitchen court with my s-s-six sons. We were . . . f-f-forced to watch."

Jao narrowed her eyes ominously. "Was this attack on you personal or was it just a warning . . . against conspiring?"

"There is no doubt about what happened here today. I have known what t-t-to expect ever since the two mothers of my sons disappeared and my friends were torn apart in the square by oxen. I am the t-t-target . . . an obstacle to the throne."

"You knew and did not tell me?" she asked.

"I cannot run to my mother when I am hurt," he said quietly. "I cannot interfere w-w-with you."

"Interfere!" she exclaimed. "What do you mean? What on earth do you mean? If your friends were not trying to conspire for my death, as I was told, what were they doing here with you?"

"We were not conspiring . . . we were d-d-discussing the poetry of our gifted young Tang authors, Sun and Li," he said sadly. He looked away from her at his sons, who were also working in the garden. "Why should I conspire for the throne when I do not even want it? Your Majesty knows this well," he continued softly.

Jao swallowed and tears came to her eyes. "You shall never again be threatened as long as I am alive. Neither you nor your sons ever again." She left his presence.

Jao lost no time in ordering Lai to drop all charges against the imperial heir—and everyone in his household—and ordered Lai himself into exile. The palace and city seemed to be freed at last from the terror of the star chamber.

Five years had passed since the inauguration of the new dynasty, and Abbot Hsueh Huai-i had gradually become dislodged from his preeminent position in Jao's life. He reacted in eccentric ways, and this served to alienate him further from her affections. Attempting to regain Jao's favor, Hsueh planned a great ceremony in the Ming Tang at Lantern Festival time to honor her. He had a two-hundred-foot Buddha painted on a banner and hung on the Tien Tang tower. Wu Jao was to be a central figure in the ceremony, but she did not come at all, either to take part or to attend the services.

Hsueh was a passionate man, and his experiences with Jao had been of a passionate nature, sustained over a long period of time. Unable to accept anything less from her than the best, Hsueh chose a windy night and set fire to the Ming Tang. I raised her up to the skies, I can now bring her down, he thought in anguish. The flames soon mounted to the top of the costly tower and for hundreds of feet above it, in a fire so intense that it lit up the whole city and sent burning brands over all the surrounding area. The Tien Tang next door caught fire as well. The wind tore down the giant Buddha inside and the fire reduced the whole to ashes which smoldered for days afterward.

Jao immediately suspected Hsueh and sent for him. After some delay, he came. She surveyed his unkempt appearance, his bloodshot eyes and his lifeless stance. He sustained her gaze quietly, as he always had, until she dropped her eyes, confused.

"I am hearing about wild orgies in the temple grounds and excesses of extremist Buddhists among your followers. I am told of their disorderly conduct and abuse of private property. What have you to say?" Jao asked.

Hsueh maintained his steady look. "No criminal conduct on my part, absolutely not. Sometimes the fervor of the multitudes of worshipers gets out of hand."

"Then much of what I have been told is untrue?" she asked.

"Probably," he answered. "It is a long time since I have seen you and I am out of touch with the latest political turns. This much I know—you and I have been traveling in opposite directions since our creative architectural days. You were then a beautiful person, worthy of the highest honors. Now you have hardened and are suspicious of everyone and everything . . . and there is the stain of the star chamber. And as for me? I have been trying to rid myself of secular trappings of all kinds—and have become in truth an unworldly fellow."

"What are the 'opposite directions' you are talking about?" Jao asked bleakly. She did not really need to be told what the opposite directions were. She knew very well.

"Yours has been to achieve the throne for yourself and keep it. Mine is to flee the palace and the trappings of secular life as much as possible," he said.

"Why did you do it?" she said in anguish. They were talking past each other but with clear understanding on both sides. "For me, it was like being burned with the Ming Tang."

"Not you . . . only the dreams of you and our life together, and our visions of the Great Cloud and of worlds beyond our ken, all gone now. In ashes."

"Oh, that is cruel of you," she cried. "Cruel beyond belief. You may be free to seek your spirituality, but I am not. Do you know what I have to do about your gigantic act of destruction? Do you know? So painful that it is unendurable to me. Unendurable."

Silence fell between them, a silence infinitely long.

"You will rebuild the Ming Tang," she said finally, the tears running down her cheeks unchecked.

"Is there time?" he asked in sadness.

Her answer was barely audible. "No, there won't be."

"You have given me everything good. What you are about to do now is right also. I must be punished. I am ready, more than ready, for my next rebirth and for what is beyond. You have my humble and eternal gratitude for giving me the best that could possibly happen to one man in his lifetime."

He bowed with deliberation, and left knowing that because of what he had done he would never see Jao again.

She sat a long time, staring into the rafters, noticing idly that there were cobwebs there and that over the door some starlings were building a nest.

"This is the lowest, the very lowest moment in my life," she told herself in despair. "All the other bad times were the fault of others. This is the fault of one only—myself."

The sites of the pagoda and the Ming Tang were raked over and a palisade of bamboo slats was erected around it to protect the new lumber and other construction materials. Hsueh arrived daily with his armed bodyguard to supervise the rebuilding of the foundations of the new Ming Tang.

One day a maid came to call him to partake of refreshments with the empress. He dropped his measuring tools and with deliberate slowness followed her. They proceeded through one gallery after another, not toward the personal palace of the empress, but away from it. He became suspicious, and when a platoon of enormous women guards appeared behind him, he attempted to turn back. He was too late. The women guards, who protected the younger palace ladies, silently blocked his path and propelled him into a remote yard, where he was overcome. He did not resist at all—in this way Jao was protecting him from humiliation and shame and physical torture in a public trial. His body was sent at once in an unmarked cart to the White Horse Monastery, where it was carefully cremated with high honors and deep affection by the monks who knew him only as one of them.

That night Wu Jao slept badly, plagued once more by nightmares with which she had to cope without Mi's help.

Gardener An leaned his bamboo rake against the wall and gave a critical look around. Nature had been kind—the May day was cloudless, the breeze over the river warm and scented, and the peonies on the terraces slanting downward to the water were at the height of perfection. An crinkled his eyes in satisfaction. He was not a smiling man and seldom spoke in praise of anyone or anything, but there were times when his emotions got the best of him and the crinkles appeared. This day he gazed at his masses of dew-sprinkled flowers in all their flamboyant colors and his eyes and mouth were pursed. "Never seen 'em better," he grunted.

"I agree," said a voice.

Startled, An bobbed his head. "Your Majesty!" he ejaculated.

Jao stood in the middle of the flagstone terrace contemplating with ardor the sight before her. "Well done, An! I see you haven't lost your skills. These peonies cannot be matched anywhere in the empire, especially those deep, velvety red ones." Jao was immaculately dressed in dark red brocade, her only jewelry the Burma rubies in her tiara. She looked like a peony herself.

An bowed deeper to hide his gratification. "Your Majesty!" he said with fervor.

"How is your stomach, An?" Jao inquired. She was not just being polite. She was interested.

"Good as new!" An stuttered.

"That's all right, then," Jao returned with satisfaction. It had been three years since she had rescued the faithful An when he had disemboweled himself in Juitsung's courtyard. "It's good to see you healthy. Good to see you at work—and what superb work it is!"

"Your Majesty!" An exclaimed while he ducked a grateful obeisance, then hastily disappeared as Chi entered the garden.

He looked around him with pleasure. Jao smiled at his appreciative glance, then said gently, "Chi, you must tell me. What is it that has made you cool to me?"

His eyes grew distant. "I can't speak of it, Your Majesty," he said.

She stiffened. "Must I command you?" she demanded.

"Very well. Your clemency to Lai—who has made a fool of you," Chi said bitterly. "And your support of the unredeemable Chengssu."

Jao was silent a long time. "This is unfair of you," she said at length. "You encouraged me to become emperor, and I couldn't have done so without their help."

"That is debatable. You underestimate yourself. You are a magnificent administrator, and in a crisis unmatchable—a true Son of Heaven at such times. What I am saying is that you don't act like an emperor at all times. You still act like a woman behind the scenes, expecting someone out there to take the responsibility if events turn out badly. There is no one out there. The emperor is you—if you will only realize the fact fully." He kowtowed forlornly.

Somewhere deep within her, Jao had known these truths, but had never had to face them. She remembered the death of her lover Hsueh, and said slowly, "When Hsueh died I had to face up to self-condemnation, but now I must face the stark and terrible condemnation of others. It is true that Lai went to extremes against anyone who might be opposing me. It is true that he used reprehensible means, but he has been punished. It is true that I have given princedoms to a score or more members of the Wu family—Chengssu is now the most powerful person in court after me—and it is true that he has destroyed his own political enemies rather than mine."

Chi listened intently but said nothing. Jao continued, "The thing to do now is to inaugurate a new era free of secret police and all that went with the hunting down of conspirators. I must restore traditional government and stability."

"Yes," Chi said in approval. "Yes . . ."

She continued, "Especially in the Office of Justice, to build a strong Censorate. That will make it impossible for Chengssu to get at his political opponents directly anymore. I have many capable new men in office—people like Dee and the redoubtable Hsu and the stalwart Wei, arrested by Lai three times and saved by me each time."

Jao saw Chi's eyes light up in approval. She took his hands between her own and pressed them. "You may go now. Once again I am able to function—as Huang, this time. There are no words good enough to thank you."

Elated, Chi left at once, and Jao summoned her secretary. "Call in a courier to send for Judge Dee at once."

Jao's eyes were warm with friendliness as she greeted Dee. *"Hau-hau!"* she said, shaking her own hand in the conventional gesture of goodwill. He bowed respectfully.

"Please be seated," Jao invited. "There, in Taitsung's favorite chair."

Dee settled in the oversized chair while looking around him curiously. The room was spacious and heated by large braziers of burning charcoal. Attendants hovered in the background, where a table was spread with breakfast delicacies. "Good food and good company!" he commented politely in his brisk manner. Jao smiled and poured his tea herself, waving the eunuchs out of earshot.

"Kaotsung wouldn't live here and so the palace decayed, but it was Taitsung's main Loyang palace, and I have had it rebuilt since becoming Huang because of its splendid location. It's comfortable now."

Dee gazed at the shining pillars, at the scrolls on the walls by Yen Lipen and Wu Taotzu, and at the great, highly polished beams overhead. "Hsueh Huai-i?" he asked.

Jao glanced defensively at him. "Hsueh supervised the carpenters, but I did all the rest." She filled her cup with hot tea and changed the subject. "Did you ever meet Yen Lipen when he was in charge of the censorate?" she asked.

"No, he was too lofty a personage for the likes of me. That was twenty years ago when I was a lowly magistrate in Changping," he answered, sipping his excellent tea with appreciation.

"You did not know him but he knew you. I have just read your file and discovered that Yen himself read all your reports because of the sensational cases you solved."

"Oh, those," said Dee disparagingly. "The case of the poisoned bride was one, I suppose."

"Yes, but the one that impressed Yen the most was the murder of a poor shopkeeper by his wife. I'll read you the passage from the report:

'The magistrate Dee Jenjer initiated and brought to a conclusion this small case, risking the loss of his rank and position, and estranging the sympathy of the people in his district. His motivation was that justice be done and the death of a miserable, small man avenged. This I consider exemplary conduct, worthy of a special citation.' "

"Oh, that one," returned Dee briefly, but he was pleased.

"There is more. That painting you see on the wall was done by Yen the night he read your report. He was staying in the home of the governor of Shantung, and he found the view of that famous seven-storied pagoda against the backdrop of mountains truly enchanting. Listen to what he said about it in his report to the governor:

> I have already painted it twice—once with the effect of the early morning haze and once trying to capture the uncertain atmosphere of twilight. The sight of a lonely sail on a moonlit lake, the sounds of a temple bell at night . . . I sometimes wonder whether these things are, after all, not more important than all the complications of official life.

Jao laid down the file and looked at Dee. "He gave the painting to the governor, who gave the painting to Kaotsung and there it is, my own favorite of the moment."

Dee studied the painting and then looked at Jao quizzically.

"You are wondering why I invited you here?" He nodded. "I want to offer you a new position."

Dee lifted his heavy black brows and waited.

Jao continued. "I want to talk about your future—and mine. First I want to ask whether you are loyal to me and whether you are a Tang loyalist."

Dee did not pretend to misunderstand. "Yes to both, Your Majesty," he stated unequivocally.

Jao studied him for a long minute. "I have called you to help me rule this empire the way it should be ruled. No, wait," she said as he moved heavily. "Hear me out. You are too good an official in the ideal Confucian way to chop and change your ideology as I have done with mine—Buddhism, Taoism, river-goddess worship and the lot. You deal in certainties in black and white. I deal in grays, in ambiguities which I balance. I often get a workable balance by not doing something, as in the Wu and Li rivalry; for instance, I do not officially name my successor. I deny to both sides the power that clear right to the throne would give them. I also deny to both sides the right to go to extremes in abuses—I confess it does happen, but I catch up with them."

"But your purges of the Tang imperial families, how can you justify them? Lai and . . . and others? All that is surely a—a—demerit on your rule," Dee replied somberly.

"You know as well as I do—better, because you were a victim—how legal all those executions were, once the confessions were obtained. And you know that I was deceived . . . but that is not what I want to talk about. I want to get, and keep, your loyalty and your total commitment to your new post, so we must discuss how it can be done. You just said 'Lai and others.' Were you referring to Wu Chengssu?"

"Yes, Your Majesty." Dee's response was almost inaudible.

"Do you know that he is in here repeatedly these days recommending, forcibly, your execution?"

"I am not surprised, Your Majesty," he replied heavily.

"He persists, no matter how often he is refused," she continued. "You are here now because I wish to tell you that he has not attained his goal."

"I thank you for your mercy. He may regard me as an enemy because I stand in his way to the throne. He may be stepping up his petitions to be named crown prince in order to force your hand."

"He will not attain his wish in that either." Jao's tone was stern.

Dee took a deep breath and then showed his profound gratitude by kowtowing. "Rise," Jao said, "I have more to say. It is more than ten years since Kaotsung died, and there has been no peace. Do you think that that has been all my fault?"

"No," he replied thoughtfully. "No, I don't."

"Do you think that I have been a wicked, unscrupulous schemer with only one thought in mind, to gain power for myself? Insanely ambitious to gain power by occupying the throne myself? Plotting night and day to become emperor and change the dynasty?"

Dee met her gaze steadily. "To tell the truth, I don't know what to think. Often your moves seem to say that you are opportunistic, playing politics as you go along, not a plotter at all. Chengssu is the one who plots . . . it appears for his own reasons."

Jao interrupted him. "He did all the hard work, clearing the way for me to be accepted as Huang, on his own volition. He has already been rewarded. I owe him nothing. Now, listen carefully about what I have to say about myself: Those same years that he and Lai were working so dishonorably, and you were away from court in the provinces, were the years that I was at the lowest ebb in political activity. I was putting heart and soul into the erection of the Ming Tang and all the other great buildings, and into fulfilling my incarnation as Maitreya, and into that genius Hsueh Huai-i . . . Heart and soul. Those were years that I was spending what little time I had for thinking, not on plots, but in gazing into space, unseeingly, many times daily while my mind wandered in daydreams. It was all excitement and emotion in those days.

"Those were years I left the big decisions to others—to Heaven, which sent me the comet, which sent the rain when Pei wanted to have me assassinated, which sent me the right wind at the battle of Kao Yu in order to end a revolt, which sent the wrong wind that prevented the rebels' escape, and which sent many other good omens as well, not manufactured omens, but real ones. Then I offered to let Juitsung be emperor. Would I offer to step down when it was my intention to step up? With hindsight you probably think so. Those were the years, however, that I would have settled for ruling in Juitsung's name if the princes' revolt and all the other conspiracies hadn't arisen. I would have given the empire good service for nothing! You don't approve of me because you think I bring disorder, but think, my friend—what I am actually doing is bringing order to this empire. My way."

Dee remained silent for so long that Jao stirred restlessly.

"Yes, I do see," Dee said finally. "And I am deeply appreciative of being told these secrets in such a way to convince me. I now understand how you have reconciled irreconcilables. May I now humbly inquire what I can do to serve Your Majesty?"

"It is time to return the empire to more traditional government, and I am asking you to help by first becoming the chief of the Censorate and then perhaps prime minister," Jao said simply.

Dee was stunned. At once he understood the significance of what he was being offered. It was overwhelming, but in answer he quipped, "Is that why you read me Yen's words about the hollowness of official life?"

Jao burst into surprised laughter. "Do you accept?" she asked.

"I do," Dee replied slowly. "I have only one one question: Do you seriously think that Wu Chengssu might one day follow you on the throne?"

"I thought I answered that question by saying that he will not attain his ambition as long as I am on the throne."

"He still has official position and he is in place for a coup. I have to have this matter clearly addressed before I can give good service in the Censorate. My concern is major. A plotter like Chengssu cannot solve problems as they arise because his mind is set in one direction and unable to cope with matters not in his focus. You, on the other hand, are able to see in all directions and can solve any problem quickly. You show the ability to improvise under pressure . . . and that is the mark of the true statesman. Chengssu has no such ability."

He paused and Jao's eyes softened with pleasure. "If you feel that I can rule—with justice," she said, "not with terror—that is what I want to hear! I want to have your full loyalty and respect. I know that you will always be loyal to the Tang imperial house somehow and loyal also to me, a Wu, because of my sons and because of our long friendship. Is this true?"

"Your Majesty always seems to know what is in people's hearts," he answered, "and for this I am your servant to command. For this reason I have found courage to write so many petitions asking you to name one or the other son crown prince, so many thousands of words."

Jao leaned over and touched his knee in a friendly way as a sign that their talk was over. "I don't read them all," she said, and they both rose in a burst of laughter.

CHAPTER TWENTY-ONE

Court life during the three years after the destruction of the Ming Tang gradually stabilized. Jao became more tolerant in her decisions, and Dee energetically settled a pileup of neglected cases and brought many capable new men into the bureaucracy. In the spring of 698, however, a new crisis arose. Jao was confronted with a genuine conspiracy and she resorted to a relative, the barbarous Wu Itsung, to deal with it. The Wu family took advantage of the situation to accuse the most prestigious men at court of treason and were able to cashier thirty-six families of Tang loyalists whom they regarded as their chief political opponents.

The situation worsened when Jao, in order to remove Itsung from the turmoil in the capital, posted him to a frontier town to protect it from Khitan invaders. They attacked at once and Wu Itsung fled, leaving the inhabitants to be massacred.

Mortified beyond words, Jao fell back upon Lai and recalled him to investigate and prosecute. He was not at all humbled by his years in exile, and returned to his old habits, more dangerous than ever. He lost no time in launching another wave of terror in his reach for supreme power. He no longer cared how high or how powerful his victims might be. He forced confessions, kidnaped women he desired, and effected wholesale confiscations. The situation confronting Jao was becoming intolerable when Lai made a fatal mistake in accusing of treason not only the most powerful of the Wus, but also all three imperial children, including Taiping.

Dee and the other high officials were obliged to act. Dee, facing his sovereign, asked her for a warrant of execution for Lai.

"Obviously, he will have to go back into exile. At once," Jao said reluctantly.

Dee's expression was granite hard. "That will not do," he said. "This time execution is your only option."

"Lai has been a faithful servant of the state—too assiduous, perhaps." Jao faltered, mortified on yet another count.

"Lai has accused the three imperial children," Dee said stiffly. "The council is unanimous in demanding the death penalty."

Jao flinched. "Yes," she said. "Yes, I suppose so."

She waited, however, for three days before she signed the warrant of execution. On the day of execution, the crowds turned out in unprecedented numbers and could not be restrained in their attack on Lai's corpse. It was mutilated beyond recognition. When Jao heard about this, she was shocked to the core. She had no inkling of the extent of popular hatred for Lai and his abominable star chamber. In acute dismay, Jao read to the court in plenary session the list of Lai's crimes which had recently been revealed to her. All the secrets of the inquisition were exposed.

She faced the court in person. "Your sovereign has supported Lai Chunchen eight years now, excluding his years in exile. There was one year in getting his system started, two in coping with real problems, and five years of flagrant abuse of office. Your sovereign was informed that Lai and Jo followed Tang law in every particular, and so they seemed to be doing when they brought their cases to the privy council for action. Lai's spy system was intended to implement the government's effort to discover the truth. Moreover, when your sovereign sent investigators to the prison to check on alleged atrocities, the prisoners all reported that they had voluntarily confessed to conspiring against the throne."

Jao's open presentation to the court appeased the officials, both Tang and Chou loyalists. They accepted her word that terrorism had ended. Her ultimate responsibility for the terrorism was not forgotten, however, and she knew it.

She asked Dee to remain in the chamber after the other officials had left. When he was seated next to her, she accepted his congratulations for her clear presentation, then turned serious. "Dee, you must listen to me. This Lai business. In the end I knew that he deserved death, but not the way he died, not the way that people hated him. It is as if they hate me personally, and I cannot tolerate that and keep my sanity. Is it your opinion that the people hate me . . . like that?"

Dee looked into the bleak eyes of his sovereign and put all his forceful personality into his words. "No, Your Majesty." He was unequivocal. "No, not at all like that."

"Thank you. You may leave now," she said and stopped, unable to speak further.

Jao was on her terrace watching the clouds whip across the face of the moon when she felt someone appear beside her. "Oh, it is you," she said with a small smile.

Taiping stood quietly beside her mother.

"There will be a storm soon . . . with thunder and rain," Jao said. "We shall be having leaks all over the palace as usual."

Her daughter grimaced. "Of course, sure to. A good thing—it will give the lazy servants something to do. Come inside," Taiping urged.

She took Jao's elbow and steered her inside the hall, where the candles were being lit.

"Respected Mother . . . what is the matter?" Taiping asked casually. "Are you in trouble?"

"Not for the first time," Jao responded wryly, lapsing into heavy silence again.

Taiping realized then that her mother was in no mood for the usual light banter. "May I say what I think?" she asked.

"When have you not?"

"First, I hate my cousins, all of them, and Chengssu most of all." She looked at Jao out of the corner of her eye.

"Why this outburst, Taiping?' Jao asked.

"The oldest son of the oldest son of your father, candidate for emperor himself—Wu Chengssu is the cause of all the trouble you are having. He expects to be formally recognized. I think that you are treating him as your heir."

Jao looked appraisingly at her daughter. "Well, you can think again. Chengssu is out of favor. He will never be named crown prince and he will never obtain the throne—if that is what you are thinking."

"Not all of what I am thinking," Tai cried rudely, sitting back on her heels. "August Mother, you moved Heaven and Earth to encourage Chengssu and he moved Heaven and Earth to support you in establishing the Chou dynasty. It was a miracle that only a miracle woman like my mother could accomplish. To help with this you created Lai's powerful service like nothing ever seen before for organization and quick results. Now you know how Lai deceived you. Worse than Lai is

Chengssu. I hear that today in audience you ate bitterness before them all about the star chamber."

Jao glanced sharply at her daughter. "I confessed that I had been betrayed by officials who committed the atrocities in my name. I told them that I had rewarded the officials who enlightened me, like Dee and Hsu and Wei, and that the reign of terror was a thing of the past. Then I had on my hands petitions from hundreds of officials who owed their positions to Lai and Wu Chengssu and were terrified as to what might befall them now. No good could come of confessions from such men, so I pardoned them all." Jao looked ravaged again and continued almost inaudibly. "They say that Lai could not have deceived me had I not wanted to listen to him. No one has ever been hated like Lai. And that means me as well . . ." Jao studied the rain pouring from the tiles. "I would like to know what you think," Jao asked as matter-of-factly as she could.

"I think," Tai said passionately, "that there are a lot of slandering fools in the world, and I think that you are wholly exonerated now that you have destroyed Lai's yamen. And you have just said that you are distancing yourself from the troublesome Wus."

Jao sighed and took a deep breath. She sighed again and felt herself eased. The rain and wind banged the doors and rattled the shutters. Somewhere a loud slam indicated that a door had blown off its hinges.

"You have created a great dynasty, and now you don't know to whom to give it," Taiping ventured. "Your children are not skilled enough—or even willing to become skilled enough—to follow you, and neither are the infernal Wus."

"You are skilled enough, but everything is black and white with you," Jao replied. "You are unwilling to balance the forces in politics to achieve necessary acceptance from all sides. Whoever sits upon the throne after me will have a great and prosperous nation to rule. This empire is the greatest in all the Four Seas. Just because I have been the means of destroying fifty or so rebellious families of Tang out of the two hundred, and two tens of my own unworthy relatives out of fifty families, does not mean that the empire is affected at all. We still have our great loyal armies and our loyal officials. The men that I have put into office over thirty years are from all ten provinces and are beholden to my administration for their prompt salaries. It is not a bad thing for this great empire of ours that it is rid of the old military families of the northwest—the area and class I come from, the Wus, the Lis, all of us. Not a bad thing. Especially as it prevents the imperial Tang families, with the thirty or so children to each family multiplying in four generations into the thousands, from all living on the state."

Taiping leapt up. She put her hands on each side of her mother's face, her favorite gesture when a child.

Jao sighed. "What are you up to now, then?"

"I'll chase away your black mood," Tai answered. "Now, tonight, I am going to call in some friends to amuse you."

Jao shuddered at the suggestion, and Tai only laughed. "Let's have more light in here and at least one musician who can play lively airs to drive off the ghosts. I know someone who can do this for us for hours without repeating himself. If you call for a tune, he can play it, anything you want, new or old, a marvelous young man."

"One of your young friends?" Jao asked dampeningly. "A common entertainer? Someone's slave? You've been so restless after the death of your husband—I'm going to find you another, Sanssu's son, maybe."

Taiping ignored the remark about a new husband. "Tatsu comes from a good family, the Changs, early supporters of the Tangs. He is very good looking. And yes, he is one of my young men."

"He won't thank you for getting him out on a night like this," Jao commented. "But send for him if you can't bear to be without him."

Taiping sped to the door and spoke to a eunuch waiting in the gallery. A maid came in with a lacquer tray containing freshly baked honey cakes and a ewer of the best Indian tea. Another brought in a smokeless lamp, which she placed behind Wu Jao so that it shone on the low settee in front of her. Finally she rearranged the silk cushions and set a pot of heavily scented summer roses in a corner.

"What is all this for?" Jao asked irritably. "It is only a dreary, rainy evening and I am only passing time. There is no need for all this."

The attendant bowed low, poured scalding tea into an ostrich-shell cup, and presented it to Jao. The fragrance of jasmine filled the air. "Princess Taiping ordered the flowers and this drink. It is tea from the jar brought by Ijing from India."

"Perhaps it will do me some good if it has been blessed by the famous priest," Jao said without enthusiasm.

Tai seated herself, her silks rustling, and poured herself some tea. A few minutes later, without ceremony, a young man with a lute slipped into the room. He kowtowed in an unassuming manner and Taiping introduced him. "Chang Changtsung—Tatsu," she said to her mother.

"Your Majesty," he said with a shy smile.

"Please join us in a drink," Jao said, automatically putting him at ease. "To refresh you after being summoned so suddenly in all this rain."

"An honor to join you in your drink—whatever it is."

"A magic potion," put in Taiping. "Made from the smallest leaves of a small plant grown only in small islands of the Southern Sea."

"Heavens!" he said, taking an experimental sip.

"That cupful that you are drinking now," Tai continued rudely, "is equal to ten ounces of gold dust."

He was just taking another sip. He lowered his cup and stared at it in consternation, making both women smile.

Tai laughed. "Drink it, idiotic man!"

He took another few sips while flashing a smile of such charm that Jao brightened. How good looking he is, she thought, and how easily he fits in here. Without pretension—lightly, like one of those immortals wafting in from the Court of the Western Queen Mother.

"Now some music, Tatsu," Taiping said after drinking five cups of tea. Jao noted her use of his informal name.

Tatsu picked up his lute. "What would you like?" he asked her while keeping his eyes on the empress. Taiping raised her elegant eyebrows in thought, so he laid the lute down again, and reaching over, caught her hand. "Don't bother to think. We'll play the finger game. You win, you choose the first thing that comes into your head. I win, I choose."

Like two children they swung their hands and simultaneously opened their fists. The princess displayed two fingers in the scissors mode and Tatsu an open palm.

"My scissors cuts your paper!" Tai said. "So sing 'Swallows Nest on Sungshan.' "

He bowed elaborately and broke into a lively melody, then brought it to a close and turned to the empress. "Your turn," he said.

Amused, Jao found herself swinging her arm and presenting a fist while Tatsu held out his palm. "My paper wraps your stone. I win, so I'll sing 'The Many Moons of Hangchow Lake.' " He plucked a few strings tentatively and then launched into the popular song.

The rain sluiced down outside, the women relaxed into their cushions, and Tatsu smiled playfully at them both as he sang.

"Make a drum out of the tabletop," he said when he finished the song, "and keep time on it with your chopsticks. I like to see your graceful fingers move." He flashed a merry look at Jao. "Please?" he insisted, and picked up her hand to put chopsticks in her fingers. He then sang a farmer's harvest song, increasing in tempo as he went along so that she had to increase her drumming in order to keep up with him. He stopped suddenly. "Now improvise while you are keeping time—this way."

The tune he played next was so catchy that the empress found herself tapping the tabletop with her fingers as well as with the chopsticks. She was out of breath and laughing by the time the song ended, and so were Tatsu and Tai.

"This is ridiculous!" Jao said, but she made no move to end the fun.

An hour passed. The wind died down but the rain was more violent than ever. Tatsu's musical laments were in keeping with the mood of the night, finally ceasing on a minor note long drawn out. He rested, then softly strummed an old-fashioned song, 'Rainbow Dancer of Kucha,' and Jao smiled. This song she knew. She had often sung it to Taitsung long ago. The years slipped away from her. She did not have any idea how enchanting she looked in her nostalgic mood. Her daughter and Tatsu stared at her, beguiled.

Jao shook herself and struck a gong. A eunuch answered, and a few minutes later ushered in servants with bowls of chicken soup and dumplings with side dishes of foods fried in batter.

Another hour slipped by while they ate, and Tatsu struck up a concert of quiet songs, one after another, his eyes never leaving the empress's face. Jao, settling into her cushions with her eyes closed, thought sleepily, he enjoys his own music just as much as we do. He is not afraid of me . . . he has no idea how flagrant it was to lay a hand on the emperor of China. How restful all this is!

Taiping yawned and asked quietly for permission to retire. Jao nodded, and not too much later, overcome by food and the monotonous beat of the rain, she withdrew to her silken bed. She left the sliding door open so that she could hear the soft and soothing music. The attendant eunuch extinguished all lights except one candle beside the singer. "Just blow it out when you leave," he instructed Tatsu. "The guard will show you to your carriage. I am going off duty now."

"Dismiss the carriage. I will go home by street chair," Tatsu replied.

He played for another hour, watching his shadow dance among the rafters. When he heard the midnight drum, he stopped in mid-tune and wrapped his lute carefully in a square of heavy silk. He snuffed the candle and went to the open door, not to the gallery, but to the bedroom, and slipped inside. He could hear the sleeping empress breathing softly. He paused, then slipped under the silk quilt and snuggled up to the silent woman. She sighed, and soon they were both deep in sleep.

The next morning dawned clear and fresh without a cloud in the sky. Jao opened her eyes to find that she had overslept and her early morning tea had grown cold. I must have tossed a lot last night! she thought as she looked at her disheveled bed.

"Is my daughter still here?" she asked her maid. But Tai was still sleeping. Jao shrugged and dressed hurriedly in preparation for meeting Minister Dee as scheduled.

He was pleased when he searched her face for signs of anxiety and hidden discontent but found only tranquillity in her eyes.

"What bad news have you for me today?" she asked mildly.

Dee smiled in return, something he rarely did during his official dealings with her. He was thinking that perhaps now was the time to get her committed to the restoration of one of her sons as emperor and to release her grip on the government.

"The ploy to arm the peasants in northern Hopei and to train militia troops against the Khitans is working well, Your Majesty."

"Thanks to you, but no thanks to those cowardly relatives of mine," she answered.

He blinked at her candor. "But not working as well as it might," he hazarded. "If we set about recruiting fresh troops in Chungtsung's name, as emperor, we could get volunteers in large numbers. Wu Sanssu raised only a thousand men in a month."

Wu Jao regarded her minister steadily. "That is going too far too fast."

Dee swallowed and decided to risk a supreme and possibly last argument in favor of restoring the Tang dynasty. "Your Majesty told me about her dream of the chess game in which she could not win. Now, I suggest that the word for chessman, *tzu,* is the same as for son. Unless you move the right *tzu* into the right spots at the right time, you lose. Is this just a dream of yours or is it a warning? How can you know how important this dream of yours might be? A nephew cannot worship at the ancestral shrine of an aunt—her name is in the shrine of her husband—but a son can attend to the important sacrifices on behalf of the spirit of his mother. One's own natural ancestors are of the utmost importance. What parent wants his spirit to wander alone in the emptiness of death without a soul to care? Without a son to worship at the ancestral shrine?"

Jao winced at his words but immediately restrained herself and sat quietly, her hands folded on her lap. Her thoughts strayed unaccountably to the ease and comfort of the night before and to a vision of a life ahead filled with music, wit, laughter, instead of the unremitting strain of her present existence.

"What if I recalled Chungtsung to the capital?"

"As what, Your Majesty?" Dee countered swiftly.

"As crown prince?" she said, so softly that he hardly caught it.

"Excellent! Hm . . . excellent! You will see, everything will change for the better for you, for all of us, for the empire! Better when the people are granted stability . . . ha! You will see . . . excellent . . . inspired!"

With a small smile Jao dismissed him, and Dee, elated beyond words to have achieved his great goal, bowed low and hurried out. There was no one else in the empire who could have settled the succession as he had just done, and he knew it.

Jao watched him go with a wry smile on her face. Dee was now indispensable to her, the only one who could meet the really great crises—the only one she dared to let take the load off her shoulders. No one else had the record of accomplishment that he had. He had cleared up seventeen thousand old cases since coming to court as first minister. Perhaps he would even be able to cope with her impossible court. And she could enjoy her life in peace at last.

"Move the right *tzu* at the right time," she said aloud while she put her feet up on a stool and rang for tea. "Time to end the Tang-Wu feud. I ended the terrorism—I can end this tangle!"

The summer was hotter than usual, and the warm weather lasted into the fall. Jao was enjoying the mild days in spite of the occasional bit of bad news from the frontier, where the Khitans and Turks seemed to be crossing the Great Wall into the farmlands of China whenever they liked. As always, Cloud was with her, and Jao had managed to get Phoenix out of the seclusion of her Changan mansion to visit her also. Chi exerted himself—he was a stalwart eighty-year-old still on light service in the palace—to see that the three ladies had every luxury that he could manage for them. He enjoyed seeing the three white heads close together, three peals of laughter frequently mingling as they talked.

They sound as they used to when they were tsairen, he thought, shaking his head. Witty girls they were, and witty old ladies they are now, he mused affectionately. The coolness between him and Jao had disappeared with her moves against Lai and the more troublesome Wus.

They were sitting around a tea table on the terrace when Wu Chengssu was announced. He had come frequently all summer, although he had grown emaciated from ulcers.

"I must run," Cloud said at once, her white hair streaming around her face in curls much as it used to. Phoenix, too, rose, so Jao reluctantly let them go and admitted him.

"Terrible news!" he shouted as soon as he came in the door. "Those Turks have taken Tingchow! And Tingchow is not really so far from Loyang! You must send another Wu general at once—that traitor Dee should be executed for failure!"

"You should rest easy," Jao said coldly. "You look ill. Your hates are consuming you."

"You must settle the succession at once. The throne is threatened because you are only a woman ruler. You must rectify that by naming me crown prince at once if Sanssu is to raise enough volunteers to drive them out!" Spittle ran down his jaw in his excitement.

"Will you have some tea?" Jao said, eyeing him speculatively.

"No. I don't want it," he said irritably. "What I want is the title. You have put me off long enough!"

"Do you know that I sent for my son Chungtsung and that he is in the palace right now?" Jao asked.

"Of course I know! Why? He failed you once, and now he has been out of things so long that he is even less capable of ruling. Shut him up with Juitsung and give me my due! You have to do something about this crisis."

"I have done something about it." Jao spoke slowly. "Today I have named my successor. Chungtsung is now crown prince."

Chengssu looked as if lightning had struck him. He shriveled before her eyes and tottered, looking suddenly so ill that Jao called her eunuchs in haste.

"Please revive my nephew and help him to his chair," she ordered. Chi had remained in attendance and hurried forward to help. Chengssu, slumped into his seat, was unable to speak. He began to recover at once, however, and accepted the assistance that the eunuchs offered. Jao watched anxiously, expecting an outburst. Instead, as Chengssu left the room, he looked back beseechingly.

This upset her. Wretched man, she thought when she saw his woebegone expression. He doesn't doubt that whatever he wants, he can have. It has done him no good to be in the palace—he can only cope with what is petty or ruthless. He should have guessed where he stood when I donated him a princedom but named Juitsung heir. All the benefits he received were payment for his services. I owe him nothing.

In his litter, Chengssu recovered somewhat, deciding, as always, that the bad news could not be permanent. Still desiring consolation, he chose to go to one of the newly fashionable brothels and obtain the services of a very young girl. The resulting exertion was too much for him, and he died in his palanquin on the way home.

Jao was informed of his death and the manner of it at once. Remorsefully, she recalled his supplicating look as he had left her the day before. Then she stiffened as she read further down the scroll and saw that the family had covered up the manner of his death by indicating that it resulted from shock at being so badly treated by her. "Just as well that he's out of it now," Jao said grimly, and she tossed the scroll on the table.

After the restoration of Chungtsung to first place in the succession, and the demotion of Juitsung—who was more than willing—the situation on the frontier did change for the better, as Chungtsung's return enabled Dee to raise fifty thousand volunteers in a few days.

Chang Tatsu was invited back to the palace by Jao, and he in turn introduced his relatives into the living rooms of Jao and her daughter. There were five Chang brothers, whose effervescence was so infectious that it spilled over into a long string of palace entertainments and into several innovative enterprises which captured Jao's sustained interest. One of these was the creation of a garden, inspired by the imagined paradise of the Western Queen Mother, which was supposed to be located somewhere in the mysterious Kunlun Mountains. This garden was designed to offer Jao both the symbol and reality of carefree leisure and release from earthly duties.

The garden paradise of Taoist myth came into being inside the imperial hunting park. Enclosed by a ten-foot fence of bamboo, it covered a two-mile-square site in which, among small hills and year-round streams, there was a large lake. Two remote islets could be reached only by boat. Trees brought in from all parts of the empire grew in well-tended plantations around the lake. Winding paths, arched bridges, and pagodas graced the grounds in carefully designed vistas. Aviaries of net were placed at sheltered spots for the exotic parrots and other birds of foreign lands, and a zoo complete with elephants and giraffes was built against the south wall.

The gate to the park had a double roof with upturned corners, an architectural innovation from southern Lingnan in striking contrast to the northern style of straight-edged rooflines.

Inside the gate a stone-paved drive curved off to the right around the lake. To the left, just out of sight from the entrance, was another gate with towers. A smaller drive led to a flight of shallow steps up to a low-walled enclosure shaded by deodars, flowering trees, and potted plants. Inside, on a double terrace of granite blocks, stood the empress's hall, with porches and hinged shutters that could be fastened up on any side for the view. Azaleas, iris, peonies, and chrysanthemums blossomed in seasonal masses around the house. There was color and fragrance and vitality in the flowering plants, but they were not allowed to grow high enough to obstruct the view. Narrow galleries ran around the building directly under the outflung eaves. They served as open-air anterooms.

"My frugal officials allowed, without complaint, ten times the amount spent on this garden to be spent for public buildings to which they had access, but they complain about this fairyland because they are not allowed here!" she told Dee with a laugh one day as he sat in her jasmine-scented courtyard enjoying a drink and a rest. "The important officials, princes, and relatives just can't bear it if they cannot gain face-to-face access to me any time they wish," she continued, chuckling. "They simply can't understand why they are not welcome here. They cannot conceive that I might be feeling tired or that I do not want to attend to their constant efforts to browbeat something out of me!"

Dee listened with an appreciative glint in his eye. He was not young either, nearly seventy. He now had some difficulty in rising after kowtowing, but still accomplished in a single day the work of three others. He was often invited to this paradise of Jao's, and he always accepted, staying long hours, often just sitting silently in her company, enjoying the quiet. He appreciated the freedom from human voices, and relished the sounds of running water and of birds everywhere. The avian chorus included raucous magpies in their flashing black and white, bluebirds, thrushes, and always the kites whistling as they circled the skies.

"It is this perfection, this calm," he agreed with a sigh, "that I have never seen elsewhere."

"*Lauban,* old friend! I believe that you have a spark of poetry in you after all," Jao teased.

"I have more than you think!" the white-haired old man said, looking at her with the mocking smile of his youth, which never failed to raise Jao's spirits.

"If I am leaning too heavily on you, you must tell me," Jao said lazily. "This last conspiracy of Governor Liu rattled me. It grew before anyone knew about it."

"Are you missing Lai?" Dee asked at once.

Jao winced. The memory of Lai's death was still a sore spot. "Not really—but being Huang leaves scars."

Judge Dee looked at her with such sincere understanding and approval that Jao lowered her eyes in elation. He gave no indication of his feelings in his stern and businesslike reply. "Better to rely on regular channels of information then, even if it seems a weak policy. Lai's sort of operation can never flush out real conspiracies. Lai never knew about those because his methods couldn't discover the truth."

"That governor thought he was destined to be emperor because a fortune-teller told him so. Can you imagine anything more insane?" Jao said, shifting the subject away from the star chamber.

Dee nodded agreeably, remembering Jao's certitude that the Bright Mansion comet was a sign of heavenly approval, but he was a wise man and raised a new subject. "The Chang brothers have done marvels not just with this garden, but with the court. They have contributed much with all their concerts and entertainments. But Your Majesty, you must see that many of the ministers do not appreciate their whimsy. There is a growing coalition against the Changs. They complain about them and about the costs of their entertainments and this garden. Do you realize this?"

Jao did not take this very seriously. "My experienced officials cannot take the antics of my lighthearted—and light-headed—artists as anything to worry about!"

"They are jealous of the Changs' access to you. Jealousy in high officials is dangerous. You must be careful to put reliable ministers like Chang Chienjer and others like him into positions of power to fend off the irresponsible elements."

"All right. I will keep what you say in mind," Jao said and smilingly dismissed him.

Dee looked over at the empress and stood up. "Only one more mountain for you to climb," he said in parting. "The effort to bring your children and your Wu relatives together in peace."

In addition to her city garden, Wu Jao had access to a mountain retreat for the hottest of the summer months, the Sanyang camp about sixty miles from Loyang. After Chungtsung and his family had moved to Loyang, Jao had all her family near her. She had taken steps to reduce rivalry by having her children take the name Wu and by marrying Taiping to a remote but acceptable relative, Wu Yuji. Now the time had come, Jao decided, to get her grandchildren acquainted with one another by taking them to that recreation area for a holiday. Chungtsung had twelve children, Juitsung seventeen—and most of these twenty-nine grandchildren she did not know very well.

Within minutes after the arrival at the meadow where the rough summer cottages were located, the area rang with childish voices and excited cries. The rushing torrents, the rugged peaks, the deep pools where trout and catfish lurked, all invited exploration and offered attractions such as fishing, wading, swimming, and hunting.

Jao had a small staff with her, including Minister Dee and two of the Chang brothers. Attendants and guests made themselves comfortable and spent their time as they pleased from first light to moonrise. There were picnics and expeditions to nearby monasteries in the daytime, and in the evenings there might be lantern-lit entertainments put on by court shadow-players, music from the Changs, or skits scrambled together by the imperial family members themselves.

Jao devoted herself to seeing that everyone had a good time. She chuckled at the antics of the small ones, and watched the older ones with keen interest, wondering idly as she watched which one might emerge as emperor. Chungtsung's children, raised in the country, were boisterous and inclined to overreact when excited. They were also in constant dispute with one another and were never restrained by their mother, the aloof Lady Wei. His oldest boy, the son of a concubine, stood apart much of the time, feeling that it was below his dignity to participate in the games of the younger ones. Chung's oldest daughter, Yungtai, openly avoided Jao, as did Lady Wei's two children, Chungjun and his sister Anlo. They were in their late teens, the same age as Juitsung's two older sons.

Juitsung's children were palace-bred, quiet and perceptive, habitually sharing with each other. The third son, Prince Lungchi, a robust fourteen, attracted Jao's attention with his unfailing good spirits, endless energy, and amicable interaction with everyone else. He's got what it takes to be Huang, said Jao to herself with satisfaction. Even though he is only Juitsung's third son, if the throne finally comes to the most able, it will come to him.

One halcyon day in August when the cicadas were singing their loudest and not a leaf stirred in the clear air, Jao, realizing that she had spent most of her time with the children, organized a picnic with her adult guests, her chief assistants, and her sons. The group of eleven also included Dee and the Chang brothers.

They gathered in a grassy glade just above a waterfall that emptied into a large jade-green pool a hundred feet below. Attendants took wine jugs down to the water to cool and built a charcoal cooking fire among the boulders some distance from the party. Jao informed her guests, to the accompaniment of much quipping, that she expected each one to compose a poem to celebrate the day—eight lines long, seven words to each line. The subject was to be Wandering on Boulder Torrent Mountain on a Summer Day.

"Women first!" Dee stipulated.

"Agreed!" Jao's eyes sparkled with animation.

The afternoon sun was low when the time came to read the poems. Everyone was relaxed after a day in the sun with plenty to eat and to drink, and all had had time to juggle his words and rhymes. Jao called her two sons first, then the others. Each one got to his feet to recite and to accept with laughter the inevitable accolade from his fellow guests.

Dee was last. He cleared his throat in a manner that brought forth chuckles and read his poem sonorously and with flourishes. There was vigorous applause and a few whistles.

"Your poem, Jenjer, is so full of literary allusions that it is like a m-m-meat dumpling—one is not sure what one is chewing," Juitsung said. "Flowery compliments for our Huang here—exquisite phrases, subtle references, a classic! Should I petition to have it, and all the others, carved on this cliff? As a memorial?"

"Do it!" Jao interrupted. "I want this day to be remembered!" She turned to Dee. "What a flamboyant, delightful bit of nonsense from you! Here you are, a stern Confucian who has closed down hundreds of what you view to be immoral, superstitious Taoist shrines, displaying yourself in poetry as a Taoist immortal who has power over rain and even death! Alluding, no doubt, to your value to the throne because of your supernatural qualities!"

A shout of laughter at Dee's expense greeted this, a laugh in which he joined heartily. The sun shone brilliantly on his white hair as he stood on the edge of the cliff, his young-old eyes twinkling with humor, his garments blowing gently in the breeze, good friend, relentless enemy, fine companion whatever the occasion. Everyone felt that his presence there at that moment was a boon, something to be remembered.

"I'll have the poems engraved on the cliff to remember this day. And let us meet again this time next year and try our hands once more at poetry-making," Jao invited cordially, in the mood of the day. There was hearty agreement to the plan.

It was not to be. Dee died during a November cold front of freezing wind and drafty palace offices. Wu Jao wept when the news was brought to her, remarking sadly to her attendants, "My court is empty now."

Motivated by her loss of Dee, and full of guilt that she had not yet succeeded in "climbing the last mountain" in healing the breach in her family, Jao decided to stage such a solemn ceremony of renunciation of feuding that no one would ever forget it. As a symbol of equality she chose the day of the spring equinox to give a formal banquet for the princes of both houses. She held it in the new Ming Tang to impress her family with the solemnity of the occasion. Officiating ministers of high rank administered a solemn oath to all by which they bound themselves from that day on, individually and collectively, to live in harmony with one another.

Jao watched their faces as each one took the oath. Juitsung's children were round-eyed and silent with seriousness. Chungtsung's children whispered and had to be hushed and urged forward when their turns came. The oldest son of Chungtsung took the oath in a sullen way, and the two children of Empress Wei boldly shuffled their feet and smirked. Jao saw Wu Yenji, the oldest son of Chengssu, exchange a glance of derision with his wife, Yungtai, daughter of Chengssu, and then both darted a swift glance at her, their faces instantly blank when they saw that she was looking. Like father, like son—they both have wanted me out of the way, Jao thought, feeling a flush of unforgiving anger surge through her at these signs of disloyalty. But she reassured herself that the law requiring the death penalty for infringement would surely stop the destructive thoughts.

When it came time for her to close the ceremony, she spoke slowly and clearly about the meaning of the oath and what it demanded. "We have just announced to Heaven and Earth in the presence of all the officials of government and of the spirits investing this sacred Ming Tang hall that each and every one of you will abide by your oath. This oath has been engraved on an iron tablet and it will be deposited in the archives as a solemn assurance of your intentions.

"The penalty for breaking such a binding commitment is the same as the penalty for treason. This is the law from this moment on. I stand here as a person in close relationship with all of you, but I am also your sovereign and myself am bound by the laws. Never forget how you must behave in obedience not only to me, but to the sovereign who follows me. Be warned and depart in eternal, and fraternal, peace." She stopped. The silence was heavy.

The two years that followed were relatively calm for Jao. Except for trouble with her heart and recurrence of a mysterious fever, she enjoyed her garden, gave parties, and was entertained by the ever-devoted Chang brothers. She saw to it that they were rewarded handsomely and that they all had some prestige coming from various honors she bestowed on them. Dee, before he had died, had been friendly to them, and after Dee's death Jao had reluctantly followed his advice to promote Chang Chienjer and the other ministers he had recommended. She was slow to do so because, although loyal to the Tang house, they were not her own supporters.

Chang versus Chang! The five Chang brothers as opposed to the five ministers—they are all retainers of mine, she told herself. I will balance them! And thus keep my court stable. However, she felt she really needed to throw her weight behind the Chang brothers whenever they got into trouble. They were so inept!

"Trouble? The trouble is," said one of Tatsu's brothers one day when he was ruefully reporting a mistake he had made, "that I recommend too many people to office."

Jao looked alert. "Tell me," she ordered.

"Well, this is the way it is. When I need money I tell a client that if he pays me fifty ounces of gold, I will find an appointment for him. Not long ago I was waylaid on my way to court by a graduate named Hsueh who had not yet found a position. He gave me his credentials and the gold, and I took the papers to the vice-chief of the civil service. The fool lost the papers and came back to me for the full name—such an irresponsible official! I told him what I thought of him! I couldn't remember the first name, so I just said 'Appoint any Hsueh', and later I heard that when the vice-chief looked in the register, he found more than sixty Hsuehs waiting for appointment, so he appointed them all. The dumb ox!"

Jao gave a gurgle of laughter and ignored the matter along with the rest of the peccadilloes of her endearing servitors.

What she did not let pass was an enormity perpetrated by Chungtsung's oldest son, when he informed against his half-brother Chungjun and his sister Yungtai, by revealing their anti-Jao attitudes and activities. Both Chungjun, a Li, and Yungtai's husband, Yenji, a Wu, were first in line for the throne in their generation. Each oldest son thought he should be first, and jealousy betrayed them all. The younger ones had all been vehement in their criticism of the Changs and in their condemnation of Jao for her relationship with them. This was the last straw for Jao. It had been her supreme goal to establish harmony between the Li and Wu camps, and here already was a deliberate flouting of her fiat by self-willed young people who recklessly ignored the law as promulgated in the oath of harmony that they had taken.

Agonized, Jao told Chungtsung and her council that all three young people must receive the severest punishment to warn the others that breaches in the harmony between the two camps would not be tolerated. When the death sentences for her grandchildren and grandnephew were carried out, Jao retreated into her palace in Loyang to recover from both the shock and an illness. There, she was waited upon by the Chang brothers, who eased her in her convalescence, ran errands for her, and amused her with their constant bantering and witticisms.

In the winter of 705, Jao became too ill to see her ministers. Only the Changs had access to her bedside, as they had for many years assumed responsibility for her care. Jao's sudden turn for the worse alarmed the ministers so much that Chang Chienjer declared a crisis and called together his colleagues to deal with it.

"We are in jeopardy!" Chienjer cried excitedly. "Wu Jao is dying and the Changs are in control—they could easily put Wu Sanssu on the throne and have us all executed!"

His colleagues nodded in agreement, looking grim.

"What do you suggest doing?" asked Minister Tsui.

"Fearing this, I have already inserted some of my men into the Palace Guard. Today I have already won over their commander, Li Totsu, and I will be approaching Li Chan, who commands the night guards of the pavilion where Jao is now in residence . . ."

Tsui nodded slowly, reluctant to agree now that he understood the way the coup was headed. "No violence, no harm to our sovereign, should come of this—I insist," he said sternly.

"No bloodshed intended—of course not! Except to the Changs, who have manipulated her," Chienjer responded harshly. "This action is urgent. Chief Censor Huan here is even more anxious about this explosive situation than I am." Huan nodded vigorously.

Tsui frowned. "Are you men sure of Chungtsung? Is he fully prepared to take his mother's place on the throne? I will only consent to this action in order to restore the Tang, and that is final!" Tsui exclaimed, pale with emotion.

"Without question Chungtsung is our man," Chienjer exclaimed hastily.

"What does his highness say about the plan?" Tsui continued, still unconvinced about employing the guards.

"No one has had time to consult him yet—but not to worry. This is a great moment for him and he will go along with anything we suggest." Chienjer was impatient.

"He must be consulted before we do anything else. We can't just jump into this dangerous situation without careful preparation. I agree with Tsui," said another minister.

"Yes, yes—I will ask for an audience immediately—at once. It will be all right. We can count on Chungtsung, I assure you," Chienjer said. He was sweating profusely.

Tsui rose. "So! I take you at your word and join you in this scheme on the conditions mentioned." He bowed formally and left. The others also left after pledging support if Chungtsung agreed to the terms.

Chienjer called his chair to take him to the crown prince.

Chungtsung received him politely, listened to him in silence, and then said, "I've heard all this before."

"But never before has your situation been so critical with those dangerous Changs in power as they are now."

"They should certainly be executed, of course. But as her majesty is so ill, we should not agitate her now. Better postpone your coup," Chungtsung said in a placid voice.

"You will come with us when the time is ripe, won't you?" urged the minster, and the crown prince, after thinking about it, nodded his lukewarm agreement.

Several days later, late in the afternoon of a cold day in February, Chang Chienjer led five hundred guards to the north gate in order to break into the palace. They waited for General Totso and Li Chan to bring Chungtsung first. It was dark by the time the two officers reached the east palace to escort the crown prince. He refused. "What is the meaning of this intrusion?" Chungtsung asked crossly.

"We remind you of your promise to help us to restore you to your throne. The time has come. It is essential for you to come now," Totso said worriedly.

"Essential? No, I am going nowhere with you," Chungtsung replied, stubbornly.

"Your father left the throne to you, but what has happened? For twenty years you have suffered exile. Heaven has at last taken pity on you. The Palace Guards are here now to remove the traitors and restore the Li family. It is the wish of the people that you now satisfy their hopes and join the officers waiting at the north gate."

"Not in the middle of the night," Chungtsung returned. "My mother wouldn't like it at all."

Li Chan stepped into the breach. "You are the only one who has the authority to disband the guards, and the ministers are now waiting to risk their lives and their families in order to protect you. I request you to ride to the north gate to tell them to postpone the plan."

Chungtsung hesitated. "Yes, I'll go then," he agreed, completely taken in by the innocent countenance of Li Chan, his mother's protégé. He mounted his horse, an officer took the bridle, and he was led through the dark streets to the north gate, which was alive with torches and noisy armed men.

As soon as he appeared, the guards broke down the gate and poured through into the palace grounds. Chungtsung was swept along before he could get explanations. The leaders knew where to go to reach Wu Jao's quarters. They broke into the front gate and caught Tatsu and one of his brothers frantically trying to escape. An order given to decapitate was quickly obeyed on the porch of the main hall while Jao's attendant eunuchs were rounded up and bound.

Hearing the uproar, Jao got up to investigate. Going into the chill night, she stopped in shock when she saw the headless corpses. Numb with grief at her loss, she neverthess controlled her tumultuous feelings enough to deal with the emergency. She stared at the suddenly silent crowd in the yard in cold anger. "You!" she exclaimed when she caught sight of her son at the back of the crowd. "Well, Chungtsung, you have now killed the two boys—you may return to the eastern palace and go back to sleep."

Hearing this, Chang Chienjer hurriedly stepped forward. "How can Emperor Chungtsung return to the palace of a crown prince? He is now emperor. He is in charge, rightfully ordering the execution of these two wicked men. We ministers expect Your Majesty to abdicate in conformity with the will of Heaven and of all mankind."

"Neither the will of Heaven nor the will of all mankind is to blame for the atrocities committed here tonight. You are. Leave my presence."

She was turning to go back into her house when she caught sight of Li Chan making himself small behind the others. "So here is the brave general with these other brave men coming here in the middle of the night to do this great deed. You whom I have helped, you and your father Li Ifu before you. I have guaranteed your careers during my entire reign, and now you repay me by bravely killing these poor lads. Ingrate that you are."

Li Chan flushed and had nothing to say. Strangely, none of the other men in the courtyard did either. They stood silent before the frail old lady. She turned her back on them and, returning to her room, lay down on her bed and quietly relinquished the reign of empire.

She had moved to the Shangyang Detached Palace, which the Changs had remodeled for her and where she could be out of the city in comfortable surroundings. She was treated with respect and consideration which she accepted as her right. The chief women of the new regime, Emperor Chungtsung's wife, Lady Wei, and his daughter Anlo, along with Waner, Jao's former secretary, who had been promoted in order to guide the uninformed emperor and empress, had called on her only once. Taiping and Tan came, not frequently, but often enough. The chief of the Wu clan, Sanssu, had not come at all. Her son Chungtsung called formally with the chief officers twice a month, an ordeal for both.

It was now December, and the garden that year had outdone itself. Jao's flowers, especially her chrysanthemums, had lasted late into the fall, delighting her. Everyone knew the empress would not last the evening, so Chi and Cloud were her only attendants. Cloud held her hand until Jao grew too restless to be still. She opened her eyes and smiled. "Chi," she said, "are you still here? You should be in bed . . . at your age." Her breath was labored but she still had a few words to say. "Cloud, my friend, you are such a comfort to me. Just to see your lovely face is enough to make me feel better. . . . Chi, you once said there's no escape, but there is, I'm escaping now. . . ."

"I will too—soon!" he said with his old half-smile. They all laughed gently.

"What are we laughing at . . . ourselves?" Jao whispered through dry lips. She clutched her old rosary from her convent days.

"No," Chi said, leaning over her so that she could hear, "at life. . . ."

On the morning of her death, gardener An pulled up all the remaining flowers in a gesture of mourning and wept while unburdening himself to his friends in his favorite tea shop. "See my scar!" he said, displaying the long blue welt across his stomach. "Old Taitai took care of me herself, had me sewn up by her own healer, she did! This is the way our lady emperor was, always for us common folk she was. There won't never be another like her!"

AUTHOR'S NOTE

During the seventh century, China became the major power in the known world. The ancient empires of India, Persia, and Rome were crumbling under barbarian invasion, and only Byzantium still flourished. The reigns of the Tang emperors Taitsung and Kaotsung were proving to be the most vigorous and farflung in the history of China, but also in the history of Asia in general. Kaotsung was only thirty-two when he was taken ill in 660, and after that his empress, Wu Jao, undertook his duties. Her success satisfied the administrators and people of China to such an extent that she was permitted to share the responsibility of government with her husband until his death in 683, and after that she continued to rule until her own death in 705. Her career in the palace lasted nearly seventy years and coincided with the years of China's greatest century, to which she contributed substantially. Her accomplishments place her among the great women of the world.

In spite of her record, she has been vilified unmercifully by most Chinese historians for no other reason than that she was a woman. The Chinese system prohibited the participation of females in government or academic life. Even the comparatively liberal Buddhism forbade women to administer important ritual. Western historians took their history from Chinese sources, and few of them ever refer to her name without using the word "notorious" without mitigation. There are exceptions. John Fairbank of Harvard stated flatly, in his widely used textbook *East Asia, Tradition and Transformation*, that Wu Tset'tien was a strong and able ruler. The sinologist, C. P. Fitzgerald of Australia, went further in *The Empress Wu* (1968, p. 157): "Without Wu Chao there would have been no long enduring T'ang dynasty which carried on the tradition of the great Tai Tsung and saved his heritage, perhaps no lasting unity of China . . . no woman ever again occupied her place, though many aspired to it."

A word should be said here about the writing of historical fiction. I have followed the dictum of the late Josephine Tey, who held that to write fiction about historic fact is very nearly impermissible except under two conditions: that the simplification of plot and the invention of detail should not falsify the general picture, and the author should state where the facts may be found. The two titles mentioned above can well be used to satisfy the second condition. The first condition I have dealt with by writing about the "probabilities," everything considered.

Another difficulty I experienced was rendering foreign words in English. I have departed from the standards of the Wade-Giles system and Pinyon in order to spell the names as simply as possible for the average reader. Tai Tsung is Taitsung and Liu Jenguei is Liu Jen. *Ch* aspirated is romanized *ch* as in church. *Ch* unaspirated becomes J, that is, Chao is Jao and Jenchieh is Jenjer. *Ti* is spelled the way it sounds, that is, Dee. So the proper romanization of Ti Jenchieh becomes Dee Jenjer in practical fiction. Van Gulick spelled it Dee Jen-chieh in his novel about Judge Dee.

Finally, a just comparison of the several hundred political executions occuring during Wu Jao's regimen which have provoked most of the criticisms against her, viewed against the excesses perpetrated by all other Tang rulers, not to mention rulers the world over, demonstrates the restraints and mitigations practiced by Wu Jao rather than the opposite. Also, the charge that that she was a usurper can also be made against the venerated Taitsung, and practically everyone else up to her time. It was a violent era. History has dealt heavily with Wu Jao. I have dealt lightly because of the evidence in her favor. Unquestionably, she had superlative qualities, with her only major political demerit being her sex, so I hope by this fictionalized account to introduce Jao to new readers and to induce today's historians to use some other word than "notorious" to describe this very great lady.

ABOUT THE AUTHOR

EVELYN MCCUNE was born in a walled city in Korea and was raised on the campuses of the first two colleges there. Her husband served the White House and armed forces as a specialist in Korean affairs. After his death, she worked for three agencies during the Korean War: the State Department, the United Nations Korean Reconstruction Agency, and the Library of Congress. She has taught and written on a variety of Asian subjects. She now lives in Hawaii.